The Painted Skin

Pu Songling

Pu Songling (1640-1715) was a renowned Chinese writer from the Qing Dynasty, known for his elegantly written supernatural stories that conveyed simple truths and morals through fascinating imagery. The seminal work *Strange Stories from a Chinese Studio* (posthumously published in 1740), which has been translated into English, Russian, German and Manchu, was attributed to him. Many tales from *Strange Stories from a Chinese Studio* have been adapted to film and television, including 'The Painted Skin', which was widely acclaimed after its English translation by Herbert A. Giles in 1880.

At T'ai-yüan there lived a man named Wang. One morning he was out walking when he met a young lady carrying a bundle and hurrying along by herself. As she moved along with some difficulty, Wang quickened his pace and caught her up, and found she was a pretty girl of about sixteen. Much smitten he inquired whither she was going so early, and no one with her. "A traveller like you," replied the girl, "cannot alleviate my distress; why trouble yourself to ask?" "What distress is it?" said Wang; "I'm sure I'll do anything I can for you." "My parents," answered she, "loved money, and they sold me as concubine into a rich family, where the wife was very jealous, and beat and abused me morning and night. It was more than I could stand, so I have run away."

Wang asked her where she was going; to which she replied that a runaway had no fixed place of abode. "My house," said Wang, "is at no great distance; what do you say to coming there?" She joyfully acquiesced; and Wang, taking up her bundle, led the way to his house. Finding no one there, she asked Wang where his family were; to which he replied that that was only the library. "And a very nice place, too," said she; "but if you are kind enough to wish to save my life, you mustn't let it be known that I am here." Wang promised he would not divulge her secret, and so she remained there for some days without anyone knowing anything about it. He then told his wife, and she, fearing the girl might belong to some influential family, advised him to send her away. This, however, he would not consent to do; when one day, going into the town, he met a Taoist priest, who looked at him in astonishment, and asked him what he had met. "I have met nothing," replied Wang. "Why," said the priest, "you are bewitched; what do you mean by not having met anything?" But Wang insisted that it was so, and the priest walked away, saying, "The fool! Some people don't seem to know when death is at hand." This startled Wang, who at first thought of the girl; but then he reflected that a pretty young thing as she was couldn't well be a witch, and began to suspect that the priest merely wanted to do a stroke of business.

When he returned, the library door was shut, and he couldn't get in, which made him suspect that something was wrong; and so he climbed over the wall, where he found the door of the inner room shut too. Softly creeping up, he looked through the window and saw a hideous devil, with a green face and jagged teeth like a saw, spreading a human skin upon the bed and painting it with a paint-brush. The devil then threw aside the brush, and giving the skin a shake out, just as you would a coat, threw it over its shoulders, when, lo! it was the girl. Terrified at this, Wang hurried away with his head down in search of the priest who had gone he knew not whither; subsequently finding him in the fields, where he threw himself on his knees and begged the priest to save him. "As to driving her away," said the priest, "the creature must be in great distress to be seeking a substitute for herself; besides, I could hardly endure to injure a living thing." However, he gave Wang a fly-brush, and bade him hang it at the door of the bedroom, agreeing to meet again at the Ch'ing-ti temple.

Wang went home, but did not dare enter the library; so he hung up the brush at the bedroom door, and before long heard a sound of footsteps outside. Not daring to move, he made his wife peep out;

51 Great Short Stories

51 Great Short Stories

Om Books International

Reprinted in 2025

Om Books International

Corporate & Editorial Office
A-12, Sector 64, Noida 201 301
Uttar Pradesh, India
Phone: +91 120 477 4100
Email: editorial@ombooks.com
Website: www.ombooksinternational.com

Sales Office
107, Ansari Road, Darya Ganj,
New Delhi 110 002, India
Phone: +91 11 4000 9000
Email: sales@ombooks.com
Website: www.ombooks.com

Compiled by: Anukriti Singh

ISBN: 9789352766789

Printed in India

10 9 8 7 6 5 4 3

Contents

and she saw the girl standing looking at the brush, afraid to pass it. She then ground her teeth and went away; but in a little while came back, and began cursing, saying, "You priest, you won't frighten me. Do you think I am going to give up what is already in my grasp?" Thereupon, she tore the brush to pieces, and bursting open the door, walked straight up to the bed, where she ripped open Wang and tore out his heart, with which she went away. Wang's wife screamed out, and the servant came in with a light; but Wang was already dead and presented a most miserable spectacle. His wife, who was in an agony of fright, hardly dared cry for fear of making a noise; and next day she sent Wang's brother to see the priest. The latter got into a great rage, and cried out, "Was it for this that I had compassion on you, devil that you are?" proceeding at once with Wang's brother to the house, from which the girl had disappeared without anyone knowing whither she had gone. But the priest, raising his head, looked all round, and said, "Luckily she's not far off." He then asked who lived in the apartments on the south side, to which Wang's brother replied that he did; whereupon the priest declared that there she would be found. Wang's brother was horribly frightened and said he did not think so; and then the priest asked him if any stranger had been to the house. To this he answered that he had been out to the Ch'ing-ti temple and couldn't possibly say; but he went off to inquire, and in a little while came back and reported that an old woman had sought service with them as a maid-of-all-work, and had been engaged by his wife. "That is she," said the priest, as Wang's brother added she was still there; and they all set out to go to the house together. Then the priest took his wooden sword, and standing in the middle of the courtyard, shouted out, "Base-born fiend, give me back my fly-brush!"

Meanwhile the new maid-of-all-work was in a great state of alarm, and tried to get away by the door; but the priest struck her and down she fell flat, the human skin dropped off, and she became a hideous devil. There she lay grunting like a pig, until the priest grasped his wooden sword and struck off her head. She then became a dense column of smoke curling up from the ground, when the priest took an uncorked gourd and threw it right into the midst of the smoke. A sucking noise was heard, and the whole column was drawn into the gourd; after which the priest corked it up closely and put it in his pouch. The skin, too, which was complete even to the eyebrows, eyes, hands, and feet, he also rolled up as if it had been a scroll, and was on the point of leaving with it, when Wang's wife stopped him, and with tears entreated him to bring her husband to life. The priest said he was unable to do that; but Wang's wife flung herself at his feet, and with loud lamentations implored his assistance. For some time he remained immersed in thought, and then replied, "My power is not equal to what you ask. I myself cannot raise the dead; but I will direct you to some one who can, and if you apply to him properly you will succeed." Wang's wife asked the priest who it was; to which he replied, "There is a maniac in the town who passes his time grovelling in the dirt. Go, prostrate yourself before him, and beg him to help you. If he insults you, shew no sign of anger." Wang's brother knew the man to whom he alluded, and accordingly bade the priest adieu, and proceeded thither with his sister-in-law.

They found the destitute creature raving away by the road side, so filthy that it was all they could do to go near him. Wang's wife approached him on her knees; at which the maniac leered at her, and cried out, "Do you love me, my beauty?" Wang's wife told him what she had come for, but he only laughed and said, "You can get plenty of other husbands. Why raise the dead one to life?" But Wang's wife entreated him to help her; whereupon he observed, "It's very strange: people apply to me to raise their dead as if I was king of the infernal regions." He then gave Wang's wife a thrashing with his staff, which she bore without a murmur, and before a gradually increasing crowd of spectators. After this he produced a loathsome pill which he told her she must swallow, but here she broke down and was quite unable to do so. However, she did manage it at last, and then the maniac crying out, "How you do love me!" got up and went away without taking any more notice of her. They followed him into a temple with loud supplications, but he had disappeared, and every effort to find him was unsuccessful. Overcome with rage and shame, Wang's wife went home, where she mourned bitterly over her dead husband, grievously repenting the steps she had taken, and wishing only to die. She then bethought herself of preparing the corpse, near which none of the servants would venture; and set to work to close up the frightful wound of which he died.

While thus employed, interrupted from time to time by her sobs, she felt a rising lump in her throat, which by-and-by came out with a pop and fell straight into the dead man's wound. Looking closely at it, she saw it was a human heart; and then it began as it were to throb, emitting a warm vapour like smoke. Much excited, she at once closed the flesh over it, and held the sides of the wound together with all her might. Very soon, however, she got tired, and finding the vapour escaping from the crevices, she tore up a piece of silk and bound it round, at the same time bringing back circulation by rubbing the body and covering it up with clothes. In the night, she removed the coverings, and found that breath was coming from the nose; and by next morning her husband was alive again, though disturbed in mind as if awaking from a dream and feeling a pain in his heart. Where he had been wounded, there was a cicatrix about as big as a cash, which soon after disappeared.

The Purple Jar

Maria Edgeworth

Maria Edgeworth (1768-1849), best-known for writing didactic children's literature, was an important writer of Victorian England. Tutored in Politics, Economics, Science and Literature by her father, Edgeworth learned Estate Management as well to help her father look after Edgeworthstown in Ireland. She grew up surrounded by intellectuals belonging to the Lunar Society and also wrote *Letters for Literary Ladies* (1795) to express her views on women's education. 'The Purple Jar' (1796) is Edgeworth's most famous children's story.

Rosamond, a little girl of about seven years old, was walking with her mother in the streets of London. As she passed along, she looked in at the windows of several shops, and she saw a great variety of different sorts of things, of which she did not know the use, or even the names. She wished to stop to look at them; but there was a great number of people in the streets, and a great many carts and carriages and wheelbarrows, and she was afraid to let go her mother's hand.

"Oh! Mother, how happy I should be," said she, as she passed a toy-shop, "if I had all these pretty things!"

"What, all! Do you wish for them all, Rosamond?"

"Yes, mamma, all."

As she spoke, they came to a milliner's shop; the windows were hung with ribbons, and lace, and festoons of artificial flowers.

"Oh! Mamma, what beautiful roses! Won't you buy some of them?"

"No, my dear."

"Why?"

"Because I don't want them, my dear."

They went a little farther, and they came to another shop, which caught Rosamond's eye. It was a jeweler's shop; and there were a great many pretty baubles, ranged in drawers behind glass.

"Mamma, you'll buy some of these?"

"Which of them, Rosamond?"

"Which? I don't know which; but any of them, for they are all pretty."

"Yes, they are all pretty; but of what use would they be to me?"

"Use! Oh, I'm sure you could find some use or other, if you would only buy them first."

"But I would rather find out the use first."

Rosamond was very sorry that her mother wanted nothing. Presently, however, they came to a shop, which appeared to her far more beautiful than the rest. It was a chemist's shop; but she did not know that.

"Oh, mother! Oh!" cried she, pulling her mother's hand. "Look! Look! Blue, green, red, yellow, and purple! Oh, mamma, what beautiful things! Won't you buy some of these?"

Still her mother answered as before, "What use would they be to me, Rosamond?"

"You might put flowers in them, mamma, and they would look so pretty on the chimney-piece. I wish I had one of them."

"You have a flower-vase," said her mother; "and that is not for flowers."

"But I could use it for a flower-vase, mamma, you know."

"Perhaps if you were to see it nearer, if you were to examine it, you might be disappointed."

"No, indeed; I'm sure I should not. I should like it exceedingly."

Rosamond kept her head turned to look at the purple vase till she could see it no longer.

"Then, mother," said she, after a pause, "perhaps you have no money."

"Yes, I have."

"Dear me! If I had money, I would buy roses, and boxes, and purple flower-pots, and everything." Rosamond was obliged to pause in the midst of her speech.

"Oh, mamma, would you stop a minute for me? I have got a stone in my shoe; it hurts me very much."

"How comes there to be a stone in your shoe?"

"Because of this great hole, mamma — it comes in there: my shoes are quite worn out; I wish you'd be so very good as to give me another pair."

"Nay, Rosamond, but I have not money enough to buy shoes, and flower-pots, and boxes, and everything."

Rosamond thought that was a great pity. But now her foot, which had been hurt by the stone, began to give her so much pain that she was obliged to hop every other step, and she could think of nothing else. They came to a shoemaker's shop soon afterwards.

"There! There! mamma, there are shoes — there are little shoes that would just fit me; and you know shoes would be really of use to me."

"Yes, so they would, Rosamond. Come in."

She followed her mother into the shop.

Mr. Sole, the shoemaker, had a great many customers, and his shop was full, so they were obliged to wait.

"Well, Rosamond," said her mother, "you don't think this shop so pretty as the rest?"

"No, not nearly; it's black and dark, and there are nothing but shoes all round; and besides, there's a very disagreeable smell."

"That smell is the smell of new leather."

"Is it? Oh!" said Rosamond, looking round, "there is a pair of little shoes; they'll just fit me, I'm sure."

"Perhaps they might, but you cannot be sure till you have tried them on, any more than you can be quite sure that you should like the purple vase exceedingly, till you have examined it more attentively."

"Why, I don't know about the shoes, certainly, till I've tried; but, mamma, I'm quite sure I should like the flower-pot."

"Well, which would you rather have, that jar, or a pair of shoes? I will buy either for you."

"Dear mamma, thank you — but if you could buy both?"

"No, not both."

"Then the jar, if you please."

"But I should tell you that I shall not give you another pair of shoes this month."

"This month! That's a very long time indeed. You can't think how these hurt me. I believe I'd better have the new shoes — but yet, that purple flower-pot — Oh, indeed, mamma, these shoes are not so very, very bad; I think I might wear them a little longer; and the month will soon be over: I can make them last to the end of the month, can't I? Don't you think so, mamma?"

"Nay, my dear, I want you to think for yourself: you will have time enough to consider about it whilst I speak to Mr. Sole about my boots."

Mr. Sole was by this time at leisure; and whilst her mother was speaking to him, Rosamond stood in profound meditation, with one shoe on, and the other in her hand.

"Well, my dear, have you decided?"

"Mamma! — Yes — I believe. If you please — I should like the flower-pot; that is, if you won't think me very silly, mamma."

"Why, as to that, I can't promise you, Rosamond; but when you are to judge for yourself, you should choose what will make you the happiest; and then it would not signify who thought you silly."

"Then, mamma, if that's all, I'm sure the flower-pot would make me the happiest," said she, putting on her old shoe again; "so I choose the flower-pot."

"Very well, you shall have it: clasp your shoe and come home."

Rosamond clasped her shoe, and ran after her mother: it was not long before the shoe came down at the heel, and many times was she obliged to stop, to take the stones out of her shoe, and often was she obliged to hop with pain; but still the thoughts of the purple flower-pot prevailed, and she persisted in her choice.

When they came to the shop with the large window, Rosamond felt her joy redouble, upon hearing her mother desire the servant, who was with them, to buy the purple jar, and bring it home. He had other commissions, so he did not return with them. Rosamond, as soon as she got in, ran to gather all her own flowers, which she had in a corner of her mother's garden.

"I'm afraid they'll be dead before the flower-pot comes, Rosamond," said her mother to her, when she was coming in with the flowers in her lap.

"No, indeed, mamma, it will come home very soon, I dare say; and shan't I be very happy putting them into the purple flower-pot?"

"I hope so, my dear."

The servant was much longer returning home than Rosamond had expected; but at length he came, and brought with him the long-wished-for jar. The moment it was set down upon the table, Rosamond ran up with an exclamation of joy.

"I may have it now, mamma?"

"Yes, my dear, it is yours."

Rosamond poured the flowers from her lap upon the carpet, and seized the purple flower-pot. "Oh, dear mother!" cried she, as soon as she had taken off the top, "but there's something dark in it — it smells very disagreeable: what is in it? I didn't want this black stuff."

"Nor I neither, my dear."

"But what shall I do with it, mamma?"

"That I cannot tell."

"But it will be of no use to me, mamma."

"That I can't help."

"But I must pour it out, and fill the flower-pot with water."

"That's as you please, my dear."

"Will you lend me a bowl to pour it into, mamma?"

"That was more than I promised you, my dear; but I will lend you a bowl."

The bowl was produced, and Rosamond proceeded to empty the purple vase. But what was her surprise and disappointment, when it was entirely empty, to find that it was no longer a purple vase! It was a plain white glass jar, which had appeared to have that beautiful color merely from the liquor with which it had been filled.

Little Rosamond burst into tears.

"Why should you cry, my dear?" said her mother; "it will be of as much use to you now as ever for a flower-vase."

"But it won't look so pretty on the chimney-piece. I am sure, if I had known that it was not really purple, I should not have wished to have it so much."

"But didn't I tell you that you had not examined it, and that perhaps you would be disappointed?"

"And so I am disappointed indeed. I wish I had believed you beforehand. Now I had much rather have the shoes, for I shall not be able to walk all this month: even walking home that little way hurt me exceedingly. Mamma, I'll give you the flower-pot back again, and that purple stuff and all, if you'll only give me the shoes."

"No, Rosamond, you must abide by your own choice; and now the best thing you can possibly do is to bear your disappointment with good-humour."

"I will bear it as well as I can," said Rosamond, wiping her eyes, and she began slowly and sorrowfully to fill the vase with flowers.

But Rosamond's disappointment did not end here: many were the difficulties and distresses into which her imprudent choice brought her before the end of the month. Every day her shoes grew worse and worse, till at last she could neither run, dance, jump, nor walk in them. Whenever Rosamond was called to see anything, she was pulling up her shoes at the heels, and was sure to be too late. Whenever her mother was going out to walk, she could not take Rosamond with her, for Rosamond had no soles to her shoes; and at length, on the very last day of the month, it happened that her father proposed to take her and her brother to a glass-house which she had long wished to see. She was very happy; but, when she was quite ready, had her hat and gloves on, and was making haste downstairs to her brother and father, who were waiting at the hall door for her, the shoe dropped off; she put it on again in a great hurry; but, as she was going across the hall, her father turned round.

"Why are you walking slipshod? No one must walk slipshod with me. Why, Rosamond," said he, looking at her shoes with disgust, "I thought that you were always neat. Go, I cannot take you with me."

Rosamond colored and retired. "Oh, mamma," said she, as she took off her hat, "how I wish that I had chosen the shoes! They would have been of so much more use to me than that jar: however, I am sure — no, not quite sure — but I hope I shall be wiser another time."

The Devil And Tom Walker

Washington Irving

Washington Irving (1783-1859) was the first American man of letters to achieve international acclaim. An American diplomat, historian and short story writer, Irving also served as Ambassador of the United States to Spain in the 1840s. For the benefit of writers, he advocated for stricter laws against copyright infringement. Besides popular short stories like 'The Legend Of Sleepy Hollow' (1820), Irving also wrote the biographies of George Washington and Oliver Goldsmith, and other important historical works. 'The Devil And Tom Walker' is from the collection *Tales of a Traveler* (1824).

A few miles from Boston in Massachusetts, there is a deep inlet, winding several miles into the interior of the country from Charles Bay, and terminating in a thickly-wooded swamp or morass. On one side of this inlet is a beautiful dark grove; on the opposite side the land rises abruptly from the water's edge into a high ridge, on which grow a few scattered oaks of great age and immense size. Under one of these gigantic trees, according to old stories, there was a great amount of treasure buried by Kidd the pirate. The inlet allowed a facility to bring the money in a boat secretly and at night to the very foot of the hill; the elevation of the place permitted a good lookout to be kept that no one was at hand; while the remarkable trees formed good landmarks by which the place might easily be found again. The old stories add, moreover, that the devil presided at the hiding of the money, and took it under his guardianship; but this, it is well known, he always does with buried treasure, particularly when it has been ill-gotten. Be that as it may, Kidd never returned to recover his wealth; being shortly after seized at Boston, sent out to England, and there hanged for a pirate.

About the year 1727, just at the time that earthquakes were prevalent in New England, and shook many tall sinners down upon their knees, there lived near this place a meagre, miserly fellow, of the name of Tom Walker. He had a wife as miserly as himself: they were so miserly that they even conspired to cheat each other. Whatever the woman could lay hands on, she hid away; a hen could not cackle but she was on the alert to secure the new-laid egg. Her husband was continually prying about to detect her secret hoards, and many and fierce were the conflicts that took place about what ought to have been common property. They lived in a forlorn-looking house that stood alone, and had an air of starvation. A few straggling savin-trees, emblems of sterility, grew near it; no smoke ever curled from its chimney; no traveller stopped at its door. A miserable horse, whose ribs were as articulate as the bars of a gridiron, stalked about a field, where a thin carpet of moss, scarcely covering the ragged beds of pudding-stone, tantalized and balked his hunger; and sometimes he would lean his head over the fence, look piteously at the passer-by, and seem to petition deliverance from this land of famine.

The house and its inmates had altogether a bad name. Tom's wife was a tall termagant, fierce of temper, loud of tongue, and strong of arm. Her voice was often heard in wordy warfare with her husband; and his face sometimes showed signs that their conflicts were not confined to words. No one ventured, however, to interfere between them. The lonely wayfarer shrunk within himself at the horrid clamour and clapper-clawing; eyed the den of discord askance; and hurried on his way, rejoicing, if a bachelor, in his celibacy.

One day that Tom Walker had been to a distant part of the neighbourhood, he took what he considered a short cut homeward, through the swamp. Like most short cuts, it was an ill-chosen route. The swamp was thickly grown with great gloomy pines and hemlocks, some of them ninety feet high, which made it dark at noonday, and a retreat for all the owls of the neighbourhood. It was full of pits and quagmires, partly covered with weeds and mosses, where the green surface often betrayed the traveller into a gulf of black, smothering mud: there were also dark and stagnant pools, the abodes of the tadpole, the bull-frog, and the water-snake; where the trunks of pines and hemlocks lay half-drowned, half-rotting, looking like alligators sleeping in the mire.

Tom had long been picking his way cautiously through this treacherous forest; stepping from tuft to tuft of rushes and roots, which afforded precarious footholds among deep sloughs; or pacing carefully, like a cat, along the prostrate trunks of trees; startled now and then by the sudden screaming of the bittern, or the quacking of a wild duck rising on the wing from some solitary pool. At length he arrived at a firm piece of ground, which ran out like a peninsula into the deep bosom of the swamp. It had been one of the strongholds of the Indians during their wars with the first colonists. Here they had thrown up a kind of fort, which they had looked upon as almost impregnable, and had used as a place of refuge for their squaws and children. Nothing remained of the old Indian fort but a few embankments, gradually sinking to the level of the surrounding earth, and already overgrown in part by oaks and other forest trees, the foliage of which formed a contrast to the dark pines and hemlocks of the swamp.

It was late in the dusk of evening when Tom Walker reached the old fort, and he paused there awhile to rest himself. Any one but he would have felt unwilling to linger in this lonely, melancholy place, for the common people had a bad opinion of it, from the stories handed down from the time of the Indian wars; when it was asserted that the savages held incantations here, and made sacrifices to the evil spirit.

Tom Walker, however, was not a man to be troubled with any fears of the kind. He reposed himself for some time on the trunk of a fallen hemlock, listening to the boding cry of the tree-toad, and delving with his walking-staff into a mound of black mould at his feet. As he turned up the soil unconsciously, his staff struck against something hard. He raked it out of the vegetable mould, and lo! a cloven skull, with an Indian tomahawk buried deep in it, lay before him. The rust on the weapon showed the time that had elapsed since this death-blow had been given. It was a dreary memento of the fierce struggle that had taken place in this last foothold of the Indian warriors.

"Humph!" said Tom Walker, as he gave it a kick to shake the dirt from it.

"Let that skull alone!" said a gruff voice. Tom lifted up his eyes, and beheld a great black man seated directly opposite him, on the stump of a tree. He was exceedingly surprised, having neither heard nor seen any one approach; and he was still more perplexed on observing, as well as the gathering gloom would permit, that the stranger was neither negro nor Indian. It is true he was dressed in a rude half Indian garb, and had a red belt or sash swathed round his body; but his face was neither black nor copper-colour, but swarthy and dingy, and begrimed with soot, as if he had been accustomed to toil among fires and forges. He had a shock of coarse black hair, that stood out from his head in all directions, and bore an ax on his shoulder.

He scowled for a moment at Tom with a pair of great red eyes.

"What are you doing on my grounds?" said the black man, with a hoarse growling voice.

"Your grounds!" said Tom, with a sneer, "no more your grounds than mine; they belong to Deacon Peabody."

"Deacon Peabody be d — d," said the stranger, "as I flatter myself he will be, if he does not look more to his own sins and less to those of his neighbours. Look yonder, and see how Deacon Peabody is faring."

Tom looked in the direction that the stranger pointed, and beheld one of the great trees, fair and flourishing without, but rotten at the core, and saw that it had been nearly hewn through, so that the first high wind was likely to blow it down. On the bark of the tree was scored the name of Deacon Peabody, an eminent man, who had waxed wealthy by driving shrewd bargains with the Indians. He now looked around, and found most of the tall trees marked with the name of some great man of the colony, and all more or less scored by the ax. The one on which he had been seated, and which had evidently just been hewn down, bore the name of Crowninshield; and he recollected a mighty rich man of that name, who made a vulgar display of wealth, which it was whispered he had acquired by buccaneering.

"He's just ready for burning!" said the black man, with a growl of triumph. "You see I am likely to have a good stock of firewood for winter."

"But what right have you," said Tom, "to cut down Deacon Peabody's timber?"

"The right of a prior claim," said the other. "This woodland belonged to me long before one of your whitefaced race put foot upon the soil."

"And pray, who are you, if I may be so bold?" said Tom.

"Oh, I go by various names. I am the wild huntsman in some countries; the black miner in others. In this neighbourhood I am known by the name of the black woodsman. I am he to whom the red men consecrated this spot, and in honour of whom they now and then roasted a white man, by way of sweet-smelling sacrifice. Since the red men have been exterminated by you white savages, I amuse myself by presiding at the persecutions of Quakers and Anabaptists; I am the great patron and prompter of slave-dealers, and the grand-master of the Salem witches."

"The upshot of all which is, that, if I mistake not," said Tom, sturdily, "you are he commonly called Old Scratch."

"The same, at your service!" replied the black man, with a half civil nod.

Such was the opening of this interview, according to the old story; though it has almost too familiar an air to be credited. One would think that to meet with such a singular personage, in this wild, lonely place, would have shaken any man's nerves; but Tom was a hard-minded fellow, not easily daunted, and he had lived so long with a termagant wife, that he did not even fear the devil.

It is said that after this commencement they had a long and earnest conversation together, as Tom returned homeward. The black man told him of great sums of money buried by Kidd the pirate, under the oak-trees on the high ridge, not far from the morass. All these were under his command, and protected by his power, so that none could find them but such as propitiated his favour. These he offered to place within Tom Walker's reach, having conceived an especial kindness for him; but they were to be had only on certain conditions. What these conditions were may be easily surmised, though Tom never disclosed them publicly. They must have been very hard, for he required time to think of them, and he was not a man to stick at trifles when money was in view. When they had reached the edge of the swamp, the stranger paused. "What proof have I that all you have been telling me is true?" said Tom. "There's my signature," said the black man, pressing his finger on Tom's forehead. So saying, he turned off among the thickets of the swamp, and seemed, as Tom said, to go down, down, down, into the earth, until nothing but his head and shoulders could be seen, and so on, until he totally disappeared.

When Tom reached home, he found the black print of a finger burnt, as it were, into his forehead, which nothing could obliterate.

The first news his wife had to tell him was the sudden death of Absalom Crowninshield, the rich buccaneer. It was announced in the papers with the usual flourish, that "A great man had fallen in Israel."

Tom recollected the tree which his black friend had just hewn down, and which was ready for burning. "Let the freebooter roast," said Tom, "who cares!" He now felt convinced that all he had heard and seen was no illusion.

He was not prone to let his wife into his confidence; but as this was an uneasy secret, he willingly shared it with her. All her avarice was awakened at the mention of hidden gold, and she urged her husband to comply with the black man's terms, and secure what would make them wealthy for life. However Tom might have felt disposed to sell himself to the Devil, he was determined not to do so to oblige his wife; so he flatly refused, out of the mere spirit of contradiction. Many and bitter were the quarrels they had on the subject; but the more she talked, the more resolute was Tom not to be damned to please her.

At length she determined to drive the bargain on her own account, and if she succeeded, to keep all the gain to herself. Being of the same fearless temper as her husband, she set off for the old Indian fort towards the close of a summer's day. She was many hours absent. When she came back, she was reserved and sullen in her replies. She spoke something of a black man, whom she had met about twilight hewing at the root of a tall tree. He was sulky, however, and would not come to terms: she was to go again with a propitiatory offering, but what it was she forbore to say.

The next evening she set off again for the swamp, with her apron heavily laden. Tom waited and waited for her, but in vain; midnight came, but she did not make her appearance: morning, noon, night returned, but still she did not come. Tom now grew uneasy for her safety, especially as he found she had carried off in her apron the silver tea-pot and spoons, and every portable article of value. Another night elapsed, another morning came; but no wife. In a word, she was never heard of more.

What was her real fate nobody knows, in consequence of so many pretending to know. It is one of those facts which have become confounded by a variety of historians. Some asserted that she lost her way among the tangled mazes of the swamp, and sank into some pit or slough; others, more charitable, hinted that she had eloped with the household booty, and made off to some other province; while others surmised that the tempter had decoyed her into a dismal quagmire, on the top of which her hat was found lying. In confirmation of this, it was said a great black man, with an ax on his shoulder, was seen late that very evening coming out of the swamp, carrying a bundle tied in a check apron, with an air of surly triumph.

The most current and probable story, however, observes, that Tom Walker grew so anxious about the fate of his wife and his property, that he set out at length to seek them both at the Indian fort. During a long summer's afternoon he searched about the gloomy place, but no wife was to be seen. He called her name repeatedly, but she was nowhere to be heard. The bittern alone responded to his voice, as he flew screaming by; or the bull-frog croaked dolefully from a neighbouring pool. At length, it is said, just in the brown hour of twilight, when the owls began to hoot, and the bats to flit about, his attention was attracted by the clamour of carrion crows hovering about a cypress-tree. He looked up, and beheld a bundle tied in a check apron, and hanging in the branches of the tree, with a great vulture perched hard by, as if keeping watch upon it. He leaped with joy; for he recognized his wife's apron, and supposed it to contain the household valuables.

"Let us get hold of the property," said he, consolingly to himself, "and we will endeavour to do without the woman."

As he scrambled up the tree, the vulture spread its wide wings, and sailed off, screaming, into the deep shadows of the forest. Tom seized the checked apron, but, woeful sight! found nothing but a heart and liver tied up in it!

Such, according to this most authentic old story, was all that was to be found of Tom's wife. She had probably attempted to deal with the black man as she had been accustomed to deal with her husband; but though a female scold is generally considered a match for the devil, yet in this instance she appears to have had the worst of it. She must have died game, however; for it is said Tom noticed many prints of cloven feet deeply stamped about the tree, and found handfuls of hair, that looked as if they had been plucked from the coarse black shock of the woodman. Tom knew his wife's prowess by experience. He shrugged his shoulders, as he looked at the signs of a fierce clapper-clawing. "Egad," said he to himself, "Old Scratch must have had a tough time of it!"

Tom consoled himself for the loss of his property, with the loss of his wife, for he was a man of fortitude. He even felt something like gratitude towards the black woodman, who, he considered, had done him a kindness. He sought, therefore, to cultivate a further acquaintance with him, but for some time without success; the old black-legs played shy, for whatever people may think, he is not always to be had for calling for: he knows how to play his cards when pretty sure of his game.

At length, it is said, when delay had whetted Tom's eagerness to the quick, and prepared him to agree to anything rather than not gain the promised treasure, he met the black man one evening in his usual woodman's dress, with his ax on his shoulder, sauntering along the swamp, and humming a tune. He affected to receive Tom's advances with great indifference, made brief replies, and went on humming his tune.

By degrees, however, Tom brought him to business, and they began to haggle about the terms on which the former was to have the pirate's treasure. There was one condition which need not be mentioned, being generally understood in all cases where the devil grants favours; but there were others about which, though of less importance, he was inflexibly obstinate. He insisted that the money found through his means should be employed in his service. He proposed, therefore, that Tom should employ it in the black traffic; that is to say, that he should fit out a slave-ship. This, however, Tom resolutely refused: he was bad enough in all conscience; but the devil himself could not tempt him to turn slave-trader.

Finding Tom so squeamish on this point, he did not insist upon it, but proposed, instead, that he should turn usurer; the devil being extremely anxious for the increase of usurers, looking upon them as his peculiar people.

To this no objections were made, for it was just to Tom's taste.

"You shall open a broker's shop in Boston next month," said the black man.

"I'll do it tomorrow, if you wish," said Tom Walker.

"You shall lend money at two per cent. a month."

"Egad, I'll charge four!" replied Tom Walker.

"You shall extort bonds, foreclose mortgages, drive the merchants to bankruptcy" —

"I'll drive them to the d — l," cried Tom Walker.

"You are the usurer for my money!" said black-legs with delight. "When will you want the rhino?"

"This very night."

"Done!" said the devil.

"Done!" said Tom Walker. — So they shook hands and struck a bargain.

A few days' time saw Tom Walker seated behind his desk in a counting-house in Boston.

His reputation for a ready-moneyed man, who would lend money out for a good consideration, soon spread abroad. Everybody remembers the time of Governor Belcher, when money was particularly scarce. It was a time of paper credit. The country had been deluged with government bills, the famous Land Bank had been established; there had been a rage for speculating; the people had run mad with schemes for new settlements; for building cities in the wilderness; land-jobbers went about with maps of grants, and townships, and Eldorados, lying nobody knew where, but which everybody was ready to purchase. In a word, the great speculating fever which breaks out every now and then in the country, had raged to an alarming degree, and everybody was dreaming of making sudden fortunes from nothing. As usual the fever had subsided; the dream had gone off, and the imaginary fortunes with it; the patients were left in doleful plight, and the whole country resounded with the consequent cry of "hard times."

At this propitious time of public distress did Tom Walker set up as usurer in Boston. His door was soon thronged by customers. The needy and adventurous; the gambling speculator; the dreaming land-jobber; the thriftless tradesman; the merchant with cracked credit; in short, every one driven to raise money by desperate means and desperate sacrifices, hurried to Tom Walker.

Thus Tom was the universal friend of the needy, and acted like a "friend in need"; that is to say, he always exacted good pay and good security. In proportion to the distress of the applicant was the hardness of his terms. He accumulated bonds and mortgages; gradually squeezed his customers closer and closer: and sent them at length, dry as a sponge, from his door.

In this way he made money hand over hand; became a rich and mighty man, and exalted his cocked hat upon "Change." He built himself, as usual, a vast house, out of ostentation; but left the greater part of it unfinished and unfurnished, out of parsimony. He even set up a carriage in the fulness of his vainglory, though he nearly starved the horses which drew it; and as the ungreased wheels groaned and screeched on the axle-trees, you would have thought you heard the souls of the poor debtors he was squeezing.

As Tom waxed old, however, he grew thoughtful. Having secured the good things of this world, he began to feel anxious about those of the next. He thought with regret on the bargain he had made with his black friend, and set his wits to work to cheat him out of the conditions. He became, therefore, all of a sudden, a violent church-goer. He prayed loudly and strenuously, as if heaven were to be taken by force of lungs. Indeed, one might always tell when he had sinned most during the week, by the clamour of his Sunday devotion. The quiet Christians who had been modestly and steadfastly travelling Zionward, were struck with self-reproach at seeing themselves so suddenly outstripped in their career by this new-made convert. Tom was as rigid in religious as in money matters; he was a stern supervisor and censurer of his neighbours, and seemed to think every sin entered up to their account became a credit on his own side of the page. He even talked of the expediency of reviving the persecution of Quakers and Anabaptists. In a word, Tom's zeal became as notorious as his riches.

Still, in spite of all this strenuous attention to forms, Tom had a lurking dread that the devil, after all, would have his due. That he might not be taken unawares, therefore, it is said he always carried a small Bible in his coat-pocket. He had also a great folio Bible on his counting-house desk, and would frequently be found reading it when people called on business; on such occasions he would lay his green spectacles in the book, to mark the place, while he turned round to drive some usurious bargain.

Some say that Tom grew a little crack-brained in his old days, and that, fancying his end approaching, he had his horse new shod, saddled and bridled, and buried with his feet uppermost; because he supposed that at the last day the world would be turned upside down; in which case he should find his horse standing ready for mounting, and he was determined at the worst to give his old friend a run for it. This, however, is probably a mere old wives' fable. If he really did take such a precaution, it was totally superfluous; at least so says the authentic old legend; which closes his story in the following manner.

One hot summer afternoon in the dog-days, just as a terrible black thunder-gust was coming up, Tom sat in his counting-house, in his white linen cap and India silk morning-gown. He was on the point of foreclosing a mortgage, by which he would complete the ruin of an unlucky land-speculator for whom he had professed the greatest friendship. The poor land-jobber begged him to grant a few months' indulgence. Tom had grown testy and irritated, and refused another day.

"My family will be ruined, and brought upon the parish," said the land-jobber. "Charity begins at home," replied Tom; "I must take care of myself in these hard times."

"You have made so much money out of me," said the speculator.

Tom lost his patience and his piety. "The devil take me," said he, "if I have made a farthing!"

Just then there were three loud knocks at the street-door. He stepped out to see who was there. A black man was holding a black horse, which neighed and stamped with impatience.

"Tom, you're come for," said the black fellow, gruffly. Tom shrank back, but too late. He had left his little Bible at the bottom of his coat-pocket, and his big Bible on the desk buried under the mortgage he was about to foreclose: never was sinner taken more unawares. The black man whisked him like a child into the saddle, gave the horse the lash, and away he galloped, with Tom on his back, in the midst of the thunder-storm. The clerks stuck their pens behind their ears, and stared after him from the windows. Away went Tom Walker, dashing down the street; his white cap bobbing up and down; his morning-gown fluttering in the wind, and his steed striking fire out of the pavement at every bound. When the clerks turned to look for the black man, he had disappeared.

Tom Walker never returned to foreclose the mortgage. A countryman, who lived on the border of the swamp, reported that in the height of the thunder-gust he had heard a great clattering of hoofs and a howling along the road, and running to the window caught sight of a figure, such as I have described, on a horse that galloped like mad across the fields, over the hills, and down into the black hemlock swamp towards the old Indian fort; and that shortly after a thunder-bolt falling in that direction seemed to set the whole forest in a blaze.

The good people of Boston shook their heads and shrugged their shoulders, but had been so much accustomed to witches and goblins, and tricks of the devil, in all kinds of shapes, from the first settlement of the colony, that they were not so much horror-struck as might have been expected. Trustees were appointed to take charge of Tom's effects. There was nothing, however, to administer upon. On searching his coffers, all his bonds and mortgages were found reduced to cinders. In place of gold and silver, his iron chest was filled with chips and shavings; two skeletons lay in his stable instead of his half-starved horses, and the very next day his great house took fire and was burnt to the ground.

Such was the end of Tom Walker and his ill-gotten wealth. Let all griping money-brokers lay this story to heart. The truth of it is not to be doubted. The very hole under the oak-trees, whence he dug Kidd's money, is to be seen to this day; and the neighbouring swamp and old Indian fort are often haunted in stormy nights by a figure on horseback, in morning-gown and white cap, which is doubtless the troubled spirit of the usurer. In fact, the story has resolved itself into a proverb, and is the origin of that popular saying, so prevalent throughout New England, of "The Devil and Tom Walker."

The Blizzard

Alexander Pushkin

Alexander Pushkin (1799-1837), considered to be the greatest Russian poet ever, belonged to the Romantic era, and wrote the two famous Romantic poems, 'The Captive of the Caucasus' (1822) and 'The Fountain of Bakhchisaray' (1824). His poem 'Ode to Liberty' brought him under the surveillance of the Tsarist regime and his literary radicalism eventually led to his exile from the capital to his mother's rural estate near Pskov in 1820. Besides writing poetry, Pushkin was also well-known for his short stories. 'The Blizzard' is from the famous collection *The Tales of the Late Ivan Petrovich Belkin* (1831).

Near the end of 1811, in the epoch highly memorable to us, there lived in his estate of Nenaradovo the kind Gavrila Gavrilovich R. He was famed throughout all the neighbourhood for his welcoming spirit and cordiality; the neighbours called by at his house every minute: to eat, drink, play Boston at five kopecks per player per hand with his wife, and some — to have a look at their daughter, Marya Gavrilovna, the slender, pale, seventeen-year-old maiden. She was viewed as a wealthy bride, and many destined her for themselves or their sons.

Marya Gavrilovna was brought up on French novels, and, consequently, was in love. The object, chosen by her, was a poor army ensign on leave in his village. It goes without saying, that the young man burned with an equal passion, and that the parents of his ladylove, on noticing their reciprocal affinity, forbade their daughter even to think of him, and him they treated worse than your retired local delegate.

Our lovers held correspondence, and each day they privately met in the pine grove or near the old chapel. There they vowed and declared eternal love for one another, lamented their fate and put forth various imaginings. Thus corresponding and talking, they (what is quite natural) had arrived at the following inference: if we cannot breathe without each other, and the will of the cruel parents interferes with our welfare, then can we not do without it? Certainly, that happy thought first came into the young man's head, and, certainly, Marya Gavrilovna's novel-impelled romantic imagination quite took to it.

Winter came and stopped their rendezvous; but their correspondence became all the livelier for it. Vladimir Nikolayevich implored her in each letter to surrender herself to him, to be wed secretly, to go into hiding for some time, then to throw themselves at the parents' feet, who will, of course, be touched at last by the heroic constancy and wretchedness of the lovers, and will by all means say to them: "Children! Come into our arms."

Marya Gavrilovna long hesitated; a multitude of elopement plans was rejected. At last she consented: on the appointed day she was to refuse supper, and to confine herself to her chamber on the excuse of a headache. Her maid was in it; they were both to go out into the garden by the back porch, and finding the ready sleigh behind the garden, to sit onto the same and go the five versts from Nenaradovo to the little town of Zhadrino, right to the church where Vladimir would presumably have been expecting them by the time.

On the eve of the critical day, Marya Gavrilovna did not sleep all night; she spent it packing up, bundling up her clothes and linen, writing a long letter to one susceptible young lady — her friend — another to her parents. In that last she bade them goodbye in the most touching expressions, excused her transgression by the irrepressible force of passion, and finished by saying that as the most blissful minute of her life would she hold that one, in which she should be allowed to fling herself at the feet of her parents most dear. Having sealed both the letters with a Tula signet bearing two flaming hearts and a suitable motto, she threw herself onto the bed just before dawn and fell into a doze, but even then the horrible dreams awakened her continually. First she dreamt that at the very moment of her getting into the sleigh to be off to the wedding, her father checked her and with excruciating rapidity dragged her across the snow and cast her into a dark and bottomless dungeon...and she fell headlong with an ineffable faintness of heart; at another time she saw Vladimir lying on the grass, pale and bloodstained. Dying, he prayed her in a shrill voice to hurry and be wed to him...some more hideous, senseless visions rushed in front of her one after another. At last she rose, paler than usual and with an unfeigned headache. Her father and mother noted her distress; their tender solicitude and incessant questions — What is the matter with you, Masha? Are you not ill, Masha? — lacerated her heart. She strove to calm them, tried to seem merry, and could not. Evening came. The thought that it was the last time she saw off the day amidst her kindred, oppressed her heart. She was barely alive; she bade goodbye secretly to all the persons and all the objects surrounding her.

Supper was served; her heart throbbed fast. With a faltering voice she declared that she did not wish to have supper, and began saying good night to her father and mother. They kissed her and, as was their custom, blessed her: she nearly wept. On reaching her room she flung herself into an armchair and burst into tears. The maid pleaded with her to calm down and take heart. All was ready. In half an hour Masha would forever part with the fold, her room, a quiet maiden's life... There was a blizzard outside; the wind howled, the shutters shook and rattled; everything boded her threat and ill omen. Soon every thing in the house went quiet and asleep. Masha wrapped herself in her shawl, put on a warm overcoat, and, holding her jewel-box in her hands, came out onto the back porch. The servant carried along her two bundles. They came down into the garden. The snowstorm did not relent; the wind blew contrarily, as if striving to stop the young transgressor. They hardly reached the end of the garden. In the road the sleigh was expecting them. Having grown cold, the horses could not stand still: Vladimir's coachman walked to and fro before the shafts, checking the ardent beasts. He helped the lady and her maid to get in and stow the bundles and the box, took hold of the reins, and the horses flew. Handing over the lady to the solicitude of fate and the skill of Teryoshka the coachman, let us turn to our young lover.

Vladimir spent the whole day riding about. In the morning he visited Zhadrino's priest, could hardly arrange the matter with him; then went to seek witnesses among the neighbouring landowners. The first to receive him, a retired cornet of forty, Dravin, agreed eagerly. This adventure, he assured, reminded him of the old time and the hussars' escapades. He talked Vladimir into staying for dinner and assured him that finding the remaining two witnesses would not be a difficulty. And indeed, right after the dinner there appeared Schmidt, a land-surveyor moustachioed and spur-clad, and a son of the local police captain, a boy of about sixteen years old who only recently enlisted with the uhlans. They not only accepted Vladimir's proposal, but even vowed their readiness to sacrifice their lives for him. Vladimir embraced them with delight and rode home to make preparations.

Twilight had long fallen. He despatched his faithful Teryoshka to Nenaradovo with his own troika and with orders detailed and thorough, and for himself he ordered to prepare a small one-horse sleigh and set off alone without driver to Zhadrino, whereto in about two hours Marya Gavrilovna was expected to have come also. He knew the way well, and it was only a twenty minutes' ride.

But no sooner had Vladimir left the boundaries of the village and found himself in an open field, than the wind rose, and such a blizzard started, as to render him completely blind. In a minute the road was covered up; the whole scope vanished in a turbid yellowish murk bespeckled with the flying hoary lumps of snow; sky blended into earth. Vladimir strayed into the field and vainly tried to gain the road: the horse only stumbled along at random and continually kept mounting the drifts or falling into pits; the sleigh toppled over each minute. Vladimir only strove to keep to the correct direction. But it seemed to him that more than half an hour had passed, and he still did not reach Zhadrino's grove. Another ten minutes or so passed; no grove was to be seen. Vladimir was riding through a field furrowed with deep gullies. The storm did not relent, the sky did not brighten up. The horse was growing weary and Vladimir was dripping with sweat despite his being continually waist-deep in snow.

Finally he saw that he had taken the wrong direction. Vladimir stopped; he began thinking, remembering, inferring, and eventually became assured that he should now steer to the right. He drove right. His horse barely moved. He had been under way for more than an hour now. Zhadrino would not be far. But as he rode, the field kept unfolding before him without end. Only snowdrifts and gullies; every minute the sleigh toppled over, every minute he set it right. More time elapsed; Vladimir was beginning to worry exceedingly.

At last something black loomed aside. Vladimir turned thither. Coming closer, he saw that it was a grove. Thank God, he thought, it cannot be far now. He rode along the grove hoping to get onto a familiar road shortly or to go round the grove: Zhadrino was situated right behind it. Soon he found the road and entered the darkness of the bare winter trees. The wind could not rage here; the road was smooth; the horse cheered up, and Vladimir grew calm.

But as he rode on for a good while, no Zhadrino met his eye; the grove had no end. Vladimir was terrified to realise that he had gone into an unknown forest. Despair engulfed him. He struck the horse; the poor animal seemingly broke into a trot, but got fatigued soon and in a quarter of an hour lapsed into a walking pace again, despite all the efforts of the unfortunate Vladimir.

Little by little the forest became scantier, and presently Vladimir got out of it; no Zhadrino was in sight. It must have been near midnight. Tears rolled from his eyes; he rode at random. The weather had abated, the dark clouds were dispersing; a plain lay before him, bedight with a white undulating carpet. It was quite a clear night. He saw a wisp of a village nearby consisting of four or five homesteads. Vladimir went that way. By the first hut he jumped out of the sleigh, ran up to the window and began knocking. In a few minutes the wooden shutter was raised, and an old man stuck out his grey beard. "What need'st thou?" — "Is Zhadrino far?" — "Zhadrino, eh, now?" — "Yes, yes! Is it far?" — "Not a good deal; can't be more'n ten verst." At this answer Vladimir seized his hair and remained motionless, like someone sentenced to death.

"Whence com'st thou, tell?" the old man spoke on. Vladimir had not the spirit to respond to queries. "Can you get me horses to Zhadrino, my old fellow?" he said. "Horses! We hain't any, not we!" said the muzhik. "Can I not at least have a guide? I will pay what he pleases to ask." — "Stay a minute," said the old man lowering the shutter, "I'll send'ee my son, he'll show thee around." Vladimir started waiting. A minute had not elapsed when he began knocking again. The shutter went up, the beard showed. "What need'st thou?" — "Where is your son, then?" — "He'll be out now, he's getting into his boots. Beest thou cold? Come up in, warm the chill off theeself!" — "Thank you, you just hurry on your son."

The gate creaked; a young fellow with a cudgel came out and went forth, at times leading, at times himself searching for the road buried under the snowdrifts. "What o'clock is it?" Vladimir asked him. "Dawn is about to set in, sooth," the young peasant replied. Vladimir did not utter a single word.

The cocks were crowing, and it was already light when they had reached Zhadrino. The church was locked. Vladimir paid the guide and rode to the priest's house. His troika was not at the yard. What tidings awaited him!

But let us return to the kind landowners of Nenaradovo and look at the goings-on there.

And nothing much to see.

The old couple wakened and came down into the drawing-room. Gavrila Gavrilovich wearing a cap and a flannel jacket, Praskovya Petrovna in a cotton-padded dressing-gown. The samovar was served, and Gavrila Gavrilovich sent a girl to enquire after Marya Gavrilovna: about her health and how well she rested. The girl returned, announcing that the lady said she rested poorly, but that now — she said — she was feeling better, and that she would presently come down. Indeed, the door opened, and Marya Gavrilovna came in to say hello to papa and mama.

"How is your head, Masha?" asked Gavrila Gavrilovich. "It is better, papa," replied Masha. — "Not but what, of yestereven you must have breathed in the poisonous fumes from the fire," said Praskovya Petrovna. — "It may be, mama," replied Masha.

The day passed without trouble, but nearer the night Masha was taken ill. They sent for the town doctor. He arrived at night and found the patient raving. A strong fever opened, and the poor diseased thing was poised on the brink of the grave for two weeks.

Nobody of the house knew about the supposed elopement. The letters that had been written by her, were burned; her maid did not tell anyone anything, fearing her lords' anger. The priest, the retired cornet, the moustachioed land-surveyor, and the little uhlan all held their peace; and deservingly indeed was it known of Teryoshka the coachman that he never let anything improper slip his tongue even when tipsy. And thus it happened that the secret was kept by more than half a dozen conspirators. But Marya Gavrilovna in her incessant ravings herself revealed her mystery. However, her words seemed so incoherent and unrelated to anything, that the mother who did not leave her sickbed, could only gather from them that her daughter was deadly in love with Vladimir Nikolayevich, and that that love was likely to have caused the illness. She consulted her husband and some of the neighbours, and eventually they decided by general consent that, evidently, such was the fate of Marya Gavrilovna, and that you cannot get around your intended on a horse, and that poverty is not a vice, and that you do not marry a man's wealth, and so forth. Moral proverbs come exceedingly useful in those cases when we ourselves have next to nothing original to offer in our defence.

In the meantime the young lady was getting over her illness. Vladimir had long ceased to visit Gavrila Gavrilovich's house: he was scared away by the customary treatment. They decided to send for him and divulge the unexpected fortune: their consent to the marriage. But the bewilderment of the Nenaradovo landowners, when in response to their invitation they received from him a half-mad letter! He declared in it that his foot would never be upon their threshold, and asked them to forget the unfortunate man for whom death remained the only hope. In several days they found out that Vladimir had enlisted in the army. That was in 1812.

For long they dared not reveal the news to the convalescent Masha. She never mentioned Vladimir. Several months later, finding his name among the merited and badly wounded at Borodino, she fainted, and they feared her fever returning. But, thank God, the swoon had no consequence.

Another misfortune came to her: Gavrila Gavrilovich passed away, leaving her the sole heir of the estate. But her inheritance did not comfort her; she sincerely shared poor Praskovya Petrovna's sorrow, swore never to part from her; together they left

Nenaradovo, the place holding the sad memories, and went to live in the estate of —.

Here also the suitors kept around the pretty and wealthy bride, but not to any one of them would she give the slightest sign of hope. Sometimes her mother tried to persuade her to choose a friend; Marya Gavrilovna would shake her head and become thoughtful. Vladimir had ceased to exist: he died in Moscow on the eve of the French occupation. His memory appeared sacred to Masha; at least, she carefully preserved everything that could remind her of him: the books he once read, his drawings, sheets of music, and poems copied by him for her. The neighbours, on learning it all, marvelled at her constancy and expected with curiosity a hero who was destined at last to triumph over the melancholy faithfulness of that virgin Artemisia.

In the meantime the war was gloriously completed. Our regiments were returning from abroad. The folk ran out to meet them. The orchestras played the trophy songs: *Vive Henri-Quatre,* the Tyrolean waltzes, and airs from *Joconde.* Joining the campaign as almost adolescents, the officers now returned, having matured in the air of battle, hung all over with crosses. The soldiers gleefully talked with each other, mixing into their speech some words of German or French all the while. The time unforgettable! The time of glory and delight! The rapid beating of the Russian heart at the word "fatherland"! The sweetest taste of the tears of meeting! The strong unanimity, with which we blended the feelings of being the pride of the folk and our love for the monarch! And for him, what a minute that was!

The women, the Russian women were then splendid like nothing before. Their usual coldness vanished. Their delight was truly ravishing when, on meeting the victors, they cried: "Hooray!"

And threw their caps into the air.

Who of the officers of that time will fail to admit that it was to the Russian woman that he owed his highest and most precious reward?..

At that spectacular time Marya Gavrilovna lived with her mother in the province of — and missed the celebrations in the two capitals on the occasion of our troops returning. However, in the smaller state units and villages the common delight could have been even stronger. The appearance of an officer in those parts was a true triumph for him, and the tail-coated civilian lover was undone by his presence.

We have related that in spite of her coldness, Marya Gavrilovna was still surrounded by applicants. But they all had to fall back when there showed in her castle the wounded hussar colonel Burmin, with St. George in his buttonhole and with "an interesting paleness", as the local young ladies put it. He was about twenty-six years old. He came on leave to his estates which were in the neighbourhood of Marya Gavrilovna's village. Marya Gavrilovna quite distinguished him. In his presence her customary pensiveness was resolved into vigour. One could not say that her bearing was coquettish, but, noting her behaviour, a poet would have said:

"Se amor non è, che dunque?"

Burmin was, in truth, a very nice young man. He had the very sort of mind that women like: the mind of propriety and observation devoid of any claims — a nonchalantly sarcastic mind. His conduct with Marya Gavrilovna was simple and free, but whatever she said or did, his soul and eyes kept following her adherently. He seemed of a quiet and modest temper, but the rumour ran that he used to be a terrible scapegrace, although that did not detract from him in Marya Gavrilovna's opinion of him, who (like all young ladies in general) was glad to excuse the mischief eliciting bravery and mettle.

But more than anything else — more than his tenderness, more than his pleasant conversation, more than his interesting paleness, more than his bandaged arm — the reserve of the young hussar most instigated her curiosity and imagination. She could not have failed to admit that he liked her very much; and likewise he, with his intelligence and experience, should probably have noticed that she distinguished him. How came it then, that she still did not hear his confession and see him kneeling at her feet? What held him? Was it timidity — the unfailing sign of true love — was it pride or a cunning Casanova scheming? That was a mystery to her. Having turned it over carefully in her mind, she decided that timidity was the sole reason for it all, and resolved to encourage him with more attention, or (depending on the circumstances) even tenderness.

She envisaged a dénouement most unforeseen and eagerly looked forward to the minute of the romantic confession. A mystery, whatever its nature, is always oppressive to a woman's heart. Her strategy had had its desired effect; at least, Burmin had grown so thoughtful, and his black eyes caught Marya Gavrilovna with such a fire in them, that the critical minute seemed to be drawing close. The neighbours talked of the wedding as of a solid fact, and the kind Praskovya Petrovna was glad that her daughter had finally found a worthy fiancé.

The good old lady once sat alone in the drawing-room laying out her solitaire, when Burmin entered the room and enquired at once about Marya Gavrilovna. "She is in the garden," the old party replied, "go to her, and I shall expect you here." Burmin went out, and the old lady crossed herself and thought: "I would it happened right today!"

Burmin found Marya Gavrilovna near the pond, under a willow, wearing a white dress and with a book in her hands: a true heroine of a novel. After the formal phrases Marya Gavrilovna had purposely stopped keeping up the conversation, thus increasing the mutual embarrassment which possibly could only be resolved through a sudden and uncompromising confession. And so it happened: Burmin feeling the difficulty of his position, declared that he long sought an occasion to open his heart to her and demanded attention. Marya Gavrilovna shut her book and lowered her glance as a sign of consent.

"I love you," said Burmin, "I love you with all passion..." (Marya Gavrilovna turned red and bowed her head even lower.) "I acted inconsiderately, indulging my sweet habit, the habit of seeing and hearing you daily..." (Marya Gavrilovna recalled the first letter of St. Preux.) "Now it is late to try to defy my fate; the memory of you, your lovely, unsurpassed image will henceforth be my life's torment and joy; but I have also this hard task to fulfil: to reveal to you a terrible mystery and to cast between us an insurmountable obstacle..." — "It has ever existed," interrupted Marya Gavrilovna vigorously, "I could never be your wife..." — "I know," he answered quietly, "I know that you loved once, but the death and the three years full of lamentations... My kind and sweet Marya Gavrilovna!

Do not deprive me of my last comfort: the thought that you would have agreed to make my happiness, if... Do not speak, for God's sake, do not speak. You torment me. Yes, I know, I feel that you would have been mine, but... A miserable wretch am I... I am married!"

Marya Gavrilovna looked at him with surprise.

"I am married," Burmin spoke on, "I have been married those three past years without knowing who my wife is, or where she is, or if I am meant to see her someday!"

"That you should say so!" — Marya Gavrilovna exclaimed, "How strange it is! Carry on, I will tell you later... Do carry on, pray."

"At the beginning of 1812," said Burmin, "I was hastily travelling to Vilna, where our regiment stood. Arriving at a station late one evening, I quickly ordered to get the horses ready as soon as possible, when suddenly a terrible blizzard started, and the station keeper and all the coachmen advised me to wait until it was over. I obeyed, but an unaccountable anxiety took hold of me; someone seemed to be pushing me on, as it were. In the meanwhile the blizzard would not relent; I lost my patience, ordered anon to get the horses ready, and so I rode off into the very rage of the storm. The driver had a mind to go by the river, which way should have saved us three versts of distance. The banks were buried in snow; the driver missed the spot where the road joined, and thus it happened that we found ourselves in an unfamiliar neighbourhood. The snowstorm did not abate; I saw a small light and ordered to steer that way. We arrived at a village; there was light in a wooden church. The church was open, there were several sleighs inside the courtyard; people walked on the parvis. 'Here! Come here!' some voices shouted. I told the driver to come close. 'Mercy, what has been deterring you?' someone told me. 'The bride is barely conscious; the priest does not know what's to be done; we were ready to go back. Do come out quickly.' Silently I jumped out of the sleigh and entered the church faintly lit with two or three candles. A girl sat on a bench in a dark corner; another was rubbing her temples. 'Thank God,' said that latter, 'at last you have come. You've all but tormented the lady into death.' The old priest came up to me with the question of: 'Do you say to begin?' — 'Yes, do begin, father,' I answered distractedly. The girl was stood up. She appeared to me not bad... The inexplicable, unforgivable irresponsibility! I stood by her in front of the lectern; the priest was in a hurry, the three men and the maid supported the bride and were busy with her only. We were wed. 'Kiss now,' they said. My wife turned her pallid face to me. I made to kiss her... She cried: 'Oh, it's not him! 'Tisn't he!' and fainted right clear. The witnesses lifted their frightened eyes onto me. I turned around, walked out of the church with no one hindering me, flung myself into the carriage and shouted 'Go!' "

"My God!" cried Marya Gavrilovna, "And you do not know what happened to your poor wife?"

"I do not," replied Burmin, "I do not know the name of the village where I was wed; I do not remember which station it was that I rode from. At the time I attached so little importance to my criminal prank that, having ridden away from the church, I fell asleep and only awakened on the morning of the next day, and it was a third station that I was passing. The servant accompanying me then has died in a march, so I have not the slightest hope of finding the one who fell victim to my cruel joke, and who has now been avenged so bitterly."

"My God! My good God!" said Marya Gavrilovna, seizing his hand. "So it was you! And you do not recognise me?"

Burmin turned pale...and cast himself at her feet...

The Mortal Immortal

Mary Shelley

Mary Shelley (1797-1851), best-known for the widely acclaimed gothic novel *Frankenstein; or, The Modern Prometheus* (1818) was a renowned English novelist, biographer and short story writer. The daughter of political philosopher William Godwin and feminist writer Mary Wollstonecraft, Shelley was highly educated and infused radical political elements in her works. 'The Mortal Immortal' (1833) is an important short story in the science fiction genre.

July 16, 1833. — This is a memorable anniversary for me; on it I complete my three hundred and twenty-third year!

The Wandering Jew? — Certainly not. More than eighteen centuries have passed over his head. In comparison with him, I am a very young Immortal.

Am I, then, immortal? This is a question which I have asked myself, by day and night, for now three hundred and three years, and yet cannot answer it. I detected a gray hair amidst my brown locks this very day — that surely signifies decay. Yet it may have remained concealed there for three hundred years—for some persons have become entirely white headed before twenty years of age.

I will tell my story, and my reader shall judge for me. I will tell my story, and so contrive to pass some few hours of a long eternity, become so wearisome to me. For ever! Can it be? to live for ever! I have heard of enchantments, in which the victims were plunged into a deep sleep, to wake, after a hundred years, as fresh as ever: I have heard of the Seven Sleepers—thus to be immortal would not be so burthensome: but, oh! the weight of never-ending time—the tedious passage of the still-succeeding hours! How happy was the fabled Nourjahad!...But to my task.

All the world has heard of Cornelius Agrippa. His memory is as immortal as his arts have made me. All the world has also heard of his scholar, who, unawares, raised the foul fiend during his master's absence, and was destroyed by him. The report, true or false, of this accident, was attended with many inconveniences to the renowned philosopher. All his scholars at once deserted him—his servants disappeared. He had no one near him to put coals on his ever-burning fires while he slept, or to attend to the changeful colours of his medicines while he studied. Experiment after experiment failed, because one pair of hands was insufficient to complete them: the dark spirits laughed at him for not being able to retain a single mortal in his service.

I was then very young—very poor—and very much. in love. I had been for about a year the pupil of Cornelius, though I was absent when this accident took place. On my return, my friends implored me not to return to the alchymist's abode. I trembled as I listened to the dire tale they told; I required no second warning; and when Cornelius came and offered me a purse of gold if I would remain under his roof, I felt as if Satan himself tempted me. My teeth chattered—my hair stood on end:—I ran off as fast as my trembling knees would permit.

My failing steps were directed whither for two years they had every evening been attracted—a gently bubbling spring of pure living waters, beside which lingered a dark-haired girl, whose beaming eyes were fixed on the path I was accustomed each night to tread. I cannot remember the hour when I did not love Bertha; we had been neighbours and playmates from infancy—her parents, like mine, were of humble life, yet respectable—our attachment had been a source of pleasure to them. In an evil hour, a malignant fever carried off both her father and mother, and Bertha became an orphan. She would have found a home beneath my paternal roof, but, unfortunately, the old lady of the near castle, rich, childless, and solitary, declared her intention to adopt her. Henceforth Bertha was clad in silk—inhabited a marble palace—and was looked on as being highly favoured by fortune. But in her new situation among her new associates, Bertha remained true to the friend of her humbler days; she often visited the cottage of my father, and when forbidden to go thither, she would stray towards the neighbouring wood, and meet me beside its shady fountain.

She often declared that she owed no duty to her new protectress equal in sanctity to that which bound us. Yet still I was too poor to marry, and she grew weary of being tormented on my account. She had a haughty but an impatient spirit, and grew angry at the obstacles that prevented our union. We met now after an absence, and she had been sorely beset while I was away; she complained bitterly, and almost reproached me for being poor. I replied hastily—

"I am honest, if I am poor!—were I not, I might soon become rich!"

This exclamation produced a thousand questions. I feared to shock her by owning the truth, but she drew it from me; and then, casting a look of disdain on me, she said—

"You pretend to love, and you fear to face the Devil for my sake!"

I protested that I had only dreaded to offend her;—while she dwelt on the magnitude of the reward that I should receive. Thus encouraged— shamed by her—led on by love and hope, laughing at my late fears, with quick steps and a light heart, I returned to accept the offers of the alchymist, and was instantly installed in my office.

A year passed away. I became possessed of no insignificant sum of money. Custom had banished my fears. In spite of the most painful vigilance, I had never detected the trace of a cloven foot; nor was the studious silence of our abode ever disturbed by demoniac howls. I still continued my stolen interviews with Bertha, and Hope dawned on me—Hope—but not perfect joy; for Bertha fancied that love and security were enemies, and her pleasure was to divide them in my bosom. Though true of heart, she was somewhat of a coquette in manner; and I was jealous as a Turk. She slighted me in a thousand ways, yet would never acknowledge herself to be in the wrong. She would drive me mad with anger, and then force me to beg her pardon. Sometimes she fancied that I was not sufficiently submissive, and then she had some story of a rival, favoured by her protectress. She was surrounded by silk-clad youths—the rich and gay—What chance had the sad-robed scholar of Cornelius compared with these?

On one occasion, the philosopher made such large demands upon my time, that I was unable to meet her as I was wont. He was engaged in some mighty work, and I was forced to remain, day and night, feeding his furnaces and watching his chemical preparations. Bertha waited for me in vain at the fountain. Her haughty spirit fired at this neglect; and when at last I stole out during the few short minutes allotted to me for slumber, and hoped to be consoled by her, she received me with disdain, dismissed me in scorn, and vowed that any man should possess her hand rather than he who could not be in two places at once for her sake. She would be revenged! — And truly she was. In my dingy retreat I heard that she had been hunting, attended by Albert Hoffer. Albert Hoffer was favoured by her protectress, and the three passed in cavalcade before my smoky window. Methought that they mentioned my name — it was followed by a laugh of derision, as her dark eyes glanced contemptuously towards my abode.

Jealousy, with all its venom, and all its misery, entered my breast. Now I shed a torrent of tears, to think that I should never call her mine; and, anon, I imprecated a thousand curses on her inconstancy. Yet, still I must stir the fires of the alchymist, still attend on the changes of his unintelligible medicines.

Cornelius had watched for three days and nights, nor closed his eyes. The progress of his alembics was slower than he expected: in spite of his anxiety, sleep weighed upon his eyelids. Again and again he threw off drowsiness with more than human energy; again and again it stole away his senses. He eyed his crucibles wistfully. "Not ready yet," he murmured; "will another night pass before the work is accomplished? Winzy, you are vigilant — you are faithful — you have slept, my boy — you slept last night. Look at that glass vessel. The liquid it contains is of a soft rose-colour: the moment it begins to change its hue, awaken me — till then I may close my eyes. First, it will turn white, and then emit golden flashes; but wait not till then; when the rose-colour fades, rouse me." I scarcely heard the last words, muttered, as they were, in sleep. Even then he did not quite yield to nature. "Winzy, my boy," he again said, "do not touch the vessel — do not put it to your lips; it is a philter — a philter to cure love; you would not cease to love your Bertha — beware to drink!"

And he slept. His venerable head sunk on his breast, and I scarce heard his regular breathing. For a few minutes I watched the vessel — the rosy hue of the liquid remained unchanged. Then my thoughts wandered — they visited the fountain, and dwelt on a thousand charming scenes never to be renewed — never! Serpents and adders were in my heart as the word "Never!" half formed itself on my lips. False girl! — False and cruel! Never more would she smile on me as that evening she smiled on Albert. Worthless, detested woman! I would not remain unrevenged — she should see Albert expire at her feet—she should die beneath my vengeance. She had smiled in disdain and triumph — she knew my wretchedness and her power. Yet what power had she? — the power of exciting my hate — my utter scorn...my...oh, all but indifference! Could I attain that — could I regard her with careless eyes, transferring my rejected love to one fairer and more true, that were indeed a victory!

A bright flash darted before my eyes. I had forgotten the medicine of the adept; I gazed on it with wonder: flashes of admirable beauty, more bright than those which the diamond emits when the sun's rays are on it, glanced from the surface of the liquid; an odour the most fragrant and grateful stole over my sense; the vessel seemed one globe of living radiance, lovely to the eye, and most inviting to the taste. The first thought, instinctively inspired by the grosser sense, was, I will...I must drink. I raised the vessel to my lips. "It will cure me of love...of torture!" Already I had quaffed half of the most delicious liquor ever tasted by the palate of man, when the philosopher stirred. I started...I dropped the glass—the fluid flamed and glanced along the floor, while I felt Cornelius's gripe at my throat, as he shrieked aloud, "Wretch! You have destroyed the labour of my life!"

The philosopher was totally unaware that I had drunk any portion of his drug. His idea was, and I gave a tacit assent to it, that I had raised the vessel from curiosity, and that, frighted at its brightness, and the flashes of intense light it gave forth, I had let it fall. I never undeceived him. The fire of the medicine was quenched—the fragrance died away—he grew calm, as a philosopher should under the heaviest trials, and dismissed me to rest.

I will not attempt to describe the sleep of glory and bliss which bathed my soul in paradise during the remaining hours of that memorable night. Words would be faint and shallow types of my enjoyment, or of the gladness that possessed my bosom when I woke. I trod air—my thoughts were in heaven. Earth appeared heaven, and my inheritance upon it was to be one trance of delight. "This it is to be cured of love," I thought; "I will see Bertha this day, and she will find her lover cold and regardless: too happy to be disdainful, yet how utterly indifferent to her!"

The hours danced away. The philosopher, secure that he had once succeeded, and believing that he might again, began to concoct the same medicine once more. He was shut up with his books and drugs, and I had a holiday. I dressed myself with care; I looked in an old but polished shield, which served me for a mirror; methought my good looks had wonderfully improved. I hurried beyond the precincts of the town, joy in my soul, the beauty of heaven and earth around me. I turned my steps towards the castle—I could look on its lofty turrets with lightness of heart, for I was cured of love. My Bertha saw me afar off, as I came up the avenue. I know not what sudden impulse animated her bosom, but at the sight, she sprung with a light fawn-like bound down the marble steps, and was hastening towards me. But I had been perceived by another person. The old high-born hag, who called herself her protectress, and was her tyrant, had seen me, also; she hobbled, panting, up the terrace; a page, as ugly as herself, held up her train, and fanned her as she hurried along, and stopped my fair girl with a "How, now, my bold mistress? Whither so fast? Back to your cage—hawks are abroad!"

Bertha clasped her hands—her eyes were still bent on my approaching figure. I saw the contest. How I abhorred the old crone who checked the kind impulses of my Bertha's softening heart. Hitherto, respect for her rank had caused me to avoid the lady of the castle; now I disdained such trivial considerations. I was cured of love, and lifted above all human fears; I hastened forwards, and soon reached the terrace. How lovely Bertha looked! her eyes flashing fire, her cheeks glowing with impatience and anger, she was a thousand times more graceful and charming than ever—I no longer loved—Oh! no, I adored—worshipped—idolised her!

She had that morning been persecuted, with more than usual vehemence, to consent to an immediate marriage with my rival.

She was reproached with the encouragement that she had shown him—she was threatened with being turned out of doors with disgrace and shame. Her proud spirit rose in arms at the threat; but when she remembered the scorn that she had heaped upon me, and how, perhaps, she had thus lost one whom she now regarded as her only friend, she wept with remorse and rage. At that moment I appeared. "O, Winzy!" she exclaimed, "take me to your mother's cot; swiftly let me leave the detested luxuries and wretchedness of this noble dwelling—take me to poverty and happiness."

I clasped her in my arms with transport. The old lady was speechless with fury, and broke forth into invective only when we were far on our road to my natal cottage. My mother received the fair fugitive, escaped from a gilt cage to nature and liberty, with tenderness and joy; my father, who loved her, welcomed her heartily; it was a day of rejoicing, which did not need the addition of the celestial potion of the alchymist to steep me in delight.

Soon after this eventful day, I became the husband of Bertha. I ceased to be the scholar of Cornelius, but I continued his friend. I always felt grateful to him for having, unawares, procured me that delicious draught of a divine elixir, which, instead of curing me of love (sad cure! Solitary and joyless remedy for evils which seem blessings to the memory), had inspired me with courage and resolution, thus winning for me an inestimable treasure in my Bertha.

I often called to mind that period of trance-like inebriation with wonder. The drink of Cornelius had not fulfilled the task for which he affirmed that it had been prepared, but its effects were more potent and blissful than words can express.

They had faded by degrees, yet they lingered long—and painted life in hues of splendour. Bertha often wondered at my lightness of heart and unaccustomed gaiety; for, before, I had been rather serious, or even sad, in my disposition. She loved me the better for my cheerful temper, and our days were winged by joy.

Five years afterwards I was suddenly summoned to the bedside of the dying Cornelius. He had sent for me in haste, conjuring my instant presence. I found him stretched on his pallet, enfeebled even to death; all of life that yet remained animated his piercing eyes, and they were fixed on a glass vessel, full of a roseate liquid.

"Behold," he said, in a broken and inward voice, "the vanity of human wishes! a second time my hopes are about to be crowned, a second time they are destroyed. Look at that liquor—you remember five years ago I had prepared the same, with the same success;—then, as now, my thirsting lips expected to taste the immortal elixir—you dashed it from me! and at present it is too late."

He spoke with difficulty, and fell back on his pillow. I could not help saying—

"How, revered master, can a cure for love restore you to life?"

A faint smile gleamed across his face as I listened earnestly to his scarcely intelligible answer. "A cure for love and for all things—the Elixir of Immortality. Ah! if now I might drink, I should live for ever!"

As he spoke, a golden flash gleamed from the fluid; a well-remembered fragrance stole over the air; he raised himself, all weak as he was— strength seemed miraculously to re-enter his frame—he stretched forth his hand—a loud explosion startled me—a ray of fire shot up from the elixir, and the glass vessel which contained it was shivered to atoms! I turned my eyes towards the philosopher; he had fallen back—his eyes were glassy—his features rigid—he was dead!

But I lived, and was to live for ever! So said the unfortunate alchymist, and for a few days I believed his words. I remembered the glorious drunkenness that had followed my stolen draught. I reflected on the change I had felt in my frame—in my soul. The bounding elasticity of the one—the buoyant lightness of the other. I surveyed myself in a mirror, and could perceive no change in my features during the space of the five years which had elapsed. I remembered the radiant hues and grateful scent of that delicious beverage—worthy the gift it was capable of bestowing…I was, then, IMMORTAL!

A few days after I laughed at my credulity. The old proverb, that "a prophet is least regarded in his own country," was true with respect to me and my defunct master. I loved him as a man—I respected him as a sage—but I derided the notion that he could command the powers of darkness, and laughed at the superstitious fears with which he was regarded by the vulgar. He was a wise philosopher, but had no acquaintance with any spirits but those clad in flesh and blood. His science was simply human; and human science, I soon persuaded myself, could never conquer nature's laws so far as to imprison the soul for ever within its carnal habitation. Cornelius had brewed a soul-refreshing drink—more inebriating than wine—sweeter and more fragrant than any fruit: it possessed probably strong medicinal powers, imparting gladness to the heart and vigor to the limbs; but its effects would wear out; already were they diminished in my frame. I was a lucky fellow to have quaffed health and joyous spirits, and perhaps long life, at my master's hands; but my good fortune ended there: longevity was far different from immortality.

I continued to entertain this belief for many years. Sometimes a thought stole across me—Was the alchymist indeed deceived? But my habitual credence was, that I should meet the fate of all the children of Adam at my appointed time—a little late, but still at a natural age. Yet it was certain that I retained a wonderfully youthful look. I was laughed at for my vanity in consulting the mirror so often, but I consulted it in vain—my brow was untrenched—my cheeks—my eyes—my whole person continued as untarnished as in my twentieth year.

I was troubled. I looked at the faded beauty of Bertha—I seemed more like her son. By degrees our neighbours began to make similar observations, and I found at last that I went by the name of the Scholar bewitched. Bertha herself grew uneasy. She became jealous and peevish, and at length she began to question me. We had no children; we were all in all to each other; and though, as she grew older, her vivacious spirit became a little allied to ill-temper, and her beauty sadly diminished, I cherished her in my heart as the mistress I had idolized, the wife I had sought and won with such perfect love.

At last our situation became intolerable: Bertha was fifty—I twenty years of age. I had, in very shame, in some measure adopted the habits of a more advanced age; I no longer mingled in the dance among the young and gay, but my heart bounded along with them while I restrained my feet; and a sorry figure I cut among the Nestors of our village. But before the time I mention, things were altered—we were universally shunned; we were—at least, I was—reported to have kept up an iniquitous acquaintance with some of my former master's supposed friends. Poor Bertha was pitied, but deserted. I was regarded with horror and detestation.

What was to be done? we sat by our winter fire—poverty had made itself felt, for none would buy the produce of my farm; and often I had been forced to journey twenty miles, to some place where I was not known, to dispose of our property. It is true we had saved something for an evil day—that day was come.

We sat by our lone fireside—the old-hearted youth and his antiquated wife. Again Bertha insisted on knowing the truth; she recapitulated all she had ever heard said about me, and added her own observations. She conjured me to cast off the spell; she described how much more comely grey hairs were than my chestnut locks; she descanted on the reverence and respect due to age—how preferable to the slight regard paid to mere children: could I imagine that the despicable gifts of youth and good looks outweighed disgrace, hatred, and scorn? Nay, in the end I should be burnt as a dealer in the black art, while she, to whom I had not deigned to communicate any portion of my good fortune, might be stoned as my accomplice. At length she insinuated that I must share my secret with her, and bestow on her like benefits to those I myself enjoyed, or she would denounce me—and then she burst into tears.

Thus beset, methought it was the best way to tell the truth. I revealed it as tenderly as I could, and spoke only of a very long life, not of immortality—which representation, indeed, coincided best with my own ideas. When I ended, I rose and said,

"And now, my Bertha, will you denounce the lover of your youth? — You will not, I know. But it is too hard, my poor wife, that you should suffer from my ill-luck and the accursed arts of Cornelius. I will leave you—you have wealth enough, and friends will return in my absence. I will go; young as I seem, and strong as I am, I can work and gain my bread among strangers, unsuspected and unknown. I loved you in youth; God is my witness that I would not desert you in age, but that your safety and happiness require it."

I took my cap and moved towards the door; in a moment Bertha's arms were round my neck, and her lips were pressed to mine. "No, my husband, my Winzy," she said, "you shall not go alone—take me with you; we will remove from this place, and, as you say, among strangers we shall be unsuspected and safe. I am not so very old as quite to shame you, my Winzy; and I dare say the charm will soon wear off, and, with the blessing of God, you will become more elderly-looking, as is fitting; you shall not leave me."

I returned the good soul's embrace heartily. "I will not, my Bertha; but for your sake I had not thought of such a thing. I will be your true, faithful husband while you are spared to me, and do my duty by you to the last."

The next day we prepared secretly for our emigration. We were obliged to make great pecuniary sacrifices—it could not be helped. We realised a sum sufficient, at least, to maintain us while Bertha lived; and, without saying adieu to any one, quitted our native country to take refuge in a remote part of western France.

It was a cruel thing to transport poor Bertha from her native village, and the friends of her youth, to a new country, new language, new customs. The strange secret of my destiny rendered this removal immaterial to me; but I compassionated her deeply, and was glad to perceive that she found compensation for her misfortunes in a variety of little ridiculous circumstances. Away from all tell-tale chroniclers, she sought to decrease the apparent disparity of our ages by a thousand feminine arts—rouge, youthful dress, and assumed juvenility of manner. I could not be angry— Did not I myself wear a mask? Why quarrel with hers, because it was less successful? I grieved deeply when I remembered that this was my Bertha, whom I had loved so fondly, and won with such transport—the dark eyed, dark-haired girl, with smiles of enchanting archness and a step like a fawn—this mincing, simpering, jealous old woman. I should have revered her gray locks and withered cheeks; but thus!…It was my, work, I knew; but I did not the less deplore this type of human weakness.

Her jealousy never slept. Her chief occupation was to discover that, in spite of outward appearances, I was myself growing old. I verily believe that the poor soul loved me truly in her heart, but never had woman so tormenting a mode of displaying fondness. She would discern wrinkles in my face and decrepitude in my walk, while I bounded along in youthful vigour, the youngest looking of twenty youths. I never dared address another woman: on one occasion, fancying that the belle of the village regarded me with favouring eyes, she bought me a gray wig. Her constant discourse among her acquaintances was, that though I looked so young, there was ruin at work within my frame; and she affirmed that the worst symptom about me was my apparent health. My youth was a disease, she said, and I ought at all times to prepare, if not for a sudden and awful death, at least to awake some morning white-headed, and bowed down with all the marks of advanced years. I let her talk—I often joined in her conjectures. Her warnings chimed in with my never-ceasing speculations concerning my state, and I took an earnest, though painful, interest in listening to all that her quick wit and excited imagination could say on the subject.

Why dwell on these minute circumstances? We lived on for many long years. Bertha became bed-rid and paralytic: I nursed her as mother might a child. She grew peevish, and still harped upon one string—of how long I should survive her. It has ever been a source of consolation to me, that I performed my duty scrupulously towards her. She had been mine in youth, she was mine in age, and at last, when I heaped the sod over her corpse, I wept to feel that I had lost all that really bound me to humanity.

Since then how many have been my cares and woes, how few and empty my enjoyments! I pause here in my history—I will pursue it no further. A sailor without rudder or compass, tossed on a stormy sea—a traveller lost on a widespread heath, without landmark or starto him—such have I been: more lost, more hopeless than either. A nearing ship, a gleam from some far cot, may save them; but I have no beacon except the hope of death.

Death! Mysterious, ill-visaged friend of weak humanity! Why alone of all mortals have you cast me from your sheltering fold? O, for the peace of the grave! The deep silence of the iron-bound tomb! That thought would cease to work in my brain, and my heart beat no more with emotions varied only by new forms of sadness!

Am I immortal? I return to my first question. In the first place, is it not more probable that the beverage of the alchymist was fraught rather with longevity than eternal life? Such is my hope. And then be it remembered that I only drank half of the potion prepared by him. Was not the whole necessary to complete the charm? To have drained half the Elixir of Immortality is but to be half immortal—my Forever is thus truncated and null.

But again, who shall number the years of the half of eternity? I often try to imagine by what rule the infinite may be divided. Sometimes I fancy age advancing upon me. One gray hair I have found. Fool! Do I lament? Yes, the fear of age and death often creeps coldly into my heart; and the more I live, the more I dread death, even while I abhor life. Such an enigma is man—born to perish—when he wars, as I do, against the established laws of his nature.

But for this anomaly of feeling surely I might die: the medicine of the alchymist would not be proof against fire—sword—and the strangling waters. I have gazed upon the blue depths of many a placid lake, and the tumultuous rushing of many a mighty river, and have said, peace inhabits those waters; yet I have turned my steps away, to live yet another day. I have asked myself, whether suicide would be a crime in one to whom thus only the portals of the other world could be opened. I have done all, except presenting myself as a soldier or duellist, an object of destruction to my—no, not my fellow-mortals, and therefore I have shrunk away. They are not my fellows. The inextinguishable power of life in my frame, and their ephemeral existence, place us wide as the poles asunder. I could not raise a hand against the meanest or the most powerful among them.

Thus I have lived on for many a year—alone, and weary of myself—desirous of death, yet never dying—a mortal immortal. Neither ambition nor avarice can enter my mind, and the ardent love that gnaws at my heart, never to be returned—never to find an equal on which to expend itself—lives there only to torment me.

This very day I conceived a design by which I may end all—without self-slaughter, without making another man a Cain—an expedition, which mortal frame can never survive, even endued with the youth and strength that inhabits mine. Thus I shall put my immortality to the test, and rest for ever—or return, the wonder and benefactor of the human species.

Before I go, a miserable vanity has caused me to pen these pages. I would not die, and leave no name behind. Three centuries have passed since I quaffed the fatal beverage: another year shall not elapse before, encountering gigantic dangers—warring with the powers of frost in their home—beset by famine, toil, and tempest—I yield this body, too tenacious a cage for a soul which thirsts for freedom, to the destructive elements of air and water—or, if I survive, my name shall be recorded as one of the most famous among the sons of men; and, my task achieved, I shall adopt more resolute means, and, by scattering and annihilating the atoms that compose my frame, set at liberty the life imprisoned within, and so cruelly prevented from soaring from this dim earth to a sphere more congenial to its immortal essence.

The Purloined Letter

Edgar Allan Poe

Edgar Allan Poe (1809-1849), a famous American poet, critic and short story writer, was the master of horror stories and science fiction tales. His powers of ratiocination were unparalleled in America. 'The Purloined Letter' (1844) features C. Auguste Dupin, the genius fictional detective from some of Poe's most popular stories, including 'The Murders In The Rue Morgue' (1841), his seminal work that remains influential even today.

I

The Search For The Letter

It was just after dark one windy evening in the autumn of 18. I was with my friend C. Auguste Dupin, in the library of his Paris apartment. For one hour at least we had been sitting in profound silence. Dupin seemed content just to watch the smoke rising from his pipe. As for myself, I was thinking about the affair of the Rue Morgue. More particularly I was thinking about how quickly Dupin had solved the case when the police could do nothing. It was therefore something of a coincidence when our old acquaintance Monsieur G of the Paris police arrived at the door.

G. explained that he had called to consult us, or rather to ask the opinion of my friend, about some official business that had caused a great deal of trouble.

"And what is the difficulty now?" I asked. "No more murders, I hope?"

"Oh no, nothing like that. The fact is, the business is very simple indeed, and I am sure we can manage it ourselves. But I thought

Dupin would like to hear the details of the case, because it is so very odd."

"Simple and odd." said Dupin.

"Yes, in a way, though not exactly. The fact is, we have all been extremely puzzled because the affair is so simple and yet... we cannot understand it."

"Perhaps it is the very simplicity of the case which you do not understand," said my friend.

"What nonsense you talk sometimes, Monsieur Dupin," said the Prefect, laughing.

"Perhaps the mystery is a little too simple," Dupin continued.

"Oh good heavens! What an absurd idea!"

"A little too obvious."

"Ha! Ha! Ha!" laughed our visitor, deeply amused by Dupin's suggestion.

"And what after all is this business all about?" I asked.

"I will tell you in a few words," said the Prefect of police, "but before I begin I must warn you that this affair demands the greatest secrecy. If anybody knew that I was telling you about it, I would probably lose my job."

"Proceed," I said.

"Well then, I have received personal information from a very high official that a certain document of the utmost importance has been purloined from the royal apartments. The individual who took it is known; he was seen to take it. It is also known that he still has the document."

"How do you know this?" asked Dupin.

"We know, because of the nature of the document, and because if it had passed out of the robber's possession it would have certain... ahem... 'dramatic' consequences. Since these consequences have not yet arrived, we can assume that the robber still has the document."

"Can't you be a little more explicit?" I said.

The policeman hesitated for a minute.

"If this document were revealed to a third person, an exalted personage whom I cannot name, it would cause grave damage to the honour and reputation of its owner, who is herself an important royal personage. This fact gives the robber power over her. He can use the document as a form of blackmail."

"But this power would depend on the robber knowing that the owner of the letter knew he had taken it."

"The thief," said G. "is the Minister D, an unscrupulous individual. The method of the theft was ingenious. The document, it is a letter to be honest, had been received by the royal personage while she was alone in the royal bedroom. As she was reading it, she was suddenly interrupted by the entrance of her husband, the other personage I mentioned before, the person that she wanted to conceal it from. She tried to throw the letter into a drawer, without success, and so she was forced to lay it, open as it was, on a table. Fortunately only the side with the address on it was visible and so the letter was not noticed. It was then that the Minister D entered. His sharp eye immediately perceived the letter and recognised the address. When he saw the anxious state of its owner, he knew at once her secret. After some routine business transactions, he produced from his pocket a letter similar to the one lying on the table and opened it, pretending to read the contents. He then casually placed his letter next to the one on the table and continued conversing with the lady and her husband about political matters. Then just before leaving the room he took the lady's letter from the table. Of course she saw him take it but she could say nothing. Her husband was standing next to her, and naturally she did not want him to know about the letter. And so the minister left the room with the vital document in his pocket, leaving his own letter, which was of no importance, upon the table."

"So it is true," said Dupin. "The robber knows that his victim saw him take the letter. He has her in his power."

"Yes," said the Prefect of Police. "And for the last few months he has been using that power for political purposes, to a very dangerous extent. The lady who was robbed is now convinced that she must get the letter back. But this cannot be done openly. That is why she has put me in charge of the case."

"Quite right," said Dupin, through the smoke. "I cannot imagine that the Paris police has a better agent."

"You flatter me," said the Prefect, "but perhaps there is some truth in what you say."

"It is clear," said I, "that the minister still has the letter in his possession. If he used it it would no longer give him any power."

"True," said G. "and that is why I decided to conduct a meticulous search of the minister's house. The problem was how to search without his knowledge. It would be extremely dangerous if he realized we were looking for the letter. Fortunately for us the minister is often absent from home all night, and he does not have many servants. The servants' bedroom is quite far from the minister's rooms, and the servants are usually drunk at night.

"As you know, I have keys which can open any room or cabinet in Paris. So every night for the last three months we have been searching his house. But after all our efforts I must now conclude that the minister is a more astute individual than I am. I can assure you that we have investigated every corner of the premises, every little space where it would be possible to conceal the letter, but still we cannot find it."

"But is it not possible," I said, "that he has hidden it somewhere else, somewhere other than his own house?"

"No, I don't think that's very likely," said Dupin. "He needs to have the document near to him. It must be instantly available so that he can produce it whenever it becomes necessary to do so."

"If that is the case, then the letter must be somewhere in the minister's house. For it is not possible that it is on his person."

"Absolutely not," said the Prefect of Police. "My men have stopped and searched him twice under my own supervision."

"Obviously the man is not a complete fool," said Dupin. "He surely knew that he would be searched."

"Not a complete fool, no," said G. "But he is a poet, which I consider to be only one grade higher than a fool."

"Tell us the details of your search," I said.

"Well, we took our time and we searched everywhere. I have a lot of experience in these matters. We divided the building into its separate rooms and for each of these rooms we spent an entire week searching. First we examined the furniture. We opened every possible drawer. To a well-trained police officer the existence of a secret drawer is impossible: there is only a certain amount of space in each cabinet. After the cabinets we examined the chairs. We probed the cushions with long needles. Then we removed the tops from the tables."

"Why did you do that?"

"Sometimes a person who wishes to conceal a document removes the top of a table and excavates one of the legs. He then pushes the document into the cavity and replaces the top. The bottoms and tops of bedposts are used in the same way."

"But you could not possibly remove, you could not dismantle all the pieces of furniture in which it would be possible to hide a letter. A letter can be rolled into a thin spiral tube, no thicker than a knitting needle. In this form it could be inserted into the rung of a chair for example. You did not dismantle all the chairs?"

"Certainly not; but we did better, we examined the rungs of every chair in the house, and indeed the jointings of every other piece of furniture, with the help of a very powerful microscope. If there had been any changes in the jointings, any disorder in the glueing, we would have noticed it immediately."

"I presume you looked at the mirrors, between the frames and the glass plates, and also the beds and bedclothes as well as the curtains and carpets?"

"Of course; and when we had finished examining the furniture we searched the house itself. We divided its surface into numbered compartments; then we scrutinized each individual square centimetre of the house, and also of the two adjoining houses."

"The two adjoining houses!" I exclaimed. "You must have had a great deal of trouble."

"Yes we had, but the reward for finding the letter is very high."

"You included the grounds around the houses?"

"All the grounds are paved with brick. It was easy to search them. We simply had to check that the grass between the bricks was undisturbed."

"Of course you looked through papers and examined his books."

"Certainly: we opened every file and turned over every page of every book. We also measured the thickness of each book cover and examined the bindings with the microscope. If any of the bindings had been altered in any way we would have noticed."

"You explored the floors beneath the carpets."

"Yes. We removed every carpet and examined the floorboards with the microscope."

"And the wallpaper?"

"Yes."

"You looked in the cellars?"

"Yes we did."

"Then." I said, "you have made a miscalculation and the letter is not in the house."

"I think you are right," said the Prefect. "And now Dupin, what do you think I should do?"

"I think you should search the house again."

"That would be absolutely pointless," said the Prefect. "I tell you, as sure as I live and breathe, the letter is not in the house."

"I have no better advice to give you," said Dupin. "I presume you have an accurate description of the letter."

"Oh yes!" said the Prefect. He took a notebook out of his pocket and began to read a detailed account of the internal, and especially of the external appearance of the stolen document. Soon afterwards, he thanked us for our time and left the apartment. He looked more depressed than I had ever seen him before.

II

Dupin's Techniques

About a month later, the Prefect paid us another visit. He found us occupied in the same manner as before. He sat down and began talking about the general business of the week.

After a few minutes I interrupted him:

"Well, but G, what about the Purloined Letter?"

The Prefect's face turned pale.

"I searched the house again, as Dupin suggested, but it was a waste of time, as I knew it would be."

"How much was the reward offered, did you say?" asked Dupin.

"A very large reward, a very liberal reward, I don't like to say how much; but I will say one thing, that I would give my own cheque for fifty thousand francs to anyone who could give me that letter. The fact is, the matter is becoming more and more urgent every day;

the reward has recently been doubled. But even if it were trebled I could do no more than I have done already."

"Do you think so?" said Dupin. "I think, that there is some more that you could do to find the letter, eh?"

"How? In what way?"

"You might, for example, take advice."

"My dear sir, I would happily pay for such advice. I would really give my fifty thousand francs to anyone who could help me."

"In that case," replied Dupin, "you can write me a cheque now. When you have signed it, I will give you the letter."

I was astonished. The Prefect appeared absolutely incredulous. For some minutes he remained silent and motionless, looking at my friend with open mouth and eyes that seemed to jump out from their sockets. Then he suddenly took a pen and after some hesitation signed a cheque for fifty thousand francs and gave it to Dupin. Dupin quickly examined the cheque and put it in his wallet. Then he opened a drawer in his desk and took a letter from it which he gave to the Prefect. The Prefect looked at the letter. His face was a perfect agony of joy as he opened it and quickly scanned its contents. Without saying another word, he ran out of the apartment still holding the letter in his hand.

When he had gone, Dupin began to explain.

"The Parisian police," he said, "are very capable in their way. They are persevering and ingenious and they know their job well.

When G recounted to us his mode of searching D's house, I was sure he had made a satisfactory investigation in as far as he was able."

"In as far as he was able?" I said.

"Yes. The techniques he used were not only the best of their kind, they were also executed to absolute perfection. If the letter had been hidden within the limits of G's search, he would certainly have discovered it."

I laughed, but Dupin seemed quite serious in all he was saying.

"The techniques," he continued, "were the best of their kind and were well executed. The problem was that they were not suitable for this case. They could not be applied to this particular thief. The Prefect has a set of extremely ingenious resources and he thinks he can use them to solve every single case in the same way.

But he continually makes the mistake of being either too deep or too superficial, for the case in question; there are many schoolboys who are better thinkers than he is. I knew one about eight years of age who had great success in the game of 'even or odd'. This game is simple and is played with marbles. One player holds in his hand a number of marbles and asks the other player whether the number is even or odd. If his guess is right, the guesser wins one: if he is wrong he loses one. The boy I refer to won all the marbles of the school. Of course he had a principle which he used to make his guesses. He observed and measured the intelligence of his opponents. For example, let's imagine his opponent is a complete idiot. The idiot holds up his closed hand and asks the boy 'are they even or odd?' Our schoolboy replies 'odd' and loses; but the next time he wins. How does he do this? He simply says to himself, 'The idiot had them even the first time and his amount of intelligence is just sufficient to make him change them to odd the second time.' So he guesses odd and wins. Now with an idiot a degree more intelligent than the first he would reason like this: 'This boy sees that the first time I guess odd. Now the second time he will immediately propose a simple variation from even to odd, like the first idiot did.' But then a second thought will tell him that this variation is too simple, and finally he will decide to keep the marbles even as before. 'I will therefore guess even,' he guesses even and wins. And so on. Now this method of reasoning which the other boys call 'luck,' what is it exactly?"

"It is simply a question of the boy trying to think like his opponent," I said.

"Precisely," said Dupin. "The boy identifies himself with his opponent's intellect."

"And the success of this identification depends on how accurately he can measure the intellect of his opponent?"

"Yes, for its practical value it depends on this," replied Dupin. "This is where the Prefect and his men make the mistake. They do not identify themselves with the intellect of their opponent. They do not even try to measure his intellect. They consider only their own ideas of ingenuity; and in searching for anything hidden, they consider only the ways in which they would have hidden it.

In part they are right to do so, for their ingenuity is an accurate representation of that of the mass; but when the intelligence of the thief is greater than their own, and often when it is lower, their investigations fail. They have no variation in principle in their methods. The most they ever do is to extend or exaggerate these old methods, without considering the principles on which they are based. Let's look at the case of D. What did G do to vary the principle of action? What is all this drilling and probing and sounding and scrutinizing with the microscope and dividing the building into numbered square centimetres? It is simply the exaggeration of the application of one set of principles, which are based on the Prefect's own ideas about human ingenuity. He thinks that all men will hide a letter in the same way, not necessarily inside the leg of a chair, but in some place which is equally difficult to reach. But such hiding places are imagined only by ordinary intellects. In all cases of concealment, it is presumed that the article will be concealed in a place which is hard to find. Thus its discovery depends not upon the intelligence of the seekers but upon their patience, perseverance and determination. You will now understand what I meant when I said that the Prefect would surely have found the letter if it had been placed within the limits of his examination, in other words, if the principle of its concealment was the same as the principle of the Prefect's investigation. But the Prefect has been mystified, and the reason for his defeat is that he believes the minister to be a fool, simply because he is a poet. The Prefect thinks: all fools are poets, but that does riot mean that all poets are necessarily fools!"

"I thought it was the minister's brother who was the poet. The minister is a mathematician, isn't he?"

"No, he is both a mathematician and a poet. If he were just a mathematician he would not be able to reason well, and the Prefect would have found the letter."

"You surprise me when you say this. Mathematical reason has for centuries been regarded as the greatest form of reason."

"That is what mathematicians have made us believe, but it is an error."

"Explain."

"Mathematical axioms are not axioms of general truth, but only of relation. And something which may be true for relation, of form and quantity for example, is often completely false in terms of morality, or of human nature in general. To put it simply, in human nature the sum of the parts is rarely equal to the whole. In life, there is always something more, some unpredictable element that cannot be reduced to an equation."

"Whatever do you mean?" I said, laughing. By now I was completely confused.

"I mean to say," said Dupin, "that if the minister had been only a mathematician, the Prefect would have been able to keep the fifty thousand francs for himself. He would certainly have found the letter. But I knew the minister was also a poet. And so I tried to think like him, considering the circumstances he was in.

"Go on," I said.

"Remember that this man is a clever politician. He obviously knew the normal police procedures. He knew he would be searched and I'm sure he also knew that the police would search his house. The Prefect said that he was fortunate that the minister was often absent from the house at night. But I think that the minister was deliberately absent. He wanted the Prefect to search the house. It was all part of his plan. He wanted to make the police think that the letter was not in the house. So he let them search it from top to bottom. Finding nothing, the police would be convinced that the letter was not there. The minister must have known how the police conducted their searches. He must have known that the police would examine all the normal hiding places, all the places the Prefect told us about. So obviously he could not hide the letter in any of these places. I realized that because of this he would be forced to choose simplicity as the principle for hiding the letter. You remember how the Prefect laughed when I suggested that the problem of the mystery was perhaps the fact that it was too obvious."

"Yes," said I, "I remember it well."

"There is a game," Dupin said, "which is played on a map. One of the players tells another to find a given word on the map, it could be the name of a town or a river or a monument, any word that appears on the map. Now a beginner immediately seeks the most difficult names with the most complicated spelling; but the expert selects those simple words which appear in huge letters and which stretch from one end of the map to the other. These, like street signs, are written in big letters, but they escape our attention, precisely because they are so excessively obvious. We simply don't see them."

"But what is the connection between this and the minister?"

"What is true of the physical world is also true of the moral world. This is something the Prefect cannot understand. He never once considered that the minister might have placed the letter right under his very nose, that he had perhaps hidden it in a very visible place, where nobody would think of looking for it. Or that perhaps the best way to hide the letter was not to hide it at all."

III
The Solution Of The Case

With these ideas in my head I went to visit the minister at his house. I wore a pair of special green spectacles to aid my vision. As the minister told me about the political business of the day, I scrutinized his large writing table on which lay several papers and letters, as well as one or two books. But there was no trace of the purloined letter itself.

"As my eyes circled around the room I noticed a card-rack hanging from the centre of the mantlepiece. In this rack, which had five or six compartments, were a few visiting cards and a solitary letter. The letter was very soiled and crumpled and it was torn at the edge. It seemed as if someone had decided to tear it up but had then changed their mind. I looked closer to see what was written on it. It was addressed to the minister himself in female handwriting. The letter had been thrown carelessly into one of the compartments.

"I knew immediately that this was the letter I was looking for. Certainly its appearance was completely different from the description of the stolen letter that the Prefect had given us. The wax seal of this letter was large and black with D's insignia inscribed on it, where as the purloined letter had a small red seal bearing the coat of arms of the Royal Family. This letter was addressed to D in a small female hand. The writing on the purloined letter was large and bold and it was addressed to a lady. But it seemed to me that these differences were excessive. The fact that this letter was almost the opposite of the letter the Prefect described made me suspicious. Then there was the fact that this letter was so clearly visible, in full view of every visitor. So visible, in fact, that nobody would see it, just like in the game I told you about."

"So what did you do?"

"I memorised the appearance of the letter and left the minister's house immediately, leaving a gold tobacco box on the writing table.

"The next morning I called at the minister's house again, saying that I had forgotten my tobacco. The minister seemed happy to see me again and we continued the conversation we had had the previous day. Suddenly we heard a loud noise coming from outside, the sound of a pistol shot followed by several screams. D ran to the window to see what was happening. In the meantime I went over to the card rack, took the letter, put it in my pocket and replaced it with a facsimile. "The disturbance in the street had been caused by a man with a gun. He had fired it above the heads of the crowd and everybody thought he was simply a lunatic or a drunk. In fact I had employed him to carry out this diversion to distract D and give me time to get the letter."

"But why didn't you simply take it on your first visit?"

D replied Dupin, "is a desperate and dangerous man. If I had taken the letter openly he would probably have had me killed before I could leave the building. But there was another reason. For eighteen months the minister has had the owner of the letter in his power. Now the situation is reversed. She has him in her power."

"How is that?"

"Because he still thinks he has the letter, thanks to my facsimile. He will proceed with his blackmail and his political career will be destroyed. It's ironic in a way too."

"In what way?"

"It was the minister who gave me the idea of the facsimile, when he stole the original letter. To get the letter back I just did the same thing he did when he stole it. You could even say that between our letters there is a perfect, ahem...correspondence."

"Very funny."

Bartleby, The Scrivener: A Story Of Wall Street

Herman Melville

Herman Melville (1819-1891), best known for his masterpiece, *Moby Dick* (1851), was an American novelist, poet and short story writer. Considered one of America's greatest writers today, he barely won much acclaim during his lifetime. 'Bartleby, The Scrivener' (1853) was written in the latter part of his writing career, and reflects the materialism and moral degradation of American society in the 19th century.

I am a rather elderly man. The nature of my avocations for the last thirty years has brought me into more than ordinary contact with what would seem an interesting and somewhat singular set of men, of whom as yet nothing that I know of has ever been written:—I mean the law-copyists or scriveners. I have known very many of them, professionally and privately, and if I pleased, could relate divers histories, at which good-natured gentlemen might smile, and sentimental souls might weep. But I waive the biographies of all other scriveners for a few passages in the life of Bartleby, who was a scrivener of the strangest I ever saw or heard of. While of other law-copyists I might write the complete life, of Bartleby nothing of that sort can be done. I believe that no materials exist for a full and satisfactory biography of this man. It is an irreparable loss to literature. Bartleby was one of those beings of whom nothing is ascertainable, except from the original sources, and in his case those are very small. What my own astonished eyes saw of Bartleby, that is all I know of him, except, indeed, one vague report which will appear in the sequel.

Ere introducing the scrivener, as he first appeared to me, it is fit I make some mention of myself, my employees, my business, my chambers, and general surroundings; because some such description is indispensable to an adequate understanding of the chief character about to be presented.

Imprimis: I am a man who, from his youth upwards, has been filled with a profound conviction that the easiest way of life is the best. Hence, though I belong to a profession proverbially energetic and nervous, even to turbulence, at times, yet nothing of that sort have I ever suffered to invade my peace. I am one of those unambitious lawyers who never addresses a jury, or in any way draws down public applause; but in the cool tranquility of a snug retreat, do a snug business among rich men's bonds and mortgages and title-deeds. All who know me, consider me an eminently safe man. The late John Jacob Astor, a personage little given to poetic enthusiasm, had no hesitation in pronouncing my first grand point to be prudence; my next, method. I do not speak it in vanity, but simply record the fact, that I was not unemployed in my profession by the late John Jacob Astor; a name which, I admit, I love to repeat, for it hath a rounded and orbicular sound to it, and rings like unto bullion. I will freely add, that I was not insensible to the late John Jacob Astor's good opinion.

Some time prior to the period at which this little history begins, my avocations had been largely increased. The good old office, now extinct in the State of New York, of a Master in Chancery, had been conferred upon me. It was not a very arduous office, but very pleasantly remunerative. I seldom lose my temper; much more seldom indulge in dangerous indignation at wrongs and outrages; but I must be permitted to be rash here and declare, that I consider the sudden and violent abrogation of the office of Master in Chancery, by the new Constitution, as a—premature act; inasmuch as I had counted upon a life-lease of the profits, whereas I only received those of a few short years. But this is by the way.

My chambers were up stairs at No. – Wall-street. At one end they looked upon the white wall of the interior of a spacious sky-light shaft, penetrating the building from top to bottom. This view might have been considered rather tame than otherwise, deficient in what landscape painters call "life." But if so, the view from the other end of my chambers offered, at least, a contrast, if nothing more. In that direction my windows commanded an unobstructed view of a lofty brick wall, black by age and everlasting shade; which wall required no spy-glass to bring out its lurking beauties, but for the benefit of all near-sighted spectators, was pushed up to within ten feet of my windowpanes. Owing to the great height of the surrounding buildings, and my chambers being on the second floor, the interval between this wall and mine not a little resembled a huge square cistern.

At the period just preceding the advent of Bartleby, I had two persons as copyists in my employment, and a promising lad as an office-boy. First, Turkey; second, Nippers; third, Ginger Nut. These may seem names, the like of which are not usually found in the Directory. In truth they were nicknames, mutually conferred upon each other by my three clerks, and were deemed expressive of their respective persons or characters. Turkey was a short, pursy Englishman of about my own age, that is, somewhere not far from sixty. In the morning, one might say, his face was of a fine florid hue, but after twelve o'clock, meridian — his dinner hour — it blazed like a grate full of Christmas coals; and continued blazing — but, as it were, with a gradual wane—till 6 o'clock, p.m. or thereabouts, after which I saw no more of the proprietor of the face, which gaining its meridian with the sun, seemed to set with it, to rise, culminate, and decline the following day, with the like regularity and undiminished glory. There are many singular coincidences I have known in the course of my life, not the least among which was the fact, that exactly when Turkey displayed his fullest beams from his red and radiant countenance, just then, too, at that critical moment, began the daily period when I considered his business capacities as seriously disturbed for the remainder of the twenty-four hours. Not that he was absolutely idle, or averse to business then; far from it. The difficulty was, he was apt to be altogether too energetic. There was a strange, inflamed, flurried, flighty recklessness of activity about him. He would be incautious in dipping his pen into his inkstand. All his blots upon my documents, were dropped there after twelve o'clock, meridian.

Indeed, not only would he be reckless and sadly given to making blots in the afternoon, but some days he went further, and was rather noisy. At such times, too, his face flamed with augmented blazonry, as if cannel coal had been heaped on anthracite. He made an unpleasant racket with his chair; spilled his sand-box; in mending his pens, impatiently split them all to pieces, and threw them on the floor in a sudden passion; stood up and leaned over his table, boxing his papers about in a most indecorous manner, very sad to behold in an elderly man like him. Nevertheless, as he was in many ways a most valuable person to me, and all the time before twelve o'clock, meridian, was the quickest, steadiest creature too, accomplishing a great deal of work in a style not easy to be matched—for these reasons, I was willing to overlook his eccentricities, though indeed, occasionally, I remonstrated with him. I did this very gently, however, because, though the civilest, nay, the blandest and most reverential of men in the morning, yet in the afternoon he was disposed, upon provocation, to be slightly rash with his tongue, in fact, insolent. Now, valuing his morning services as I did, and resolved not to lose them; yet, at the same time made uncomfortable by his inflamed ways after twelve o'clock; and being a man of peace, unwilling by my admonitions to call forth unseemly retorts from him; I took upon me, one Saturday noon (he was always worse on Saturdays), to hint to him, very kindly, that perhaps now that he was growing old, it might be well to abridge his labors; in short, he need not come to my chambers after twelve o'clock, but, dinner over, had best go home to his lodgings and rest himself till teatime. But no; he insisted upon his afternoon devotions. His countenance became intolerably fervid, as he oratorically assured me—gesticulating with a long ruler at the other end of the room—that if his services in the morning were useful, how indispensable, then, in the afternoon?

"With submission, sir," said Turkey on this occasion, "I consider myself your right-hand man. In the morning I but marshal and deploy my columns; but in the afternoon I put myself at their head, and gallantly charge the foe, thus!" — and he made a violent thrust with the ruler.

"But the blots, Turkey," intimated I.

"True—but, with submission, sir, behold these hairs! I am getting old. Surely, sir, a blot or two of a warm afternoon is not to be severely urged against gray hairs. Old age—even if it blot the page—is honorable. With submission, sir, we both are getting old."

This appeal to my fellow-feeling was hardly to be resisted. At all events, I saw that go he would not. So I made up my mind to let him stay, resolving, nevertheless, to see to it, that during the afternoon he had to do with my less important papers.

Nippers, the second on my list, was a whiskered, sallow, and, upon the whole, rather piratical-looking young man of about five and twenty. I always deemed him the victim of two evil powers—ambition and indigestion. The ambition was evinced by a certain impatience of the duties of a mere copyist, an unwarrantable usurpation of strictly professional affairs, such as the original drawing up of legal documents. The indigestion seemed betokened in an occasional nervous testiness and grinning irritability, causing the teeth to audibly grind together over mistakes committed in copying; unnecessary maledictions, hissed, rather than spoken, in the heat of business; and especially by a continual discontent with the height of the table where he worked. Though of a very ingenious mechanical turn, Nippers could never get this table to suit him. He put chips under it, blocks of various sorts, bits of pasteboard, and at last went so far as to attempt an exquisite adjustment by final pieces of folded blotting paper. But no invention would answer. If, for the sake of easing his back, he brought the table lid at a sharp angle well up towards his chin, and wrote there like a man using the steep roof of a Dutch house for his desk:—then he declared that it stopped the circulation in his arms. If now he lowered the table to his waistbands, and stooped over it in writing, then there was a sore aching in his back. In short, the truth of the matter was, Nippers knew not what he wanted. Or, if he wanted any thing, it was to be rid of a scrivener's table altogether. Among the manifestations of his diseased ambition was a fondness he had for receiving visits from certain ambiguous-looking fellows in seedy coats, whom he called his clients. Indeed I was aware that not only was he, at times, considerable of a ward-politician, but he occasionally did a little business at the Justices' courts, and was not unknown on the steps of the Tombs. I have good reason to believe, however, that one individual who called upon him at my chambers, and who, with a grand air, he insisted was his client, was no other than a dun, and the alleged title-deed, a bill. But with all his failings, and the annoyances he caused me, Nippers, like his compatriot Turkey, was a very useful man to me; wrote a neat, swift hand; and, when he chose, was not deficient in a gentlemanly sort of deportment. Added to this, he always dressed in a gentlemanly sort of way; and so, incidentally, reflected credit upon my chambers. Whereas with respect to Turkey, I had much ado to keep him from being a reproach to me. His clothes were apt to look oily and smell of eating-houses. He wore his pantaloons very loose and baggy in summer. His coats were execrable; his hat not to be handled. But while the hat was a thing of indifference to me, inasmuch as his natural civility and deference, as a dependent Englishman, always led him to doff it the moment he entered the room, yet his coat was another matter. Concerning his coats, I reasoned with him; but with no effect. The truth was, I suppose, that a man of so small an income, could not afford to sport such a lustrous face and a lustrous coat at one and the same time. As Nippers once observed, Turkey's money went chiefly for red ink. One winter day I presented Turkey with a highly-respectable looking coat of my own, a padded gray coat, of a most comfortable warmth, and which buttoned straight up from the knee to the neck. I thought Turkey would appreciate the favor, and abate his rashness and obstreperousness of afternoons. But no. I verily believe that buttoning himself up in so downy and blanket-like a coat had a pernicious effect upon him; upon the same principle that too much oats are bad for horses.

In fact, precisely as a rash, restive horse is said to feel his oats, so Turkey felt his coat. It made him insolent. He was a man whom prosperity harmed.

Though concerning the self-indulgent habits of Turkey I had my own private surmises, yet touching Nippers I was well persuaded that whatever might be his faults in other respects, he was, at least, a temperate young man. But indeed, nature herself seemed to have been his vintner, and at his birth charged him so thoroughly with an irritable, brandy-like disposition, that all subsequent potations were needless. When I consider how, amid the stillness of my chambers, Nippers would sometimes impatiently rise from his seat, and stooping over his table, spread his arms wide apart, seize the whole desk, and move it, and jerk it, with a grim, grinding motion on the floor, as if the table were a perverse voluntary agent, intent on thwarting and vexing him; I plainly perceive that for Nippers, brandy and water were altogether superfluous.

It was fortunate for me that, owing to its peculiar cause—indigestion—the irritability and consequent nervousness of Nippers, were mainly observable in the morning, while in the afternoon he was comparatively mild. So that Turkey's paroxysms only coming on about twelve o'clock, I never had to do with their eccentricities at one time. Their fits relieved each other like guards. When Nippers' was on, Turkey's was off; and vice versa. This was a good natural arrangement under the circumstances.

Ginger Nut, the third on my list, was a lad some twelve years old. His father was a carman, ambitious of seeing his son on the bench instead of a cart, before he died. So he sent him to my office as student at law, errand boy, and cleaner and sweeper, at the rate of one dollar a week. He had a little desk to himself, but he did not use it much. Upon inspection, the drawer exhibited a great array of the shells of various sorts of nuts. Indeed, to this quick-witted youth the whole noble science of the law was contained in a nut-shell. Not the least among the employments of Ginger Nut, as well as one which he discharged with the most alacrity, was his duty as cake and apple purveyor for Turkey and Nippers. Copying law papers being proverbially dry, husky sort of business, my two scriveners were fain to moisten their mouths very often with Spitzenbergs to be had at the numerous stalls nigh the Custom House and Post Office. Also, they sent Ginger Nut very frequently for that peculiar cake—small, flat, round, and very spicy—after which he had been named by them. Of a cold morning when business was but dull, Turkey would gobble up scores of these cakes, as if they were mere wafers—indeed they sell them at the rate of six or eight for a penny—the scrape of his pen blending with the crunching of the crisp particles in his mouth. Of all the fiery afternoon blunders and flurried rashnesses of Turkey, was his once moistening a ginger-cake between his lips, and clapping it on to a mortgage for a seal. I came within an ace of dismissing him then. But he mollified me by making an oriental bow, and saying— "With submission, sir, it was generous of me to find you in stationery on my own account."

Now my original business—that of a conveyancer and title hunter, and drawer-up of recondite documents of all sorts—was considerably increased by receiving the master's office. There was now great work for scriveners. Not only must I push the clerks already with me, but I must have additional help. In answer to my advertisement, a motionless young man one morning, stood upon my office threshold, the door being open, for it was summer. I can see that figure now—pallidly neat, pitiably respectable, incurably forlorn! It was Bartleby.

After a few words touching his qualifications, I engaged him, glad to have among my corps of copyists a man of so singularly sedate an aspect, which I thought might operate beneficially upon the flighty temper of Turkey, and the fiery one of Nippers.

I should have stated before that ground glass folding-doors divided my premises into two parts, one of which was occupied by my scriveners, the other by myself. According to my humor I threw open these doors, or closed them. I resolved to assign Bartleby a corner by the folding-doors, but on my side of them, so as to have this quiet man within easy call, in case any trifling thing was to be done. I placed his desk close up to a small side-window in that part of the room, a window which originally had afforded a lateral view of certain grimy backyards and bricks, but which, owing to subsequent erections, commanded at present no view at all, though it gave some light. Within three feet of the panes was a wall, and the light came down from far above, between two lofty buildings, as from a very small opening in a dome. Still further to a satisfactory arrangement, I procured a high green folding screen, which might entirely isolate Bartleby from my sight, though not remove him from my voice. And thus, in a manner, privacy and society were conjoined.

At first Bartleby did an extraordinary quantity of writing. As if long famishing for something to copy, he seemed to gorge himself on my documents. There was no pause for digestion. He ran a day and night line, copying by sunlight and by candle-light. I should have been quite delighted with his application, had he been cheerfully industrious. But he wrote on silently, palely, mechanically.

It is, of course, an indispensable part of a scrivener's business to verify the accuracy of his copy, word by word. Where there are two or more scriveners in an office, they assist each other in this examination, one reading from the copy, the other holding the original. It is a very dull, wearisome, and lethargic affair. I can readily imagine that to some sanguine temperaments it would be altogether intolerable. For example, I cannot credit that the mettlesome poet Byron would have contentedly sat down with Bartleby to examine a law document of, say five hundred pages, closely written in a crimpy hand.

Now and then, in the haste of business, it had been my habit to assist in comparing some brief document myself, calling Turkey or Nippers for this purpose. One object I had in placing Bartleby so handy to me behind the screen, was to avail myself of his services on such trivial occasions. It was on the third day, I think, of his being with me, and before any necessity had arisen for having his own writing examined, that, being much hurried to complete a small affair I had in hand, I abruptly called to Bartleby. In my haste and natural expectancy of instant compliance, I sat with my head bent over the original on my desk, and my right hand sideways, and somewhat nervously extended with the copy, so that immediately upon emerging from his retreat, Bartleby might snatch it and proceed to business without the least delay.

In this very attitude did I sit when I called to him, rapidly stating what it was I wanted him to do—namely, to examine a small paper with me. Imagine my surprise, nay, my consternation, when without moving from his privacy, Bartleby in a singularly mild, firm voice, replied, "I would prefer not to."

I sat awhile in perfect silence, rallying my stunned faculties. Immediately it occurred to me that my ears had deceived me, or Bartleby had entirely misunderstood my meaning. I repeated my request in the clearest tone I could assume. But in quite as clear a one came the previous reply, "I would prefer not to."

"Prefer not to," echoed I, rising in high excitement, and crossing the room with a stride. "What do you mean? Are you moon-struck?

I want you to help me compare this sheet here—take it," and I thrust it towards him.

"I would prefer not to," said he.

I looked at him steadfastly. His face was leanly composed; his gray eye dimly calm. Not a wrinkle of agitation rippled him. Had there been the least uneasiness, anger, impatience or impertinence in his manner; in other words, had there been any thing ordinarily human about him, doubtless I should have violently dismissed him from the premises. But as it was, I should have as soon thought of turning my pale plaster-of-paris bust of Cicero out of doors. I stood gazing at him awhile, as he went on with his own writing, and then reseated myself at my desk. This is very strange, thought I. What had one best do? But my business hurried me. I concluded to forget the matter for the present, reserving it for my future leisure. So calling Nippers from the other room, the paper was speedily examined.

A few days after this, Bartleby concluded four lengthy documents, being quadruplicates of a week's testimony taken before me in my High Court of Chancery. It became necessary to examine them. It was an important suit, and great accuracy was imperative. Having all things arranged I called Turkey, Nippers and Ginger Nut from the next room, meaning to place the four copies in the hands of my four clerks, while I should read from the original. Accordingly Turkey, Nippers and Ginger Nut had taken their seats in a row, each with his document in hand, when I called to Bartleby to join this interesting group.

"Bartleby! Quick, I am waiting."

I heard a slow scrape of his chair legs on the uncarpeted floor, and soon he appeared standing at the entrance of his hermitage.

"What is wanted?" said he mildly.

"The copies, the copies," said I hurriedly. "We are going to examine them. There" — and I held towards him the fourth quadruplicate.

"I would prefer not to," he said, and gently disappeared behind the screen. For a few moments I was turned into a pillar of salt, standing at the head of my seated column of clerks. Recovering myself, I advanced towards the screen, and demanded the reason for such extraordinary conduct.

"Why do you refuse?"

"I would prefer not to."

With any other man I should have flown outright into a dreadful passion, scorned all further words, and thrust him ignominiously from my presence. But there was something about Bartleby that not only strangely disarmed me, but in a wonderful manner touched and disconcerted me. I began to reason with him.

"These are your own copies we are about to examine. It is labor saving to you, because one examination will answer for your four papers. It is common usage. Every copyist is bound to help examine his copy. Is it not so? Will you not speak? Answer!"

"I prefer not to," he replied in a flute-like tone. It seemed to me that while I had been addressing him, he carefully revolved every statement that I made; fully comprehended the meaning; could not gainsay the irresistible conclusions; but, at the same time, some paramount consideration prevailed with him to reply as he did.

"You are decided, then, not to comply with my request — a request made according to common usage and common sense?"

He briefly gave me to understand that on that point my judgment was sound. Yes: his decision was irreversible.

It is not seldom the case that when a man is browbeaten in some unprecedented and violently unreasonable way, he begins to stagger in his own plainest faith. He begins, as it were, vaguely to surmise that, wonderful as it may be, all the justice and all the reason is on the other side. Accordingly, if any disinterested persons are present, he turns to them for some reinforcement for his own faltering mind.

"Turkey," said I, "what do you think of this? Am I not right?"

"With submission, sir," said Turkey, with his blandest tone, "I think that you are."

"Nippers," said I, "what do you think of it?" "I think I should kick him out of the office."

(The reader of nice perceptions will here perceive that, it being morning, Turkey's answer is couched in polite and tranquil terms, but Nippers replies in ill-tempered ones. Or, to repeat a previous sentence, Nippers' ugly mood was on duty and Turkey's off.)

"Ginger Nut," said I, willing to enlist the smallest suffrage in my behalf, "what do you think of it?"

"I think, sir, he's a little *luny*," replied Ginger Nut with a grin.

"You hear what they say," said I, turning towards the screen, "come forth and do your duty."

But he vouchsafed no reply. I pondered a moment in sore perplexity. But once more business hurried me. I determined again to postpone the consideration of this dilemma to my future leisure. With a little trouble we made out to examine the papers without Bartleby, though at every page or two, Turkey deferentially dropped his opinion that this proceeding was quite out of the common; while Nippers, twitching in his chair with a dyspeptic nervousness, ground out between his set teeth occasional hissing maledictions against the stubborn oaf behind the screen. And for his (Nippers') part, this was the first and the last time he would do another man's business without pay.

Meanwhile Bartleby sat in his hermitage, oblivious to every thing but his own peculiar business there.

Some days passed, the scrivener being employed upon another lengthy work. His late remarkable conduct led me to regard his ways narrowly. I observed that he never went to dinner; indeed that he never went any where. As yet I had never of my personal knowledge known him to be outside of my office. He was a perpetual sentry in the corner. At about eleven o'clock though, in the morning, I noticed that Ginger Nut would advance toward the opening in Bartleby's screen, as if silently beckoned thither by a gesture invisible to me where I sat. The boy would then leave the office jingling a few pence, and reappear with a handful of ginger-nuts which he delivered in the hermitage, receiving two of the cakes for his trouble.

He lives, then, on ginger-nuts, thought I; never eats a dinner, properly speaking; he must be a vegetarian then; but no; he never eats even vegetables, he eats nothing but ginger-nuts. My mind then ran on in reveries concerning the probable effects upon the human constitution of living entirely on ginger-nuts. Ginger-nuts are so called because they contain ginger as one of their peculiar constituents, and the final flavoring one. Now what was ginger? A hot, spicy thing. Was Bartleby hot and spicy? Not at all. Ginger, then, had no effect upon Bartleby. Probably he preferred it should have none.

Nothing so aggravates an earnest person as a passive resistance. If the individual so resisted be of a not inhumane temper, and the resisting one perfectly harmless in his passivity; then, in the better moods of the former, he will endeavor charitably to construe to his imagination what proves impossible to be solved by his judgment. Even so, for the most part, I regarded Bartleby and his ways. Poor fellow! thought I, he means no mischief; it is plain he intends no insolence; his aspect sufficiently evinces that his eccentricities are involuntary. He is useful to me. I can get along with him. If I turn him away, the chances are he will fall in with some less indulgent employer, and then he will be rudely treated, and perhaps driven forth miserably to starve. Yes. Here I can cheaply purchase a delicious self-approval. To befriend Bartleby; to humor him in his strange willfulness, will cost me little or nothing, while I lay up in my soul what will eventually prove a sweet morsel for my conscience. But this mood was not invariable with me. The passiveness of Bartleby sometimes irritated me. I felt strangely goaded on to encounter him in new opposition, to elicit some angry spark from him answerable to my own. But indeed I might as well have essayed to strike fire with my knuckles against a bit of Windsor soap. But one afternoon the evil impulse in me mastered me, and the following little scene ensued:

"Bartleby," said I, "when those papers are all copied, I will compare them with you."

"I would prefer not to."

"How? Surely you do not mean to persist in that mulish vagary?" No answer.

I threw open the folding-doors near by, and turning upon Turkey and Nippers, exclaimed in an excited manner—

"He says, a second time, he won't examine his papers. What do you think of it, Turkey?"

It was afternoon, be it remembered. Turkey sat glowing like a brass boiler, his bald head steaming, his hands reeling among his blotted papers.

"Think of it?" roared Turkey; "I think I'll just step behind his screen, and black his eyes for him!"

So saying, Turkey rose to his feet and threw his arms into a pugilistic position. He was hurrying away to make good his promise, when I detained him, alarmed at the effect of incautiously rousing Turkey's combativeness after dinner.

"Sit down, Turkey," said I, "and hear what Nippers has to say. What do you think of it, Nippers? Would I not be justified in immediately dismissing Bartleby?"

"Excuse me, that is for you to decide, sir. I think his conduct quite unusual, and indeed unjust, as regards Turkey and myself. But it may only be a passing whim."

"Ah," exclaimed I, "you have strangely changed your mind then—you speak very gently of him now."

"All beer," cried Turkey; "gentleness is effects of beer—Nippers and I dined together today. You see how gentle I am, sir. Shall I go and black his eyes?"

"You refer to Bartleby, I suppose. No, not today, Turkey," I replied; "pray, put up your fists."

I closed the doors, and again advanced towards Bartleby. I felt additional incentives tempting me to my fate. I burned to be rebelled against again. I remembered that Bartleby never left the office.

"Bartleby," said I, "Ginger Nut is away; just step round to the Post Office, won't you? (it was but a three minute walk,) and see if there is any thing for me."

"I would prefer not to." "You will not?"

"I prefer not."

I staggered to my desk, and sat there in a deep study. My blind inveteracy returned. Was there any other thing in which I could procure myself to be ignominiously repulsed by this lean, penniless wight?—my hired clerk? What added thing is there, perfectly reasonable, that he will be sure to refuse to do?

"Bartleby!" No answer.

"Bartleby," in a louder tone. No answer.

"Bartleby," I roared.

Like a very ghost, agreeably to the laws of magical invocation, at the third summons, he appeared at the entrance of his hermitage.

"Go to the next room, and tell Nippers to come to me."

"I prefer not to," he respectfully and slowly said, and mildly disappeared. "Very good, Bartleby," said I, in a quiet sort of serenely severe self-possessed tone, intimating the unalterable purpose of some terrible retribution very close at hand. At the moment I half intended something of the kind. But upon the whole, as it was drawing towards my dinner-hour, I thought it best to put on my hat and walk home for the day, suffering much from perplexity and distress of mind.

Shall I acknowledge it? The conclusion of this whole business was, that it soon became a fixed fact of my chambers, that a pale young scrivener, by the name of Bartleby, had a desk there; that he copied for me at the usual rate of four cents a folio (one hundred words); but he was permanently exempt from examining the work done by him, that duty being transferred to Turkey and Nippers, one of compliment doubtless to their superior acuteness; moreover, said Bartleby was never on any account to be dispatched on the most trivial errand of any sort; and that even if entreated to take upon him such a matter, it was generally understood that he would prefer not to—in other words, that he would refuse pointblank.

As days passed on, I became considerably reconciled to Bartleby. His steadiness, his freedom from all dissipation, his incessant industry (except when he chose to throw himself into a standing revery behind his screen), his great, stillness, his unalterableness of demeanor under all circumstances, made him a valuable acquisition. One prime thing was this—he was always there;—first in the morning, continually through the day, and the last at night. I had a singular confidence in his honesty. I felt my most precious papers perfectly safe in his hands. Sometimes to be sure I could not, for the very soul of me, avoid falling into sudden spasmodic passions with him. For it was exceeding difficult to bear in mind all the time those strange peculiarities, privileges, and unheard of exemptions, forming the tacit stipulations on Bartleby's part under which he remained in my office. Now and then, in the eagerness of dispatching pressing business, I would inadvertently summon Bartleby, in a short, rapid tone, to put his finger, say, on the incipient tie of a bit of red tape with which I was about compressing some papers. Of course, from behind the screen the usual answer, "I prefer not to," was sure to come; and then, how could a human creature with the common infirmities of our nature, refrain from bitterly exclaiming upon such perverseness — such unreasonableness. However, every added repulse of this sort which I received only tended to lessen the probability of my repeating the inadvertence.

Here it must be said, that according to the custom of most legal gentlemen occupying chambers in densely-populated law buildings, there were several keys to my door. One was kept by a woman residing in the attic, which person weekly scrubbed and daily swept and dusted my apartments. Another was kept by Turkey for convenience sake. The third I sometimes carried in my own pocket. The fourth I knew not who had.

Now, one Sunday morning I happened to go to Trinity Church, to hear a celebrated preacher, and finding myself rather early on the ground, I thought I would walk around to my chambers for a while. Luckily I had my key with me; but upon applying it to the lock, I found it resisted by something inserted from the inside. Quite surprised, I called out; when to my consternation a key was turned from within; and thrusting his lean visage at me, and holding the door ajar, the apparition of Bartleby appeared, in his shirt sleeves, and otherwise in a strangely tattered dishabille, saying quietly that he was sorry, but he was deeply engaged just then, and—preferred not admitting me at present. In a brief word or two, he moreover added, that perhaps I had better walk round the block two or three times, and by that time he would probably have concluded his affairs.

Now, the utterly unsurmised appearance of Bartleby, tenanting my law-chambers of a Sunday morning, with his cadaverously gentlemanly nonchalance, yet withal firm and self-possessed, had such a strange effect upon me, that incontinently I slunk away from my own door, and did as desired. But not without sundry twinges of impotent rebellion against the mild effrontery of this unaccountable scrivener. Indeed, it was his wonderful mildness chiefly, which not only disarmed me, but unmanned me, as it were. For I consider that one, for the time, is a sort of unmanned when he tranquilly permits his hired clerk to dictate to him, and order him away from his own premises. Furthermore, I was full of uneasiness as to what Bartleby could possibly be doing in my office in his shirt sleeves, and in an otherwise dismantled condition of a Sunday morning. Was any thing amiss going on? Nay, that was out of the question. It was not to be thought of for a moment that Bartleby was an immoral person. But what could he be doing there?—Copying? Nay again, whatever might be his eccentricities, Bartleby was an eminently decorous person. He would be the last man to sit down to his desk in any state approaching to nudity. Besides, it was Sunday; and there was something about Bartleby that forbade the supposition that he would by any secular occupation violate the proprieties of the day.

Nevertheless, my mind was not pacified; and full of a restless curiosity, at last I returned to the door. Without hindrance I inserted my key, opened it, and entered. Bartleby was not to be seen. I looked round anxiously, peeped behind his screen; but it was very plain that he was gone. Upon more closely examining the place, I surmised that for an indefinite period Bartleby must have ate, dressed, and slept in my office, and that too without plate, mirror, or bed. The cushioned seat of a rickety old sofa in one corner bore the faint impress of a lean, reclining form. Rolled away under his desk, I found a blanket; under the empty grate, a blacking box and brush; on a chair, a tin basin, with soap and a ragged towel; in a newspaper a few crumbs of ginger-nuts and a morsel of cheese. Yes, thought I, it is evident enough that Bartleby has been making his home here, keeping bachelor's hall all by himself. Immediately then the thought came sweeping across me, What miserable friendlessness and loneliness are here revealed! His poverty is great; but his solitude, how horrible! Think of it. Of a Sunday, Wall-street is deserted as Petra; and every night of every day it is an emptiness. This building too, which of weekdays hums with industry and life, at nightfall echoes with sheer vacancy, and all through Sunday is forlorn. And here Bartleby makes his home; sole spectator of a solitude which he has seen all populous—a sort of innocent and transformed Marius brooding among the ruins of Carthage!

For the first time in my life a feeling of overpowering stinging melancholy seized me. Before, I had never experienced aught but a not-unpleasing sadness. The bond of a common humanity now drew me irresistibly to gloom. A fraternal melancholy! For both I and Bartleby were sons of Adam. I remembered the bright silks and sparkling faces I had seen that day, in gala trim, swan-like sailing down the Mississippi of Broadway; and I contrasted them with the pallid copyist, and thought to myself, Ah, happiness courts the light, so we deem the world is gay; but misery hides aloof, so we deem that misery there is none. These sad fancyings—chimeras, doubtless, of a sick and silly brain—led on to other and more special thoughts, concerning the eccentricities of Bartleby. Presentiments of strange discoveries hovered round me. The scrivener's pale form appeared to me laid out, among uncaring strangers, in its shivering winding sheet.

Suddenly I was attracted by Bartleby's closed desk, the key in open sight left in the lock.

I mean no mischief, seek the gratification of no heartless curiosity, thought I; besides, the desk is mine, and its contents too, so I will make bold to look within. Every thing was methodically arranged, the papers smoothly placed. The pigeon holes were deep, and removing the files of documents, I groped into their recesses. Presently I felt something there, and dragged it out. It was an old bandanna handkerchief, heavy and knotted. I opened it, and saw it was a savings' bank.

I now recalled all the quiet mysteries which I had noted in the man. I remembered that he never spoke but to answer; that though at intervals he had considerable time to himself, yet I had never seen him reading—no, not even a newspaper; that for long periods he would stand looking out, at his pale window behind the screen, upon the dead brick wall; I was quite sure he never visited any refectory or eating house; while his pale face clearly indicated that he never drank beer like Turkey, or tea and coffee even, like other men; that he never went any where in particular that I could learn; never went out for a walk, unless indeed that was the case at present; that he had declined telling who he was, or whence he came, or whether he had any relatives in the world; that though so thin and pale, he never complained of ill health. And more than all, I remembered a certain unconscious air of pallid—how shall I call it?—of pallid haughtiness, say, or rather an austere reserve about him, which had positively awed me into my tame compliance with his eccentricities, when I had feared to ask him to do the slightest incidental thing for me, even though I might know, from his long-continued motionlessness, that behind his screen he must be standing in one of those dead-wall reveries of his.

Revolving all these things, and coupling them with the recently discovered fact that he made my office his constant abiding place and home, and not forgetful of his morbid moodiness; revolving all these things, a prudential feeling began to steal over me. My first emotions had been those of pure melancholy and sincerest pity; but just in proportion as the forlornness of Bartleby grew and grew to my imagination, did that same melancholy merge into fear, that pity into repulsion. So true it is, and so terrible too, that up to a certain point the thought or sight of misery enlists our best affections; but, in certain special cases, beyond that point it does not. They err who would assert that invariably this is owing to the inherent selfishness of the human heart. It rather proceeds from a certain hopelessness of remedying excessive and organic ill. To a sensitive being, pity is not seldom pain. And when at last it is perceived that such pity cannot lead to effectual succor, common sense bids the soul rid of it. What I saw that morning persuaded me that the scrivener was the victim of innate and incurable disorder. I might give alms to his body; but his body did not pain him; it was his soul that suffered, and his soul I could not reach.

I did not accomplish the purpose of going to Trinity Church that morning. Somehow, the things I had seen disqualified me for the time from church-going. I walked homeward, thinking what I would do with Bartleby. Finally, I resolved upon this;—I would put certain calm questions to him the next morning, touching his history, etc., and if he declined to answer them openly and unreservedly (and I supposed he would prefer not), then to give him a twenty dollar bill over and above whatever I might owe him, and tell him his services were no longer required; but that if in any other way I could assist him, I would be happy to do so, especially if he desired to return to his native place, wherever that might be, I would willingly help to defray the expenses. Moreover, if, after reaching home, he found himself at any time in want of aid, a letter from him would be sure of a reply.

The next morning came.

"Bartleby," said I, gently calling to him behind his screen. No reply.

"Bartleby," said I, in a still gentler tone, "come here; I am not going to ask you to do any thing you would prefer not to do—I simply wish to speak to you."

Upon this he noiselessly slid into view.

"Will you tell me, Bartleby, where you were born?" "I would prefer not to."

"Will you tell me any thing about yourself?" "I would prefer not to."

"But what reasonable objection can you have to speak to me? I feel friendly towards you."

He did not look at me while I spoke, but kept his glance fixed upon my bust of Cicero, which as I then sat, was directly behind me, some six inches above my head.

"What is your answer, Bartleby?" said I, after waiting a considerable time for a reply, during which his countenance remained immovable, only there was the faintest conceivable tremor of the white attenuated mouth.

"At present I prefer to give no answer," he said, and retired into his hermitage.

It was rather weak in me I confess, but his manner on this occasion nettled me. Not only did there seem to lurk in it a certain calm disdain, but his perverseness seemed ungrateful, considering the undeniable good usage and indulgence he had received from me.

Again I sat ruminating what I should do. Mortified as I was at his behavior, and resolved as I had been to dismiss him when I entered my offices, nevertheless I strangely felt something superstitious knocking at my heart, and forbidding me to carry out my purpose, and denouncing me for a villain if I dared to breathe one bitter word against this forlornest of mankind. At last, familiarly drawing my chair behind his screen, I sat down and said: "Bartleby, never mind then about revealing your history; but let me entreat you, as a friend, to comply as far as may be with the usages of this office. Say now you will help to examine papers tomorrow or next day: in short, say now that in a day or two you will begin to be a little reasonable:—say so, Bartleby."

"At present I would prefer not to be a little reasonable," was his mildly cadaverous reply.

Just then the folding-doors opened, and Nippers approached. He seemed suffering from an unusually bad night's rest, induced by severer indigestion then common. He overheard those final words of Bartleby.

"Prefer not, eh?" gritted Nippers — "I'd prefer him, if I were you, sir," addressing me — "I'd prefer him; I'd give him preferences, the stubborn mule! What is it, sir, pray, that he prefers not to do now?"

Bartleby moved not a limb.

"Mr. Nippers," said I, "I'd prefer that you would withdraw for the present." Somehow, of late I had got into the way of involuntarily using this word "prefer" upon all sorts of not exactly suitable occasions. And I trembled to think that my contact with the scrivener had already and seriously affected me in a mental way. And what further and deeper aberration might it not yet produce? This apprehension had not been without efficacy in determining me to summary means.

As Nippers, looking very sour and sulky, was departing, Turkey blandly and deferentially approached.

"With submission, sir," said he, "yesterday I was thinking about Bartleby here, and I think that if he would but prefer to take a quart of good ale every day, it would do much towards mending him, and enabling him to assist in examining his papers."

"So you have got the word too," said I, slightly excited.

"With submission, what word, sir," asked Turkey, respectfully crowding himself into the contracted space behind the screen, and by so doing, making me jostle the scrivener. "What word, sir?"

"I would prefer to be left alone here," said Bartleby, as if offended at being mobbed in his privacy.

"That's the word, Turkey," said I — "that's it."

"Oh, prefer? Oh yes—queer word. I never use it myself. But, sir, as I was saying, if he would but prefer—"

"Turkey," interrupted I, "you will please withdraw." "Oh certainly, sir, if you prefer that I should."

As he opened the folding-door to retire, Nippers at his desk caught a glimpse of me, and asked whether I would prefer to have a certain paper copied on blue paper or white. He did not in the least roguishly accent the word prefer. It was plain that it involuntarily rolled form his tongue. I thought to myself, surely I must get rid of a demented man, who already has in some degree turned the tongues, if not the heads of myself and clerks. But I thought it prudent not to break the dismission at once.

The next day I noticed that Bartleby did nothing but stand at his window in his dead-wall revery. Upon asking him why he did not write, he said that he had decided upon doing no more writing.

"Why, how now? What next?" exclaimed I, "Do no more writing?"

"No more."

"And what is the reason?"

"Do you not see the reason for yourself," he indifferently replied.

I looked steadfastly at him, and perceived that his eyes looked dull and glazed. Instantly it occurred to me, that his unexampled diligence in copying by his dim window for the first few weeks of his stay with me might have temporarily impaired his vision.

I was touched. I said something in condolence with him. I hinted that of course he did wisely in abstaining from writing for a while; and urged him to embrace that opportunity of taking wholesome exercise in the open air. This, however, he did not do. A few days after this, my other clerks being absent, and being in a great hurry to dispatch certain letters by the mail, I thought that, having nothing else earthly to do, Bartleby would surely be less inflexible than usual, and carry these letters to the post-office. But he blankly declined. So, much to my inconvenience, I went myself.

Still added days went by. Whether Bartleby's eyes improved or not, I could not say. To all appearance, I thought they did. But when I asked him if they did, he vouchsafed no answer. At all events, he would do no copying. At last, in reply to my urgings, he informed me that he had permanently given up copying.

"What!" exclaimed I; "suppose your eyes should get entirely well— better than ever before—would you not copy then?"

"I have given up copying," he answered, and slid aside.

He remained as ever, a fixture in my chamber. Nay—if that were possible—he became still more of a fixture than before. What was to be done? He would do nothing in the office: why should he stay there? In plain fact, he had now become a millstone to me, not only useless as a necklace, but afflictive to bear. Yet I was sorry for him. I speak less than truth when I say that, on his own account, he occasioned me uneasiness. If he would but have named a single relative or friend, I would instantly have written, and urged their taking the poor fellow away to some convenient retreat. But he seemed alone, absolutely alone in the universe. A bit of wreck in the mid Atlantic. At length, necessities connected with my business tyrannized over all other considerations. Decently as I could, I told Bartleby that in six days' time he must unconditionally leave the office. I warned him to take measures, in the interval, for procuring some other abode. I offered to assist him in this endeavor, if he himself would but take the first step towards a removal. "And when you finally quit me, Bartleby," added I, "I shall see that you go not away entirely unprovided. Six days from this hour, remember."

At the expiration of that period, I peeped behind the screen, and lo! Bartleby was there.

I buttoned up my coat,balanced myself; advanced slowly towards him, touched his shoulder, and said, "The time has come; you must quit this place; I am sorry for you; here is money; but you must go."

"I would prefer not," he replied, with his back still towards me.

"You must."

He remained silent.

Now I had an unbounded confidence in this man's common honesty. He had frequently restored to me sixpences and shillings carelessly dropped upon the floor, for I am apt to be very reckless in such shirt-button affairs. The proceeding then which followed will not be deemed extraordinary.

"Bartleby," said I, "I owe you twelve dollars on account; here are thirty-two; the odd twenty are yours.—Will you take it?" and I handed the bills towards him.

But he made no motion.

"I will leave them here then," putting them under a weight on the table. Then taking my hat and cane and going to the door I tranquilly turned and added— "After you have removed your things from these offices, Bartleby, you will of course lock the door—since every one is now gone for the day but you—and if you please, slip your key underneath the mat, so that I may have it in the morning. I shall not see you again; so goodbye to you. If hereafter in your new place of abode I can be of any service to you, do not fail to advise me by letter. Goodbye, Bartleby, and fare you well."

But he answered not a word; like the last column of some ruined temple, he remained standing mute and solitary in the middle of the otherwise deserted room.

As I walked home in a pensive mood, my vanity got the better of my pity. I could not but highly plume myself on my masterly management in getting rid of Bartleby. Masterly I call it, and such it must appear to any dispassionate thinker. The beauty of my procedure seemed to consist in its perfect quietness. There was no vulgar bullying, no bravado of any sort, no choleric hectoring, and striding to and fro across the apartment, jerking out vehement commands for Bartleby to bundle himself off with his beggarly traps. Nothing of the kind. Without loudly bidding Bartleby depart—as an inferior genius might have done—I assumed the ground that depart he must; and upon that assumption built all I had to say. The more I thought over my procedure, the more I was charmed with it. Nevertheless, next morning, upon awakening, I had my doubts—I had somehow slept off the fumes of vanity. One of the coolest and wisest hours a man has, is just after he awakes in the morning. My procedure seemed as sagacious as ever — but only in theory. How it would prove in practice — there was the rub. It was truly a beautiful thought to have assumed Bartleby's departure; but, after all, that assumption was simply my own, and none of Bartleby's. The great point was, not whether I had assumed that he would quit me, but whether he would prefer so to do. He was more a man of preferences than assumptions.

After breakfast, I walked down town, arguing the probabilities pro and con. One moment I thought it would prove a miserable failure, and Bartleby would be found all alive at my office as usual; the next moment it seemed certain that I should see his chair empty. And so I kept veering about. At the corner of Broadway and Canal-street, I saw quite an excited group of people standing in earnest conversation.

"I'll take odds he doesn't," said a voice as I passed. "Doesn't go?—Done!" said I, "put up your money."

I was instinctively putting my hand in my pocket to produce my own, when I remembered that this was an election day. The words

I had overheard bore no reference to Bartleby, but to the success or non-success of some candidate for the mayoralty. In my intent frame of mind, I had, as it were, imagined that all Broadway shared in my excitement, and were debating the same question with me. I passed on, very thankful that the uproar of the street screened my momentary absent-mindedness.

As I had intended, I was earlier than usual at my office door. I stood listening for a moment. All was still. He must be gone. I tried the knob. The door was locked. Yes, my procedure had worked to a charm; he indeed must be vanished. Yet a certain melancholy mixed with this: I was almost sorry for my brilliant success. I was fumbling under the door mat for the key, which Bartleby was to have left there for me, when accidentally my knee knocked against a panel, producing a summoning sound, and in response a voice came to me from within— "Not yet; I am occupied."

It was Bartleby.

I was thunderstruck. For an instant I stood like the man who, pipe in mouth, was killed one cloudless afternoon long ago in Virginia, by a summer lightning; at his own warm open window he was killed, and remained leaning out there upon the dreamy afternoon, till some one touched him, when he fell.

"Not gone!" I murmured at last. But again obeying that wondrous ascendancy which the inscrutable scrivener had over me, and from which ascendancy, for all my chafing, I could not completely escape, I slowly went down stairs and out into the street, and while walking round the block, considered what I should next do in this unheard-of perplexity. Turn the man out by an actual thrusting I could not; to drive him away by calling him hard names would not do; calling in the police was an unpleasant idea; and yet, permit him to enjoy his cadaverous triumph over me—this too I could not think of. What was to be done? Or, if nothing could be done, was there any thing further that I could assume in the matter? Yes, as before I had prospectively assumed that Bartleby would depart, so now I might retrospectively assume that departed he was. In the legitimate carrying out of this assumption, I might enter my office in a great hurry, and pretending not to see Bartleby at all, walk straight against him as if he were air. Such a proceeding would in a singular degree have the appearance of a home-thrust. It was hardly possible that Bartleby could withstand such an application of the doctrine of assumptions. But upon second thoughts the success of the plan seemed rather dubious. I resolved to argue the matter over with him again.

"Bartleby," said I, entering the office, with a quietly severe expression, "I am seriously displeased. I am pained, Bartleby. I had thought better of you. I had imagined you of such a gentlemanly organization, that in any delicate dilemma a slight hint would suffice—in short, an assumption. But it appears I am deceived. Why," I added, unaffectedly starting, "you have not even touched that money yet," pointing to it, just where I had left it the evening previous.

He answered nothing.

"Will you, or will you not, quit me?" I now demanded in a sudden passion, advancing close to him.

"I would prefer not to quit you," he replied, gently emphasizing the not. "What earthly right have you to stay here? Do you pay any rent? Do you pay my taxes? Or is this property yours?" He answered nothing.

"Are you ready to go on and write now? Are your eyes recovered? Could you copy a small paper for me this morning? Or help examine a few lines? Or step round to the post-office? In a word, will you do any thing at all, to give a coloring to your refusal to depart the premises?"

He silently retired into his hermitage.

I was now in such a state of nervous resentment that I thought it but prudent to check myself at present from further demonstrations. Bartleby and I were alone. I remembered the tragedy of the unfortunate Adams and the still more unfortunate Colt in the solitary office of the latter; and how poor Colt, being dreadfully incensed by Adams, and imprudently permitting himself to get wildly excited, was at unawares hurried into his fatal act—an act which certainly no man could possibly deplore more than the actor himself. Often it had occurred to me in my ponderings upon the subject, that had that altercation taken place in the public street, or at a private residence, it would not have terminated as it did. It was the circumstance of being alone in a solitary office, up stairs, of a building entirely unhallowed by humanizing domestic associations—an uncarpeted office, doubtless, of a dusty, haggard sort of appearance;—this it must have been, which greatly helped to enhance the irritable desperation of the hapless Colt.

But when this old Adam of resentment rose in me and tempted me concerning Bartleby, I grappled him and threw him. How? Why, simply by recalling the divine injunction: "A new commandment give I unto you, that ye love one another." Yes, this it was that saved me. Aside from higher considerations, charity often operates as a vastly wise and prudent principle—a great safeguard to its possessor. Men have committed murder for jealousy's sake, and anger's sake, and hatred's sake, and selfishness' sake, and spiritual pride's sake; but no man that ever I heard of, ever committed a diabolical murder for sweet charity's sake. Mere self-interest, then, if no better motive can be enlisted, should, especially with high-tempered men, prompt all beings to charity and philanthropy. At any rate, upon the occasion in question, I strove to drown my exasperated feelings towards the scrivener by benevolently construing his conduct. Poor fellow, poor fellow! thought I, he don't mean any thing; and besides, he has seen hard times, and ought to be indulged.

I endeavored also immediately to occupy myself, and at the same time to comfort my despondency. I tried to fancy that in the course of the morning, at such time as might prove agreeable to him. Bartleby, of his own free accord, would emerge from his hermitage, and take up some decided line of march in the direction of the door. But no. Half-past twelve o'clock came; Turkey began to glow in the face, overturn his inkstand, and become generally obstreperous; Nippers abated down into quietude and courtesy; Ginger Nut munched his noon apple; and Bartleby remained standing at his window in one of his profoundest dead-wall reveries. Will it be credited? Ought I to acknowledge it? That afternoon I left the office without saying one further word to him.

Some days now passed, during which, at leisure intervals I looked a little into "Edwards on the Will," and "Priestly on Necessity." Under the circumstances, those books induced a salutary feeling. Gradually I slid into the persuasion that these troubles of mine touching the scrivener, had been all predestinated from eternity, and

Bartleby was billeted upon me for some mysterious purpose of an all-wise Providence, which it was not for a mere mortal like me to fathom. Yes, Bartleby, stay there behind your screen, thought i; I shall persecute you no more; you are harmless and noiseless as any of these old chairs; in short, I never feel so private as when I know you are here. At last I see it, I feel it; I penetrate to the predestinated purpose of my life. I am content. Others may have loftier parts to enact; but my mission in this world, Bartleby, is to furnish you with office-room for such period as you may see fit to remain.

I believe that this wise and blessed frame of mind would have continued with me, had it not been for the unsolicited and uncharitable remarks obtruded upon me by my professional friends who visited the rooms. But thus it often is, that the constant friction of illiberal minds wears out at last the best resolves of the more generous. Though to be sure, when I reflected upon it, it was not strange that people entering my office should be struck by the peculiar aspect of the unaccountable Bartleby, and so be tempted to throw out some sinister observations concerning him. Sometimes an attorney having business with me, and calling at my office and finding no one but the scrivener there, would undertake to obtain some sort of precise information from him touching my whereabouts; but without heeding his idle talk, Bartleby would remain standing immovable in the middle of the room. So after contemplating him in that position for a time, the attorney would depart, no wiser than he came.

Also, when a Reference was going on, and the room full of lawyers and witnesses and business was driving fast; some deeply occupied legal gentleman present, seeing Bartleby wholly unemployed, would request him to run round to his (the legal gentleman's) office and fetch some papers for him. Thereupon, Bartleby would tranquilly decline, and yet remain idle as before. Then the lawyer would give a great stare, and turn to me. And what could I say? At last I was made aware that all through the circle of my professional acquaintance, a whisper of wonder was running round, having reference to the strange creature I kept at my office. This worried me very much. And as the idea came upon me of his possibly turning out a long-lived man, and keep occupying my chambers, and denying my authority; and perplexing my visitors; and scandalizing my professional reputation; and casting a general gloom over the premises; keeping soul and body together to the last upon his savings (for doubtless he spent but half a dime a day), and in the end perhaps outlive me, and claim possession of my office by right of his perpetual occupancy: as all these dark anticipations crowded upon me more and more, and my friends continually intruded their relentless remarks upon the apparition in my room; a great change was wrought in me. I resolved to gather all my faculties together, and for ever rid me of this intolerable incubus.

Ere revolving any complicated project, however, adapted to this end, I first simply suggested to Bartleby the propriety of his permanent departure. In a calm and serious tone, I commended the idea to his careful and mature consideration. But having taken three days to meditate upon it, he apprised me that his original determination remained the same; in short, that he still preferred to abide with me.

What shall I do? I now said to myself, buttoning up my coat to the last button. What shall I do? What ought I to do? What does conscience say I should do with this man, or rather ghost. Rid myself of him, I must; go, he shall. But how? You will not thrust him, the poor, pale, passive mortal, — you will not thrust such a helpless creature out of your door? You will not dishonor yourself by such cruelty? No, I will not, I cannot do that. Rather would I let him live and die here, and then mason up his remains in the wall. What then will you do? For all your coaxing, he will not budge. Bribes he leaves under your own paperweight on your table; in short, it is quite plain that he prefers to cling to you.

Then something severe, something unusual must be done. What! Surely you will not have him collared by a constable, and commit his innocent pallor to the common jail? And upon what ground could you procure such a thing to be done? — A vagrant, is he? What! He a vagrant, a wanderer, who refuses to budge? It is because he will not be a vagrant, then, that you seek to count him as a vagrant. That is too absurd. No visible means of support: there I have him. Wrong again: for indubitably he does support himself, and that is the only unanswerable proof that any man can show of his possessing the means so to do. No more then. Since he will not quit me, I must quit him. I will change my offices; I will move elsewhere; and give him fair notice, that if I find him on my new premises I will then proceed against him as a common trespasser.

Acting accordingly, next day I thus addressed him: "I find these chambers too far from the City Hall; the air is unwholesome. In a word, I propose to remove my offices next week, and shall no longer require your services. I tell you this now, in order that you may seek another place."

He made no reply, and nothing more was said.

On the appointed day I engaged carts and men, proceeded to my chambers, and having but little furniture, every thing was removed in a few hours. Throughout, the scrivener remained standing behind the screen, which I directed to be removed the last thing. It was withdrawn; and being folded up like a huge folio, left him the motionless occupant of a naked room. I stood in the entry watching him a moment, while something from within me upbraided me.

I re-entered, with my hand in my pocket—and—and my heart in my mouth. "Goodbye, Bartleby; I am going—goodbye, and God some way bless you; and take that," slipping something in his hand. But it dropped upon the floor, and then—strange to say—I tore myself from him whom I had so longed to be rid of.

Established in my new quarters, for a day or two I kept the door locked, and started at every footfall in the passages. When I returned to my rooms after any little absence, I would pause at the threshold for an instant, and attentively listen, ere applying my key. But these fears were needless. Bartleby never came nigh me.

I thought all was going well, when a perturbed looking stranger visited me, inquiring whether I was the person who had recently occupied rooms at No. – Wall-street.

Full of forebodings, I replied that I was.

"Then sir," said the stranger, who proved a lawyer, "you are responsible for the man you left there. He refuses to do any copying; he refuses to do any thing; he says he prefers not to; and he refuses to quit the premises."

"I am very sorry, sir," said I, with assumed tranquility, but an inward tremor, "but, really, the man you allude to is nothing to me—he is no relation or apprentice of mine, that you should hold me responsible for him."

"In mercy's name, who is he?"

"I certainly cannot inform you. I know nothing about him. Formerly I employed him as a copyist; but he has done nothing for me now for some time past."

"I shall settle him then—good morning, sir."

Several days passed, and I heard nothing more; and though I often felt a charitable prompting to call at the place and see poor Bartleby, yet a certain squeamishness of I know not what withheld me.

All is over with him, by this time, thought I at last, when through another week no further intelligence reached me. But coming to my room the day after, I found several persons waiting at my door in a high state of nervous excitement. "That's the man—here he comes," cried the foremost one, whom I recognized as the lawyer who had previously called upon me alone.

"You must take him away, sir, at once," cried a portly person among them, advancing upon me, and whom I knew to be the landlord of No. — Wall-street. "These gentlemen, my tenants, cannot stand it any longer; Mr. B—" pointing to the lawyer, "has turned him out of his room, and he now persists in haunting the building generally, sitting upon the banisters of the stairs by day, and sleeping in the entry by night. Every body is concerned; clients are leaving the offices; some fears are entertained of a mob; something you must do, and that without delay." Aghast at this torrent, I fell back before it, and would fain have locked myself in my new quarters. In vain I persisted that Bartleby was nothing to me—no more than to any one else. In vain:—I was the last person known to have any thing to do with him, and they held me to the terrible account. Fearful then of being exposed in the papers (as one person present obscurely threatened) I considered the matter, and at length said, that if the lawyer would give me a confidential interview with the scrivener, in his (the lawyer's) own room, I would that afternoon strive my best to rid them of the nuisance they complained of.

Going up stairs to my old haunt, there was Bartleby silently sitting upon the banister at the landing.

"What are you doing here, Bartleby?" said I. "Sitting upon the banister," he mildly replied.

I motioned him into the lawyer's room, who then left us.

"Bartleby," said I, "are you aware that you are the cause of great tribulation to me, by persisting in occupying the entry after being dismissed from the office?"

No answer.

"Now one of two things must take place. Either you must do something, or something must be done to you. Now what sort of business would you like to engage in? Would you like to re-engage in copying for some one?"

"No; I would prefer not to make any change."

"Would you like a clerkship in a dry-goods store?"

"There is too much confinement about that. No, I would not like a clerkship; but I am not particular."

"Too much confinement," I cried, "why you keep yourself confined all the time!"

"I would prefer not to take a clerkship," he rejoined, as if to settle that little item at once.

"How would a bartender's business suit you? There is no trying of the eyesight in that."

"I would not like it at all; though, as I said before, I am not particular." His unwonted wordiness inspirited me. I returned to the charge.

"Well then, would you like to travel through the country collecting bills for the merchants? That would improve your health."

"No, I would prefer to be doing something else."

"How then would going as a companion to Europe, to entertain some young gentleman with your conversation, — how would that suit you?"

"Not at all. It does not strike me that there is any thing definite about that. I like to be stationary. But I am not particular."

"Stationary you shall be then," I cried, now losing all patience, and for the first time in all my exasperating connection with him fairly flying into a passion. "If you do not go away from these premises before night, I shall feel bound— indeed I am bound—to—to—to quit the premises myself!" I rather absurdly concluded, knowing not with what possible threat to try to frighten his immobility into compliance. Despairing of all further efforts, I was precipitately leaving him, when a final thought occurred to me—one which had not been wholly unindulged before.

"Bartleby," said I, in the kindest tone I could assume under such exciting circumstances, "will you go home with me now—not to my office, but my dwelling—and remain there till we can conclude upon some convenient arrangement for you at our leisure? Come, let us start now, right away."

"No: at present I would prefer not to make any change at all."

I answered nothing; but effectually dodging every one by the suddenness and rapidity of my flight, rushed from the building, ran up Wall-street towards Broadway, and jumping into the first omnibus was soon removed from pursuit. As soon as tranquility returned I distinctly perceived that I had now done all that I possibly could, both in respect to the demands of the landlord and his tenants, and with regard to my own desire and sense of duty, to benefit Bartleby, and shield him from rude persecution. I now strove to be entirely care-free and quiescent; and my conscience justified me in the attempt; though indeed it was not so successful as I could have wished. So fearful was I of being again hunted out by the incensed landlord and his exasperated tenants, that, surrendering my business to Nippers, for a few days I drove about the upper part of the town and through the suburbs, in my rockaway; crossed over to Jersey City and Hoboken, and paid fugitive visits to Manhattanville and Astoria. In fact I almost lived in my rockaway for the time.

When again I entered my office, lo, a note from the landlord lay upon the desk. I opened it with trembling hands. It informed me that the writer had sent to the police, and had Bartleby removed to the Tombs as a vagrant. Moreover, since I knew more about him than any one else, he wished me to appear at that place, and make a suitable statement of the facts. These tidings had a conflicting effect upon me. At first I was indignant; but at last almost approved. The landlord's energetic, summary disposition had led him to adopt a procedure which I do not think I would have decided upon myself; and yet as a last resort, under such peculiar circumstances, it seemed the only plan.

As I afterwards learned, the poor scrivener, when told that he must be conducted to the Tombs, offered not the slightest obstacle, but in his pale unmoving way, silently acquiesced.

Some of the compassionate and curious bystanders joined the party; and headed by one of the constables arm in arm with Bartleby, the silent procession filed its way through all the noise, and heat, and joy of the roaring thoroughfares at noon.

The same day I received the note I went to the Tombs, or to speak more properly, the Halls of Justice. Seeking the right officer, I stated the purpose of my call, and was informed that the individual I described was indeed within. I then assured the functionary that Bartleby was a perfectly honest man, and greatly to be compassionated, however unaccountably eccentric. I narrated all I knew, and closed by suggesting the idea of letting him remain in as indulgent confinement as possible till something less harsh might be done—though indeed I hardly knew what. At all events, if nothing else could be decided upon, the alms-house must receive him. I then begged to have an interview.

Being under no disgraceful charge, and quite serene and harmless in all his ways, they had permitted him freely to wander about the prison, and especially in the inclosed grass-platted yard thereof. And so I found him there, standing all alone in the quietest of the yards, his face towards a high wall, while all around, from the narrow slits of the jail windows, I thought I saw peering out upon him the eyes of murderers and thieves.

"Bartleby!"

"I know you," he said, without looking round, — "and I want nothing to say to you."

"It was not I that brought you here, Bartleby," said I, keenly pained at his implied suspicion. "And to you, this should not be so vile a place. Nothing reproachful attaches to you by being here. And see, it is not so sad a place as one might think. Look, there is the sky, and here is the grass."

"I know where I am," he replied, but would say nothing more, and so I left him.

As I entered the corridor again, a broad meat-like man, in an apron, accosted me, and jerking his thumb over his shoulder said—"Is that your friend?"

"Yes."

"Does he want to starve? If he does, let him live on the prison fare, that's all." "Who are you?" asked I, not knowing what to make of such an unofficially speaking person in such a place.

"I am the grub-man. Such gentlemen as have friends here, hire me to provide them with something good to eat."

"Is this so?" said I, turning to the turnkey.

He said it was.

"Well then," said I, slipping some silver into the grub-man's hands (for so they called him). "I want you to give particular attention to my friend there; let him have the best dinner you can get. And you must be as polite to him as possible." "Introduce me, will you?" said the grub-man, looking at me with an expression which seemed to say he was all impatience for an opportunity to give a specimen of his breeding.

Thinking it would prove of benefit to the scrivener, I acquiesced; and asking the grub-man his name, went up with him to Bartleby.

"Bartleby, this is Mr. Cutlets; you will find him very useful to you."

"Your sarvant, sir, your sarvant," said the grub-man, making a low salutation behind his apron. "Hope you find it pleasant here, sir;—spacious grounds—cool apartments, sir—hope you'll stay with us some time—try to make it agreeable. May Mrs. Cutlets and I have the pleasure of your company to dinner, sir, in Mrs. Cutlets' private room?"

"I prefer not to dine today," said Bartleby, turning away. "It would disagree with me; I am unused to dinners." So saying he slowly moved to the other side of the inclosure, and took up a position fronting the dead-wall.

"How's this?" said the grub-man, addressing me with a stare of astonishment. "He's odd, aint he?"

"I think he is a little deranged," said I, sadly.

"Deranged? Deranged is it? Well now, upon my word, I thought that friend of yourn was a gentleman forger; they are always pale and genteel-like, them forgers. I can't pity'em—can't help it, sir. Did you know Monroe Edwards?" he added touchingly, and paused. Then, laying his hand pityingly on my shoulder, sighed, "he died of consumption at Sing-Sing. So you weren't acquainted with

Monroe?" "No, I was never socially acquainted with any forgers. But I cannot stop longer. Look to my friend yonder. You will not lose by it. I will see you again." Some few days after this, I again obtained admission to the Tombs, and went through the corridors in quest of Bartleby; but without finding him.

"I saw him coming from his cell not long ago," said a turnkey, "may be he's gone to loiter in the yards."

So I went in that direction.

"Are you looking for the silent man?" said another turnkey passing me. "Yonder he lies—sleeping in the yard there. 'Tis not twenty minutes since I saw him lie down."

The yard was entirely quiet. It was not accessible to the common prisoners. The surrounding walls, of amazing thickness, kept off all sounds behind them. The Egyptian character of the masonry weighed upon me with its gloom. But a soft imprisoned turf grew under foot. The heart of the eternal pyramids, it seemed, wherein, by some strange magic, through the clefts, grass-seed, dropped by birds, had sprung.

Strangely huddled at the base of the wall, his knees drawn up, and lying on his side, his head touching the cold stones, I saw the wasted Bartleby. But nothing stirred. I paused; then went close up to him; stooped over, and saw that his dim eyes were open; otherwise he seemed profoundly sleeping. Something prompted me to touch him. I felt his hand, when a tingling shiver ran up my arm and down my spine to my feet.

The round face of the grub-man peered upon me now. "His dinner is ready. Won't he dine today, either? Or does he live without dining?"

"Lives without dining," said I, and closed his eyes. "Eh!—He's asleep, aint he?"

"With kings and counselors," murmured I.

~

There would seem little need for proceeding further in this history. Imagination will readily supply the meager recital of poor Bartleby's interment. But ere parting with the reader, let me say, that if this little narrative has sufficiently interested him, to awaken curiosity as to who Bartleby was, and what manner of life he led prior to the present narrator's making his acquaintance, I can only reply, that in such curiosity I fully share, but am wholly unable to gratify it. Yet here I hardly know whether I should divulge one little item of rumor, which came to my ear a few months after the scrivener's decease. Upon what basis it rested, I could never ascertain; and hence, how true it is I cannot now tell. But inasmuch as this vague report has not been without certain strange suggestive interest to me, however sad, it may prove the same with some others; and so I will briefly mention it. The report was this: that Bartleby had been a subordinate clerk in the Dead Letter Office at Washington, from which he had been suddenly removed by a change in the administration. When I think over this rumor, I cannot adequately express the emotions which seize me. Dead letters! Does it not sound like dead men? Conceive a man by nature and misfortune prone to a pallid hopelessness, can any business seem more fitted to heighten it than that of continually handling these dead letters, and assorting them for the flames? For by the cart-load they are annually burned. Sometimes from out the folded paper the pale clerk takes a ring:—the finger it was meant for, perhaps, moulders in the grave; a bank-note sent in swiftest charity:—he whom it would relieve, nor eats nor hungers any more; pardon for those who died despairing; hope for those who died unhoping; good tidings for those who died stifled by unrelieved calamities. On errands of life, these letters speed to death.

Ah Bartleby! Ah humanity!

The Signal-Man

Charles Dickens

Charles Dickens (1812-1870) was arguably the greatest writer of the Victorian era. Besides writing some of the most popular novels of the 19th century such as *A Christmas Carol* (1844) and *David Copperfield* (1850), this English author also wrote short stories such as 'The Signal-Man', which was first published in *Mugby Junction*, the Christmas edition of his periodical *All the Year Round* (1866).

"Halloa! Below there!"

When he heard a voice thus calling to him, he was standing at the door of his box, with a flag in his hand, furled round its short pole. One would have thought, considering the nature of the ground, that he could not have doubted from what quarter the voice came; but, instead of looking up to where I stood on the top of the steep cutting nearly over his head, he turned himself about and looked down the Line. There was something remarkable in his manner of doing so, though I could not have said, for my life, what. But, I know it was remarkable enough to attract my notice, even though his figure was foreshortened and shadowed, down in the deep trench, and mine was high above him, so steeped in the glow of an angry sunset that I had shaded my eyes with my hand before I saw him at all.

"Halloa! Below!"

From looking down the Line, he turned himself about again, and, raising his eyes, saw my figure high above him.

"Is there any path by which I can come down and speak to you?"

He looked up at me without replying, and I looked down at him without pressing him too soon with a repetition of my idle question.

Just then, there came a vague vibration in the earth and air, quickly changing into a violent pulsation, and an oncoming rush that caused me to start back, as though it had force to draw me down. When such vapour as rose to my height from this rapid train, had passed me and was skimming away over the landscape, I looked down again, and saw him re-furling the flag he had shown while the train went by.

I repeated my inquiry. After a pause, during which he seemed to regard me with fixed attention, he motioned with his rolled-up flag towards a point on my level, some two or three hundred yards distant. I called down to him, "All right!" and made for that point. There, by dint of looking closely about me, I found a rough zig-zag descending path notched out: which I followed.

The cutting was extremely deep, and unusually precipitate. It was made through a clammy stone that became oozier and wetter as I went down. For these reasons, I found the way long enough to give me time to recall a singular air of reluctance or compulsion with which he had pointed out the path.

When I came down low enough upon the zig-zag descent, to see him again, I saw that he was standing between the rails on the way by which the train had lately passed, in an attitude as if he were waiting for me to appear. He had his left hand at his chin, and that left elbow rested on his right hand crossed over his breast. His attitude was one of such expectation and watchfulness, that I stopped a moment, wondering at it.

I resumed my downward way, and, stepping out upon the level of the railroad and drawing nearer to him, saw that he was a dark sallow man, with a dark beard and rather heavy eyebrows. His post was in as solitary and dismal a place as ever I saw. On either side, a dripping-wet wall of jagged stone, excluding all view but a strip of sky; the perspective one way, only a crooked prolongation of this great dungeon; the shorter perspective in the other direction, terminating in a gloomy red light, and the gloomier entrance to a black tunnel, in whose massive architecture there was a barbarous, depressing, and forbidding air. So little sunlight ever found its way to this spot, that it had an earthy deadly smell; and so much cold wind rushed through it, that it struck chill to me, as if I had left the natural world.

Before he stirred, I was near enough to him to have touched him. Not even then removing his eyes from mine, he stepped back one step, and lifted his hand.

This was a lonesome post to occupy (I said), and it had riveted my attention when I looked down from up yonder. A visitor was a rarity, I should suppose; not an unwelcome rarity, I hoped? In me, he merely saw a man who had been shut up within narrow limits all his life, and who, being at last set free, had a newly-awakened interest in these great works. To such purpose I spoke to him; but I am far from sure of the terms I used, for, besides that I am not happy in opening any conversation, there was something in the man that daunted me.

He directed a most curious look towards the red light near the tunnel's mouth, and looked all about it, as if something were missing from it, and then looked at me.

That light was part of his charge? Was it not?

He answered in a low voice: "Don't you know it is?"

The monstrous thought came into my mind as I perused the fixed eyes and the saturnine face, that this was a spirit, not a man. I have speculated since, whether there may have been infection in his mind.

In my turn, I stepped back. But in making the action, I detected in his eyes some latent fear of me. This put the monstrous thought to flight.

"You look at me," I said, forcing a smile, "as if you had a dread of me."

"I was doubtful," he returned, "whether I had seen you before."

"Where?"

He pointed to the red light he had looked at.

"There?" I said.

Intently watchful of me, he replied (but without sound), Yes.

"My good fellow, what should I do there? However, be that as it may, I never was there, you may swear." "I think I may," he rejoined. "Yes. I am sure I may."

His manner cleared, like my own. He replied to my remarks with readiness, and in well-chosen words. Had he much to do there? Yes; that was to say, he had enough responsibility to bear; but exactness and watchfulness were what was required of him, and of actual work—manual labour he had next to none. To change that signal, to trim those lights, and to turn this iron handle now and then, was all he had to do under that head. Regarding those many long and lonely hours of which I seemed to make so much, he could only say that the routine of his life had shaped itself into that form, and he had grown used to it. He had taught himself a language down here—if only to know it by sight, and to have formed his own crude ideas of its pronunciation, could be called learning it. He had also worked at fractions and decimals, and tried a little algebra; but he was, and had been as a boy, a poor hand at figures. Was it necessary for him when on duty, always to remain in that channel of damp air, and could he never rise into the sunshine from between those high stone walls? Why, that depended upon times and circumstances. Under some conditions there would be less upon the Line than under others, and the same held good as to certain hours of the day and night. In bright weather, he did choose occasions for getting a little above these lower shadows; but, being at all times liable to be called by his electric bell, and at such times listening for it with redoubled anxiety, the relief was less than I would suppose.

He took me into his box, where there was a fire, a desk for an official book in which he had to make certain entries, a telegraphic instrument with its dial face and needles, and the little bell of which he had spoken. On my trusting that he would excuse the remark that he had been well-educated, and (I hoped I might say without offence), perhaps educated above that station, he observed that instances of slight incongruity in such-wise would rarely be found wanting among large bodies of men; that he had heard it was so in workhouses, in the police force, even in that last desperate resource, the army; and that he knew it was so, more or less, in any great railway staff. He had been, when young (if I could believe it, sitting in that, hut; he scarcely could), a student of natural philosophy, and had attended lectures; but he had run wild, misused his opportunities, gone down, and never risen again. He had no complaint to offer about that. He had made his bed and he lay upon it. It was far too late to make another.

All that I have here condensed, he said in a quiet manner, with his grave dark regards divided between me and the fire. He threw in the word "Sir" from time to time, and especially when he referred to his youth: as though to request me to understand that he claimed to be nothing but what I found him. He was several times interrupted by the little bell, and had to read off messages, and send replies. Once, he had to stand without the door, and display a flag as a train passed, and make some verbal communication to the driver. In the discharge of his duties I observed him to be remarkably exact and vigilant, breaking off his discourse at a syllable, and remaining silent until what he had to do was done.

In a word, I should have set this man down as one of the safest of men to be employed in that capacity, but for the circumstance that while he was speaking to me he twice broke off with a fallen colour, turned his face towards the little bell when it did NOT ring, opened the door of the hut (which was kept shut to exclude the unhealthy damp), and looked out towards the red light near the mouth of the tunnel. On both of those occasions, he came back to the fire with the inexplicable air upon him which I had remarked, without being able to define, when we were so far asunder.

Said I when I rose to leave him: "You almost make me think that I have met with a contented man."

(I am afraid I must acknowledge that I said it to lead him on.)

"I believe I used to be so," he rejoined, in the low voice in which he had first spoken; "but I am troubled, sir, I am troubled."

He would have recalled the words if he could. He had said them, however, and I took them up quickly.

"With what? What is your trouble?"

"It is very difficult to impart, sir. It is very, very difficult to speak of. If ever you make me another visit, I will try to tell you."

"But I expressly intend to make you another visit. Say, when shall it be?"

"I go off early in the morning, and I shall be on again at ten tomorrow night, sir." "I will come at eleven."

He thanked me, and went out at the door with me. "I'll show my white light, sir," he said, in his peculiar low voice, "till you have found the way up. When you have found it, don't call out! And when you are at the top, don't call out!"

His manner seemed to make the place strike colder to me, but I said no more than "Very well."

"And when you come down tomorrow night, don't call out! Let me ask you a parting question. What made you cry 'Halloa! Below there!' tonight?"

"Heaven knows," said I. "I cried something to that effect…"

"Not to that effect, sir. Those were the very words. I know them well."

"Admit those were the very words. I said them, no doubt, because I saw you below."

"For no other reason?"

"What other reason could I possibly have!"

"You had no feeling that they were conveyed to you in any supernatural way?"

"No."

He wished me good night, and held up his light. I walked by the side of the down Line of rails (with a very disagreeable sensation of a train coming behind me), until I found the path. It was easier to mount than to descend, and I got back to my inn without any adventure.

Punctual to my appointment, I placed my foot on the first notch of the zig-zag next night, as the distant clocks were striking eleven. He was waiting for me at the bottom, with his white light on. "I have not called out," I said, when we came close together; "may I speak now?" "By all means, sir." "Good night then, and here's my hand." "Good night, sir, and here's mine." With that, we walked side by side to his box, entered it, closed the door, and sat down by the fire.

"I have made up my mind, sir," he began, bending forward as soon as we were seated, and speaking in a tone but a little above a whisper, "that you shall not have to ask me twice what troubles me. I took you for someone else yesterday evening. That troubles me."

"That mistake?"

"No. That someone else."

"Who is it?"

"I don't know."

"Like me?"

"I don't know. I never saw the face. The left arm is across the face, and the right arm is waved. Violently waved. This way."

I followed his action with my eyes, and it was the action of an arm gesticulating with the utmost passion and vehemence: "For God's sake clear the way!"

"One moonlight night," said the man, "I was sitting here, when I heard a voice cry "Halloa! Below there!" I started up, looked from that door, and saw this Some one else standing by the red light near the tunnel, waving as I just now showed you. The voice seemed hoarse with shouting, and it cried, "Look out! Look out!" And then again "Halloa! Below there! Look out!" I caught up my lamp, turned it on red, and ran towards the figure, calling, "What's wrong? What has happened? Where?" It stood just outside the blackness of the tunnel. I advanced so close upon it that I wondered at its keeping the sleeve across its eyes. I ran right up at it, and had my hand stretched out to pull the sleeve away, when it was gone."

"Into the tunnel," said I.

"No. I ran on into the tunnel, five hundred yards. I stopped and held my lamp above my head, and saw the figures of the measured distance, and saw the wet stains stealing down the walls and trickling through the arch. I ran out again, faster than I had run in (for I had a mortal abhorrence of the place upon me), and I looked all round the red light with my own red light, and I went up the iron ladder to the gallery atop of it, and I came down again, and ran back here. I telegraphed both ways, 'An alarm has been given. Is anything wrong?' The answer came back, both ways: 'All well.'"

Resisting the slow touch of a frozen finger tracing out my spine, I showed him how that this figure must be a deception of his sense of sight, and how that figures, originating in disease of the delicate nerves that minister to the functions of the eye, were known to have often troubled patients, some of whom had become conscious of the nature of their affliction, and had even proved it by experiments upon themselves. "As to an imaginary cry," said I, "do but listen for a moment to the wind in this unnatural valley while we speak so low, and to the wild harp it makes of the telegraph wires!"

That was all very well, he returned, after we had sat listening for a while, and he ought to know something of the wind and the wires, he who so often passed long winter nights there, alone and watching. But he would beg to remark that he had not finished.

I asked his pardon, and he slowly added these words, touching my arm: "Within six hours after the Appearance, the memorable accident on this Line happened, and within ten hours the dead and wounded were brought along through the tunnel over the spot where the figure had stood."

A disagreeable shudder crept over me, but I did my best against it. It was not to be denied, I rejoined, that this was a remarkable coincidence, calculated deeply to impress his mind. But it was unquestionable that remarkable coincidences did continually occur, and they must be taken into account in dealing with such a subject. Though to be sure I must admit, I added (for I thought I saw that he was going to bring the objection to bear upon me), men of common sense did not allow much for coincidences in making the ordinary calculations of life.

He again begged to remark that he had not finished.

I again begged his pardon for being betrayed into interruptions.

"This," he said, again laying his hand upon my arm, and glancing over his shoulder with hollow eyes, "was just a year ago. Six or seven months passed, and I had recovered from the surprise and shock, when one morning, as the day was breaking, I, standing at that door, looked towards the red light, and saw the spectre again." He stopped, with a fixed look at me.

"Did it cry out?"

"No. It was silent."

"Did it wave its arm?"

"No. It leaned against the shaft of the light, with both hands before the face. Like this."

Once more, I followed his action with my eyes. It was an action of mourning. I have seen such an attitude in stone figures on tombs.

"Did you go up to it?"

"I came in and sat down, partly to collect my thoughts, partly because it had turned me faint. When I went to the door again, daylight was above me, and the ghost was gone."

"But nothing followed? Nothing came of this?"

He touched me on the arm with his forefinger twice or thrice, giving a ghastly nod each time: "That very day, as a train came out of the tunnel, I noticed, at a carriage window on my side, what looked like a confusion of hands and heads, and something waved. I saw it, just in time to signal the driver, Stop! He shut off, and put his brake on, but the train drifted past here a hundred and fifty yards or more. I ran after it, and, as I went along, heard terrible screams and cries. A beautiful young lady had died instantaneously in one of the compartments, and was brought in here, and laid down on this floor between us."

Involuntarily, I pushed my chair back, as I looked from the boards at which he pointed, to himself.

"True, sir. True. Precisely as it happened, so I tell it you."

I could think of nothing to say, to any purpose, and my mouth was very dry. The wind and the wires took up the story with a long lamenting wail.

He resumed. "Now, sir, mark this, and judge how my mind is troubled. The spectre came back, a week ago. Ever since, it has been there, now and again, by fits and starts."

"At the light?"

"At the Danger-light."

"What does it seem to do?"

He repeated, if possible with increased passion and vehemence, that former gesticulation of "For God's sake clear the way!"

Then, he went on. "I have no peace or rest for it. It calls to me, for many minutes together, in an agonised manner, "Below there! Look out! Look out!" It stands waving to me. It rings my little bell…"

I caught at that. "Did it ring your bell yesterday evening when I was here, and you went to the door?"

"Twice."

"Why, see," said I, "how your imagination misleads you. My eyes were on the bell, and my ears were open to the bell, and if I am a living man, it did NOT ring at those times. No, nor at any other time, except when it was rung in the natural course of physical things by the station communicating with you."

He shook his head. "I have never made a mistake as to that, yet, sir. I have never confused the spectre's ring with the man's. The ghost's ring is a strange vibration in the bell that it derives from nothing else, and I have not asserted that the bell stirs to the eye. I don't wonder that you failed to hear it. But I heard it."

"And did the spectre seem to be there, when you looked out?"

"It was there."

"Both times?"

He repeated firmly: "Both times."

"Will you come to the door with me, and look for it now?"

He bit his under-lip as though he were somewhat unwilling, but arose. I opened the door, and stood on the step, while he stood in the doorway. There, was the Danger-light. There, was the dismal mouth of the tunnel. There, were the high wet stone walls of the cutting. There, were the stars above them.

"Do you see it?" I asked him, taking particular note of his face. His eyes were prominent and strained; but not very much more so, perhaps, than my own had been when I had directed them earnestly towards the same spot.

"No," he answered. "It is not there.'

"Agreed," said I.

We went in again, shut the door, and resumed our seats. I was thinking how best to improve this advantage, if it might be called one, when he took up the conversation in such a matter of course way, so assuming that there could be no serious question of fact between us, that I felt myself placed in the weakest of positions.

"By this time you will fully understand, sir," he said, "that what troubles me so dreadfully, is the question, What does the spectre mean?"

I was not sure, I told him, that I did fully understand.

"What is its warning against?" he said, ruminating, with his eyes on the fire, and only by times turning them on me. "What is the danger? Where is the danger? There is danger overhanging, somewhere on the Line. Some dreadful calamity will happen. It is not to be doubted this third time, after what has gone before. But surely this is a cruel haunting of me. What can I do?"

He pulled out his handkerchief, and wiped the drops from his heated forehead.

"If I telegraph Danger, on either side of me, or on both, I can give no reason for it," he went on, wiping the palms of his hands. "I should get into trouble, and do no good. They would think I was mad. This is the way it would work:—Message: "Danger! Take care!" Answer: "What danger? Where?" Message: "Don't know. But for God's sake take care!" They would displace me. What else could they do?"

His pain of mind was most pitiable to see. It was the mental torture of a conscientious man, oppressed beyond endurance by an unintelligible responsibility involving life.

"When it first stood under the Danger-light," he went on, putting his dark hair back from his head, and drawing his hands outward across and across his temples in an extremity of feverish distress, "why not tell me where that accident was to happen—if it must happen? Why not tell me how it could be averted—if it could have been averted? When on its second coming it hid its face, why not tell me instead: "She is going to die. Let them keep her at home"? If it came, on those two occasions, only to show me that its warnings were true, and so to prepare me for the third, why not warn me plainly now? And I, Lord help me! A mere poor signal-man on this solitary station! Why not go to somebody with credit to be believed, and power to act!"

When I saw him in this state, I saw that for the poor man's sake, as well as for the public safety, what I had to do for the time was, to compose his mind. Therefore, setting aside all question of reality or unreality between us, I represented to him that whoever thoroughly discharged his duty, must do well, and that at least it was his comfort that he understood his duty, though he did not understand these confounding Appearances. In this effort I succeeded far better than in the attempt to reason him out of his conviction. He became calm; the occupations incidental to his post as the night advanced, began to make larger demands on his attention; and I left him at two in the morning. I had offered to stay through the night, but he would not hear of it.

That I more than once looked back at the red light as I ascended the pathway, that I did not like the red light, and that I should have slept but poorly if my bed had been under it, I see no reason to conceal. Nor, did I like the two sequences of the accident and the dead girl. I see no reason to conceal that, either.

But, what ran most in my thoughts was the consideration how ought I to act, having become the recipient of this disclosure? I had proved the man to be intelligent, vigilant, painstaking, and exact; but how long might he remain so, in his state of mind? Though in a subordinate position, still he held a most important trust, and would I (for instance) like to stake my own life on the chances of his continuing to execute it with precision?

Unable to overcome a feeling that there would be something treacherous in my communicating what he had told me, to his superiors in the Company, without first being plain with himself and proposing a middle course to him, I ultimately resolved to offer to accompany him (otherwise keeping his secret for the present) to the wisest medical practitioner we could hear of in those parts, and to take his opinion. A change in his time of duty would come round next night, he had apprised me, and he would be off an hour or two after sunrise, and on again soon after sunset. I had appointed to return accordingly.

Next evening was a lovely evening, and I walked out early to enjoy it. The sun was not yet quite down when I traversed the field-path near the top of the deep cutting. I would extend my walk for an hour, I said to myself, half an hour on and half an hour back, and it would then be time to go to my signal-man's box.

Before pursuing my stroll, I stepped to the brink, and mechanically looked down, from the point from which I had first seen him. I cannot describe the thrill that seized upon me, when, close at the mouth of the tunnel, I saw the appearance of a man, with his left sleeve across his eyes, passionately waving his right arm.

The nameless horror that oppressed me, passed in a moment, for in a moment I saw that this appearance of a man was a man indeed, and that there was a little group of other men standing at a short distance, to whom he seemed to be rehearsing the gesture he made. The Danger-light was not yet lighted. Against its shaft, a little low hut, entirely new to me, had been made of some wooden supports and tarpaulin. It looked no bigger than a bed.

With an irresistible sense that something was wrong—with a flashing self-reproachful fear that fatal mischief had come of my leaving the man there, and causing no one to be sent to overlook or correct what he did—I descended the notched path with all the speed I could make.

"What is the matter?" I asked the men.

"Signal-man killed this morning, sir."

"Not the man belonging to that box?"

"Yes, sir."

"Not the man I know?"

"You will recognise him, sir, if you knew him," said the man who spoke for the others, solemnly uncovering his own head and raising an end of the tarpaulin, "for his face is quite composed."

"O! How did this happen, how did this happen?" I asked, turning from one to another as the hut closed in again.

"He was cut down by an engine, sir. No man in England knew his work better. But somehow he was not clear of the outer rail. It was just at broad day. He had struck the light, and had the lamp in his hand. As the engine came out of the tunnel, his back was towards her, and she cut him down. That man drove her, and was showing how it happened. Show the gentleman, Tom."

The man, who wore a rough dark dress, stepped back to his former place at the mouth of the tunnel!

"Coming round the curve in the tunnel, sir," he said, 'I saw him at the end, like as if I saw him down a perspective-glass. There was no time to check speed, and I knew him to be very careful. As he didn't seem to take heed of the whistle, I shut it off when we were running down upon him, and called to him as loud as I could call."

"What did you say?"

"I said, Below there! Look out! Look out! For God's sake clear the way!"

I started.

"Ah! it was a dreadful time, sir. I never left off calling to him. I put this arm before my eyes, not to see, and I waved this arm to the last; but it was no use."

Without prolonging the narrative to dwell on any one of its curious circumstances more than on any other, I may, in closing it, point out the coincidence that the warning of the Engine-Driver included, not only the words which the unfortunate Signal-man had repeated to me as haunting him, but also the words which I myself—not he—had attached, and that only in my own mind, to the gesticulation he had imitated.

God Sees The Truth, But Waits

Leo Tolstoy

Leo Tolstoy (1828-1910) was regarded as one of the greatest novelists of the world. Best known for works such as *War and Peace* (1867) and *Anna Karenina* (1877), the Russian author was considered a master of realistic fiction. Besides writing novels, Tolstoy also wrote short stories such as 'God Sees The Truth, But Waits' (1872) which was translated to English by Aylmer Maude, who was instrumental in generating interest in Tolstoy's works.

In the town of Vladimir lived a young merchant named Ivan Dmitrich Aksionov. He had two shops and a house of his own.

Aksionov was a handsome, fair-haired, curly-headed fellow, full of fun, and very fond of singing. When quite a young man he had been given to drink, and was riotous when he had had too much; but after he married he gave up drinking, except now and then.

One summer Aksionov was going to the Nizhny Fair, and as he bade goodbye to his family, his wife said to him, "Ivan Dmitrich, do not start today; I have had a bad dream about you."

Aksionov laughed, and said, "You are afraid that when I get to the fair I shall go on a spree."

His wife replied: "I do not know what I am afraid of; all I know is that I had a bad dream. I dreamt you returned from the town, and when you took off your cap I saw that your hair was quite grey."

Aksionov laughed. "That's a lucky sign," said he. "See if I don't sell out all my goods, and bring you some presents from the fair."

So he said goodbye to his family, and drove away.

When he had travelled halfway, he met a merchant whom he knew, and they put up at the same inn for the night. They had some tea together, and then went to bed in adjoining rooms.

It was not Aksionov's habit to sleep late, and, wishing to travel while it was still cool, he aroused his driver before dawn, and told him to put in the horses.

Then he made his way across to the landlord of the inn (who lived in a cottage at the back), paid his bill, and continued his journey.

When he had gone about twenty-five miles, he stopped for the horses to be fed. Aksionov rested awhile in the passage of the inn, then he stepped out into the porch, and, ordering a samovar to be heated, got out his guitar and began to play.

Suddenly a troika drove up with tinkling bells and an official alighted, followed by two soldiers. He came to Aksionov and began to question him, asking him who he was and whence he came. Aksionov answered him fully, and said, "Won't you have some tea with me?" But the official went on cross-questioning him and asking him. "Where did you spend last night? Were you alone, or with a fellow-merchant? Did you see the other merchant this morning? Why did you leave the inn before dawn?"

Aksionov wondered why he was asked all these questions, but he described all that had happened, and then added, "Why do you cross-question me as if I were a thief or a robber? I am travelling on business of my own, and there is no need to question me."

Then the official, calling the soldiers, said, "I am the police-officer of this district, and I question you because the merchant with whom you spent last night has been found with his throat cut. We must search your things."

They entered the house. The soldiers and the police-officer unstrapped Aksionov's luggage and searched it. Suddenly the officer drew a knife out of a bag, crying, "Whose knife is this?"

Aksionov looked, and seeing a blood-stained knife taken from his bag, he was frightened.

"How is it there is blood on this knife?"

Aksionov tried to answer, but could hardly utter a word, and only stammered: "I—don't know—not mine." Then the police-officer said: "This morning the merchant was found in bed with his throat cut. You are the only person who could have done it. The house was locked from inside, and no one else was there. Here is this blood-stained knife in your bag and your face and manner betray you! Tell me how you killed him, and how much money you stole?"

Aksionov swore he had not done it; that he had not seen the merchant after they had had tea together; that he had no money except eight thousand rubles of his own, and that the knife was not his. But his voice was broken, his face pale, and he trembled with fear as though he went guilty.

The police-officer ordered the soldiers to bind Aksionov and to put him in the cart. As they tied his feet together and flung him into the cart, Aksionov crossed himself and wept. His money and goods were taken from him, and he was sent to the nearest town and imprisoned there. Enquiries as to his character were made in Vladimir. The merchants and other inhabitants of that town said that in former days he used to drink and waste his time, but that he was a good man. Then the trial came on: he was charged with murdering a merchant from Ryazan, and robbing him of twenty thousand rubles.

His wife was in despair, and did not know what to believe. Her children were all quite small; one was a baby at her breast. Taking them all with her, she went to the town where her husband was in jail. At first she was not allowed to see him; but after much begging, she obtained permission from the officials, and was taken to him. When she saw her husband in prison-dress and in chains, shut up with thieves and criminals, she fell down, and did not come to her senses for a long time. Then she drew her children to her, and sat down near him. She told him of things at home, and asked about what had happened to him. He told her all, and she asked, "What can we do now?"

"We must petition the Czar not to let an innocent man perish."

His wife told him that she had sent a petition to the Czar, but it had not been accepted. Aksionov did not reply, but only looked downcast.

Then his wife said, "It was not for nothing I dreamt your hair had turned grey. You remember? You should not have started that day."

And passing her fingers through his hair, she said: "Vanya dearest, tell your wife the truth; was it not you who did it?"

"So you, too, suspect me!" said Aksionov, and, hiding his face in his hands, he began to weep. Then a soldier came to say that the wife and children must go away; and Aksionov said goodbye to his family for the last time.

When they were gone, Aksionov recalled what had been said, and when he remembered that his wife also had suspected him, he said to himself, "It seems that only God can know the truth; it is to Him alone we must appeal, and from Him alone expect mercy."

And Aksionov wrote no more petitions; gave up all hope, and only prayed to God. Aksionov was condemned to be flogged and sent to the mines. So he was flogged with a knot, and when the wounds made by the knot were healed, he was driven to Siberia with other convicts.

For twenty-six years Aksionov lived as a convict in Siberia. His hair turned white as snow, and his beard grew long, thin, and grey. All his mirth went; he stooped; he walked slowly, spoke little, and never laughed, but he often prayed.

In prison Aksionov learnt to make boots, and earned a little money, with which he bought *The Lives of the Saints*. He read this book when there was light enough in the prison; and on Sundays in the prison-church he read the lessons and sang in the choir; for his voice was still good.

The prison authorities liked Aksionov for his meekness, and his fellow-prisoners respected him: they called him "Grandfather," and "The Saint." When they wanted to petition the prison authorities about anything, they always made Aksionov their spokesman, and when there were quarrels among the prisoners they came to him to put things right, and to judge the matter.

No news reached Aksionov from his home, and he did not even know if his wife and children were still alive.

One day a fresh gang of convicts came to the prison. In the evening the old prisoners collected round the new ones and asked them what towns or villages they came from, and what they were sentenced for. Among the rest Aksionov sat down near the newcomers, and listened with downcast air to what was said.

One of the new convicts, a tall, strong man of sixty, with a closely-cropped grey beard, was telling the others what be had been arrested for.

"Well, friends," he said, "I only took a horse that was tied to a sledge, and I was arrested and accused of stealing. I said I had only taken it to get home quicker, and had then let it go; besides, the driver was a personal friend of mine. So I said, 'It's all right.' 'No,' said they, 'you stole it.' But how or where I stole it they could not say. I once really did something wrong, and ought by rights to have come here long ago, but that time I was not found out. Now I have been sent here for nothing at all... Eh, but it's lies I'm telling you; I've been to Siberia before, but I did not stay long."

"Where are you from?" asked some one.

"From Vladimir. My family are of that town. My name is Makar, and they also call me Semyonich."

Aksionov raised his head and said: "Tell me, Semyonich, do you know anything of the merchants Aksionov of Vladimir? Are they still alive?"

"Know them? Of course I do. The Aksionovs are rich, though their father is in Siberia: a sinner like ourselves, it seems! As for you, Gran'dad, how did you come here?"

Aksionov did not like to speak of his misfortune. He only sighed, and said, "For my sins I have been in prison these twenty-six years."
"What sins?" asked Makar Semyonich.

But Aksionov only said, "Well, well—I must have deserved it!" He would have said no more, but his companions told the newcomers how Aksionov came to be in Siberia; how some one had killed a merchant, and had put the knife among Aksionov's things, and Aksionov had been unjustly condemned.

When Makar Semyonich heard this, he looked at Aksionov, slapped his *own* knee, and exclaimed, "Well, this is wonderful! Really wonderful! But how old you've grown, Gran'dad!"

The others asked him why he was so surprised, and where he had seen Aksionov before; but Makar Semyonich did not reply. He only said: "It's wonderful that we should meet here, lads!"

These words made Aksionov wonder whether this man knew who had killed the merchant; so he said, "Perhaps, Semyonich, you have heard of that affair, or maybe you've seen me before?"

"How could I help hearing? The world's full of rumours. But it's a long time ago, and I've forgotten what I heard."

"Perhaps you heard who killed the merchant?" asked Aksionov.

Makar Semyonich laughed, and replied: "It must have been him in whose bag the knife was found! If someone else hid the knife there, 'He's not a thief till he's caught,' as the saying is. How could anyone put a knife into your bag while it was under your head? It would surely have woke you up."

When Aksionov heard these words, he felt sure this was the man who had killed the merchant. He rose and went away. All that night Aksionov lay awake. He felt terribly unhappy, and all sorts of images rose in his mind. There was the image of his wife as she was when he parted from her to go to the fair. He saw her as if she were present; her face and her eyes rose before him; he heard her speak and laugh. Then he saw his children, quite little, as they were at that time: one with a little cloak on, another at his mother's breast. And then he remembered himself as he used to be-young and merry. He remembered how he sat playing the guitar in the porch of the inn where he was arrested, and how free from care he had been. He saw, in his mind, the place where he was flogged, the executioner, and the people standing around; the chains, the convicts, all the twenty-six years of his prison life, and his premature old age. The thought of it all made him so wretched that he was ready to kill himself.

"And it's all that villain's doing!" thought Aksionov. And his anger was so great against Makar Semyonich that he longed for vengeance, even if he himself should perish for it. He kept repeating prayers all night, but could get no peace. During the day he did not go near Makar Semyonich, nor even look at him.

A fortnight passed in this way. Aksionov could not sleep at night, and was so miserable that he did not know what to do.

One night as he was walking about the prison he noticed some earth that came rolling out from under one of the shelves on which the prisoners slept. He stopped to see what it was. Suddenly Makar Semyonich crept out from under the shelf, and looked up at Aksionov with frightened face. Aksionov tried to pass without looking at him, but Makar seized his hand and told him that he had dug a hole under the wall, getting rid of the earth by putting it into his high-boots, and emptying it out every day on the road when the prisoners were driven to their work.

"Just you keep quiet, old man, and you shall get out too. If you blab, they'll flog the life out of me, but I will kill you first."

Aksionov trembled with anger as he looked at his enemy. He drew his hand away, saying, "I have no wish to escape, and you have no need to kill me; you killed me long ago! As to telling of you—I may do so or not, as God shall direct."

Next day, when the convicts were led out to work, the convoy soldiers noticed that one or other of the prisoners emptied some earth out of his boots. The prison was searched and the tunnel found. The Governor came and questioned all the prisoners to find out who had dug the hole. They all denied any knowledge of it. Those who knew would not betray Makar Semyonich, knowing he would be flogged almost to death. At last the Governor turned to Aksionov whom he knew to be a just man, and said:

"You are a truthful old man; tell me, before God, who dug the hole?"

Makar Semyonich stood as if he were quite unconcerned, looking at the Governor and not so much as glancing at Aksionov. Aksionov's lips and hands trembled, and for a long time he could not utter a word. He thought, "Why should I screen him who ruined my life? Let him pay for what I have suffered. But if I tell, they will probably flog the life out of him, and maybe I suspect him wrongly. And, after all, what good would it be to me?"

"Well, old man," repeated the Governor, "tell me the truth: who has been digging under the wall?"

Aksionov glanced at Makar Semyonich, and said, "I cannot say, your honour. It is not God's will that I should tell! Do what you like with me; I am your hands."

However much the Governor tried, Aksionov would say no more, and so the matter had to be left.

That night, when Aksionov was lying on his bed and just beginning to doze, some one came quietly and sat down on his bed. He peered through the darkness and recognised Makar.

"What more do you want of me?" asked Aksionov. "Why have you come here?"

Makar Semyonich was silent. So Aksionov sat up and said, "What do you want? Go away, or I will call the guard!"

Makar Semyonich bent close over Aksionov, and whispered, "Ivan Dmitrich, forgive me!"

"What for?" asked Aksionov.

"It was I who killed the merchant and hid the knife among your things. I meant to kill you too, but I heard a noise outside, so I hid the knife in your bag and escaped out of the window."

Aksionov was silent, and did not know what to say. Makar Semyonich slid off the bed-shelf and knelt upon the ground. "Ivan Dmitrich," said he, "forgive me! For the love of God, forgive me! I will confess that it was I who killed the merchant, and you will be released and can go to your home."

"It is easy for you to talk," said Aksionov, "but I have suffered for you these twenty-six years. Where could I go to now? ... My wife is dead, and my children have forgotten me. I have nowhere to go ...."

Makar Semyonich did not rise, but beat his head on the floor. "Ivan Dmitrich, forgive me!" he cried. "When they flogged me with the knot it was not so hard to bear as it is to see you now...yet you had pity on me, and did not tell. For Christ's sake forgive me, wretch that I am!" And he began to sob.

When Aksionov heard him sobbing he, too, began to weep. "God will forgive you!" said he. "Maybe I am a hundred times worse than you." And at these words his heart grew light, and the longing for home left him. He no longer had any desire to leave the prison, but only hoped for his last hour to come.

In spite of what Aksionov had said, Makar Semyonich confessed, his guilt. But when the order for his release came, Aksionov was already dead.

The Child Spy

Alphonse Daudet

Alphonse Daudet (1840-1897) was an important French man of letters of the 19th century. His earlier works such as 'The Last Idol' (1862), a play and *Letters from My Mill* (1869), a collection of short stories, won considerable acclaim. Daudet's literary sensibility was deeply affected by the Franco-Prussian War (1870-71)—apparent in the short story 'The Child Spy' (1873).

His name was Stenne, little Stenne.

He was a child of Paris, sickly and pale, who might have been ten years old, perhaps fifteen; with those urchins one can never tell. His mother was dead; his father, formerly in the navy, was keeper of a square in he Temple quarter. Babies, nurse-maids, old ladies in reclining-chairs, poor mothers, all of toddling Paris that seeks shelter from vehicles in those flower-gardens bordered by paths, knew Father Stenne and adored him. They knew that beneath that rough mustache, the terror of dogs and of loiterers, lay concealed a kind, melting, almost maternal smile, and that, in order to see that smile one had only to ask the good man:

How is your little boy?

Father Stenne was so fond of his boy! He was so happy in the afternoon, after school, when the little fellow came for him and they made together the circuit of the paths, stopping at each bench to salute the occupants and to answer their kind words.

Unfortunately with the siege everything changed. Father Stenne's square was closed, petroleum was stored there, and the poor man, forced to keep watch all the time, passed his life among the deserted and neglected shrubs, alone, unable to smoke, and without the company of his boy except very late at night, at home. So that you should have seen his mustache when he mentioned the Prussians. As for little Stenne, he did not complain' very much of that new life.

A siege! It is such an amusing thing for urchins. No school! No lessons! Vacation all the time and the street like a fair.

The child stayed out of doors, wandering about until night. He followed the battalions of the quarter when they went to the fortifications, choosing by preference those which had a good band; and upon that subject little Stenne was well posted. He could tell you that the band of the 96th did not amount to much, but that in the 55th they had a fine one. At other times he watched the troops go through the drill; then there were the lines at the shopdoors. With his basket on his arm, he stood in the long lines that formed in the dark winter mornings, without gas, at the doors of the butchers' and bakers' shops. There, with their feet in the water, people became acquainted, talked politics, and every one asked his advice, as M. Stenne's son. But the games of *bouchon* were the most amusing thing of all, and that famous game of *galoche,* which the Breton militia had brought into fashion during the siege. When little Stenne was not at the fortifications, or at the baker's, you were sure to find him at the game on Place du Château d'Eau. He did not play, you understand; it required too much money. He contented himself with watching the players, with such eyes!

One especially, a tall youth in a blue blouse, who bet nothing less than five-franc pieces, aroused his admiration. When he ran you could hear the money jingling in his pockets.

One day, as he picked up a coin which had rolled to little Stenne's feet, the tall youth said to him in an undertone:

"That makes you squint, eh? Well, I will tell you where they are to be found, if you want."

When the game was ended he led him to a corner of the square and proposed to him to go with him to sell newspapers to the Prussians; he received thirty francs per trip. At first Stenne refused, highly indignant; and he actually stayed away from the game for three days. Three terrible days. He did not eat, he did not sleep. At night, he saw piles of *galoches* at the foot of his bed, and five-franc pieces lying flat, all glistening. The temptation was too great. On the fourth day he returned to the Château d'Eau, saw the tall youth again, and allowed himself to be persuaded.

They set out one snowy morning, a canvas bag over their shoulders and newspapers hidden under their blouses, When they reached the Flanders gate it was barely light. The tall youth took Stenne by the hand, and, approaching the sentry, an honest volunteer with a red nose and a good-natured expression, he said to him in the whining voice of a pauper:

"Let us pass, my kind monsieur. Our mother is sick, papa is dead, I am going out with my little brother to pick up potatoes in the fields."

And he wept. Stenne, covered with shame, hung his head. The sentry looked at them a moment, and cast a glance at the deserted road.

"Hurry up," he said, stepping aside; and there they were upon the Aubervilliers Road. How the tall fellow laughed!

Confusedly, as in a dream, little Stenne saw factories transformed into barracks, abandoned barricades covered with wet rags, long chimneys cutting the mist and rising into the sky, smokeless and broken. At intervals, a sentry, beplumed officers looking into the distance with field-glasses, and small tents drenched with melted snow in front of dying fires. The tall fellow knew the roads and cut across the fields to avoid the outposts. However, they fell in with a patrol of sharp-shooters, whom they could not avoid. The sharp-shooters were in their little cabins, perched on the edge of a ditch filled with water, along the Soissons railroad. That time the tall fellow repeated his story in vain; they would not allow them to pass. Then, while he was complaining, an old sergeant, all wrinkled and grizzled, who resembled Father Stenne, came out of the guardhouse to the road.

"Come, little brats, I wouldn't cry!" he said to the children; "we'll let you go to get your potatoes, but come in and warm yourselves a little first. This little fellow looks as if he was frozen!"

Alas! It was not with cold that little Stenne was trembling;it was with fear, with shame. In the guard-house they found several soldiers crouching about a paltry fire, a genuine widow's fire, by the heat of which they were thawing out biscuit on the points of their bayonets. They moved closer together to make room for the children. They gave them a little coffee. While they have were drinking, an officer came to the door, called to the sergeant, spoke to him in an undertone and hurried away.

"MY boys," said the sergeant, returning with a radiant face, "there will be something up tonight. They have found out the Prussians' countersign. I believe that this time we shall capture that infernal Bourget again."

There was a explosion of cheers and laughter. They danced and sang and brandished their sword-bayonets; and the children, taking advantage of the tumult, disappeared.

When they had passed the railway there was nothing before them but a level plain, and in the distance a long, blank wall, riddled with loopholes. It was towards that wall that they bent their steps, stooping constantly to make it appear that they were picking up potatoes.

"Let's go back, let's not go on," said little Stenne again and again.

The other shrugged his shoulders and kept on. Suddenly they heard the click of a gun being cocked.

"Lie down!" said the tall fellow, throwing himself on the ground.

When they were down, he whistled. Another whistled. Another whistle answered over the snow. They crawled on. In front of the wall, level with the ground, appeared a pair of yellow mustaches beneath a soiled cap. The tall youth jumped into the trench, beside the Prussian.

"This is my brother," he said, pointing to his companion.

Little Stenne was so little, that at the sight of him the Prussian began to laugh, and he was obliged to take him in his arms to lift him up to the breach.

On the other side of the wall were great piles of earth, felled trees, black holes in the snow, and in each hole the same dirty cap and the same yellow mustaches, laughing when they saw the children pass.

In the corner was a gardener's house casemated with trunks of trees. The lower room was full of soldiers playing cards, and cooking soup over a big, blazing fire. The cabbages and pork smelled good;

what a contrast to the bivouac of the sharp-shooters! Above were the officers. They could hear them playing the piano and opening champagne. When the Parisian entered, a joyous cheer greeted them. They produced their newspapers; then they were given drink and were induced to talk. All the officers had a haughty and disdainful manner; but the tall youth amused them with his faubourgian wit, his street Arab's vocabulary. They laughed, repeated his phrases after him, and wallowed with delight in the Parisian mud which he brought them.

Little Stenne would have liked to talk too, to prove that he was not stupid, but something embarrassed him. Opposite him, apart from the rest, was an older and graver Prussian, who was reading, or rather seemed to be reading, for his eyes did not leave little Stenne. Affection and reproach were in his glance as if he had at home a child of the same age as Stenne, and as if he were saying to himself:

"I would rather die than see my son engaged in such business."

From that moment Stenne felt as it were a hand resting on his heart, which prevented it from beating.

To escape that torture, he began to drink. Soon everything about him whirled around. He heard vaguely, amid loud laughter, his comrade making fun of the National Guards, of their manner of drilling; he imitated a call to arms in the Marais, a night alarm on the ramparts. Then the tall fellow lowered his voice, the officers drew nearer to him, and their faces became serious. The villain was warning them of the attack of the sharp-shooters.

At that little Stenne sprang to his feet in a rage, thoroughly sober:

"Not that! I won't have it!"

But the other simply laughed and kept on. Before he had finished, all the officers were standing. One of them pointed to the door and said to the children:

"Clear out!"

And they began to talk among themselves very rapidly, in German.

The tall youth went out as proud as a prince, jingling his money. Stenne followed him, hanging his head; and when he passed the Prussian whose glance had embarrassed him so, he heard a sad voice say:

"Not a nice thing to do, that. Not a nice thing."

Tears came to his eyes.

Once in the field, the children began to run and returned quickly to the city. Their bag was full of potatoes which the Prussians had given them. With them they passed unhindered to the trench of the sharp-shooters. There they were preparing for the night attack. Troops came up silently and massed behind the walls. The old sergeant was there, busily engaged in posting his men, with such a happy expression. When the children passed, he recognised them and bestowed a pleasant smile upon them.

Oh! How that smile hurt little Stenne! For a moment he was tempted to call out:

"Don't go there; we have betrayed you."

But the other had told him: "If you speak we shall be shot"; and fear restrained him.

At La Courneuve, they entered an abandoned house to divide the money. Truth compels me to state that the division was made honestly, and that little Stenne's crime did not seem so terrible to him when he heard the coins jingling under his blouse, and thought of the games of *galoche* which he had in prospect.

But when he was alone, the wretched child! When the tall fellow had left him at the gate, then his pockets began to be very heavy, and the hand that grasped his heart grasped it tighter than ever. Paris did not seem the same to him. The people who passed gazed sternly at him as if they knew whence he came. He heard the word "spy" in the rumbling of the wheels, in the beating of the drums along the canal. At last he reached home, and, overjoyed to find that his father was not there, he went quickly up to their room, to hide under his pillow that money that weighed so heavily upon him.

Never had Father Stenne been so joyous and so good-humoured as when he returned that night. News had been received from the provinces: affairs were looking better. As he ate, the old soldier looked at his musket hanging on the wall, and said to the child with his hearty laugh:

"I say, my boy, how you would go at the Prussians if you were big!"

Above eight o'clock, they heard cannon.

"That is Aubervilliers. They are fighting at Bourget," said the good man, who knew all the forts. Little Stenne turned pale, and, on the plea that he was very tired, he went to bed; but he did not sleep. The cannon still roared. He imagined the sharp-shooters arriving in the dark to surprise the Prussians, and themselves falling into an ambush. He remembered the sergeant who had smiled at him and he saw him stretched out on the snow, and many others with him. The price of all that blood was concealed there under his pillow, and it was he, the son of Monsieur Stenne, of a soldier—tears choked him. In the adjoining room he heard his father walk to the window and open it. Below on the square, the recall was sounding; and a battalion was forming to leave the city. Evidently it was a real battle. The unhappy child cloud not restrain a sob.

"What's the matter with you?" asked Father Stenne as he entered the room.

The child could not stand it any longer; he leaped out of bed and threw himself at his father's feet. At the movement that he made the silver pieces rolled on the floor.

"What is all this? Have you been stealing?" demanded the old man, trembling.

Thereupon, without pausing for breath, little Stenne told him that he had been to the Prussian quarters and of what he had done there.

As he spoke, his heart felt freer; it relieved him to accuse himself. Father Stenne listened, with a terrible face. When it was at an end, he hid face in his hands and wept.

"Father, father—" the child began.

The old man pushed him away without replying, and picked up the money.

"Is this all?" he asked.

Little Stenne motioned that it was all. The old man took down his musket and cartridge box, and said as he put the money in his pocket:

"All right; I am going to return it to them."

And without another word, without even turning his head, he went down and joined the troops who were marching away in the darkness. He was never seen again.

A Simple Heart

Gustave Flaubert

Gustave Flaubert (1821-1880), the founding father of French realism, wrote the masterpiece *Madame Bovary* (1857). Popular for his slow and painstaking method of composition, he often placed beauty over morality in his creative works. 'A Simple Heart' is a part of his sole collection of short stories known as *Trois Contes* (1877), which was translated to English by Arthur Mcdowall as *Three Tales*.

I

For fifty years the ladies of Pont-l'Évêque envied Madame Aubain her servant Felicity.

For a hundred francs a year she cooked, and cleaned, sewed, washed, ironed, could harness a horse, fatten up poultry, churn butter; and she remained loyal to her mistress who, all the same, was not an agreeable person.

Madame Aubain had married a fine young fellow without a fortune, who died at the beginning of 1809, leaving her two very young children, and a great number of debts. Then she sold her real estate, except the farm of Toucques, and the farm of Geffosses, whose rents amounted to five thousand francs at the outside, and she quitted the house at Saint-Milaine to settle in another one less costly, which had belonged to her ancestors, and was situated behind the market-place.

This house, covered with tiles, was set between a lane and an alley that gave on the river. Inside, its ground levels were unequal, and were the cause of frequent stumbles. A narrow vestibule separated the kitchen from the living-room, where Madame Aubain passed the whole day, seated near the window casement on a straw-bottomed chair. Against the wainscoting, painted white, were lined up eight mahogany chairs. An old piano carried, under a barometer, a heaped pyramid of wooden and cardboard boxes. Two deep armchairs, tapestry covered, flanked the yellow marble mantelpiece in the style of Louis XV. The clock in the middle represented a temple of Vesta, and the whole room smelled slightly musty, for the floor was lower than the garden.

On the first floor there was, first of all, 'Madame's' room, very big, hung with a wallpaper with pale flowers, and containing the portrait of 'Monsieur' in the costume of a *muscadin*. It communicated with a smaller room, where two children's couches were to be seen without their mattresses. Then came the drawing-room, always shut up, and filled with furniture covered with a sheet. Then a corridor led to a study: books and papers filled the shelves of a book-case surrounding with its three sides a large blackwood desk. The two end panels were invisible beneath pen-and-ink sketches, landscapes in body colour, and Audran's engravings, souvenirs of better times and vanished luxury. A dormer window on the second story lighted Felicity's room, looking out on the fields.

She rose with the dawn so as not to miss Mass, and worked without stopping until evening; then, dinner being finished, the dishes put away and the door fast shut, she covered the faggots with ashes, and fell asleep before the hearth, her rosary in her hand. Nobody in her marketing could show more obstinacy. As to her cleanliness, the polish on her saucepans was the despair of other servants. Thrifty, she ate slowly, and gathered up from the table with her fingers the crumbs of the loaf—a twelve-pound loaf, baked specially for her, which lasted twenty days.

All through the year she carried a cotton handkerchief fixed at her back by a pin, a bonnet that hid her hair, grey stockings, a red skirt, and over her bodice an apron with a bib like a hospital nurse.

Her face was thin and her voice sharp. At twenty-five years of age you would have guessed her to be forty. After her fiftieth year she showed no traces of any age at all; and, always silent, upright in carriage, and measured in gesture, she seemed a woman made of wood, functioning automatically.

II

She had had, like anyone else, her love story.

Her father, a mason, had been killed in falling from a scaffolding. Then her mother died, her sisters scattered; a farmer took her in, and employed her, while still a little girl, in guarding cows in the fields. She shivered under her rags, drank flat on her stomach the water of the pools, for no pretext at all was beaten, and finally was dismissed for a theft of thirty pence which she had not committed. She took service in another farm, became hen girl there, and, as she pleased her employers, her comrades were jealous of her.

One day in the month of August (she was eighteen then) they took her with them to the fair at Colleville. Straightway she was bewildered, stupefied by the noise of the fiddlers, the lights in the trees, the motley of the costumes, the laces, the gold crosses—this mass of people who leapt simultaneously. She was keeping modestly in the background when a young man, well-to-do in appearance, smoking his pipe, with his two elbows on the pole of a small wagon, came to invite her to dance. He recompensed her with cider, with coffee, with cake, with a scarf, and offered to lead her out again. She did not know what to answer, and wanted to run away. He departed.

Another evening on the road to Beaumont she wanted to pass a big wagon of hay that was going along slowly, and as she brushed past the wheels she recognized Theodore.

At once he spoke of the harvests and the notables of the district, for his father had left Colleville for the farm of Écots, so that now they were neighbours. "Ah," she said. He added that they wanted to set him up for himself. Yet he wasn't in a hurry; he was waiting for a wife to his taste. She hung her head. Then he asked her if she was thinking of marriage. She answered, smiling, that it wasn't right to laugh at her. "But I'm not, I give you my word!" and with his left arm he encircled her waist: she walked on, held up by his embrace: they went more slowly. The wind was soft, the stars shone, the huge wagon-load of hay swayed before them, and the four horses, dragging their feet, raised the dust. Then, without being told, they turned to the right. He hugged her again. She disappeared into the shadows. Theodore, the following week, got her to promise to meet him.

They met at the far end of the courtyard, under an isolated tree. She was not innocent, in the fashion of ladies, but common sense and the instinct of honour kept her from yielding. This resistance exasperated Theodore's love so much that in order to satisfy it (or perhaps quite ingenuously) he proposed to marry her. She hesitated to believe him. He swore great oaths.

Soon he admitted something annoying; his parents last year had bought him off conscription; but any day they could take him again. The idea of serving terrified him. This cowardice was in Felicity's eyes a proof of affection; her own redoubled. She stole out at night, and when she got to the meeting place Theodore tortured her with his anxiety and his entreaties.

At last he announced that he would go himself to headquarters to get information, and that he would bring her word on the following Sunday between eleven and twelve at night.

When the moment came she ran to her lover.

In his place she found one of his friends. He told her that she would not see him again. To assure himself from conscription Theodore had married a very rich old woman, Madame Lehoussais, of Toucques.

She gave way to a burst of extravagant grief. She threw herself on the ground, cried aloud, called on the good God, and groaned, all alone in the country till sunrise. Then she went back to the farm, and declared her intention of leaving it, and at the end of a month, having received her wages, she tied all her little belongings in a handkerchief, and went to Pont-l'Évêque.

In front of the inn she asked some questions of a lady in a widow's cap, who happened at the time to be looking for a cook. The girl did not know much, but she seemed so anxious to please and to have so few unreasonable demands, that Madame Aubain finished by saying:

"All right, I'll take you."

Felicity a quarter of an hour afterwards was settled in her house.

At first she lived there in a sort of tremor caused by the 'kind of house', and the memory of 'Monsieur' hovering over everything. Paul and Virginia, one aged seven, the other hardly four, seemed to her to be made of precious stuff; she carried them on her back like a horse, and Madame Aubain forbade her to kiss them every minute, and that mortified her. Yet she was happy. The gentleness of the environment had melted her sorrow.

Every Thursday friends came to take a hand at boston-whist. Felicity prepared in advance the cards and the footwarmers. They arrived at eight o'clock very punctually, and went away before the stroke of eleven.

Each Monday morning the second-hand dealer who lodged under the alley spread out his scrap iron on the ground. Then the town was filled with a hum of voices, in which were mingled the neighing of horses, the bleating of sheep, the grunting of pigs, and the dry rattle of traps on the road. About midday, at the height of the market, could be seen on the threshold a tall old peasant, his cap pulled down, his nose hooked, and who was Robelin, the farmer of Geffosses. A short time after it was Liébard, the farmer of Toucques, small, red, fat, wearing a grey jacket and leggings fitted with spurs.

Both of them offered their landlady fowls or cheeses. Felicity invariably baffled their tricks, and they went away full of consideration for her.

On indeterminate occasions Madame Aubain received a visit from the Marquis de Germanville, one of her uncles, ruined by debauchery, who lived at Falaise, on the last morsel of his property. He arrived always at lunch time, with a frightful little dog, whose paws dirtied all the furniture. In spite of his efforts to appear a gentleman, even going so far as to lift his hat every time he said: "My late father," his old habits got the better of him; he poured out for himself glass after glass, and let out some rather free stories. Felicity would push him outside politely: "You've had enough of it, Monsieur de Germanville! We'll see you another time!" And she shut the door.

She opened it with pleasure to Monsieur Bourais, an ex-solicitor. His white cravat, and his bald head, the frill of his shirt, his wide brown frockcoat, his way of taking snuff, making a circle with his arm, his whole personality produced in her the excitement into which the sight of extraordinary men throws us.

As he managed the estate of 'Madame' he shut himself up with her for hours in monsieur's study: he was always afraid of compromising himself, he had a great respect for the magistracy, and had pretensions to Latin.

To instruct the children in a pleasant fashion he made them a present of a geography with engravings. They represented different scenes in the world, cannibals with feathers in their hair, a monkey carrying off a young lady, Bedouins in the desert, a whale being harpooned, etc.

Paul explained these engravings to Felicity. This, in fact, was all her literary education.

The children's education was taken in hand by Guyot, a poor wretch employed at the Town Hall, famous for his fine handwriting, a man who sharpened his penknife on his boot.

When the weather was clear they would go early in the morning to the farm of Geffosses.

The courtyard is sloping, the house in the middle: and the sea, in the distance, appears like a grey stain.

Felicity took out of her basket slices of cold meat, and they lunched in a room attached to the dairy. It was the only remnant of a pleasure house which had not disappeared. The wall-paper hung in rags, and trembled in the draughts. Madame Aubain leant forward, overwhelmed with memories: the children did not dare to speak. "But go out and play," she would say. They decamped.

Paul went up into the barn, caught birds, played ducks and drakes with stones on the pond, or with a stick hit the big casks that resounded like drums.

Virginia fed the rabbits, rushed to gather cornflowers, and the swift motion of her legs showed her little embroidered drawers.

One autumn evening they came back through the meadows.

The moon in its first quarter lit up a part of the sky, and a mist was floating like a veil on the windings of the River Toucques. Oxen, stretched amid the turf, tranquilly watched those four people pass. In the third meadow some of them rose, and formed a circle before them. "Don't be afraid," said Felicity, and murmuring a sort of low song she patted the one who was nearest on the spine; he turned round, the others imitated him. But when the succeeding field was crossed a formidable bellowing arose. It was a bull that the fog had concealed. He advanced towards the two women. Madame Aubain was going to run. "No, no, not so quick!" They quickened their steps all the same, and heard behind them a sonorous breathing coming nearer them. His hoofs, like hammers, beat the grass of the fields; there, he was galloping now! Felicity turned round and tore up with her two hands clods of earth which she threw in his eyes. He lowered his muzzle, shook his horns, and trembled with fury, bellowing horribly. Madame Aubain, at the end of the grass with her two children, was madly seeking how to get over the high bank. Felicity retired steadily before the bull, and continually flung bits of turf that blinded him, while she cried: "Hurry up, hurry up!" Madame Aubain climbed over the ditch, pushed Virginia up, then Paul, fell several times in trying to climb over the slope, and by dint of courage succeeded.

The bull had driven Felicity into a corner against an opening in the hedge; his slaver sprayed on her face, a second more and he would have gored her. She had time to slip between two bars, and the big beast, quite surprised, stopped short.

This event for many years was a topic of conversation at Pont-l'Évêque. Felicity felt no pride about it, not even considering that she had done anything heroic.

Virginia took up all her time, for she suffered, as a result of her fright, from an affection of the nerves, and Monsieur Pourpart, the doctor, advised sea baths at Trouville.

In those days they were not crowded. Madame Aubain made inquiries, consulted Bourais, and made preparations as for a long journey.

Her luggage went off the night before in Liébard's cart. The next day he brought two horses, one of which had a woman's saddle fitted with a velvet backrest; and on the croup of the second a coat, rolled up, formed a sort of seat. Madame Aubain mounted there behind him. Felicity took charge of Virginia, and Paul straddled Monsieur Lechaptois's donkey, lent on condition they would take great care of it.

The road was so bad that the eight kilometres took two hours. The horses sank up to the pasterns in the mud, and to free themselves made brusque movements with their haunches; or else they stumbled against the hedges; other times they had to jump over them. Liébard's mare, at certain spots, stopped suddenly. Liébard waited patiently until she resumed her walk, and he talked about the people whose estates bordered the road, adding moral reflections to their story. Thus, in the middle of Toucques as they passed under windows surrounded by nasturtiums, he said with a shrug of his shoulders: "There's a Madame Lehoussais lives there, who, instead of taking a young husband—" Felicity did not hear the rest: the horses trotted, the donkey galloped; they all went in single file up a path; a gate swung round, two stable boys appeared, they got down beside the dung water on the very threshold of the door.

Mother Liébard, seeing her mistress, was prodigal in demonstrations of joy. She served them a lunch where there was roast beef, tripe, black sausage, a fricassee of chicken, sparkling cider, a fruit tart, and plums in brandy, accompanying the whole with polite observations to Madame, who seemed in better health, to mademoiselle, become 'magnificent', to Mr. Paul, grown singularly 'stout' without forgetting their late grandparents, whom the Liébards had known, being in the service of the family for several generations. The farm had, like them, an old-time character. The beams of the roof were worm-eaten, the walls black with smoke, the tiles grey with dust. An oak dresser carried all sorts of utensils, jugs, plates, pewter, basins, wolf traps, sheep shears; an enormous syringe made the children laugh. Not a tree in the three courtyards but had mushrooms at its base, or in its branches a bunch of mistletoe. The wind had thrown down several. They had sprouted again in the middle, and all were bent under the number of their apples. The thatch roofs, like brown velvet, and all unequal in thickness, resisted the strongest gales. Yet the wagon-shed was falling in ruins. Madame Aubain said she would see about it, and bade them reharness the beasts.

They were half an hour yet before they reached Trouville. The little caravan dismounted to pass the Écores Hill; it was a rock overhanging the ships; and three minutes later, at the end of the quay, they entered the courtyard of the Golden Lamb, Mother David's inn.

Virginia, from the beginning, felt herself more robust, the result of the change of air and the action of the baths. She took them in her chemise, for lack of a bathing costume; and her maid dressed her afterwards in the shed of a customs man who looked after the bathers.

In the afternoon they would go with the donkey past the Black Rocks in the direction of Hennequeville. The path at first rose between land undulating like the lawns of a gentleman's estate, then arrived at a plateau, where alternated pasture ground and cultivated fields. At the edge of the road, among the clusters of reeds, grew holly bushes; here and there a tall dead tree made zigzags with its branches on the blue air.

Almost always they rested in a meadow, with Deauville on their left, Havre on their right, and in front the open sea. It was brilliant in the sunshine, smooth like a mirror, so gentle that its murmur could scarcely be heard. Hidden sparrows chirped, and the immense vault of the sky formed a cover for all. Madame Aubain, seated, would work at her sewing; Virginia beside her, plaited reeds; Felicity pulled up lavender; Paul, who was bored, wanted to go away.

Other times they crossed the River Toucques in a boat, and looked for shells. The low tide left uncovered sea urchins, scallops, jellyfish; and the children ran to catch the puffs of foam that the wind carried up. The sleepy waves, falling on the sand, rolled in along the beach; they stretched as far as eye could see, but on the landward side had for limit the dunes separating it from the Marais, a wide meadow, shaped like a hippodrome. When they were coming back that way Trouville, at the foot of its sloping hillock, grew bigger at each step, and with all its different-sized houses, seemed to spread out in gay disorder.

The days on which it was too hot they did not leave their room. The dazzling brightness outside plastered bars of light between the slats of the shutters. No noise in the village. Down below on the pavement, nobody. This widespread silence increased everything's tranquillity. In the distance the hammers of the caulkers plugged the keels, and a heavy breeze brought a scent of tar.

The principal amusement was the homecoming of the ships. As soon as they had passed the buoys they began to tack. Their sails dropped to two-thirds of the masts: and the foresail swelling like a balloon they came on, gliding in the plashing of the waves, to the middle of the harbour, where the anchor suddenly fell. Then the boat drew up beside the quay. The sailors threw over the edge the quivering fish; a row of carts was waiting, and women in cotton bonnets ran forward to take the baskets and embrace their men.

One of the women one day accosted Felicity, who a little while afterwards came into the room full of joy. She had refound a sister: and Nastasie Barette, wife of Leroux, appeared, holding a baby at her breast, another child clinging to her right hand, and at her left a little fellow with his fists on his hips, and his beret over one ear.

At the end of a quarter of an hour Madame Aubain dismissed her.

They were always to be met hanging about the kitchen, or on the walks they took. The husband did not show himself.

Felicity took a liking to them. She bought them bedclothes, shirts, a cooking stove; evidently they were exploiting her. This weakness irritated Madame Aubain, who, besides, didn't like the familiarities of the nephew, for he talked to her son as to an equal; and, as Virginia had a cough, and the weather was no longer good, she returned to Pont-l'Évêque.

Monsieur Bourais gave her advice on the choice of a school. The one at Caen was considered the best. Paul was sent there, and said goodbye stoutly, pleased to go and live in a house where he would have comrades.

Madame Aubain resigned herself to the separation from her son because it was indispensable. Virginia thought of it less and less. Felicity missed the noise he made. But an occupation came along to distract her. Starting at Christmas, she took the little girl every day to Catechism.

III

When she had made a genuflexion at the door she walked on under the high nave between the double row of chairs, opened Madame Aubain's pew, sat down, and looked all round her. The boys on the right, the girls on the left, filled the stalls of the choir; the priest stood near the lectern; on a stained-glass window in the apse the Holy Ghost hovering over the virgin; another showed her on her knees before the Infant Jesus, and behind the ciborium a group carved in wood represented Saint Michael subduing the dragon.

The priest gave them first a short account of Sacred History. She thought she saw Paradise, the deluge, the tower of Babel, cities in flames, peoples dying, idols overthrown; and she retained from this state of amazement respect for the Most High, and fear of His wrath. Then she wept, listening to the Passion. Why had they crucified Him, this One who loved the children, who fed the multitudes, who cured the blind, and had desired, in His gentleness, to be born amid the poor, on the dung of a stable? Seed time, harvest, the winepress, all the familiar things of which the Gospel speaks, existed in her life; the passage of God had sanctified them; and she loved the lambs more tenderly for love of the Lamb of God, the doves because of the Holy Ghost.

She had trouble in imagining its shape; for it was not only a bird, but besides that, a fire, and at other times a breath. Maybe it was its light that flickered at nights on the edge of the marshes, its breath that pushed the clouds, its voice that made the bells ring sweetly; and she stayed in adoration, enjoying the freshness of the walls and the tranquillity of the church.

As to the dogmas, she understood none of them, did not even try to understand them. The priest discoursed, the children recited, she finished by going to sleep; and woke up suddenly when, as they came out, their wooden shoes clattered on the flagstones.

It was in this way, by dint of hearing it, that she learned the catechism, her religious education having been neglected in her youth; and from that time she imitated all the practices of Virginia, fasting as she did, going to confession with her. On Corpus Christi day together they erected a street altar.

She worried about the first communion in advance. She was in a flutter about the slippers, about the wreath, about the book, about the gloves. With what inner tremblings she helped her mother dress her!

All through the Mass she was in an agony. Monsieur Bourais hid a part of the choir from her; but just in front the flock of girls, wearing their white crowns over their lowered veils, formed as it were a field of snow; and she recognized from afar her dear little one by her dainty neck and contemplative attitude. The bells rang out: heads bent: there was a silence. To an outburst of organ music the choristers and the congregation began to sing the Agnus Dei; then the march past of the boys began; and after them the girls rose. Step by step, and hands joined in prayer, they went towards the altar, ablaze with candles, knelt on the first step, received in turn the wafer, and in the same order returned and knelt in their places. When it was Virginia's turn Felicity bent forward to see her, and with the imagination which true tenderness bestows, it seemed to her that she herself was this child. Virginia's face became her own, her dress clothed her; her heart beat in her breast; at the moment when she opened her mouth, shutting her eyes, she almost fainted.

Next day, early, she presented herself in the vestry so that the priest might give her communion. She received it devoutly, but did not taste the same delights.

Madame Aubain wanted to make her daughter accomplished: and as Guyot could not teach either English or music, she resolved to send her to the boarding school of the Ursulines at Honfleur.

The child made no objections. Felicity sighed, finding Madame hard-hearted. Then she thought that her mistress, perhaps, was right. These matters went beyond her province.

Finally, one day, an old van stopped before the door, and from it stepped a nun, who had come to get mademoiselle. Felicity lifted the baggage on to the top, gave injunctions to the coachman, and placed under the seat six pots of jam, and a dozen pears, with a bunch of violets.

Virginia, at the last moment, was shaken by a huge sob; she embraced her mother, who kissed her on the forehead, repeating: "Come now, courage, courage!" The steps were drawn up, the carriage set out.

Then Madame Aubain fainted: and in the evening all her friends, the Lormeau household, Madame Lechaptois, *those* ladies Rochefeuille, Monsieur de Houpeville, and Bourais put in an appearance to console her.

The loss of her daughter was at first very grievous. But three times a week she got a letter from her, the other days she wrote to her, walked in her garden, read a little, and in this way filled the emptiness of the hours.

In the morning, from habit, Felicity went into Virginia's room and looked at the walls. She missed not having her hair to comb, her boots to lace, to tuck her in her bed—and not seeing continually her pretty face, not having to hold her hand when they went out together. Not having enough work to do, she tried to make lace. Her fingers were too clumsy and broke the threads. She was good for nothing, could not sleep, to use her own expression was 'a wreck'.

To 'cheer herself up' she asked permission to have a visit from her nephew Victor.

He arrived on Sunday after mass, with rosy cheeks, his chest bare, breathing the odour of the country he had passed through. At once she set his place. They had lunch facing each other: and herself eating as little as possible to keep down the expense, she stuffed him with food to such an extent that he finished by going to sleep. At the first stroke of the bell for vespers she woke him, brushed his trousers, tied his tie, and went to church, leaning on his arm in maternal pride.

His parents charged him always to bring something home, maybe a packet of brown sugar, soap, brandy, sometimes even money. He brought his clothes to be mended, and she accepted this task, glad of the chance which forced him to come back.

In August his father took him with him on the coasting trade.

It was holiday time. The arrival of the children consoled her. But Paul had become capricious, and Virginia was no longer young enough to be spoken to as an equal, and that put a feeling of constraint, a barrier between them.

Victor went in turn to Morlaix, to Dunkirk, and to Brighton. On his return from each voyage he made her a present. The first time it was a box covered with shells; the second a coffee cup; the third a big gingerbread man. He grew handsome, with a good carriage, nice frank eyes, and a little leather cap worn well to the front like a pilot. He amused her by telling her stories mixed with nautical terms.

On Monday, 14th July 1819 (she did not forget the date), Victor announced that he was engaged for a trip and, during the night of the day after next, by the Honfleur steamer, he would go to join his schooner, which was going to sail from Havre quite soon. He would be, maybe, away for two years.

The prospect of such an absence grieved Felicity; and to say another goodbye to him on Wednesday evening, after Madame's dinner, she put on her clogs and hurried down the four leagues which separated Pont-l'Évêque from Honfleur.

When she was at the crossroads before the Calvary, instead of taking the path to the left she took the one to the right, lost herself in the yards, and came back on her tracks; the people she accosted advised her to hurry. She walked right round the harbour, stumbled over ropes; then the land dropped before her, lights intersected each other, and she thought herself mad, perceiving horses in the air.

On the edge of the quay others whinnied, terrified of the sea. The tackle that lifted them set them down in a boat where travellers elbowed one another among casks of cider, baskets of cheese, sacks of grain; you could hear hens cackling, the captain was swearing; and a boy was standing leaning on the cathead, indifferent to all that. Felicity, who had not recognized him, screamed "Victor!" He raised his head; she rushed forward, when the gangway was suddenly pulled back.

The steamer which was towed by women, singing, left the port. Its timbers creaked, heavy waves whipped its prow. The vessel had turned, nobody was seen any longer—and, on the sea silvered by the moon, it made a black spot that steadily paled, sank, disappeared.

Felicity, passing near the Calvary, wanted to recommend to God that which she cherished most. And she prayed a long time, standing, her face bathed in tears, her eyes towards the clouds. The town slept, customs officials walked about, and the water fell without ceasing through the holes of the sluice. Two o'clock struck.

The reception room of the convent did not open before day-break. A delay, quite certainly, would annoy Madame; and, in spite of her desire to embrace the other child, she returned. The servant girls at the inn were waking as she entered Pont-l'Évêque.

The poor lad was going to roll about on the waves for months. His former voyages had not frightened her. From England and Brittany people came back; but America, the Colonies, the West Indies, that was to be lost in an uncertain land, at the other end of the world.

From that time on Felicity thought exclusively of her nephew. On sunny days she tormented herself with thirst; when a storm came on she feared the thunder for him. Listening to the wind which howled in the chimney and blew off the tiles, she saw him beaten by the same tempest, at the top of a shattered mast, all his body thrown back under a sheet of foam; or else—souvenirs of the geography engravings—he was devoured by savages, captured in a wood by monkeys, was dying along a deserted seashore. And never did she speak of her anxieties.

Madame Aubain had others for her daughter. The good sisters found that she was affectionate but delicate. The slightest emotion unnerved her. The piano had to be given up.

Her mother required a regular correspondence from the convent. One morning that the postman did not come she was impatient: and she walked about the living-room from her chair to the window. It was really extraordinary! For four days no news.

So that she might find comfort in her example Felicity said to her:

"Look at me, Madame, it's six months since I've had any!"

"From whom?"

The servant replied gently:

"But—from my nephew!"

"Oh—your nephew!" and, shrugging her shoulders, Madame Aubain went on with her walking as if to say: "I did not think about him! Moreover, I don't care! A cabin boy, a beggar, a fine business—while my daughter—Think of it!"

Felicity, although brought up on rudeness, was indignant against Madame, then forgot.

It seemed to her quite easy to lose one's head about the little girl's concerns.

The two children had an equal importance; one of her heart-strings united them, and their destinies should be the same.

The chemist told her that Victor's boat had arrived at Havana. He had read the information in a gazette.

Because of the cigars she imagined Havana a country where nothing else was done but smoke, and Victor moving among the niggers in a cloud of tobacco. Could he 'in case of need' come back by land? What distance was it from Pont-l'Évêque? To learn that she asked Monsieur Bourais.

He got his atlas, then began explanations about the longitudes, and he had a fine pedant's smile in face of Felicity's bewilderment. At length with his pocket pencil he showed her the indentations on an oval mark, a black imperceptible point, adding: "That's it". She leaned over the map; this network of coloured lines tired her eyes, without teaching her anything; and, Bourais inviting her to say what was worrying her, she begged him to show her the house where Victor was living. Bourais raised his arms, sneezed, laughed enormously; such ingenuousness excited his joy: and Felicity did not understand the cause of it—she who was expecting, perhaps, even to see a photograph of her nephew, so limited was her intelligence.

It was a fortnight afterwards that Liébard, at the hour when the market was on, as was his custom, came into the kitchen and gave her a letter which her brother-in-law had sent. Since neither of the two know how to read, she had recourse to her mistress.

Madame Aubain, who was counting stitches in her knitting, put her work down beside her, unsealed the letter, trembled, and in a low voice with a serious look:

"It's bad news…you are being told of. Your nephew—" He was dead. They told her no more.

Felicity fell on a chair, leaning her head on the wall, and shut her eyes, and her eyelids suddenly grew pink. Then, her head drooping, her eyes fixed, she repeated at intervals:

"Poor little chap! Poor little chap!"

Liébard looked at her, emitting deep sighs. Madame Aubain was trembling slightly. She proposed to her to go and see her sister at Trouville.

Felicity answered by a gesture that she had no need to go there.

There was a silence. Good old Liébard thought it proper to go away. Then she said:

"It's nothing to them!"

Her head sank down again; and mechanically she lifted, from time to time, the long knitting-needles on the work-table.

Some women passed in the courtyard with a barrow heaped with dripping linen.

As she saw them through the windowpanes she remembered her washing; she had soaked it the night before, today it had to be rinsed, and she left the room.

Her washboard and her tub were on the brink of the River Toucques. She flung on the bank a heap of chemises, tucked up her sleeves, took up her beating-stick; and the heavy blows she gave were heard in the other gardens alongside. The fields were empty, the wind rippled the river; at the bottom long weeds swept over like the hair of dead men floating in the water. She restrained her sorrow till evening, was very brave; but, in her room she abandoned herself to it, lying flat, face down on her mattress, her eyes in her pillow, and her fists against her temples.

Much later, from Victor's captain himself, she learnt the circumstances of his death. He had been bled too much at the hospital for yellow fever. Four doctors were looking after him at once. He died immediately, and the chief had said:

"Tut, tut, that's another one!"

His parents had always treated him barbarously. She preferred not to see them again; and they made no advances, either through forgetfulness or the callousness of the wretched poor.

Virginia grew weaker.

Shortness of breath, a cough, a continual fever, and red spots on her cheekbones revealed some deep-seated affection. Monsieur Pourpart had advised a stay in Provence. Madame Aubain made up her mind to go there, and would have immediately recalled her daughter home except for the climate of Pont-l'Évêque.

She made an arrangement with a man who hired carriages to take her to the convent every Thursday. There is in the gardens a terrace from which you can discern the Seine. Virginia would walk there on her arm, on the fallen grapevine leaves. Sometimes the sun, shining through the clouds, made her blink her eyelids, when she looked at the sails in the distance, and all the horizon from the château of Tancarville to the lighthouse at Havre. Then they rested in the arbour. Her mother had got a little barrel of an excellent Malaga wine; and, laughing at the idea of being drunk, she would drink two fingers of it, not more.

Her strength improved. The autumn slipped away quietly. Felicity reassured Madame Aubain. But one evening that she had been on an errand in the neighbourhood she met before the door Monsieur Pourpart's gig: and he himself was in the vestibule. Madame Aubain was tying on her hat.

"Give me my foot warmer, my purse, my gloves: be quicker, can't you?" Virginia had an inflammation of the lungs: it was perhaps hopeless.

"Not yet," said the doctor, and the two of them got into the carriage under the snowflakes which eddied around. Night was about to fall. It was very cold.

Felicity rushed into the church to light a candle. Then she ran after the gig, which she rejoined an hour later, leaped lightly up behind, where she was holding on by the twisted cords, when a reflection came to her. "The courtyard is not shut. If robbers get in?" and she got down.

Next day at sunrise she presented herself at the doctor's. He had come in, and gone out again to the country. Then she stayed in the inn, thinking that strangers would bring her a letter. At length at dawn she took the coach to Lisieux.

The convent was situated at the end of a steep lane. About the middle she heard strange sounds, a death knell. 'It's for other people,' she thought, and Felicity pulled violently at the knocker.

At the end of several minutes slippers dragged along, the door half opened, and a nun appeared.

The good sister said with an air of compunction that "she had just passed". At the same time the knell of Saint Leonard's redoubled its peal.

Felicity arrived at the second story.

From the threshold of the room she saw Virginia, stretched on her back, her hands joined, her mouth open, and her head thrown back under a black cross bending towards her, between motionless curtains, less white than her face. Madame Aubain, at the foot of the couch which she clasped with her hands, uttered sobs of agony. The Mother Superior was standing on the right. Three candlesticks on the chest of drawers made red splashes, and the mist whitened the windows. Nuns took away Madame Aubain.

For two nights Felicity did not leave the dead girl. She repeated the same prayers, threw holy water on the sheets, came back and sat down, and looked at her. At the end of the first watch she noticed that the face had got yellow, the lips blue, the nose pinched, the eyes sunk. She kissed them several times, and would not have felt an immense astonishment if Virginia had reopened them: for souls like hers the supernatural is quite simple. She dressed her, wrapped her in her shroud, lifted her into her coffin, placed a wreath on her, spread out her hair. Her hair was fair, of an extraordinary length for her age. Felicity cut off a thick lock, the half of which she slipped into her bosom, resolved never to part with it.

The body was carried back to Pont-l'Évêque, in obedience to the wishes of Madame Aubain, who followed the hearse in a closed carriage.

After the mass they took another three-quarters of an hour to reach the cemetery. Paul walked in front and sobbed. Monsieur Bourais was behind, then the principal inhabitants, the women covered in black mantles, and Felicity. She thought of her nephew, and not having been able to render him these honours, felt an increase of grief as if they were burying him with the other.

Madame Aubain's despair was without bounds.

First she revolted against God, finding Him unjust for having taken her daughter, she who had never done any wrong, and whose conscience was so pure. But no! She should have taken her south. Other doctors would have saved her! She accused herself, wanted to join her, cried out in distress amid her dreams. One dream, above all, obsessed her. Her husband, clad like a sailor, was coming back from a long voyage, and said to her weeping, that he had got orders to take away Virginia. Then they arranged to find a hiding place somewhere.

One day she came in from the garden completely upset. The father and daughter (she pointed out the place) had appeared to her just now, one after the other, and they did nothing; they looked at her.

For several months she remained in her room inert. Felicity lectured her gently; she must keep herself for her son, and for the other, in memory of 'her'.

"Her," took up Madame Aubain, as if awakening, "oh, yes! yes! You do not forget her!" An allusion to the cemetery which it had been scrupulously forbidden to mention.

Felicity went there every day.

At four o'clock exactly she passed alongside the houses, climbed the slope, opened the gate, and arrived at Virginia's tomb. It was a little column of rose marble, with a flagstone at the base, and chains around, framing a little garden. The flower-beds were invisible under a coverlet of flowers. She watered their leaves, renewed the sand, knelt down the better to work the earth. Madame Aubain, when she could come there, felt some comfort, a kind of consolation.

Then years slipped by, all alike, and without other episodes than the return of the great feasts: Easter, the Assumption, All Saints. Inside happenings marked the dates which they used for reference later on. Thus in 1825 two glaziers white-washed the vestibule; in 1827 a bit of the roof, falling into the courtyard, almost killed a man. In the summer of 1828 it was Madame's turn to provide the sacred bread for Mass. Bourais, about this time, absented himself mysteriously; and the old acquaintances, little by little, passed away; Guyot, Liébard, Madame Lechaptois, Robelin, Uncle Germanville, paralysed a long time ago.

One night the driver of the mail coach announced in Pont-l'Évêque the July Revolution. A new sub-prefect was appointed a few days afterwards; the Baron de Larsonnière, an ex-consul in America, who had living with him, besides his wife, his sister-in-law, with three young ladies, already pretty big. They were seen on their lawn, dressed in floating blouses; they possessed a negro and a parrot. Madame Aubain received a visit from them, and did not fail to return it. When they appeared in the farthest distance Felicity ran to warn her. But one thing was alone capable of moving her, her son's letters.

He could not follow any career, being wrapped up in taverns. She paid his debts; he ran up others; and the sighs which Madame Aubain uttered, knitting near her window, could be heard by Felicity, turning her spinning-wheel in the kitchen.

They took walks together beside the wall where the pears grew; and talked always of Virginia, asking each other if such and such a thing would have pleased her; on such an occasion what would she probably have said?

All her little possessions occupied a press in the room with the two beds. Madame Aubain inspected them as seldom as possible. One summer day she resigned herself to it, and moths flew from the wardrobe.

Her dresses were there in a row under a shelf, on which there were three dolls, hoops, doll's furniture, the washbowl she had used. They took out as well underskirts, stockings, handkerchiefs, and spread them on the two couches before folding them up again. The sun shone on those poor objects, showing up the stains and the folds made by the body's movements. The air was hot and blue, a blackbird chirped, everything seemed alive in a deep sweetness. They found a little plush hat, with long hair, chestnut coloured; but it was all eaten by insects. Felicity claimed it for herself. Their eyes met, filled with tears; finally the mistress opened her arms, the servant flung herself into them; and they clung together, satisfying their grief in a kiss that equalized them.

It was the first time in their lives, Madame Aubain not being of an expansive nature. Felicity was grateful for it, as for a kindness, and henceforth cherished her with an animal devotion and a religious veneration.

The kindness of her heart developed.

When she heard in the street the drums of a regiment on the march she stationed herself before the door with a jug of cider, and offered the soldiers a drink. She looked after the victims of cholera. She protected the Poles; and there was even one of them who declared he wanted to marry her. But they quarrelled: for one morning, coming in from the Angelus, she found him in her kitchen, into which he had made his way, and fixed himself up a dish of meat with vinegar sauce which he was eating quietly.

After the Poles there was old Father Colmiche, an old man, who passed for having done terrible things in '93. He lived on the riverside, in the ruins of a pigsty. Urchins used to peer at him through the chinks in the wall, and threw stones which fell on the wretched bed where he lay, continually shaken by a cold, with very long hair, inflamed eyelids, and on his arm a tumour bigger than his head. She got linen for him, tried to clean out his hovel, had dreams of settling him in the washhouse, without annoying Madame. When cancer knocked him out she bandaged him every day, sometimes brought him cake, put him in the sun on a bundle of hay; and the poor old man, drooling and trembling, thanked her in his feeble voice, fearing to lose her, stretching out his hands when he saw her going off. He died: she had a Mass said for the repose of his soul.

That day a great happiness came to her; just at dinner-time Madame de Larsonnières's negro presented himself, holding the parrot in its cage, with the stand, the chain, and the padlock. A note from the baroness announced to Madame Aubain that, her husband being raised to the prefecture, they were leaving that evening; and she begged her to accept the bird as a souvenir, and in token of her respect.

For a long time he had filled Felicity's imagination, for he came from America, and this word recalled Victor, so much so that she had made inquiries about it from the negro. Once even she had said:

"Madame would like to have it!"

The negro had repeated the remark to his mistress who, not being able to take the bird with her, had got rid of it in this way.

IV

He was called Loulou. His body was green, the tips of his wings rose, his front blue, and his throat golden.

But he had the tiresome mania of biting his stand, pulling out his feathers, spilling the water from his bath. Madame Aubain, whom he bored, gave him for good to Felicity.

She undertook to instruct him. Soon he repeated: "Nice boy!" "Your servant, sir!"

"Hail Mary!" He was placed beside the door, and some people were astonished that he did not answer to the name of Jacquot, since all parrots are called Jacquot. He was compared to a goose, to a blockhead: so many dagger blows for Felicity! Strange obstinacy of Loulou not speaking at the time people were looking.

Nevertheless he courted company; for on Sundays, when *those* ladies Rochefeuille, Monsieur de Houpeville, and some new friends—Onfroy the apothecary, Monsieur Varin, and Captain Mathieu—were making up their party at cards, he knocked on the windowpanes with his wings, and thrashed about so violently that it was impossible to hear oneself.

Bourais's face, no doubt, seemed to him very funny. As soon as he saw him he began to laugh, to laugh with all his might. The peals of his voice rebounded in the courtyard, the echoes repeated them, the neighbours came to their windows laughing too; and so as not to be seen by the parrot, Monsieur Bourais slipped along the wall, hiding his profile with his hat, reached the river, then entered by the garden gate; and the glances he directed at the bird lacked tenderness.

The butcher's boy had snapped his fingers at Loulou, who had ventured to thrust his head into his basket; and since then he had always tried to pinch him through his shirt. Fabu threatened to wring his neck, although he was not cruel, in spite of the tattooing on his arm, and his thick whiskers. On the contrary he had rather a liking for the parrot, wanting, in a jovial mood, to teach him swear words. Felicity, who was frightened at this kind of behaviour, put him in the kitchen. His little chain was taken off, and he moved about the house.

When he came down the stairs he leaned the curve of his beak on the steps, raised his right claw, then the left, and she was afraid that such gymnastics would make him dizzy. He became ill, was not able to speak or eat. There was a growth under his tongue, as there sometimes is in hens. She cured him, tearing out the lump with her nails. Monsieur Paul one day was imprudent enough to puff the smoke of a cigar into his nostrils; another time that Madame Lormeau annoyed him with the end of her sunshade he snapped the ferule off; finally he got lost.

She had put him on the grass to let him refresh himself, went away for a moment; and when she came back, no parrot. At first she looked for him in the bushes, at the water edge, and on the roofs, without heeding her mistress who cried to her:

"Take care. You are mad!" Then she inspected all the gardens of Pont-l'Évêque: and she stopped the passers-by: "You haven't seen anywhere, by chance, my parrot?" To those who did not know the parrot she described him. Suddenly she thought she distinguished, behind the mill, at the bottom of the slope, a green thing fluttering about. But at the top of the hill, nothing! A pedlar affirmed that he had just met it in Saint-Milaine in Mother Simon's shop. She ran there. Nobody knew what she meant. Finally she came back, worn out, her slippers in rags, death in her soul; and, seated in the centre of the garden seat, near Madame, she was recounting all her adventures, when a light weight fell on her shoulder—Loulou! What the deuce had he done? Maybe he had taken a stroll in the neighbourhood.

She had trouble in recovering from it, or rather, she never did recover.

As a result of a chill she got a sore throat; a little after, an ear-ache. Three years after, she was deaf; and she spoke very loud, even in the church. Although her sins might have been broadcast to all the corners of the parish, without dishonouring her, or inconveniencing the world, the priest thought it right to receive her confession only in the vestry.

Illusory buzzings in the ear completely confused her. Often her mistress would say: "Gracious! How stupid you are!" And she would reply: "Yes, Madame," looking for something round her.

The little circle of her ideas narrowed still more, and the ringing of the bells, the lowing of the herds no longer existed. All creatures functioned in ghostly silence.

One noise alone now reached her ears, the voice of the parrot.

As if to amuse her, he would reproduce the tick-tack of the turnspit, the shrill cry of the fishmonger, the saw of the carpenter who lived opposite: and when the bell rang, imitated Madame Aubain: "Felicity! The door! The door!"

They had dialogues together; he reeling off to satiety the three phrases of his repertory, and she answering by words without coherence but in which her soul unbosomed itself. Loulou, in her isolation, was almost a son, a lover. He climbed up her fingers, nibbled at her lips, hung on to her neckerchief; and as she bent her forehead, shaking her head as children's nurses do, the big wings of her bonnet and the wings of the bird shook together.

When the clouds gathered and the thunder growled, he would utter cries, recalling perhaps the deluges of his native forests.

The trickling of water excited him almost to delirium: he fluttered about madly, rose to the roof, turned over everything, and went through the window to dabble in the garden; but came back quickly to one of the andirons and, hopping about to dry his wings, showed now his tail, and now his beak.

One morning of the terrible winter of 1837, when she had put him before the hearth because of the cold, she found him dead in the middle of his cage, his head down, his claws in the wire meshing. A congestion had killed him, no doubt. She believed he had been poisoned by parsley; and, in spite of the absence of all proof, her suspicions centred on Fabu.

She wept so much that her mistress said to her: "Well, then, have him stuffed." She asked advice from the chemist, who had always been good to the parrot.

He wrote to Havre. A certain Fellacher undertook the business. But, as the stage coach sometimes mislaid parcels, she resolved to carry it herself as far as Honfleur.

Apple trees bare of leaves, one after another, bordered the sides of the road. Ice covered the ditches. Dogs barked around the farms; and, her hands under her cloak, with her little black wooden shoes and her basket, she walked quickly in the centre of the road.

She crossed the forest, passed Haut Chêne, reached Saint Gatien.

Behind her, in a cloud of dust, and carried away by its own impetus on the hill, a mailcoach at a full gallop rushed on her like a whirlwind. Seeing this woman, who did not get out of the way, the driver stood up on the hood, and the postilion shouted too, while the four horses that he could not hold back went quicker than ever; the two first just grazed her; with a twist of the reins he drew them to the side of the road, but in a temper, raised his arm, and with a full swing, with his big whip, gave her such a lash from stomach to the twist of hair at the nape of her neck, that she fell on her back.

Her first gesture, when she came back to consciousness, was to open her basket. Loulou was not hurt, fortunately. She felt a burning on her right cheek: she raised her hands to it, and they were red. Blood was flowing.

She sat down on a pile of road metal, patted her face with her handkerchief, then she ate a crust of bread, put in her basket by way of precaution, and consoled herself for her wound in looking at the bird.

When she reached the heights of Ecquemauville she saw the lights of Honfleur sparkling in the night like a cluster of stars; the sea, farther off, stretched out vaguely. Then a feeling of faintness stopped her, and the wretchedness of her childhood, the disappointment of her first love, the departure of her nephew, the death of Virginia, like the waves of a tide, returning all at once, and rising to her throat, choked her.

Then she wanted to speak to the captain of the boat, and without telling him what she was sending, she gave him careful orders.

Fellacher kept the parrot a long time. He always promised it for the next week; at the end of six months he announced the shipping of a box, and there was no more question of it. She could only think that Loulou would never come back.

"They'll have stolen him from me," she thought.

Finally he arrived—and splendid, upright on the branch of a tree, which was screwed in a mahogany base, one claw in the air, his head sideways, and biting a nut which the birdstuffer had gilded through love of the grandiose.

She shut it up in her room.

This spot, to which she admitted few people, had the look at once of a chapel and a bazaar, it contained so many religious objects and heteroclite things.

A big wardrobe was in the way when one opened the door. In front of the window, overhanging the garden, a round window looked out at the courtyard; a table near the truckle bed bore a water jug, two combs, and a cube of blue soap on a chipped plate. On the walls were seen strings of beads, medals, several Holy Virgins, a holy-water basin of coconut; on the chest of drawers covered with a cloth like an altar, the shellbox that Victor had given her: then a watering pot and a balloon, writing exercise books, the geography with engravings, a pair of boots; and on the nail which held up the mirror, hung by its ribbons, the little plush hat. Felicity even pushed this kind of respect so far as to keep one of monsieur's coats. All the old stuff that Madame Aubain did not want any more she took for her room. That was why there were artificial flowers at the side of the drawers, and the picture of the Count of Artois in the recess of the dormer window.

By way of shelf, Loulou was established on a part of the chimney-piece which jutted into the room. Every morning as she waked up she saw him in the light of dawn, and recalled then the days that were gone, insignificant actions, down to their least detail, without grief, full of tranquillity.

Communicating with no one, she lived in the torpor of the sleep-walker. The processions of Corpus Christi day roused her. She went to beg from the neighbours torches and straw matting to embellish the altar set up in the street.

At the church she contemplated steadily the Holy Ghost, and noticed that it had a look of the parrot. The resemblance seemed to her still more noticeable on an Épinal picture, representing the baptism of Our Lord. With its purple wings and emerald body it was really the portrait of Loulou.

Having bought it she hung it in the place of the Count of Artois, so that with the same look she could see them both. They became associated in her thoughts, the parrot becoming sanctified by this union with the Holy Ghost, which became more alive and intelligible in her eyes. The Father, to give utterance to his will, had not chosen a dove, since these beasts have no voice, but rather one of the ancestors of Loulou. And Felicity said her prayers, looking at the picture, but from time to time turned a little to the bird.

She wanted to join the Sisters of the Virgin; Madame Aubain dissuaded her. An event of some importance took place: Paul's marriage.

After having been at first a notary clerk, then in business, in the Customs, in the Treasury, and having even taken some steps to get into the Water and Forests Department, at the age of thirty-six, suddenly, by a heaven-sent inspiration, he had discovered his real road: the Registry Office. And he had shown such high talents that an auditor had offered him his daughter, promising him his protection.

Paul, become serious minded, brought her to his mother.

She looked down on the customs of Pont-l'Évêque, behaved like a princess, hurt Felicity. Madame Aubain, when she went away, felt relieved.

The following week they learned of the death of Monsieur Bourais, in Lower Brittany, in an inn. The rumour of suicide was confirmed: doubts rose about his honesty. Madame Aubain studied her accounts, and was not long in finding the whole list of his evil deeds; embezzlement of arrears, pretended sales of wood, false receipts, etc.

These acts of baseness afflicted her greatly. In March 1853 she was seized by a pain in the chest; her tongue seemed covered with smoke; leeches did not calm the fever; and on the eighth day she died, being exactly seventy-two years old.

She was considered younger, because of her brown hair, whose folds surrounded her pale face, marked with the smallpox. Few friends mourned her, her way of living had displayed a haughtiness which kept people at a distance.

Felicity wept for her, as masters are not wept for. That Madame should die before her upset her ideas, seemed to her contrary to the order of things, inadmissible and monstrous.

Ten days after (the time to rush to Besançon) the heirs arrived; the daughter-in-law went through the drawers, chose the best of the furniture, sold the rest; then they went down to the Registry Office again.

Madame's chair, her table, her foot warmer, the eight chairs were gone. The place of the engravings was marked by yellow squares on the walls. They had taken away the two little beds, with their mattresses, and in the cupboard none of Virginia's belongings were seen any more. Felicity climbed the stairs, drunk with grief.

The next day there was a notice on the door: the apothecary shouted in her ear that the house was for sale.

She staggered and was obliged to sit down.

What distressed her most was leaving her room, so convenient for poor Loulou. Enveloping him with a look of anguish she implored the Holy Ghost, and contracted the idolatrous habit of saying her prayers on her knees before the parrot. Sometimes the sun, entering through the dormer window, fell on his glass eye, and caused it to shoot out a fine luminous beam, which put her in ecstasies.

She had an income of three hundred and eighty francs, a legacy from her mistress. The garden furnished her with vegetables. As to dresses, she possessed enough of them to clothe her to the end of her days, and she saved light by going to bed at dusk.

She hardly ever went out, so as to avoid the second-hand dealer's shop, where was displayed some of the old furniture. Since her attack of dizziness she limped in one leg, and, her strength diminishing, Mother Simon, ruined in the grocery business, came every morning to cut her wood and to pump her water.

Her eyes grew weaker. The shutters were no longer opened. Many years passed. And the house was not let, nor sold.

In terror lest she should be sent away Felicity did not ask for any repairs. The laths of the roof were rotting. During the whole of one winter, her pillow was damp. After Easter she spat blood.

Then Mother Simon had recourse to a doctor. Felicity wanted to know what was the matter with her. But, too deaf to hear, a single word reached her, "Pneumonia!" It was one she knew, and she replied quietly: "Ah, like Madame," finding it natural to follow her mistress.

The time for setting up the street altars drew near. The first was always at the foot of the hill, the second before the posthouse, the third about the middle of the road. There were rival factions about that one; and the parishioners finally chose Madame Aubain's courtyard.

Her difficulty in breathing and fever grew worse. Felicity was wretched at doing nothing for the altar. If she had had something to put there at least! Then she thought of the parrot. It was not suitable, the neighbours objected. But the priest granted permission for it; she was so happy that she begged him to accept, when she should be dead, Loulou, her only treasure.

From Tuesday to Saturday, the eve of Corpus Christi, she coughed more frequently. In the evening, her face drawn, her lips stuck to her gums, vomitings made their appearance; and the next day, at daybreak, feeling herself very low, she got them to call the priest.

Three old women surrounded her during the extreme unction. Then she declared that she required to speak to Fabu.

He arrived in his Sunday clothes, ill at ease in this lugubrious atmosphere.

"Forgive me," she said, with an effort to stretch out her arm, 'I thought it was you who had killed him!'

What was the meaning of gossip like that? To suspect him of a murder, a man like him! And he was indignant, was going to make a row.

"She hasn't her wits, you can see that easily enough."

Felicity from time to time spoke to the ghosts. The old women went away. Madame Simon had her breakfast.

A little later she took Loulou, and lifting him close to Felicity: "Come, then! Say goodbye!"

Although he was not a corpse the worms were devouring him; one of his wings was broken, the stuffing protruded from his stomach. But blind now, she kissed him on the head, and pressed him against her cheek. Mother Simon took him, to put him on the street altar.

V

From the grass was wafted up the scent of summer; the flies buzzed; the sun glinted on the river, and warmed the roofs. Mother Simon returned to the room and slept peacefully.

Church bells woke her; people were coming out from vespers. Felicity's delirium dropped. Thinking of the procession, she saw it, just as if she were following it.

All the school children, the choristers, and the fire brigade were marching along the pavements, while in the middle of the road were advancing, first the head beadle, armed with his halberd, the under-beadle with his big cross, the teacher supervising the boys, the nun anxious for her little girls; three of the prettiest, curly-haired like angles, were throwing petals of roses into the air; the deacon with outspread arms conducted the music; and two censer swingers turned at each step to the Holy Sacrament, which, under a dais of flaming red velvet, upheld by four churchwardens, the priest in his fine chasuble was carrying. A crowd of people jostled behind, between the white cloths covering the house walls; and the foot of the hill was reached.

A cold sweat wet Felicity's temples. Mother Simon sponged it with a towel, saying that one day we must all go that way. The murmur of the crowd grew, was very loud for a moment, died away.

A volley shook the windowpanes. It was the postilions saluting the Monstrance. Felicity rolled her eyeballs, and said, as loud as she could: "Does he look all right?" tormented by the parrot.

Her death agony began. A rattle, more and more hurried, caused her sides to heave. Bubbles of foam came to the corners of her mouth, and all her body trembled.

Soon the blare of ophicleides was distinguished, the clear voices of the children, the deep voices of the men. All was still at intervals, and the tramp of feet which the flowers muffled made the noise of a flock on the turf.

The clergy appeared in the courtyard. Madame Simon climbed on a chair to reach the round window, and in this way commanded a view of the altar.

Green garlands were hanging on the altar, adorned with a flounce in English point lace. There was in the centre a little box enclosing the relics, two orange trees at the corners, and, all its length, silver candlesticks and porcelain vases, whence sprang sunflowers, lilies, peonies, foxgloves, bunches of hortensias.

This mass of dazzling colours descended in a sloping line from the table to the carpet, trailing on the paving-stones; and rare objects drew the eye. A silver-gilt sugar basin had a crown of violets, earrings in Alencon quartz gleamed in the moss, two Chinese screens displayed their landscapes. Loulou, hidden under the roses, only showed his blue front like a sheet of lapis-lazuli.

The churchwardens, the choristers, the children ranged themselves on three sides of the courtyard. The priest slowly mounted the steps, and placed on the lace his huge, glittering "Golden Sun". Everybody knelt. There was a great silence. And the censers, swinging in full flight, slipped on their chains.

An azure vapour rose into Felicity's room. She distended her nostrils, scenting it with a mystic sensuality: then she shut her eyes. Her lips smiled. The beats of her heart slowed one by one, more unsteady each time, more gentle like a fountain that is exhausted, like an echo that disappears; and when she breathed her last breath she thought she saw in the heavens as they opened, a gigantic parrot, flying above her head.

The Dream Of A Ridiculous Man

Fyodor Dostoevsky

Fyodor Dostoevsky (1821-1881) was a Russian novelist and short story writer known for his 'novels of ideas' such as *Crime and Punishment* (1866) and *The Idiot* (1869). He was regarded as one of the finest writers who ever lived. Through glimpses into the interiority of his complex characters, Dostoevsky rendered accurate psychological analyses to the reader and closely examined how social conditions affect the human mind. Dostoevsky also explored the themes of nihilism, existentialism and psychoanalysis in 'The Dream Of A Ridiculous Man' (1877), which was translated to English by the notable translator of Russian literature, Constance Garnett.

I

I am a ridiculous man. They call me mad now. That wouldbe a step up in rank, if I did not still remain as ridiculous to them as before. But now I'm no longer angry, now they are all dear to me, and even when they laugh at me, then, too, they are even somehow especially dear to me. I would laugh with them, not really at myself, but for love of them, if it weren't so sad for me to look at them. Sad because they don't know the truth, and I do know the truth. Ah, how hard it is to be the only one who knows the truth! But they won't understand that. No, they won't understand it.

Before, it caused me great anguish that I seemed ridiculous. Not seemed, but was. I was always ridiculous, and I know it, maybe right from birth. Maybe from the age of seven I already knew I was ridiculous. Then I went to school, then to the university, and what, the more I studied, the more I learned that I was ridiculous.

So that for me, all my university education existed ultimately as if only to prove and explain to me, the deeper I went into it, that I was ridiculous. And as with learning, so with life. Every passing year the same consciousness grew and strengthened in me that my appearance was in all respects ridiculous. I was ridiculed by everyone and always. But none of them knew or suspected that if there was one man on earth who was more aware than anyone else of my ridiculousness, it was I myself, and this was the most vexing thing for me, that they didn't know it, but here I myself was to blame: I was always so proud that I would never confess it to anyone for anything. This pride grew in me over the years, and if it had so happened that I allowed myself to confess to anyone at all that I was ridiculous, I think that same evening I'd have blown my head off with a revolver. Oh, how I suffered in my youth over being unable to help myself and suddenly somehow confessing it to my comrades. But once I reached early manhood, I became a bit calmer for some reason, though with ever passing year I learned more and more about my terrible quality. Precisely for some reason, because to this day I cannot determine why. Maybe because a dreadful anguish was growing in my soul over one circumstance which was infinitely higher than the whole of me: namely, the conviction was overtaking me that everywhere in the world it *made no difference*. I had had a presentiment of this for a very long time, but the full conviction came during the last year somehow suddenly. I suddenly felt that it would *make no difference* to me whether the world existed or there was nothing anywhere. I began to feel and know with my whole being that *with me there was nothing*. At first I kept thinking that instead there had been a lot before, but then I realized that there had been nothing before either, it only seemed so for some reason. Little by little I became convinced that there would never be anything. Then I suddenly stopped being angry with people and began almost not to notice them. Indeed, this was manifest even in the smallest trifles: it would happen, for instance, that I'd walk down the street and bump into people. It wasn't really because I was lost in thought: what could I have been thinking about, I had completely ceased to think then: it made no difference to me. And it would have been fine if I had resolved questions, oh, I never resolved a single one, and there were so many! But it began to *make no difference* to me, and the questions all went away.

And then, after that, I learned the truth. I learned the truth last November, precisely on the third of November, and since that time I remember my every moment. It was a gloomy evening, as gloomy as could be. I was returning home then, between ten and eleven o'clock, and I remember I precisely thought that there could not be a gloomier time. Even in the physical respect. Rain had poured down all day, and it was the coldest and gloomiest rain, even some sort of menacing rain, I remember that, with an obvious hostility to people, and now, between ten and eleven, it suddenly stopped, and a terrible dampness set in, damper and colder than when it was raining, and a sort of steam rose from everything, from every stone in the street and from every alleyway, if you looked far into its depths from the street. I suddenly imagined that if the gaslights went out everywhere, it would be more cheerful, and that with the gaslights it was sadder for the heart, because they threw light on it all. I'd had almost no dinner that day, and had spent since early evening sitting at some engineer's, with two more friends siting there as well. I kept silent, and they seemed to be sick of me. They talked about something provocative and suddenly even grew excited. But it made no difference to them, I could see that, and they got excited just so. I suddenly told them that: "Gentlemen," I said, "it makes no difference to you." They weren't offended, but they all started laughing at me. It was because I said it without any reproach and simply because it made no difference to me. And they could see that it made no difference to me, and found that amusing.

When I thought in the street about the gaslights, I looked up at the sky. The sky was terribly dark, but one could clearly make out the torn clouds and the bottomless black spots between them. Suddenly in one of these spots I noticed a little star and began gazing at it intently. Because this little star gave me an idea: I resolved to kill myself that night. I had firmly resolved on it two months earlier, and, poor as I was, had bought an excellent revolver and loaded it that same day. But two months had passed and it was still lying in the drawer; but it made so little difference to me that

I wished finally to seize a moment when it was less so, why, I didn't know. And thus, during those two months, returning home each night, I thought I was going to shoot myself. I kept waiting for the moment. And so now this little star gave me the idea, and I resolved that it would be that night *without fail*. And why the star gave me the idea, I don't know.

And so, as I was looking at the sky, this girl suddenly seized me by the elbow. The street was empty, and almost no one was about. Far off a coachman was sleeping in his droshky. The girl was about eight years old, in a kerchief and just a little dress, all wet, but I especially remembered her wet, torn shoes, and remember them now. They especially flashed before my eyes. She suddenly started pulling me by the elbow and calling out. She didn't cry, but somehow abruptly shouted some words, which she was unable to pronounce properly because she was chilled and shivering all over. She was terrified by something and shouted desperately: "Mama! Mama!" I turned my face to her, but did not say a word and went on walking, but she was running and pulling at me, and in her voice there was the sound which in very frightened children indicates despair. I know that sound. Though she did not speak all the words out, I understood that her mother was dying somewhere, or something had happened with them there, and she had run out to call someone, to find something so as to help her mother. But I did not go with her and, on the contrary suddenly had the idea of chasing her away. First I told her to go and find a policeman. But she suddenly pressed her hands together and, sobbing, choking, kept running beside me and wouldn't leave me. It was then that I stamped my feet at her and shouted. She only cried out: "Mister! Mister!..." but suddenly she dropped me and ran headlong across the street: some other passerby appeared there, and she apparently rushed from me to him.

I went up to my fifth floor. I live in a rented room, a furnished one. It's a poor and small room, with a half-round garret window. I have an oilcloth sofa, and a table with books on it, two chairs, and an armchair, as old as can be, but a Voltaire one. I sat down, lighted a candle, and began to think. Next door, in another room, behind a partition, there was a bedlam. It had been going on for two days. A retired captain lived there, and he had guests, some six scurvy fellows, drinking vodka and playing blackjack with used cards. The previous night they'd had a fight, and I know that two of them had pulled each other's hair for a long time. The landlady wanted to lodge a complaint, but she's terribly afraid of the captain. The only other tenants in our furnished rooms are a small, thin lady, an army wife and out-of-towner, with three small children who had already fallen ill in our rooms. She and her children are afraid of the captain to the point of fainting, and spend whole nights trembling and crossing themselves, and the smallest child had some sort of fit from fear. This captain, I know for certain, sometimes stops passersby on Nevsky Prospect and begs money from them. They won't take him into any kind of service, yet, strangely (this is what I've been driving at), in the whole month that he had been living with us, the captain had never aroused any vexation in me. Of course, I avoided making his acquaintance from the very start, and he himself got bored with me from the first, yet no matter how they shouted behind their partition, and however many they were, it never made any difference to me. I sit the whole night and don't really hear them, so far do I forget about them. I don't sleep at night until dawn, and that for a year now. I sit all night at the table in the armchair and do nothing. I read books only during the day. I sit and don't even think, just so, some thoughts wander about and I let them go. A whole candle burns down overnight. I quietly sat down at the table, took out the revolver, and placed it in front of me. As I placed it there, I remember asking myself: "Is it so?" and answering myself quite affirmatively: "It is." Meaning I would shoot myself. I knew that I would shoot myself that night for certain, but how long I would stay sitting at the table before then, that I did not know. And of course I would have shot myself if it hadn't been for that girl.

II

You see: though it made no difference to me, I did still feel pain, for instance. If someone hit me, I would feel pain. The same in the moral respect: if something very pitiful happened, I would feel pity, just as when it still made a difference to me in life. And I felt pity that night: I certainly would have helped a child. Why, then, had

I not helped the little girl? From an idea that had come along then: as she was pulling and calling to me, a question suddenly arose before me, and I couldn't resolve it. The question was an idle one, but I got angry. I got angry owing to the conclusion that, if I had already resolved to kill myself that night, it followed that now more than ever everything in the world should make no difference to me. Why, then, did I suddenly feel that it did make a difference, and that I pitied the girl? I remember that I pitied her very much; even to the point of some strange pain, even quite incredible in my situation. Really, I'm unable to express the fleeting feeling I had then any better, but the feeling continued at home as well, when I had already settled at my table, and I was extremely vexed, as I hadn't been for a long time. Reasoning flowed from reasoning. It seemed clear that, if I was a man and not yet a zero, then, as long as I did not turn into a zero, I was alive, and consequently could suffer, be angry, and feel shame for my actions. Good. But if I was going to kill myself in two hours, for instance, then what was the girl to me and what did I care then about shame or anything in the world? I turned into a zero, an absolute zero. And could it be that the awareness that I would presently cease to exist *altogether,* and that therefore nothing would exist, could not have the slightest influence either on my feeling of pity of the girl, or upon the feeling of shame after the meanness I had committed? And I had stamped and shouted at the unfortunate child in a savage voice precisely because, "you see, not only do I feel no pity, but even if I commit some inhuman meanness, I can do so now, because in two hours everything will be extinguished." Do you believe this was why I shouted? I'm now almost convinced of it. It seemed clear that life and the world were now as if dependent on me. One might even say that the world was now as if made for me alone: I'd shoot myself and there would be no more world, at least for me. Not to mention that maybe there would indeed be nothing for anyone after me, and that as soon as my consciousness was extinguished, the whole world would be extinguished at once, like a phantom, like a mere accessory of my consciousness, it would be done away with, for maybe all this world and all these people were, just myself alone. I remember that, sitting and reasoning, I turned all these new questions, which came crowding one after another, even in quite a different direction and invented something quite new. For instance, there suddenly came to me a strange consideration, that if I had once lived on the moon or on Mars, and had committed some most shameful and dishonorable act there, such as can only be imagined, and had been abused and dishonored for it as one can only perhaps feel and imagine in a dream, a nightmare, and if, ending up later on earth, I continued to preserve an awareness of what I had done on the other planet, and knew at the same time that I would never ever return there, then, looking from the earth to the moon, would it *make any difference* to me, or not? Would I feel shame for that act, or not? The questions were idle and superfluous, since the revolver was already lying in front of me, and I knew with my whole being that *this* was certain to be, but they excited me, and I was getting furious. It was as if I couldn't die now without first resolving something. In short, this girl saved me, because with the questions I postponed the shot. Meanwhile, everything was also quieting down at the captain's: they had ended their card game and were settling down to sleep, grumbling and lazily finishing their squabbles. It was then that I suddenly fell asleep, something that had never happened to me before, at the table, in the armchair. I fell asleep quite imperceptibly to myself. Dreams, as is known, are extremely strange: one thing is pictured with the most terrible clarity, with a jeweler's thoroughness in the finish of its details, and over other things you skip as if without noticing them at all, for instance, over space and time. Dreams apparently proceed not from reason but from desire, not from the head but from the heart, and yet what clever things my reason has sometimes performed in sleep! And yet quite inconceivable things happen with it in sleep. My brother, for instance, died five years ago. Sometimes I see him in my dreams: he takes part in my doings, we are both very interested, and yet I remember and am fully aware, throughout the whole dream, that my brother is dead and buried. Why, then, am I not surprised that, though he is dead, he is still here by me and busy with me? Why does my reason fully admit all this? But enough. I'll get down to my dream. Yes, I had this dream then, my dream of the third of November! They tease me now that it was just a dream. But does it make any difference whether it was a dream or not, if this dream proclaimed the Truth to me? For if you once knew the truth and saw it, then you know that it is the truth and there is and can be no other, whether you're asleep or alive. So let it be a dream, let it be, but this life, which you extol so much, I wanted to extinguish by suicide, while my dream, my dream, oh, it proclaimed to me a new, great, renewed strong life!

Listen.

III

I said that I fell asleep imperceptibly and even as if while continuing to reason about the same matters. Suddenly I dreamed that I took the revolver and, sitting there, aimed it straight at my heart, my heart, not my head; thought I had resolved earlier to shoot myself in the head, and precisely in the right temple. Having aimed it at my chest, I waited for a second or two, and my candle, the table, and the wall facing me suddenly started moving and heaving. I hastily fired.

In dreams you sometimes fall from a height, or are stabbed, or beaten, but you never feel pain except when you are somehow really hurt in bed, then you do feel pain and it almost always wakes you up. So it was in my d ream: I felt no pain, but I imagined that, as I fired, everything shook inside me and everything suddenly went out, and it became terribly black around me. I became as if blind and dumb, and now I'm lying on something hard, stretched out on my back, I don't see anything and can't make the slightest movement. Around me there is walking and shouting, there is the captain's bass and the landlady's shrieking, and suddenly another break, and now I'm being carried in a closed coffin. And I feel the coffin heave and I start reasoning about that, when suddenly for the first time I'm struck by the idea that I'm dead, quite dead, I know this and do not doubt it, I can't see, I can't move, yet I feel and reason. But I quickly come to terms with it and, as is usual in dreams accept the reality without arguing.

And now, they bury me in the ground. Everyone leaves, I'm alone, completely alone. I can't move. Always before, whenever I actually imagined to myself how I would be buried in the grave, my only association with the grave proper was the feeling of dampness and cold. So now, too, I felt that I was very cold, especially the tips of my toes, but I didn't feel anything else.

I lay there and, strangely, didn't expect anything, accepting without argument that a dead man has nothing to expect. But it was damp. I don't know how much time passed, an hour, or a few days, or many days. But then suddenly a drop of water that had seeped through the lid of the coffin fell on my closed left eye, another followed it in a minute, then a third a minute later, and so on and so on, with a minute's interval. A deep indignation suddenly blazed up in my heart, and suddenly I felt physical pain in it. "It's my wound," I thought, "it's my shot, there's a bullet there…" The drop kept dripping, each minute and straight onto my closed eye. And I suddenly called out, not in a voice, for I was motionless, but with my whole being, to the master of all that was coming to pass with me.

"Whoever you are, if you're there, and if there exists anything more reasonable than what is coming to pass now, allow it to be here, too. And if you are taking revenge on me for my unreasonable suicide by the ugliness and absurdity of my subsequent existence, know, then, that no matter what torment befalls me, it will never equal the contempt I am silently going to feel, even if the torment were to last a million years!…"

I called out and fell silent. For almost a whole minute the deep silence lasted, and one more drop even fell, but I knew, boundlessly and inviolably, I knew and believed that everything was certain to change presently. And then suddenly my grave gaped wide. That is, I don't know whether it was opened and dug up, but I was taken by some dark being unknown to me, and we found ourselves in space. I suddenly could see again: it was deep night, and never, never has there been such darkness! We were rushing through space far from earth. I did not ask the one carrying me about anything, I waited and was proud. I assured myself that I was not afraid and swooned with delight at the thought that I was not afraid. I don't remember how long we rushed like that, and cannot imagine it: everything was happening as it always does in dreams, when you leap over space and time and over laws of being and reason, and pause only on the points of the heart's reverie. I remember that I suddenly saw a little star in the darkness. "Is that Sirius?" I asked, suddenly unable to restrain myself, for I did not want to ask about anything. "No, it is the very star you saw between the clouds, as you were returning home," the being who was carrying me replied. I knew that it had as if a human countenance. Strangely, I did not like this being, I even felt a deep revulsion. I had expected complete nonexistence and with that had shot myself in the heart. And here I am in the hands of a being, not a human one, of course, but who *is,* who exists: "Ah, so there is life beyond the grave!" I thought with the strange light-mindedness of dreams, but the essence of my heart remained with me in all its depth: "And if I must *be* again," I thought, "and live again according to someone's ineluctable will, I don't want to be defeated and humiliated!" "You know I'm afraid of you, and you despise me for it," I said suddenly to my companion, unable to hold back the humiliating question, which contained a confession, and feeling my humiliation like the prick of a needle in my heart. He did not answer my question, but I suddenly felt that I was not despised or laughed at, and not even pitied, and that our journey had an unknown and mysterious purpose which concerned me alone. Fear was growing in my heart. Something was being communicated to me, mutely but tormentingly, from my silent companion, and was as if penetrating me. We were rushing through dark and unknown spaces. I had long ceased to see constellations familiar to the eye. I knew that in the heavenly spaces there were stars whose light reached the earth only after thousands or millions of years. Maybe we were already flying through those spaces. I awaited something in a terrible anguish that wrung my heart. And suddenly the call of some highly familiar feeling shook me:

I suddenly saw our sun! I knew it could not be *our* sun, which had generated *our* earth, and that we were at an infinite distance from our sun, but for some reason I recognized, with my whole being, that it was absolutely the same as our sun, its replica and double. The call of a sweet feeling sounded delightfully in my soul: the native power of light, the same light that gave birth to me, echoed in my heart and resurrected it, and I felt life, the former life, for the first time after my grave.

"But if this is the sun, if this is absolutely the same as our sun," I cried out, "then where is the earth?" And my companion pointed to the little star that shone in the darkness with an emerald brilliance. We were rushing straight toward her.

"And are such replicas really possible in the universe, is that really the law of nature? ... And if that is the earth there, is it really the same as our earth ... absolutely the same, unfortunate, poor, but dear and eternally beloved, giving birth to the same tormenting love for herself even in her most ungrateful children? ... " I cried out, shaking with irrepressible, rapturous love for that former native earth I had abandoned. The image of the poor little girl whom I had offended flashed before me.

"You will see all," my companion replied, and some sadness sounded in his words. But we were quickly approaching the planet. It was growing before my eyes, I could already make out the ocean, the outlines of Europe, and suddenly a strange feeling of some great, holy jealousy blazed up in my heart: "How can there be such a replica, and what for? I love, I can love, only the earth I left, where the stains of my blood were left, when I, the ungrateful one, extinguished my life with a shot in the heart. But never, never did I cease to love that earth, and even on that night, as I was parting from her, I perhaps loved her more tormentingly than ever before. Is there suffering on this new earth? On our earth we can love truly only with suffering and through suffering! We're unable to love otherwise and we know no other love. I want suffering, in order to love. I want, I thirst, to kiss, this very minute, pouring out tears, that one earth alone which I left, and I do not want, I do not accept life on any other! ... "

But my companion had already left me. Suddenly, as if quite imperceptibly, I came to stand on this other earth, in the bright light of a sunny day, lovely as paradise. I was standing, it seems, on one of those islands which on our earth make up the Greek archipelago, or somewhere on the coast of the mainland adjacent to that archipelago. Oh, everything was exactly as with us, but seemed everywhere to radiate some festivity and a great, holy, and finally attained triumph. The gentle emerald sea splashed softly against the shores and kissed them with love, plain, visible, almost conscious.

Tall, beautiful trees stood in all the luxury of their flowering, and their numberless leaves, I was convinced, greeted me with their soft, gentle sound, as if uttering words of love. The grass glittered with bright, fragrant flowers. Flocks of birds flew about in the air and, fearless of me, landed on my shoulders and arms, joyfully beating me with their dear, fluttering wings. And finally I got to see and know the people of that happy earth. They came to me themselves, they surrounded me, kissed me. Children of the sun, children of their sun, oh, how beautiful they were! Never on earth have I seen such beauty in man. Maybe only in our children, in their first years, can one find a remote, though faint, glimmer of that beauty. The eyes of these happy people shone with clear brightness. Their faces radiated reason and a sort of consciousness fulfilled to the point of serenity, yet they were mirthful faces; a childlike joy sounded in the words and voices of these people. Oh, at once, with the first glance at their faces, I understood everything, everything! This was the earth undefiled by the fall, the people who lived on it had not sinned, they lived in the same paradise in which, according to the legends of all mankind, our fallen forefathers lived, with the only difference that the whole earth here was everywhere one and the same paradise. These people, laughing joyfully, crowded around me and caressed me; they took me with them and each of them wished to set me at ease. Oh, they didn't ask me about anything, but it seemed to me as if they already knew everything, and wished quickly to drive the torment from my face.

IV

You see, once again: well, let it be only a dream! But the feeling of love from these innocent and beautiful people remained in me ever after, and I feel that their love pours upon me from there even now. I saw them myself, I knew them and was convinced, I loved them, I suffered for them afterward. Oh I at once understood, even then, that in many ways I would never understand them; to me, a modern Russian progressive and vile Petersburger, it seemed insoluble, for instance, that they, while knowing so much, did not have our science. But I soon realized that their knowledge was fulfilled and nourished by different insights than on our earth, and that their aspirations were also quite different. They did not wish for anything and were at peace, they did not aspire to a knowledge of life, as we do, because their life was fulfilled. But their knowledge was deeper and loftier than our science; for our science seeks to explain what life is it aspires to comprehend it, in order to teach others to live; but they know how to live even without science, and I understood that, but I could not understand their knowledge. They pointed out their trees to me, and I could not understand the extent of the love with which they looked at them: as if they were talking with creatures of their own kind. And you know, perhaps I wouldn't be mistaken if I said that they did talk to them! Yes, they had found their language, and I'm convinced that the trees understood them. They looked at the whole of nature in the same way, at the animals, who lived in peace with them, did not attack them, and loved them, won over by their love. They pointed out the stars to me and talked of them with me about something I couldn't understand, but I'm convinced that they had some contact, as it were, with the heavenly stars, not just in thought, but in some living way. Oh, these people did not even try to make me understand them, they loved me even without that, but on the other hand I knew that they would also never understand me, and therefor I hardly ever spoke to them about our earth. I only kissed before them that earth on which they lived and wordlessly adored them, and they saw it allowed me to adore them without being ashamed of my adoring them, because they loved much themselves. They did not suffer for me when sometimes, in tears, I kissed their feet, joyfully knowing at heart with what force of love they would respond to me. At times I asked myself in astonishment: how could they manage, all this while, not to insult a man such as I, and never once provoke in a man such as I any feeling of jealousy or envy? Many times I asked myself how I, a braggart and a liar, could manage not to speak to them about my knowledge, of which they, of course, had no notion, not to wish to astonish them with it, if only out of love for them? They were frisky and gay as children. They wandered through their beautiful groves and forests, they sang their beautiful songs, they ate their light food, fruit from their trees, honey from their forests, and milk from the animals who loved them.

For their food and clothing they labored little and but lightly. There was love among them, and children were born, but I never observed in them any impulses of that *cruel* sensuality that overtakes almost everyone on our earth, each and every one, and is the only source of almost all the sins of our mankind. They rejoiced in the children they had as new partakers of their bliss. Among them there was no quarreling or jealousy, they did not even understand what it meant. Their children were everyone's children, because they all constituted one family. They had almost no illnesses, though there was death; but their old people died quietly, as if falling asleep, surrounded by those bidding them farewell, blessing them, smiling at them, and receiving bright parting smiles themselves. I saw no sorrow or tears at that, there was only love increased as if to the point of rapture, but a rapture that was calm, fulfilled, contemplative. One might think they were in touch with their dead even after their death and that the earthly union between them was not interrupted by death. They barely understood me when I asked them about eternal life, but they were apparently so convinced of it unconsciously that it did not constitute a question for them. They had no temples, but they had some essential, living, and constant union with the Entirety of the universe; they had no faith, but instead had a firm knowledge that when their earthly joy was fulfilled to the limits of earthly nature, there would then come for them, both for the living and for the dead, a still greater expansion of their contract with the Entirety of the universe. They waited for this moment with joy, but without haste, without suffering over it, but as if already having it in the presages of their hearts, which they conveyed to one another. In the evenings, before going to sleep, they liked to sing in balanced, harmonious choruses. In these songs they expressed all the feelings that the departing day had given them, praised it, and bade it farewell. They praised nature, the earth, the sea, the forest. They liked to compose songs about each other and praised each other like children; these were the most simple songs, but they flowed from the heart and penetrated hearts. And not in songs only, but it seemed they spent their whole life only in admiring each other. It was a sort of mutual being-in-love, total, universal. And some of their songs, solemn and rapturous, I hardly understood at all. While

I understood the words, I was never able to penetrate their full meaning. It remained as if inaccessible to my mind, yet my heart was as if unconsciously pervaded by it more and more. I often told them that I had long ago had a presentiment of all this, that all this joy and glory had already spoken to me on our earth in a anguished call, sometimes reaching the point of unbearable sorrow; that I had a presentiment of them all and of their glory in the dreams of my heart and the reveries of my mind, that I had often been unable, on our earth, to watch the setting sun without tears... That my hatred of the people of our earth always contained anguish: why am I unable to hate them without loving them, why am I unable not to forgive them, and why is there anguish in my love for them: why am I unable to love them without hating them? They listened to me, and I saw that they could not imagine what I was talking about, but I did not regret talking to them about it: I knew they understood all the intensity of my anguish for those whom I had abandoned. Yes, when they looked at me with their dear eyes pervaded by love, when I felt that in their presence my heart, too, became as innocent and truthful as theirs, I did not regret not understanding them. The feeling of the fullness of life took my breath away, and I silently worshipped them.

Oh, everyone laughs in my face now and assures me that even in dreams one cannot see such details as I'm now telling, that in my dream I saw or felt only a certain sensation generated by my own heart in delirium, and that I invented the details when I woke up. And when I disclosed to them that perhaps it was actually so, God, what laughter they threw in my face, and what fun they had at my expense! Oh, yes, of course, I was overcome just by the sensation of that dream, and it alone survived in the bloody wound of my heart: yet the real images and forms of my dream, that is, those that I actually saw at the time of my dreaming, were fulfilled so harmoniously, they were so enchanting and beautiful, and so true, that having awakened, I was, of course, unable to embody them in our weak words, so that they must have been as if effaced in my mind, and therefore, indeed, perhaps I myself unconsciously was forced to invent the details afterward; and of course distorted them, especially with my so passionate desire to hurry and tell them at least somehow. And yet how can I not believe that it all really was? And was, perhaps a thousand times better, brighter, and more joyful than I'm telling? Let it be a dream, still it all could not but be. You know, I'll tell you a secret: perhaps it wasn't a dream at all! For here a certain thing happened, something so terribly true that it couldn't have been imagined in a dream. Let my dream have been generated by my heart, but was my heart alone capable of generating the terrible truth that happened to me afterward? How could I myself invent or imagine it in my heart? Can it be that my paltry heart and capricious, insignificant mind were able to rise to such a revelation of the truth! Oh, judge for yourselves: I've concealed it so far, but now I'll finish telling this truth as well. The thing was that I ... corrupted them all!

V

Yes, yes, it ended with me corrupting them all! How it could have happened I don't know, but I remember it clearly. The dream flew through thousands of years and left in me just a sense of the whole. I know only that the cause of the fall was I. Like a foul trichina, like an atom of plague infecting whole countries, so I infected that whole happy and previously sinless earth with myself. They learned to lie and began to love the lie and knew the beauty of the lie. Oh, maybe it started *innocently*, with a joke, with coquetry, with amorous play, maybe, indeed, with an atom, but this atom of lie penetrated their hearts, and they liked it. Then sensuality was quickly born, sensuality generated jealousy, and jealousy, cruelty ... Oh, I don't know, I don't remember, but soon, very soon, the first blood was shed; they were astonished and horrified, and began to part, to separate. Alliances appeared, but against each other now. Rebukes, reproaches began. They knew shame, and shame was made into a virtue. The notion of honor was born, and each alliance raised its own banner. They began tormenting animals, and the animals withdrew from them into the forests and became their enemies. There began the struggle for separation, for isolation, for the personal, for mine and yours. They started speaking different languages. They knew sorrow and came to love sorrow, they thirsted for suffering and said that truth is attained only through suffering. Then science appeared among them. When they became wicked, they began to talk of brotherhood and humaneness and understood these ideas. When they became criminal, they invented justice and prescribed whole codices for themselves in order to maintain it, and to ensure the codices they set up the guillotine. They just barely remembered what they had lost, and did not even want to believe that they had once been innocent and happy. They even laughed at the possibility of the former happiness and called it a dream. They couldn't even imagine it in forms and images, but, strange and wonderful thing, having lost all belief in their former happiness, having called it a fairy tale, they wised so much to be innocent and happy again, once more, that they fell down before their hearts' desires like children, they deified their desire, they built temples and started praying to their own idea, their own "desire," all the while fully believing in its unrealizability and unfeasibility, but adoring it in tears and worshipping it. And yet, if it had so happened that they could have returned to that innocent and happy condition which they had lost, or if someone had suddenly shown it to them again and asked them: did they want to go back to it? They would certainly have refused. They used to answer me: "Granted we're deceitful, wicked and unjust, we *know* that and weep for it, and we torment ourselves over it, and torture and punish ourselves perhaps even more than that merciful judge who will judge us and whose name we do not know. But we have science, and through it we shall again find the truth, but we shall now accept it consciously, knowledge is higher than feelings, the consciousness of life is higher than life. Science will give us wisdom, wisdom will discover laws, and knowledge of the laws of happiness is higher than happiness." That's what they used to say, and after such words each of them loved himself more than anyone else, and they couldn't have done otherwise. Each of them became so jealous of his own person that he tried as hard as he could to humiliate and belittle it in others, and gave his life to that. Slavery appeared, even voluntary slavery: the weak willingly submitted to the strong, only so as to help them crush those still weaker than themselves. Righteous men appeared, who came to these people in tears and spoke to them of their pride, their lack of measure and harmony, their loss of shame. They were derided or stoned. Holy blood was spilled on the thresholds of temples. On the other hand, people began to appear who started inventing ways for everyone to unite again so that each of them, without ceasing to love himself more than anyone else, would at the same time not hinder others, and thus live all together in a harmonious society, as it were. Whole wars arose because of this idea. At the same time, the warring sides all firmly believed that science, wisdom, and the sense of self-preservation would finally force men to unite in a harmonious and reasonable society, and therefore, to speed things up meanwhile, the "wise" tried quickly to exterminate all the "unwise," who did not understand their idea, so that they would not hinder its triumph. But the sense of self-preservation quickly began to weaken, proud men and sensualists appeared who directly demanded everything or nothing. To acquire everything, they resorted to evildoing, and if that did not succeed, to suicide. Religions appeared with a cult of non-being and self-destruction for the sake of eternal peace in nothingness. Finally, these people grew weary in meaningless toil, and suffering appeared on their faces, and these people proclaimed that suffering is beauty, for only in suffering is there thought. They sang suffering in their songs. I walked among them, wringing my hands, and wept over them, but I loved them perhaps still more than before, when there was as yet no suffering on their faces and they were innocent and so beautiful. I loved their defiled earth still more than when it had been a paradise, only because grief had appeared on it. Alas, I had always loved grief and sorrow, but only for myself, for myself, while over them I wept, pitying them. I stretched out my arms to them, in despair accusing, cursing, and despising myself. I told them that I, I alone, had done it all; that it was I who had brought them depravity, infection, and the lie! I beseeched them to crucify me on a cross, I taught them how to make a cross. I couldn't, I hadn't the strength to kill myself, but I wanted to take the suffering from them, I longed for suffering, I longed to shed my blood to the last drop in this suffering. But they just laughed at me and in the end began to consider me some sort of holy fool. They vindicated me, they said they had received only what they themselves had wanted, and that everything could not but be as it was. Finally, they announced to me that I was becoming dangerous for them and that they would put me in a madhouse if I didn't keep quiet. Here sorrow entered my soul with such force that my heart was wrung, and I felt I was going to die, and here ... well, here I woke up.

It was already morning, that is, not light yet, but it was about six o'clock. I came to my senses in the same armchair, my candle had burned all the way down, everyone was asleep at the captain's, and around me was a silence rare in our apartment. First of all, I jumped up extremely surprised; nothing like that had ever happened to me, even down to trifling little details: for instance, never before had I fallen asleep in my armchair like that. Here suddenly, while I was standing and coming to my senses, suddenly my revolver flashed before me, ready, loaded, but I instantly pushed it away from me! Oh, life, life now! I lifted up my arms and called out to the eternal truth; did not call out, but wept; rapture, boundless rapture, elevated my whole being. Yes, life and, preaching! I decided on preaching that same moment, and, of course, for the rest of my life! I'm going out to preach, I want to preach, what? The truth, for I saw it, saw it with my own eyes, saw all its glory!

And so, since then I've been preaching! What's more, I love those who laugh at me more than all the rest. Why that's so I don't know and can't explain, but let it be so. They say I'm already getting confused now, that is, if I'm already so confused now, how will it be later? The veritable truth: I'm getting confused now, and maybe it will be worse later. And of course I'm going to get confused a few times before I discover how to preach, that is, in what words and in what deeds, because it's very hard to do. I see it clear as day even now, but listen: is there anyone who doesn't get confused? And yet everyone goes toward one and the same thing, at least everyone strives for one and the same thing, from the sage to the last robber, only by different paths. This is an old truth, but what is new here is this: I cannot get very confused. Because I saw the truth, I saw and I know that people can be beautiful and happy without losing the ability to live on earth. I will not and cannot believe that evil is the normal condition of people. And they all laugh merely at this belief of mine. But how can I not believe: I saw the truth, it's not that my mind invented it, but I saw it, I saw it, and its *living image* filled my soul for all time. I saw it in such fulfilled wholeness that I cannot believe it is impossible for people to have it. And so, how could I get confused? I'll wander off, of course, even several times, and will maybe even speak in other people's words, but not for long: the living image of what I saw will always be with me and will always correct and direct me. Oh, I'm hale, I'm fresh, I'm going, going, even if it's for a thousand years. You know, I even wanted to conceal, at first, that I corrupted them all, but that was a mistake, already the first mistake! But truth whispered to me that I was *lying,* and guarded and directed me. But how to set up paradise, I don't know, because I'm unable to put it into words. After my dream, I lost words. At least all the main words, the most necessary ones. But so be it: I'll go and I'll keep talking, tirelessly, because after all I saw it with my own eyes, thought I can't recount what I saw. But that is what the scoffers don't understand: "He had a dream," they say, "a delirium, a hallucination." Eh! As if that's so clever? And how proud they are! A dream? What is a dream? And is our life not a dream? I'll say more: let it never, let it never come true, and let there be no paradise (that I can understand!), well, but I will preach all the same. And yet it's so simple: in one day, *in one hour,* it could all be set up at once! The main thing is, love others as yourself, that's the main thing, and it's everything, there's no need for anything else at all: it will immediately be discovered how to set things up. And yet this is merely an old truth, repeated and read a billion times, but still it has never taken root! "The consciousness of life is higher than life, the knowledge of the laws of happiness is higher than happiness," that is what must be fought! And I will. If only everyone wants it, everything can be set up at once.

And I found that little girl… And I'll go! I'll go!

Two Friends

Guy de Maupassant

Guy de Maupassant (1850-1893) was known as the greatest short story writer of France. He often infused naturalist elements in his writings, marked by the economy of expression and simplicity of style. Maupassant volunteered for the Franco-Prussian War (1870-71), and much of his writings stemmed from his war experience. His poignant story 'Two Friends' (1882) is also set during the Franco-Prussian War.

The following story is set during the Franco-Prussian War. Beginning on July 19, 1870, the war had resulted from the Prussian prime minister Otto von Bismarck's belief that a war with France would strengthen the bond between the German states, along with French emperor Napoleon III's feeling that a successful conflict with Prussia would help him to gain support among the French people. As it turned out, the French army was no match for the German forces. After a series of victories, one of which ended in the capture of Napoleon III, the German army established a blockade around Paris on September 19, 1870. Led by a provisional govern-ment, Paris managed to hold out until January 28, 1871, though the city's inhabitants were plagued by famine and a sense of hopelessness. As de Maupasant's story begins, the city is on the verge of surrender.

Paris was blockaded, starved, in its death agony. Sparrows were becoming scarcer and scarcer on the rooftops and the sewers were being depopulated. One ate whatever one could get.

As he was strolling sadly along the outer boulevard one bright January morning, his hands in his trousers pockets and his stomach empty, M.1 Morissot, watchmaker by trade but local militiaman for the time being, stopped short before a fellow militiaman whom he recognized as a friend. It was M. Sauvage, a riverside acquaintance.

Every Sunday, before the war, Morissot left at dawn, a bamboo pole in his hand, a tin box on his back. He would take the Argenteuil' railroad, get off at Colombes, and walk to Marante Island. As soon as he arrived at this ideal spot he would start to fish; he fished until nightfall.

Every Sunday he would meet a stout, jovial little man, M. Sauvage, a haberdasher in Rue Notre-Dame-de-Lorette, another ardent fisherman. Often they spent half a day side by side, line in hand and feet dangling above the current. Inevitably they had struck up a friendship.

Some days they did not speak. Sometimes they did; but they understood one another admirably without saying anything because they had similar tastes and responded to their surroundings in exactly the same way.

On a spring morning, toward ten o'clock, when the young sun was drawing up from the tranquil stream wisps of haze which floated off in the direction of the current and was pouring down its vernal warmth on the backs of the two fanatical anglers, Morissot would sometimes say to his neighbor, "Nice, isn't it?" and M. Sauvage would answer, "There's nothing like it." And that was enough for them to understand and appreciate each other.

On an autumn afternoon, when the sky, reddened by the setting sun, cast reflections of its scarlet clouds on the water, made the whole river crimson, lighted up the horizon, made the two friends look as ruddy as fire, and gilded the trees which were already brown and beginning to tremble with a wintery shiver, M. Sauvage would look at Morissot with a smile and say, "Fine sight!" And Morissot, awed, would answer, "It's better than the city, isn't it?" without taking his eyes from his float.

As soon as they recognized one another they shook hands energetically, touched at meeting under such changed circumstances. M. Sauvage, with a sigh, grumbled, "What goings-on!" Morissot groaned dismally, "And what weather! This is the first fine day of the year."

The sky was, in fact, blue and brilliant.

They started to walk side by side, absent-minded and sad. Morissot went on, "And fishing! Ah! Nothing but a pleasant memory."

"When'll we get back to it?" asked M. Sauvage.

They went into a little cafe and had an absinthe, then resumed their stroll along the sidewalks. Morissot stopped suddenly, "How about another, eh?" M. Sauvage agreed, "If you want." And they entered another wine shop.

On leaving they felt giddy, muddled, as one does after drinking on an empty stomach. It was mild. A caressing breeze touched their faces.

The warm air completed what the absinthe had begun. M. Sauvage stopped.

"Suppose we went?"

"Went where?"

"Fishing, of course."

"But where?"

"Why, on our island. The French outposts are near Colombes. I know Colonel Dumoulin; they'll let us pass without any trouble."

Morissot trembled with eagerness: "Done! I'm with you." And they went off to get their tackle.

An hour later they were walking side by side on the highway. They reached the villa which the Colonel occupied. He smiled at their request and gave his consent to their whim. They started off again, armed with a pass.

Soon they passed the outposts, went through the abandoned village of Colombes, and reached the edge of the little vineyards which slope toward the Seine. It was about eleven.

Opposite, the village of Argenteuil seemed dead. The heights of Orgemont and Sannois dominated the whole countryside. The broad plain which stretches as far as Nanterre was empty, absolutely empty, with its bare cherry trees and its colorless fields.

Pointing up to the heights, M. Sauvage murmured, "The Prussians are up there!" And a feeling of uneasiness paralyzed the two friends as they faced this deserted region.

"The Prussians!" They had never seen any, but for months they had felt their presence—around Paris, ruining France, pillaging, massacring, starving the country, invisible and all-powerful. And a kind of superstitious terror was superimposed on the hatred which they felt for this unknown and victorious people.

Morissot stammered, "Say, suppose we met some of them?"

His Parisian jauntiness coming to the surface in spite of everything, M. Sauvage answered, "We'll offer them some fish."

But they hesitated to venture into the country, frightened by the silence all about them.

Finally M. Sauvage pulled himself together: "Come on! On our way! But let's go carefully." And they climbed over into a vineyard, bent double, crawling, taking advantage of the vines to conceal themselves, watching, listening.

A stretch of bare ground had to be crossed to reach the edge of the river. They began to run, and when they reached the bank they plunged down among the dry reeds.

Morissot glued his ear to the ground and listened for sounds of anyone walking in the vicinity. He heard nothing. They were indeed alone, all alone. Reassured, they started to fish.

Opposite them Marante Island, deserted, hid them from the other bank. The little building which had housed a restaurant was shut up and looked as if it had been abandoned for years.

M. Sauvage caught the first gudgeon. Morissot got the second, and from then on they pulled in their lines every minute or two with a silvery little fish squirming on the end, a truly miraculous draught.

Skillfully they slipped the fish into a sack made of fine net which they had hung in the water at their feet. And happiness pervaded their whole being, the happiness which seizes upon you when you regain a cherished pleasure of which you have long been deprived.

The good sun was pouring down its warmth on their backs. They heard nothing more; they no longer thought about anything at all; they forgot about the rest of the world—they were fishing!

But suddenly a dull sound which seemed to come from under ground made the earth tremble. The cannon were beginning.

Morissot turned and saw, over the bank to the left, the great silhouette of Mount Valerien wearing a white plume on its brow, powdersmoke which it had just spit out.

And almost at once a second puff of smoke rolled from the summit, and a few seconds after the roar still another explosion was heard.

Then more followed, and time after time the mountain belched forth death-dealing breath, breathed out milky-white vapor which rose slowly in the calm sky and formed a cloud above the summit.

M. Sauvage shrugged his shoulders. "There they go again," he said.

As he sat anxiously watching his float bob up and down, Morissot was suddenly seized by the wrath which a peace-loving man will feel toward madmen who fight, and grumbled, "Folks sure are stupid to kill one another like that."

M. Sauvage answered, "They're worse than animals."

And Morissot, who had just pulled in a bleak, went on, "And to think that it will always be like this as long as there are governments."

M. Sauvage stopped him: "The Republic wouldn't have declared war—"

Morissot interrupted: "Under kings you have war abroad; under the Republic you have war at home." And they started a leisurely discussion, unraveling great political problems with the sane reasonableness of easygoing, limited individuals, and found themselves in agreement on the point that men would never be free. And Mount Valerien thundered unceasingly, demolishing French homes with its cannon, crushing out lives, putting an end to the dreams which many had dreamt, the joys which many had been waiting for, the happiness which many had hoped for, planting in wives' hearts, in maidens' hearts, in mothers' hearts, over there, in other lands, sufferings which would never end.

"That's life for you," opined M. Sauvage. "You'd better say 'That's death for you,'" laughed Morissot.

But they shuddered in terror when they realized that someone had just come up behind them, and looking around they saw four men standing almost at their elbows, four tall men, armed and bearded, dressed like liveried' servants, with flat caps on their heads, pointing rifles at them.

The two fish lines dropped from their hands and floated off down stream.

In a few seconds they were seized, trussed up, carried off, thrown into a rowboat and taken over to the island.

And behind the building which they had thought deserted they saw a score of German soldiers.

A kind of hairy giant who was seated astride a chair smoking a porcelain pipe asked them in excellent

French: "Well, gentlemen, have you had good fishing?"

Then a soldier put down at the officer's feet the sack full of fish which he had carefully brought along. The Prussian smiled: "Aha! I see that it didn't go badly. But we have to talk about another little matter. Listen to me and don't get excited.

"As far as I am concerned, you are two spies sent to keep an eye on me. I catch you and I shoot you. You were pretending to fish in order to conceal your business. You have fallen into my hands, so much the worse for you. War is like that.

"But—since you came out past the outposts you have, of course, the password to return. Tell me that password and I will pardon you."

The two friends, side by side, pale, kept silent. A slight nervous trembling shook their hands.

The officer went on: "No one will ever know. You will go back placidly. The secret will disappear with you. If you refuse, it is immediate death. Choose."

They stood motionless, mouths shut.

The Prussian quietly went on, stretching out his hand toward the stream: "Remember that within five minutes you will be at the bottom of that river. Within five minutes! You have relatives, of course?"

Mount Valerien kept thundering.

The two fishermen stood silent. The German gave orders in his own language. Then he moved his chair so as not to be near the prisoners and twelve men took their places, twenty paces distant, rifles grounded.

The officer went on: "I give you one minute, not two seconds more."

Then he rose suddenly, approached the two Frenchmen, took Morissot by the arm, dragged him aside, whispered to him, "Quick, the password? Your friend won't know. I'll pretend to relent."

Morissot answered not a word.

The Prussian drew M. Sauvage aside and put the same question. M. Sauvage did not answer.

They stood side by side again.

And the officer began to give commands. The soldiers raised their rifles.

Then Morissot's glance happened to fall on the sack full of gudgeons which was lying on the grass a few steps away.

A ray of sunshine made the little heap of still squirming fish gleam. And he almost weakened. In spite of his efforts his eyes filled with tears.

He stammered, "Farewell, Monsieur Sauvage." M. Sauvage answered, "Farewell, Monsieur Morissot." They shook hands, trembling from head to foot with a shudder which they could not control.

The officer shouted, "Fire!"

The twelve shots rang out together.

M. Sauvage fell straight forward, like a log. Morissot, who was taller, tottered, half turned, and fell crosswise on top of his comrade, face up, as the blood spurted from his torn shirt.

The German gave more orders.

His men scattered, then returned with rope and stones which they tied to the dead men's feet. Then they carried them to the bank.

Mount Valerien continued to roar, its summit hidden now in a mountainous cloud of smoke.

Two soldiers took Morissot by the head and the feet, two others seized M. Sauvage. They swung the bodies for a moment then let go. They described an arc and plunged into the river feet first, for the weights made them seem to be standing upright.

There was a splash, the water trembled, then grew calm, while tiny wavelets spread to both shores.

A little blood remained on the surface.

The officer, still calm, said in a low voice: "Now the fish will have their turn." And he went back to the house.

And all at once he caught sight of the sack of gudgeons in the grass. He picked it up, looked at it, smiled, shouted, "Wilhelm!"

A soldier in a white apron ran out. And the Prussian threw him the catch of the two and said: "Fry these little animals right away while they are still alive. They will be delicious."

Then he lighted his pipe again.

Olalla

R.L. Stevenson

Robert Louis Stevenson (1850-1894) was a renowned Scottish essayist, poet, travel writer and short story writer, best known for his novels *Treasure Island* (1881) and *The Strange Case of Dr. Jekyll and Mr. Hyde* (1886). Besides writing travelogues and romantic novels, Stevenson also wrote horror stories with moral undertones. 'Olalla' was first published in the Christmas issue of *The Court and Society Review* (1885).

"Now," said the doctor, "my part is done, and, I may say, with some vanity, well done. It remains only to get you out of this cold and poisonous city, and to give you two months of a pure air and an easy conscience. The last is your affair. To the first I think I can help you. It fells indeed rather oddly; it was but the other day the Padre came in from the country; and as he and I are old friends, although of contrary professions, he applied to me in a matter of distress among some of his parishioners. This was a family—but you are ignorant of Spain, and even the names of our grandees are hardly known to you; suffice it, then, that they were once great people, and are now fallen to the brink of destitution. Nothing now belongs to them but the residencia, and certain leagues of desert mountain, in the greater part of which not even a goat could support life. But the house is a fine old place, and stands at a great height among the hills, and most salubriously; and I had no sooner heard my friend's tale, than I remembered you. I told him I had a wounded officer, wounded in the good cause, who was now able to make a change; and I proposed that his friends should take you for a lodger. Instantly the Padre's face grew dark, as I had maliciously foreseen it would. It was out of the question, he said. Then let them starve, said I, for I have no sympathy with tatterdemalion pride. Thereupon we separated, not very content with one another; but yesterday, to my wonder, the Padre returned and made a submission: the difficulty, he said, he had found upon enquiry to be less than he had feared; or, in other words, these proud people had put their pride in their pocket. I closed with the offer; and, subject to your approval, I have taken rooms for you in the residencia. The air of these mountains will renew your blood; and the quiet in which you will there live is worth all the medicines in the world."

"Doctor," said I, "you have been throughout my good angel, and your advice is a command. But tell me, if you please, something of the family with which I am to reside."

"I am coming to that," replied my friend; "and, indeed, there is a difficulty in the way. These beggars are, as I have said, of very high descent and swollen with the most baseless vanity; they have lived for some generations in a growing isolation, drawing away, on either hand, from the rich who had now become too high for them, and from the poor, whom they still regarded as too low; and even today, when poverty forces them to unfasten their door to a guest, they cannot do so without a most ungracious stipulation. You are to remain, they say, a stranger; they will give you attendance, but they refuse from the first the idea of the smallest intimacy."

I will not deny that I was piqued, and perhaps the feeling strengthened my desire to go, for I was confident that I could break down that barrier if I desired. "There is nothing offensive in such a stipulation," said I; "and I even sympathise with the feeling that inspired it."

"It is true they have never seen you," returned the doctor politely; "and if they knew you were the handsomest and the most pleasant man that ever came from England (where I am told that handsome men are common, but pleasant ones not so much so), they would doubtless make you welcome with a better grace. But since you take the thing so well, it matters not. To me, indeed, it seems discourteous. But you will find yourself the gainer. The family will not much tempt you. A mother, a son, and a daughter; an old woman said to be half-witted, a country lout, and a country girl, who stands very high with her confessor, and is, therefore," chuckled the physician, "most likely plain; there is not much in that to attract the fancy of a dashing officer."

"And yet you say they are high-born," I objected.

"Well, as to that, I should distinguish," returned the doctor. "The mother is; not so the children. The mother was the last representative of a princely stock, degenerate both in parts and fortune. Her father was not only poor, he was mad: and the girl ran wild about the residencia till his death. Then, much of the fortune having died with him, and the family being quite extinct, the girl ran wilder than ever, until at last she married, Heaven knows whom, a muleteer some say, others a smuggler; while there are some who uphold there was no marriage at all, and that Felipe and are bastards. The union, such as it was, was tragically dissolved some years ago; but they live in such seclusion, and the country at that time was in so much disorder, that the precise manner of the man's end is known only to the priest—if even to him."

"I begin to think I shall have strange experiences," said I.

"I would not romance, if I were you," replied the doctor; "you will find, I fear, a very grovelling and commonplace reality. Felipe, for instance, I have seen. And what am I to say? He is very rustic, very cunning, very loutish, and, I should say, an innocent; the others are probably to match. No, no, senor commandante, you must seek congenial society among the great sights of our mountains; and in these at least, if you are at all a lover of the works of nature, I promise you will not be disappointed."

The next day Felipe came for me in a rough country cart, drawn by a mule; and a little before the stroke of noon, after I had said farewell to the doctor, the innkeeper, and different good souls who had befriended me during my sickness, we set forth out of the city by the Eastern gate, and began to ascend into the Sierra. I had been so long a prisoner, since I was left behind for dying after the loss of the convoy, that the mere smell of the earth set me smiling. The country through which we went was wild and rocky, partially covered with rough woods, now of the cork-tree, and now of the great Spanish chestnut, and frequently intersected by the beds of mountain torrents. The sun shone, the wind rustled joyously;

and we had advanced some miles, and the city had already shrunk into an inconsiderable knoll upon the plain behind us, before my attention began to be diverted to the companion of my drive. To the eye, he seemed but a diminutive, loutish, well-made country lad, such as the doctor had described, mighty quick and active, but devoid of any culture; and this first impression was with most observers final. What began to strike me was his familiar, chattering talk; so strangely inconsistent with the terms on which I was to be received; and partly from his imperfect enunciation, partly from the sprightly incoherence of the matter, so very difficult to follow clearly without an effort of the mind. It is true I had before talked with persons of a similar mental constitution; persons who seemed to live (as he did) by the senses, taken and possessed by the visual object of the moment and unable to discharge their minds of that impression. His seemed to me (as I sat, distantly giving ear) a kind of conversation proper to drivers, who pass much of their time in a great vacancy of the intellect and threading the sights of a familiar country. But this was not the case of Felipe; by his own account, he was a home—keeper; "I wish I was there now," he said; and then, spying a tree by the wayside, he broke off to tell me that he had once seen a crow among its branches.

"A crow?" I repeated, struck by the ineptitude of the remark, and thinking I had heard imperfectly.

But by this time he was already filled with a new idea; hearkening with a rapt intentness, his head on one side, his face puckered; and he struck me rudely, to make me hold my peace. Then he smiled and shook his head.

"What did you hear?" I asked.

"O, it is all right," he said; and began encouraging his mule with cries that echoed unhumanly up the mountain walls.

I looked at him more closely. He was superlatively well-built, light, and lithe and strong; he was well-featured; his yellow eyes were very large, though, perhaps, not very expressive; take him altogether, he was a pleasant-looking lad, and I had no fault to find with him, beyond that he was of a dusky hue, and inclined to hairyness; two characteristics that I disliked. It was his mind that puzzled, and yet attracted me. The doctor's phrase—an innocent—came back to me;

and I was wondering if that were, after all, the true description, when the road began to go down into the narrow and naked chasm of a torrent. The waters thundered tumultuously in the bottom; and the ravine was filled full of the sound, the thin spray, and the claps of wind, that accompanied their descent. The scene was certainly impressive; but the road was in that part very securely walled in; the mule went steadily forward; and I was astonished to perceive the paleness of terror in the face of my companion. The voice of that wild river was inconstant, now sinking lower as if in weariness, now doubling its hoarse tones; momentary freshets seemed to swell its volume, sweeping down the gorge, raving and booming against the barrier walls; and I observed it was at each of these accessions to the clamour, that my driver more particularly winced and blanched. Some thoughts of Scottish superstition and the river Kelpie, passed across my mind; I wondered if perchance the like were prevalent in that part of Spain; and turning to Felipe, sought to draw him out.

"What is the matter?" I asked.

"O, I am afraid," he replied.

"Of what are you afraid?" I returned. "This seems one of the safest places on this very dangerous road."

"It makes a noise," he said, with a simplicity of awe that set my doubts at rest.

The lad was but a child in intellect; his mind was like his body, active and swift, but stunted in development; and I began from that time forth to regard him with a measure of pity, and to listen at first with indulgence, and at last even with pleasure, to his disjointed babble.

By about four in the afternoon we had crossed the summit of the mountain line, said farewell to the western sunshine, and began to go down upon the other side, skirting the edge of many ravines and moving through the shadow of dusky woods. There rose upon all sides the voice of falling water, not condensed and formidable as in the gorge of the river, but scattered and sounding gaily and musically from glen to glen. Here, too, the spirits of my driver mended, and he began to sing aloud in a falsetto voice, and with a singular bluntness of musical perception, never true either to melody or key, but wandering at will, and yet somehow with an effect that was natural and pleasing, like that of the of birds. As the dusk increased, I fell more and more under the spell of this artless warbling, listening and waiting for some articulate air, and still disappointed; and when at last I asked him what it was he sang—"O," cried he, "I am just singing!" Above all, I was taken with a trick he had of unweariedly repeating the same note at little intervals; it was not so monotonous as you would think, or, at least, not disagreeable; and it seemed to breathe a wonderful contentment with what is, such as we love to fancy in the attitude of trees, or the quiescence of a pool.

Night had fallen dark before we came out upon a plateau, and drew up a little after, before a certain lump of superior blackness which I could only conjecture to be the residencia. Here, my guide, getting down from the cart, hooted and whistled for a long time in vain; until at last an old peasant man came towards us from somewhere in the surrounding dark, carrying a candle in his hand. By the light of this I was able to perceive a great arched doorway of a Moorish character: it was closed by iron-studded gates, in one of the leaves of which Felipe opened a wicket. The peasant carried off the cart to some out-building; but my guide and I passed through the wicket, which was closed again behind us; and by the glimmer of the candle, passed through a court, up a stone stair, along a section of an open gallery, and up more stairs again, until we came at last to the door of a great and somewhat bare apartment. This room, which I understood was to be mine, was pierced by three windows, lined with some lustrous wood disposed in panels, and carpeted with the skins of many savage animals. A bright fire burned in the chimney, and shed abroad a changeful flicker; close up to the blaze there was drawn a table, laid for supper; and in the far end a bed stood ready. I was pleased by these preparations, and said so to Felipe; and he, with the same simplicity of disposition that I held already remarked in him, warmly re-echoed my praises. "A fine room," he said; "a very fine room. And fire, too; fire is good; it melts out the pleasure in your bones. And the bed," he continued, carrying over the candle in that direction—"see what fine sheets—how soft, how smooth, smooth;" and he passed his hand again and again over their texture, and then laid down his head and rubbed his cheeks among them with a grossness of content that somehow offended me. I took the candle from his hand (for I feared he would set the bed on fire) and walked back to the supper-table, where, perceiving a measure of wine, I poured out a cup and called to him to come and drink of it. He started to his feet at once and ran to me with a strong expression of hope; but when he saw the wine, he visibly shuddered.

"Oh, no," he said, "not that; that is for you. I hate it."

"Very well, Senor," said I; "then I will drink to your good health, and to the prosperity of your house and family. Speaking of which," I added, after I had drunk, "shall I not have the pleasure of laying my salutations in person at the feet of the Senora, your mother?"

But at these words all the childishness passed out of his face, and was succeeded by a look of indescribable cunning and secrecy. He backed away from me at the same time, as though I were an animal about to leap or some dangerous fellow with a weapon, and when he had got near the door, glowered at me sullenly with contracted pupils. "No," he said at last, and the next moment was gone noiselessly out of the room; and I heard his footing die away downstairs as light as rainfall, and silence closed over the house.

After I had supped I drew up the table nearer to the bed and began to prepare for rest; but in the new position of the light, I was struck by a picture on the wall. It represented a woman, still young. To judge by her costume and the mellow unity which reigned over the canvas, she had long been dead; to judge by the vivacity of the attitude, the eyes and the features, I might have been beholding in a mirror the image of life. Her figure was very slim and strong, and of a just proportion; red tresses lay like a crown over her brow; her eyes, of a very golden brown, held mine with a look; and her face, which was perfectly shaped, was yet marred by a cruel, sullen, and sensual expression. Something in both face and figure, something exquisitely intangible, like the echo of an echo, suggested the features and bearing of my guide; and I stood awhile, unpleasantly attracted and wondering at the oddity of the resemblance. The common, carnal stock of that race, which had been originally designed for such high dames as the one now looking on me from the canvas, had fallen to baser uses, wearing country clothes, sitting on the shaft and holding the reins of a mule cart, to bring home a lodger. Perhaps an actual link subsisted; perhaps some scruple of the delicate flesh that was once clothed upon with the satin and brocade of the dead lady, now winced at the rude contact of Felipe's frieze.

The first light of the morning shone full upon the portrait, and, as I lay awake, my eyes continued to dwell upon it with growing complacency; its beauty crept about my heart insidiously, silencing my scruples one after another; and while I knew that to love such a woman were to sign and seal one's own sentence of degeneration, I still knew that, if she were alive, I should love her. Day after day the double knowledge of her wickedness and of my weakness grew clearer. She came to be the heroine of many day-dreams, in which her eyes led on to, and sufficiently rewarded, crimes. She cast a dark shadow on my fancy; and when I was out in the free air of heaven, taking vigorous exercise and healthily renewing the current of my blood, it was often a glad thought to me that my enchantress was safe in the grave, her wand of beauty broken, her lips closed in silence, her philtre spilt. And yet I had a half-lingering terror that she might not be dead after all, but re-arisen in the body of some descendant.

Felipe served my meals in my own apartment; and his resemblance to the portrait haunted me. At times it was not; at times, upon some change of attitude or flash of expression, it would leap out upon me like a ghost. It was above all in his ill tempers that the likeness triumphed. He certainly liked me; he was proud of my notice, which he sought to engage by many simple and childlike devices; he loved to sit close before my fire, talking his broken talk or singing his odd, endless, wordless songs, and sometimes drawing his hand over my clothes with an affectionate manner of caressing that never failed to cause in me an embarrassment of which I was ashamed. But for all that, he was capable of flashes of causeless anger and fits of sturdy sullenness. At a word of reproof, I have seen him upset the dish of which I was about to eat, and this not surreptitiously, but with defiance; and similarly at a hint of inquisition. I was not unnaturally curious, being in a strange place and surrounded by string people; but at the shadow of a question, he shrank back, lowering and dangerous. Then it was that, for a fraction of a second, this rough lad might have been the brother of the lady in the frame. But these humours were swift to pass; and the resemblance died along with them.

In these first days I saw nothing of any one but Felipe, unless the portrait is to be counted; and since the lad was plainly of weak mind, and had moments of passion, it may be wondered that I bore his dangerous neighbourhood with equanimity. As a matter of fact, it was for some time irksome; but it happened before long that I obtained over him so complete a mastery as set my disquietude at rest.

It fell in this way. He was by nature slothful, and much of a vagabond, and yet he kept by the house, and not only waited upon my wants, but laboured every day in the garden or small farm to the south of the residencia. Here he would be joined by the peasant whom I had seen on the night of my arrival, and who dwelt at the far end of the enclosure, about half a mile away, in a rude out—house; but it was plain to me that, of these two, it was Felipe who did most; and though I would sometimes see him throw down his spade and go to sleep among the very plants he had been digging, his constancy and energy were admirable in themselves, and still more so since I was well assured they were foreign to his disposition and the fruit of an ungrateful effort. But while I admired, I wondered what had called forth in a lad so shuttle-witted this enduring sense of duty. How was it sustained? I asked myself, and to what length did it prevail over his instincts? The priest was possibly his inspirer; but the priest came one day to the residencia. I saw him both come and go after an interval of close upon an hour, from a knoll where I was sketching, and all that time Felipe continued to labour undisturbed in the garden.

At last, in a very unworthy spirit, I determined to debauch the lad from his good resolutions, and, way-laying him at the gate, easily pursuaded him to join me in a ramble. It was a fine day, and the woods to which I led him were green and pleasant and sweet-smelling and alive with the hum of insects. Here he discovered himself in a fresh character, mounting up to heights of gaiety that abashed me, and displaying an energy and grace of movement that delighted the eye. He leaped, he ran round me in mere glee; he would stop, and look and listen, and seem to drink in the world like a cordial; and then he would suddenly spring into a tree with one bound, and hang and gambol there like one at home. Little as he said to me, and that of not much import, I have rarely enjoyed more stirring company; the sight of his delight was a continual feast; the speed and accuracy of his movements pleased me to the heart; and I might have been so thoughtlessly unkind as to make a habit of these wants, had not chance prepared a very rude conclusion to my pleasure. By some swiftness or dexterity the lad captured a squirrel in a tree top. He was then some way ahead of me, but I saw him drop to the ground and crouch there, crying aloud for pleasure like a child. The sound stirred my sympathies, it was so fresh and innocent; but as I bettered my pace to draw near, the cry of the squirrel knocked upon my heart. I have heard and seen much of the cruelty of lads, and above all of peasants; but what I now beheld struck me into a passion of anger. I thrust the fellow aside, plucked the poor brute out of his hands, and with swift mercy killed it. Then I turned upon the torturer, spoke to him long out of the heat of my indignation, calling him names at which he seemed to wither; and at length, pointing toward the residencia, bade him begone and leave me, for I chose to walk with men, not with vermin. He fell upon his knees, and, the words coming to him with more cleanness than usual, poured out a stream of the most touching supplications, begging me in mercy to forgive him, to forget what he had done, to look to the future. "O, I try so hard," he said. "O, commandante, bear with Felipe this once; he will never be a brute again!" Thereupon, much more affected than I cared to show, I suffered myself to be persuaded, and at last shook hands with him and made it up. But the squirrel, by way of penance, I made him bury; speaking of the poor thing's beauty, telling him what pains it had suffered, and how base a thing was the abuse of strength. "See, Felipe," said I, "you are strong indeed; but in my hands you are as helpless as that poor thing of the trees. Give me your hand in mine. You cannot remove it. Now suppose that I were cruel like you, and took a pleasure in pain. I only tighten my hold, and see how you suffer." He screamed aloud, his face stricken ashy and dotted with needle points of sweat; and when I set him free, he fell to the earth and nursed his hand and moaned over it like a baby. But he took the lesson in good part; and whether from that, or from what I had said to him, or the higher notion he now had of my bodily strength, his original affection was changed into a dog-like, adoring fidelity.

Meanwhile I gained rapidly in health. The residencia stood on the crown of a stony plateau; on every side the mountains hemmed it about; only from the roof, where was a bartizan, there might be seen between two peaks, a small segment of plain, blue with extreme distance. The air in these altitudes moved freely and largely; great clouds congregated there, and were broken up by the wind and left in tatters on the hilltops; a hoarse, and yet faint rumbling of torrents rose from all round; and one could there study all the ruder and more ancient characters of nature in something of their pristine force. I delighted from the first in the vigorous scenery and changeful weather; nor less in the antique and dilapidated mansion where I dwelt. This was a large oblong, flanked at two opposite corners by bastion-like projections, one of which commanded the door, while both were loopholed for musketry. The lower storey was, besides, naked of windows, so that the building, if garrisoned, could not be carried without artillery. It enclosed an open court planted with pomegranate trees. From this a broad flight of marble stairs ascended to an open gallery, running all round and resting, towards the court, on slender pillars. Thence again, several enclosed stairs led to the upper storeys of the house, which were thus broken up into distinct divisions. The windows, both within and without, were closely shuttered; some of the stone-work in the upper parts had fallen; the roof, in one place, had been wrecked in one of the flurries of wind which were common in these mountains; and the whole house, in the strong, beating sunlight, and standing out above a grove of stunted cork—trees, thickly laden and discoloured with dust, looked like the sleeping palace of the legend. The court, in particular, seemed the very home of slumber. A hoarse cooing of doves haunted about the eaves; the winds were excluded, but when they blew outside, the mountain dust fell here as thick as rain, and veiled the red bloom of the pomegranates; shuttered windows and the closed doors of numerous cellars, and the vacant, arches of the gallery, enclosed it; and all day long the sun made broken profiles on the four sides, and paraded the shadow of the pillars on the gallery floor. At the ground level there was, however, a certain pillared recess, which bore the marks of human habitation. Though it was open in front upon the court, it was yet provided with a chimney, where a wood fire would he always prettily blazing; and the tile floor was littered with the skins of animals.

It was in this place that I first saw my hostess. She had drawn one of the skins forward and sat in the sun, leaning against a pillar. It was her dress that struck me first of all, for it was rich and brightly coloured, and shone out in that dusty courtyard with something of the same relief as the flowers of the pomegranates. At a second look it was her beauty of person that took hold of me. As she sat back—watching me, I thought, though with invisible eyes—and wearing at the same time an expression of almost imbecile good-humour and contentment, she showed a perfectness of feature and a quiet nobility of attitude that were beyond a statue's. I took off my hat to her in passing, and her face puckered with suspicion as swiftly and lightly as a pool ruffles in the breeze; but she paid no heed to my courtesy. I went forth on my customary walk a trifle daunted, her idol-like impassivity haunting me; and when I returned, although she was still in much the same posture, I was half surprised to see that she had moved as far as the next pillar, following the sunshine. This time, however, she addressed me with some trivial salutation, civilly enough conceived, and uttered in the same deep-chested, and yet indistinct and lisping tones, that had already baffled the utmost niceness of my hearing from her son. I answered rather at a venture; for not only did I fail to take her meaning with precision, but the sudden disclosure of her eyes disturbed me. They were unusually large, the iris golden like Felipe's, but the pupil at that moment so distended that they seemed almost black; and what affected me was not so much their size as (what was perhaps its consequence) the singular insignificance of their regard. A look more blankly stupid I have never met. My eyes dropped before it even as I spoke, and I went on my way upstairs to my own room, at once baffled and embarrassed. Yet, when I came there and saw the face of the portrait, I was again reminded of the miracle of family descent. My hostess was, indeed, both older and fuller in person; her eyes were of a different colour; her face, besides, was not only free from the ill-significance that offended and attracted me in the painting; it was devoid of either good or bad—a moral blank expressing literally naught. And yet there was a likeness, not so much speaking as immanent, not so much in any particular feature as upon the whole. It should seem, I thought, as if when the master set his signature to that grave canvas, he had not only caught the image of one smiling and false-eyed woman, but stamped the essential quality of a race.

From that day forth, whether I came or went, I was sure to find the Senora seated in the sun against a pillar, or stretched on a rug before the fire; only at times she would shift her station to the top round of the stone staircase, where she lay with the same nonchalance right across my path. In all these days, I never knew her to display the least spark of energy beyond what she expended in brushing and re-brushing her copious copper-coloured hair, or in lisping out, in the rich and broken hoarseness of her voice, her customary idle salutations to myself. These, I think, were her two chief pleasures, beyond that of mere quiescence. She seemed always proud of her remarks, as though they had been witticisms: and, indeed, though they were empty enough, like the conversation of many respectable persons, and turned on a very narrow range of subjects, they were never meaningless or incoherent; nay, they had a certain beauty of their own, breathing, as they did, of her entire contentment. Now she would speak of the warmth, in which (like her son) she greatly delighted; now of the flowers of the pomegranate trees, and now of the white doves and long-winged swallows that fanned the air of the court. The birds excited her. As they raked the eaves in their swift flight, or skimmed sidelong past her with a rush of wind, she would sometimes stir, and sit a little up, and seem to awaken from her doze of satisfaction. But for the rest of her days she lay luxuriously folded on herself and sunk in sloth and pleasure. Her invincible content at first annoyed me, but I came gradually to find repose in the spectacle, until at last it grew to be my habit to sit down beside her four times in the day, both coming and going, and to talk with her sleepily, I scarce knew of what. I had come to like her dull, almost animal neighbourhood; her beauty and her stupidity soothed and amused me. I began to find a kind of transcendental good sense in her remarks, and her unfathomable good nature moved me to admiration and envy. The liking was returned; she enjoyed my presence half-unconsciously, as a man in deep meditation may enjoy the babbling of a brook. I can scarce say she brightened when I came, for satisfaction was written on her face eternally, as on some foolish statue's; but I was made conscious of her pleasure by some more intimate communication than the sight. And one day, as I set within reach of her on the marble step, she suddenly shot forth one of her hands and patted mine. The thing was done, and she was back in her accustomed attitude, before my mind had received intelligence of the caress; and when I turned to look her in the face I could perceive no answerable sentiment. It was plain she attached no moment to the act, and I blamed myself for my own more uneasy consciousness.

The sight and (if I may so call it) the acquaintance of the mother confirmed the view I had already taken of the son. The family blood had been impoverished, perhaps by long inbreeding, which I knew to be a common error among the proud and the exclusive. No decline, indeed, was to be traced in the body, which had been handed down unimpaired in shapeliness and strength; and the faces of today were struck as sharply from the mint, as the face of two centuries ago that smiled upon me from the portrait. But the intelligence (that more precious heirloom) was degenerate; the treasure of ancestral memory ran low; and it had required the potent, plebeian crossing of a muleteer or mountain contrabandista to raise, what approached hebetude in the mother, into the active oddity of the son. Yet of the two, it was the mother I preferred. Of Felipe, vengeful and placable, full of starts and shyings, inconstant as a hare, I could even conceive as a creature possibly noxious. Of the mother I had no thoughts but those of kindness. And indeed, as spectators are apt ignorantly to take sides, I grew something of a partisan in the enmity which I perceived to smoulder between them. True, it seemed mostly on the mother's part. She would sometimes draw in her breath as he came near, and the pupils of her vacant eyes would contract as if with horror or fear. Her emotions, such as they were, were much upon the surface and readily shared; and this latent repulsion occupied my mind, and kept me wondering on what grounds it rested, and whether the son was certainly in fault.

I had been about ten days in the residencia, when there sprang up a high and harsh wind, carrying clouds of dust. It came out of malarious lowlands, and over several snowy sierras. The nerves of those on whom it blew were strung and jangled; their eyes smarted with the dust; their legs ached under the burthen of their body; and the touch of one hand upon another grew to be odious. The wind, besides, came down the gullies of the hills and stormed about the house with a great, hollow buzzing and whistling that was wearisome to the ear and dismally depressing to the mind. It did not so much blow in gusts as with the steady sweep of a waterfall, so that there was no remission of discomfort while it blew. But higher upon the mountain, it was probably of a more variable strength, with accesses of fury; for there came down at times a far-off wailing, infinitely grievous to hear; and at times, on one of the high shelves or terraces, there would start up, and then disperse, a tower of dust, like the smoke of in explosion.

I no sooner awoke in bed than I was conscious of the nervous tension and depression of the weather, and the effect grew stronger as the day proceeded. It was in vain that I resisted; in vain that I set forth upon my customary morning's walk; the irrational, unchanging fury of the storm had soon beat down my strength and wrecked my temper; and I returned to the residencia, glowing with dry heat, and foul and gritty with dust. The court had a forlorn appearance; now and then a glimmer of sun fled over it; now and then the wind swooped down upon the pomegranates, and scattered the blossoms, and set the window shutters clapping on the wall. In the recess the Senora was pacing to and fro with a flushed countenance and bright eyes; I thought, too, she was speaking to herself, like one in anger. But when I addressed her with my customary salutation, she only replied by a sharp gesture and continued her walk. The weather had distempered even this impassive creature; and as I went on upstairs I was the less ashamed of my own discomposure.

All day the wind continued; and I sat in my room and made a feint of reading, or walked up and down, and listened to the riot overhead. Night fell, and I had not so much as a candle. I began to long for some society, and stole down to the court. It was now plunged in the blue of the first darkness; but the recess was redly lighted by the fire. The wood had been piled high, and was crowned by a shock of flames, which the draught of the chimney brandished to and fro. In this strong and shaken brightness the Senora continued pacing from wall to wall with disconnected gestures, clasping her hands, stretching forth her arms, throwing back her head as in appeal to heaven. In these disordered movements the beauty and grace of the woman showed more clearly; but there was a light in her eye that struck on me unpleasantly; and when I had looked on awhile in silence, and seemingly unobserved, I turned tail as I had come, and groped my way back again to my own chamber.

By the time Felipe brought my supper and lights, my nerve was utterly gone; and, had the lad been such as I was used to seeing him, I should have kept him (even by force had that been necessary) to take off the edge from my distasteful solitude. But on Felipe, also, the wind had exercised its influence. He had been feverish all day; now that the night had come he was fallen into a low and tremulous humour that reacted on my own. The sight of his scared face, his starts and pallors and sudden harkenings, unstrung me; and when he dropped and broke a dish, I fairly leaped out of my seat.

"I think we are all mad today," said I, affecting to laugh.

"It is the black wind," he replied dolefully. "You feel as if you must do something, and you don't know what it is."

I noted the aptness of the description; but, indeed, Felipe had sometimes a strange felicity in rendering into words the sensations of the body. "And your mother, too," said I; "she seems to feel this weather much. Do you not fear she may be unwell?"

He stared at me a little, and then said, "No," almost defiantly; and the next moment, carrying his hand to his brow, cried out lamentably on the wind and the noise that made his head go round like a millwheel. "Who can be well?" he cried; and, indeed, I could only echo his question, for I was disturbed enough myself.

I went to bed early, wearied with day-long restlessness, but the poisonous nature of the wind, and its ungodly and unintermittent uproar, would not suffer me to sleep. I lay there and tossed, my nerves and senses on the stretch. At times I would doze, dream horribly, and wake again; and these snatches of oblivion confused me as to time. But it must have been late on in the night, when I was suddenly startled by an outbreak of pitiable and hateful cries. I leaped from my bed, supposing I had dreamed; but the cries still continued to fill the house, cries of pain, I thought, but certainly of rage also, and so savage and discordant that they shocked the heart. It was no illusion; some living thing, some lunatic or some wild animal, was being foully tortured. The thought of Felipe and the squirrel flashed into my mind, and I ran to the door, but it had been locked from the outside; and I might shake it as I pleased, I was a fast prisoner. Still the cries continued. Now they would dwindle down into a moaning that seemed to be articulate, and at these times I made sure they must be human; and again they would break forth and fill the house with ravings worthy of hell. I stood at the door and gave ear to them, till at, last they died away. Long after that, I still lingered and still continued to hear them mingle in fancy with the storming of the wind; and when at last I crept to my bed, it was with a deadly sickness and a blackness of horror on my heart.

It was little wonder if I slept no more. Why had I been locked in? What had passed? Who was the author of these indescribable and shocking cries? A human being? It was inconceivable. A beast? The cries were scarce quite bestial; and what animal, short of a lion or a tiger, could thus shake the solid walls of the residencia? And while I was thus turning over the elements of the mystery, it came into my mind that I had not yet set eyes upon the daughter of the house. What was more probable than that the daughter of the Senora, and the sister of Felipe, should be herself insane? Or, what more likely than that these ignorant and half—witted people should seek to manage an afflicted kinswoman by violence? Here was a solution; and yet when I called to mind the cries (which I never did without a shuddering chill) it seemed altogether insufficient: not even cruelty could wring such cries from madness. But of one thing I was sure: I could not live in a house where such a thing was half conceivable, and not probe the matter home and, if necessary, interfere.

The next day came, the wind had blown itself out, and there was nothing to remind me of the business of the night. Felipe came to my bedside with obvious cheerfulness; as I passed through the court, the Senora was sunning herself with her accustomed immobility; and when I issued from the gateway, I found the whole face of nature austerely smiling, the heavens of a cold blue, and sown with great cloud islands, and the mountain-sides mapped forth into provinces of light and shadow. A short walk restored me to myself, and renewed within me the resolve to plumb this mystery; and when, from the vantage of my knoll, I had seen Felipe pass forth to his labours in the garden, I returned at once to the residencia to put my design in practice. The Senora appeared plunged in slumber; I stood awhile and marked her, but she did not stir; even if my design were indiscreet, I had little to fear from such a guardian; and turning away, I mounted to the gallery and began my exploration of the house.

All morning I went from one door to another, and entered spacious and faded chambers, some rudely shuttered, some receiving their full charge of daylight, all empty and unhomely. It was a rich house, on which Time had breathed his tarnish and dust had scattered disillusion. The spider swung there; the bloated tarantula scampered on the cornices; ants had their crowded highways on the floor of halls of audience; the big and foul fly, that lives on carrion and is often the messenger of death, had set up his nest in the rotten woodwork, and buzzed heavily about the rooms. Here and there a stool or two, a couch, a bed, or a great carved chair remained behind, like islets on the bare floors, to testify of man's bygone habitation; and everywhere the walls were set with the portraits of the dead. I could judge, by these decaying effigies, in the house of what a great and what a handsome race I was then wandering. Many of the men wore orders on their breasts and had the port of noble offices; the women were all richly attired; the canvases most of them by famous hands. But it was not so much these evidences of greatness that took hold upon my mind, even contrasted, as they were, with the present depopulation and decay of that great house. It was rather the parable of family life that I read in this succession of fair faces and shapely bodies. Never before had I so realised the miracle of the continued race, the creation and recreation, the weaving and changing and handing down of fleshly elements. That a child should be born of its mother, that it should grow and clothe itself (we know not how) with humanity, and put on inherited looks, and turn its head with the manner of one ascendant, and offer its hand with the gesture of another, are wonders dulled for us by repetition. But in the singular unity of look, in the common features and common bearing, of all these painted generations on the walls of the residencia, the miracle started out and looked me in the face. And an ancient mirror falling opportunely in my way, I stood and read my own features a long while, tracing out on either hand the filaments of descent and the bonds that knit me with my family.

At last, in the course of these investigations, I opened the door of a chamber that bore the marks of habitation. It was of large proportions and faced to the north, where the mountains were most wildly figured. The embers of a fire smouldered and smoked upon the hearth, to which a chair had been drawn close. And yet the aspect of the chamber was ascetic to the degree of sternness; the chair was uncushioned; the floor and walls were naked; and beyond the books which lay here and there in some confusion, there was no instrument of either work or pleasure. The sight of books in the house of such a family exceedingly amazed me; and I began with a great hurry, and in momentary fear of interruption, to go from one to another and hastily inspect their character. They were of all sorts, devotional, historical, and scientific, but mostly of a great age and in the Latin tongue. Some I could see to bear the marks of constant study; others had been torn across and tossed aside as if in petulance or disapproval. Lastly, as I cruised about that empty chamber, I espied some papers written upon with pencil on a table near the window. An unthinking curiosity led me to take one up. It bore a copy of verses, very roughly metred in the original Spanish, and which I may render somewhat thus—

Pleasure approached with pain and shame, Grief with a wreath of lilies came. Pleasure showed the lovely sun; Jesu dear, how sweet it shone! Grief with her worn hand pointed on, Jesu dear, to thee!

Shame and confusion at once fell on me; and, laying down the paper, I beat an immediate retreat from the apartment. Neither Felipe nor his mother could have read the books nor written these rough but feeling verses. It was plain I had stumbled with sacrilegious feet into the room of the daughter of the house. God knows, my own heart most sharply punished me for my indiscretion. The thought that I had thus secretly pushed my way into the confidence of a girl so strangely situated, and the fear that she might somehow come to hear of it, oppressed me like guilt. I blamed myself besides for my suspicions of the night before; wondered that I should ever have attributed those shocking cries to one of whom I now conceived as of a saint, spectral of mien, wasted with maceration, bound up in the practices of a mechanical devotion, and dwelling in a great isolation of soul with her incongruous relatives; and as I leaned on the balustrade of the gallery and looked down into the bright close of pomegranates and at the gaily dressed and somnolent woman, who just then stretched herself and delicately licked her lips as in the very sensuality of sloth, my mind swiftly compared the scene with the cold chamber looking northward on the mountains, where the daughter dwelt.

That same afternoon, as I sat upon my knoll, I saw the Padre enter the gates of the residencia. The revelation of the daughter's character had struck home to my fancy, and almost blotted out the horrors of the night before; but at sight of this worthy man the memory revived. I descended, then, from the knoll, and making a circuit among the woods, posted myself by the wayside to await his passage. As soon as he appeared I stepped forth and introduced myself as the lodger of the residencia. He had a very strong, honest countenance, on which it was easy to read the mingled emotions with which he regarded me, as a foreigner, a heretic, and yet one who had been wounded for the good cause. Of the family at the residencia he spoke with reserve, and yet with respect. I mentioned that I had not yet seen the daughter, whereupon he remarked that that was as it should be, and looked at me a little askance. Lastly, I plucked up courage to refer to the cries that had disturbed me in the night. He heard me out in silence, and then stopped and partly turned about, as though to mark beyond doubt that he was dismissing me.

"Do you take tobacco powder?" said he, offering his snuff-box; and then, when I had refused, "I am an old man," he added, "and I may be allowed to remind you that you are a guest."

"I have, then, your authority," I returned, firmly enough, although I flushed at the implied reproof, "to let things take their course, and not to interfere?"

He said "yes," and with a somewhat uneasy salute turned and left me where I was. But he had done two things: he had set my conscience at rest, and he had awakened my delicacy. I made a great effort, once more dismissed the recollections of the night, and fell once more to brooding on my saintly poetess. At the same time, I could not quite forget that I had been locked in, and that night when Felipe brought me my supper I attacked him warily on both points of interest.

"I never see your sister," said I casually.

"Oh, no," said he; "she is a good, good girl," and his mind instantly veered to something else.

"Your sister is pious, I suppose?" I asked in the next pause.

"Oh!" he cried, joining his hands with extreme fervour, "a saint; it is she that keeps me up."

"You are very fortunate," said I, "for the most of us, I am afraid, and myself among the number, are better at going down."

"Senor," said Felipe earnestly, "I would not say that. You should not tempt your angel. If one goes down, where is he to stop?"

"Why, Felipe," said I, "I had no guess you were a preacher, and I may say a good one; but I suppose that is your sister's doing?"

He nodded at me with round eyes.

"Well, then," I continued, "she has doubtless reproved you for your sin of cruelty?"

"Twelve times!" he cried; for this was the phrase by which the odd creature expressed the sense of frequency. "And I told her you had done so—I remembered that," he added proudly—"and she was pleased."

"Then, Felipe," said I, "what were those cries that I heard last night? For surely they were cries of some creature in suffering."

"The wind," returned Felipe, looking in the fire.

I took his hand in mine, at which, thinking it to be a caress, he smiled with a brightness of pleasure that came near disarming my resolve. But I trod the weakness down. "The wind," I repeated; "and yet I think it was this hand," holding it up, "that had first locked me in." The lad shook visibly, but answered never a word. "Well," said I, "I am a stranger and a guest. It is not my part either to meddle or to judge in your affairs; in these you shall take your sister's counsel, which I cannot doubt to be excellent. But in so far as concerns my own I will be no man's prisoner, and I demand that key." Half an hour later my door was suddenly thrown open, and the key tossed ringing on the floor.

A day or two after I came in from a walk a little before the point of noon. The Senora was lying lapped in slumber on the threshold of the recess; the pigeons dozed below the eaves like snowdrifts; the house was under a deep spell of noontide quiet; and only a wandering and gentle wind from the mountain stole round the galleries, rustled among the pomegranates, and pleasantly stirred the shadows. Something in the stillness moved me to imitation, and I went very lightly across the court and up the marble staircase. My foot was on the topmost round, when a door opened, and I found myself face to face with . Surprise transfixed me; her loveliness struck to my heart; she glowed in the deep shadow of the gallery, a gem of colour; her eyes took hold upon mine and clung there, and bound us together like the joining of hands; and the moments we thus stood face to face, drinking each other in, were sacramental and the wedding of souls. I know not how long it was before I awoke out of a deep trance, and, hastily bowing, passed on into the upper stair. She did not move, but followed me with her great, thirsting eyes; and as I passed out of sight it seemed to me as if she paled and faded.

In my own room, I opened the window and looked out, and could not think what change had come upon that austere field of mountains that it should thus sing and shine under the lofty heaven. I had seen her—! And the stone crags answered, Olalla! And the dumb, unfathomable azure answered, Olalla! The pale saint of my dreams had vanished for ever; and in her place I beheld this maiden on whom God had lavished the richest colours and the most exuberant energies of life, whom he had made active as a deer, slender as a reed, and in whose great eyes he had lighted the torches of the soul. The thrill of her young life, strung like a wild animal's, had entered into me; the force of soul that had looked out from her eyes and conquered mine, mantled about my heart and sprang to my lips in singing. She passed through my veins: she was one with me.

I will not say that this enthusiasm declined; rather my soul held out in its ecstasy as in a strong castle, and was there besieged by cold and sorrowful considerations. I could not doubt but that I loved her at first sight, and already with a quivering ardour that was strange to my experience. What then was to follow? She was the child of an afflicted house, the Senora's daughter, the sister of Felipe; she bore it even in her beauty. She had the lightness and swiftness of the one, swift as an arrow, light as dew; like the other, she shone on the pale background of the world with the brilliancy of flowers. I could not call by the name of brother that half-witted lad, nor by the name of mother that immovable and lovely thing of flesh, whose silly eyes and perpetual simper now recurred to my mind like something hateful. And if I could not marry, what then? She was helplessly unprotected; her eyes, in that single and long glance which had been all our intercourse, had confessed a weakness equal to my own; but in my heart I knew her for the student of the cold northern chamber, and the writer of the sorrowful lines; and this was a knowledge to disarm a brute. To flee was more than I could find courage for; but I registered a vow of unsleeping circumspection.

As I turned from the window, my eyes alighted on the portrait. It had fallen dead, like a candle after sunrise; it followed me with eyes of paint. I knew it to be like, and marvelled at the tenacity of type in that declining race; but the likeness was swallowed up in difference. I remembered how it had seemed to me a thing unapproachable in the life, a creature rather of the painter's craft than of the modesty of nature, and I marvelled at the thought, and exulted in the image of . Beauty I had seen before, and not been charmed, and I had been often drawn to women, who were not beautiful except to me; but in Olalla all that I desired and had not dared to imagine was united.

I did not see her the next day, and my heart ached and my eyes longed for her, as men long for morning. But the day after, when I returned, about my usual hour, she was once more on the gallery, and our looks once more met and embraced. I would have spoken, I would have drawn near to her; but strongly as she plucked at my heart, drawing me like a magnet, something yet more imperious withheld me; and I could only bow and pass by; and she, leaving my salutation unanswered, only followed me with her noble eyes.

I had now her image by rote, and as I conned the traits in memory it seemed as if I read her very heart. She was dressed with something of her mother's coquetry, and love of positive colour. Her robe, which I know she must have made with her own hands, clung about her with a cunning grace. After the fashion of that country, besides, her bodice stood open in the middle, in a long slit, and here, in spite of the poverty of the house, a gold coin, hanging by a ribbon, lay on her brown bosom. These were proofs, had any been needed, of her inborn delight in life and her own loveliness. On the other hand, in her eyes that hung upon mine, I could read depth beyond depth of passion and sadness, lights of poetry and hope, blacknesses of despair, and thoughts that were above the earth. It was a lovely body, but the inmate, the soul, was more than worthy of that lodging. Should I leave this incomparable flower to wither unseen on these rough mountains? Should I despise the great gift offered me in the eloquent silence of her eyes? Here was a soul immured; should I not burst its prison? All side considerations fell off from me; were she the child of Herod I swore I should make her mine; and that very evening I set myself, with a mingled sense of treachery and disgrace, to captivate the brother. Perhaps I read him with more favourable eyes, perhaps the thought of his sister always summoned up the better qualities of that imperfect soul; but he had never seemed to me so amiable, and his very likeness to , while it annoyed, yet softened me.

A third day passed in vain—an empty desert of hours. I would not lose a chance, and loitered all afternoon in the court where (to give myself a countenance) I spoke more than usual with the Senora. God knows it was with a most tender and sincere interest that I now studied her; and even as for Felipe, so now for the mother, I was conscious of a growing warmth of toleration. And yet I wondered. Even while I spoke with her, she would doze off into a little sleep, and presently awake again without embarrassment; and this composure staggered me. And again, as I marked her make infinitesimal changes in her posture, savouring and lingering on the bodily pleasure of the movement, I was driven to wonder at this depth of passive sensuality. She lived in her body; and her consciousness was all sunk into and disseminated through her members, where it luxuriously dwelt. Lastly, I could not grow accustomed to her eyes. Each time she turned on me these great beautiful and meaningless orbs, wide open to the day, but closed against human inquiry—each time I had occasion to observe the lively changes of her pupils which expanded and contracted in a breath—I know not what it was came over me, I can find no name for the mingled feeling of disappointment, annoyance, and distaste that jarred along my nerves. I tried her on a variety of subjects, equally in vain; and at last led the talk to her daughter. But even there she proved indifferent; said she was pretty, which (as with children) was her highest word of commendation, but was plainly incapable of any higher thought; and when I remarked that seemed silent, merely yawned in my face and replied that speech was of no great use when you had nothing to say. "People speak much, very much," she added, looking at me with expanded pupils; and then again yawned and again showed me a mouth that was as dainty as a toy. This time I took the hint, and, leaving her to her repose, went up into my own chamber to sit by the open window, looking on the hills and not beholding them, sunk in lustrous and deep dreams, and hearkening in fancy to the note of a voice that I had never heard.

I awoke on the fifth morning with a brightness of anticipation that seemed to challenge fate. I was sure of myself, light of heart and foot, and resolved to put my love incontinently to the touch of knowledge. It should lie no longer under the bonds of silence, a dumb thing, living by the eye only, like the love of beasts; but should now put on the spirit, and enter upon the joys of the complete human intimacy. I thought of it with wild hopes, like a voyager to El Dorado; into that unknown and lovely country of her soul, I no longer trembled to adventure. Yet when I did indeed encounter her, the same force of passion descended on me and at once submerged my mind; speech seemed to drop away from me like a childish habit; and I but drew near to her as the giddy man draws near to the margin of a gulf. She drew back from me a little as I came; but her eyes did not waver from mine, and these lured me forward. At last, when I was already within reach of her, I stopped. Words were denied me; if I advanced I could but clasp her to my heart in silence; and all that was sane in me, all that was still unconquered, revolted against the thought of such an accost. So we stood for a second, all our life in our eyes, exchanging salvos of attraction and yet each resisting; and then, with a great effort of the will, and conscious at the same time of a sudden bitterness of disappointment, I turned and went away in the same silence.

What power lay upon me that I could not speak? And she, why was she also silent? Why did she draw away before me dumbly, with fascinated eyes? Was this love? Or was it a mere brute attraction, mindless and inevitable, like that of the magnet for the steel? We had never spoken, we were wholly strangers: and yet an influence, strong as the grasp of a giant, swept us silently together. On my side, it filled me with impatience; and yet I was sure that she was worthy; I had seen her books, read her verses, and thus, in a sense, divined the soul of my mistress. But on her side, it struck me almost cold. Of me, she knew nothing but my bodily favour; she was drawn to me as stones fall to the earth; the laws that rule the earth conducted her, unconsenting, to my arms; and I drew back at the thought of such a bridal, and began to be jealous for myself. It was not thus that I desired to be loved. And then I began to fall into a great pity for the girl herself. I thought how sharp must be her mortification, that she, the student, the recluse, Felipe's saintly monitress, should have thus confessed an overweening weakness for a man with whom she had never exchanged a word. And at the coming of pity, all other thoughts were swallowed up; and I longed only to find and console and reassure her; to tell her how wholly her love was returned on my side, and how her choice, even if blindly made, was not unworthy.

The next day it was glorious weather; depth upon depth of blue over-canopied the mountains; the sun shone wide; and the wind in the trees and the many falling torrents in the mountains filled the air with delicate and haunting music. Yet I was prostrated with sadness. My heart wept for the sight of , as a child weeps for its mother. I sat down on a boulder on the verge of the low cliffs that bound the plateau to the north. Thence I looked down into the wooded valley of a stream, where no foot came. In the mood I was in, it was even touching to behold the place untenanted; it lacked Olalla; and I thought of the delight and glory of a life passed wholly with her in that strong air, and among these rugged and lovely surroundings, at first with a whimpering sentiment, and then again with such a fiery joy that I seemed to grow in strength and stature, like a Samson.

And then suddenly I was aware of drawing near. She appeared out of a grove of cork-trees, and came straight towards me; and I stood up and waited. She seemed in her walking a creature of such life and fire and lightness as amazed me; yet she came quietly and slowly. Her energy was in the slowness; but for inimitable strength, I felt she would have run, she would have flown to me. Still, as she approached, she kept her eyes lowered to the ground; and when she had drawn quite near, it was without one glance that she addressed me. At the first note of her voice I started. It was for this I had been waiting; this was the last test of my love. And lo, her enunciation was precise and clear, not lisping and incomplete like that of her family; and the voice, though deeper than usual with women, was still both youthful and womanly. She spoke in a rich chord; golden contralto strains mingled with hoarseness, as the red threads were mingled with the brown among her tresses. It was not only a voice that spoke to my heart directly; but it spoke to me of her. And yet her words immediately plunged me back upon despair.

"You will go away," she said, "today."

Her example broke the bonds of my speech; I felt as lightened of a weight, or as if a spell had been dissolved. I know not in what words I answered; but, standing before her on the cliffs, I poured out the whole ardour of my love, telling her that I lived upon the thought of her, slept only to dream of her loveliness, and would gladly forswear my country, my language, and my friends, to live for ever by her side. And then, strongly commanding myself, I changed the note; I reassured, I comforted her; I told her I had divined in her a pious and heroic spirit, with which I was worthy to sympathise, and which I longed to share and lighten. "Nature," I told her, "was the voice of God, which men disobey at peril; and if we were thus humbly drawn together, ay, even as by a miracle of love, it must imply a divine fitness in our souls; we must be made," I said—"made for one another. We should be mad rebels," I cried out—"mad rebels against God, not to obey this instinct."

She shook her head. "You will go today," she repeated, and then with a gesture, and in a sudden, sharp note—"no, not today," she cried, "tomorrow!"

But at this sign of relenting, power came in upon me in a tide. I stretched out my arms and called upon her name; and she leaped to me and clung to me. The hills rocked about us, the earth quailed; a shock as of a blow went through me and left me blind and dizzy. And the next moment she had thrust me back, broken rudely from my arms, and fled with the speed of a deer among the cork-trees.

I stood and shouted to the mountains; I turned and went back towards the residencia, waltzing upon air. She sent me away, and yet I had but to call upon her name and she came to me. These were but the weaknesses of girls, from which even she, the strangest of her sex, was not exempted. Go? Not I, —O, not I, Olalla, my Olalla! A bird sang near by; and in that season, birds were rare. It bade me be of good cheer. And once more the whole countenance of nature, from the ponderous and stable mountains down to the lightest leaf and the smallest darting fly in the shadow of the groves, began to stir before me and to put on the lineaments of life and wear a face of awful joy. The sunshine struck upon the hills, strong as a hammer on the anvil, and the hills shook; the earth, under that vigorous insulation, yielded up heady scents; the woods smouldered in the blaze. I felt the thrill of travail and delight run through the earth. Something elemental, something rude, violent, and savage, in the love that sang in my heart, was like a key to nature's secrets; and the very stones that rattled under my feet appeared alive and friendly. Olalla! Her touch had quickened, and renewed, and strung me up to the old pitch of concert with the rugged earth, to a swelling of the soul that men learn to forget in their polite assemblies. Love burned in me like rage; tenderness waxed fierce; I hated, I adored, I pitied, I revered her with ecstasy. She seemed the link that bound me in with dead things on the one hand, and with our pure and pitying God upon the other: a thing brutal and divine, and akin at once to the innocence and to the unbridled forces of the earth.

My head thus reeling, I came into the courtyard of the residencia, and the sight of the mother struck me like a revelation. She sat there, all sloth and contentment, blinking under the strong sunshine, branded with a passive enjoyment, a creature set quite apart, before whom my ardour fell away like a thing ashamed. I stopped a moment, and, commanding such shaken tones as I was able, said a word or two. She looked at me with her unfathomable kindness; her voice in reply sounded vaguely out of the realm of peace in which she slumbered, and there fell on my mind, for the first time, a sense of respect for one so uniformly innocent and happy, and I passed on in a kind of wonder at myself, that I should be so much disquieted.

On my table there lay a piece of the same yellow paper I had seen in the north room; it was written on with pencil in the same hand, Olalla's hand, and I picked it up with a sudden sinking of alarm, and read, "If you have any kindness for Olalla, if you have any chivalry for a creature sorely wrought, go from here today; in pity, in honour, for the sake of Him who died, I supplicate that you shall go." I looked at this awhile in mere stupidity, then I began to awaken to a weariness and horror of life; the sunshine darkened outside on the bare hills, and I began to shake like a man in terror. The vacancy thus suddenly opened in my life unmanned me like a physical void. It was not my heart, it was not my happiness, it was life itself that was involved. I could not lose her. I said so, and stood repeating it. And then, like one in a dream, I moved to the window, put forth my hand to open the casement, and thrust it through the pane. The blood spurted from my wrist; and with an instantaneous quietude and command of myself, I pressed my thumb on the little leaping fountain, and reflected what to do. In that empty room there was nothing to my purpose; I felt, besides, that I required assistance. There shot into my mind a hope that Olalla herself might be my helper, and I turned and went down stairs, still keeping my thumb upon the wound.

There was no sign of either or Felipe, and I addressed myself to the recess, whither the Senora had now drawn quite back and sat dozing close before the fire, for no degree of heat appeared too much for her.

"Pardon me," said I, "if I disturb you, but I must apply to you for help."

She looked up sleepily and asked me what it was, and with the very words I thought she drew in her breath with a widening of the nostrils and seemed to come suddenly and fully alive.

"I have cut myself," I said, "and rather badly. See!" And I held out my two hands from which the blood was oozing and dripping.

Her great eyes opened wide, the pupils shrank into points; a veil seemed to fall from her face, and leave it sharply expressive and yet inscrutable. And as I still stood, marvelling a little at her disturbance, she came swiftly up to me, and stooped and caught me by the hand; and the next moment my hand was at her mouth, and she had bitten me to the bone. The pang of the bite, the sudden spurting of blood, and the monstrous horror of the act, flashed through me all in one, and I beat her back; and she sprang at me again and again, with bestial cries, cries that I recognised, such cries as had awakened me on the night of the high wind. Her strength was like that of madness; mine was rapidly ebbing with the loss of blood; my mind besides was whirling with the abhorrent strangeness of the onslaught, and I was already forced against the wall, when ran betwixt us, and Felipe, following at a bound, pinned down his mother on the floor.

A trance-like weakness fell upon me; I saw, heard, and felt, but I was incapable of movement. I heard the struggle roll to and fro upon the floor, the yells of that catamount ringing up to Heaven as she strove to reach me. I felt clasp me in her arms, her hair falling on my face, and, with the strength of a man, raise and half drag, half carry me upstairs into my own room, where she cast me down upon the bed. Then I saw her hasten to the door and lock it, and stand an instant listening to the savage cries that shook the residencia. And then, swift and light as a thought, she was again beside me, binding up my hand, laying it in her bosom, moaning and mourning over it with dove-like sounds. They were not words that came to her, they were sounds more beautiful than speech, infinitely touching, infinitely tender; and yet as I lay there, a thought stung to my heart, a thought wounded me like a sword, a thought, like a worm in a flower, profaned the holiness of my love. Yes, they were beautiful sounds, and they were inspired by human tenderness; but was their beauty human?

All day I lay there. For a long time the cries of that nameless female thing, as she struggled with her half-witted whelp, resounded through the house, and pierced me with despairing sorrow and disgust. They were the death-cry of my love; my love was murdered; was not only dead, but an offence to me; and yet, think as I pleased, feel as I must, it still swelled within me like a storm of sweetness, and my heart melted at her looks and touch. This horror that had sprung out, this doubt upon , this savage and bestial strain that ran not only through the whole behaviour of her family, but found a place in the very foundations and story of our love—though it appalled, though it shocked and sickened me, was yet not of power to break the knot of my infatuation.

When the cries had ceased, there came a scraping at the door, by which I knew Felipe was without; and went and spoke to him—I know not what. With that exception, she stayed close beside me, now kneeling by my bed and fervently praying, now sitting with her eyes upon mine. So then, for these six hours I drank in her beauty, and silently perused the story in her face. I saw the golden coin hover on her breaths; I saw her eyes darken and brighter, and still speak no language but that of an unfathomable kindness; I saw the faultless face, and, through the robe, the lines of the faultless body. Night came at last, and in the growing darkness of the chamber, the sight of her slowly melted; but even then the touch of her smooth hand lingered in mine and talked with me. To lie thus in deadly weakness and drink in the traits of the beloved, is to reawake to love from whatever shock of disillusion. I reasoned with myself; and I shut my eyes on horrors, and again I was very bold to accept the worst. What mattered it, if that imperious sentiment survived; if her eyes still beckoned and attached me; if now, even as before, every fi bre of my dull body yearned and turned to her? Late on in the night some strength revived in me, and I spoke:—

"Olalla," I said, "nothing matters; I ask nothing; I am content; I love you."

She knelt down awhile and prayed, and I devoutly respected her devotions. The moon had begun to shine in upon one side of each of the three windows, and make a misty clearness in the room, by which I saw her indistinctly. When she rearose she made the sign of the cross.

"It is for me to speak," she said, "and for you to listen. I know; you can but guess. I prayed, how I prayed for you to leave this place. I begged it of you, and I know you would have granted me even this; or if not, O let me think so!"

"I love you," I said.

"And yet you have lived in the world," she said; after a pause, "you are a man and wise; and I am but a child. Forgive me, if I seem to teach, who am as ignorant as the trees of the mountain; but those who learn much do but skim the face of knowledge; they seize the laws, they conceive the dignity of the design—the horror of the living fact fades from their memory. It is we who sit at home with evil who remember, I think, and are warned and pity. Go, rather, go now, and keep me in mind. So I shall have a life in the cherished places of your memory: a life as much my own, as that which I lead in this body."

"I love you," I said once more; and reaching out my weak hand, took hers, and carried it to my lips, and kissed it. Nor did she resist, but winced a little; and I could see her look upon me with a frown that was not unkindly, only sad and baffled. And then it seemed she made a call upon her resolution; plucked my hand towards her, herself at the same time leaning somewhat forward, and laid it on the beating of her heart. "There," she cried, "you feel the very footfall of my life. It only moves for you; it is yours. But is it even mine? It is mine indeed to offer you, as I might take the coin from my neck, as I might break a live branch from a tree, and give it you. And yet not mine! I dwell, or I think I dwell (if I exist at all), somewhere apart, an impotent prisoner, and carried about and deafened by a mob that I disown. This capsule, such as throbs against the sides of animals, knows you at a touch for its master; ay, it loves you! But my soul, does my soul? I think not; I know not, fearing to ask. Yet when you spoke to me your words were of the soul; it is of the soul that you ask—it is only from the soul that you would take me."

"Olalla," I said, "the soul and the body are one, and mostly so in love. What the body chooses, the soul loves; where the body clings, the soul cleaves; body for body, soul to soul, they come together at God's signal; and the lower part (if we can call aught low) is only the footstool and foundation of the highest."

"Have you," she said, "seen the portraits in the house of my fathers? Have you looked at my mother or at Felipe? Have your eyes never rested on that picture that hangs by your bed? She who sat for it died ages ago; and she did evil in her life. But, look—again: there is my hand to the least line, there are my eyes and my hair. What is mine, then, and what am I? If not a curve in this poor body of mine (which you love, and for the sake of which you dotingly dream that you love me) not a gesture that I can frame, not a tone of my voice, not any look from my eyes, no, not even now when I speak to him I love, but has belonged to others? Others, ages dead, have wooed other men with my eyes; other men have heard the pleading of the same voice that now sounds in your ears. The hands of the dead are in my bosom; they move me, they pluck me, they guide me; I am a puppet at their command; and I but reinform features and attributes that have long been laid aside from evil in the quiet of the grave. Is it me you love, friend? Or the race that made me? The girl who does not know and cannot answer for the least portion of herself? Or the stream of which she is a transitory eddy, the tree of which she is the passing fruit? The race exists; it is old, it is ever young, it carries its eternal destiny in its bosom; upon it, like waves upon the sea, individual succeeds to individual, mocked with a semblance of self-control, but they are nothing. We speak of the soul, but the soul is in the race."

"You fret against the common law," I said. "You rebel against the voice of God, which he has made so winning to convince, so imperious to command. Hear it, and how it speaks between us! Your hand clings to mine, your heart leaps at my touch, the unknown elements of which we are compounded awake and run together at a look; the clay of the earth remembers its independent life and yearns to join us; we are drawn together as the stars are turned about in space, or as the tides ebb and flow, by things older and greater than we ourselves."

"Alas!" she said, "what can I say to you? My fathers, eight hundred years ago, ruled all this province: they were wise, great, cunning, and cruel; they were a picked race of the Spanish; their flags led in war; the king called them his cousin; the people, when the rope was slung for them or when they returned and found their hovels smoking, blasphemed their name. Presently a change began. Man has risen; if he has sprung from the brutes, he can descend again to the same level. The breath of weariness blew on their humanity and the cords relaxed; they began to go down; their minds fell on sleep, their passions awoke in gusts, heady and senseless like the wind in the gutters of the mountains; beauty was still handed down, but no longer the guiding wit nor the human heart; the seed passed on, it was wrapped in flesh, the flesh covered the bones, but they were the bones and the flesh of brutes, and their mind was as the mind of flies. I speak to you as I dare; but you have seen for yourself how the wheel has gone backward with my doomed race. I stand, as it were, upon a little rising ground in this desperate descent, and see both before and behind, both what we have lost and to what we are condemned to go farther downward. And shall I—I that dwell apart in the house of the dead, my body, loathing its ways—shall I repeat the spell? Shall I bind another spirit, reluctant as my own, into this bewitched and tempest-broken tenement that I now suffer in? Shall I hand down this cursed vessel of humanity, charge it with fresh life as with fresh poison, and dash it, like a fire, in the faces of posterity? But my vow has been given; the race shall cease from off the earth. At this hour my brother is making ready; his foot will soon be on the stair; and you will go with him and pass out of my sight for ever. Think of me sometimes as one to whom the lesson of life was very harshly told, but who heard it with courage; as one who loved you indeed, but who hated herself so deeply that her love was hateful to her; as one who sent you away and yet would have longed to keep you for ever; who had no dearer hope than to forget you, and no greater fear than to be forgotten."

She had drawn towards the door as she spoke, her rich voice sounding softer and farther away; and with the last word she was gone, and I lay alone in the moonlit chamber. What I might have done had not I lain bound by my extreme weakness, I know not; but as it was there fell upon me a great and blank despair. It was not long before there shone in at the door the ruddy glimmer of a lantern, and Felipe coming, charged me without a word upon his shoulders, and carried me down to the great gate, where the cart was waiting. In the moonlight the hills stood out sharply, as if they were of cardboard; on the glimmering surface of the plateau, and from among the low trees which swung together and sparkled in the wind, the great black cube of the residencia stood out bulkily, its mass only broken by three dimly lighted windows in the northern front above the gate. They were 's windows, and as the cart jolted onwards I kept my eyes fixed upon them till, where the road dipped into a valley, they were lost to my view forever. Felipe walked in silence beside the shafts, but from time to time he would cheek the mule and seem to look back upon me; and at length drew quite near and laid his hand upon my head. There was such kindness in the touch, and such a simplicity, as of the brutes, that tears broke from me like the bursting of an artery.

"Felipe," I said, "take me where they will ask no questions."

He said never a word, but he turned his mule about, end for end, retraced some part of the way we had gone, and, striking into another path, led me to the mountain village, which was, as we say in Scotland, the kirkton of that thinly peopled district. Some broken memories dwell in my mind of the day breaking over the plain, of the cart stopping, of arms that helped me down, of a bare room into which I was carried, and of a swoon that fell upon me like sleep.

The next day and the days following the old priest was often at my side with his snuff-box and prayer book, and after a while, when I began to pick up strength, he told me that I was now on a fair way to recovery, and must as soon as possible hurry my departure; whereupon, without naming any reason, he took snuff and looked at me sideways. I did not affect ignorance; I knew he must have seen. "Sir," said I, "you know that I do not ask in wantonness. What of that family?"

He said they were very unfortunate; that it seemed a declining race, and that they were very poor and had been much neglected.

"But she has not," I said. "Thanks, doubtless, to yourself, she is instructed and wise beyond the use of women."

"Yes," he said; "the Senorita is well-informed. But the family has been neglected."

"The mother?" I queried.

"Yes, the mother too," said the Padre, taking snuff. "But Felipe is a well-intentioned lad."

"The mother is odd?" I asked.

"Very odd," replied the priest.

"I think, sir, we beat about the bush," said I. "You must know more of my affairs than you allow. You must know my curiosity to be justified on many grounds. Will you not be frank with me?"

"My son," said the old gentleman, "I will be very frank with you on matters within my competence; on those of which I know nothing it does not require much discretion to be silent. I will not fence with you, I take your meaning perfectly; and what can I say, but that we are all in God's hands, and that His ways are not as our ways? I have even advised with my superiors in the church, but they, too, were dumb. It is a great mystery."

"Is she mad?" I asked.

"I will answer you according to my belief. She is not," returned the Padre, "or she was not. When she was young—God help me, I fear I neglected that wild lamb—she was surely sane; and yet, although it did not run to such heights, the same strain was already notable; it had been so before her in her father, ay, and before him, and this inclined me, perhaps, to think too lightly of it. But these things go on growing, not only in the individual but in the race."

"When she was young," I began, and my voice failed me for a moment, and it was only with a great effort that I was able to add, "was she like ?"

"Now God forbid!" exclaimed the Padre. "God forbid that any man should think so slightingly of my favourite penitent. No, no; the Senorita (but for her beauty, which I wish most honestly she had less of) has not a hair's resemblance to what her mother was at the same age. I could not bear to have you think so; though, Heaven knows, it were, perhaps, better that you should."

At this, I raised myself in bed, and opened my heart to the old man; telling him of our love and of her decision, owning my own horrors, my own passing fancies, but telling him that these were at an end; and with something more than a purely formal submission, appealing to his judgment.

He heard me very patiently and without surprise; and when I had done, he sat for some time silent. Then he began: "The church," and instantly broke off again to apologise. "I had forgotten, my child, that you were not a Christian," said he. "And indeed, upon a point so highly unusual, even the church can scarce be said to have decided. But would you have my opinion? The Senorita is, in a matter of this kind, the best judge; I would accept her judgment."

On the back of that he went away, nor was he thenceforward so assiduous in his visits; indeed, even when I began to get about again, he plainly feared and deprecated my society, not as in distaste but much as a man might be disposed to flee from the riddling sphinx. The villagers, too, avoided me; they were unwilling to be my guides upon the mountain. I thought they looked at me askance, and I made sure that the more superstitious crossed themselves on my approach. At first I set this down to my heretical opinions; but it began at length to dawn upon me that if I was thus redoubted it was because I had stayed at the residencia. All men despise the savage notions of such peasantry; and yet I was conscious of a chill shadow that seemed to fall and dwell upon my love. It did not conquer, but I may not deify that it restrained my ardour.

Some miles westward of the village there was a gap in the sierra, from which the eye plunged direct upon the residencia; and thither it became my daily habit to repair. A wood crowned the summit; and just where the pathway issued from its fringes, it was overhung by a considerable shelf of rock, and that, in its turn, was surmounted by a crucifix of the size of life and more than usually painful in design. This was my perch; thence, day after day, I looked down upon the plateau, and the great old house, and could see Felipe, no bigger than a fly, going to and fro about the garden. Sometimes mists would draw across the view, and be broken up again by mountain winds; sometimes the plain slumbered below me in unbroken sunshine; it would sometimes be all blotted out by rain. This distant post, these interrupted sights of the place where my life had been so strangely changed, suited the indecision of my humour. I passed whole days there, debating with myself the various elements of our position; now leaning to the suggestions of love, now giving an ear to prudence, and in the end halting irresolute between the two.

One day, as I was sitting on my rock, there came by that way a somewhat gaunt peasant wrapped in a mantle. He was a stranger, and plainly did not know me even by repute; for, instead of keeping the other side, he drew near and sat down beside me, and we had soon fallen in talk. Among other things he told me he had been a muleteer, and in former years had much frequented these mountains; later on, he had followed the army with his mules, had realised a competence, and was now living retired with his family.

"Do you know that house?" I inquired, at last, pointing to the residencia, for I readily wearied of any talk that kept me from the thought of.

He looked at me darkly and crossed himself.

"Too well," he said, "it was there that one of my comrades sold himself to Satan; the Virgin shield us from temptations! He has paid the price; he is now burning in the reddest place in Hell!"

A fear came upon me; I could answer nothing; and presently the man resumed, as if to himself: "Yes," he said, "O yes, I know it. I have passed its doors. There was snow upon the pass, the wind was driving it; sure enough there was death that night upon the mountains, but there was worse beside the hearth. I took him by the arm, Senor, and dragged him to the gate; I conjured him, by all he loved and respected, to go forth with me; I went on my knees before him in the snow; and I could see he was moved by my entreaty. And just then she came out on the gallery, and called him by his name; and he turned, and there was she standing with a lamp in her hand and smiling on him to come back. I cried out aloud to God, and threw my arms about him, but he put me by, and left me alone. He had made his choice; God help us. I would pray for him, but to what end? There are sins that not even the Pope can loose."

"And your friend," I asked, "what became of him?"

"Nay, God knows," said the muleteer. "If all be true that we hear, his end was like his sin, a thing to raise the hair."

"Do you mean that he was killed?" I asked.

"Sure enough, he was killed," returned the man. "But how? Ay, how? But these are things that it is sin to speak of."

"The people of that house..." I began.

But he interrupted me with a savage outburst. "The people?" he cried. "What people? There are neither men nor women in that house of Satan's! What? Have you lived here so long, and never heard?" And here he put his mouth to my ear and whispered, as if even the fowls of the mountain might have overheard and been stricken with horror.

What he told me was not true, nor was it even original; being, indeed, but a new edition, vamped up again by village ignorance and superstition, of stories nearly as ancient as the race of man. It was rather the application that appalled me. In the old days, he said, the church would have burned out that nest of basilisks; but the arm of the church was now shortened; his friend Miguel had been unpunished by the hands of men, and left to the more awful judgment of an offended God. This was wrong; but it should be so no more. The Padre was sunk in age; he was even bewitched himself; but the eyes of his flock were now awake to their own danger; and some day—ay, and before long—the smoke of that house should go up to heaven.

He left me filled with horror and fear. Which way to turn I knew not; whether first to warn the Padre, or to carry my ill-news direct to the threatened inhabitants of the residencia. Fate was to decide for me; for, while I was still hesitating, I beheld the veiled figure of a woman drawing near to me up the pathway. No veil could deceive my penetration; by every line and every movement I recognised Olalla; and keeping hidden behind a corner of the rock, I suffered her to gain the summit. Then I came forward. She knew me and paused, but did not speak; I, too, remained silent; and we continued for some time to gaze upon each other with a passionate sadness.

"I thought you had gone," she said at length. "It is all that you can do for me—to go. It is all I ever asked of you. And you still stay. But do you know, that every day heaps up the peril of death, not only on your head, but on ours? A report has gone about the mountain; it is thought you love me, and the people will not suffer it."

I saw she was already informed of her danger, and I rejoiced at it. "Olalla," I said, "I am ready to go this day, this very hour, but not alone."

She stepped aside and knelt down before the crucifix to pray, and I stood by and looked now at her and now at the object of her adoration, now at the living figure of the penitent, and now at the ghastly, daubed countenance, the painted wounds, and the projected ribs of the image. The silence was only broken by the wailing of some large birds that circled sidelong, as if in surprise or alarm, about the summit of the hills. Presently rose again, turned towards me, raised her veil, and, still leaning with one hand on the shaft of the crucifix, looked upon me with a pale and sorrowful countenance.

"I have laid my hand upon the cross," she said. "The Padre says you are no Christian; but look up for a moment with my eyes, and behold the face of the Man of Sorrows. We are all such as He was—the inheritors of sin; we must all bear and expiate a past which was not ours; there is in all of us—ay, even in me—a sparkle of the divine. Like Him, we must endure for a little while, until morning returns bringing peace. Suffer me to pass on upon my way alone; it is thus that I shall be least lonely, counting for my friend Him who is the friend of all the distressed; it is thus that I shall be the most happy, having taken my farewell of earthly happiness, and willingly accepted sorrow for my portion."

I looked at the face of the crucifix, and, though I was no friend to images, and despised that imitative and grimacing art of which it was a rude example, some sense of what the thing implied was carried home to my intelligence. The face looked down upon me with a painful and deadly contraction; but the rays of a glory encircled it, and reminded me that the sacrifice was voluntary. It stood there, crowning the rock, as it still stands on so many highway sides, vainly preaching to passers-by, an emblem of sad and noble truths; that pleasure is not an end, but an accident; that pain is the choice of the magnanimous; that it is best to suffer all things and do well. I turned and went down the mountain in silence; and when I looked back for the last time before the wood closed about my path, I saw still leaning on the crucifix.

The Happy Prince

Oscar Wilde

Oscar Wilde (1854-1900) was an Irish wit, poet and playwright who also wrote the famous novel *The Picture of Dorian Gray* (1890), which he vehemently defended using the concept of making 'art for art's sake'. His aesthetic sensibilities mixed with his wit were apparent in notable plays such as *The Importance of Being Earnest* (1895) and *Lady Windermere's Fan* (1893). 'The Happy Prince' is the title story of *The Happy Prince and Other Tales* (1888), a collection of short stories for children.

High above the city, on a tall column, stood the statue of the Happy Prince. He was gilded all over with thin leaves of fine gold, for eyes he had two bright sapphires, and a large red ruby glowed on his sword-hilt.

He was very much admired indeed. "He is as beautiful as a weathercock," remarked one of the Town Councillors who wished to gain a reputation for having artistic tastes; "only not quite so useful," he added, fearing lest people should think him unpractical, which he really was not.

"Why can't you be like the Happy Prince?" asked a sensible mother of her little boy who was crying for the moon. "The Happy Prince never dreams of crying for anything."

"I am glad there is someone in the world who is quite happy," muttered a disappointed man as he gazed at the wonderful statue.

"He looks just like an angel," said the Charity Children as they came out of the cathedral in their bright scarlet cloaks and their clean white pinafores.

"How do you know?" said the Mathematical Master, "you have never seen one."

"Ah! But we have, in our dreams," answered the children; and the Mathematical Master frowned and looked very severe, for he did not approve of children dreaming.

One night there flew over the city a little Swallow. His friends had gone away to Egypt six weeks before, but he had stayed behind, for he was in love with the most beautiful Reed. He had met her early in the spring as he was flying down the river after a big yellow moth, and had been so attracted by her slender waist that he had stopped to talk to her.

"Shall I love you?" said the Swallow, who liked to come to the point at once, and the Reed made him a low bow. So he flew round and round her, touching the water with his wings, and making silver ripples. This was his courtship, and it lasted all through the summer.

"It is a ridiculous attachment," twittered the other Swallows; "she has no money, and far too many relations;" and indeed the river was quite full of Reeds. Then, when the autumn came they all flew away.

After they had gone he felt lonely, and began to tire of his lady-love. "She has no conversation," he said, "and I am afraid that she is a coquette, for she is always flirting with the wind." And certainly, whenever the wind blew, the Reed made the most graceful curtseys. "I admit that she is domestic," he continued, "but I love travelling, and my wife, consequently, should love travelling also."

"Will you come away with me?" he said finally to her; but the Reed shook her head, she was so attached to her home.

"You have been trifling with me," he cried. "I am off to the Pyramids. Goodbye!" and he flew away.

All day long he flew, and at night-time he arrived at the city. "Where shall I put up?" he said; "I hope the town has made preparations."

Then he saw the statue on the tall column.

"I will put up there," he cried; "it is a fine position, with plenty of fresh air." So he alighted just between the feet of the Happy Prince.

"I have a golden bedroom," he said softly to himself as he looked round, and he prepared to go to sleep; but just as he was putting his head under his wing a large drop of water fell on him. "What a curious thing!" he cried; "there is not a single cloud in the sky, the stars are quite clear and bright, and yet it is raining. The climate in the north of Europe is really dreadful. The Reed used to like the rain, but that was merely her selfishness."

Then another drop fell.

"What is the use of a statue if it cannot keep the rain off?" he said; "I must look for a good chimney-pot," and he determined to fly away.

But before he had opened his wings, a third drop fell, and he looked up, and saw—Ah! What did he see?

The eyes of the Happy Prince were filled with tears, and tears were running down his golden cheeks. His face was so beautiful in the moonlight that the little Swallow was filled with pity.

"Who are you?" he said.

"I am the Happy Prince."

"Why are you weeping then?" asked the Swallow; "you have quite drenched me."

"When I was alive and had a human heart," answered the statue, "I did not know what tears were, for I lived in the Palace of Sans-Souci, where sorrow is not allowed to enter. In the daytime I played with my companions in the garden, and in the evening I led the dance in the Great Hall. Round the garden ran a very lofty wall, but I never cared to ask what lay beyond it, everything about me was so beautiful. My courtiers called me the Happy Prince, and happy indeed I was, if pleasure be happiness. So I lived, and so I died. And now that I am dead they have set me up here so high that I can see all the ugliness and all the misery of my city, and though my heart is made of lead yet I cannot chose but weep."

"What! Is he not solid gold?" said the Swallow to himself. He was too polite to make any personal remarks out loud.

"Far away," continued the statue in a low musical voice, "far away in a little street there is a poor house. One of the windows is open, and through it I can see a woman seated at a table. Her face is thin and worn, and she has coarse, red hands, all pricked by the needle, for she is a seamstress. She is embroidering passion-flowers on a satin gown for the loveliest of the Queen's maids-of-honour to wear at the next Court-ball. In a bed in the corner of the room her little boy is lying ill. He has a fever, and is asking for oranges. His mother has nothing to give him but river water, so he is crying. Swallow, Swallow, little Swallow, will you not bring her the ruby out of my sword-hilt? My feet are fastened to this pedestal and I cannot move."

"I am waited for in Egypt," said the Swallow. "My friends are flying up and down the Nile, and talking to the large lotus-flowers. Soon they will go to sleep in the tomb of the great King. The King is there himself in his painted coffin. He is wrapped in yellow linen, and embalmed with spices. Round his neck is a chain of pale green jade, and his hands are like withered leaves."

"Swallow, Swallow, little Swallow," said the Prince, "will you not stay with me for one night, and be my messenger? The boy is so thirsty, and the mother so sad."

"I don't think I like boys," answered the Swallow. "Last summer, when I was staying on the river, there were two rude boys, the miller's sons, who were always throwing stones at me. They never hit me, of course; we swallows fly far too well for that, and besides, I come of a family famous for its agility; but still, it was a mark of disrespect."

But the Happy Prince looked so sad that the little Swallow was sorry. "It is very cold here," he said; "but I will stay with you for one night, and be your messenger."

"Thank you, little Swallow," said the Prince.

So the Swallow picked out the great ruby from the Prince's sword, and flew away with it in his beak over the roofs of the town.

He passed by the cathedral tower, where the white marble angels were sculptured. He passed by the palace and heard the sound of dancing. A beautiful girl came out on the balcony with her lover. "How wonderful the stars are," he said to her, "and how wonderful is the power of love!"

"I hope my dress will be ready in time for the State-ball," she answered; "I have ordered passion-flowers to be embroidered on it; but the seamstresses are so lazy."

He passed over the river, and saw the lanterns hanging to the masts of the ships. He passed over the Ghetto, and saw the old Jews bargaining with each other, and weighing out money in copper scales. At last he came to the poor house and looked in. The boy was tossing feverishly on his bed, and the mother had fallen asleep, she was so tired. In he hopped, and laid the great ruby on the table beside the woman's thimble. Then he flew gently round the bed, fanning the boy's forehead with his wings. "How cool I feel," said the boy, "I must be getting better"; and he sank into a delicious slumber.

Then the Swallow flew back to the Happy Prince, and told him what he had done. "It is curious," he remarked, "but I feel quite warm now, although it is so cold."

"That is because you have done a good action," said the Prince. And the little Swallow began to think, and then he fell asleep. Thinking always made him sleepy.

When day broke he flew down to the river and had a bath. "What a remarkable phenomenon," said the Professor of Ornithology as he was passing over the bridge. "A swallow in winter!" And he wrote a long letter about it to the local newspaper. Every one quoted it, it was full of so many words that they could not understand.

"Tonight I go to Egypt," said the Swallow, and he was in high spirits at the prospect. He visited all the public monuments, and sat a long time on top of the church steeple. Wherever he went the Sparrows chirruped, and said to each other, "What a distinguished stranger!" so he enjoyed himself very much.

When the moon rose he flew back to the Happy Prince. "Have you any commissions for Egypt?" he cried; "I am just starting."

"Swallow, Swallow, little Swallow," said the Prince, "will you not stay with me one night longer?"

"I am waited for in Egypt," answered the Swallow. "Tomorrow my friends will fly up to the Second Cataract. The river-horse couches there among the bulrushes, and on a great granite throne sits the God Memnon. All night long he watches the stars, and when the morning star shines he utters one cry of joy, and then he is silent. At noon the yellow lions come down to the water's edge to drink. They have eyes like green beryls, and their roar is louder than the roar of the cataract."

"Swallow, Swallow, little Swallow," said the Prince, "far away across the city I see a young man in a garret. He is leaning over a desk covered with papers, and in a tumbler by his side there is a bunch of withered violets. His hair is brown and crisp, and his lips are red as a pomegranate, and he has large and dreamy eyes. He is trying to finish a play for the Director of the Theatre, but he is too cold to write any more. There is no fire in the grate, and hunger has made him faint."

"I will wait with you one night longer," said the Swallow, who really had a good heart. "Shall I take him another ruby?"

"Alas! I have no ruby now," said the Prince; "my eyes are all that I have left. They are made of rare sapphires, which were brought out of India a thousand years ago. Pluck out one of them and take it to him. He will sell it to the jeweller, and buy food and firewood, and finish his play."

"Dear Prince," said the Swallow, "I cannot do that"; and he began to weep.

"Swallow, Swallow, little Swallow," said the Prince, "do as I command you."

So the Swallow plucked out the Prince's eye, and flew away to the student's garret. It was easy enough to get in, as there was a hole in the roof. Through this he darted, and came into the room. The young man had his head buried in his hands, so he did not hear the flutter of the bird's wings, and when he looked up he found the beautiful sapphire lying on the withered violets.

"I am beginning to be appreciated," he cried; "this is from some great admirer. Now I can finish my play," and he looked quite happy.

The next day the Swallow flew down to the harbour. He sat on the mast of a large vessel and watched the sailors hauling big chests out of the hold with ropes. "Heave a-hoy!" they shouted as each chest came up. "I am going to Egypt"! cried the Swallow, but nobody minded, and when the moon rose he flew back to the Happy Prince.

"I am come to bid you goodbye," he cried.

"Swallow, Swallow, little Swallow," said the Prince, "will you not stay with me one night longer?"

"It is winter," answered the Swallow, "and the chill snow will soon be here. In Egypt the sun is warm on the green palm-trees, and the crocodiles lie in the mud and look lazily about them. My companions are building a nest in the Temple of Baalbec, and the pink and white doves are watching them, and cooing to each other. Dear Prince, I must leave you, but I will never forget you, and next spring I will bring you back two beautiful jewels in place of those you have given away. The ruby shall be redder than a red rose, and the sapphire shall be as blue as the great sea."

"In the square below," said the Happy Prince, "there stands a little match-girl. She has let her matches fall in the gutter, and they are all spoiled. Her father will beat her if she does not bring home some money, and she is crying. She has no shoes or stockings, and her little head is bare. Pluck out my other eye, and give it to her, and her father will not beat her."

"I will stay with you one night longer," said the Swallow, "but I cannot pluck out your eye. You would be quite blind then."

"Swallow, Swallow, little Swallow," said the Prince, "do as I command you."

So he plucked out the Prince's other eye, and darted down with it. He swooped past the match-girl, and slipped the jewel into the palm of her hand. "What a lovely bit of glass," cried the little girl; and she ran home, laughing.

Then the Swallow came back to the Prince. "You are blind now," he said, "so I will stay with you always."

"No, little Swallow," said the poor Prince, "you must go away to Egypt."

"I will stay with you always," said the Swallow, and he slept at the Prince's feet.

All the next day he sat on the Prince's shoulder, and told him stories of what he had seen in strange lands. He told him of the red ibises, who stand in long rows on the banks of the Nile, and catch gold-fish in their beaks; of the Sphinx, who is as old as the world itself, and lives in the desert, and knows everything; of the merchants, who walk slowly by the side of their camels, and carry amber beads in their hands; of the King of the Mountains of the Moon, who is as black as ebony, and worships a large crystal; of the great green snake that sleeps in a palm-tree, and has twenty priests to feed it with honey-cakes; and of the pygmies who sail over a big lake on large flat leaves, and are always at war with the butterflies.

"Dear little Swallow," said the Prince, "you tell me of marvellous things, but more marvellous than anything is the suffering of men and of women. There is no Mystery so great as Misery. Fly over my city, little Swallow, and tell me what you see there."

So the Swallow flew over the great city, and saw the rich making merry in their beautiful houses, while the beggars were sitting at the gates. He flew into dark lanes, and saw the white faces of starving children looking out listlessly at the black streets. Under the archway of a bridge two little boys were lying in one another's arms to try and keep themselves warm. "How hungry we are!" they said. "You must not lie here," shouted the Watchman, and they wandered out into the rain.

Then he flew back and told the Prince what he had seen.

"I am covered with fine gold," said the Prince, "you must take it off, leaf by leaf, and give it to my poor; the living always think that gold can make them happy."

Leaf after leaf of the fine gold the Swallow picked off, till the Happy Prince looked quite dull and grey. Leaf after leaf of the fine gold he brought to the poor, and the children's faces grew rosier, and they laughed and played games in the street. "We have bread now!" they cried.

Then the snow came, and after the snow came the frost. The streets looked as if they were made of silver, they were so bright and glistening; long icicles like crystal daggers hung down from the eaves of the houses, everybody went about in furs, and the little boys wore scarlet caps and skated on the ice.

The poor little Swallow grew colder and colder, but he would not leave the Prince, he loved him too well. He picked up crumbs outside the baker's door when the baker was not looking and tried to keep himself warm by flapping his wings.

But at last he knew that he was going to die. He had just strength to fly up to the Prince's shoulder once more. "Goodbye, dear Prince!" he murmured, "will you let me kiss your hand?"

"I am glad that you are going to Egypt at last, little Swallow," said the Prince, "you have stayed too long here; but you must kiss me on the lips, for I love you."

"It is not to Egypt that I am going," said the Swallow. "I am going to the House of Death. Death is the brother of Sleep, is he not?"

And he kissed the Happy Prince on the lips, and fell down dead at his feet.

At that moment a curious crack sounded inside the statue, as if something had broken. The fact is that the leaden heart had snapped right in two. It certainly was a dreadfully hard frost.

Early the next morning the Mayor was walking in the square below in company with the Town Councillors. As they passed the column he looked up at the statue: "Dear me! How shabby the Happy Prince looks!" he said.

"How shabby indeed!" cried the Town Councillors, who always agreed with the Mayor; and they went up to look at it.

"The ruby has fallen out of his sword, his eyes are gone, and he is golden no longer," said the Mayor in fact, "he is litttle better than a beggar!"

"Little better than a beggar," said the Town Councillors.

"And here is actually a dead bird at his feet!" continued the Mayor. "We must really issue a proclamation that birds are not to be allowed to die here." And the Town Clerk made a note of the suggestion.

So they pulled down the statue of the Happy Prince. "As he is no longer beautiful he is no longer useful," said the Art Professor at the University.

Then they melted the statue in a furnace, and the Mayor held a meeting of the Corporation to decide what was to be done with the metal. "We must have another statue, of course," he said, "and it shall be a statue of myself."

"Of myself," said each of the Town Councillors, and they quarrelled. When I last heard of them they were quarrelling still.

"What a strange thing!" said the overseer of the workmen at the foundry. "This broken lead heart will not melt in the furnace. We must throw it away." So they threw it on a dust-heap where the dead Swallow was also lying.

"Bring me the two most precious things in the city," said God to one of His Angels; and the Angel brought Him the leaden heart and the dead bird.

"You have rightly chosen," said God, "for in my garden of Paradise this little bird shall sing for evermore, and in my city of gold the Happy Prince shall praise me."

The Boarded Window

Ambrose Bierce

Ambrose Bierce (1842-1914) was an American journalist, satirist and author who was popular for writing horror and mystery short stories. He volunteered for the American Civil War (1861-65) and later became a renowned newspaper columnist, initiating sharp attacks on dishonest politicians, amateur poets and impostors of all sorts. However, he was renowned for his finely composed short stories such as 'The Boarded Window' (1891).

In eighteen thirty, only a few miles away from what is now the great city of Cincinnati, Ohio, lay a huge and almost endless forest.

The area had a few settlements established by people of the frontier. Many of them had already left the area for settlements further to the west. But among those remaining was a man who had been one of the first people to arrive there.

He lived alone in a house of logs surrounded on all sides by the great forest. He seemed a part of the darkness and silence of the forest, for no one had ever known him to smile or speak an unnecessary word. His simple needs were supplied by selling or trading the skins of wild animals in the town.

His little log house had a single door. Directly opposite was a window. The window was boarded up. No one could remember a time when it was not. And no one knew why it had been closed. I imagine there are few people living today who ever knew the secret of that window. But I am one, as you shall see.

The man's name was said to be Murlock. He appeared to be seventy years old, but he was really fifty. Something other than years had been the cause of his aging.

His hair and long, full beard were white. His gray, lifeless eyes were sunken. His face was wrinkled. He was tall and thin with drooping shoulders—like someone with many problems.

I never saw him. These details I learned from my grandfather. He told me the man's story when I was a boy. He had known him when living nearby in that early day.

One day Murlock was found in his cabin, dead. It was not a time and place for medical examiners and newspapers. I suppose it was agreed that he had died from natural causes or I should have been told, and should remember.

I know only that the body was buried near the cabin, next to the burial place of his wife. She had died so many years before him that local tradition noted very little of her existence.

That closes the final part of this true story, except for the incident that followed many years later. With a fearless spirit I went to the place and got close enough to the ruined cabin to throw a stone against it. I ran away to avoid the ghost which every well-informed boy in the area knew haunted the spot.

But there is an earlier part to this story supplied by my grandfather.

When Murlock built his cabin he was young, strong and full of hope. He began the hard work of creating a farm. He kept a gun—a rifle—for hunting to support himself.

He had married a young woman, in all ways worthy of his honest love and loyalty. She shared the dangers of life with a willing spirit and a light heart. There is no known record of her name or details about her. They loved each other and were happy.

One day Murlock returned from hunting in a deep part of the forest. He found his wife sick with fever and confusion. There was no doctor or neighbor within miles. She was in no condition to be left alone while he went to find help. So Murlock tried to take care of his wife and return her to good health. But at the end of the third day she fell into unconsciousness and died.

From what we know about a man like Murlock, we may try to imagine some of the details of the story told by my grandfather.

When he was sure she was dead, Murlock had sense enough to remember that the dead must be prepared for burial. He made a mistake now and again while performing this special duty. He did certain things wrong. And others which he did correctly were done over and over again.

He was surprised that he did not cry — surprised and a little ashamed. Surely it is unkind not to cry for the dead.

"Tomorrow," he said out loud, "I shall have to make the coffin and dig the grave; and then I shall miss her, when she is no longer in sight. But now — she is dead, of course, but it is all right — it must be all right, somehow. Things cannot be as bad as they seem."

He stood over the body of his wife in the disappearing light. He fixed the hair and made finishing touches to the rest. He did all of this without thinking but with care. And still through his mind ran a feeling that all was right — that he should have her again as before, and everything would be explained.

Murlock had no experience in deep sadness. His heart could not contain it all. His imagination could not understand it. He did not know he was so hard struck. That knowledge would come later and never leave.

Deep sadness is an artist of powers that affects people in different ways. To one it comes like the stroke of an arrow, shocking all the emotions to a sharper life. To another, it comes as the blow of a crushing strike. We may believe Murlock to have been affected that way.

Soon after he had finished his work he sank into a chair by the side of the table upon which the body lay. He noted how white his wife's face looked in the deepening darkness. He laid his arms upon the table's edge and dropped his face into them, tearless and very sleepy.

At that moment a long, screaming sound came in through the open window. It was like the cry of a lost child in the far deep of the darkening forest! But the man did not move. He heard that unearthly cry upon his failing sense, again and nearer than before. Maybe it was a wild animal or maybe it was a dream. For Murlock was asleep.

Some hours later, he awoke, lifted his head from his arms and listened closely. He knew not why. There in the black darkness by the side of the body, he remembered everything without a shock. He strained his eyes to see, he knew not what.

His senses were all alert. His breath was suspended. His blood was still as if to assist the silence. Who — what had awakened him and where was it!

Suddenly the table shook under his arms. At the same time he heard, or imagined he heard, a light, soft step and then another. The sounds were as bare feet walking upon the floor!

He was afraid beyond the power to cry out or move. He waited—waited there in the darkness through what seemed like centuries of such fear. Fear as one may know, but yet live to tell. He tried but failed to speak the dead woman's name. He tried but failed to stretch his hand across the table to learn if she was there. His throat was powerless. His arms and hands were like lead.

Then something most frightful happened. It seemed as if a heavy body was thrown against the table with a force that pushed against his chest. At the same time he heard and felt the fall of something upon the floor. It was so violent a crash that the whole house shook. A fight followed and a confusion of sounds impossible to describe.

Murlock had risen to his feet. Extreme fear had caused him to lose control of his senses. He threw his hands upon the table. Nothing was there!

There is a point at which fear may turn to insanity; and insanity incites to action. With no definite plan and acting like a madman, Murlock ran quickly to the wall. He seized his loaded rifle and without aim fired it.

The flash from the rifle lit the room with a clear brightness. He saw a huge fierce panther dragging the dead woman toward the window. The wild animal's teeth were fixed on her throat! Then there was darkness blacker than before, and silence.

When he returned to consciousness the sun was high and the forest was filled with the sounds of singing birds. The body lay near the window, where the animal had left it when frightened away by the light and sound of the rifle.

The clothing was ruined. The long hair was in disorder. The arms and legs lay in a careless way. And a pool of blood flowed from the horribly torn throat. The ribbon he had used to tie the wrists was broken. The hands were tightly closed.

And between the teeth was a piece of the animal's ear.

The Postmaster

Rabindranath Tagore

Rabindranath Tagore (1861-1941) was the first non-European winner of the Nobel Prize for Literature (1913). A Bengali poet, essayist, playwright, short story writer, lyricist and painter, his short stories are often poignant tales about country dwellers and their ordinary lives and struggles. 'The Postmaster' was first published as part of the collection *Mashi and Other Stories* (1891).

The postmaster first took up his duties in the village of Ulapur. Though the village was a small one, there was an indigo factory near by, and the proprietor, an Englishman, had managed to get a post office established.

Our postmaster belonged to Calcutta. He felt like a fish out of water in this remote village. His office and living-room were in a dark thatched shed, not far from a green, slimy pond, surrounded on all sides by a dense growth.

The men employed in the indigo factory had no leisure; moreover, they were hardly desirable companions for decent folk. Nor is a Calcutta boy an adept in the art of associating with others. Among strangers he appears either proud or ill at ease. At any rate, the postmaster had but little company; nor had he much to do.

At times he tried his hand at writing a verse or two. That the movement of the leaves and the clouds of the sky were enough to fill life with joy—such were the sentiments to which he sought to give expression. But God knows that the poor fellow would have felt it as the gift of a new life, if some genie of the Arabian Nights had in one night swept away the trees, leaves and all, and replaced them with a macadamised road, hiding the clouds from view with rows of tall houses.

The postmaster's salary was small. He had to cook his own meals, which he used to share with Ratan, an orphan girl of the village, who did odd jobs for him.

When in the evening the smoke began to curl up from the village cowsheds, and the cicalas chirped in every bush; when the mendicants of the Baül sect sang their shrill songs in their daily meeting-place, when any poet, who had attempted to watch the movement of the leaves in the dense bamboo thickets, would have felt a ghostly shiver run down his back, the postmaster would light his little lamp, and call out "Ratan."

Ratan would sit outside waiting for this call, and, instead of coming in at once, would reply, "Did you call me, sir?"

"What are you doing?" the postmaster would ask.

"I must be going to light the kitchen fire," would be the answer.

And the postmaster would say: "Oh, let the kitchen fire be for awhile; light me my pipe first."

At last Ratan would enter, with puffed-out cheeks, vigorously blowing into a flame a live coal to light the tobacco. This would give the postmaster an opportunity of conversing. "Well, Ratan," perhaps he would begin, "do you remember anything of your mother?" That was a fertile subject. Ratan partly remembered, and partly didn't. Her father had been fonder of her than her mother; him she recollected more vividly. He used to come home in the evening after his work, and one or two evenings stood out more clearly than others, like pictures in her memory. Ratan would sit on the floor near the postmaster's feet, as memories crowded in upon her. She called to mind a little brother that she had—and how on some bygone cloudy day she had played at fishing with him on the edge of the pond, with a twig for a make-believe fishing-rod. Such little incidents would drive out greater events from her mind. Thus, as they talked, it would often get very late, and the postmaster would feel too lazy to do any cooking at all. Ratan would then hastily light the fire, and toast some unleavened bread, which, with the cold remnants of the morning meal, was enough for their supper.

On some evenings, seated at his desk in the corner of the big empty shed, the postmaster too would call up memories of his own home, of his mother and his sister, of those for whom in his exile his heart was sad—memories which were always haunting him, but which he could not talk about with the men of the factory, though he found himself naturally recalling them aloud in the presence of the simple little girl. And so it came about that the girl would allude to his people as mother, brother, and sister, as if she had known them all her life. In fact, she had a complete picture of each one of them painted in her little heart.

One noon, during a break in the rains, there was a cool soft breeze blowing; the smell of the damp grass and leaves in the hot sun felt like the warm breathing of the tired earth on one's body. A persistent bird went on all the afternoon repeating the burden of its one complaint in Nature's audience chamber.

The postmaster had nothing to do. The shimmer of the freshly washed leaves, and the banked-up remnants of the retreating rain-clouds were sights to see; and the postmaster was watching them and thinking to himself: "Oh, if only some kindred soul were near—just one loving human being whom I could hold near my heart!" This was exactly, he went on to think, what that bird was trying to say, and it was the same feeling which the murmuring leaves were striving to express. But no one knows, or would believe, that such an idea might also take possession of an ill-paid village postmaster in the deep, silent mid-day interval of his work.

The postmaster sighed, and called out "Ratan." Ratan was then sprawling beneath the guava-tree, busily engaged in eating unripe guavas. At the voice of her master, she ran up breathlessly, saying: "Were you calling me, Dada?" "I was thinking," said the postmaster, "of teaching you to read." And then for the rest of the afternoon he taught her the alphabet.

Thus, in a very short time, Ratan had got as far as the double consonants.

It seemed as though the showers of the season would never end. Canals, ditches, and hollows were all overflowing with water. Day and night the patter of rain was heard, and the croaking of frogs.

The village roads became impassable, and marketing had to be done in punts.

One heavily clouded morning, the postmaster's little pupil had been long waiting outside the door for her call, but, not hearing it as usual, she took up her dog-eared book, and slowly entered the room. She found her master stretched out on his bed, and, thinking that he was resting, she was about to retire on tip-toe, when she suddenly heard her name — "Ratan!" She turned at once and asked: "Were you sleeping, Dada?" The postmaster in a plaintive voice said: "I am not well. Feel my head; is it very hot?"

In the loneliness of his exile, and in the gloom of the rains, his ailing body needed a little tender nursing. He longed to remember the touch on the forehead of soft hands with tinkling bracelets, to imagine the presence of loving womanhood, the nearness of mother and sister. And the exile was not disappointed. Ratan ceased to be a little girl. She at once stepped into the post of mother, called in the village doctor, gave the patient his pills at the proper intervals, sat up all night by his pillow, cooked his gruel for him, and every now and then asked: "Are you feeling a little better, Dada?"

It was some time before the postmaster, with weakened body, was able to leave his sick-bed. "No more of this," said he with decision. "I must get a transfer." He at once wrote off to Calcutta an application for a transfer, on the ground of the unhealthiness of the place.

Relieved from her duties as nurse, Ratan again took up her old place outside the door. But she no longer heard the same old call. She would sometimes peep inside furtively to find the postmaster sitting on his chair, or stretched on his bed, and staring absent-mindedly into the air. While Ratan was awaiting her call, the postmaster was awaiting a reply to his application. The girl read her old lessons over and over again—her great fear was lest, when the call came, she might be found wanting in the double consonants. At last, after a week, the call did come one evening. With an overflowing heart Ratan rushed into the room with her — "Were you calling me, Dada?"

The postmaster said: "I am going away tomorrow, Ratan."

"Where are you going, Dada?"

"I am going home."

"When will you come back?"

"I am not coming back."

Ratan asked no other question. The postmaster, of his own accord, went on to tell her that his application for a transfer had been rejected, so he had resigned his post and was going home.

For a long time neither of them spoke another word. The lamp went on dimly burning, and from a leak in one corner of the thatch water dripped steadily into an earthen vessel on the floor beneath it.

After a while Ratan rose, and went off to the kitchen to prepare the meal; but she was not so quick about it as on other days. Many new things to think of had entered her little brain. When the postmaster had finished his supper, the girl suddenly asked him: "Dada, will you take me to your home?"

The postmaster laughed. "What an idea!" said he; but he did not think it necessary to explain to the girl wherein lay the absurdity.

That whole night, in her waking and in her dreams, the postmaster's laughing reply haunted her — "What an idea!"

On getting up in the morning, the postmaster found his bath ready. He had stuck to his Calcutta habit of bathing in water drawn and kept in pitchers, instead of taking a plunge in the river as was the custom of the village. For some reason or other, the girl could not ask him about the time of his departure, so she had fetched the water from the river long before sunrise, that it should be ready as early as he might want it. After the bath came a call for Ratan. She entered noiselessly, and looked silently into her master's face for orders. The master said: "You need not be anxious about my going away, Ratan; I shall tell my successor to look after you." These words were kindly meant, no doubt: but inscrutable are the ways of a woman's heart!

Ratan had borne many a scolding from her master without complaint, but these kind words she could not bear. She burst out weeping, and said: "No, no, you need not tell anybody anything at all about me; I don't want to stay on here."

The postmaster was dumbfounded. He had never seen Ratan like this before.

The new incumbent duly arrived, and the postmaster, having given over charge, prepared to depart. Just before starting he called

Ratan and said: "Here is something for you; I hope it will keep you for some little time." He brought out from his pocket the whole of his month's salary, retaining only a trifle for his travelling expenses. Then Ratan fell at his feet and cried: "Oh, Dada, I pray you, don't give me anything, don't in any way trouble about me," and then she ran away out of sight.

The postmaster heaved a sigh, took up his carpet bag, put his umbrella over his shoulder, and, accompanied by a man carrying his many-coloured tin trunk, he slowly made for the boat.

When he got in and the boat was under way, and the rain-swollen river, like a stream of tears welling up from the earth, swirled and sobbed at her bows, then he felt a pain at heart; the grief-stricken face of a village girl seemed to represent for him the great unspoken pervading grief of Mother Earth herself. At one time he had an impulse to go back, and bring away along with him that lonesome waif, forsaken of the world. But the wind had just filled the sails, the boat had got well into the middle of the turbulent current, and already the village was left behind, and its outlying burning-ground came in sight.

So the traveller, borne on the breast of the swift-flowing river, consoled himself with philosophical reflections on the numberless meetings and partings going on in the world—on death, the great parting, from which none returns.

But Ratan had no philosophy. She was wandering about the post office in a flood of tears. It may be that she had still a lurking hope in some corner of her heart that her Dada would return, and that is why she could not tear herself away. Alas for our foolish human nature! Its fond mistakes are persistent. The dictates of reason take a long time to assert their own sway. The surest proofs meanwhile are disbelieved. False hope is clung to with all one's might and main, till a day comes when it has sucked the heart dry and it forcibly breaks through its bonds and departs. After that comes the misery of awakening, and then once again the longing to get back into the maze of the same mistakes.

A Scandal In Bohemia

Sir Arthur Conan Doyle

Sir Arthur Conan Doyle (1859-1930) was a world-renowned detective fiction writer, who created the most popular detective of English crime fiction, Sherlock Holmes. The popularity of Sherlock Holmes stories overshadowed the merit of his historical fiction such as *The White Company* (1891) and *Sir Nigel* (1906) as well as his semi-autobiographical works like *The Firm of Girdlestone* (1890) and *The Stark Munro Letters* (1895). 'A Scandal In Bohemia' (1891) is one of the most popular stories in the Sherlock Holmes series.

I

To Sherlock Holmes she is always *the* woman. I have seldom heard him mention her under any other name. In his eyes she eclipses and predominates the whole of her sex. It was not that he felt any emotion akin to love for Irene Adler. All emotions, and that one particularly, were abhorrent to his cold, precise but admirably balanced mind. He was, I take it, the most perfect reasoning and observing machine that the world has seen, but as a lover he would have placed himself in a false position. He never spoke of the softer passions, save with a gibe and a sneer. They were admirable things for the observer—excellent for drawing the veil from men's motives and actions. But for the trained reasoner to admit such intrusions into his own delicate and finely adjusted temperament was to introduce a distracting factor which might throw a doubt upon all his mental results. Grit in a sensitive instrument, or a crack in one of his own high-power lenses, would not be more disturbing than a strong emotion in a nature such as his. And yet there was but one woman to him, and that woman was the late Irene Adler, of dubious and questionable memory.

I had seen little of Holmes lately. My marriage had drifted us away from each other. My own complete happiness, and the home-centred interests which rise up around the man who first finds himself master of his own establishment, were sufficient to absorb all my attention, while Holmes, who loathed every form of society with his whole Bohemian soul, remained in our lodgings in Baker Street, buried among his old books, and alternating from week to week between cocaine and ambition, the drowsiness of the drug, and the fierce energy of his own keen nature. He was still, as ever, deeply attracted by the study of crime, and occupied his immense faculties and extraordinary powers of observation in following out those clues, and clearing up those mysteries which had been abandoned as hopeless by the official police. From time to time I heard some vague account of his doings: of his summons to Odessa in the case of the Trepoff murder, of his clearing up of the singular tragedy of the Atkinson brothers at Trincomalee, and finally of the mission which he had accomplished so delicately and successfully for the reigning family of Holland. Beyond these signs of his activity, however, which I merely shared with all the readers of the daily press, I knew little of my former friend and companion.

One night—it was on the twentieth of March, 1888—I was returning from a journey to a patient (for I had now returned to civil practice), when my way led me through Baker Street. As I passed the well-remembered door, which must always be associated in my mind with my wooing, and with the dark incidents of the Study in Scarlet, I was seized with a keen desire to see Holmes again, and to know how he was employing his extraordinary powers. His rooms were brilliantly lit, and, even as I looked up, I saw his tall, spare figure pass twice in a dark silhouette against the blind. He was pacing the room swiftly, eagerly, with his head sunk upon his chest and his hands clasped behind him. To me, who knew his every mood and habit, his attitude and manner told their own story. He was at work again. He had risen out of his drug-created dreams and was hot upon the scent of some new problem. I rang the bell and was shown up to the chamber which had formerly been in part my own.

His manner was not effusive. It seldom was; but he was glad, I think, to see me. With hardly a word spoken, but with a kindly eye, he waved me to an armchair, threw across his case of cigars, and indicated a spirit case and a gasogene in the corner. Then he stood before the fire and looked me over in his singular introspective fashion.

"Wedlock suits you," he remarked. "I think, Watson, that you have put on seven and a half pounds since I saw you."

"Seven!" I answered.

"Indeed, I should have thought a little more. Just a trifle more, I fancy, Watson. And in practice again, I observe. You did not tell me that you intended to go into harness."

"Then, how do you know?"

"I see it, I deduce it. How do I know that you have been getting yourself very wet lately, and that you have a most clumsy and careless servant girl?"

"My dear Holmes," said I, "this is too much. You would certainly have been burned, had you lived a few centuries ago. It is true that I had a country walk on Thursday and came home in a dreadful mess, but as I have changed my clothes I can't imagine how you deduce it. As to Mary Jane, she is incorrigible, and my wife has given her notice, but there, again, I fail to see how you work it out."

He chuckled to himself and rubbed his long, nervous hands together.

"It is simplicity itself," said he; "my eyes tell me that on the inside of your left shoe, just where the firelight strikes it, the leather is scored by six almost parallel cuts. Obviously they have been caused by someone who has very carelessly scraped round the edges of the sole in order to remove crusted mud from it. Hence, you see, my double deduction that you had been out in vile weather, and that you had a particularly malignant boot-slitting specimen of the London slavery. As to your practice, if a gentleman walks into my rooms smelling of iodoform, with a black mark of nitrate of silver upon his right forefinger, and a bulge on the right side of his top-hat to show where he has secreted his stethoscope, I must be dull, indeed, if I do not pronounce him to be an active member of the medical profession."

I could not help laughing at the ease with which he explained his process of deduction. "When I hear you give your reasons,"

I remarked, "the thing always appears to me to be so ridiculously simple that I could easily do it myself, though at each successive instance of your reasoning I am baffled until you explain your process. And yet I believe that my eyes are as good as yours."

"Quite so," he answered, lighting a cigarette, and throwing himself down into an armchair. "You see, but you do not observe. The distinction is clear. For example, you have frequently seen the steps which lead up from the hall to this room."

"Frequently."

"How often?"

"Well, some hundreds of times."

"Then how many are there?"

"How many? I don't know."

"Quite so! You have not observed. And yet you have seen. That is just my point. Now, I know that there are seventeen steps, because I have both seen and observed. By the way, since you are interested in these little problems, and since you are good enough to chronicle one or two of my trifling experiences, you may be interested in this." He threw over a sheet of thick, pink-tinted notepaper which had been lying open upon the table. "It came by the last post," said he. "Read it aloud."

The note was undated, and without either signature or address.

"There will call upon you tonight, at a quarter to eight o'clock," it said, "a gentleman who desires to consult you upon a matter of the very deepest moment. Your recent services to one of the royal houses of Europe have shown that you are one who may safely be trusted with matters which are of an importance which can hardly be exaggerated. This account of you we have from all quarters received. Be in your chamber then at that hour, and do not take it amiss if your visitor wear a mask."

"This is indeed a mystery," I remarked. "What do you imagine that it means?"

"I have no data yet. It is a capital mistake to theorise before one has data. Insensibly one begins to twist facts to suit theories, instead of theories to suit facts. But the note itself. What do you deduce from it?"

I carefully examined the writing, and the paper upon which it was written.

"The man who wrote it was presumably well to do," I remarked, endeavouring to imitate my companion's processes. "Such paper could not be bought under half a crown a packet. It is peculiarly strong and stiff."

"Peculiar—that is the very word," said Holmes. "It is not an English paper at all. Hold it up to the light."

I did so, and saw a large "E" with a small "g," a "P," and a large "G" with a small "t" woven into the texture of the paper.

"What do you make of that?" asked Holmes.

"The name of the maker, no doubt; or his monogram, rather."

"Not at all. The "G" with the small "t" stands for "Gesellschaft," which is the German for "Company." It is a customary contraction like our "Co." 'P," of course, stands for "Papier." Now for the "Eg." Let us glance at our Continental Gazetteer." He took down a heavy brown volume from his shelves. "Eglow, Eglonitz—here we are, Egria. It is in a German-speaking country—in Bohemia, not far from Carlsbad. 'Remarkable as being the scene of the death of Wallenstein, and for its numerous glass-factories and paper-mills.' Ha, ha, my boy, what do you make of that?" His eyes sparkled, and he sent up a great blue triumphant cloud from his cigarette.

"The paper was made in Bohemia," I said.

"Precisely. And the man who wrote the note is a German. Do you note the peculiar construction of the sentence—'This account of you we have from all quarters received.' A Frenchman or Russian could not have written that. It is the German who is so uncourteous to his verbs. It only remains, therefore, to discover what is wanted by this German who writes upon Bohemian paper and prefers wearing a mask to showing his face. And here he comes, if I am not mistaken, to resolve all our doubts."

As he spoke there was the sharp sound of horses' hoofs and grating wheels against the curb, followed by a sharp pull at the bell. Holmes whistled.

"A pair, by the sound," said he. "Yes," he continued, glancing out of the window. "A nice little brougham and a pair of beauties. A hundred and fifty guineas apiece. There's money in this case, Watson, if there is nothing else."

"I think that I had better go, Holmes."

"Not a bit, Doctor. Stay where you are. I am lost without my Boswell. And this promises to be interesting. It would be a pity to miss it."

"But your client—"

"Never mind him. I may want your help, and so may he. Here he comes. Sit down in that armchair, Doctor, and give us your best attention."

A slow and heavy step, which had been heard upon the stairs and in the passage, paused immediately outside the door. Then there was a loud and authoritative tap.

"Come in!" said Holmes.

A man entered who could hardly have been less than six feet six inches in height, with the chest and limbs of a Hercules. His dress was rich with a richness which would, in England, be looked upon as akin to bad taste. Heavy bands of astrakhan were slashed across the sleeves and fronts of his double-breasted coat, while the deep blue cloak which was thrown over his shoulders was lined with flame-coloured silk and secured at the neck with a brooch which consisted of a single flaming beryl. Boots which extended halfway up his calves, and which were trimmed at the tops with rich brown fur, completed the impression of barbaric opulence which was suggested by his whole appearance. He carried a broad-brimmed hat in his hand, while he wore across the upper part of his face, extending down past the cheekbones, a black vizard mask, which he had apparently adjusted that very moment, for his hand was still raised to it as he entered. From the lower part of the face he appeared to be a man of strong character, with a thick, hanging lip, and a long, straight chin suggestive of resolution pushed to the length of obstinacy.

"You had my note?" he asked with a deep harsh voice and a strongly marked German accent. "I told you that I would call." He looked from one to the other of us, as if uncertain which to address.

"Pray take a seat," said Holmes. "This is my friend and colleague, Dr. Watson, who is occasionally good enough to help me in my cases. Whom have I the honour to address?"

"You may address me as the Count Von Kramm, a Bohemian nobleman. I understand that this gentleman, your friend, is a man of honour and discretion, whom I may trust with a matter of the most extreme importance. If not, I should much prefer to communicate with you alone."

I rose to go, but Holmes caught me by the wrist and pushed me back into my chair. "It is both, or none," said he. "You may say before this gentleman anything which you may say to me."

The Count shrugged his broad shoulders. "Then I must begin," said he, "by binding you both to absolute secrecy for two years; at the end of that time the matter will be of no importance. At present it is not too much to say that it is of such weight it may have an influence upon European history."

"I promise," said Holmes.

"And I."

"You will excuse this mask," continued our strange visitor. "The august person who employs me wishes his agent to be unknown to you, and I may confess at once that the title by which I have just called myself is not exactly my own."

"I was aware of it," said Holmes dryly.

"The circumstances are of great delicacy, and every precaution has to be taken to quench what might grow to be an immense scandal and seriously compromise one of the reigning families of Europe. To speak plainly, the matter implicates the great House of Ormstein, hereditary kings of Bohemia."

"I was also aware of that," murmured Holmes, settling himself down in his armchair and closing his eyes.

Our visitor glanced with some apparent surprise at the languid, lounging figure of the man who had been no doubt depicted to him as the most incisive reasoner and most energetic agent in Europe. Holmes slowly reopened his eyes and looked impatiently at his gigantic client.

"If your Majesty would condescend to state your case," he remarked, "I should be better able to advise you."

The man sprang from his chair and paced up and down the room in uncontrollable agitation. Then, with a gesture of desperation, he tore the mask from his face and hurled it upon the ground. "You are right," he cried; "I am the King. Why should I attempt to conceal it?"

"Why, indeed?" murmured Holmes. "Your Majesty had not spoken before I was aware that I was addressing Wilhelm Gottsreich Sigismond von Ormstein, Grand Duke of Cassel-Felstein, and hereditary King of Bohemia."

"But you can understand," said our strange visitor, sitting down once more and passing his hand over his high white forehead, "you can understand that I am not accustomed to doing such business in my own person. Yet the matter was so delicate that I could not confide it to an agent without putting myself in his power. I have come *incognito* from Prague for the purpose of consulting you."

"Then, pray consult," said Holmes, shutting his eyes once more.

"The facts are briefly these: Some five years ago, during a lengthy visit to Warsaw, I made the acquaintance of the well-known adventuress, Irene Adler. The name is no doubt familiar to you."

"Kindly look her up in my index, Doctor," murmured Holmes without opening his eyes. For many years he had adopted a system of docketing all paragraphs concerning men and things, so that it was difficult to name a subject or a person on which he could not at once furnish information. In this case I found her biography sandwiched in between that of a Hebrew rabbi and that of a staff-commander who had written a monograph upon the deep-sea fishes.

"Let me see!" said Holmes. "Hum! Born in New Jersey in the year 1858. Contralto—hum! La Scala, hum! Prima donna Imperial Opera of Warsaw—yes! Retired from operatic stage—ha! Living in London—quite so! Your Majesty, as I understand, became entangled with this young person, wrote her some compromising letters, and is now desirous of getting those letters back."

"Precisely so. But how—"

"Was there a secret marriage?"

"None."

"No legal papers or certificates?"

"None."

"Then I fail to follow your Majesty. If this young person should produce her letters for blackmailing or other purposes, how is she to prove their authenticity?"

"There is the writing."

"Pooh, pooh! Forgery."

"My private note-paper."

"Stolen."

"My own seal."

"Imitated."

"My photograph."

"Bought."

"We were both in the photograph."

"Oh, dear! That is very bad! Your Majesty has indeed committed an indiscretion."

"I was mad—insane."

"You have compromised yourself seriously."

"I was only Crown Prince then. I was young. I am but thirty now."

"It must be recovered."

"We have tried and failed."

"Your Majesty must pay. It must be bought."

"She will not sell."

"Stolen, then."

"Five attempts have been made. Twice burglars in my pay ransacked her house. Once we diverted her luggage when she travelled. Twice she has been waylaid. There has been no result."

"No sign of it?"

"Absolutely none."

Holmes laughed. "It is quite a pretty little problem," said he.

"But a very serious one to me," returned the King reproachfully.

"Very, indeed. And what does she propose to do with the photograph?"

"To ruin me."

"But how?"

"I am about to be married."

"So I have heard."

"To Clotilde Lothman von Saxe-Meningen, second daughter of the King of Scandinavia. You may know the strict principles of her family. She is herself the very soul of delicacy. A shadow of a doubt as to my conduct would bring the matter to an end."

"And Irene Adler?"

"Threatens to send them the photograph. And she will do it. I know that she will do it. You do not know her, but she has a soul of steel. She has the face of the most beautiful of women, and the mind of the most resolute of men. Rather than I should marry another woman, there are no lengths to which she would not go—none."

"You are sure that she has not sent it yet?"

"I am sure."

"And why?"

"Because she has said that she would send it on the day when the betrothal was publicly proclaimed. That will be next Monday."

"Oh, then we have three days yet," said Holmes with a yawn. "That is very fortunate, as I have one or two matters of importance to look into just at present. Your Majesty will, of course, stay in London for the present?"

"Certainly. You will find me at the Langham under the name of the Count Von Kramm."

"Then I shall drop you a line to let you know how we progress."

"Pray do so. I shall be all anxiety."

"Then, as to money?"

"You have *carte blanche*."

"Absolutely?"

"I tell you that I would give one of the provinces of my kingdom to have that photograph."

"And for present expenses?"

The King took a heavy chamois leather bag from under his cloak and laid it on the table.

"There are three hundred pounds in gold and seven hundred in notes," he said.

Holmes scribbled a receipt upon a sheet of his notebook and handed it to him.

"And Mademoiselle's address?" he asked.

"Is Briony Lodge, Serpentine Avenue, St. John's Wood."

Holmes took a note of it. "One other question," said he. "Was the photograph a cabinet?"

"It was."

"Then, good night, your Majesty, and I trust that we shall soon have some good news for you. And good night, Watson," he added, as the wheels of the royal brougham rolled down the street. "If you will be good enough to call tomorrow afternoon at three o'clock I should like to chat this little matter over with you."

II

At three o'clock precisely I was at Baker Street, but Holmes had not yet returned. The landlady informed me that he had left the house shortly after eight o'clock in the morning. I sat down beside the fire, however, with the intention of awaiting him, however long he might be. I was already deeply interested in his inquiry, for, though it was surrounded by none of the grim and strange features which were associated with the two crimes which I have already recorded, still, the nature of the case and the exalted station of his client gave it a character of its own. Indeed, apart from the nature of the investigation which my friend had on hand, there was something in his masterly grasp of a situation, and his keen, incisive reasoning, which made it a pleasure to me to study his system of work, and to follow the quick, subtle methods by which he disentangled the most inextricable mysteries. So accustomed was I to his invariable success that the very possibility of his failing had ceased to enter into my head.

It was close upon four before the door opened, and a drunken-looking groom, ill-kempt and side-whiskered, with an inflamed face and disreputable clothes, walked into the room. Accustomed as I was to my friend's amazing powers in the use of disguises, I had to look three times before I was certain that it was indeed he. With a nod he vanished into the bedroom, whence he emerged in five minutes tweed-suited and respectable, as of old. Putting his hands into his pockets, he stretched out his legs in front of the fire and laughed heartily for some minutes.

"Well, really!" he cried, and then he choked and laughed again until he was obliged to lie back, limp and helpless, in the chair.

"What is it?"

"It's quite too funny. I am sure you could never guess how I employed my morning, or what I ended by doing."

"I can't imagine. I suppose that you have been watching the habits, and perhaps the house, of Miss Irene Adler."

"Quite so; but the sequel was rather unusual. I will tell you, however. I left the house a little after eight o'clock this morning in the character of a groom out of work. There is a wonderful sympathy and freemasonry among horsey men. Be one of them, and you will know all that there is to know. I soon found Briony Lodge. It is a *bijou* villa, with a garden at the back, but built out in front right up to the road, two stories. Chubb lock to the door. Large sitting-room on the right side, well furnished, with long windows almost to the floor, and those preposterous English window fasteners which a child could open. Behind there was nothing remarkable, save that the passage window could be reached from the top of the coach-house. I walked round it and examined it closely from every point of view, but without noting anything else of interest.

"I then lounged down the street and found, as I expected, that there was a mews in a lane which runs down by one wall of the garden. I lent the ostlers a hand in rubbing down their horses, and received in exchange twopence, a glass of half-and-half, two fills of shag tobacco, and as much information as I could desire about Miss Adler, to say nothing of half a dozen other people in the neighbourhood in whom I was not in the least interested, but whose biographies I was compelled to listen to."

"And what of Irene Adler?" I asked.

"Oh, she has turned all the men's heads down in that part. She is the daintiest thing under a bonnet on this planet. So say the Serpentine-mews, to a man. She lives quietly, sings at concerts, drives out at five every day, and returns at seven sharp for dinner. Seldom goes out at other times, except when she sings. Has only one male visitor, but a good deal of him. He is dark, handsome, and dashing, never calls less than once a day, and often twice. He is a Mr. Godfrey Norton, of the Inner Temple. See the advantages of a cabman as a confidant. They had driven him home a dozen times from Serpentine-mews, and knew all about him. When I had listened to all they had to tell, I began to walk up and down near Briony Lodge once more, and to think over my plan of campaign.

"This Godfrey Norton was evidently an important factor in the matter. He was a lawyer. That sounded ominous. What was the relation between them, and what the object of his repeated visits?

Was she his client, his friend, or his mistress? If the former, she had probably transferred the photograph to his keeping. If the latter, it was less likely. On the issue of this question depended whether I should continue my work at Briony Lodge, or turn my attention to the gentleman's chambers in the Temple. It was a delicate point, and it widened the field of my inquiry. I fear that I bore you with these details, but I have to let you see my little difficulties, if you are to understand the situation."

"I am following you closely," I answered.

"I was still balancing the matter in my mind when a hansom cab drove up to Briony Lodge, and a gentleman sprang out. He was a remarkably handsome man, dark, aquiline, and moustached—evidently the man of whom I had heard. He appeared to be in a great hurry, shouted to the cabman to wait, and brushed past the maid who opened the door with the air of a man who was thoroughly at home.

"He was in the house about half an hour, and I could catch glimpses of him in the windows of the sitting-room, pacing up and down, talking excitedly, and waving his arms. Of her I could see nothing. Presently he emerged, looking even more flurried than before. As he stepped up to the cab, he pulled a gold watch from his pocket and looked at it earnestly, 'Drive like the devil,' he shouted, 'first to Gross & Hankey's in Regent Street, and then to the Church of St. Monica in the Edgeware Road. Half a guinea if you do it in twenty minutes!'

"Away they went, and I was just wondering whether I should not do well to follow them when up the lane came a neat little landau, the coachman with his coat only half-buttoned, and his tie under his ear, while all the tags of his harness were sticking out of the buckles. It hadn't pulled up before she shot out of the hall door and into it. I only caught a glimpse of her at the moment, but she was a lovely woman, with a face that a man might die for.

"'The Church of St. Monica, John,' she cried, 'and half a sovereign if you reach it in twenty minutes.'

"This was quite too good to lose, Watson. I was just balancing whether I should run for it, or whether I should perch behind her landau when a cab came through the street. The driver looked twice at such a shabby fare, but I jumped in before he could object. 'The Church of St. Monica,' said I, 'and half a sovereign if you reach it in twenty minutes.' It was twenty-five minutes to twelve, and of course it was clear enough what was in the wind.

"My cabby drove fast. I don't think I ever drove faster, but the others were there before us. The cab and the landau with their steaming horses were in front of the door when I arrived. I paid the man and hurried into the church. There was not a soul there save the two whom I had followed and a surpliced clergyman, who seemed to be expostulating with them. They were all three standing in a knot in front of the altar. I lounged up the side aisle like any other idler who has dropped into a church. Suddenly, to my surprise, the three at the altar faced round to me, and Godfrey Norton came running as hard as he could towards me.

"'Thank God,' he cried. 'You'll do. Come! Come!'

"'What then?' I asked.

"'Come, man, come, only three minutes, or it won't be legal.'

"I was half-dragged up to the altar, and before I knew where I was I found myself mumbling responses which were whispered in my ear, and vouching for things of which I knew nothing, and generally assisting in the secure tying up of Irene Adler, spinster, to Godfrey Norton, bachelor. It was all done in an instant, and there was the gentleman thanking me on the one side and the lady on the other, while the clergyman beamed on me in front. It was the most preposterous position in which I ever found myself in my life, and it was the thought of it that started me laughing just now. It seems that there had been some informality about their license, that the clergyman absolutely refused to marry them without a witness of some sort, and that my lucky appearance saved the bridegroom from having to sally out into the streets in search of a best man. The bride gave me a sovereign, and I mean to wear it on my watch chain in memory of the occasion."

"This is a very unexpected turn of affairs," said I; "and what then?"

"Well, I found my plans very seriously menaced. It looked as if the pair might take an immediate departure, and so necessitate very prompt and energetic measures on my part. At the church door, however, they separated, he driving back to the Temple, and she to her own house. 'I shall drive out in the park at five as usual,' she said as she left him. I heard no more. They drove away in different directions, and I went off to make my own arrangements."

"Which are?"

"Some cold beef and a glass of beer," he answered, ringing the bell. "I have been too busy to think of food, and I am likely to be busier still this evening. By the way, Doctor, I shall want your cooperation."

"I shall be delighted."

"You don't mind breaking the law?"

"Not in the least."

"Nor running a chance of arrest?"

"Not in a good cause."

"Oh, the cause is excellent!"

"Then I am your man."

"I was sure that I might rely on you."

"But what is it you wish?"

"When Mrs. Turner has brought in the tray I will make it clear to you. Now," he said as he turned hungrily on the simple fare that our landlady had provided, "I must discuss it while I eat, for I have not much time. It is nearly five now. In two hours we must be on the scene of action. Miss Irene, or Madame, rather, returns from her drive at seven. We must be at Briony Lodge to meet her."

"And what then?"

"You must leave that to me. I have already arranged what is to occur. There is only one point on which I must insist. You must not interfere, come what may. You understand?"

"I am to be neutral?"

"To do nothing whatever. There will probably be some small unpleasantness. Do not join in it. It will end in my being conveyed into the house. Four or five minutes afterwards the sitting-room window will open. You are to station yourself close to that open window."

"Yes."

"You are to watch me, for I will be visible to you."

"Yes."

"And when I raise my hand—so—you will throw into the room what I give you to throw, and will, at the same time, raise the cry of fire. You quite follow me?"

"Entirely."

"It is nothing very formidable," he said, taking a long cigar-shaped roll from his pocket. "It is an ordinary plumber's smoke-rocket, fitted with a cap at either end to make it self-lighting. Your task is confined to that. When you raise your cry of fire, it will be taken up by quite a number of people. You may then walk to the end of the street, and I will rejoin you in ten minutes. I hope that I have made myself clear?"

"I am to remain neutral, to get near the window, to watch you, and at the signal to throw in this object, then to raise the cry of fire, and to wait you at the corner of the street."

"Precisely."

"Then you may entirely rely on me."

"That is excellent. I think, perhaps, it is almost time that I prepare for the new role I have to play."

He disappeared into his bedroom and returned in a few minutes in the character of an amiable and simple-minded Nonconformist clergyman. His broad black hat, his baggy trousers, his white tie, his sympathetic smile, and general look of peering and benevolent curiosity were such as Mr. John Hare alone could have equalled. It was not merely that Holmes changed his costume. His expression, his manner, his very soul seemed to vary with every fresh part that he assumed. The stage lost a fine actor, even as science lost an acute reasoner, when he became a specialist in crime.

It was a quarter past six when we left Baker Street, and it still wanted ten minutes to the hour when we found ourselves in Serpentine Avenue. It was already dusk, and the lamps were just being lighted as we paced up and down in front of Briony Lodge, waiting for the coming of its occupant. The house was just such as I had pictured it from Sherlock Holmes' succinct description, but the locality appeared to be less private than I expected. On the contrary, for a small street in a quiet neighbourhood, it was remarkably animated. There was a group of shabbily dressed men smoking and laughing in a corner, a scissors-grinder with his wheel, two guardsmen who were flirting with a nurse-girl, and several well-dressed young men who were lounging up and down with cigars in their mouths.

"You see," remarked Holmes, as we paced to and fro in front of the house, "this marriage rather simplifies matters. The photograph becomes a double-edged weapon now. The chances are that she would be as averse to its being seen by Mr. Godfrey Norton, as our client is to its coming to the eyes of his princess. Now the question is, Where are we to find the photograph?"

"Where, indeed?"

"It is most unlikely that she carries it about with her. It is cabinet size. Too large for easy concealment about a woman's dress. She knows that the King is capable of having her waylaid and searched. Two attempts of the sort have already been made. We may take it, then, that she does not carry it about with her."

"Where, then?"

"Her banker or her lawyer. There is that double possibility. But I am inclined to think neither. Women are naturally secretive, and they like to do their own secreting. Why should she hand it over to anyone else? She could trust her own guardianship, but she could not tell what indirect or political influence might be brought to bear upon a business man. Besides, remember that she had resolved to use it within a few days. It must be where she can lay her hands upon it. It must be in her own house."

"But it has twice been burgled."

"Pshaw! They did not know how to look."

"But how will you look?"

"I will not look."

"What then?"

"I will get her to show me."

"But she will refuse."

"She will not be able to. But I hear the rumble of wheels. It is her carriage. Now carry out my orders to the letter."

As he spoke the gleam of the sidelights of a carriage came round the curve of the avenue. It was a smart little landau which rattled up to the door of Briony Lodge. As it pulled up, one of the loafing men at the corner dashed forward to open the door in the hope of earning a copper, but was elbowed away by another loafer, who had rushed up with the same intention. A fierce quarrel broke out, which was increased by the two guardsmen, who took sides with one of the loungers, and by the scissors-grinder, who was equally hot upon the other side. A blow was struck, and in an instant the lady, who had stepped from her carriage, was the centre of a little knot of flushed and struggling men, who struck savagely at each other with their fists and sticks. Holmes dashed into the crowd to protect the lady; but, just as he reached her, he gave a cry and dropped to the ground, with the blood running freely down his face. At his fall the guardsmen took to their heels in one direction and the loungers in the other, while a number of better dressed people, who had watched the scuffle without taking part in it, crowded in to help the lady and to attend to the injured man. Irene Adler, as I will still call her, had hurried up the steps; but she stood at the top with her superb figure outlined against the lights of the hall, looking back into the street.

"Is the poor gentleman much hurt?" she asked.

"He is dead," cried several voices.

"No, no, there's life in him!" shouted another. "But he'll be gone before you can get him to hospital."

"He's a brave fellow," said a woman. "They would have had the lady's purse and watch if it hadn't been for him. They were a gang, and a rough one, too. Ah, he's breathing now."

"He can't lie in the street. May we bring him in, marm?"

"Surely. Bring him into the sitting-room. There is a comfortable sofa. This way, please!"

Slowly and solemnly he was borne into Briony Lodge and laid out in the principal room, while I still observed the proceedings from my post by the window. The lamps had been lit, but the blinds had not been drawn, so that I could see Holmes as he lay upon the couch. I do not know whether he was seized with compunction at that moment for the part he was playing, but I know that I never felt more heartily ashamed of myself in my life than when I saw the beautiful creature against whom I was conspiring, or the grace and kindliness with which she waited upon the injured man. And yet it would be the blackest treachery to Holmes to draw back now from the part which he had intrusted to me. I hardened my heart, and took the smoke-rocket from under my ulster. After all, I thought, we are not injuring her. We are but preventing her from injuring another.

Holmes had sat up upon the couch, and I saw him motion like a man who is in need of air. A maid rushed across and threw open the window. At the same instant I saw him raise his hand and at the signal I tossed my rocket into the room with a cry of "Fire!" The word was no sooner out of my mouth than the whole crowd of spectators, well dressed and ill—gentlemen, ostlers, and servant maids—joined in a general shriek of "Fire!" Thick clouds of smoke curled through the room and out at the open window. I caught a glimpse of rushing figures, and a moment later the voice of Holmes from within assuring them that it was a false alarm. Slipping through the shouting crowd I made my way to the corner of the street, and in ten minutes was rejoiced to find my friend's arm in mine, and to get away from the scene of uproar. He walked swiftly and in silence for some few minutes until we had turned down one of the quiet streets which lead towards the Edgeware Road.

"You did it very nicely, Doctor," he remarked. "Nothing could have been better. It is all right."

"You have the photograph?"

"I know where it is."

"And how did you find out?"

"She showed me, as I told you she would."

"I am still in the dark."

"I do not wish to make a mystery," said he, laughing. "The matter was perfectly simple. You, of course, saw that everyone in the street was an accomplice. They were all engaged for the evening."

"I guessed as much."

"Then, when the row broke out, I had a little moist red paint in the palm of my hand. I rushed forward, fell down, clapped my hand to my face, and became a piteous spectacle. It is an old trick."

"That also I could fathom."

"Then they carried me in. She was bound to have me in. What else could she do? And into her sitting-room, which was the very room which I suspected. It lay between that and her bedroom, and I was determined to see which. They laid me on a couch, I motioned for air, they were compelled to open the window, and you had your chance."

"How did that help you?"

"It was all-important. When a woman thinks that her house is on fire, her instinct is at once to rush to the thing which she values most. It is a perfectly overpowering impulse, and I have more than once taken advantage of it. In the case of the Darlington Substitution Scandal it was of use to me, and also in the Arnsworth Castle business. A married woman grabs at her baby; an unmarried one reaches for her jewel-box. Now it was clear to me that our lady of today had nothing in the house more precious to her than what we are in quest of. She would rush to secure it. The alarm of fire was admirably done. The smoke and shouting were enough to shake nerves of steel. She responded beautifully. The photograph is in a recess behind a sliding panel just above the right bell-pull. She was there in an instant, and I caught a glimpse of it as she half drew it out. When I cried out that it was a false alarm, she replaced it, glanced at the rocket, rushed from the room, and I have not seen her since. I rose, and, making my excuses, escaped from the house. I hesitated whether to attempt to secure the photograph at once; but the coachman had come in, and as he was watching me narrowly, it seemed safer to wait. A little over-precipitance may ruin all."

"And now?" I asked.

"Our quest is practically finished. I shall call with the King tomorrow, and with you, if you care to come with us. We will be shown into the sitting-room to wait for the lady, but it is probable that when she comes she may find neither us nor the photograph. It might be a satisfaction to his Majesty to regain it with his own hands."

"And when will you call?"

"At eight in the morning. She will not be up, so that we shall have a clear field. Besides, we must be prompt, for this marriage may mean a complete change in her life and habits. I must wire to the King without delay."

We had reached Baker Street and had stopped at the door. He was searching his pockets for the key when someone passing said:

"Good night, Mister Sherlock Holmes."

There were several people on the pavement at the time, but the greeting appeared to come from a slim youth in an ulster who had hurried by.

"I've heard that voice before," said Holmes, staring down the dimly lit street. "Now, I wonder who the deuce that could have been."

III

I slept at Baker Street that night, and we were engaged upon our toast and coffee in the morning when the King of Bohemia rushed into the room.

"You have really got it!" he cried, grasping Sherlock Holmes by either shoulder and looking eagerly into his face.

"Not yet."

"But you have hopes?"

"I have hopes."

"Then, come. I am all impatience to be gone."

"We must have a cab."

"No, my brougham is waiting."

"Then that will simplify matters." We descended and started off once more for Briony Lodge.

"Irene Adler is married," remarked Holmes.

"Married! When?"

"Yesterday."

"But to whom?"

"To an English lawyer named Norton."

"But she could not love him."

"I am in hopes that she does."

"And why in hopes?"

"Because it would spare your Majesty all fear of future annoyance. If the lady loves her husband, she does not love your Majesty. If she does not love your Majesty, there is no reason why she should interfere with your Majesty's plan."

"It is true. And yet—! Well! I wish she had been of my own station! What a queen she would have made!" He relapsed into a moody silence, which was not broken until we drew up in Serpentine Avenue.

The door of Briony Lodge was open, and an elderly woman stood upon the steps. She watched us with a sardonic eye as we stepped from the brougham.

"Mr. Sherlock Holmes, I believe?" said she.

"I am Mr. Holmes," answered my companion, looking at her with a questioning and rather startled gaze.

"Indeed! My mistress told me that you were likely to call. She left this morning with her husband by the 5:15 train from Charing Cross for the Continent."

"What!" Sherlock Holmes staggered back, white with chagrin and surprise. "Do you mean that she has left England?"

"Never to return."

"And the papers?" asked the King hoarsely. "All is lost."

"We shall see." He pushed past the servant and rushed into the drawing-room, followed by the King and myself. The furniture was scattered about in every direction, with dismantled shelves and open drawers, as if the lady had hurriedly ransacked them before her flight. Holmes rushed at the bell-pull, tore back a small sliding shutter, and, plunging in his hand, pulled out a photograph and a letter. The photograph was of Irene Adler herself in evening dress, the letter was superscribed to "Sherlock Holmes, Esq. To be left till called for." My friend tore it open, and we all three read it together. It was dated at midnight of the preceding night and ran in this way:

"MY DEAR MR. SHERLOCK HOLMES—You really did it very well. You took me in completely. Until after the alarm of fire, I had not a suspicion. But then, when I found how I had betrayed myself, I began to think. I had been warned against you months ago. I had been told that, if the King employed an agent, it would certainly be you. And your address had been given me. Yet, with all this, you made me reveal what you wanted to know. Even after I became suspicious, I found it hard to think evil of such a dear, kind old clergyman. But, you know, I have been trained as an actress myself. Male costume is nothing new to me. I often take advantage of the freedom which it gives. I sent John, the coachman, to watch you, ran upstairs, got into my walking clothes, as I call them, and came down just as you departed.

"Well, I followed you to your door, and so made sure that I was really an object of interest to the celebrated Mr. Sherlock Holmes. Then I, rather imprudently, wished you good night, and started for the Temple to see my husband.

"We both thought the best resource was flight, when pursued by so formidable an antagonist; so you will find the nest empty when you call tomorrow. As to the photograph, your client may rest in peace. I love and am loved by a better man than he. The King may do what he will without hindrance from one whom he has cruelly wronged. I keep it only to safeguard myself, and to preserve a weapon which will always secure me from any steps which he might take in the future. I leave a photograph which he might care to possess; and I remain, dear Mr. Sherlock Holmes,

"Very truly yours,
"IRENE NORTON, *née* ADLER."

"What a woman—oh, what a woman!" cried the King of Bohemia, when we had all three read this epistle. "Did I not tell you how quick and resolute she was? Would she not have made an admirable queen? Is it not a pity that she was not on my level?"

"From what I have seen of the lady, she seems, indeed, to be on a very different level to your Majesty," said Holmes coldly. "I am sorry that I have not been able to bring your Majesty's business to a more successful conclusion."

"On the contrary, my dear sir," cried the King; "nothing could be more successful. I know that her word is inviolate. The photograph is now as safe as if it were in the fire."

"I am glad to hear your Majesty say so."

"I am immensely indebted to you. Pray tell me in what way I can reward you. This ring—" He slipped an emerald snake ring from his finger and held it out upon the palm of his hand.

"Your Majesty has something which I should value even more highly," said Holmes.

"You have but to name it."

"This photograph!"

The King stared at him in amazement.

"Irene's photograph!" he cried. "Certainly, if you wish it."

"I thank your Majesty. Then there is no more to be done in the matter. I have the honour to wish you a very good morning." He bowed, and, turning away without observing the hand which the King had stretched out to him, he set off in my company for his chambers.

And that was how a great scandal threatened to affect the kingdom of Bohemia, and how the best plans of Mr. Sherlock Holmes were beaten by a woman's wit. He used to make merry over the cleverness of women, but I have not heard him do it of late. And when he speaks of Irene Adler, or when he refers to her photograph, it is always under the honourable title of *the* woman.

The Yellow Wallpaper

Charlotte Perkins Gilman

Charlotte Perkins Gilman (1860-1935) was an influential American feminist, lecturer and short story writer who played a significant role in the women's movement in the United States. She argued for women's economic independence and challenged the limiting role of motherhood and womanhood that was prescribed for women by society. Moreover, her stories such as 'The Yellow Wallpaper' (1892), stress on the importance of mental health and the problems that plague women in a patriarchal society.

It is very seldom that mere ordinary people like John and myself secure ancestral halls for the summer.

A colonial mansion, a hereditary estate, I would say a haunted house, and reach the height of romantic felicity—but that would be asking too much of fate!

Still I will proudly declare that there is something queer about it.

Else, why should it be let so cheaply? And why have stood so long untenanted?

John laughs at me, of course, but one expects that in marriage.

John is practical in the extreme. He has no patience with faith, an intense horror of superstition, and he scoffs openly at any talk of things not to be felt and seen and put down in figures.

John is a physician, and *perhaps*—(I would not say it to a living soul, of course, but this is dead paper and a great relief to my mind)—perhaps that is one reason I do not get well faster.

You see, he does not believe I am sick!

And what can one do?

If a physician of high standing, and one's own husband, assures friends and relatives that there is really nothing the matter with one but temporary nervous depression—a slight hysterical tendency—what is one to do?

My brother is also a physician, and also of high standing, and he says the same thing.

So I take phosphates or phosphites—whichever it is, and tonics, and journeys, and air, and exercise, and am absolutely forbidden to "work" until I am well again.

Personally, I disagree with their ideas.

Personally, I believe that congenial work, with excitement and change, would do me good.

But what is one to do?

I did write for a while in spite of them; but it *does* exhaust me a good deal—having to be so sly about it, or else meet with heavy opposition.

I sometimes fancy that in my condition if I had less opposition and more society and stimulus—but John says the very worst thing I can do is to think about my condition, and I confess it always makes me feel bad.

So I will let it alone and talk about the house.

The most beautiful place! It is quite alone, standing well back from the road, quite three miles from the village. It makes me think of English places that you read about, for there are hedges and walls and gates that lock, and lots of separate little houses for the gardeners and people.

There is a *delicious* garden! I never saw such a garden—large and shady, full of box-bordered paths, and lined with long grape-covered arbors with seats under them.

There were greenhouses, too, but they are all broken now.

There was some legal trouble, I believe, something about the heirs and co-heirs; anyhow, the place has been empty for years.

That spoils my ghostliness, I am afraid; but I don't care—there is something strange about the house—I can feel it.

I even said so to John one moonlight evening, but he said what I felt was a draught, and shut the window.

I get unreasonably angry with John sometimes. I'm sure I never used to be so sensitive. I think it is due to this nervous condition.

But John says if I feel so I shall neglect proper self-control; so I take pains to control myself—before him, at least—and that makes me very tired.

I don't like our room a bit. I wanted one downstairs that opened on the piazza and had roses all over the window, and such pretty old-fashioned chintz hangings! But John would not hear of it.

He said there was only one window and not room for two beds, and no near room for him if he took another.

He is very careful and loving, and hardly lets me stir without special direction.

I have a schedule prescription for each hour in the day; he takes all care from me, and so I feel basely ungrateful not to value it more.

He said we came here solely on my account, that I was to have perfect rest and all the air I could get. "Your exercise depends on your strength, my dear," said he, "and your food somewhat on your appetite; but air you can absorb all the time." So we took the nursery, at the top of the house.

It is a big, airy room, the whole floor nearly, with windows that look all ways, and air and sunshine galore. It was nursery first and then playground and gymnasium, I should judge; for the windows are barred for little children, and there are rings and things in the walls.

The paint and paper look as if a boys' school had used it. It is stripped off—the paper—in great patches all around the head of my bed, about as far as I can reach, and in a great place on the other side of the room low down. I never saw a worse paper in my life.

One of those sprawling flamboyant patterns committing every artistic sin.

It is dull enough to confuse the eye in following, pronounced enough to constantly irritate, and provoke study, and when you follow the lame, uncertain curves for a little distance they suddenly commit suicide—plunge off at outrageous angles, destroy themselves in unheard-of contradictions.

The color is repellant, almost revolting; a smouldering, unclean yellow, strangely faded by the slow-turning sunlight.

It is a dull yet lurid orange in some places, a sickly sulphur tint in others.

No wonder the children hated it! I should hate it myself if I had to live in this room long.

There comes John, and I must put this away—he hates to have me write a word.

We have been here two weeks, and I haven't felt like writing before, since that first day.

I am sitting by the window now, up in this atrocious nursery, and there is nothing to hinder my writing as much as I please, save lack of strength.

John is away all day, and even some nights when his cases are serious.

I am glad my case is not serious!

But these nervous troubles are dreadfully depressing.

John does not know how much I really suffer. He knows there is no *reason* to suffer, and that satisfies him.

Of course it is only nervousness. It does weigh on me so not to do my duty in any way!

I meant to be such a help to John, such a real rest and comfort, and here I am a comparative burden already!

Nobody would believe what an effort it is to do what little I am able—to dress and entertain, and order things.

It is fortunate Mary is so good with the baby. Such a dear baby!

And yet I *cannot* be with him, it makes me so nervous.

I suppose John never was nervous in his life. He laughs at me so about this wallpaper!

At first he meant to repaper the room, but afterwards he said that I was letting it get the better of me, and that nothing was worse for a nervous patient than to give way to such fancies.

He said that after the wallpaper was changed it would be the heavy bedstead, and then the barred windows, and then that gate at the head of the stairs, and so on.

"You know the place is doing you good," he said, "and really, dear, I don't care to renovate the house just for a three months' rental."

"Then do let us go downstairs," I said, "there are such pretty rooms there."

Then he took me in his arms and called me a blessed little goose, and said he would go down cellar if I wished, and have it whitewashed into the bargain.

But he is right enough about the beds and windows and things.

It is as airy and comfortable a room as any one need wish, and, of course, I would not be so silly as to make him uncomfortable just for a whim.

I'm really getting quite fond of the big room, all but that horrid paper.

Out of one window I can see the garden, those mysterious deep-shaded arbors, the riotous old-fashioned flowers, and bushes and gnarly trees.

Out of another I get a lovely view of the bay and a little private wharf belonging to the estate. There is a beautiful shaded lane that runs down there from the house. I always fancy I see people walking in these numerous paths and arbors, but John has cautioned me not to give way to fancy in the least. He says that with my imaginative power and habit of story-making a nervous weakness like mine is sure to lead to all manner of excited fancies, and that I ought to use my will and good sense to check the tendency. So I try.

I think sometimes that if I were only well enough to write a little it would relieve the press of ideas and rest me.

But I find I get pretty tired when I try.

It is so discouraging not to have any advice and companionship about my work. When I get really well John says we will ask Cousin Henry and Julia down for a long visit; but he says he would as soon put fireworks in my pillow-case as to let me have those stimulating people about now.

I wish I could get well faster.

But I must not think about that. This paper looks to me as if it *knew* what a vicious influence it had!

There is a recurrent spot where the pattern lolls like a broken neck and two bulbous eyes stare at you upside-down.

I get positively angry with the impertinence of it and the everlastingness. Up and down and sideways they crawl, and those absurd, unblinking eyes are everywhere. There is one place where two breadths didn't match, and the eyes go all up and down the line, one a little higher than the other.

I never saw so much expression in an inanimate thing before, and we all know how much expression they have! I used to lie awake as a child and get more entertainment and terror out of blank walls and plain furniture than most children could find in a toy-store.

I remember what a kindly wink the knobs of our big old bureau used to have, and there was one chair that always seemed like a strong friend.

I used to feel that if any of the other things looked too fierce I could always hop into that chair and be safe.

The furniture in this room is no worse than inharmonious, however, for we had to bring it all from downstairs. I suppose when this was used as a playroom they had to take the nursery things out, and no wonder! I never saw such ravages as the children have made here.

The wallpaper, as I said before, is torn off in spots, and it sticketh closer than a brother—they must have had perseverance as well as hatred.

Then the floor is scratched and gouged and splintered, the plaster itself is dug out here and there, and this great heavy bed, which is all we found in the room, looks as if it had been through the wars.

But I don't mind it a bit—only the paper.

There comes John's sister. Such a dear girl as she is, and so careful of me! I must not let her find me writing.

She is a perfect, and enthusiastic housekeeper, and hopes for no better profession. I verily believe she thinks it is the writing which made me sick!

But I can write when she is out, and see her a long way off from these windows.

There is one that commands the road, a lovely, shaded, winding road, and one that just looks off over the country. A lovely country, too, full of great elms and velvet meadows.

This wallpaper has a kind of sub-pattern in a different shade, a particularly irritating one, for you can only see it in certain lights, and not clearly then.

But in the places where it isn't faded, and where the sun is just so, I can see a strange, provoking, formless sort of figure, that seems to sulk about behind that silly and conspicuous front design.

There's sister on the stairs!

Well, the Fourth of July is over! The people are gone and I am tired out. John thought it might do me good to see a little company, so we just had mother and Nellie and the children down for a week.

Of course I didn't do a thing. Jennie sees to everything now.

But it tired me all the same.

John says if I don't pick up faster he shall send me to Weir Mitchell in the fall.

But I don't want to go there at all. I had a friend who was in his hands once, and she says he is just like John and my brother, only more so!

Besides, it is such an undertaking to go so far.

I don't feel as if it was worth while to turn my hand over for anything, and I'm getting dreadfully fretful and querulous.

I cry at nothing, and cry most of the time.

Of course I don't when John is here, or anybody else, but when I am alone.

And I am alone a good deal just now. John is kept in town very often by serious cases, and Jennie is good and lets me alone when I want her to.

So I walk a little in the garden or down that lovely lane, sit on the porch under the roses, and lie down up here a good deal.

I'm getting really fond of the room in spite of the wallpaper. Perhaps *because* of the wallpaper.

It dwells in my mind so!

I lie here on this great immovable bed—it is nailed down, I believe—and follow that pattern about by the hour. It is as good as gymnastics, I assure you. I start, we'll say, at the bottom, down in the corner over there where it has not been touched, and I determine for the thousandth time that I *will* follow that pointless pattern to some sort of a conclusion.

I know a little of the principle of design, and I know this thing was not arranged on any laws of radiation, or alternation, or repetition, or symmetry, or anything else that I ever heard of.

It is repeated, of course, by the breadths, but not otherwise.

Looked at in one way each breadth stands alone, the bloated curves and flourishes—a kind of "debased Romanesque" with *delirium tremens*—go waddling up and down in isolated columns of fatuity.

But, on the other hand, they connect diagonally, and the sprawling outlines run off in great slanting waves of optic horror, like a lot of wallowing seaweeds in full chase.

The whole thing goes horizontally, too, at least it seems so, and I exhaust myself in trying to distinguish the order of its going in that direction.

They have used a horizontal breadth for a frieze, and that adds wonderfully to the confusion.

There is one end of the room where it is almost intact, and there, when the cross-lights fade and the low sun shines directly upon it, I can almost fancy radiation after all—the interminable grotesques seem to form around a common centre and rush off in headlong plunges of equal distraction.

It makes me tired to follow it. I will take a nap, I guess.

I don't know why I should write this.

I don't want to.

I don't feel able.

And I know John would think it absurd. But I *must* say what I feel and think in some way—it is such a relief!

But the effort is getting to be greater than the relief.

Half the time now I am awfully lazy, and lie down ever so much.

John says I musn't lose my strength, and has me take cod-liver oil and lots of tonics and things, to say nothing of ale and wine and rare meat.

Dear John! He loves me very dearly, and hates to have me sick. I tried to have a real earnest reasonable talk with him the other day, and tell him how I wish he would let me go and make a visit to Cousin Henry and Julia.

But he said I wasn't able to go, nor able to stand it after I got there; and I did not make out a very good case for myself, for I was crying before I had finished.

It is getting to be a great effort for me to think straight. Just this nervous weakness, I suppose.

And dear John gathered me up in his arms, and just carried me upstairs and laid me on the bed, and sat by me and read to me till it tired my head.

He said I was his darling and his comfort and all he had, and that I must take care of myself for his sake, and keep well.

He says no one but myself can help me out of it, that I must use my will and self-control and not let any silly fancies run away with me.

There's one comfort, the baby is well and happy, and does not have to occupy this nursery with the horrid wallpaper.

If we had not used it that blessed child would have! What a fortunate escape! Why, I wouldn't have a child of mine, an impressionable little thing, live in such a room for worlds.

I never thought of it before, but it is lucky that John kept me here after all. I can stand it so much easier than a baby, you see.

Of course I never mention it to them any more—I am too wise—but I keep watch of it all the same.

There are things in that paper that nobody knows but me, or ever will.

Behind that outside pattern the dim shapes get clearer every day.

It is always the same shape, only very numerous.

And it is like a woman stooping down and creeping about behind that pattern. I don't like it a bit. I wonder—I begin to think—I wish John would take me away from here!

It is so hard to talk with John about my case, because he is so wise, and because he loves me so.

But I tried it last night.

It was moonlight. The moon shines in all around, just as the sun does.

I hate to see it sometimes, it creeps so slowly, and always comes in by one window or another.

John was asleep and I hated to waken him, so I kept still and watched the moonlight on that undulating wallpaper till I felt creepy.

The faint figure behind seemed to shake the pattern, just as if she wanted to get out.

I got up softly and went to feel and see if the paper *did* move, and when I came back John was awake.

"What is it, little girl?" he said. "Don't go walking about like that—you'll get cold."

I though it was a good time to talk, so I told him that I really was not gaining here, and that I wished he would take me away.

"Why darling!" said he, "our lease will be up in three weeks, and I can't see how to leave before.

"The repairs are not done at home, and I cannot possibly leave town just now. Of course if you were in any danger I could and would, but you really are better, dear, whether you can see it or not. I am a doctor, dear, and I know. You are gaining flesh and color, your appetite is better. I feel really much easier about you."

"I don't weigh a bit more," said I, "nor as much; and my appetite may be better in the evening, when you are here, but it is worse in the morning when you are away."

"Bless her little heart!" said he with a big hug; "she shall be as sick as she pleases! But now let's improve the shining hours by going to sleep, and talk about it in the morning!"

"And you won't go away?" I asked gloomily.

"Why, how can I, dear? It is only three weeks more and then we will take a nice little trip of a few days while Jennie is getting the house ready. Really, dear, you are better!"

"Better in body perhaps"—I began, and stopped short, for he sat up straight and looked at me with such a stern, reproachful look that I could not say another word.

"My darling," said he, "I beg of you, for my sake and for our child's sake, as well as for your own, that you will never for one instant let that idea enter your mind! There is nothing so dangerous, so fascinating, to a temperament like yours. It is a false and foolish fancy. Can you not trust me as a physician when I tell you so?"

So of course I said no more on that score, and we went to sleep before long. He thought I was asleep first, but I wasn't—I lay there for hours trying to decide whether that front pattern and the back pattern really did move together or separately.

On a pattern like this, by daylight, there is a lack of sequence, a defiance of law, that is a constant irritant to a normal mind.

The color is hideous enough, and unreliable enough, and infuriating enough, but the pattern is torturing.

You think you have mastered it, but just as you get well under way in following, it turns a back somersault and there you are. It slaps you in the face, knocks you down, and tramples upon you. It is like a bad dream.

The outside pattern is a florid arabesque, reminding one of a fungus. If you can imagine a toadstool in joints, an interminable string of toadstools, budding and sprouting in endless convolutions—why, that is something like it.

That is, sometimes!

There is one marked peculiarity about this paper, a thing nobody seems to notice but myself, and that is that it changes as the light changes.

When the sun shoots in through the east window—I always watch for that first long, straight ray—it changes so quickly that I never can quite believe it.

That is why I watch it always.

By moonlight—the moon shines in all night when there is a moon—I wouldn't know it was the same paper.

At night in any kind of light, in twilight, candlelight, lamplight, and worst of all by moonlight, it becomes bars! The outside pattern I mean, and the woman behind it is as plain as can be.

I didn't realize for a long time what the thing was that showed behind—that dim sub-pattern—but now I am quite sure it is a woman.

By daylight she is subdued, quiet. I fancy it is the pattern that keeps her so still. It is so puzzling. It keeps me quiet by the hour.

I lie down ever so much now. John says it is good for me, and to sleep all I can.

Indeed, he started the habit by making me lie down for an hour after each meal.

It is a very bad habit, I am convinced, for, you see, I don't sleep.

And that cultivates deceit, for I don't tell them I'm awake—oh, no!

The fact is, I am getting a little afraid of John.

He seems very queer sometimes, and even Jennie has an inexplicable look.

It strikes me occasionally, just as a scientific hypothesis, that perhaps it is the paper!

I have watched John when he did not know I was looking, and come into the room suddenly on the most innocent excuses, and I've caught him several times *looking at the paper!* And Jennie too. I caught Jennie with her hand on it once.

She didn't know I was in the room, and when I asked her in a quiet, a very quiet voice, with the most restrained manner possible, what she was doing with the paper she turned around as if she had been caught stealing, and looked quite angry—asked me why I should frighten her so!

Then she said that the paper stained everything it touched, that she had found yellow smooches on all my clothes and John's, and she wished we would be more careful!

Did not that sound innocent? But I know she was studying that pattern, and I am determined that nobody shall find it out but myself!

Life is very much more exciting now than it used to be. You see I have something more to expect, to look forward to, to watch. I really do eat better, and am more quiet than I was.

John is so pleased to see me improve! He laughed a little the other day, and said I seemed to be flourishing in spite of my wallpaper.

I turned it off with a laugh. I had no intention of telling him it was *because* of the wallpaper—he would make fun of me. He might even want to take me away.

I don't want to leave now until I have found it out. There is a week more, and I think that will be enough.

I'm feeling ever so much better! I don't sleep much at night, for it is so interesting to watch developments; but I sleep a good deal in the daytime.

In the daytime it is tiresome and perplexing.

There are always new shoots on the fungus, and new shades of yellow all over it. I cannot keep count of them, though I have tried conscientiously.

It is the strangest yellow, that wallpaper! It makes me think of all the yellow things I ever saw—not beautiful ones like buttercups, but old foul, bad yellow things.

But there is something else about that paper—the smell! I noticed it the moment we came into the room, but with so much air and sun it was not bad. Now we have had a week of fog and rain, and whether the windows are open or not, the smell is here.

It creeps all over the house.

I find it hovering in the dining-room, skulking in the parlor, hiding in the hall, lying in wait for me on the stairs.

It gets into my hair.

Even when I go to ride, if I turn my head suddenly and surprise it—there is that smell!

Such a peculiar odor, too! I have spent hours in trying to analyze it, to find what it smelled like.

It is not bad—at first, and very gentle, but quite the subtlest, most enduring odor I ever met.

In this damp weather it is awful. I wake up in the night and find it hanging over me.

It used to disturb me at first. I thought seriously of burning the house—to reach the smell.

But now I am used to it. The only thing I can think of that it is like is the *color* of the paper! A yellow smell.

There is a very funny mark on this wall, low down, near the mopboard. A streak that runs round the room. It goes behind every piece of furniture, except the bed, a long, straight, even *smooch*, as if it had been rubbed over and over.

I wonder how it was done and who did it, and what they did it for. Round and round and round—round and round and round—it makes me dizzy!

I really have discovered something at last.

Through watching so much at night, when it changes so, I have finally found out.

The front pattern *does* move—and no wonder! The woman behind shakes it!

Sometimes I think there are a great many women behind, and sometimes only one, and she crawls around fast, and her crawling shakes it all over.

Then in the very bright spots she keeps still, and in the very shady spots she just takes hold of the bars and shakes them hard.

And she is all the time trying to climb through. But nobody could climb through that pattern—it strangles so; I think that is why it has so many heads.

They get through, and then the pattern strangles them off and turns them upside-down, and makes their eyes white!

If those heads were covered or taken off it would not be half so bad.

I think that woman gets out in the daytime!

And I'll tell you why—privately—I've seen her!

I can see her out of every one of my windows!

It is the same woman, I know, for she is always creeping, and most women do not creep by daylight.

I see her on that long shaded lane, creeping up and down. I see her in those dark grape arbors, creeping all around the garden.

I see her on that long road under the trees, creeping along, and when a carriage comes she hides under the blackberry vines.

I don't blame her a bit. It must be very humiliating to be caught creeping by daylight!

I always lock the door when I creep by daylight. I can't do it at night, for I know John would suspect something at once.

And John is so queer now, that I don't want to irritate him. I wish he would take another room! Besides, I don't want anybody to get that woman out at night but myself.

I often wonder if I could see her out of all the windows at once.

But, turn as fast as I can, I can only see out of one at one time.

And though I always see her she *may* be able to creep faster than I can turn!

I have watched her sometimes away off in the open country, creeping as fast as a cloud shadow in a high wind.

If only that top pattern could be gotten off from the under one! I mean to try it, little by little.

I have found out another funny thing, but I shan't tell it this time! It does not do to trust people too much.

There are only two more days to get this paper off, and I believe John is beginning to notice. I don't like the look in his eyes.

And I heard him ask Jennie a lot of professional questions about me. She had a very good report to give.

She said I slept a good deal in the daytime.

John knows I don't sleep very well at night, for all I'm so quiet!

He asked me all sorts of questions, too, and pretended to be very loving and kind.

As if I couldn't see through him!

Still, I don't wonder he acts so, sleeping under this paper for three months.

It only interests me, but I feel sure John and Jennie are secretly affected by it.

Hurrah! This is the last day, but it is enough. John is to stay in town over night, and won't be out until this evening.

Jennie wanted to sleep with me—the sly thing! But I told her I should undoubtedly rest better for a night all alone.

That was clever, for really I wasn't alone a bit! As soon as it was moonlight, and that poor thing began to crawl and shake the pattern, I got up and ran to help her.

I pulled and she shook, I shook and she pulled, and before morning we had peeled off yards of that paper.

A strip about as high as my head and half around the room.

And then when the sun came and that awful pattern began to laugh at me I declared I would finish it today!

We go away tomorrow, and they are moving all my furniture down again to leave things as they were before.

Jennie looked at the wall in amazement, but I told her merrily that I did it out of pure spite at the vicious thing.

She laughed and said she wouldn't mind doing it herself, but I must not get tired.

How she betrayed herself that time!

But I am here, and no person touches this paper but me—not *alive!*

She tried to get me out of the room—it was too patent! But I said it was so quiet and empty and clean now that I believed I would lie down again and sleep all I could; and not to wake me even for dinner—I would call when I woke.

So now she is gone, and the servants are gone, and the things are gone, and there is nothing left but that great bedstead nailed down, with the canvas mattress we found on it.

We shall sleep downstairs tonight, and take the boat home tomorrow.

I quite enjoy the room, now it is bare again.

How those children did tear about here!

This bedstead is fairly gnawed!

But I must get to work.

I have locked the door and thrown the key down into the front path.

I don't want to go out, and I don't want to have anybody come in, till John comes.

I want to astonish him.

I've got a rope up here that even Jennie did not find. If that woman does get out, and tries to get away, I can tie her!

But I forgot I could not reach far without anything to stand on!

This bed will *not* move!

I tried to lift and push it until I was lame, and then I got so angry I bit off a little piece at one corner—but it hurt my teeth.

Then I peeled off all the paper I could reach standing on the floor. It sticks horribly and the pattern just enjoys it! All those strangled heads and bulbous eyes and waddling fungus growths just shriek with derision!

I am getting angry enough to do something desperate. To jump out of the window would be admirable exercise, but the bars are too strong even to try.

Besides I wouldn't do it. Of course not. I know well enough that a step like that is improper and might be misconstrued.

I don't like to *look* out of the windows even—there are so many of those creeping women, and they creep so fast.

I wonder if they all come out of that wallpaper as I did?

But I am securely fastened now by my well-hidden rope—you don't get *me* out in the road there!

I suppose I shall have to get back behind the pattern when it comes night, and that is hard!

It is so pleasant to be out in this great room and creep around as I please!

I don't want to go outside. I won't, even if Jennie asks me to.

For outside you have to creep on the ground, and everything is green instead of yellow.

But here I can creep smoothly on the floor, and my shoulder just fits in that long smooch around the wall, so I cannot lose my way.

Why, there's John at the door!

It is no use, young man, you can't open it!

How he does call and pound!

Now he's crying for an axe.

It would be a shame to break down that beautiful door!

"John dear!" said I in the gentlest voice, "the key is down by the front steps, under a plantain leaf!"

That silenced him for a few moments.

Then he said—very quietly indeed, "Open the door, my darling!"

"I can't," said I. "The key is down by the front door under a plantain leaf!"

And then I said it again, several times, very gently and slowly, and said it so often that he had to go and see, and he got it, of course, and came in. He stopped short by the door.

"What is the matter?" he cried. "For God's sake, what are you doing!"

I kept on creeping just the same, but I looked at him over my shoulder.

"I've got out at last," said I, "in spite of you and Jane! And I've pulled off most of the paper, so you can't put me back!"

Now why should that man have fainted? But he did, and right across my path by the wall, so that I had to creep over him every time!

The Woman's Rose

Olive Schreiner

Olive Schreiner (1855-1920) was a prominent South African writer and feminist who wrote the first great South African novel *The Story of an African Farm* (1883), which was semi-autobiographical in nature. Writing under the pseudonym Ralph Iron, she was popular for her feminist, liberal and often anti-Christian views. 'The Woman's Rose' (1893) is also feminist in its approach.

I have an old, brown carved box; the lid is broken and tied with a string. In it I keep little squares of paper, with hair inside, and a little picture which hung over my brother's bed when we were children, and other things as small. I have in it a rose. Other women also have such boxes where they keep such trifles, but no one has my rose.

When my eye is dim, and my heart grows faint, and my faith in woman flickers, and her present is an agony to me, and her future a despair, the scent of that dead rose, withered for twelve years, comes back to me. I know there will be spring; as surely as the birds know it when they see above the snow two tiny, quivering green leaves. Spring cannot fail us.

There were other flowers in the box once; a bunch of white acacia flowers, gathered by the strong hand of a man, as we passed down a village street on a sultry afternoon, when it had rained, and the drops fell on us from the leaves of the acacia trees. The flowers were damp; they made mildew marks on the paper I folded them in. After many years I threw them away. There is nothing of them left in the box now, but a faint, strong smell of dried acacia, that recalls that sultry summer afternoon; but the rose is in the box still.

It is many years ago now; I was a girl of fifteen, and I went to visit in a small up-country town. It was young in those days, and two days' journey from the nearest village; the population consisted mainly of men. A few were married, and had their wives and children, but most were single. There was only one young girl there when I came. She was about seventeen, fair, and rather fully-fleshed; she had large dreamy blue eyes, and wavy light hair; full, rather heavy lips, until she smiled; then her face broke into dimples, and all her white teeth shone. The hotel-keeper may have had a daughter, and the farmer in the outskirts had two, but we never saw them. She reigned alone. All the men worshipped her. She was the only woman they had to think of. They talked of her on the stoep, at the market, at the hotel; they watched for her at street corners; they hated the man she bowed to or walked with down the street. They brought flowers to the front door; they offered her their horses; they begged her to marry them when they dared. Partly, there was something noble and heroic in this devotion of men to the best woman they knew; partly there was something natural in it, that these men, shut off from the world, should pour at the feet of one woman the worship that otherwise would have been given to twenty; and partly there was something mean in their envy of one another. If she had raised her little finger, I suppose, she might have married any one out of twenty of them.

Then I came. I do not think I was prettier; I do not think I was so pretty as she was. I was certainly not as handsome. But I was vital, and I was new, and she was old—they all forsook her and followed me. They worshipped me. It was to my door that the flowers came; it was I had twenty horses offered me when I could only ride one; it was for me they waited at street corners; it was what I said and did that they talked of. Partly I liked it. I had lived alone all my life; no one ever had told me I was beautiful and a woman. I believed them. I did not know it was simply a fashion, which one man had set and the rest followed unreasoningly. I liked them to ask me to marry them, and to say, No. I despised them. The mother heart had not swelled in me yet; I did not know all men were my children, as the large woman knows when her heart is grown. I was too small to be tender. I liked my power. I was like a child with a new whip, which it goes about cracking everywhere, not caring against what.

I could not wind it up and put it away. Men were curious creatures, who liked me, I could never tell why. Only one thing took from my pleasure; I could not bear that they had deserted her for me. I liked her great dreamy blue eyes, I liked her slow walk and drawl; when I saw her sitting among men, she seemed to me much too good to be among them; I would have given all their compliments if she would once have smiled at me as she smiled at them, with all her face breaking into radiance, with her dimples and flashing teeth. But I knew it never could be; I felt sure she hated me; that she wished I was dead; that she wished I had never come to the village. She did not know, when we went out riding, and a man who had always ridden beside her came to ride beside me, that I sent him away; that once when a man thought to win my favour by ridiculing her slow drawl before me I turned on him so fiercely that he never dared come before me again. I knew she knew that at the hotel men had made a bet as to which was the prettier, she or I, and had asked each man who came in, and that the one who had staked on me won. I hated them for it, but I would not let her see that I cared about what she felt towards me.

She and I never spoke to each other.

If we met in the village street we bowed and passed on; when we shook hands we did so silently, and did not look at each other. But I thought she felt my presence in a room just as I felt hers.

At last the time for my going came. I was to leave the next day. Some one I knew gave a party in my honour, to which all the village was invited.

It was midwinter. There was nothing in the gardens but a few dahlias and chrysanthemums, and I suppose that for two hundred miles round there was not a rose to be bought for love or money. Only in the garden of a friend of mine, in a sunny corner between the oven and the brick wall, there was a rose tree growing which had on it one bud. It was white, and it had been promised to the fair haired girl to wear at the party.

The evening came; when I arrived and went to the waiting-room, to take off my mantle, I found the girl there already. She was dressed in pure white, with her great white arms and shoulders showing, and her bright hair glittering in the candle-light, and the white rose fastened at her breast. She looked like a queen. I said "Good evening," and turned away quickly to the glass to arrange my old black scarf across my old black dress.

Then I felt a hand touch my hair.

"Stand still," she said.

I looked in the glass. She had taken the white rose from her breast, and was fastening it in my hair.

"How nice dark hair is; it sets off flowers so." She stepped back and looked at me. "It looks much better there!"

I turned round.

"You are so beautiful to me," I said.

"Y-e-s," she said, with her slow Colonial drawl; "I'm so glad."

We stood looking at each other.

Then they came in and swept us away to dance. All the evening we did not come near to each other. Only once, as she passed, she smiled at me.

The next morning I left the town.

I never saw her again.

Years afterwards I heard she had married and gone to America; it may or may not be so—but the rose—the rose is in the box still! When my faith in woman grows dim, and it seems that for want of love and magnanimity she can play no part in any future heaven; then the scent of that small withered thing comes back:—spring cannot fail us.

Matjesfontein, South Africa.

A Story Of A Wedding Tour

Margaret Oliphant

Margaret Oliphant (1828-1897) was a Scottish novelist, biographer and historian. A prolific writer, she authored over 100 books, often humorous portrayals of the lives of small town people. In an era marked by scant respect for women writers as professionals, she supported her own and her brother's children by writing. 'A Story Of A Wedding Tour' was first published in 1894.

I

They had been married exactly a week when this incident occurred.

It was not a love marriage. The man, indeed, had been universally described as "very much in love," but the girl was not by any one supposed to be in that desirable condition. She was a very lonely little girl, without parents, almost without relations. Her guardian was a man who had been engaged in business relations with her father, and who had accepted the charge of the little orphan as his duty. But neither he nor his wife had any love to expend upon her, and they did not feel that such visionary sentiments came within the line of duty. He was a very honourable man, and took charge of her small…very small…property with unimpeachable care.

If anything, he wronged himself rather than Janey, charging her nothing for the transfers which he made of her farthing's worth of stock from time to time, to get a scarcely appreciable rise of interest and income for her. The whole thing was scarcely appreciable, and to a large-handed man like Mr Midhurst, dealing with hundreds of thousands, it was almost ridiculous to give a moment's attention to what a few hundreds might produce. But he did so; and if there is any angel who has to do with trade affairs, I hope it was carefully put to his account to balance some of the occasions on which he was not perhaps so particular. Nor did Mrs Midhurst shrink from her duty in all substantial and real good offices to the girl. She, who spent hundreds at the dressmaker's every year on account of her many daughters, did not disdain to get Janey's serge frocks at a cheaper shop, and to have them made by an inexpensive workwoman, so that the girl should have the very utmost she could get for her poor little money.

Was not this real goodness, real honesty, and devotion to their duty? But to love a little thing like that with no real claim upon them, and nothing that could be called specially attractive about her, who could be expected to do it? They had plenty…almost more than enough…of children of their own. These children were big boys and girls, gradually growing, in relays, into manhood and womanhood, when this child came upon their hands. There was no room for her in the full and noisy house. When she was grown up most of the Midhurst children were married, but there was one son at home, who, in the well-known contradictiousness of young people…it being a very wrong and, indeed, impossible thing…was quite capable of falling in love with Janey…and one daughter, with whom it was also possible that Janey might come into competition.

The young Midhursts were nice-looking young people enough; but Janey was very pretty. If Providence did but fully consider all the circumstances, it cannot but be felt that Providence would not carry out, as often is done, such ridiculous arrangements. Janey was very pretty. Could anything more inconvenient, more inappropriate, be conceived?

The poor little girl had, accordingly, spent most of her life at school, where she had, let it not be doubted, made many friendships and little loves; but these were broken up by holidays, by the returning home of the other pupils, while she stayed for ever at school: and not at one school, but several…for in his extreme conscientiousness her guardian desired to do her "every justice," as he said, and prepare her fully for the life…probably that of a governess…which lay before her.

Therefore, when she had become proficient in one part of her education she was carried on to another, with the highest devotion to her commercial value no doubt, but a sublime indifference to her little feelings. Thus, she had been in France for two years, and in Germany for two years, so as to be able to state that French and German acquired in these countries were among the list of her accomplishments. English, of course, was the foundation of all; and Janey had spent some time at a famous academy of music… her guardian adding something out of his own pocket to her scanty means, that she might be fully equipped for her profession. And then she was brought, I will not say home: Janey fondly said home, but she knew very well it did not mean home. And it was while Mrs Midhurst was actually writing out the advertisement for 'The Times,' and the 'Morning Post,' and 'The Guardian,' which was to announce to all the world that a young lady desired an engagement as governess, that her husband burst in with the extraordinary news that Mr Rosendale, who had chanced to travel with Janey from Flushing, on her return, and who had afterwards, by a still greater chance, met her when asked to lunch at the Midhursts', and stared very much at her, as they all remarked… had fallen in love with, and wanted to marry, this humble little girl.

"Fallen in love with Janey!" Mrs Midhurst cried. "Fallen in love with you, Janey!" said Agnes Midhurst, with a little emphasis on the pronoun. He was not, indeed, quite good enough to have permitted himself the luxury of falling in love with Mr Midhurst's daughter, but he was an astonishing match for Janey. He was a man who was very well off: he could afford himself such a caprice as that. He was not handsome. There was a strain of Jewish blood in him. He was a thick-set little man, and did not dress or talk in perfect taste; but…in love! These two words made all the difference. Nobody had ever loved her, much less been "in love" with her. Janey consented willingly enough for the magic of these two words. She felt that she was going to be like the best of women at last…to have some one who loved her, some one who was in love with her. He might not be "joli, joli," as they say in France. She might not feel any very strong impulse on her own part towards him; but if he was in love with her…in love! Romeo was no more than that with Juliet. The thought went to Janey's head. She married him quite willingly for the sake of this.

I am afraid that Janey, being young, and shy, and strange, was a good deal frightened, horrified, and even revolted, by her first discoveries of what it meant to be in love. She had made tremendous discoveries in the course of a week. She had found out that Mr Rosendale, her husband, was in love with her beauty, but as indifferent to herself as any of the persons she had quitted to give herself to him. He did not care at all what she thought, how she felt, what she liked or disliked. He did not care even for her comfort, or that she should be pleased and happy, which, in the first moment even of such a union, and out of pure self-regard to make a woman more agreeable to himself, a man…even the most brutal… generally regards more or less. He was, perhaps, not aware that he did not regard it. He took it for granted that, being his wife, she would naturally be pleased with what pleased him, and his mind went no further than this.

Therefore, as far as Janey liked the things he liked, all went well enough. She had these, but no other. Her wishes were not consulted further, nor did he know that he failed in any way towards her. He had little to say to her, except expressions of admiration. When he was not telling her that she was a little beauty, or admiring her pretty hair, her pretty eyes, the softness of her skin, and the smallness of her waist, he had nothing to say. He read his paper, disappearing behind it in the morning; he went to sleep after his midday meal (for the weather was warm;) he played billiards in the evening in the hotels to which he took her on their wedding journey; or he overwhelmed her with caresses from which she shrank in disgust, almost in terror. That was all that being in love meant, she found; and to say that she was disappointed cruelly was to express in the very mildest way the dreadful downfall of all her expectations and hopes which happened to Janey before she had been seven days a wife. It is not disagreeable to be told that you are a little beauty, prettier than any one else. Janey would have been very well pleased to put up with that; but to be petted like a little lapdog and then left as a lapdog is… to be quiet and not to trouble in the intervals of petting…was to the poor little girl, unaccustomed to love and athirst for it, who had hoped to be loved, and to find a companion to whom she would be truly dear, a disenchantment and disappointment which was almost more than flesh and blood could bear.

She was in the full bitterness of these discoveries when the strange incident occurred which was of so much importance in her life. They were travelling through France in one of those long night journeys to which we are all accustomed nowadays; and Janey, pale and tired, had been contemplating for some time the figure of her husband thrown back in the corner opposite, snoring complacently with his mouth open, and looking the worst that a middle-aged man can look in the utter abandonment of self-indulgence and rude comfort, when the train began to slacken its speed, and to prepare to enter one of those large stations which look so ghastly in the desertion of the night.

Rosendale jumped up instinctively, only half awake, as the train stopped. The other people in the carriage were leaving it, having attained the end of their journey, but he pushed through them and their baggage to get out, with the impatience which some men show at any pause of the kind, and determination to stretch their legs, or get something to drink, which mark the breaks in the journey. He did not even say anything to Janey as he forced his way out, but she was so familiar with his ways by this time that she took no notice. She did take notice, however when, her fellow-passengers and their packages having all been cleared away, she suddenly became sensible that the train was getting slowly into motion again without any sign of her husband.

She thought she caught a glimpse of him strolling about on the opposite platform before she was quite sure of what was happening. And then there was a scurry of hurrying feet, a slamming of doors, and as she rose and ran to the window bewildered, she saw him, along with some other men, running at full speed, but quite hopelessly, to catch the train. The last she saw was his face, fully revealed by the light of the lamp, convulsed with rage and astonishment, evidently with a yell of denunciation on the lips. Janey trembled at the sight. There was that in him, too, though as yet in her submissiveness she had never called it forth, a temper as unrestrained as his love-making, and as little touched by any thought save that of his own gratification. Her first sensation was fright, a terror that she was in fault and was about to be crushed to pieces in his rage: and then Janey sank back in her corner, and a flood of feeling of quite another kind took possession of her breast.

Was it possible that she was alone? Was it possible that for the first time since that terrible moment of her marriage she was more safely by herself than any locked door or even watchful guardian could keep her, quite unapproachable in the isolation of the train? Alone!

"Safe!" Janey ventured to say to herself, clasping her hands together with a mingled sensation of excitement and terror and tremulous delight which words could not tell.

She did not know what to think at first. The sound of the train plunging along through the darkness, through the unknown country, filled her mind as if some one was talking to her. And she was fluttered by the strangeness of the incident and disturbed by alarms. There was a fearful joy in thus being alone, in having a few hours, perhaps a whole long tranquil night, to herself: whatever came of it, that was always so much gained. But then she seemed to see him in the morning coming in upon her heated and angry. She had always felt that the moment would come when he would be angry, and more terrible to confront than any governess, or even principal of a ladies' college. He would come in furious, accusing her of being the cause of the accident, of doing something to set the train in motion; or else he would come in fatigued and dusty, claiming her services as if she were his valet…a thing which had, more or less, happened already, and against which Janey's pride and her sense of what was fit had risen in arms. She thought of this for a little time with trouble, and of the difficulties she would have in arriving, and where she would go to, and what she would say. It was an absurd story to tell, not to his advantage, "I lost my husband at Montbard." How could she say it? The hotel people would think she was a deceiver. Perhaps they would not take her in. And how would he know where to find her when he arrived? He would feel that he had lost her, as much as she had lost him.

Just as this idea rose in her mind, like a new thing full of strange suggestions, the train began to shorten speed again, and presently stopped once more. She felt it to do so with a pang of horror. No doubt he had climbed up somewhere, at the end or upon the engine, and was now to be restored to his legitimate place, to fall upon her either in fondness or in rage, delighted to get back to her, or angry with her for leaving him behind: she did not know which would be the worst. Her heart began to beat with fright and anticipation. But to her great relief it was only the guard who came to the door. He wanted to know if Madame was the lady whose husband had been left behind; and to offer a hundred apologies and explanations. One of those fools at Montbard had proclaimed twenty minutes' pause when there were but five. If he had but heard he would have put it right, but he was at the other end of the train. But Madame must not be too much distressed; a few hours would put it all right.

"Then there is another train?" said Janey, her poor little head buzzing between excitement and relief.

"Not for some hours," said the guard. "Madame will understand that there is not more than one rapide in the middle of the night; but in the morning quite early there is the train omnibus. Oh, very early, at five o'clock. Before Madame is ready for her dinner monsieur will be at her side."

"Not till evening, then?" said Janey, with again a sudden acceleration of the movement of her heart.

The guard was desolated. "Not before evening. But if Madame will remain quietly in the carriage when the train arrives at the station, I will find the omnibus of the hotel for her…I will see to everything! Madame, no doubt, knows which hotel to go to?"

Janey, as a matter of fact, did not know. Her husband had told her none of the details of the journey; but she said with a quick breath of excitement…

"I will go to the one that is nearest, the one at the Gare. There will be no need, for any omnibus."

"And the baggage? Madame has her ticket?"

"I have nothing," cried Janey, "except my travelling-bag. You must explain that for me. But otherwise…otherwise, I think I can manage."

"Madame speaks French so well," the man said, with admiration. It was, indeed, a piece of good fortune that she had been made to acquire the language in the country: that she was not frightened to find herself in a foreign place, and surrounded by people speaking a strange tongue, as many a young English bride would have been. There was a moment of tremendous excitement and noise at the station while all was explained to a serious chef de Gare, and a gesticulating band of porters and attendants, whose loud voices, as they all spoke together, would have frightened an ordinary English girl out of her wits. But Janey, in the strange excitement which had taken possession of her, and in her fortunate acquaintance with the language, stood still as a little rock amid all the confusion. "I will wait at the hotel till my husband comes," she said, taking out the travelling-bag and her wraps, and maintaining a composure worthy of all admiration. Not a tear, not an outcry. How astonishing are these English, cried the little crowd, with that swift classification which the Frenchman loves.

Janey walked into the hotel with her little belongings, not knowing whether she was indeed walking upon her feet or floating upon wings. She was quite composed. But if any one could only have seen the commotion within that youthful bosom! She locked the door of the little delightful solitary room in which she was placed. It was not delightful at all; but to Janey it was a haven of peace, as sweet, as secluded from everything alarming and terrible, as any bower. Not till evening could he by any possibility arrive... the man who had caused such a revolution in her life. She had some ten hours of divine quiet before her, of blessed solitude, of thought. She did not refuse to take the little meal that was brought to her, the breakfast of which she stood in need; and she was glad to be able to bathe her face, to take off her dusty dress, and put on the soft and fresh one, which, happily, had folded into very small space, and therefore could be put into her bag. Her head still buzzed with the strangeness of the position, yet began to settle a little. When she had made all these little arrangements she sat down to consider. Perhaps you will think there was very little to consider, nothing but how to wait till the next train brought him, which, after all, was not a very great thing to do. Appalling, perhaps, to a little inexperienced bride; but not to Janey, who had travelled alone so often, and knew the language, and all that.

But whoever had been able to look into Janey's mind would have seen that something more was there...a very, very different thing from the question of how best to await his coming back. Oh, if he had loved her, Janey would have put up with many things! She would have schooled herself out of all her private repugnances; she would have been so grateful to him, so touched by the affection which nobody had ever bestowed upon her before! But he did not love her. He cared nothing about herself, Janey; did not even know her, or want to know her, or take into consideration her ways or her wishes. He was in love with her pretty face, her fresh little beauty, her power of pleasing him. If ever that power ceased, which it was sure to do, sooner or later, she would be to him less than nothing, the dreary little wife whom everybody has seen attached to a careless man: Janey felt that this was what was in store for her. She felt the horror of him, and his kind of loving, which had been such a miserable revelation to her. She felt the relief, the happiness, ah, the bliss, of having lost him for a moment, of being alone.

She took out her purse from her pocket, which was full of the change she had got in Paris of one of the ten-pound notes which her guardian had given her when she left his house on her wedding morning. She took out the clumsy pocket-book, an old one, in which there were still nine ten-pound notes. It was all her fortune, except a very, very small investment which brought her in some seven pounds a year. This was the remainder of another small investment which had been withdrawn in order to provide her with her simple trousseau, leaving this sum of a hundred pounds which her guardian had given her, advising her to place it at once for security in her husband's hands. Janey had not done this, she scarcely could tell why. She spread them on the table…the nine notes, the twelve napoleons of shining French money. A hundred pounds: she had still the twelve francs which made up the sum. She had spent nothing. There were even the few coppers over for the agio. She spread them all out, and counted them from right to left, and again from left to right. Nine ten-pound notes, twelve and a-half French napoleons…or louis, as people call them nowadays… making a hundred pounds. A hundred pounds is a large sum in the eyes of a girl. It may not be much to you and me, who know that it means only ten times ten pounds, and that ten pounds goes like the wind as soon as you begin to spend it. But to Janey! Why, she could live upon a hundred pounds for…certainly for two years: for two long delightful years, with nobody to trouble her, nobody to scold, nobody to interfere. Something mounted to her head like the fumes of wine. Everything began to buzz again, to turn round, to sweep her away as on a rapidly mounting current. She put back all the money in the pocket-book…her fortune, the great sum that made her independent; and she put back her things into the bag. A sudden energy of resolution seized her. She put on her hat again, and as she looked at herself in the glass encountered the vision of a little face which was new to her. It was not that of Janey, the little governess-pupil; it was not young Mrs Rosendale. It was full of life, and meaning, and energy, and strength. Who was it? Janey? Janey herself, the real woman, whom nobody had ever seen before.

II

It is astonishing how many things can be done in sudden excitement and passion which could not be possible under any other circumstances. Janey was by nature a shy girl and easily frightened, accustomed indeed to do many things for herself, and to move quietly without attracting observation through the midst of a crowd; but she had never taken any initiative, and since her marriage had been reduced to such a state of complete dependence on her husband's wishes and plans that she had not attempted the smallest step on her own impulse.

Now, however, she moved about with a quiet assurance and decision which astonished herself. She carried her few possessions back again to the railway station, leaving the small gold piece of ten francs to pay, and much overpay, her hour's shelter and entertainment at the hotel.

Nobody noticed her as she went through the bustle of the place and back to the crowded station, where a little leisurely local train was about starting…a slow train occupied by peasants and country folk, and which stopped at every station along the line. English people abound in that place at all hours, except at this particular moment, when the rapide going towards Italy had but newly left and the little country train was preparing in peace. Nobody seemed to notice Janey as she moved about with her bag on her arm. She took her ticket in her irreproachable French "acquired in the country," which attracted no attention. She got into a second-class carriage in which there were already various country people, and especially a young mother with a baby, and its nurse in a white round cap with long streaming ribbons. Janey's heart went out to these people. She wondered if the young woman was happy, if her husband loved her, if it was not very sweet to have a child…a child must love you; it would not mind whether your cheeks were rosy or pale, whether you were pretty or not, whether you had accomplishments or languages acquired in the country.

Looking at this baby, Janey almost forgot that she was going out upon the world alone, and did not know where. It is a tremendous thing to do this, to separate from all the world you are acquainted with, to plunge into the unknown. Men do it often enough, though seldom without some clue, some link of connection with the past and way of return. Janey was about to cut herself off as by the Fury's shears from everything. She would never join her husband again. She would never fear her guardian again. She must drop out of sight like a stone into the sea. There was no longing love to search for her, no pardon to be offered, no one who would be heart-struck at the thought of the little girl lost and unhappy. Only anger would be excited by her running away, and a desire to punish, to shake her little fragile person to pieces, to make her suffer. She knew that if she did it at all, it must be final. But this did not overwhelm her. What troubled Janey a great deal more than the act of severance which she was about to accomplish, was the inevitable fib or fibs she must tell in order to account for her appearance in the unknown. She did not like to tell a fib, even a justifiable one. It was against all her traditions, against her nature. She felt that she could never do it anything but badly, never without exciting suspicions; and she must needs have some story, some way of accounting for herself.

This occupied her mind while the slow train crawled from station to station. It was the most friendly, idle, gossiping little train. It seemed to stop at the merest signal-box to have a talk, to drink as it were a social glass administered through that black hose, with a friend; it stopped wherever there were a few houses, it carried little parcels, it took up a leisurely passenger going next door, and the little electric bell went on tingling, and the guard cried "En voiture!" and the little bugle sounded. Janey was amused by all these little sounds and sights, and the country all flooded with sunshine, and the flowers everywhere, though it was only March, and dark black weather when she had left home.

Left home! And she had no home now, anywhere, no place to take refuge in, nobody to write to, to appeal to, to tell if she was happy or unhappy. But Janey did not care! She felt a strange elation of ease and relief. All alone, but everybody smiling upon her, the young mother opposite beginning to chatter, the baby to crow to her, the nurse to smile and approve of the bonne petite dame who took so much notice of the child. Her head was swimming, but with pleasure, and the blessed sensation of freedom…pleasure tinctured with the exhilaration of escape, and the thrill of fright which added to the excitement. Yet at that moment she was certainly in no danger. He was toiling along, no doubt, fuming and perhaps swearing, on another slow train on the other side of Marseilles. Janey laughed to herself a little guiltily at the thought.

And she had escaped! It was not her doing primarily. She might have gone on all her life till she had died, but for that accident which was none of her doing. It was destiny that had done it, fate. The cage door had been opened and the bird had flown away. And how nice it would be to settle down, with this little mother, just about her own age, for a neighbour, and to help to bring the baby up! The kind, sweet faces they all had, mother and baby and bonne all smiling upon her! When Janey looked out on the other side she saw the sea flashing in the sunshine, the red porphyry rocks reflecting themselves in the brilliant blue, and village after village perched upon a promontory or in the hollow of a bay. She had never in all her life before felt that sensation of blessedness, of being able to do what she liked, of having no one to call her to account. She did not know where she was going, but that was part of the pleasure. She did not want to know where she was going.

Then suddenly this sentiment changed, and she saw in a moment a place that smiled at her like the smiling of the mother and baby. It was one of those villages in a bay: a range of blue mountains threw forth a protecting arm into the sea to shield it: the roofs were red, the houses were white, they were all blazing in the sun. Soft olives and palms fringed the deep green of the pines that rolled back in waves of verdure over the country behind, and strayed down in groups and scattered files to the shore below. Oh, what a cheerful, delightsome place! And this was where the little group with the baby were preparing to get out. "I will go too," said Janey to herself; and her heart gave a little bound of pleasure. She was delighted to reach the place where she was going to stay…just as she had been delighted to go on in the little pottering train, not knowing where she was going, and not wishing to know.

This was how Janey settled herself on the day of her flight from the world. She scarcely knew what story it was she told to the young woman whose face had so charmed her, and whom she asked whether she would be likely to find lodgings anywhere, lodgings that would not be too expensive.

"My husband is…at sea," Janey heard herself saying. She could scarcely tell what it was that put those words into her head.

"Oh, but yes," the other young woman cried with rapture. Nothing was more easy to get than a lodging in St Honorat, which was beginning to try to be a winter resort, and was eager to attract strangers. Janey had dreamed of a cottage and a garden, but she was not dissatisfied when she found herself in a sunbright room on the second floor of a tall white house facing the sea. It had a little balcony all to itself. The water rippled on the shore just over the road, the curve of the blue mountains was before her eyes.

I do not say that when she had settled down, when the thrill of movement was no longer in her brain, Janey was not without a shiver at the thought of what she had done. When the sun set, and that little chill which comes into the air of the south at the moment of its setting breathed a momentary cold about her, and when the woman of the house carefully closed the shutters and shut out the shining of the bay, and she was left alone with her candle, something sank in Janey's heart…something of the unreasonable elation, the fantastic happiness, of the day. She thought of "Mr Rosendale" (she had never got so near her husband as to call him by any other name) arriving, of the fuss there would be about her and the inquiries.

Was it rash to have come to a place so near as this…within an hour or two of where he was? Was there a danger that some one might have seen her? That it might be found out that she had taken her ticket? But then she had taken her ticket for a place much farther along the coast. She thought she could see him arrive all flaming with anger and eagerness, and the group that would gather round him, and how he would be betrayed by his bad French, and the rage he would get into! Again she laughed guiltily; but then got very grave again trying to count up all the chances…how some porter might have noticed and might betray her, how he might yet come down upon her furiously, to wreak upon her all the fury of his discomfiture. Janey knew by instinct that though it was in no way her fault, her husband would wreak his vengeance upon her even for being left behind by the train. She became desperate as she sat and thought it all over. It would be better for her to leap from the window, to throw herself into the sea, than to fall into his hands. There would be no forgiveness for her if he once laid hands upon her. Now that she had taken this desperate step, she must stand by it to the death.

III

Ten years had passed away since the time of that wedding tour.

Ten years! It is a very long time in a life. It makes a young man middle-aged, and a middle-aged man old. It takes away the bloom of youth, and the ignorance of the most inexperienced; and yet what a little while it is!…no more than a day when you look back upon it. The train from Marseilles to Nice, which is called the rapide, goes every day, and most people one time or another have travelled by it.

One day last winter one of the passengers in this train, established very comfortably in the best corner of a sleeping carriage in which he had passed the night luxuriously, and from which he was now looking out upon the shining sea, the red rocks, the many bays and headlands of the coast, suddenly received such a shock and sensation as seldom occurs to any one. He was a man of middle-age and not of engaging aspect. His face was red, and his eyes were dull yet fiery. He had the air of a man who had indulged himself much and all his inclinations, had loved good living and all the joys of the flesh, had denied himself nothing...and was now paying the penalties. Such men, to tell the truth, are not at all unusual apparitions on that beautiful coast or in the train rapide. No doubt appearances are deceitful, and it is not always a bad man who bears that aspect or who pays those penalties: but in this case few people would have doubted.

His eyes were bloodshot, he had a scowl upon his brow, his foot was supported upon a cushion. He had a servant with him to whom he rarely spoke but with an insult. Not an agreeable man...and the life he was now leading, whatever it had been, was not an agreeable life. He was staring out at the window upon the curves of the coast, sometimes putting up the collar of his fur coat over his ears, though it was a warm morning, and the sun had all the force of April. What he was thinking of it would be difficult to divine...perhaps of the good dinner that awaited him at Monte Carlo when he got there, perhaps of his good luck in being out of England when the east winds began to blow, perhaps of something quite different...some recollection of his past. The rapide does not stop at such small places as St Honorat, which indeed had not succeeded in making itself a winter resort. It was still a very small place. There were a few people on the platform when the train rushed through. It seemed to pass like a whirlwind, yet notwithstanding, in that moment two things happened. The gentleman in the corner of the carriage started in his seat, and flung himself half out of the window, with a sudden roar which lost itself in the tunnel into which the train plunged. There was an awful minute in that tunnel: for the servant thought his master had taken a fit, and there was no light to see what convulsions he might have fallen into, while at the same time he fought furiously against the man's efforts to loose his wrappings and place him in a recumbent position, exclaiming furiously all the time. He had not taken a fit, but when the train emerged into the light he was as near to it as possible...purple-red in his face, and shouting with rage and pain.

"Stop the train! Stop the train!" he shouted. "Do you hear, you fool? Stop the train! Ring the bell or whatever it is! Break the... thing! Stop the train!"

"Sir, sir! If you will only be quiet, I will get your medicine in a moment!"

"Medicine, indeed!" cried the master, indignantly, and every furious name that he could think of mounted to his lips…fool, idiot, ass, swine…there was no end to his epithets. "I tell you I saw her, I saw her!" he shouted. "Stop the train! Stop the train!"

On the other hand, among the few insignificant persons, peasants and others, who had been standing on the platform at St Honorat when the rapide dashed past, there had been a woman and a child. The woman was not a peasant: she was very simply dressed in black, with one of the small bonnets which were a few years ago so distinctively English, and with an air which corresponded to that simple coiffure. She was young, and yet had the air of responsibility and motherhood which marks a woman who is no longer in the first chapter of life. The child, a boy of nine or ten, standing close by her side, had seized her hand just as the train appeared impatiently to call her attention to something else; but, by some strange spell of attraction or coincidence, her eyes fixed upon that window out of which the gouty traveller was looking. She saw him as he saw her, and fell back dragging the boy with her as if she would have sunk into the ground. It was only a moment and the rapide was gone, screaming and roaring into the tunnel, making too much noise with the rush and sweep of its going to permit the shout of the passenger to be heard.

Ten years, ten long years, during which life had undergone so many changes! They all seemed to fly away in a moment, and the girl who had arrived at the little station of St Honorat alone, a fugitive, elated and intoxicated with her freedom, suddenly felt herself again the little Janey who had emancipated herself so strangely…though she had for a long time been frightened by every train that passed and every stranger who came near.

In the course of these long years all this had changed. Her baby had been born, her forlorn state had called forth great pity, great remark and criticism, in the village where she had found refuge… great censure also, for the fact of her marriage was not believed by everybody. But she was so lonely, so modest, and so friendly, that the poor little English stranger was soon forgiven. Perhaps her simple neighbours were glad to find that a prim Englishwoman, supposed to stand so fierce on her virtue, was in reality so fallible…or perhaps pity put all other sentiments out of court. She told her real story to the priest when the boy was baptised, and though he tried to persuade her to return to her husband, he only half believed in that husband, since the story was told not under any seal of confession. Janey never became absolutely one of his flock. She was a prim little Protestant in her heart, standing strong against the saints, but devoutly attending church, believing with simple religiousness that to go to church was better than not to go to church, whatever the rites might be, and reading her little English service steadily through all the prayers of the Mass, which she never learned to follow. But her boy was like the other children of St Honorat, and learned his catechism and said his lessons with the rest.

There were various things which she did to get a living, and got it very innocently and sufficiently, though in the humblest way. She taught English to the children of some of the richer people in the village: she taught them music. She had so much credit in this latter branch, that she often held the organ in church on a holiday and pleased everybody. Then she worked very well with her needle, and would help on an emergency at first for pure kindness, and then, as her faculties and her powers of service became known, for pay, with diligence and readiness. She found a niche in the little place which she filled perfectly, though only accident seemed to have made it for her. She had fifty pounds of her little fortune laid by for the boy. She had a share of a cottage in a garden…not an English cottage indeed, but the upper floor of a two-storeyed French house; and she and her boy did much in the garden, cultivating prettinesses which do not commend themselves much to the villagers of St Honorat. Whether she ever regretted the step she had taken nobody ever knew. She might have been a lady with a larger house than any in St Honorat, and servants at her call. Perhaps she sometimes thought of that; perhaps she felt herself happier as she was; sometimes, I think, she felt that if she had known the boy was coming she might have possessed her soul in patience, and borne even with Mr Rosendale. But then at the time the decisive step was taken she did not know.

She hurried home in a great fright, not knowing what to do; then calmed herself with the thought that even if he had recognised her, there were many chances against his following her, or at least finding her, with no clue, and after so many years. And then a dreadful panic seized her at the thought that he might take her boy from her. He had known nothing about the boy: but if he discovered that fact it would make a great difference. He could not compel Janey to return to him, but he could take the boy. When this occurred to her she started up again, having just sat down, and put on her bonnet and called the child.

"Are you going out again, mother?" he cried.

"Yes, directly, directly: come, John, come, come!" she said, putting his cap upon his head and seizing him by the hand. She led him straight to the presbytery, and asked for the cure, and went in to the good priest in great agitation, leaving the boy with his housekeeper.

"M. l'Abbe," she said, with what the village called her English directness, "I have just seen my husband go past in the train!"

"Not possible!" said M. l'Abbe, who only half believed there was a husband at all.

"And he saw me. He will come back, and I am afraid he will find me. I want you to do something for me."

"With pleasure," said the priest; "I will come and meet Monsieur your husband, and I will explain…"

"That is not what I want you to do. I want you to let John stay with you, to keep him here till…till…He will want to take him away from me!" she cried.

"He will want to take you both away, chère petite dame. He has a right to do so."

"No, no! But I do not ask you what is his right. I ask you to keep John safe; to keep him here…till the danger has passed away!"

The priest tried to reason, to entreat, to persuade her that a father, not to say a husband, had his rights. But Janey would hear no reason: had she heard reason either from herself or another, she would not have been at St Honorat now. And he gave at last a reluctant consent. There was perhaps no harm in it after all. If a man came to claim his rights, he would not certainly go away again without some appeal to the authorities…which was a thing it must come to sooner or later…if there was indeed a husband at all, and the story was true.

Janey then went back to her home. She thought she could await him there and defy him. "I will not go with you," she would say. "I may be your wife, but I am not your slave. You have left me alone for ten years. I will not go with you now!" She repeated this to herself many times, but it did not subdue the commotion in her being. She went out again when it became too much for her, locking her door with a strange sense that she might never come back again. She walked along the sea shore, repeating these words to herself, and then she walked up and down the streets, and went into the church and made the round of it, passing all the altars and wondering if the saints did pay any attention to the poor women who were there, as always, telling St Joseph or the Blessed Mary all about it. She sank down in a dark corner, and said…

"Oh, my God! Oh, my God!"

She could not tell Him about it in her agitation, with her heart beating so, but only call His attention, as the woman in the Bible touched the Redeemer's robe. And then she went out and walked up and down again. I cannot tell what drew her back to the station… what fascination, what dreadful spell. Before she knew what she was doing she found herself there, walking up and down, up and down.

As if she were waiting for some one! "You have come to meet a friend?" someone said to her, with an air of suspicion. And she first nodded and then shook her head; but still continued in spite of herself to walk up and down. Then she said to herself that it was best so…that to get it over would be a great thing, now John was out of the way; he would be sure to find her sooner or later…far better to get it over! When the train came in, the slow local train, coming from the side of Italy, she drew herself back a little to watch. There was a great commotion when it drew up at the platform. A man got out and called all the loungers about to help to lift out a gentleman who was ill…who had had a bad attack in the train.

"Is there anywhere here we can take him to? Is there any decent hotel? Is there a room fit to put my master in?" he cried.

He was English with not much French at his command, and in great distress. Janey, forgetting herself and her terrors, and strong in the relief of the moment that he whom she feared had not come, went up to offer her help. She answered the man's questions; she called the right people to help him; she summoned the chef de Gare to make some provision for carrying the stricken man to the hotel.

"I will go with you," she said to the servant, who felt as if an angel speaking English had suddenly come to his help. She stood by full of pity, as they lifted that great inert mass out of the carriage. Then she gave a great cry and fell back against the wall.

It was a dreadful sight the men said afterwards, enough to overcome the tender heart of any lady, especially of one so kind as Madame Jeanne. A huge man, helpless, unconscious, with a purple countenance, staring eyes, breathing so that you could hear him a mile off. No wonder that she covered her eyes with her hands not to see him; and then covered her ears with her hands not to hear him: but finally she hurried away to the hotel to prepare for him, and to call the doctor, that no time should be lost. Janey felt as if she was restored for the moment to life when there was something she could do. The questions were all postponed. She did not think of flight or concealment, or even of John at the presbytery. "He is my husband," she said, with awe in her heart.

This was how the train brought back to Janey the man whom the train had separated from her ten years before. The whole tragedy was of the railway, the noisy carriages, the snorting locomotives. He was taken to the hotel, but he never came to himself again, and died there next day, without being able to say what his object was, or why he had got out of the rapide, though unable to walk, and insisted on returning to St Honorat. It cost him his life; but then his life was not worth a day's purchase, all the doctors said, in the condition in which he was.

Friends had to be summoned, and men of business, and it was impossible but that Janey's secret should be made known. When she found herself and her son recognised, and that there could be no doubt that the boy was his father's heir, she was struck with a great horror which she never quite got over all her life. She had not blamed herself before; but now seemed to herself no less than the murderer of her husband: and could not forgive herself, nor get out of her eyes the face she had seen, nor out of her ears the dreadful sound of that labouring breath.

The Absent-Minded Man

Jerome K. Jerome

Jerome Klapka Jerome (1859-1927) was a famous English novelist, playwright and humorist. Initially, Jerome wrote short stories and satirical essays that he sent to various magazines. Later, *Idle Thoughts of an Idle Fellow* (1886) *Three Men in a Boat* (1889) turned Jerome into one of the most influential and celebrated English authors. 'The Absent-Minded Man' (1897) is one of Jerome's most cherished short stories.

You ask him to dine with you on Thursday to meet a few people who are anxious to know him.

"Now don't make a muddle of it," you say, recollectful of former mishaps, "and come on the Wednesday." He laughs good-naturedly as he hunts through the room for his diary.

"Shan't be able to come Wednesday," he says, "shall be at the Mansion House, sketching dresses, and on Friday I start for Scotland, so as to be at the opening of the Exhibition on Saturday. It's bound to be all right this time. Where the deuce is that diary! Never mind, I'll make a note of it on this—you can see me do it."

You stand over him while he writes the appointment down on a sheet of foolscap, and watch him pin it up over his desk. Then you come away contented.

"I do hope he'll turn up," you say to your wife on the Thursday evening, while dressing.

"Are you sure you made it clear to him?" she replies, suspiciously, and you instinctively feel that whatever happens she is going to blame you for it.

Eight o'clock arrives, and with it the other guests. At half-past eight your wife is beckoned mysteriously out of the room, where the parlour-maid informs her that the cook has expressed a determination, in case of further delay, to wash her hands, figuratively speaking, of the whole affair.

Your wife, returning, suggests that if the dinner is to be eaten at all it had better be begun. She evidently considers that in pretending to expect him you have been merely playing a part, and that it would have been manlier and more straightforward for you to have admitted at the beginning that you had forgotten to invite him.

During the soup and the fish you recount anecdotes of his unpunctuality. By the time the entrée arrives the empty chair has begun to cast a gloom over the dinner, and with the joint the conversation drifts into talk about dead relatives.

On Friday, at a quarter past eight, he dashes to the door and rings violently. Hearing his voice in the hall, you go to meet him.

"Sorry I'm late," he sings out cheerily. "Fool of a cabman took me to Alfred Place instead of—"

"Well, what do you want now you are come?" you interrupt, feeling anything but genially inclined towards him. He is an old friend, so you can be rude to him.

He laughs, and slaps you on the shoulder. "Why, my dinner, my dear boy, I'm starving."

"Oh," you grunt in reply. "Well, you go and get it somewhere else, then. You're not going to have it here." "What the devil do you mean?" he says. "You asked me to dinner."

"I did nothing of the kind," you tell him. "I asked you to dinner on Thursday, not on Friday." He stares at you incredulously.

"How did I get Friday fixed in my mind?" inquiringly.

"Because yours is the sort of mind that would get Friday firmly fixed into it, when Thursday was the day," you explain. "I thought you had to be off to Edinburgh tonight," you add.

"Great Scott!" he cries, "so I have."

And without another word he dashes out, and you hear him rushing down the road, shouting for the cab he has just dismissed.

As you return to your study you reflect that he will have to travel all the way to Scotland in evening dress, and will have to send out the hotel porter in the morning to buy him a suit of ready-made clothes, and are glad.

Matters work out still more awkwardly when it is he who is the host. I remember being with him on his house-boat one day. It was a little after twelve, and we were sitting on the edge of the boat, dangling our feet in the river—the spot was a lonely one, halfway between Wallingford and Day's Lock. Suddenly round the bend appeared two skiffs, each one containing six elaborately-dressed persons. As soon as they caught sight of us they began waving handkerchiefs and parasols.

"Hullo!" I said, "here's some people hailing you."

"Oh, they all do that about here," he answered, without looking up. "Some beanfeast from Abingdon, I expect."

The boats draw nearer. When about two hundred yards off an elderly gentleman raised himself up in the prow of the leading one and shouted to us.

McQuae heard his voice, and gave a start that all but pitched him into the water. "Good God!" he cried, "I'd forgotten all about it."

"About what?" I asked.

"Why, it's the Palmers and the Grahams and the Hendersons. I've asked them all over to lunch, and there's not a blessed thing on board but two mutton chops and a pound of potatoes, and I've given the boy a holiday."

Another day I was lunching with him at the Junior Hogarth, when a man named Hallyard, a mutual friend, strolled across to us.

"What are you fellows going to do this afternoon?" he asked, seating himself the opposite side of the table. "I'm going to stop here and write letters," I answered.

"Come with me if you want something to do," said McQuae. "I'm going to drive Leena down to Richmond." ("Leena" was the young lady he recollected being engaged to. It transpired afterwards that he was engaged to three girls at the time. The other two he had forgotten all about.) "It's a roomy seat at the back."

"Oh, all right," said Hallyard, and they went away together in a hansom.

An hour and a half later Hallyard walked into the smoking-room looking depressed and worn, and flung himself into a chair.

"I thought you were going to Richmond with McQuae," I said.

"So did I," he answered.

"Had an accident?" I asked. "Yes."

He was decidedly curt in his replies. "Cart upset?" I continued.

"No, only me."

His grammar and his nerves seemed thoroughly shaken. I waited for an explanation, and after a while he gave it.

"We got to Putney," he said, "with just an occasional run into a tram-car, and were going up the hill, when suddenly he turned a corner. You know his style at a corner—over the curb, across the road, and into the opposite lamp post. Of course, as a rule one is prepared for it, but I never reckoned on his turning up there, and the first thing I recollect is finding myself sitting in the middle of the street with a dozen fools grinning at me.

"It takes a man a few minutes in such a case to think where he is and what has happened, and when I got up they were some distance away. I ran after them for a quarter of a mile, shouting at the top of my voice, and accompanied by a mob of boys, all yelling like hell on a Bank Holiday. But one might as well have tried to hail the dead, so I took the 'bus back.

"They might have guessed what had happened," he added, "by the shifting of the cart, if they'd had any sense. I'm not a light-weight."

He complained of soreness, and said he would go home. I suggested a cab, but he replied that he would rather walk.

I met McQuae in the evening at the St. James's Theatre. It was a first night, and he was taking sketches for The Graphic. The moment he saw me he made his way across to me.

"The very man I wanted to see," he said. "Did I take Hallyard with me in the cart to Richmond this afternoon?"

"You did," I replied.

"So Leena says," he answered, greatly bewildered, "but I'll swear he wasn't there when we got to the Queen's Hotel."

"It's all right," I said, "you dropped him at Putney."

"Dropped him at Putney!" he repeated. "I've no recollection of doing so." "He has," I answered. "You ask him about it. He's full of it."

Everybody said he never would get married; that it was absurd to suppose he ever would remember the day, the church, and the girl, all in one morning; that if he did get as far as the altar he would forget what he had come for, and would give the bride away to his own best man. Hallyard had an idea that he was already married, but that the fact had slipped his memory. I myself felt sure that if he did marry he would forget all about it the next day.

But everybody was wrong. By some miraculous means the ceremony got itself accomplished, so that if Hallyard's idea be correct (as to which there is every possibility), there will be trouble. As for my own fears, I dismissed them the moment I saw the lady. She was a charming, cheerful little woman, but did not look the type that would let him forget all about it.

I had not seen him since his marriage, which had happened in the spring. Working my way back from Scotland by easy stages, I stopped for a few days at Scarboro. After table d'hôte I put on my mackintosh, and went out for a walk. It was raining hard, but after a month in Scotland one does not notice English weather, and I wanted some air. Struggling along the dark beach with my head against the wind, I stumbled over a crouching figure, seeking to shelter itself a little from the storm under the lee of the Spa wall.

I expected it to swear at me, but it seemed too broken-spirited to mind anything. "I beg your pardon," I said. "I did not see you."

At the sound of my voice it started to its feet. "Is that you, old man?" it cried.

"McQuae!" I exclaimed.

"By Jove!" he said, "I was never so glad to see a man in all my life before." And he nearly shook my hand off.

"But what in thunder!" I said, "are you doing here? Why, you're drenched to the skin." He was dressed in flannels and a tennis-coat.

"Yes," he answered. "I never thought it would rain. It was a lovely morning." I began to fear he had overworked himself into a brain fever.

"Why don't you go home?" I asked.

"I can't," he replied. "I don't know where I live. I've forgotten the address."

"For heaven's sake," he said, "take me somewhere, and give me something to eat. I'm literally starving."

"Haven't you any money?" I asked him, as we turned towards the hotel.

"Not a sou," he answered. "We got in here from York, the wife and I, about eleven. We left our things at the station, and started to hunt for apartments. As soon as we were fixed, I changed my clothes and came out for a walk, telling Maud I should be back at one to lunch. Like a fool, I never took the address, and never noticed the way I was going.

"It's an awful business," he continued. "I don't see how I'm ever going to find her. I hoped she might stroll down to the Spa in the evening, and I've been hanging about the gates ever since six. I hadn't the threepence to go in."

"But have you no notion of the sort of street or the kind of house it was?" I enquired. "Not a ghost," he replied. "I left it all to Maud, and didn't trouble."

"Have you tried any of the lodging-houses?" I asked.

"Tried!" he exclaimed bitterly. "I've been knocking at doors, and asking if Mrs. McQuae lives there steadily all the afternoon, and they slam the door in my face, mostly without answering. I told a policeman—I thought perhaps he might suggest something—but the idiot only burst out laughing, and that made me so mad that I gave him a black eye, and had to cut. I expect they're on the lookout for me now."

"I went into a restaurant," he continued gloomily, "and tried to get them to trust me for a steak. But the proprietress said she'd heard that tale before, and ordered me out before all the other customers. I think I'd have drowned myself if you hadn't turned up."

After a change of clothes and some supper, he discussed the case more calmly, but it was really a serious affair. They had shut up their flat, and his wife's relatives were travelling abroad. There was no one to whom he could send a letter to be forwarded; there was no one with whom she would be likely to communicate. Their chance of meeting again in this world appeared remote.

Nor did it seem to me—fond as he was of his wife, and anxious as he undoubtedly was to recover her—that he looked forward to the actual meeting, should it ever arrive, with any too pleasurable anticipation.

"She will think it strange," he murmured reflectively, sitting on the edge of the bed, and thoughtfully pulling off his socks. "She is sure to think it strange."

The following day, which was Wednesday, we went to a solicitor, and laid the case before him, and he instituted inquiries among all the lodging-house keepers in Scarborough, with the result that on Thursday afternoon McQuae was restored (after the manner of an Adelphi hero in the last act) to his home and wife.

I asked him next time I met him what she had said. "Oh, much what I expected," he replied.

But he never told me what he had expected.

A Pair Of Silk Stockings

Kate Chopin

Kate Chopin (1851-1904) was an American novelist and short story writer. Her finely crafted short stories are acclaimed for their strong feminist undercurrents and modern sensibility. 'A Pair Of Silk Stockings' (1897) is a fine example of the complexity and subtlety of Chopin's craft.

Little Mrs. Sommers one day found herself the unexpected possessor of fifteen dollars. It seemed to her a very large amount of money, and the way in which it stuffed and bulged her worn old *porte-monnaie* gave her a feeling of importance such as she had not enjoyed for years.

The question of investment was one that occupied her greatly. For a day or two she walked about apparently in a dreamy state, but really absorbed in speculation and calculation. She did not wish to act hastily, to do anything she might afterward regret. But it was during the still hours of the night when she lay awake revolving plans in her mind that she seemed to see her way clearly toward a proper and judicious use of the money.

A dollar or two should be added to the price usually paid for Janie's shoes, which would insure their lasting an appreciable time longer than they usually did. She would buy so and so many yards of percale for new shirt waists for the boys and Janie and Mag. She had intended to make the old ones do by skillful patching. Mag should have another gown. She had seen some beautiful patterns, veritable bargains in the shop windows. And still there would be left enough for new stockings, two pairs apiece, and what darning that would save for a while! She would get caps for the boys and sailor-hats for the girls. The vision of her little brood looking fresh and dainty and new for once in their lives excited her and made her restless and wakeful with anticipation.

The neighbors sometimes talked of certain "better days" that little Mrs. Sommers had known before she had ever thought of being Mrs. Sommers. She herself indulged in no such morbid retrospection. She had no time, no second of time to devote to the past. The needs of the present absorbed her every faculty. A vision of the future like some dim, gaunt monster sometimes appalled her, but luckily tomorrow never comes.

Mrs. Sommers was one who knew the value of bargains; who could stand for hours making her way inch by inch toward the desired object that was selling below cost. She could elbow her way if need be; she had learned to clutch a piece of goods and hold it and stick to it with persistence and determination till her turn came to be served, no matter when it came.

But that day she was a little faint and tired. She had swallowed a light luncheon, no! when she came to think of it, between getting the children fed and the place righted, and preparing herself for the shopping bout, she had actually forgotten to eat any luncheon at all!

She sat herself upon a revolving stool before a counter that was comparatively deserted, trying to gather strength and courage to charge through an eager multitude that was besieging breast-works of shirting and figured lawn. An all-gone limp feeling had come over her and she rested her hand aimlessly upon the counter. She wore no gloves. By degrees she grew aware that her hand had encountered something very soothing, very pleasant to touch. She looked down to see that her hand lay upon a pile of silk stockings. A placard near by announced that they had been reduced in price from two dollars and fifty cents to one dollar and ninety-eight cents; and a young girl who stood behind the counter asked her if she wished to examine their line of silk hosiery. She smiled, just as if she had been asked to inspect a tiara of diamonds with the ultimate view of purchasing it. But she went on feeling the soft, sheeny luxurious things, with both hands now, holding them up to see them glisten, and to feel the glide serpent-like through her fingers.

Two hectic blotches came suddenly into her pale cheeks. She looked up at the girl.

"Do you think there are any eights-and-a-half among these?"

There were any number of eights-and-a-half. In fact, there were more of that size than any other. Here was a light-blue pair; there were some lavender, some all black and various shades of tan and gray. Mrs. Sommers selected a black pair and looked at them very long and closely. She pretended to be examining their texture, which the clerk assured her was excellent.

"A dollar and ninety-eight cents," she mused aloud. "Well, I'll take this pair." She handed the girl a five-dollar bill and waited for her change and for her parcel. What a very small parcel it was. It seemed lost in the depths of her shabby old shopping-bag.

Mrs. Sommers after that did not move in the direction of the bargain counter. She took the elevator, which carried her to an upper floor into the region of the ladies' waiting-rooms. Here, in a retired corner, she exchanged her cotton stockings for the new silk ones which she had just bought. She was not going through any acute mental process or reasoning with herself, nor was she striving to explain to her satisfaction the motive of her action. She was not thinking at all. She seemed for the time to be taking a rest from that laborious and fatiguing function and to have abandoned herself to some mechanical impulse that directed her actions and freed her of responsibility.

How good was the touch of the raw silk to her flesh! She felt like lying back in the cushioned chair and reveling for a while in the luxury of it. She did for a little while. Then she replaced her shoes, rolled the cotton stockings together and thrust them into her bag. After doing this she crossed straight over to the shoe department and took her seat to be fitted.

She was fastidious. The clerk could not make her out; he could not reconcile her shoes with her stockings, and she was not too easily pleased. She held back her skirts and turned her feet one way and her head another way as she glanced down at the polished, pointed-tipped boots. Her foot and ankle looked very pretty. She could not realize that they belonged to her and were a part of herself. She wanted an excellent and stylish fit, she told the young fellow who served her, and she did not mind the difference of a dollar or two more in the price so long as she got what she desired.

It was a long time since Mrs. Sommers had been fitted with gloves. On rare occasions when she had bought a pair they were always "bargains", so cheap that it would have been preposterous and unreasonable to have expected them to be fitted to the hand.

Now she rested her elbow on the cushion of the glove counter, and a pretty, pleasant young creature, delicate and deft of touch, drew a long-wristed "kid" over Mrs. Sommers' hand. She smoothed it down over the wrist and buttoned it neatly, and both lost themselves for a second or two in admiring contemplation of the little symmetrical gloved hand. But there were other places where money might be spent.

There were books and magazines piled up in the window of a stall a few paces down the street. Mrs. Sommers bought two high-priced magazines such as she had been accustomed to read in the days when she had been accustomed to other pleasant things. She carried them without wrapping. As well as she could she lifted her skirts at the crossings. Her stockings and boots and well-fitting gloves had worked marvels in her bearing, had given her a feeling of assurance, a sense of belonging to the well-dressed multitude.

She was very hungry. Another time she would have stifled the cravings for food until reaching her own home, where she would have brewed herself a cup of tea and taken a snack of anything that was available. But the impulse that was guiding her would not suffer her to entertain any such thought.

There was a restaurant at the corner. She had never entered its doors; from the outside she had sometimes caught glimpses of spotless damask and shining crystal, and soft-stepping waiters serving people of fashion.

When she entered her appearance created no surprise, no consternation, as she had half feared it might. She seated herself at a small table alone, and an attentive waiter at once approached to take her order. She did not want a profusion; she craved a nice and tasty bite, a half-dozen blue points, a plump chop with cress, a something sweet, crème-frappèe, for instance; a glass of Rhine wine, and after all a small cup of black coffee.

While waiting to be served she removed her gloves very leisurely and laid them beside her. Then she picked up a magazine and glanced through it, cutting the pages with a blunt edge of her knife. It was all very agreeable. The damask was even more spotless than it had seemed through the window, and the crystal more sparkling. There were quiet ladies and gentlemen, who did not notice her, lunching at the small tables like her own. A soft, pleasing strain of music could be heard, and a gentle breeze was blowing through the window. She tasted a bite, and she read a word or two, and she sipped the amber wine and wiggled her toes in the silk stockings. The price of it made no difference. She counted the money out to the waiter and left an extra coin on his tray, whereupon he bowed before her as before a princess of royal blood.

There was still money in her purse, and her next temptation presented itself in the shape of a matinèe poster.

It was a little later when she entered the theatre, the play had begun and the house seemed to her to be packed. But there were vacant seats here and there, and into one of them she was ushered, between brilliantly dressed women who had gone there to kill time and eat candy and display their gaudy attire. There were many others who were there solely for the play and acting. It is safe to say there was no one present who bore quite the attitude which Mrs. Sommers did to her surroundings. She gathered in the whole, stage and players and people in one wide impression, and absorbed it and enjoyed it. She laughed at the comedy and wept, she and the gaudy woman next to her wept over the tragedy. And they talked a little together over it. And the gaudy woman wiped her eyes and sniffed on a tiny square of filmy, perfumed lace and passed little Mrs. Sommers her box of candy.

The play was over, the music ceased, the crowd filed out. It was like a dream ended. People scattered in all directions. Mrs. Sommers went to the corner and waited for the cable car.

A man with keen eyes, who sat opposite to her, seemed to like the study of her small, pale face. It puzzled him to decipher what he saw there. In truth he saw nothing, unless he were wizard enough to detect a poignant wish, a powerful longing that the cable car would never stop anywhere, but go on and on with her forever.

A Case Of Trespass

Lucy Maud Montgomery

Lucy Maud Montgomery (1874-1942) was a Canadian writer who wrote the famous *Anne of Green Gables* (1908). Besides writing a host of novels on the *Anne* series and other individual novels, Montgomery was also a prolific short story writer, with over 500 short stories published during her lifetime. 'A Case Of Trespass' (1897) is one of the earliest short stories by Montgomery.

It was the forenoon of a hazy, breathless day, and Dan Phillips was trouting up one of the back creeks of the Carleton pond. It was somewhat cooler up the creek than out on the main body of water, for the tall birches and willows, crowding down to the brim, threw cool, green shadows across it and shut out the scorching glare, while a stray breeze now and then rippled down the wooded slopes, rustling the beech leaves with an airy, pleasant sound.

Out in the pond the glassy water creamed and shimmered in the hot sun, unrippled by the faintest breath of air. Across the soft, pearly tints of the horizon blurred the smoke of the big factory chimneys that were owned by Mr. Walters, to whom the pond and adjacent property also belonged.

Mr. Walters was a comparative stranger in Carleton, having but recently purchased the factories from the heirs of the previous owner; but he had been in charge long enough to establish a reputation for sternness and inflexibility in all his business dealings.

One or two of his employees, who had been discharged by him on what they deemed insufficient grounds, helped to deepen the impression that he was an unjust and arbitrary man, merciless to all offenders, and intolerant of the slightest infringement of his cast-iron rules.

Dan Phillips had been on the pond ever since sunrise. The trout had risen well in the early morning, but as the day wore on, growing hotter and hotter, they refused to bite, and for half an hour Dan had not caught one.

He had a goodly string of them already, however, and he surveyed them with satisfaction as he rowed his leaky little skiff to the shore of the creek.

"Pretty good catch," he soliloquized. "Best I've had this summer, so far. That big spotted one must weigh near a pound. He's a beauty. They're a good price over at the hotels now, too. I'll go home and get my dinner and go straight over with them. That'll leave me time for another try at them about sunset. Whew, how hot it is! I must take Ella May home a bunch of them blue flags. They're real handsome!"

He tied his skiff under the crowding alders, gathered a big bunch of the purple flag lilies with their silky petals, and started homeward, whistling cheerily as he stepped briskly along the fern-carpeted wood path that wound up the hill under the beeches and firs.

He was a freckled, sunburned lad of thirteen years. His neighbours all said that Danny was "as smart as a steel trap," and immediately added that they wondered where he got his smartness from—certainly not from his father!

The elder Phillips had been denominated "shiftless and slack-twisted" by all who ever had any dealings with him in his unlucky, aimless life—one of those improvident, easygoing souls who sit contentedly down to breakfast with a very faint idea where their dinner is to come from.

When he had died, no one had missed him, unless it were his patient, sad-eyed wife, who bravely faced her hard lot, and toiled unremittingly to keep a home for her two children—Dan and a girl two years younger, who was a helpless cripple, suffering from some form of spinal disease.

Dan, who was old and steady for his years, had gone manfully to work to assist his mother. Though he had been disappointed in all his efforts to obtain steady employment, he was active and obliging, and earned many a small amount by odd jobs around the village, and by helping the Carleton farmers in planting and harvest.

For the last two years, however, his most profitable source of summer income had been the trout pond. The former owner had allowed anyone who wished to fish in his pond, and Dan made a regular business of it, selling his trout at the big hotels over at Mosquito Lake. This, in spite of its unattractive name, was a popular summer resort, and Dan always found a ready market for his catch.

When Mr. Walters purchased the property it somehow never occurred to Dan that the new owner might not be so complaisant as his predecessor in the matter of the best trouting pond in the country.

To be sure, Dan often wondered why it was the pond was so deserted this summer. He could not recall having seen a single person on it save himself. Still, it did not cross his mind that there could be any particular reason for this.

He always fished up in the cool, dim creeks, which long experience had taught him were best for trout, and came and went by a convenient wood path; but he had no thought of concealment in so doing. He would not have cared had all Carleton seen him.

He had done very well with his fish so far, and prices for trout at the Lake went up every day. Dan was an enterprising boy, and a general favourite with the hotel owners. They knew that he could always be depended on.

Mrs. Phillips met him at the door when he reached home.

"See, Mother," said Dan exultantly, as he held up his fish. "Just look at that fellow, will you? A pound if he's an ounce! I ought to get a good price for these, I can tell you. Let me have my dinner now, and I'll go right over to the Lake with them."

"It's a long walk for you, Danny," replied his mother pityingly, "and it's too hot to go so far. I'm afraid you'll get sun-struck or something. You'd better wait till the cool of the evening. You're looking real pale and thin this while back."

"Oh, I'm all right, Mother," assured Dan cheerfully. "I don't mind the heat a bit. A fellow must put up with some inconveniences. Wait till I bring home the money for these fish. And I mean to have another catch tonight. It's you that's looking tired. I wish you didn't have to work so hard, Mother. If I could only get a good place you could take it easier. Sam French says that Mr. Walters wants a boy up there at the factory, but I know I wouldn't do. I ain't big enough. Perhaps something will turn up soon though. When our ship comes in, Mother, we'll have our good times."

He picked up his flags and went into the little room where his sister lay.

"See what I've brought you, Ella May!" he said, as he thrust the cool, moist clusters into her thin, eager hands. "Did you ever see such beauties?"

"Oh, Dan, how lovely they are! Thank you ever so much! If you are going over to the Lake this afternoon, will you please call at Mrs. Henny's and get those nutmeg geranium slips she promised me? Just look how nice my others are growing. The pink one is going to bloom."

"I'll bring you all the geranium slips at the Lake, if you like. When I get rich, Ella May, I'll build you a big conservatory, and I'll get every flower in the world in it for you. You shall just live and sleep among posies. Is dinner ready, Mother? Trouting's hungry work, I tell you. What paper is this?"

He picked up a folded newspaper from the table.

"Oh, that's only an old Lake Advertiser," answered Mrs. Phillips, as she placed the potatoes on the table and wiped her moist, hot face with the corner of her gingham apron. "Letty Mills brought it in around a parcel this morning. It's four weeks old, but I kept it to read if I ever get time. It's so seldom we see a paper of any kind nowadays. But I haven't looked at it yet. Why, Danny, what on earth is the matter?"

For Dan, who had opened the paper and glanced over the first page, suddenly gave a choked exclamation and turned pale, staring stupidly at the sheet before him.

"See, Mother," he gasped, as she came up in alarm and looked over his shoulder. This is what they read: Notice

Anyone found fishing on my pond at Carleton after date will be prosecuted according to law, without respect of persons.

June First. H.C. Walters. "Oh, Danny, what does it mean?"

Dan went and carefully closed the door of Ella May's room before he replied. His face was pale and his voice shaky.

"Mean? Well, Mother, it just means that I've been stealing Mr. Walters's trout all summer—stealing them. That's what it means."

"Oh, Danny! But you didn't know."

"No, but I ought to have remembered that he was the new owner, and have asked him. I never thought. Mother, what does 'prosecuted according to law' mean?"

"I don't know, I'm sure, Danny. But if this is so, there's only one thing to be done. You must go straight to Mr. Walters and tell him all about it."

"Mother, I don't dare to. He is a dreadfully hard man. Sam French's father says—"

"I wouldn't believe a word Sam French's father says about Mr. Walters!" said Mrs. Phillips firmly. "He's got a spite against him because he was dismissed. Besides, Danny, it's the only right thing to do. You know that. We're poor, but we have never done anything underhand yet."

"Yes, Mother, I know," said Dan, gulping his fear bravely down. "I'll go, of course, right after dinner. I was only scared at first. I'll tell you what I'll do. I'll clean these trout nicely and take them to Mr. Walters, and tell him that, if he'll only give me time, I'll pay him back every cent of money I got for all I sold this summer. Then maybe he'll let me off, seeing as I didn't know about the notice."

"I'll go with you, Danny."

"No, I'll go alone, Mother. You needn't go with me," said Dan heroically. To himself he said that his mother had troubles enough. He would never subject her to the added ordeal of an interview with the stern factory owner. He would beard the lion in his den himself, if it had to be done.

"Don't tell Ella May anything about it. It would worry her. And don't cry, Mother, I guess it'll be all right. Let me have my dinner now and I'll go straight off."

Dan ate his dinner rapidly; then he carefully cleaned his trout, put them in a long basket, with rhubarb leaves over them, and started with an assumed cheerfulness very far from his real feelings.

He had barely passed the gate when another boy came shuffling along—a tall, raw-boned lad, with an insinuating smile and shifty, cunning eyes. The newcomer nodded familiarly to Dan.

"Hello, sonny. Going over to the Lake with your catch, are you? You'll fry up before you get there. There'll be nothing left of you but a crisp."

"No, I'm not going to the Lake. I'm going up to the factory to see Mr. Walters."

Sam French gave a long whistle of surprise.

"Why, Dan, what's taking you there? You surely ain't thinking of trying for that place, are you? Walters wouldn't look at you. Why, he wouldn't take me! You haven't the ghost of a chance."

"No, I'm not going for that. Sam, did you know that Mr. Walters had a notice in the Lake Advertiser that nobody could fish in his pond this summer?"

"Course I did—the old skinflint! He's too mean to live, that's what.

He never goes near the pond himself. Regular dog in the manger, he is.

Dad says—"

"Sam, why didn't you tell me about that notice?"

"Gracious, didn't you know? I s'posed everybody did, and here I've been taking you for the cutest chap this side of sunset—fishing away up in that creek where no one could see you, and cutting home through the woods on the sly. You don't mean to tell me you never saw that notice?"

"No, I didn't. Do you think I'd have gone near the pond if I had? I never saw it till today, and I'm going straight to Mr. Walters now to tell him about it."

Sam French stopped short in the dusty road and stared at Dan in undisguised amazement.

"Dan Phillips," he ejaculated, "have you plum gone out of your mind? Boy alive, you needn't be afraid that I'd peach on you. I'm too blamed glad to see anyone get the better of that old Walters, smart as he thinks himself. Gee! To dream of going to him and telling him you've been fishing in his pond! Why, he'll put you in jail. You don't know what sort of a man he is. Dad says—"

"Never mind what your dad says, Sam. My mind's made up."

"Dan, you chump, listen to me. That notice says 'prosecuted according to law.' Why, Danny, he'll put you in prison, or fine you, or something dreadful."

"I can't help it if he does," said Danny stoutly. "You get out of here, Sam French, and don't be trying to scare me. I mean to be honest, and how can I be if I don't own up to Mr. Walters that I've been stealing his trout all summer?"

"Stealing, fiddlesticks! Dan, I used to think you were a chap with some sense, but I see I was mistaken. You ain't done no harm. Walters will never miss them trout. If you're so dreadful squeamish that you won't fish no more, why, you needn't. But just let the matter drop and hold your tongue about it. That's my advice."

"Well, it isn't my mother's, then. I mean to go by hers. You needn't argue no more, Sam. I'm going."

"Go, then!" said Sam, stopping short in disgust. "You're a big fool, Dan, and serve you right if Walters lands you off to jail; but I don't wish you no ill. If I can do anything for your family after you're gone, I will, and I'll try and give your remains Christian burial—if there are any remains. So long, Danny! Give my love to old Walters!"

Dan was not greatly encouraged by this interview. He shrank more than ever from the thought of facing the stern factory owner. His courage had almost evaporated when he entered the office at the factory and asked shakily for Mr. Walters.

"He's in his office there," replied the clerk, "but he's very busy. Better leave your message with me."

"I must see Mr. Walters himself, please," said Dan firmly, but with inward trepidation.

The clerk swung himself impatiently from his stool and ushered Dan into Mr. Walters's private office.

"Boy to see you, sir," he said briefly, as he closed the ground-glass door behind him.

Dan, dizzy and trembling, stood in the dreaded presence. Mr. Walters was writing at a table covered with a businesslike litter of papers.

He laid down his pen and looked up with a frown as the clerk vanished. He was a stern-looking man with deep-set grey eyes and a square, clean-shaven chin. There was not an ounce of superfluous flesh on his frame, and his voice and manner were those of the decided, resolute, masterful man of business.

He pointed to a capacious leather chair and said concisely, "What is your business with me, boy?"

Dan had carefully thought out a statement of facts beforehand, but every word had vanished from his memory. He had only a confused, desperate consciousness that he had a theft to confess and that it must be done as soon as possible. He did not sit down.

"Please, Mr. Walters," he began desperately, "I came to tell you—your notice—I never saw it before—and I've been fishing on your pond all summer—but I didn't know—honest—I've brought you all I caught today—and I'll pay back for them all—some time."

An amused, puzzled expression crossed Mr. Walters's noncommittal face. He pushed the leather chair forward.

"Sit down, my boy," he said kindly. "I don't quite understand this somewhat mixed-up statement of yours. You've been fishing on my pond, you say. Didn't you see my notice in the Advertiser?"

Dan sat down more composedly. The revelation was over and he was still alive.

"No, sir. We hardly ever see an Advertiser, and nobody told me. I'd always been used to fishing there, and I never thought but what it was all right to keep on. I know I ought to have remembered and asked you, but truly, sir, I didn't mean to steal your fish. I used to sell them over at the hotels. We saw the notice today, Mother and me, and I came right up. I've brought you the trout I caught this morning, and—if only you won't prosecute me, sir, I'll pay back every cent I got for the others—every cent, sir—if you'll give me time."

Mr. Walters passed his hand across his mouth to conceal something like a smile.

"Your name is Dan Phillips, isn't it?" he said irrelevantly, "and you live with your mother, the Widow Phillips, down there at Carleton Corners, I understand."

"Yes, sir," said Dan, wondering how Mr. Walters knew so much about him, and if these were the preliminaries of prosecution.

Mr. Walters took up his pen and drew a blank sheet towards him.

"Well, Dan, I put that notice in because I found that many people who used to fish on my pond, irrespective of leave or licence, were accustomed to lunch or camp on my property, and did not a little damage. I don't care for trouting myself; I've no time for it.

However, I hardly think you'll do much damage. You can keep on fishing there. I'll give you a written permission, so that if any of my men see you they won't interfere with you. As for these trout here, I'll buy them from you at Mosquito Lake prices, and will say no more about the matter. How will that do?"

"Thank you, sir," stammered Dan. He could hardly believe his ears. He took the slip of paper Mr. Walters handed to him and rose to his feet.

"Wait a minute, Dan. How was it you came to tell me this? You might have stopped your depredations, and I should not have been any the wiser."

"That wouldn't have been honest, sir," said Dan, looking squarely at him.

There was a brief silence. Mr. Walters thrummed meditatively on the table. Dan waited wonderingly.

Finally the factory owner said abruptly, "There's a vacant place for a boy down here. I want it filled as soon as possible. Will you take it?"

"Mr. Walters! Me!" Dan thought the world must be turning upside down.

"Yes, you. You are rather young, but the duties are not hard or difficult to learn. I think you'll do. I was resolved not to fill that place until I could find a perfectly honest and trustworthy boy for it. I believe I have found him. I discharged the last boy because he lied to me about some trifling offence for which I would have forgiven him if he had told the truth. I can bear with incompetency, but falsehood and deceit I cannot and will not tolerate," he said, so sternly that Dan's face paled. "I am convinced that you are incapable of either. Will you take the place, Dan?"

"I will if you think I can fill it, sir. I will do my best."

"Yes, I believe you will. Perhaps I know more about you than you think. Businessmen must keep their eyes open. We'll regard this matter as settled then. Come up tomorrow at eight o'clock. And one word more, Dan. You have perhaps heard that I am an unjust and hard master. I am not the former, and you will never have occasion to find me the latter if you are always as truthful and straightforward as you have been today. You might easily have deceived me in this matter. That you did not do so is the best and only recommendation I require. Take those trout up to my house and leave them. That will do. Good afternoon."

Dan somehow got his dazed self through the glass door and out of the building. The whole interview had been such a surprise to him that he was hardly sure whether or not he had dreamed it all.

"I feel as if I were some person else," he said to himself, as he started down the hot white road. "But Mother was right. I'll stick to her motto. I wonder what Sam will say to this."

The Lagoon

Joseph Conrad

Joseph Conrad (1857-1924) was a notable short story writer and novelist, having authored famous works such as *Heart of Darkness* (1899) and *Nostromo: A Tale of the Seaboard* (1904). His stories often have a maritime setting and deal with the exploration of the human psyche. Even though English was Conrad's third language, he was considered one of the greatest English novelists. 'The Lagoon' was first published in the January issue of *Cornhill Magazine* in 1897.

The white man, leaning with both arms over the roof of the little house in the stern of the boat, said to the steersman—

"We will pass the night in Arsat's clearing. It is late."

The Malay only grunted, and went on looking fixedly at the river. The white man rested his chin on his crossed arms and gazed at the wake of the boat. At the end of the straight avenue of forests cut by the intense glitter of the river, the sun appeared unclouded and dazzling, poised low over the water that shone smoothly like a band of metal. The forests, sombre and dull, stood motionless and silent on each side of the broad stream. At the foot of big, towering trees, trunkless nipa palms rose from the mud of the bank, in bunches of leaves enormous and heavy, that hung unstirring over the brown swirl of eddies. In the stillness of the air every tree, every leaf, every bough, every tendril of creeper and every petal of minute blossoms seemed to have been bewitched into an immobility perfect and final. Nothing moved on the river but the eight paddles that rose flashing regularly, dipped together with a single splash; while the steersman swept right and left with a periodic and sudden flourish of his blade describing a glinting semicircle above his head. The churned-up water frothed alongside with a confused murmur. And the white man's canoe, advancing upstream in the short-lived disturbance of its own making, seemed to enter the portals of a land from which the very memory of motion had forever departed.

The white man, turning his back upon the setting sun, looked along the empty and broad expanse of the sea-reach. For the last three miles of its course the wandering, hesitating river, as if enticed irresistibly by the freedom of an open horizon, flows straight into the sea, flows straight to the east—to the east that harbours both light and darkness. Astern of the boat the repeated call of some bird, a cry discordant and feeble, skipped along over the smooth water and lost itself, before it could reach the other shore, in the breathless silence of the world.

The steersman dug his paddle into the stream, and held hard with stiffened arms, his body thrown forward. The water gurgled aloud; and suddenly the long straight reach seemed to pivot on its centre, the forests swung in a semicircle, and the slanting beams of sunset touched the broadside of the canoe with a fiery glow, throwing the slender and distorted shadows of its crew upon the streaked glitter of the river. The white man turned to look ahead. The course of the boat had been altered at right-angles to the stream, and the carved dragon-head of its prow was pointing now at a gap in the fringing bushes of the bank. It glided through, brushing the overhanging twigs, and disappeared from the river like some slim and amphibious creature leaving the water for its lair in the forests.

The narrow creek was like a ditch: tortuous, fabulously deep; filled with gloom under the thin strip of pure and shining blue of the heaven. Immense trees soared up, invisible behind the festooned draperies of creepers. Here and there, near the glistening blackness of the water, a twisted root of some tall tree showed amongst the tracery of small ferns, black and dull, writhing and motionless, like an arrested snake. The short words of the paddlers reverberated loudly between the thick and sombre walls of vegetation. Darkness oozed out from between the trees, through the tangled maze of the creepers, from behind the great fantastic and unstirring leaves; the darkness, mysterious and invincible; the darkness scented and poisonous of impenetrable forests.

The men poled in the shoaling water. The creek broadened, opening out into a wide sweep of a stagnant lagoon. The forests receded from the marshy bank, leaving a level strip of bright green, reedy grass to frame the reflected blueness of the sky. A fleecy pink cloud drifted high above, trailing the delicate colouring of its image under the floating leaves and the silvery blossoms of the lotus. A little house, perched on high piles, appeared black in the distance. Near it, two tall nibong palms, that seemed to have come out of the forests in the background, leaned slightly over the ragged roof, with a suggestion of sad tenderness and care in the droop of their leafy and soaring heads.

The steersman, pointing with his paddle, said, "Arsat is there. I see his canoe fast between the piles."

The polers ran along the sides of the boat glancing over their shoulders at the end of the day's journey. They would have preferred to spend the night somewhere else than on this lagoon of weird aspect and ghostly reputation. Moreover, they disliked Arsat, first as a stranger, and also because he who repairs a ruined house, and dwells in it, proclaims that he is not afraid to live amongst the spirits that haunt the places abandoned by mankind. Such a man can disturb the course of fate by glances or words; while his familiar ghosts are not easy to propitiate by casual wayfarers upon whom they long to wreak the malice of their human master. White men care not for such things, being unbelievers and in league with the Father of Evil, who leads them unharmed through the invisible dangers of this world. To the warnings of the righteous they oppose an offensive pretence of disbelief. What is there to be done?

So they thought, throwing their weight on the end of their long poles. The big canoe glided on swiftly, noiselessly, and smoothly, towards Arsat's clearing, till, in a great rattling of poles thrown down, and the loud murmurs of "Allah be praised!" it came with a gentle knock against the crooked piles below the house.

The boatmen with uplifted faces shouted discordantly, "Arsat! O Arsat!" Nobody came. The white man began to climb the rude ladder giving access to the bamboo platform before the house. The juragan of the boat said sulkily, "We will cook in the sampan, and sleep on the water."

"Pass my blankets and the basket," said the white man, curtly.

He knelt on the edge of the platform to receive the bundle. Then the boat shoved off, and the white man, standing up, confronted Arsat, who had come out through the low door of his hut. He was a man young, powerful, with broad chest and muscular arms. He had nothing on but his sarong. His head was bare. His big, soft eyes stared eagerly at the white man, but his voice and demeanour were composed as he asked, without any words of greeting—

"Have you medicine, Tuan?"

"No," said the visitor in a startled tone. "No. Why? Is there sickness in the house?"

"Enter and see," replied Arsat, in the same calm manner, and turning short round, passed again through the small doorway. The white man, dropping his bundles, followed.

In the dim light of the dwelling he made out on a couch of bamboos a woman stretched on her back under a broad sheet of red cotton cloth. She lay still, as if dead; but her big eyes, wide open, glittered in the gloom, staring upwards at the slender rafters, motionless and unseeing. She was in a high fever, and evidently unconscious. Her cheeks were sunk slightly, her lips were partly open, and on the young face there was the ominous and fixed expression—the absorbed, contemplating expression of the unconscious who are going to die. The two men stood looking down at her in silence.

"Has she been long ill?" asked the traveller.

"I have not slept for five nights," answered the Malay, in a deliberate tone. "At first she heard voices calling her from the water and struggled against me who held her. But since the sun of today rose she hears nothing—she hears not me. She sees nothing. She sees not me—me!"

He remained silent for a minute, then asked softly—

"Tuan, will she die?"

"I fear so," said the white man, sorrowfully. He had known Arsat years ago, in a far country in times of trouble and danger, when no friendship is to be despised. And since his Malay friend had come unexpectedly to dwell in the hut on the lagoon with a strange woman, he had slept many times there, in his journeys up and down the river. He liked the man who knew how to keep faith in council and how to fight without fear by the side of his white friend. He liked him—not so much perhaps as a man likes his favourite dog—but still he liked him well enough to help and ask no questions, to think sometimes vaguely and hazily in the midst of his own pursuits, about the lonely man and the long-haired woman with audacious face and triumphant eyes, who lived together hidden by the forests—alone and feared.

The white man came out of the hut in time to see the enormous conflagration of sunset put out by the swift and stealthy shadows that, rising like a black and impalpable vapour above the tree-tops, spread over the heaven, extinguishing the crimson glow of floating clouds and the red brilliance of departing daylight. In a few moments all the stars came out above the intense blackness of the earth and the great lagoon gleaming suddenly with reflected lights resembled an oval patch of night sky flung down into the hopeless and abysmal night of the wilderness. The white man had some supper out of the basket, then collecting a few sticks that lay about the platform, made up a small fire, not for warmth, but for the sake of the smoke, which would keep off the mosquitos. He wrapped himself in the blankets and sat with his back against the reed wall of the house, smoking thoughtfully.

Arsat came through the doorway with noiseless steps and squatted down by the fire. The white man moved his outstretched legs a little.

"She breathes," said Arsat in a low voice, anticipating the expected question. "She breathes and burns as if with a great fire. She speaks not; she hears not—and burns!"

He paused for a moment, then asked in a quiet, incurious tone—

"Tuan… will she die?"

The white man moved his shoulders uneasily and muttered in a hesitating manner—

"If such is her fate."

"No, Tuan," said Arsat, calmly. "If such is my fate. I hear, I see, I wait. I remember … Tuan, do you remember the old days? Do you remember my brother?"

"Yes," said the white man. The Malay rose suddenly and went in. The other, sitting still outside, could hear the voice in the hut. Arsat said: "Hear me! Speak!" His words were succeeded by a complete silence. "O Diamelen!" he cried, suddenly. After that cry there was a deep sigh. Arsat came out and sank down again in his old place.

They sat in silence before the fire. There was no sound within the house, there was no sound near them; but far away on the lagoon they could hear the voices of the boatmen ringing fitful and distinct on the calm water. The fire in the bows of the sampan shone faintly in the distance with a hazy red glow. Then it died out. The voices ceased. The land and the water slept invisible, unstirring and mute. It was as though there had been nothing left in the world but the glitter of stars streaming, ceaseless and vain, through the black stillness of the night.

The white man gazed straight before him into the darkness with wide-open eyes. The fear and fascination, the inspiration and the wonder of death—of death near, unavoidable, and unseen, soothed the unrest of his race and stirred the most indistinct, the most intimate of his thoughts. The ever-ready suspicion of evil, the gnawing suspicion that lurks in our hearts, flowed out into the stillness round him—into the stillness profound and dumb, and made it appear untrustworthy and infamous, like the placid and impenetrable mask of an unjustifiable violence. In that fleeting and powerful disturbance of his being the earth enfolded in the starlight peace became a shadowy country of inhuman strife, a battlefield of phantoms terrible and charming, august or ignoble, struggling ardently for the possession of our helpless hearts. An unquiet and mysterious country of inextinguishable desires and fears.

A plaintive murmur rose in the night; a murmur saddening and startling, as if the great solitudes of surrounding woods had tried to whisper into his ear the wisdom of their immense and lofty indifference. Sounds hesitating and vague floated in the air round him, shaped themselves slowly into words; and at last flowed on gently in a murmuring stream of soft and monotonous sentences. He stirred like a man waking up and changed his position slightly. Arsat, motionless and shadowy, sitting with bowed head under the stars, was speaking in a low and dreamy tone—

"... for where can we lay down the heaviness of our trouble but in a friend's heart? A man must speak of war and of love. You, Tuan, know what war is, and you have seen me in time of danger seek death as other men seek life! A writing may be lost; a lie may be written; but what the eye has seen is truth and remains in the mind!"

"I remember," said the white man, quietly. Arsat went on with mournful composure—

"Therefore I shall speak to you of love. Speak in the night. Speak before both night and love are gone—and the eye of day looks upon my sorrow and my shame; upon my blackened face; upon my burnt-up heart."

A sigh, short and faint, marked an almost imperceptible pause, and then his words flowed on, without a stir, without a gesture.

"After the time of trouble and war was over and you went away from my country in the pursuit of your desires, which we, men of the islands, cannot understand, I and my brother became again, as we had been before, the sword-bearers of the Ruler. You know we were men of family, belonging to a ruling race, and more fit than any to carry on our right shoulder the emblem of power. And in the time of prosperity Si Dendring showed us favour, as we, in time of sorrow, had showed to him the faithfulness of our courage. It was a time of peace. A time of deer-hunts and cock-fights; of idle talks and foolish squabbles between men whose bellies are full and weapons are rusty. But the sower watched the young rice-shoots grow up without fear, and the traders came and went, departed lean and returned fat into the river of peace. They brought news, too. Brought lies and truth mixed together, so that no man knew when to rejoice and when to be sorry. We heard from them about you also. They had seen you here and had seen you there. And I was glad to hear, for I remembered the stirring times, and I always remembered you, Tuan, till the time came when my eyes could see nothing in the past, because they had looked upon the one who is dying there—in the house."

He stopped to exclaim in an intense whisper, "O Mara bahia! O Calamity!" then went on speaking a little louder:

"There's no worse enemy and no better friend than a brother, Tuan, for one brother knows another, and in perfect knowledge is strength for good or evil. I loved my brother. I went to him and told him that I could see nothing but one face, hear nothing but one voice. He told me: 'Open your heart so that she can see what is in it—and wait. Patience is wisdom. Inchi Midah may die or our Ruler may throw off his fear of a woman!' … I waited! … You remember the lady with the veiled face, Tuan, and the fear of our Ruler before her cunning and temper. And if she wanted her servant, what could I do? But I fed the hunger of my heart on short glances and stealthy words. I loitered on the path to the bath-houses in the daytime, and when the sun had fallen behind the forest I crept along the jasmine hedges of the women's courtyard. Unseeing, we spoke to one another through the scent of flowers, through the veil of leaves, through the blades of long grass that stood still before our lips; so great was our prudence, so faint was the murmur of our great longing. The time passed swiftly … and there were whispers amongst women—and our enemies watched—my brother was gloomy, and I began to think of killing and of a fierce death …. We are of a people who take what they want—like you whites. There is a time when a man should forget loyalty and respect. Might and authority are given to rulers, but to all men is given love and strength and courage. My brother said, 'You shall take her from their midst. We are two who are like one.' And I answered, 'Let it be soon, for I find no warmth in sunlight that does not shine upon her.' Our time came when the Ruler and all the great people went to the mouth of the river to fish by torchlight. There were hundreds of boats, and on the white sand, between the water and the forests, dwellings of leaves were built for the households of the Rajahs. The smoke of cooking-fires was like a blue mist of the evening, and many voices rang in it joyfully. While they were making the boats ready to beat up the fish, my brother came to me and said, 'Tonight!' I looked to my weapons, and when the time came our canoe took its place in the circle of boats carrying the torches. The lights blazed on the water, but behind the boats there was darkness. When the shouting began and the excitement made them like mad we dropped out. The water swallowed our fire, and we floated back to the shore that was dark with only here and there the glimmer of embers. We could hear the talk of slave-girls amongst the sheds. Then we found a place deserted and silent. We waited there. She came. She came running along the shore, rapid and leaving no trace, like a leaf driven by the wind into the sea. My brother said gloomily, 'Go and take her; carry her into our boat.' I lifted her in my arms. She panted. Her heart was beating against my breast. I said, 'I take you from those people. You came to the cry of my heart, but my arms take you into my boat against the will of the great!' 'It is right,' said my brother. 'We are men who take what we want and can hold it against many. We should have taken her in daylight.' I said, 'Let us be off,' for since she was in my boat I began to think of our Ruler's many men. 'Yes. Let us be off,' said my brother. 'We are cast out and this boat is our country now—and the sea is our refuge.' He lingered with his foot on the shore, and I entreated him to hasten, for I remembered the strokes of her heart against my breast and thought that two men cannot withstand a hundred. We left, paddling downstream close to the bank; and as we passed by the creek where they were fishing, the great shouting had ceased, but the murmur of voices was loud like the humming of insects flying at noonday. The boats floated, clustered together, in the red light of torches, under a black roof of smoke; and men talked of their sport. Men that boasted, and praised, and jeered—men that would have been our friends in the morning, but on that night were already our enemies. We paddled swiftly past. We had no more friends in the country of our birth. She sat in the middle of the canoe with covered face; silent as she is now; unseeing as she is now—and I had no regret at what I was leaving because I could hear her breathing close to me—as I can hear her now."

He paused, listened with his ear turned to the doorway, then shook his head and went on:

"My brother wanted to shout the cry of challenge—one cry only—to let the people know we were freeborn robbers who trusted our arms and the great sea. And again I begged him in the name of our love to be silent. Could I not hear her breathing close to me? I knew the pursuit would come quick enough. My brother loved me. He dipped his paddle without a splash. He only said, 'There is half a man in you now—the other half is in that woman. I can wait. When you are a whole man again, you will come back with me here to shout defiance. We are sons of the same mother.' I made no answer. All my strength and all my spirit were in my hands that held the paddle—for I longed to be with her in a safe place beyond the reach of men's anger and of women's spite. My love was so great, that I thought it could guide me to a country where death was unknown, if I could only escape from Inchi Midah's fury and from our Ruler's sword. We paddled with haste, breathing through our teeth. The blades bit deep into the smooth water. We passed out of the river; we flew in clear channels amongst the shallows. We skirted the black coast; we skirted the sand beaches where the sea speaks in whispers to the land; and the gleam of white sand flashed back past our boat, so swiftly she ran upon the water. We spoke not. Only once I said, 'Sleep, Diamelen, for soon you may want all your strength.' I heard the sweetness of her voice, but I never turned my head. The sun rose and still we went on. Water fell from my face like rain from a cloud. We flew in the light and heat. I never looked back, but I knew that my brother's eyes, behind me, were looking steadily ahead, for the boat went as straight as a bushman's dart, when it leaves the end of the sumpitan. There was no better paddler, no better steersman than my brother. Many times, together, we had won races in that canoe. But we never had put out our strength as we did then—then, when for the last time we paddled together! There was no braver or stronger man in our country than my brother. I could not spare the strength to turn my head and look at him, but every moment I heard the hiss of his breath getting louder behind me. Still he did not speak. The sun was high. The heat clung to my back like a flame of fire. My ribs were ready to burst, but I could no longer get enough air into my chest. And then I felt I must cry out with my last breath, 'Let us rest!' … 'Good!' he answered; and his voice was firm. He was strong. He was brave. He knew not fear and no fatigue… My brother!"

A murmur powerful and gentle, a murmur vast and faint; the murmur of trembling leaves, of stirring boughs, ran through the tangled depths of the forests, ran over the starry smoothness of the lagoon, and the water between the piles lapped the slimy timber once with a sudden splash. A breath of warm air touched the two men's faces and passed on with a mournful sound—a breath loud and short like an uneasy sigh of the dreaming earth.

Arsat went on in an even, low voice.

"We ran our canoe on the white beach of a little bay close to a long tongue of land that seemed to bar our road; a long wooded cape going far into the sea. My brother knew that place. Beyond the cape a river has its entrance, and through the jungle of that land there is a narrow path. We made a fire and cooked rice. Then we lay down to sleep on the soft sand in the shade of our canoe, while she watched. No sooner had I closed my eyes than I heard her cry of alarm. We leaped up. The sun was halfway down the sky already, and coming in sight in the opening of the bay we saw a prau manned by many paddlers. We knew it at once; it was one of our Rajah's praus. They were watching the shore, and saw us. They beat the gong, and turned the head of the prau into the bay. I felt my heart become weak within my breast. Diamelen sat on the sand and covered her face. There was no escape by sea. My brother laughed. He had the gun you had given him, Tuan, before you went away, but there was only a handful of powder. He spoke to me quickly: 'Run with her along the path. I shall keep them back, for they have no firearms, and landing in the face of a man with a gun is certain death for some. Run with her. On the other side of that wood there is a fisherman's house—and a canoe. When I have fired all the shots I will follow. I am a great runner, and before they can come up we shall be gone. I will hold out as long as I can, for she is but a woman—that can neither run nor fight, but she has your heart in her weak hands.' He dropped behind the canoe. The prau was coming. She and I ran, and as we rushed along the path I heard shots. My brother fired—once—twice—and the booming of the gong ceased. There was silence behind us. That neck of land is narrow. Before I heard my brother fire the third shot I saw the shelving shore, and I saw the water again; the mouth of a broad river. We crossed a grassy glade. We ran down to the water. I saw a low hut above the black mud, and a small canoe hauled up. I heard another shot behind me. I thought, 'That is his last charge.' We rushed down to the canoe; a man came running from the hut, but I leaped on him, and we rolled together in the mud. Then I got up, and he lay still at my feet. I don't know whether I had killed him or not. I and Diamelen pushed the canoe afloat. I heard yells behind me, and I saw my brother run across the glade. Many men were bounding after him, I took her in my arms and threw her into the boat, then leaped in myself. When I looked back I saw that my brother had fallen. He fell and was up again, but the men were closing round him. He shouted, 'I am coming!' The men were close to him. I looked. Many men. Then I looked at her. Tuan, I pushed the canoe! I pushed it into deep water. She was kneeling forward looking at me, and I said, 'Take your paddle,' while I struck the water with mine. Tuan, I heard him cry. I heard him cry my name twice; and I heard voices shouting, 'Kill! Strike!' I never turned back. I heard him calling my name again with a great shriek, as when life is going out together with the voice—and I never turned my head. My own name!... My brother! Three times he called—but I was not afraid of life. Was she not there in that canoe? And could I not with her find a country where death is forgotten—where death is unknown!"

The white man sat up. Arsat rose and stood, an indistinct and silent figure above the dying embers of the fire. Over the lagoon a mist drifting and low had crept, erasing slowly the glittering images of the stars. And now a great expanse of white vapour covered the land: it flowed cold and gray in the darkness, eddied in noiseless whirls round the tree-trunks and about the platform of the house, which seemed to float upon a restless and impalpable illusion of a sea. Only far away the tops of the trees stood outlined on the twinkle of heaven, like a sombre and forbidding shore—a coast deceptive, pitiless and black.

Arsat's voice vibrated loudly in the profound peace.

"I had her there! I had her! To get her I would have faced all mankind. But I had her—and—"

His words went out ringing into the empty distances. He paused, and seemed to listen to them dying away very far—beyond help and beyond recall. Then he said quietly—

"Tuan, I loved my brother."

A breath of wind made him shiver. High above his head, high above the silent sea of mist the drooping leaves of the palms rattled together with a mournful and expiring sound. The white man stretched his legs. His chin rested on his chest, and he murmured sadly without lifting his head—

"We all love our brothers."

Arsat burst out with an intense whispering violence—

"What did I care who died? I wanted peace in my own heart."

He seemed to hear a stir in the house—listened—then stepped in noiselessly. The white man stood up. A breeze was coming in fitful puffs. The stars shone paler as if they had retreated into the frozen depths of immense space. After a chill gust of wind there were a few seconds of perfect calm and absolute silence. Then from behind the black and wavy line of the forests a column of golden light shot up into the heavens and spread over the semicircle of the eastern horizon. The sun had risen. The mist lifted, broke into drifting patches, vanished into thin flying wreaths; and the unveiled lagoon lay, polished and black, in the heavy shadows at the foot of the wall of trees. A white eagle rose over it with a slanting and ponderous flight, reached the clear sunshine and appeared dazzlingly brilliant for a moment, then soaring higher, became a dark and motionless speck before it vanished into the blue as if it had left the earth forever. The white man, standing gazing upwards before the doorway, heard in the hut a confused and broken murmur of distracted words ending with a loud groan. Suddenly Arsat stumbled out with outstretched hands, shivered, and stood still for some time with fixed eyes. Then he said—

"She burns no more."

Before his face the sun showed its edge above the tree-tops rising steadily. The breeze freshened; a great brilliance burst upon the lagoon, sparkled on the rippling water. The forests came out of the clear shadows of the morning, became distinct, as if they had rushed nearer—to stop short in a great stir of leaves, of nodding boughs, of swaying branches. In the merciless sunshine the whisper of unconscious life grew louder, speaking in an incomprehensible voice round the dumb darkness of that human sorrow. Arsat's eyes wandered slowly, then stared at the rising sun.

"I can see nothing," he said half aloud to himself.

"There is nothing," said the white man, moving to the edge of the platform and waving his hand to his boat. A shout came faintly over the lagoon and the sampan began to glide towards the abode of the friend of ghosts.

"If you want to come with me, I will wait all the morning," said the white man, looking away upon the water.

"No, Tuan," said Arsat, softly. "I shall not eat or sleep in this house, but I must first see my road. Now I can see nothing—see nothing! There is no light and no peace in the world; but there is death—death for many. We are sons of the same mother—and I left him in the midst of enemies; but I am going back now."

He drew a long breath and went on in a dreamy tone:

"In a little while I shall see clear enough to strike—to strike. But she has died, and… now… darkness."

He flung his arms wide open, let them fall along his body, then stood still with unmoved face and stony eyes, staring at the sun. The white man got down into his canoe. The polers ran smartly along the sides of the boat, looking over their shoulders at the beginning of a weary journey. High in the stern, his head muffled up in white rags, the juragan sat moody, letting his paddle trail in the water. The white man, leaning with both arms over the grass roof of the little cabin, looked back at the shining ripple of the boat's wake. Before the sampan passed out of the lagoon into the creek he lifted his eyes. Arsat had not moved. He stood lonely in the searching sunshine; and he looked beyond the great light of a cloudless day into the darkness of a world of illusions.

The Auction

Stephen Crane

Stephen Crane (1871-1900) was an American novelist, poet and short story writer who was popular for writing novels that touched upon various social problems. *The Red Badge of Courage* (1895) was praised by war veterans for the accuracy with which it portrayed the experiences of a soldier. Two years later, in 1897, Crane also served as a war correspondent. 'The Auction' is from the notable collection *The Open Boat and Other Stories* (1898).

Some said that Ferguson gave up sailoring because he was tired of the sea. Some said that it was because he loved a woman. In truth it was because he was tired of the sea and because he loved a woman.

He saw the woman once, and immediately she became for him the symbol of all things unconnected with the sea. He did not trouble to look again at the grey old goddess, the muttering slave of the moon. Her splendours, her treacheries, her smiles, her rages, her vanities, were no longer on his mind. He took heels after a little human being, and the woman made his thought spin at all times like a top; whereas the ocean had only made him think when he was on watch.

He developed a grin for the power of the sea, and, in derision, he wanted to sell the red and green parrot which had sailed four voyages with him. The woman, however, had a sentiment concerning the bird's plumage, and she commanded Ferguson to keep it in order, as it happened, that she might forget to put food in its cage.

The parrot did not attend the wedding. It stayed at home and blasphemed at a stock of furniture, bought on the installment plan, and arrayed for the reception of the bride and groom.

As a sailor, Ferguson had suffered the acute hankering for port; and being now always in port, he tried to force life to become an endless picnic. He was not an example of diligent and peaceful citizenship. Ablution became difficult in the little apartment, because Ferguson kept the wash-basin filled with ice and bottles of beer: and so, finally, the dealer in second-hand furniture agreed to auction the household goods on commission. Owing to an exceedingly liberal definition of a term, the parrot and cage were included. "On the level?" cried the parrot, "On the level? On the level? On the level?"

On the way to the sale, Ferguson's wife spoke hopefully. "You can't tell, Jim," she said. "Perhaps some of 'em will get to biddin', and we might get almost as much as we paid for the things."

The auction room was in a cellar. It was crowded with people and with house furniture; so that as the auctioneer's assistant moved from one piece to another he caused a great shuffling. There was an astounding number of old women in curious bonnets. The rickety stairway was thronged with men who wished to smoke and be free from the old women. Two lamps made all the faces appear yellow as parchment. Incidentally they could impart a lustre of value to very poor furniture.

The auctioneer was a fat, shrewd-looking individual, who seemed also to be a great bully. The assistant was the most imperturbable of beings, moving with the dignity of an image on rollers. As the Fergusons forced their way down the stairway, the assistant roared: "Number twenty-one!"

"Number twenty-one!" cried the auctioneer. "Number twenty-one! A fine new handsome bureau! Two dollars? Two dollars is bid! Two and a half! Two and a half! Three? Three is bid. Four! Four dollars! A fine new handsome bureau at four dollars! Four dollars! Four dollars! F-o-u-r d-o-l-l-a-r-s! Sold at four dollars."

"On the level?" cried the parrot, muffled somewhere among furniture and carpets. "On the level? On the level?" Every one tittered.

Mrs. Ferguson had turned pale, and gripped her husband's arm. "Jim! Did you hear? The bureau—four dollars—"

Ferguson glowered at her with the swift brutality of a man afraid of a scene. "Shut up, can't you!"

Mrs. Ferguson took a seat upon the steps; and hidden there by the thick ranks of men, she began to softly sob. Through her tears appeared the yellowish mist of the lamplight, streaming about the monstrous shadows of the spectators. From time to time these latter whispered eagerly: "See, that went cheap!" In fact when anything was bought at a particularly low price, a murmur of admiration arose for the successful bidder.

The bedstead was sold for two dollars, the mattresses and springs for one dollar and sixty cents. This figure seemed to go through the woman's heart. There was derision in the sound of it. She bowed her head in her hands. "Oh, God, a dollar-sixty! Oh, God, a dollar-sixty!"

The parrot was evidently under heaps of carpet, but the dauntless bird still raised the cry, "On the level?"

Some of the men near Mrs. Ferguson moved timidly away upon hearing her low sobs. They perfectly understood that a woman in tears is formidable.

The shrill voice went like a hammer, beat and beat, upon the woman's heart. An odour of varnish, of the dust of old carpets, assailed her and seemed to possess a sinister meaning. The golden haze from the two lamps was an atmosphere of shame, sorrow, greed. But it was when the parrot called that a terror of the place and of the eyes of the people arose in her so strongly that she could not have lifted her head any more than if her neck had been of iron.

At last came the parrot's turn. The assistant fumbled until he found the ring of the cage, and the bird was drawn into view. It adjusted its feathers calmly and cast a rolling wicked eye over the crowd.

"Oh, the good ship Sarah sailed the seas,And the wind it blew all day—"

This was the part of a ballad which Ferguson had tried to teach it. With a singular audacity and scorn, the parrot bawled these lines at the auctioneer as if it considered them to bear some particular insult.

The throng in the cellar burst into laughter. The auctioneer attempted to start the bidding, and the parrot interrupted with a repetition of the lines. It swaggered to and fro on its perch, and gazed at the faces of the crowd, with so much rowdy understanding and derision that even the auctioneer could not confront it. The auction was brought to a halt; a wild hilarity developed, and every one gave jeering advice.

Ferguson looked down at his wife and groaned. She had cowered against the wall, hiding her face. He touched her shoulder and she arose. They sneaked softly up the stairs with heads bowed.

Out in the street, Ferguson gripped his fists and said: "Oh, but wouldn't I like to strangle it!"

His wife cried in a voice of wild grief: "It—it m—made us a laughing-stock in—in front of all that crowd!"

For the auctioning of their household goods, the sale of their home—this financial calamity lost its power in the presence of the social shame contained in a crowd's laughter.

The Muse's Tragedy

Edith Wharton

Edith Wharton (1862-1937) was an American novelist and short story writer best known for *The House of Mirth* (1905) and *The Age of Innocence* (1920). She wrote about the upper-class New England society she belonged to. Like her literary model, Henry James, ethical issues were preponderant in her works. This is also evident in 'The Muse's Tragedy' (1899), which has feminist concerns at its core.

I

Danyers afterwards liked to fancy that he had recognized Mrs. Anerton at once; but that, of course, was absurd, since he had seen no portrait of her—she affected a strict anonymity, refusing even her photograph to the most privileged—and from Mrs. Memorall, whom he revered and cultivated as her friend, he had extracted but the one impressionist phrase: "Oh, well, she's like one of those old prints where the lines have the value of color."

He was almost certain, at all events, that he had been thinking of Mrs. Anerton as he sat over his breakfast in the empty hotel restaurant, and that, looking up on the approach of the lady who seated herself at the table near the window, he had said to himself, "That might be she."

Ever since his Harvard days—he was still young enough to think of them as immensely remote—Danyers had dreamed of Mrs. Anerton, the Silvia of Vincent Rendle's immortal sonnet-cycle, the Mrs. A. of the Life and Letters. Her name was enshrined in some of the noblest English verse of the nineteenth century—and of all past or future centuries, as Danyers, from the stand-point of a maturer judgment, still believed. The first reading of certain poems—of the Antinous, the Pia Tolomei, the Sonnets to Silvia,—had been epochs in Danyers's growth, and the verse seemed to gain in mellowness, in amplitude, in meaning as one brought to its interpretation more experience of life, a finer emotional sense. Where, in his boyhood, he had felt only the perfect, the almost austere beauty of form, the subtle interplay of vowel-sounds, the rush and fulness of lyric emotion, he now thrilled to the close-packed significance of each line, the allusiveness of each word—his imagination lured hither and thither on fresh trails of thought, and perpetually spurred by the sense that, beyond what he had already discovered, more marvellous regions lay waiting to be explored. Danyers had written, at college, the prize essay on Rendle's poetry (it chanced to be the moment of the great man's death); he had fashioned the fugitive verse of his own storm-and-stress period on the forms which Rendle had first given to English metre; and when two years later the Life and Letters appeared, and the Silvia of the sonnets took substance as Mrs. A., he had included in his worship of Rendle the woman who had inspired not only such divine verse but such playful, tender, incomparable prose.

Danyers never forgot the day when Mrs. Memorall happened to mention that she knew Mrs. Anerton. He had known Mrs. Memorall for a year or more, and had somewhat contemptuously classified her as the kind of woman who runs cheap excursions to celebrities; when one afternoon she remarked, as she put a second lump of sugar in his tea:

"Is it right this time? You're almost as particular as Mary Anerton."

"Mary Anerton?"

"Yes, I never can remember how she likes her tea. Either it's lemon with sugar, or lemon without sugar, or cream without either, and whichever it is must be put into the cup before the tea is poured in; and if one hasn't remembered, one must begin all over again. I suppose it was Vincent Rendle's way of taking his tea and has become a sacred rite."

"Do you know Mrs. Anerton?" cried Danyers, disturbed by this careless familiarity with the habits of his divinity.

"'And did I once see Shelley plain?' Mercy, yes! She and I were at school together—she's an American, you know. We were at a pension near Tours for nearly a year; then she went back to New York, and I didn't see her again till after her marriage. She and Anerton spent a winter in Rome while my husband was attached to our Legation there, and she used to be with us a great deal." Mrs. Memorall smiled reminiscently. "It was the winter."

"The winter they first met?"

"Precisely—but unluckily I left Rome just before the meeting took place. Wasn't it too bad? I might have been in the Life and Letters. You know he mentions that stupid Madame Vodki, at whose house he first saw her."

"And did you see much of her after that?"

"Not during Rendle's life. You know she has lived in Europe almost entirely, and though I used to see her off and on when I went abroad, she was always so engrossed, so preoccupied, that one felt one wasn't wanted. The fact is, she cared only about his friends—she separated herself gradually from all her own people. Now, of course, it's different; she's desperately lonely; she's taken to writing to me now and then; and last year, when she heard I was going abroad, she asked me to meet her in Venice, and I spent a week with her there."

"And Rendle?"

Mrs. Memorall smiled and shook her head. "Oh, I never was allowed a peep at him; none of her old friends met him, except by accident. Ill-natured people say that was the reason she kept him so long. If one happened in while he was there, he was hustled into Anerton's study, and the husband mounted guard till the inopportune visitor had departed. Anerton, you know, was really much more ridiculous about it than his wife. Mary was too clever to lose her head, or at least to show she'd lost it—but Anerton couldn't conceal his pride in the conquest. I've seen Mary shiver when he spoke of Rendle as our poet. Rendle always had to have a certain seat at the dinner-table, away from the draught and not too near the fire, and a box of cigars that no one else was allowed to touch, and a writing-table of his own in Mary's sitting-room—and Anerton was always telling one of the great man's idiosyncrasies: how he never would cut the ends of his cigars, though Anerton himself had given him a gold cutter set with a star-sapphire, and how untidy his writing-table was, and how the house- maid had orders always to bring the waste-paper basket to her mistress before emptying it, lest some immortal verse should be thrown into the dust-bin."

"The Anertons never separated, did they?"

"Separated? Bless you, no. He never would have left Rendle! And besides, he was very fond of his wife."

"And she?"

"Oh, she saw he was the kind of man who was fated to make himself ridiculous, and she never interfered with his natural tendencies."

From Mrs. Memorall, Danyers further learned that Mrs. Anerton, whose husband had died some years before her poet, now divided her life between Rome, where she had a small apartment, and England, where she occasionally went to stay with those of her friends who had been Rendle's. She had been engaged, for some time after his death, in editing some juvenilia which he had bequeathed to her care; but that task being accomplished, she had been left without definite occupation, and Mrs. Memorall, on the occasion of their last meeting, had found her listless and out of spirits.

"She misses him too much—her life is too empty. I told her so—I told her she ought to marry."

"Oh!"

"Why not, pray? She's a young woman still—what many people would call young," Mrs. Memorall interjected, with a parenthetic glance at the mirror. "Why not accept the inevitable and begin over again? All the King's horses and all the King's men won't bring Rendle to life-and besides, she didn't marry him when she had the chance."

Danyers winced slightly at this rude fingering of his idol. Was it possible that Mrs. Memorall did not see what an anti-climax such a marriage would have been? Fancy Rendle "making an honest woman" of Silvia; for so society would have viewed it! How such a reparation would have vulgarized their past—it would have been like "restoring" a masterpiece; and how exquisite must have been the perceptions of the woman who, in defiance of appearances, and perhaps of her own secret inclination, chose to go down to posterity as Silvia rather than as Mrs. Vincent Rendle!

Mrs. Memorall, from this day forth, acquired an interest in Danyers's eyes. She was like a volume of unindexed and discursive memoirs, through which he patiently plodded in the hope of finding embedded amid layers of dusty twaddle some precious allusion to the subject of his thought. When, some months later, he brought out his first slim volume, in which the remodelled college essay on Rendle figured among a dozen, somewhat overstudied "appreciations," he offered a copy to Mrs. Memorall; who surprised him, the next time they met, with the announcement that she had sent the book to Mrs. Anerton.

Mrs. Anerton in due time wrote to thank her friend. Danyers was privileged to read the few lines in which, in terms that suggested the habit of "acknowledging" similar tributes, she spoke of the author's "feeling and insight," and was "so glad of the opportunity," etc. He went away disappointed, without clearly knowing what else he had expected.

The following spring, when he went abroad, Mrs. Memorall offered him letters to everybody, from the Archbishop of Canterbury to Louise Michel. She did not include Mrs. Anerton, however, and Danyers knew, from a previous conversation, that Silvia objected to people who "brought letters." He knew also that she travelled during the summer, and was unlikely to return to Rome before the term of his holiday should be reached, and the hope of meeting her was not included among his anticipations.

The lady whose entrance broke upon his solitary repast in the restaurant of the Hotel Villa d'Este had seated herself in such a way that her profile was detached against the window; and thus viewed, her domed forehead, small arched nose, and fastidious lip suggested a silhouette of Marie Antoinette. In the lady's dress and movements—in the very turn of her wrist as she poured out her coffee—Danyers thought he detected the same fastidiousness, the same air of tacitly excluding the obvious and unexceptional. Here was a woman who had been much bored and keenly interested. The waiter brought her a Secolo, and as she bent above it Danyers noticed that the hair rolled back from her forehead was turning gray; but her figure was straight and slender, and she had the invaluable gift of a girlish back.

The rush of Anglo-Saxon travel had not set toward the lakes, and with the exception of an Italian family or two, and a hump-backed youth with an abbe, Danyers and the lady had the marble halls of the Villa d'Este to themselves.

When he returned from his morning ramble among the hills he saw her sitting at one of the little tables at the edge of the lake. She was writing, and a heap of books and newspapers lay on the table at her side. That evening they met again in the garden. He had strolled out to smoke a last cigarette before dinner, and under the black vaulting of ilexes, near the steps leading down to the boat-landing, he found her leaning on the parapet above the lake. At the sound of his approach she turned and looked at him. She had thrown a black lace scarf over her head, and in this sombre setting her face seemed thin and unhappy. He remembered afterwards that her eyes, as they met his, expressed not so much sorrow as profound discontent.

To his surprise she stepped toward him with a detaining gesture. "Mr. Lewis Danyers, I believe?"

He bowed.

"I am Mrs. Anerton. I saw your name on the visitors' list and wished to thank you for an essay on Mr. Rendle's poetry—or rather to tell you how much I appreciated it. The book was sent to me last winter by Mrs. Memorall."

She spoke in even melancholy tones, as though the habit of perfunctory utterance had robbed her voice of more spontaneous accents; but her smile was charming. They sat down on a stone bench under the ilexes, and she told him how much pleasure his essay had given her. She thought it the best in the book—she was sure he had put more of himself into it than into any other; was she not right in conjecturing that he had been very deeply influenced by Mr. Rendle's poetry? Pour comprendre il faut aimer, and it seemed to her that, in some ways, he had penetrated the poet's inner meaning more completely than any other critic. There were certain problems, of course, that he had left untouched; certain aspects of that many-sided mind that he had perhaps failed to seize—

"But then you are young," she concluded gently, "and one could not wish you, as yet, the experience that a fuller understanding would imply."

II

She stayed a month at Villa d'Este, and Danyers was with her daily. She showed an unaffected pleasure in his society; a pleasure so obviously founded on their common veneration of Rendle, that the young man could enjoy it without fear of fatuity. At first he was merely one more grain of frankincense on the altar of her insatiable divinity; but gradually a more personal note crept into their intercourse. If she still liked him only because he appreciated Rendle, she at least perceptibly distinguished him from the herd of Rendle's appreciators.

Her attitude toward the great man's memory struck Danyers as perfect. She neither proclaimed nor disavowed her identity. She was frankly Silvia to those who knew and cared; but there was no trace of the Egeria in her pose. She spoke often of Rendle's books, but seldom of himself; there was no posthumous conjugality, no use of the possessive tense, in her abounding reminiscences. Of the master's intellectual life, of his habits of thought and work, she never wearied of talking. She knew the history of each poem; by what scene or episode each image had been evoked; how many times the words in a certain line had been transposed; how long a certain adjective had been sought, and what had at last suggested it; she could even explain that one impenetrable line, the torment of critics, the joy of detractors, the last line of The Old Odysseus.

Danyers felt that in talking of these things she was no mere echo of Rendle's thought. If her identity had appeared to be merged in his it was because they thought alike, not because he had thought for her. Posterity is apt to regard the women whom poets have sung as chance pegs on which they hung their garlands; but Mrs. Anerton's mind was like some fertile garden wherein, inevitably, Rendle's imagination had rooted itself and flowered. Danyers began to see how many threads of his complex mental tissue the poet had owed to the blending of her temperament with his; in a certain sense Silvia had herself created the Sonnets to Silvia.

To be the custodian of Rendle's inner self, the door, as it were, to the sanctuary, had at first seemed to Danyers so comprehensive a privilege that he had the sense, as his friendship with Mrs. Anerton advanced, of forcing his way into a life already crowded. What room was there, among such towering memories, for so small an actuality as his? Quite suddenly, after this, he discovered that Mrs. Memorall knew better: his fortunate friend was bored as well as lonely.

"You have had more than any other woman!" he had exclaimed to her one day; and her smile flashed a derisive light on his blunder. Fool that he was, not to have seen that she had not had enough! That she was young still—do years count?—tender, human, a woman; that the living have need of the living.

After that, when they climbed the alleys of the hanging park, resting in one of the little ruined temples, or watching, through a ripple of foliage, the remote blue flash of the lake, they did not always talk of Rendle or of literature. She encouraged Danyers to speak of himself; to confide his ambitions to her; she asked him the questions which are the wise woman's substitute for advice.

"You must write," she said, administering the most exquisite flattery that human lips could give.

Of course he meant to write—why not to do something great in his turn? His best, at least; with the resolve, at the outset, that his best should be the best. Nothing less seemed possible with that mandate in his ears. How she had divined him; lifted and disentangled his groping ambitions; laid the awakening touch on his spirit with her creative Let there be light!

It was his last day with her, and he was feeling very hopeless and happy.

"You ought to write a book about him," she went on gently.

Danyers started; he was beginning to dislike Rendle's way of walking in unannounced.

"You ought to do it," she insisted. "A complete interpretation—a summing- up of his style, his purpose, his theory of life and art. No one else could do it as well."

He sat looking at her perplexedly. Suddenly—dared he guess?

"I couldn't do it without you," he faltered.

"I could help you—I would help you, of course."

They sat silent, both looking at the lake.

It was agreed, when they parted, that he should rejoin her six weeks later in Venice. There they were to talk about the book.

III

Lago d'Iseo, August 14th.

When I said goodbye to you yesterday I promised to come back to Venice in a week: I was to give you your answer then. I was not honest in saying that; I didn't mean to go back to Venice or to see you again. I was running away from you—and I mean to keep on running! If you won't, I must. Somebody must save you from marrying a disappointed woman of—well, you say years don't count, and why should they, after all, since you are not to marry me?

That is what I dare not go back to say. You are not to marry me. We have had our month together in Venice (such a good month, was it not?) and now you are to go home and write a book—any book but the one we—didn't talk of!—and I am to stay here, attitudinizing among my memories like a sort of female Tithonus. The dreariness of this enforced immortality!

But you shall know the truth. I care for you, or at least for your love, enough to owe you that.

You thought it was because Vincent Rendle had loved me that there was so little hope for you. I had had what I wanted to the full; wasn't that what you said? It is just when a man begins to think he understands a woman that he may be sure he doesn't! It is because Vincent Rendle didn't love me that there is no hope for you. I never had what I wanted, and never, never, never will I stoop to wanting anything else.

Do you begin to understand? It was all a sham then, you say? No, it was all real as far as it went. You are young—you haven't learned, as you will later, the thousand imperceptible signs by which one gropes one's way through the labyrinth of human nature; but didn't it strike you, sometimes, that I never told you any foolish little anecdotes about him? His trick, for instance, of twirling a paper-knife round and round between his thumb and forefinger while he talked; his mania for saving the backs of notes; his greediness for wild strawberries, the little pungent Alpine ones; his childish delight in acrobats and jugglers; his way of always calling me you—dear you, every letter began—I never told you a word of all that, did I? Do you suppose I could have helped telling you, if he had loved me? These little things would have been mine, then, a part of my life—of our life—they would have slipped out in spite of me (it's only your unhappy woman who is always reticent and dignified). But there never was any "our life;" it was always "our lives" to the end....

If you knew what a relief it is to tell some one at last, you would bear with me, you would let me hurt you! I shall never be quite so lonely again, now that some one knows.

Let me begin at the beginning. When I first met Vincent Rendle I was not twenty-five. That was twenty years ago. From that time until his death, five years ago, we were fast friends. He gave me fifteen years, perhaps the best fifteen years, of his life. The world, as you know, thinks that his greatest poems were written during those years; I am supposed to have "inspired" them, and in a sense I did. From the first, the intellectual sympathy between us was almost complete; my mind must have been to him (I fancy) like some perfectly tuned instrument on which he was never tired of playing. Some one told me of his once saying of me that I "always understood;" it is the only praise I ever heard of his giving me. I don't even know if he thought me pretty, though I hardly think my appearance could have been disagreeable to him, for he hated to be with ugly people. At all events he fell into the way of spending more and more of his time with me. He liked our house; our ways suited him. He was nervous, irritable; people bored him and yet he disliked solitude. He took sanctuary with us. When we travelled he went with us; in the winter he took rooms near us in Rome. In England or on the continent he was always with us for a good part of the year. In small ways I was able to help him in his work; he grew dependent on me. When we were apart he wrote to me continually—he liked to have me share in all he was doing or thinking; he was impatient for my criticism of every new book that interested him; I was a part of his intellectual life. The pity of it was that I wanted to be something more. I was a young woman and I was in love with him—not because he was Vincent Rendle, but just because he was himself!

People began to talk, of course—I was Vincent Rendle's Mrs. Anerton; when the Sonnets to Silvia appeared, it was whispered that I was Silvia. Wherever he went, I was invited; people made up to me in the hope of getting to know him; when I was in London my doorbell never stopped ringing. Elderly peeresses, aspiring hostesses, love-sick girls and struggling authors overwhelmed me with their assiduities. I hugged my success, for I knew what it meant—they thought that Rendle was in love with me! Do you know, at times, they almost made me think so too? Oh, there was no phase of folly I didn't go through. You can't imagine the excuses a woman will invent for a man's not telling her that he loves her—pitiable arguments that she would see through at a glance if any other woman used them! But all the while, deep down, I knew he had never cared. I should have known it if he had made love to me every day of his life. I could never guess whether he knew what people said about us—he listened so little to what people said; and cared still less, when he heard. He was always quite honest and straightforward with me; he treated me as one man treats another; and yet at times I felt he must see that with me it was different. If he did see, he made no sign. Perhaps he never noticed—I am sure he never meant to be cruel. He had never made love to me; it was no fault of his if I wanted more than he could give me. The Sonnets to Silvia, you say? But what are they? A cosmic philosophy, not a love-poem; addressed to Woman, not to a woman!

But then, the letters? Ah, the letters! Well, I'll make a clean breast of it. You have noticed the breaks in the letters here and there, just as they seem to be on the point of growing a little—warmer? The critics, you may remember, praised the editor for his commendable delicacy and good taste (so rare in these days!) in omitting from the correspondence all personal allusions, all those details intimes which should be kept sacred from the public gaze. They referred, of course, to the asterisks in the letters to Mrs. A. Those letters I myself prepared for publication; that is to say, I copied them out for the editor, and every now and then I put in a line of asterisks to make it appear that something had been left out. You understand? The asterisks were a sham—there was nothing to leave out.

No one but a woman could understand what I went through during those years—the moments of revolt, when I felt I must break away from it all, fling the truth in his face and never see him again; the inevitable reaction, when not to see him seemed the one unendurable thing, and I trembled lest a look or word of mine should disturb the poise of our friendship; the silly days when I hugged the delusion that he must love me, since everybody thought he did; the long periods of numbness, when I didn't seem to care whether he loved me or not. Between these wretched days came others when our intellectual accord was so perfect that I forgot everything else in the joy of feeling myself lifted up on the wings of his thought. Sometimes, then, the heavens seemed to be opened....

~

All this time he was so dear a friend! He had the genius of friendship, and he spent it all on me. Yes, you were right when you said that I have had more than any other woman. Il faut de l'adresse pour aimer, Pascal says; and I was so quiet, so cheerful, so frankly affectionate with him, that in all those years I am almost sure I never bored him. Could I have hoped as much if he had loved me?

You mustn't think of him, though, as having been tied to my skirts. He came and went as he pleased, and so did his fancies. There was a girl once (I am telling you everything), a lovely being who called his poetry "deep" and gave him Lucile on his birthday. He followed her to Switzerland one summer, and all the time that he was dangling after her (a little too conspicuously, I always thought, for a Great Man), he was writing to me about his theory of vowel-combinations—or was it his experiments in English hexameter? The letters were dated from the very places where I knew they went and sat by waterfalls together and he thought out adjectives for her hair. He talked to me about it quite frankly afterwards. She was perfectly beautiful and it had been a pure delight to watch her; but she would talk, and her mind, he said, was "all elbows." And yet, the next year, when her marriage was announced, he went away alone, quite suddenly ... and it was just afterwards that he published Love's Viaticum. Men are queer!

After my husband died—I am putting things crudely, you see—I had a return of hope. It was because he loved me, I argued, that he had never spoken; because he had always hoped some day to make me his wife; because he wanted to spare me the "reproach." Rubbish! I knew well enough, in my heart of hearts, that my one chance lay in the force of habit. He had grown used to me; he was no longer young; he dreaded new people and new ways; il avait pris son pli. Would it not be easier to marry me?

I don't believe he ever thought of it. He wrote me what people call "a beautiful letter;" he was kind; considerate, decently commiserating; then, after a few weeks, he slipped into his old way of coming in every afternoon, and our interminable talks began again just where they had left off. I heard later that people thought I had shown "such good taste" in not marrying him.

So we jogged on for five years longer. Perhaps they were the best years, for I had given up hoping. Then he died.

After his death—this is curious—there came to me a kind of mirage of love. All the books and articles written about him, all the reviews of the "Life," were full of discreet allusions to Silvia. I became again the Mrs. Anerton of the glorious days. Sentimental girls and dear lads like you turned pink when somebody whispered, "that was Silvia you were talking to." Idiots begged for my autograph—publishers urged me to write my reminiscences of him—critics consulted me about the reading of doubtful lines. And I knew that, to all these people, I was the woman Vincent Rendle had loved.

After a while that fire went out too and I was left alone with my past. Alone—quite alone; for he had never really been with me. The intellectual union counted for nothing now. It had been soul to soul, but never hand in hand, and there were no little things to remember him by.

Then there set in a kind of Arctic winter. I crawled into myself as into a snow-hut. I hated my solitude and yet dreaded any one who disturbed it. That phase, of course, passed like the others. I took up life again, and began to read the papers and consider the cut of my gowns. But there was one question that I could not be rid of, that haunted me night and day. Why had he never loved me? Why had I been so much to him, and no more? Was I so ugly, so essentially unlovable, that though a man might cherish me as his mind's comrade, he could not care for me as a woman? I can't tell you how that question tortured me. It became an obsession.

My poor friend, do you begin to see? I had to find out what some other man thought of me. Don't be too hard on me! Listen first—consider. When I first met Vincent Rendle I was a young woman, who had married early and led the quietest kind of life; I had had no "experiences." From the hour of our first meeting to the day of his death I never looked at any other man, and never noticed whether any other man looked at me. When he died, five years ago, I knew the extent of my powers no more than a baby. Was it too late to find out? Should I never know why?

Forgive me—forgive me. You are so young; it will be an episode, a mere "document," to you so soon! And, besides, it wasn't as deliberate, as cold-blooded as these disjointed lines have made it appear. I didn't plan it, like a woman in a book. Life is so much more complex than any rendering of it can be. I liked you from the first—I was drawn to you (you must have seen that)—I wanted you to like me; it was not a mere psychological experiment. And yet in a sense it was that, too—I must be honest. I had to have an answer to that question; it was a ghost that had to be laid.

At first I was afraid—oh, so much afraid—that you cared for me only because I was Silvia, that you loved me because you thought Rendle had loved me. I began to think there was no escaping my destiny.

How happy I was when I discovered that you were growing jealous of my past; that you actually hated Rendle! My heart beat like a girl's when you told me you meant to follow me to Venice.

After our parting at Villa d'Este my old doubts reasserted themselves. What did I know of your feeling for me, after all? Were you capable of analyzing it yourself? Was it not likely to be two-thirds vanity and curiosity, and one-third literary sentimentality? You might easily fancy that you cared for Mary Anerton when you were really in love with Silvia— the heart is such a hypocrite! Or you might be more calculating than I had supposed. Perhaps it was you who had been flattering my vanity in the hope (the pardonable hope!) of turning me, after a decent interval, into a pretty little essay with a margin.

When you arrived in Venice and we met again—do you remember the music on the lagoon, that evening, from my balcony?—I was so afraid you would begin to talk about the book—the book, you remember, was your ostensible reason for coming. You never spoke of it, and I soon saw your one fear was I might do so—might remind you of your object in being with me. Then I knew you cared for me! yes, at that moment really cared! We never mentioned the book once, did we, during that month in Venice?

I have read my letter over; and now I wish that I had said this to you instead of writing it. I could have felt my way then, watching your face and seeing if you understood. But, no, I could not go back to Venice; and I could not tell you (though I tried) while we were there together. I couldn't spoil that month—my one month. It was so good, for once in my life, to get away from literature....

You will be angry with me at first—but, alas! not for long. What I have done would have been cruel if I had been a younger woman; as it is, the experiment will hurt no one but myself. And it will hurt me horribly (as much as, in your first anger, you may perhaps wish), because it has shown me, for the first time, all that I have missed....

Talma Gordon

Pauline Hopkins

Pauline Hopkins (1859-1930) was an influential African-American journalist, editor, novelist and playwright. The wonderful mix of Hopkins's stories deals with issues of slavery, racism, murder and revenge. Her debut novel *Contending Forces: A Romance Illustrative of Negro Life North and South* (1900) was the first of many novels on slavery and other social themes, which were to make Hopkins an important and powerful editor. 'Talma Gordon' (1900) is one of Hopkins' celebrated short stories.

The Canterbury Club of Boston was holding its regular monthly meeting at the palatial Beacon Street residence of Dr. William Thornton, expert medical practitioner and specialist. All the members were present, because some rare opinions were to be aired by men of profound thought on a question of vital importance to the life of the Republic, and because the club celebrated its anniversary in a home usually closed to society. The Doctor's winters, since his marriage, were passed at his summer home near his celebrated sanitarium. This winter found him in town with his wife and two boys. We had heard much of the beauty of the former, who was entirely unknown to social life, and about whose life and marriage we felt sure a romantic interest attached. The Doctor himself was too bright a luminary of the professional world to remain long hidden without creating comment. We had accepted the invitation to dine with alacrity, knowing that we should be welcomed to a banquet that would feast both eye and palate; but we had not been favored by even a glimpse of the hostess. The subject for discussion was "Expansion: Its Effect Upon the

Future Development of the Anglo-Saxon Throughout the World." Dinner was over, but we still sat about the social board discussing the question of the hour. The Hon. Herbert Clapp, eminent jurist and politician, had painted in glowing colors the advantages to be gained by the increase of wealth and the exalted position which expansion would give the United States in the councils of the great governments of the world. In smoothly flowing sentences marshaled in rhetorical order, with compact ideas, and incisive argument, he drew an effective picture with all the persuasive eloquence of the trained orator.

Joseph Whitman, the theologian of worldwide fame, accepted the arguments of Mr. Clapp, but subordinated all to the great opportunity which expansion would give to the religious enthusiast. None could doubt the sincerity of this man, who looked once into the idealized face on which heaven had set the seal of consecration.

Various opinions were advanced by the twenty-five men present, but the host said nothing; he glanced from one to another with a look of amusement in his shrewd gray-blue eyes. "Wonderful eyes," said his patients who came under their magic spell. "A wonderful man and a wonderful mind," agreed his contemporaries, as they heard in amazement of some great cure of chronic or malignant disease which approached the supernatural.

"What do you think of this question, Doctor?" finally asked the president, turning to the silent host.

"Your arguments are good; they would convince almost anyone."

"But not Doctor Thornton," laughed the theologian. "I acquiesce whichever way the result turns. Still, I like to view both sides of a question. We have considered but one tonight. Did you ever think that in spite of our prejudices against amalgamation, some of our descendants, indeed many of them, will inevitably intermarry among those far-off tribes of dark-skinned peoples, if they become a part of this great Union?"

"Among the lower classes that may occur, but not to any great extent," remarked a college president.

"My experience teaches me that it will occur among all classes, and to an appalling extent," replied the doctor. "You don't believe in intermarriage with other races?"

"Yes, most emphatically, when they possess decent moral development and physical perfection, for then we develop a superior being in the progeny born of the intermarriage. But if we are not ready to receive and assimilate the new material which will be brought to mingle with our pure Anglo-Saxon stream, we should call a halt in our expansion policy."

"I must confess, Doctor, that in the idea of amalgamation you present a new thought to my mind. Will you not favor us with a few of your main points?" asked the president of the club, breaking the silence which followed the Doctor's remarks.

"Yes, Doctor, give us your theories on the subject. We may not agree with you, but we are all open to conviction." The Doctor removed the half-consumed cigar from his lips, drank what remained in his glass of the choice Burgundy, and leaning back in his chair contemplated the earnest faces before him.

"We may make laws, but laws are but straws in the hands of Omnipotence.

There's a divinity that shapes our ends, Rough-hew them how we will.

And no man may combat fate. Given a man, propinquity, opportunity, fascinating femininity, and there you are. Black, white, green, yellow—nothing will prevent intermarriage. Position, wealth, family, friends—all sink into insignificance before the God-implanted instinct that made Adam, awakening from a deep sleep and finding the woman beside him, accept Eve as bone of his bone; he cared not nor questioned whence she came. So it is with the sons of Adam ever since, through the law of heredity which makes us all one common family. And so it will be with us in our re-formation of this old Republic. Perhaps I can make my meaning clearer by illustration, and with your permission I will tell you a story which came under my observation as a practitioner.

"Doubtless all of you heard of the terrible tragedy which occurred at Gordonville, Mass., some years ago, when Capt. Jonathan Gordon, his wife, and little son were murdered. I suppose that I am the only man on this side of the Atlantic, outside of the police, who can tell you the true story of that crime.

"I knew Captain Gordon well; it was through his persuasions that I bought a place in Gordonville and settled down to spending my summers in that charming rural neighborhood. I had rendered the Captain what he was pleased to call valuable medical help, and I became his family physician. Captain Gordon was a retired sea captain, formerly engaged in the East India trade. All his ancestors had been such; but when the bottom fell out of that business he established the Gordonville Mills with his first wife's money, and settled down as a money-making manufacturer of cotton cloth. The Gordons were old New England Puritans who had come over in the *Mayflower*; they had owned Gordon Hall for more than a hundred years. It was a baronial-like pile of granite with towers, standing on a hill which commanded a superb view of Massachusetts Bay and the surrounding country. I imagine the Gordon star was under a cloud about the time Captain Jonathan married his first wife, Miss Isabel Franklin of Boston, who brought to him the money which mended the broken fortunes of the Gordon house, and restored this old Puritan stock to its rightful position. In the person of Captain Gordon the austerity of manner and indomitable willpower that he had inherited were combined with a temper that brooked no contradiction. "The first wife died at the birth of her third child, leaving him two daughters, Jeannette and Talma. Very soon after her death the Captain married again. I have heard it rumored that the Gordon girls did not get on very well with their stepmother. She was a woman with no fortune of her own, and envied the large portion left by the first Mrs. Gordon to her daughters.

"Jeannette was tall, dark, and stern like her father; Talma was like her dead mother, and possessed of great talent, so great that her father sent her to the American Academy at Rome, to develop the gift. It was the hottest of July days when her friends were bidden to an afternoon party on the lawn and a dance in the evening, to welcome Talma Gordon among them again. I watched her as she moved about among her guests, a fairylike blonde in floating white draperies, her face a study in delicate changing tints, like the heart of a flower, sparkling in smiles about the mouth to end in merry laughter in the clear blue eyes. There were all the subtle allurements of birth, wealth, and culture about the exquisite creature:

'Smiling, frowning evermore, Thou art perfect in love-lore, Ever varying Madeline,' quoted a celebrated writer as he stood apart with me, gazing upon the scene before us. He sighed as he looked at the girl.

"'Doctor, there is genius and passion in her face. Sometime our little friend will do wonderful things. But is it desirable to be singled out for special blessings by the gods? Genius always carries with it intense capacity for suffering: "Whom the gods love die young."'

"'Ah,' I replied, 'do not name death and Talma Gordon together. Cease your dismal croakings; such talk is rank heresy.'

"The dazzling daylight dropped slowly into summer twilight. The merriment continued; more guests arrived; the great dancing pagoda built for the occasion was lighted by myriads of Japanese lanterns. The strains from the band grew sweeter and sweeter, and 'all went merry as a marriage bell.' It was a rare treat to have this party at Gordon Hall, for Captain Jonathan was not given to hospitality. We broke up shortly before midnight, with expressions of delight from all the guests.

"I was a bachelor then, without ties. Captain Gordon insisted upon my having a bed at the Hall. I did not fall asleep readily; there seemed to be something in the air that forbade it. I was still awake when a distant clock struck the second hour of the morning. Suddenly the heavens were lighted by a sheet of ghastly light; a terrific midsummer thunderstorm was breaking over the sleeping town. A lurid flash lit up all the landscape, painting the trees in grotesque shapes against the murky sky, and defining clearly the sullen blackness of the waters of the bay breaking in grandeur against the rocky coast. I had arisen and put back the draperies from the windows, to have an unobstructed view of the grand scene. A low muttering coming nearer and nearer, a terrific roar, and then a tremendous downpour. The storm had burst.

"Now the uncanny howling of a dog mingled with the rattling volleys of thunder. I heard the opening and closing of doors; the servants were about looking after things. It was impossible to sleep. The lightning was more vivid. There was a blinding flash of a greenish-white tinge mingled with the crash of falling timbers. Then before my startled gaze arose columns of red flames reflected against the sky. 'Heaven help us!' I cried; 'it is the left tower; it has been struck and is on fire!'

"I hurried on my clothes and stepped into the corridor; the girls were there before me. Jeannette came up to me instantly with anxious face. 'Oh, Doctor Thornton, what shall we do? Papa and Mamma and little Johnny are in the old left tower. It is on fire. I have knocked and knocked, but get no answer.'

"'Don't be alarmed,' said I soothingly. 'Jenkins, ring the alarm bell,' I continued, turning to the butler who was standing near; 'the rest follow me. We will force the entrance to the Captain's room.'

"Instantly, it seemed to me, the bell boomed out upon the now silent air, for the storm had died down as quickly as it arose; and as our little procession paused before the entrance to the old left tower, we could distinguish the sound of the fire engines already on their way from the village.

"The door resisted all our efforts; there seemed to be a barrier against it which nothing could move. The flames were gaining headway. Still the same deathly silence within the rooms.

"'Oh, will they never get here?' cried Talma, ringing her hands in terror. Jeannette said nothing, but her face was ashen. The servants were huddled together in a panic-stricken group. I can never tell you what a relief it was when we heard the first sound of the firemen's voices, saw their quick movements, and heard the ringing of the axes with which they cut away every obstacle to our entrance to the rooms. The neighbors who had just enjoyed the hospitality of the house were now gathered around offering all the assistance in their power. In less than fifteen minutes the fire was out, and the men began to bear the unconscious inmates from the ruins. They carried them to the pagoda so lately the scene of mirth and pleasure, and I took up my station there, ready to assume my professional duties. The Captain was nearest me; and as I stooped to make the necessary examination I reeled away from the ghastly sight which confronted me—*gentlemen, across the Captain's throat was a deep gash that severed the jugular vein!*"

The Doctor paused, and the hand with which he refilled his glass trembled violently.

"'What is it, Doctor?' cried the men, gathering about me. 'Take the women away; this is murder!'

"'Murder!' cried Jeannette, as she fell against the side of the pagoda.

"'Murder!' screamed Talma, staring at me as if unable to grasp my meaning.

"I continued my examination of the bodies, and found that the same thing had happened to Mrs. Gordon and to little Johnny.

"The police were notified; and when the sun rose over the dripping town he found them in charge of Gordon Hall, the servants standing in excited knots talking over the crime, the friends of the family confounded, and the two girls trying to comfort each other and realize the terrible misfortune that had overtaken them.

"Nothing in the rooms of the left tower seemed to have been disturbed. The door of communications between the rooms of the husband and wife was open, as they had arranged it for the night. Little Johnny's crib was placed beside his mother's bed. In it he was found as though never awakened by the storm. It was quite evident that the assassin was no common ruffian. The chief gave strict orders for a watch to be kept on all strangers or suspicious characters who were seen in the neighborhood. He made inquiries among the servants, seeing each one separately, but there was nothing gained from them. No one had heard anything suspicious; all had been awakened by the storm. The chief was puzzled. Here was a triple crime for which no motive could be assigned.

"'What do you think of it?' I asked him, as we stood together on the lawn.

"'It is my opinion that the deed was committed by one of the higher classes, which makes the mystery more difficult to solve. I tell you, Doctor, there are mysteries that never come to light, and this, I think, is one of them.' "While we were talking Jenkins, the butler, an old and trusted servant, came up to the chief and saluted respectfully. 'Want to speak with me, Jenkins?' he asked. The man nodded, and they walked away together.

"The story of the inquest was short, but appalling. It was shown that Talma had been allowed to go abroad to study because she and Mrs. Gordon did not get on well together. From the testimony of Jenkins it seemed that Talma and her father had quarreled bitterly about her lover, a young artist whom she had met at Rome, who was unknown to fame, and very poor. There had been terrible things said by each, and threats even had passed, all of which now rose up in judgment against the unhappy girl. The examination of the family solicitor revealed the fact that Captain Gordon intended to leave his daughters only a small annuity, the bulk of the fortune going to his son Jonathan, junior. This was a monstrous injustice, as everyone felt. In vain Talma protested her innocence. Someone must have done it. No one would be benefited so much by these deaths as she and her sister. Moreover, the will, together with other papers, was nowhere to be found. Not the slightest clue bearing upon the disturbing elements in this family, if any there were, was to be found. As the only surviving relatives, Jeannette and Talma became joint heirs to an immense fortune, which only for the bloody tragedy just enacted would, in all probability, have passed them by. Here was the motive. The case was very black against Talma. The foreman stood up. The silence was intense: We 'find that Captain Jonathan Gordon, Mary E. Gordon, and Jonathan Gordon, junior, all deceased, came to their deaths by means of a knife or other sharp instrument in the hands of Talma Gordon.' The girl was like one stricken with death. The flowerlike mouth was drawn and pinched; the great sapphire-blue eyes were black with passionate anguish, terror, and despair. She was placed in jail to await her trial at the fall session of the criminal court. The excitement in the hitherto quiet town rose to fever heat. Many points in the evidence seemed incomplete to thinking men. The weapon could not be found, nor could it be divined what had become of it. No reason could be given for the murder except the quarrel between Talma and her father and the ill will which existed between the girl and her stepmother.

"When the trial was called Jeannette sat beside Talma in the prisoner's dock; both were arrayed in deepest mourning. Talma was pale and careworn, but seemed uplifted, spiritualized, as it were. Upon Jeannette the full realization of her sister's peril seemed to weigh heavily. She had changed much too: hollow cheeks, tottering steps, eyes blazing with fever, all suggestive of rapid and premature decay. From far-off Italy Edward Turner, growing famous in the art world, came to stand beside his girl-love in this hour of anguish.

"The trial was a memorable one. No additional evidence had been collected to strengthen the prosecution; when the attorney-general rose to open the case against Talma he knew, as everyone else did, that he could not convict solely on the evidence adduced. What was given did not always bear upon the case, and brought out strange stories of Captain Jonathan's methods. Tales were told of sailors who had sworn to take his life, in revenge for injuries inflicted upon them by his hand. One or two clues were followed, but without avail. The judge summed up the evidence impartially, giving the prisoner the benefit of the doubt. The points in hand furnished valuable collateral evidence, but were not direct proof. Although the moral presumption was against the prisoner, legal evidence was lacking to actually convict. The jury found the prisoner 'Not Guilty,' owing to the fact that the evidence was entirely circumstantial. The verdict was received in painful silence; then a murmur of discontent ran through the great crowd.

"'She must have done it,' said one; 'who else has been benefited by the horrible deed?'

"'A poor woman would not have fared so well at the hands of the jury, nor a homely one either, for that matter,' said another.

"The great Gordon trial was ended; innocent or guilty, Talma Gordon could not be tried again. She was free; but her liberty, with blasted prospects and fair fame gone forever, was valueless to her. She seemed to have but one object in her mind: to find the murderer or murderers of her parents and half brother. By her direction the shrewdest of detectives were employed and money flowed like water, but to no purpose; the Gordon tragedy remained a mystery. I had consented to act as one of the trustees of the immense Gordon estates and business interests, and by my advice the Misses Gordon went abroad. A year later I received a letter from Edward Turner, saying that Jeannette Gordon had died suddenly at Rome, and that Talma, after refusing all his entreaties for an early marriage, had disappeared, leaving no clue as to her whereabouts. I could give the poor fellow no comfort, although I had been duly notified of the death of Jeannette by Talma, in a letter telling me where to forward her remittances, and at the same time requesting me to keep her present residence secret, especially from Edward.

"I had established a sanitarium for the cure of chronic diseases at Gordonville, and absorbed in the cares of my profession I gave little thought to the Gordons. I seemed fated to be involved in mysteries.

"A man claiming to be an Englishman, and fresh from the California gold fields, engaged board and professional service at my retreat. I found him suffering in the grasp of the tubercle fiend—the last stages. He called himself Simon Cameron. Seldom have I seen so fascinating and wicked a face. The lines of the mouth were cruel, the eyes cold and sharp, the smile mocking and evil. He had money in plenty but seemed to have no friends, for he had received no letters and had had no visitors in the time he had been with us. He was an enigma to me; and his nationality puzzled me, for of course I did not believe his story of being English. The peaceful influence of the house seemed to soothe him in a measure, and make his last steps to the mysterious valley as easy as possible. For a time he improved, and would sit or walk about the grounds and sing sweet songs for the pleasure of the other inmates. Strange to say, his malady only affected his voice at times. He sang quaint songs in a silvery tenor of great purity and sweetness that was delicious to the listening ear:

'A wet sheet and a flowing sea,
A wind that follows fast,
And fills the white and rustling sail
And bends the gallant mast;
And bends the gallant mast, my boys;
While like the eagle free,
Away the good ship flies, and leaves Old England on the lea.'

"There are few singers on the lyric stage who could surpass Simon Cameron.

"One night, a few weeks after Cameron's arrival, I sat in my office making up my accounts when the door opened and closed; I glanced up, expecting to see a servant. A lady advanced toward me. She threw back her veil, and then I saw that Talma Gordon, or her ghost, stood before me. After the first excitement of our meeting was over, she told me she had come direct from Paris, to place herself in my care. I had studied her attentively during the first moments of our meeting, and I felt that she was right; unless something unforeseen happened to arouse her from the stupor into which she seemed to have fallen, the last Gordon was doomed to an early death. The next day I told her I had cabled Edward Turner to come to her.

"'It will do no good; I cannot marry him,' was her only comment.

"'Have you no feeling of pity for that faithful fellow?' I asked her sternly, provoked by her seeming indifference. I shall never forget the varied emotions depicted on her speaking face. Fully revealed to my gaze was the sight of a human soul tortured beyond the point of endurance; suffering all things, enduring all things, in the silent agony of despair.

"In a few days Edward arrived, and Talma consented to see him and explain her refusal to keep her promise to him. 'You must be present, Doctor; it is due your long, tried friendship to know that I have not been fickle, but have acted from the best and strongest motives.'

"I shall never forget that day. It was directly after lunch that we met in the library. I was greatly excited, expecting I knew not what. Edward was agitated, too. Talma was the only calm one. She handed me what seemed to be a letter, with the request that I would read it. Even now I think I can repeat every word of the document, so indelibly are the words engraved upon my mind:

"'MY DARLING SISTER TALMA:

When you read these lines I shall be no more, for I shall not live to see your life blasted by the same knowledge that has blighted mine.

"'One evening, about a year before your expected return from Rome, I climbed into a hammock in one corner of the veranda outside the breakfast-room windows, intending to spend the twilight hours in lazy comfort, for it was very hot, enervating August weather. I fell asleep. I was awakened by voices. Because of the heat the rooms had been left in semi-darkness. As I lay there, lazily enjoying the beauty of the perfect summer night, my wandering thoughts were arrested by words spoken by our father to Mrs. Gordon, for they were the occupants of the breakfast room.

"'"Never fear, Mary; Johnny shall have it all—money, houses, land, and business."

"'"But if you do go first, Jonathan, what will happen if the girls contest the will? People will think that they ought to have the money as it appears to be theirs by law. I never could survive the terrible disgrace of the story."

"'"Don't borrow trouble; all you would need to do would be to show them papers I have drawn up, and they would be glad to take their annuity and say nothing. After all, I do not think it is so bad. Jeannette can teach; Talma can paint; six hundred dollars a year is quite enough for them."

"'I had been somewhat mystified by the conversation until now. This last remark solved the riddle. What could he mean? Teach, paint, six hundred a year! With my usual impetuosity I sprang from my resting place, and in a moment stood in the room confronting my father, and asking what he meant. I could see plainly that both were disconcerted by my unexpected appearance.

"'"Ah, wretched girl! You have been listening. But what could I expect of your mother's daughter?"

"'At these words I felt the indignant blood rush to my head in a torrent. So it had been all my life. Before you could remember, Talma, I had felt my little heart swell with anger at the disparaging hints and slurs concerning our mother. Now was my time. I determined that tonight I would know why she was looked upon as an outcast, and her children subjected to every humiliation. So I replied to my father in bitter anger:

"'"I was not listening; I fell asleep in the hammock. What do you mean by a paltry six hundred a year each to Talma and to me? 'My mother's daughter' demands an explanation from you, sir, of the meaning of the monstrous injustice that you have always practiced toward my sister and me."

"'"Speak more respectfully to your father, Jeannette," broke in Mrs. Gordon.

"'"How is it, madam, that you look for respect from one whom you have delighted to torment ever since you came into this most unhappy family?"

"'"Hush, both of you," said Captain Gordon, who seemed to have recovered from the dismay into which my sudden appearance and passionate words had plunged him. "I think I may as well tell you as to wait. Since you know so much, you may as well know the whole miserable story." He motioned me to a seat. I could see that he was deeply agitated. I seated myself in a chair he pointed out, in wonder and expectation—expectation of I knew not what. I trembled. This was a supreme moment in my life; I felt it. The air was heavy with the intense stillness that had settled over us as the common sounds of day gave place to the early quiet of the rural evening. I could see Mrs. Gordon's face as she sat within the radius of the lighted hallway. There was a smile of triumph upon it. I clinched my hands and bit my lips until the blood came, in the effort to keep from screaming. What was I about to hear? At last he spoke:

""I was disappointed at your birth, and also at the birth of Talma. I wanted a male heir. When I knew that I should again be a father I was torn by hope and fear, but I comforted myself with the thought that luck would be with me in the birth of the third child. When the doctor brought me word that a son was born to the house of Gordon, I was wild with delight, and did not notice his disturbed countenance. In the midst of my joy he said to me:

"""Captain Gordon, there is something strange about this birth. I want you to see this child.'

""Quelling my exultation I followed him to the nursery, and there, lying in the cradle, I saw a child dark as a mulatto, with the characteristic features of the Negro! I was stunned. Gradually it dawned upon me that there was something radically wrong. I turned to the doctor for an explanation.

"""There is but one explanation, Captain Gordon; there is Negro blood in this child.'

"""There is no Negro blood in my veins,' I said proudly. Then I paused—*the mother!*—I glanced at the doctor. He was watching me intently. The same thought was in his mind. I must have lived a thousand years in that cursed five seconds that I stood there confronting the physician and trying to think. 'Come,' said I to him, 'let us end this suspense.' Without thinking of consequences, I hurried away to your mother and accused her of infidelity to her marriage vows. I raved like a madman. Your mother fell into convulsions; her life was despaired of. I sent for Mr. and Mrs. Franklin, and then I learned the truth. They were childless. One year while on a Southern tour, they befriended an octoroon girl who had been abandoned by her white lover. Her child was a beautiful girl baby. They, being Northern born, thought little of caste distinction because the child showed no trace of Negro blood. They determined to adopt it. They went abroad, secretly sending back word to their friends at a proper time of the birth of a little daughter. No one doubted the truth of the statement. They made Isabel their heiress, and all went well until the birth of your brother. Your mother and the unfortunate babe died. This is the story which, if known, would bring dire disgrace upon the Gordon family.

""""To appease my righteous wrath, Mr. Franklin left a codicil to his will by which all the property is left at my disposal save a small annuity to you and your sister."

"'I sat there after he had finished the story, stunned by what I had heard. I understood, now, Mrs. Gordon's half contemptuous toleration and lack of consideration for us both. As I rose from my seat to leave the room I said to Captain Gordon:

""""Still, in spite of it all, sir, I am a Gordon, legally born. I will not tamely give up my birthright."

"'I left that room a broken-hearted girl, filled with a desire for revenge upon this man, my father, who by his manner disowned us without a regret. Not once in that remarkable interview did he speak of our mother as his wife; he quietly repudiated her and us with all the cold cruelty of relentless caste prejudice. I heard the treatment of your lover's proposal; I knew why Captain Gordon's consent to your marriage was withheld.

"'The night of the reception and dance was the chance for which I had waited, planned, and watched. I crept from my window into the ivy vines, and so down, down, until I stood upon the windowsill of Captain Gordon's room in the old left tower. How did I do it, you ask? I do not know. The house was silent after the revel; the darkness of the gathering storm favored me, too. The lawyer was there that day. The will was signed and put safely away among my father's papers. I was determined to have the will and the other documents bearing upon the case, and I would have revenge, too, for the cruelties we had suffered. With the old East Indian dagger firmly grasped I entered the room and found—that my revenge had been forestalled! The horror of the discovery I made that night restored me to reason and a realization of the crime I meditated.

Scarce knowing what I did, I sought and found the papers, and crept back to my room as I had come. Do you wonder that my disease is past medical aid?'

"I looked at Edward as I finished. He sat, his face covered with his hands. Finally he looked up with a glance of haggard despair: 'God! Doctor, but this is too much. I could stand the stigma of murder, but add to that the pollution of Negro blood! No man is brave enough to face such a situation.'

"'It is as I thought it would be,' said Talma sadly, while the tears poured over her white face. 'I do not blame you, Edward.'

"He rose from his chair, wrung my hand in a convulsive clasp, turned to Talma and bowed profoundly, with his eyes fixed upon the floor, hesitated, turned, paused, bowed again, and abruptly left the room. So those two who had been lovers parted. I turned to Talma, expecting her to give way. She smiled a pitiful smile, and said: 'You see, Doctor, I knew best.'

"From that on she failed rapidly. I was restless. If only I could rouse her to an interest in life, she might live to old age. So rich, so young, so beautiful, so talented, so pure; I grew savage thinking of the injustice of the world. I had not reckoned on the power that never sleeps. Something was about to happen.

"On visiting Cameron next morning I found him approaching the end. He had been sinking for a week very rapidly. As I sat by the bedside holding his emaciated hand, he fixed his bright, wicked eyes on me, and asked:

'How long have I got to live?'

"'Candidly, but a few hours.'

"'Thank you; well, I want death; I am not afraid do die. Doctor, Cameron is not my name.'

"'I never supposed it was.'

"'No? You are sharper than I thought. I heard all your talk yesterday with Talma Gordon. Curse the whole race!'

"He clasped his bony fingers around my arm and gasped: *'I murdered the Gordons!'*

"Had I the pen of a Dumas I could not paint Cameron as he told his story. It is a question with me whether this wheedling planet, home of the suffering, doubting, dying, may not hold worse agonies on its smiling surface than those of the conventional hell. I sent for Talma and a lawyer. We gave him stimulants, and then with broken intervals of coughing and prostration we got the story of the Gordon murder. I give it to you in a few words:

"'I am an East Indian, but my name does not matter, Cameron is as good as any. There is many a soul crying in heaven and hell for vengeance on Jonathan Gordon. Gold was his idol; and many a good man walked the plank, and many a gallant ship was stripped of her treasure, to satisfy his lust for gold. His blackest crime was the murder of my father, who was his friend, and had sailed with him for many a year as mate. One night these two went ashore together to bury their treasure. My father never returned from that expedition. His body was afterward found with a bullet through the heart on the shore where the vessel stopped that night. It was the custom then among pirates for the captain to kill the men who helped bury their treasure. Captain Gordon was no better than a pirate. An East Indian never forgets, and I swore by my mother's deathbed to hunt Captain Gordon down until I had avenged my father's murder. I had the plans of the Gordon estate, and fixed on the night of the reception in honor of Talma as the time for my vengeance. There is a secret entrance from the shore to the chambers where Captain Gordon slept; no one knew of it save the Captain and trusted members of his crew. My mother gave me the plans, and entrance and escape were easy.'

"So the great mystery was solved. In a few hours Cameron was no more. We placed the confession in the hands of the police, and there the matter ended."

"But what became of Talma Gordon?" questioned the president. "Did she die?"

"Gentlemen," said the Doctor, rising to his feet and sweeping the faces of the company with his eagle gaze, "gentlemen, if you will follow me to the drawing room, I shall have much pleasure in introducing you to my wife—née Talma Gordon."

One Autumn Night

Maxim Gorky

Maxim Gorky (1868-1936) was one of the most important literary figures of Russia. His novels and short stories are known for their sympathetic portrayal of tramps, criminals and other social outcasts. Gorky lived in extreme poverty throughout his childhood and adolescence, which was perhaps a reason for his sympathetic outlook. As a result, he was often known as the greatest 'proletarian' of Russian literature. 'One Autumn Night' (1902) has naturalistic elements so characteristic of Gorky.

Once in the autumn I happened to be in a very unpleasant and inconvenient position. In the town where I had just arrived and where I knew not a soul, I found myself without a farthing in my pocket and without a night's lodging.

Having sold during the first few days every part of my costume without which it was still possible to go about, I passed from the town into the quarter called "Yste," where were the steamship wharves—a quarter which during the navigation season fermented with boisterous, laborious life, but now was silent and deserted, for we were in the last days of October.

Dragging my feet along the moist sand, and obstinately scrutinising it with the desire to discover in it any sort of fragment of food, I wandered alone among the deserted buildings and warehouses, and thought how good it would be to get a full meal.

In our present state of culture hunger of the mind is more quickly satisfied than hunger of the body. You wander about the streets, you are surrounded by buildings not bad-looking from the outside and—you may safely say it—not so badly furnished inside, and the sight of them may excite within you stimulating ideas about architecture, hygiene, and many other wise and high-flying subjects. You may meet warmly and neatly dressed folks—all very polite, and turning away from you tactfully, not wishing offensively to notice the lamentable fact of your existence. Well, well, the mind of a hungry man is always better nourished and healthier than the mind of the well-fed man; and there you have a situation from which you may draw a very ingenious conclusion in favour of the ill fed.

The evening was approaching, the rain was falling, and the wind blew violently from the north. It whistled in the empty booths and shops, blew into the plastered windowpanes of the taverns, and whipped into foam the wavelets of the river which splashed noisily on the sandy shore, casting high their white crests, racing one after another into the dim distance, and leaping impetuously over one another's shoulders. It seemed as if the river felt the proximity of winter, and was running at random away from the fetters of ice which the north wind might well have flung upon her that very night. The sky was heavy and dark; down from it swept incessantly scarcely visible drops of rain, and the melancholy elegy in nature all around me was emphasised by a couple of battered and misshapen willow-trees and a boat, bottom upwards, that was fastened to their roots.

The overturned canoe with its battered keel and the miserable old trees rifled by the cold wind—everything around me was bankrupt, barren, and dead, and the sky flowed with undryable tears... Everything around was waste and gloomy ... it seemed as if everything were dead, leaving me alone among the living, and for me also a cold death waited.

I was then eighteen years old—a good time!

I walked and walked along the cold wet sand, making my chattering teeth warble in honour of cold and hunger, when suddenly, as I was carefully searching for something to eat behind one of the empty crates, I perceived behind it, crouching on the ground, a figure in woman's clothes dank with the rain and clinging fast to her stooping shoulders. Standing over her, I watched to see what she was doing. It appeared that she was digging a trench in the sand with her hands—digging away under one of the crates.

"Why are you doing that?" I asked, crouching down on my heels quite close to her.

She gave a little scream and was quickly on her legs again. Now that she stood there staring at me, with her wide-open grey eyes full of terror, I perceived that it was a girl of my own age, with a very pleasant face embellished unfortunately by three large blue marks. This spoilt her, although these blue marks had been distributed with a remarkable sense of proportion, one at a time, and all were of equal size—two under the eyes, and one a little bigger on the forehead just over the bridge of the nose. This symmetry was evidently the work of an artist well inured to the business of spoiling the human physiognomy.

The girl looked at me, and the terror in her eyes gradually died out... She shook the sand from her hands, adjusted her cotton head-gear, cowered down, and said:

"I suppose you too want something to eat? Dig away then! My hands are tired. Over there"—she nodded her head in the direction of a booth—"there is bread for certain ... and sausages too ... That booth is still carrying on business."

I began to dig. She, after waiting a little and looking at me, sat down beside me and began to help me.

We worked in silence. I cannot say now whether I thought at that moment of the criminal code, of morality, of proprietorship, and all the other things about which, in the opinion of many experienced persons, one ought to think every moment of one's life. Wishing to keep as close to the truth as possible, I must confess that apparently I was so deeply engaged in digging under the crate that I completely forgot about everything else except this one thing: What could be inside that crate?

The evening drew on. The grey, mouldy, cold fog grew thicker and thicker around us. The waves roared with a hollower sound than before, and the rain pattered down on the boards of that crate more loudly and more frequently. Somewhere or other the night-watchman began springing his rattle.

"Has it got a bottom or not?" softly inquired my assistant. I did not understand what she was talking about, and I kept silence.

"I say, has the crate got a bottom? If it has we shall try in vain to break into it. Here we are digging a trench, and we may, after all, come upon nothing but solid boards. How shall we take them off? Better smash the lock; it is a wretched lock."

Good ideas rarely visit the heads of women, but, as you see, they do visit them sometimes. I have always valued good ideas, and have always tried to utilise them as far as possible.

Having found the lock, I tugged at it and wrenched off the whole thing. My accomplice immediately stooped down and wriggled like a serpent into the gaping-open, four cornered cover of the crate whence she called to me approvingly, in a low tone:

"You're a brick!"

Nowadays a little crumb of praise from a woman is dearer to me than a whole dithyramb from a man, even though he be more eloquent than all the ancient and modern orators put together. Then, however, I was less amiably disposed than I am now, and, paying no attention to the compliment of my comrade, I asked her curtly and anxiously:

"Is there anything?"

In a monotonous tone she set about calculating our discoveries.

"A basketful of bottles—thick furs—a sunshade—an iron pail."

All this was uneatable. I felt that my hopes had vanished... But suddenly she exclaimed vivaciously:

"Aha! Here it is!"

"What?"

"Bread ... a loaf ... it's only wet ... take it!"

A loaf flew to my feet and after it herself, my valiant comrade. I had already bitten off a morsel, stuffed it in my mouth, and was chewing it...

"Come, give me some too!... And we mustn't stay here ... Where shall we go?" she looked inquiringly about on all sides ... It was dark, wet, and boisterous.

"Look! There's an upset canoe yonder ... let us go there."

"Let us go then!" And off we set, demolishing our booty as we went, and filling our mouths with large portions of it ... The rain grew more violent, the river roared; from somewhere or other resounded a prolonged mocking whistle—just as if Someone great who feared nobody was whistling down all earthly institutions and along with them this horrid autumnal wind and us its heroes. This whistling made my heart throb painfully, in spite of which I greedily went on eating, and in this respect the girl, walking on my left hand, kept even pace with me.

"What do they call you?" I asked her—why I know not.

"Natasha," she answered shortly, munching loudly.

I stared at her. My heart ached within me; and then I stared into the mist before me, and it seemed to me as if the inimical countenance of my Destiny was smiling at me enigmatically and coldly.

~

The rain scourged the timbers of the skiff incessantly, and its soft patter induced melancholy thoughts, and the wind whistled as it flew down into the boat's battered bottom through a rift, where some loose splinters of wood were rattling together—a disquieting and depressing sound. The waves of the river were splashing on the shore, and sounded so monotonous and hopeless, just as if they were telling something unbearably dull and heavy, which was boring them into utter disgust, something from which they wanted to run away and yet were obliged to talk about all the same. The sound of the rain blended with their splashing, and a long-drawn sigh seemed to be floating above the overturned skiff—the endless, labouring sigh of the earth, injured and exhausted by the eternal changes from the bright and warm summer to the cold misty and damp autumn. The wind blew continually over the desolate shore and the foaming river—blew and sang its melancholy songs...

Our position beneath the shelter of the skiff was utterly devoid of comfort; it was narrow and damp, tiny cold drops of rain dribbled through the damaged bottom; gusts of wind penetrated it. We sat in silence and shivered with cold. I remembered that I wanted to go to sleep. Natasha leaned her back against the hull of the boat and curled herself up into a tiny ball. Embracing her knees with her hands, and resting her chin upon them, she stared doggedly at the river with wide-open eyes; on the pale patch of her face they seemed immense, because of the blue marks below them. She never moved, and this immobility and silence—I felt it—gradually produced within me a terror of my neighbour. I wanted to talk to her, but I knew not how to begin.

It was she herself who spoke.

"What a cursed thing life is!" she exclaimed plainly, abstractedly, and in a tone of deep conviction.

But this was no complaint. In these words there was too much of indifference for a complaint. This simple soul thought according to her understanding—thought and proceeded to form a certain conclusion which she expressed aloud, and which I could not confute for fear of contradicting myself. Therefore I was silent, and she, as if she had not noticed me, continued to sit there immovable.

"Even if we croaked ... what then...?" Natasha began again, this time quietly and reflectively, and still there was not one note of complaint in her words. It was plain that this person, in the course of her reflections on life, was regarding her own case, and had arrived at the conviction that in order to preserve herself from the mockeries of life, she was not in a position to do anything else but simply "croak"—to use her own expression.

The clearness of this line of thought was inexpressibly sad and painful to me, and I felt that if I kept silence any longer I was really bound to weep ... And it would have been shameful to have done this before a woman, especially as she was not weeping herself. I resolved to speak to her.

"Who was it that knocked you about?" I asked. For the moment I could not think of anything more sensible or more delicate.

"Pashka did it all," she answered in a dull and level tone.

"And who is he?"

"My lover ... He was a baker."

"Did he beat you often?"

"Whenever he was drunk he beat me ... Often!"

And suddenly, turning towards me, she began to talk about herself, Pashka, and their mutual relations. He was a baker with red moustaches and played very well on the banjo. He came to see her and greatly pleased her, for he was a merry chap and wore nice clean clothes. He had a vest which cost fifteen rubles and boots with dress tops. For these reasons she had fallen in love with him, and he became her "creditor." And when he became her creditor he made it his business to take away from her the money which her other friends gave to her for bonbons, and, getting drunk on this money, he would fall to beating her; but that would have been nothing if he hadn't also begun to "run after" other girls before her very eyes.

"Now, wasn't that an insult? I am not worse than the others. Of course that meant that he was laughing at me, the blackguard. The day before yesterday I asked leave of my mistress to go out for a bit, went to him, and there I found Dimka sitting beside him drunk. And he, too, was half seas over. I said, 'You scoundrel, you!' And he gave me a thorough hiding. He kicked me and dragged me by the hair. But that was nothing to what came after. He spoiled everything I had on—left me just as I am now! How could I appear before my mistress? He spoiled everything ... my dress and my jacket too—it was quite a new one; I gave a fiver for it ... and tore my kerchief from my head ... Oh, Lord! What will become of me now?" she suddenly whined in a lamentable overstrained voice.

The wind howled, and became ever colder and more boisterous ... Again my teeth began to dance up and down, and she, huddled up to avoid the cold, pressed as closely to me as she could, so that I could see the gleam of her eyes through the darkness.

"What wretches all you men are! I'd burn you all in an oven; I'd cut you in pieces. If any one of you was dying I'd spit in his mouth, and not pity him a bit. Mean skunks! You wheedle and wheedle, you wag your tails like cringing dogs, and we fools give ourselves up to you, and it's all up with us! Immediately you trample us underfoot ... Miserable loafers'"

She cursed us up and down, but there was no vigour, no malice, no hatred of these "miserable loafers" in her cursing that I could hear. The tone of her language by no means corresponded with its subject-matter, for it was calm enough, and the gamut of her voice was terribly poor.

Yet all this made a stronger impression on me than the most eloquent and convincing pessimistic bocks and speeches, of which I had read a good many and which I still read to this day. And this, you see, was because the agony of a dying person is much more natural and violent than the most minute and picturesque descriptions of death.

I felt really wretched—more from cold than from the words of my neighbour. I groaned softly and ground my teeth.

Almost at the same moment I felt two little arms about me—one of them touched my neck and the other lay upon my face—and at the same time an anxious, gentle, friendly voice uttered the question:

"What ails you?"

I was ready to believe that some one else was asking me this and not Natasha, who had just declared that all men were scoundrels, and expressed a wish for their destruction. But she it was, and now she began speaking quickly, hurriedly.

"What ails you, eh? Are you cold? Are you frozen? Ah, what a one you are, sitting there so silent like a little owl! Why, you should have told me long ago that you were cold. Come ... lie on the ground ... stretch yourself out and I will lie ... there! How's that? Now put your arms round me? ... tighter! How's that? You shall be warm very soon now... And then we'll lie back to back ... The night will pass so quickly, see if it won't. I say ... have you too been drinking?... Turned out of your place, eh?... It doesn't matter."

And she comforted me ... She encouraged me.

May I be thrice accursed! What a world of irony was in this single fact for me! Just imagine! Here was I, seriously occupied at this very time with the destiny of humanity, thinking of the re-organisation of the social system, of political revolutions, reading all sorts of devilishly-wise books whose abysmal profundity was certainly unfathomable by their very authors—at this very time. I say, I was trying with all my might to make of myself "a potent active social force." It even seemed to me that I had partially accomplished my object; anyhow, at this time, in my ideas about myself, I had got so far as to recognise that I had an exclusive right to exist, that I had the necessary greatness to deserve to live my life, and that I was fully competent to play a great historical part therein. And a woman was now warming me with her body, a wretched, battered, hunted creature, who had no place and no value in life, and whom I had never thought of helping till she helped me herself, and whom I really would not have known how to help in any way even if the thought of it had occurred to me.

Ah! I was ready to think that all this was happening to me in a dream—in a disagreeable, an oppressive dream.

But, ugh! It was impossible for me to think that, for cold drops of rain were dripping down upon me, the woman was pressing close to me, her warm breath was fanning my face, and—despite a slight odor of vodka—it did me good. The wind howled and raged, the rain smote upon the skiff, the waves splashed, and both of us, embracing each other convulsively, nevertheless shivered with cold. All this was only too real, and I am certain that nobody ever dreamed such an oppressive and horrid dream as that reality.

But Natasha was talking all the time of something or other, talking kindly and sympathetically, as only women can talk. Beneath the influence of her voice and kindly words a little fire began to burn up within me, and something inside my heart thawed in consequence.

Then tears poured from my eyes like a hailstorm, washing away from my heart much that was evil, much that war, stupid, much sorrow and dirt which had fastened upon it before that night. Natasha comforted me.

"Come, come, that will do, little one! Don't take on! That'll do! God will give you another chance ... you will right yourself and stand in your proper place again ... and it will be all right..."

And she kept kissing me ... many kisses did she give me ... burning kisses ... and all for nothing...

Those were the first kisses from a woman that had ever been bestowed upon me, and they were the best kisses too, for all the subsequent kisses cost me frightfully dear, and really gave me nothing at all in exchange.

"Come, don't take on so, funny one! I'll manage for you tomorrow if you cannot find a place." Her quiet persuasive whispering sounded in my ears as if it came through a dream...

There we lay till dawn...

And when the dawn came, we crept from behind the skiff and went into the town ... Then we took friendly leave of each other and never met again, although for half a year I searched in every hole and corner for that kind Natasha, with whom I spent the autumn night just described.

If she be already dead—and well for her if it were so—may she rest in peace! And if she be alive ... still I say "Peace to her soul!" And may the consciousness of her fall never enter her soul ... for that would be a superfluous and fruitless suffering if life is to be lived ...

Gooseberries

Anton Chekhov

Anton Chekhov (1860-1904) was the Russian master of the modern short story as well as a successful playwright. He was notable for the economy of expression, apparent simplicity of scenarios and the underlying complexity in his works. 'Gooseberries' (1903) is from the latter phase of his writing career, which was more serious, satirical and sombre in tone. Chekhov was regarded as one of the foremost writers of Russian realism.

From early morning the sky had been overcast with clouds; the day was still, cool, and wearisome, as usual on grey, dull days when the clouds hang low over the fields and it looks like rain, which never comes. Ivan Ivanich, the veterinary surgeon, and Bourkin, the schoolmaster, were tired of walking and the fields seemed endless to them. Far ahead they could just see the windmills of the village of Mirousky, to the right stretched away to disappear behind the village a line of hills, and they knew that it was the bank of the river; meadows, green willows, farmhouses; and from one of the hills there could be seen a field as endless, telegraphposts, and the train, looking from a distance like a crawling caterpillar, and in clear weather even the town. In the calm weather when all Nature seemed gentle and melancholy, Ivan Ivanich and Bourkin were filled with love for the fields and thought how grand and beautiful the country was.

"Last time, when we stopped in Prokofyi's shed," said Bourkin, "you were going to tell me a story."

"Yes. I wanted to tell you about my brother."

Ivan Ivanich took a deep breath and lighted his pipe before beginning his story, but just then the rain began to fall. And in about five minutes it came pelting down and showed no signs of stopping. Ivan Ivanich stopped and hesitated; the dogs, wet through, stood with their tails between their legs and looked at them mournfully.

"We ought to take shelter," said Bourkin. "Let us go to Aliokhin. It is close by." "Very well."

They took a short cut over a stubble-field and then bore to the right, until they came to the road. Soon there appeared poplars, a garden, the red roofs of granaries; the river began to glimmer and they came to a wide road with a mill and a white bathing-shed. It was Sophino, where Aliokhin lived.

The mill was working, drowning the sound of the rain, and the dam shook. Round the carts stood wet horses, hanging their heads, and men were walking about with their heads covered with sacks. It was wet, muddy, and unpleasant, and the river looked cold and sullen. Ivan Ivanich and Bourkin felt wet and uncomfortable through and through; their feet were tired with walking in the mud, and they walked past the dam to the barn in silence as though they were angry with each other.

In one of the barns a winnowing-machine was working, sending out clouds of dust. On the threshold stood Aliokhin himself, a man of about forty, tall and stout, with long hair, more like a professor or a painter than a farmer. He was wearing a grimy white shirt and rope belt, and pants instead of trousers; and his boots were covered with mud and straw. His nose and eyes were black with dust. He recognised Ivan Ivanich and was apparently very pleased.

"Please, gentlemen," he said, "go to the house. I'll be with you in a minute."

The house was large and two-storied. Aliokhin lived downstairs in two vaulted rooms with little windows designed for the farmhands; the farmhouse was plain, and the place smelled of rye bread and vodka, and leather. He rarely used the reception-rooms, only when guests arrived. Ivan Ivanich and Bourkin were received by a chambermaid; such a pretty young woman that both of them stopped and exchanged glances.

"You cannot imagine how glad I am to see you, gentlemen," said Aliokhin, coming after them into the hall. "I never expected you. Pelagueya," he said to the maid, "give my friends a change of clothes. And I will change, too. But I must have a bath. I haven't had one since the spring. Wouldn't you like to come to the bathing-shed? And meanwhile our things will be got ready."

Pretty Pelagueya, dainty and sweet, brought towels and soap, and Aliokhin led his guests to the bathing-shed.

"Yes," he said, "it is a long time since I had a bath. My bathing-shed is all right, as you see. My father and I put it up, but somehow I have no time to bathe."

He sat down on the step and lathered his long hair and neck, and the water round him became brown.

"Yes. I see," said Ivan Ivanich heavily, looking at his head.

"It is a long time since I bathed," said Aliokhin shyly, as he soaped himself again, and the water round him became dark blue, like ink.

Ivan Ivanich came out of the shed, plunged into the water with a splash, and swam about in the rain, flapping his arms, and sending waves back, and on the waves tossed white lilies; he swam out to the middle of the pool and dived, and in a minute came up again in another place and kept on swimming and diving, trying to reach the bottom. "Ah! How delicious!" he shouted in his glee. "How delicious!" He swam to the mill, spoke to the peasants, and came back, and in the middle of the pool he lay on his back to let the rain fall on his face. Bourkin and Aliokin were already dressed and ready to go, but he kept on swimming and diving.

"Delicious," he said. "Too delicious!' "You've had enough," shouted Bourkin.

They went to the house. And only when the lamp was lit in the large drawing room upstairs, and Bourkin and Ivan Ivanich, dressed in silk dressing-gowns and warm slippers, lounged in chairs, and Aliokhin himself, washed and brushed, in a new frock coat, paced up and down evidently delighting in the warmth and cleanliness and dry clothes and slippers, and pretty Pelagueya, noiselessly tripping over the carpet and smiling sweetly, brought in tea and jam on a tray, only then did Ivan Ivanich begin his story, and it was as though he was being listened to not only by Bourkin and Aliokhin, but also by the old and young ladies and the officer who looked down so staidly and tranquilly from the golden frames.

"We are two brothers," he began, "I, Ivan Ivanich, and Nicholai Ivanich, two years younger. I went in for study and became a veterinary surgeon, while Nicholai was at the Exchequer Court when he was nineteen. Our father, Tchimsha-Himalaysky, was a cantonist, but he died with an officer's rank and left us his title of nobility and a small estate. After his death the estate went to pay his debts. However, we spent our childhood there in the country. We were just like peasant's children, spent days and nights in the fields and the woods, minded the horses, barked the lime-trees, fished, and so on... And you know once a man has fished, or watched the thrushes hovering in flocks over the village in the bright, cool, autumn days, he can never really be a townsman, and to the day of his death he will be drawn to the country. My brother pined away in the Exchequer. Years passed and he sat in the same place, wrote out the same documents, and thought of one thing, how to get back to the country. And little by little his distress became a definite disorder, a fixed idea to buy a small farm somewhere by the bank of a river or a lake.

"He was a good fellow and I loved him, but I never sympathised with the desire to shut oneself up on one's own farm. It is a common saying that a man needs only six feet of land. But surely a corpse wants that, not a man. And I hear that our intellectuals have a longing for the land and want to acquire farms. But it all comes down to the six feet of land. To leave town, and the struggle and the swim of life, and go and hide yourself in a farmhouse is not life it is egoism, laziness; it is a kind of monasticism, but monasticism without action. A man needs, not six feet of land, not a farm, but the whole earth, all Nature, where in full liberty he can display all the properties and qualities of the free spirit.

"My brother Nicholai, sitting in his office, would dream of eating his own *schi*, with its savoury smell floating across the farmyard; and of eating out in the open air, and of sleeping in the sun, and of sitting for hours together on a seat by the gate and gazing at the fields and the forest. Books on agriculture and the hints in almanacs were his joy, his favourite spiritual food; and he liked reading newspapers, but only the advertisements of land to be sold, so many acres of arable and grass land, with a farmhouse, river, garden, mill, and millpond. And he would dream of garden-walls, flowers, fruits, nests, carp in the pond, don't you know, and all the rest of it. These fantasies of his used to vary according to the advertisements he found, but somehow there was always a gooseberry-bush in every one. Not a house, not a romantic spot could he imagine without its gooseberry-bush.

"'Country life has its advantages,' he used to say. 'You sit on the veranda drinking tea and your ducklings swim on the pond, and everything smells good … and there are gooseberries.'

"He used to draw out a plan of his estate and always the same things were shown on it: (a) Farmhouse, (b) cottage, (c) vegetable garden, (d) gooseberry-bush. He used to live meagrely and never had enough to eat and drink, dressed God knows how, exactly like a beggar, and always saved and put his money into the bank. He was terribly stingy. It used to hurt me to see him, and I used to give him money to go away for a holiday, but he would put that away, too. Once a man gets a fixed idea, there's nothing to be done.

"Years passed; he was transferred to another province. He completed his fortieth year and was still reading advertisements in the papers and saving up his money. Then I heard he was married. Still with the same idea of buying a farmhouse with a gooseberry-bush, he married an elderly, ugly widow, not out of any feeling for her, but because she had money. With her he still lived stingily, kept her half-starved, and put the money into the bank in his own name. She had been the wife of a postmaster and was used to good living, but with her second husband she did not even have enough black bread; she pined away in her new life, and in three years or so gave up her soul to God. And my brother never for a moment thought himself to blame for her death. Money, like vodka, can play queer tricks with a man. Once in our town a merchant lay dying. Before his death he asked for some honey, and he ate all his notes and scrip with the honey so that nobody should get it. Once I was examining a herd of cattle at a station and a horse-jobber fell under the engine, and his foot was cut off. We carried him into the waiting-room, with the blood pouring down a terrible business and all the while he kept asking anxiously for his foot; he had twenty-five roubles in his boot and did not want to lose them."

"Keep to your story," said Bourkin.

"After the death of his wife," Ivan Ivanich continued, after a long pause, "my brother began to look out for an estate. Of course you may search for five years, and even then buy a pig in a poke. Through an agent my brother Nicholai raised a mortgage and bought three hundred acres with a farmhouse, a cottage, and a park, but there was no orchard, no gooseberry-bush, no duckpond; there was a river but the water in it was coffee-coloured because the estate lay between a brickyard and a gelatine factory. But my brother Nicholai was not worried about that; he ordered twenty gooseberry-bushes and settled down to a country life.

"Last year I paid him a visit. I thought I'd go and see how things were with him. In his letters my brother called his estate Tchimbarshov Corner, or Himalayskoe. I arrived at Himalayskoe in the afternoon. It was hot. There were ditches, fences, hedges, rows of young fir-trees, trees everywhere, and there was no telling how to cross the yard or where to put your horse. I went to the house and was met by a red-haired dog, as fat as a pig. He tried to bark but felt too lazy. Out of the kitchen came the cook, barefooted, and also as fat as a pig, and said that the master was having his afternoon rest. I went in to my brother and found him sitting on his bed with his knees covered with a blanket; he looked old, stout, flabby; his cheeks, nose, and lips were pendulous. I half expected him to grunt like a pig.

"We embraced and shed a tear of joy and also of sadness to think that we had once been young, but were now both going grey and nearing death. He dressed and took me to see his estate.

"'Well? How are you getting on?' I asked.

"'All right, thank God. I am doing very well.'

"He was no longer the poor, tired official, but a real landowner and a person of consequence. He had got used to the place and liked it, ate a great deal, took Russian baths, was growing fat, had already gone to law with the parish and the two factories, and was much offended if the peasants did not call him 'Your Lordship.' And, like a good landowner, he looked after his soul and did good works pompously, never simply. What good works? He cured the peasants of all kinds of diseases with soda and castor-oil, and on his birthday he would have a thanksgiving service held in the middle of the village, and would treat the peasants to half a bucket of vodka, which he thought the right thing to do. Ah! These horrible buckets of vodka. One day a greasy landowner will drag the peasants before the Zembro Court for trespass, and the next, if it's a holiday, he will give them a bucket of vodka, and they drink and shout Hooray! and lick his boots in their drunkenness. A change to good eating and idleness always fills a Russian with the most preposterous self-conceit. Nicholai Ivanich who, when he was in the Exchequer, was terrified to have an opinion of his own, now imagined that what he said was law. 'Education is necessary for the masses, but they are not fit for it.' 'Corporal punishment is generally harmful, but in certain cases it is useful and indispensable.'

"'I know the people and I know how to treat them,' he would say. 'The people love me. I have only to raise my finger and they will do as I wish.'

"And all this, mark you, was said with a kindly smile of wisdom. He was constantly saying: 'We noblemen,' or 'I, as a nobleman.' Apparently he had forgotten that our grandfather was a peasant and our father a common soldier. Even our family name, Tchimacha-Himalaysky, which is really an absurd one, seemed to him full-sounding, distinguished, and very pleasing.

"But my point does not concern him so much as myself. I want to tell you what a change took place in me in those few hours while I was in his house. In the evening, while we were having tea, the cook laid a plateful of gooseberries on the table. They had not been bought, but were his own gooseberries, plucked for the first time since the bushes were planted. Nicholai Ivanich laughed with joy and for a minute or two he looked in silence at the gooseberries with tears in his eyes. He could not speak for excitement, then put one into his mouth, glanced at me in triumph, like a child at last being given its favourite toy, and said:

"'How good they are!'

"He went on eating greedily, and saying all the while:

"'How good they are! Do try one!'

"It was hard and sour, but, as Poushkin said, the illusion which exalts us is dearer to us than ten thousand truths. I saw a happy man, one whose dearest dream had come true, who had attained his goal in life, who had got what he wanted, and was pleased with his destiny and with himself. In my idea of human life there is always some alloy of sadness, but now at the sight of a happy man I was filled with something like despair. And at night it grew on me. A bed was made up for me in the room near my brother's and I could hear him, unable to sleep, going again and again to the plate of gooseberries. I thought: 'After all, what a lot of contented, happy people there must be! What an overwhelming power that means! I look at this life and see the arrogance and the idleness of the strong, the ignorance and bestiality of the weak, the horrible poverty everywhere, overcrowding, drunkenness, hypocrisy, falsehood... Meanwhile in all the houses, all the streets, there is peace; out of fifty thousand people who live in our town there is not one to kick against it all. Think of the people who go to the market for food: during the day they eat; at night they sleep, talk nonsense, marry, grow old, piously follow their dead to the cemetery; one never sees or hears those who suffer, and all the horror of life goes on somewhere behind the scenes. Everything is quiet, peaceful, and against it all there is only the silent protest of statistics; so many go mad, so many gallons are drunk, so many children die of starvation.... And such a state of things is obviously what we want; apparently a happy man only feels so because the unhappy bear their burden in silence, but for which happiness would be impossible. It is a general hypnosis. Every happy man should have some one with a little hammer at his door to knock and remind him that there are unhappy people, and that, however happy he may be, life will sooner or later show its claws, and some misfortune will befall him illness, poverty, loss, and then no one will see or hear him, just as he now neither sees nor hears others. But there is no man with a hammer, and the happy go on living, just a little fluttered with the petty cares of every day, like an aspentree in the wind and everything is all right.'

"That night I was able to understand how I, too, had been content and happy," Ivan Ivanich went on, getting up. "I, too, at meals or out hunting, used to lay down the law about living, and religion, and governing the masses. I, too, used to say that teaching is light, that education is necessary, but that for simple folk reading and writing is enough for the present. Freedom is a boon, I used to say, as essential as the air we breathe, but we must wait. Yes I used to say so, but now I ask: 'Why do we wait?'" Ivan Ivanich glanced angrily at Bourkin. "Why do we wait, I ask you? What considerations keep us fast? I am told that we cannot have everything at once, and that every idea is realised in time. But who says so? Where is the proof that it is so? You refer me to the natural order of things, to the law of cause and effect, but is there order or natural law in that I, a living, thinking creature, should stand by a ditch until it fills up, or is narrowed, when I could jump it or throw a bridge over it? Tell me, I say, why should we wait? Wait, when we have no strength to live, and yet must live and are full of the desire to live!

"I left my brother early the next morning, and from that time on I found it impossible to live in town. The peace and quiet of it oppress me. I dare not look in at the windows, for nothing is more dreadful to see than the sight of a happy family, sitting round a table, having tea. I am an old man now and am no good for the struggle. I commenced late. I can only grieve within my soul, and fret and sulk. At night my head buzzes with the rush of my thoughts and I cannot sleep… Ah! If I were young!"

Ivan Ivanich walked excitedly up and down the room and repeated, "If I were young."

He suddenly walked up to Aliokhin and shook him first by one hand and then by the other.

"Pavel Koustantinich," he said in a voice of entreaty, "don't be satisfied, don't let yourself be lulled to sleep! While you are young, strong, wealthy, do not cease to do good! Happiness does not exist, nor should it, and if there is any meaning or purpose in life, they are not in our peddling little happiness, but in something reasonable and grand. Do good!"

Ivan Ivanich said this with a piteous supplicating smile, as though he were asking a personal favour.

Then they all three sat in different corners of the drawing-room and were silent. Ivan Ivanich's story had satisfied neither Bourkin nor Aliokhin. With the generals and ladies looking down from their gilt frames, seeming alive in the firelight, it was tedious to hear the story of a miserable official who ate gooseberries.... Somehow they had a longing to hear and to speak of charming people, and of women. And the mere fact of sitting in the drawing-room where everything the lamp with its coloured shade, the chairs, and the carpet under their feet told how the very people who now looked down at them from their frames once walked, and sat and had tea there, and the fact that pretty Pelagueya was near was much better than any story.

Aliokhin wanted very much to go to bed; he had to get up for his work very early, about two in the morning, and now his eyes were closing, but he was afraid of his guests saying something interesting without his hearing it, so he would not go. He did not trouble to think whether what Ivan Ivanich had been saying was clever or right; his guests were talking of neither groats, nor hay, nor tar, but of something which had no bearing on his life, and he liked it and wanted them to go on....

"However, it's time to go to bed," said Bourkin, getting up. "I will wish you good night."

Aliokhin said good night and went downstairs, and left his guests. Each had a large room with an old wooden bed and carved ornaments; in the corner was an ivory crucifix; and their wide, cool beds, made by pretty Pelagueya, smelled sweetly of clean linen.

Ivan Ivanich undressed in silence and lay down.

"God forgive me, a wicked sinner," he murmured, as he drew the clothes over his head.

A smell of burning tobacco came from his pipe which lay on the table, and Bourkin could not sleep for a long time and was worried because he could not make out where the unpleasant smell came from.

The rain beat against the windows all night long.

The Country Of The Blind

H.G. Wells

Herbert George Wells (1866-1946) was an English novelist, sociologist, journalist and historian, who wrote the very popular science fiction novels—*The Invisible Man* (1897) and *The War of the Worlds* (1898). Despite being regarded as a pioneer of the science fiction genre, he eventually progressed towards writing comic novels and his work became more sociological and historical in nature. 'The Country Of The Blind' (1904), however, belongs to the genre of science fiction and fantasy so characteristic of Wells.

Three hundred miles and more from Chimborazo, one hundred from the snows of Cotopaxi, in the wildest wastes of Ecuador's Andes, there lies that mysterious mountain valley, cut off from the world of men, the Country of the Blind. Long years ago that valley lay so far open to the world that men might come at last through frightful gorges and over an icy pass into its equable meadows; and thither indeed men came, a family or so of Peruvian half-breeds fleeing from the lust and tyranny of an evil Spanish ruler. Then came the stupendous outbreak of Mindobamba, when it was night in Quito for seventeen days, and the water was boiling at Yaguachi and all the fish floating dying even as far as Guayaquil; everywhere along the Pacific slopes there were land-slips and swift thawings and sudden floods, and one whole side of the old Arauca crest slipped and came down in thunder, and cut off the Country of the Blind for ever from the exploring feet of men. But one of these early settlers had chanced to be on the hither side of the gorges when the world had so terribly shaken itself, and he perforce had to forget his wife and his child and all the friends and possessions he had left up there, and start life over again in the lower world. He started it again but ill, blindness overtook him, and he died of punishment in the mines; but the story he told begot a legend that lingers along the length of the Cordilleras of the Andes to this day.

He told of his reason for venturing back from that fastness, into which he had first been carried lashed to a llama, beside a vast bale of gear, when he was a child. The valley, he said, had in it all that the heart of man could desire—sweet water, pasture, and even climate, slopes of rich brown soil with tangles of a shrub that bore an excellent fruit, and on one side great hanging forests of pine that held the avalanches high. Far overhead, on three sides, vast cliffs of grey-green rock were capped by cliffs of ice; but the glacier stream came not to them but flowed away by the farther slopes, and only now and then huge ice masses fell on the valley side. In this valley it neither rained nor snowed, but the abundant springs gave a rich green pasture, that irrigation would spread over all the valley space. The settlers did well indeed there. Their beasts did well and multiplied, and but one thing marred their happiness. Yet it was enough to mar it greatly. A strange disease had come upon them, and had made all the children born to them there—and indeed, several older children also—blind. It was to seek some charm or antidote against this plague of blindness that he had with fatigue and danger and difficulty returned down the gorge. In those days, in such cases, men did not think of germs and infections but of sins; and it seemed to him that the reason of this affliction must lie in the negligence of these priestless immigrants to set up a shrine so soon as they entered the valley. He wanted a shrine—a handsome, cheap, effectual shrine—to be erected in the valley; he wanted relics and such-like potent things of faith, blessed objects and mysterious medals and prayers. In his wallet he had a bar of native silver for which he would not account; he insisted there was none in the valley with something of the insistence of an inexpert liar. They had all clubbed their money and ornaments together, having little need for such treasure up there, he said, to buy them holy help against their ill. I figure this dim-eyed young mountaineer, sunburnt, gaunt, and anxious, hat-brim clutched feverishly, a man all unused to the ways of the lower world, telling this story to some keen-eyed, attentive priest before the great convulsion; I can picture him presently seeking to return with pious and infallible remedies against that trouble, and the infinite dismay with which he must have faced the tumbled vastness where the gorge had once come out. But the rest of his story of mischances is lost to me, save that I know of his evil death after several years. Poor stray from that remoteness! The stream that had once made the gorge now bursts from the mouth of a rocky cave, and the legend his poor, ill-told story set going developed into the legend of a race of blind men somewhere "over there" one may still hear to-day.

And amidst the little population of that now isolated and forgotten valley the disease ran its course. The old became groping and purblind, the young saw but dimly, and the children that were born to them saw never at all. But life was very easy in that snow-rimmed basin, lost to all the world, with neither thorns nor briars, with no evil insects nor any beasts save the gentle breed of llamas they had lugged and thrust and followed up the beds of the shrunken rivers in the gorges up which they had come. The seeing had become purblind so gradually that they scarcely noted their loss. They guided the sightless youngsters hither and thither until they knew the whole Valley marvellously, and when at last sight died out among them the race lived on. They had even time to adapt themselves to the blind control of fire, which they made carefully in stoves of stone. They were a simple strain of people at the first, unlettered, only slightly touched with the Spanish civilisation, but with something of a tradition of the arts of old Peru and of its lost philosophy. Generation followed generation. They forgot many things; they devised many things. Their tradition of the greater world they came from became mythical in colour and uncertain. In all things save sight they were strong and able, and presently the chance of birth and heredity sent one who had an original mind and who could talk and persuade among them, and then afterwards another. These two passed, leaving their effects, and the little community grew in numbers and in understanding, and met and settled social and economic problems that arose. Generation followed generation. Generation followed generation. There came a time when a child was born who was fifteen generations from that ancestor who went out of the valley with a bar of silver to seek God's aid, and who never returned. Thereabouts it chanced that a man came into this community from the outer world. And this is the story of that man.

He was a mountaineer from the country near Quito, a man who had been down to the sea and had seen the world, a reader of books in an original way, an acute and enterprising man, and he was taken on by a party of Englishmen who had come out to Ecuador to climb mountains, to replace one of their three Swiss guides who had fallen ill. He climbed here and he climbed there, and then came the attempt on Parascotopetl, the Matterhorn of the Andes, in which he was lost to the outer world. The story of the accident has been written a dozen times. Pointer's narrative is the best. He tells how the little party worked their difficult and almost vertical way up to the very foot of the last and greatest precipice, and how they built a night shelter amidst the snow upon a little shelf of rock, and, with a touch of real dramatic power, how presently they found Nunez had gone from them. They shouted, and there was no reply; shouted and whistled, and for the rest of that night they slept no more.

As the morning broke they saw the traces of his fall. It seems impossible he could have uttered a sound. He had slipped eastward towards the unknown side of the mountain; far below he had struck a steep slope of snow, and ploughed his way down it in the midst of a snow avalanche. His track went straight to the edge of a frightful precipice, and beyond that everything was hidden. Far, far below, and hazy with distance, they could see trees rising out of a narrow, shut-in valley—the lost Country of the Blind. But they did not know it was the lost Country of the Blind, nor distinguish it in any way from any other narrow streak of upland valley. Unnerved by this disaster, they abandoned their attempt in the afternoon, and Pointer was called away to the war before he could make another attack. To this day Parascotopetl lifts an unconquered crest, and Pointer's shelter crumbles unvisited amidst the snows.

And the man who fell survived.

At the end of the slope he fell a thousand feet, and came down in the midst of a cloud of snow upon a snow slope even steeper than the one above. Down this he was whirled, stunned and insensible, but without a bone broken in his body; and then at last came to gentler slopes, and at last rolled out and lay still, buried amidst a softening heap of the white masses that had accompanied and saved him. He came to himself with a dim fancy that he was ill in bed; then realised his position with a mountaineer's intelligence, and worked himself loose and, after a rest or so, out until he saw the stars. He rested flat upon his chest for a space, wondering where he was and what had happened to him. He explored his limbs, and discovered that several of his buttons were gone and his coat turned over his head. His knife had gone from his pocket and his hat was lost, though he had tied it under his chin. He recalled that he had been looking for loose stones to raise his piece of the shelter wall. His ice-axe had disappeared.

He decided he must have fallen, and looked up to see, exaggerated by the ghastly light of the rising moon, the tremendous flight he had taken. For a while he lay, gazing blankly at that vast pale cliff towering above, rising moment by moment out of a subsiding tide of darkness. Its phantasmal, mysterious beauty held him for a space, and then he was seized with a paroxysm of sobbing laughter…

After a great interval of time he became aware that he was near the lower edge of the snow. Below, down what was now a moonlit and practicable slope, he saw the dark and broken appearance of rock-strewn turf. He struggled to his feet, aching in every joint and limb, got down painfully from the heaped loose snow about him, went downward until he was on the turf, and there dropped rather than lay beside a boulder, drank deep from the flask in his inner pocket, and instantly fell asleep…

He was awakened by the singing of birds in the trees far below.

He sat up and perceived he was on a little alp at the foot of a vast precipice, that was grooved by the gully down which he and his snow had come. Over against him another wall of rock reared itself against the sky. The gorge between these precipices ran east and west and was full of the morning sunlight, which lit to the westward the mass of fallen mountain that closed the descending gorge. Below him it seemed there was a precipice equally steep, but behind the snow in the gully he found a sort of chimney-cleft dripping with snow-water down which a desperate man might venture. He found it easier than it seemed, and came at last to another desolate alp, and then after a rock climb of no particular difficulty to a steep slope of trees. He took his bearings and turned his face up the gorge, for he saw it opened out above upon green meadows, among which he now glimpsed quite distinctly a cluster of stone huts of unfamiliar fashion. At times his progress was like clambering along the face of a wall, and after a time the rising sun ceased to strike along the gorge, the voices of the singing birds died away, and the air grew cold and dark about him. But the distant valley with its houses was all the brighter for that. He came presently to talus, and among the rocks he noted—for he was an observant man—an unfamiliar fern that seemed to clutch out of the crevices with intense green hands. He picked a frond or so and gnawed its stalk and found it helpful.

About midday he came at last out of the throat of the gorge into the plain and the sunlight. He was stiff and weary; he sat down in the shadow of a rock, filled up his flask with water from a spring and drank it down, and remained for a time resting before he went on to the houses.

They were very strange to his eyes, and indeed the whole aspect of that valley became, as he regarded it, queerer and more unfamiliar. The greater part of its surface was lush green meadow, starred with many beautiful flowers, irrigated with extraordinary care, and bearing evidence of systematic cropping piece by piece. High up and ringing the valley about was a wall, and what appeared to be a circumferential water-channel, from which the little trickles of water that fed the meadow plants came, and on the higher slopes above this flocks of llamas cropped the scanty herbage. Sheds, apparently shelters or feeding-places for the llamas, stood against the boundary wall here and there. The irrigation streams ran together into a main channel down the centre of the valley, and this was enclosed on either side by a wall breast high. This gave a singularly urban quality to this secluded place, a quality that was greatly enhanced by the fact that a number of paths paved with black and white stones, and each with a curious little kerb at the side, ran hither and thither in an orderly manner. The houses of the central village were quite unlike the casual and higgledy-piggledy agglomeration of the mountain villages he knew; they stood in a continuous row on either side of a central street of astonishing cleanness; here and there their particoloured facade was pierced by a door, and not a solitary window broke their even frontage. They were particoloured with extraordinary irregularity, smeared with a sort of plaster that was sometimes grey, sometimes drab, sometimes slate-coloured or dark brown; and it was the sight of this wild plastering first brought the word "blind" into the thoughts of the explorer. "The good man who did that," he thought, "must have been as blind as a bat."

He descended a steep place, and so came to the wall and channel that ran about the valley, near where the latter spouted out its surplus contents into the deeps of the gorge in a thin and wavering thread of cascade. He could now see a number of men and women resting on piled heaps of grass, as if taking a siesta, in the remoter part of the meadow, and nearer the village a number of recumbent children, and then nearer at hand three men carrying pails on yokes along a little path that ran from the encircling wall towards the houses. These latter were clad in garments of llama cloth and boots and belts of leather, and they wore caps of cloth with back and ear flaps. They followed one another in single file, walking slowly and yawning as they walked, like men who have been up all night. There was something so reassuringly prosperous and respectable in their bearing that after a moment's hesitation Nunez stood forward as conspicuously as possible upon his rock, and gave vent to a mighty shout that echoed round the valley.

The three men stopped, and moved their heads as though they were looking about them. They turned their faces this way and that, and Nunez gesticulated with freedom. But they did not appear to see him for all his gestures, and after a time, directing themselves towards the mountains far away to the right, they shouted as if in answer. Nunez bawled again, and then once more, and as he gestured ineffectually the word "blind" came up to the top of his thoughts. "The fools must be blind," he said.

When at last, after much shouting and wrath, Nunez crossed the stream by a little bridge, came through a gate in the wall, and approached them, he was sure that they were blind. He was sure that this was the Country of the Blind of which the legends told.

Conviction had sprung upon him, and a sense of great and rather enviable adventure. The three stood side by side, not looking at him, but with their ears directed towards him, judging him by his unfamiliar steps. They stood close together like men a little afraid, and he could see their eyelids closed and sunken, as though the very balls beneath had shrunk away. There was an expression near awe on their faces.

"A man," one said, in hardly recognisable Spanish—"a man it is—a man or a spirit—coming down from the rocks."

But Nunez advanced with the confident steps of a youth who enters upon life. All the old stories of the lost valley and the Country of the Blind had come back to his mind, and through his thoughts ran this old proverb, as if it were a refrain—

"In the Country of the Blind the One-eyed Man is King."

"In the Country of the Blind the One-eyed Man is King."

And very civilly he gave them greeting. He talked to them and used his eyes.

"Where does he come from, brother Pedro?" asked one.

"Down out of the rocks."

"Over the mountains I come," said Nunez, "out of the country beyond there—where men can see. From near Bogota, where there are a hundred thousands of people, and where the city passes out of sight."

"Sight?" muttered Pedro. "Sight?"

"He comes," said the second blind man, "out of the rocks."

The cloth of their coats Nunez saw was curiously fashioned, each with a different sort of stitching.

They startled him by a simultaneous movement towards him, each with a hand outstretched. He stepped back from the advance of these spread fingers.

"Come hither," said the third blind man, following his motion and clutching him neatly.

And they held Nunez and felt him over, saying no word further until they had done so.

"Carefully," he cried, with a finger in his eye, and found they thought that organ, with its fluttering lids, a queer thing in him. They went over it again.

"A strange creature, Correa," said the one called Pedro. "Feel the coarseness of his hair. Like a llama's hair."

"Rough he is as the rocks that begot him," said Correa, investigating Nunez's unshaven chin with a soft and slightly moist hand. "Perhaps he will grow finer." Nunez struggled a little under their examination, but they gripped him firm.

"Carefully," he said again.

"He speaks," said the third man. "Certainly he is a man."

"Ugh!" said Pedro, at the roughness of his coat.

"And you have come into the world?" asked Pedro.

"*Out* of the world. Over mountains and glaciers; right over above there, half-way to the sun. Out of the great big world that goes down, twelve days' journey to the sea."

They scarcely seemed to heed him. "Our fathers have told us men may be made by the forces of Nature," said Correa. "It is the warmth of things and moisture, and rottenness—rottenness."

"Let us lead him to the elders," said Pedro.

"Shout first," said Correa, "lest the children be afraid... This is a marvellous occasion."

So they shouted, and Pedro went first and took Nunez by the hand to lead him to the houses.

He drew his hand away. "I can see," he said.

"See?" said Correa.

"Yes, see," said Nunez, turning towards him, and stumbled against Pedro's pail.

"His senses are still imperfect," said the third blind man. "He stumbles, and talks unmeaning words. Lead him by the hand."

"As you will," said Nunez, and was led along, laughing.

It seemed they knew nothing of sight.

Well, all in good time he would teach them.

He heard people shouting, and saw a number of figures gathering together in the middle roadway of the village.

He found it tax his nerve and patience more than he had anticipated, that first encounter with the population of the Country of the Blind. The place seemed larger as he drew near to it, and the smeared plasterings queerer, and a crowd of children and men and women (the women and girls, he was pleased to note, had some of them quite sweet faces, for all that their eyes were shut and sunken) came about him, holding on to him, touching him with soft, sensitive hands, smelling at him, and listening at every word he spoke. Some of the maidens and children, however, kept aloof as if afraid, and indeed his voice seemed coarse and rude beside their softer notes. They mobbed him. His three guides kept close to him with an effect of proprietorship, and said again and again, "A wild man out of the rock."

"Bogota," he said. "Bogota. Over the mountain crests."

"A wild man—using wild words," said Pedro. "Did you hear that—*Bogota*? His mind is hardly formed yet. He has only the beginnings of speech."

A little boy nipped his hand. "Bogota!" he said mockingly.

"Ay! A city to your village. I come from the great world—where men have eyes and see."

"His name's Bogota," they said.

"He stumbled," said Correa, "stumbled twice as we came hither."

"Bring him to the elders."

And they thrust him suddenly through a doorway into a room as black as pitch, save at the end there faintly glowed a fire. The crowd closed in behind him and shut out all but the faintest glimmer of day, and before he could arrest himself he had fallen headlong over the feet of a seated man. His arm, outflung, struck the face of someone else as he went down; he felt the soft impact of features and heard a cry of anger, and for a moment he struggled against a number of hands that clutched him. It was a one-sided fight. An inkling of the situation came to him, and he lay quiet.

"I fell down," he said; "I couldn't see in this pitchy darkness."

There was a pause as if the unseen persons about him tried to understand his words. Then the voice of Correa said: "He is but newly formed. He stumbles as he walks and mingles words that mean nothing with his speech."

Others also said things about him that he heard or understood imperfectly.

"May I sit up?" he asked, in a pause. "I will not struggle against you again."

They consulted and let him rise.

The voice of an older man began to question him, and Nunez found himself trying to explain the great world out of which he had fallen, and the sky and mountains and sight and such-like marvels, to these elders who sat in darkness in the Country of the Blind. And they would believe and understand nothing whatever he told them, a thing quite outside his expectation. They would not even understand many of his words. For fourteen generations these people had been blind and cut off from all the seeing world; the names for all the things of sight had faded and changed; the story of the outer world was faded and changed to a child's story; and they had ceased to concern themselves with anything beyond the rocky slopes above their circling wall. Blind men of genius had arisen among them and questioned the shreds of belief and tradition they had brought with them from their seeing days, and had dismissed all these things as idle fancies, and replaced them with new and saner explanations. Much of their imagination had shrivelled with their eyes, and they had made for themselves new imaginations with their ever more sensitive ears and finger-tips. Slowly Nunez realised this; that his expectation of wonder and reverence at his origin and his gifts was not to be borne out; and after his poor attempt to explain sight to them had been set aside as the confused version of a new-made being describing the marvels of his incoherent sensations, he subsided, a little dashed, into listening to their instruction. And the eldest of the blind men explained to him life and philosophy and religion, how that the world (meaning their valley) had been first an empty hollow in the rocks, and then had come, first, inanimate things without the gift of touch, and llamas and a few other creatures that had little sense, and then men, and at last angels, whom one could hear singing and making fluttering sounds, but whom no one could touch at all, which puzzled Nunez greatly until he thought of the birds.

He went on to tell Nunez how this time had been divided into the warm and the cold, which are the blind equivalents of day and night, and how it was good to sleep in the warm and work during the cold, so that now, but for his advent, the whole town of the blind would have been asleep. He said Nunez must have been specially created to learn and serve the wisdom, they had acquired, and that for all his mental incoherency and stumbling behaviour he must have courage, and do his best to learn, and at that all the people in the doorway murmured encouragingly. He said the night—for the blind call their day night—was now far gone, and it behoved every one to go back to sleep. He asked Nunez if he knew how to sleep, and Nunez said he did, but that before sleep he wanted food.

They brought him food—llama's milk in a bowl, and rough salted bread—and led him into a lonely place, to eat out of their hearing, and afterwards to slumber until the chill of the mountain evening roused them to begin their day again. But Nunez slumbered not at all.

Instead, he sat up in the place where they had left him, resting his limbs and turning the unanticipated circumstances of his arrival over and over in his mind.

Every now and then he laughed, sometimes with amusement, and sometimes with indignation.

"Unformed mind!" he said. "Got no senses yet! They little know they've been insulting their heaven-sent king and master. I see I must bring them to reason. Let me think—let me think."

He was still thinking when the sun set.

Nunez had an eye for all beautiful things, and it seemed to him that the glow upon the snowfields and glaciers that rose about the valley on every side was the most beautiful thing he had ever seen. His eyes went from that inaccessible glory to the village and irrigated fields, fast sinking into the twilight, and suddenly a wave of emotion took him, and he thanked God from the bottom of his heart that the power of sight had been given him.

He heard a voice calling to him from out of the village. "Ya ho there, Bogota! Come hither!"

At that he stood up smiling. He would show these people once and for all what sight would do for a man. They would seek him, but not find him.

"You move not, Bogota," said the voice.

He laughed noiselessly, and made two stealthy steps aside from the path.

"Trample not on the grass, Bogota; that is not allowed."

Nunez had scarcely heard the sound he made himself. He stopped amazed.

The owner of the voice came running up the piebald path towards him.

He stepped back into the pathway. "Here I am," he said.

"Why did you not come when I called you?" said the blind man. "Must you be led like a child? Cannot you hear the path as you walk?"

Nunez laughed. "I can see it," he said.

"There is no such word as *see,*" said the blind man, after a pause. "Cease this folly, and follow the sound of my feet."

Nunez followed, a little annoyed.

"My time will come," he said.

"You'll learn," the blind man answered. "There is much to learn in the world."

"Has no one told you, 'In the Country of the Blind the One-eyed Man is King'?"

"What is blind?" asked the blind man carelessly over his shoulder.

Four days passed, and the fifth found the King of the Blind still incognito, as a clumsy and useless stranger among his subjects.

It was, he found, much more difficult to proclaim himself than he had supposed, and in the meantime, while he meditated his *coup d'état,* he did what he was told and learnt the manners and customs of the Country of the Blind. He found working and going about at night a particularly irksome thing, and he decided that that should be the first thing he would change.

They led a simple, laborious life, these people, with all the elements of virtue and happiness, as these things can be understood by men. They toiled, but not oppressively; they had food and clothing sufficient for their needs; they had days and seasons of rest; they made much of music and singing, and there was love among them, and little children.

It was marvellous with what confidence and precision they went about their ordered world. Everything, you see, had been made to fit their needs; each of the radiating paths of the valley area had a constant angle to the others, and was distinguished by a special notch upon its kerbing; all obstacles and irregularities of path or meadow had long since been cleared away; all their methods and procedure arose naturally from their special needs. Their senses had become marvellously acute; they could hear and judge the slightest gesture of a man a dozen paces away—could hear the very beating of his heart. Intonation had long replaced expression with them, and touches gesture, and their work with hoe and spade and fork was as free and confident as garden work can be. Their sense of smell was extraordinarily fine; they could distinguish individual differences as readily as a dog can, and they went about the tending of the llamas, who lived among the rocks above and came to the wall for food and shelter, with ease and confidence. It was only when at last Nunez sought to assert himself that he found how easy and confident their movements could be.

He rebelled only after he had tried persuasion.

He tried at first on several occasions to tell them of sight. "Look you here, you people," he said. "There are things you do not understand in me."

Once or twice one or two of them attended to him; they sat with faces downcast and ears turned intelligently towards him, and he did his best to tell them what it was to see. Among his hearers was a girl, with eyelids less red and sunken than the others, so that one could almost fancy she was hiding eyes, whom especially he hoped to persuade. He spoke of the beauties of sight, of watching the mountains, of the sky and the sunrise, and they heard him with amused incredulity that presently became condemnatory. They told him there were indeed no mountains at all, but that the end of the rocks where the llamas grazed was indeed the end of the world; thence sprang a cavernous roof of the universe, from which the dew and the avalanches fell; and when he maintained stoutly the world had neither end nor roof such as they supposed, they said his thoughts were wicked. So far as he could describe sky and clouds and stars to them it seemed to them a hideous void, a terrible blankness in the place of the smooth roof to things in which they believed—it was an article of faith with them that the cavern roof was exquisitely smooth to the touch. He saw that in some manner he shocked them, and gave up that aspect of the matter altogether, and tried to show them the practical value of sight. One morning he saw Pedro in the path called Seventeen and coming towards the central houses, but still too far off for hearing or scent, and he told them as much. "In a little while," he prophesied, "Pedro will be here." An old man remarked that Pedro had no business on path Seventeen, and then, as if in confirmation, that individual as he drew near turned and went transversely into path Ten, and so back with nimble paces towards the outer wall. They mocked Nunez when Pedro did not arrive, and afterwards, when he asked Pedro questions to clear his character, Pedro denied and outfaced him, and was afterwards hostile to him.

Then he induced them to let him go a long way up the sloping meadows towards the wall with one complacent individual, and to him he promised to describe all that happened among the houses. He noted certain goings and comings, but the things that really seemed to signify to these people happened inside of or behind the windowless houses—the only things they took note of to test him by—and of these he could see or tell nothing; and it was after the failure of this attempt, and the ridicule they could not repress, that he resorted to force. He thought of seizing a spade and suddenly smiting one or two of them to earth, and so in fair combat showing the advantage of eyes. He went so far with that resolution as to seize his spade, and then he discovered a new thing about himself, and that was that it was impossible for him to hit a blind man in cold blood.

He hesitated, and found them all aware that he had snatched up the spade. They stood alert, with their heads on one side, and bent ears towards him for what he would do next.

"Put that spade down," said one, and he felt a sort of helpless horror. He came near obedience.

Then he thrust one backwards against a house wall, and fled past him and out of the village.

He went athwart one of their meadows, leaving a track of trampled grass behind his feet, and presently sat down by the side of one of their ways. He felt something of the buoyancy that comes to all men in the beginning of a fight, but more perplexity. He began to realise that you cannot even fight happily with creatures who stand upon a different mental basis to yourself. Far away he saw a number of men carrying spades and sticks come out of the street of houses, and advance in a spreading line along the several paths towards him. They advanced slowly, speaking frequently to one another, and ever and again the whole cordon would halt and sniff the air and listen.

The first time they did this Nunez laughed. But afterwards he did not laugh.

One struck his trail in the meadow grass, and came stooping and feeling his way along it.

For five minutes he watched the slow extension of the cordon, and then his vague disposition to do something forthwith became frantic. He stood up, went a pace or so towards the circumferential wall, turned, and went back a little way. There they all stood in a crescent, still and listening.

He also stood still, gripping his spade very tightly in both hands. Should he charge them?

The pulse in his ears ran into the rhythm of "In the Country of the Blind the One-eyed Man is King!"

Should he charge them?

He looked back at the high and unclimbable wall behind—unclimbable because of its smooth plastering, but withal pierced with many little doors, and at the approaching line of seekers. Behind these others were now coming out of the street of houses.

Should he charge them?

"Bogota!" called one. "Bogota! where are you?"

He gripped his spade still tighter, and advanced down the meadows towards the place of habitations, and directly he moved they converged upon him. "I'll hit them if they touch me," he swore; "by Heaven, I will. I'll hit." He called aloud, "Look here, I'm going to do what I like in this valley. Do you hear? I'm going to do what I like and go where I like!"

They were moving in upon him quickly, groping, yet moving rapidly. It was like playing blind man's buff, with everyone blindfolded except one. "Get hold of him!" cried one. He found himself in the arc of a loose curve of pursuers. He felt suddenly he must be active and resolute.

"You don't understand," he cried in a voice that was meant to be great and resolute, and which broke. "You are blind, and I can see. Leave me alone!"

"Bogota! Put down that spade, and come off the grass!"

The last order, grotesque in its urban familiarity, produced a gust of anger.

"I'll hurt you," he said, sobbing with emotion. "By Heaven, I'll hurt you. Leave me alone!"

He began to run, not knowing clearly where to run. He ran from the nearest blind man, because it was a horror to hit him. He stopped, and then made a dash to escape from their closing ranks. He made for where a gap was wide, and the men on either side, with a quick perception of the approach of his paces, rushed in on one another. He sprang forward, and then saw he must be caught, and *swish*! the spade had struck. He felt the soft thud of hand and arm, and the man was down with a yell of pain, and he was through.

Through! And then he was close to the street of houses again, and blind men, whirling spades and stakes, were running with a sort of reasoned swiftness hither and thither.

He heard steps behind him just in time, and found a tall man rushing forward and swiping at the sound of him. He lost his nerve, hurled his spade a yard wide at his antagonist, and whirled about and fled, fairly yelling as he dodged another.

He was panic-stricken. He ran furiously to and fro, dodging when there was no need to dodge, and in his anxiety to see on every side of him at once, stumbling. For a moment he was down and they heard his fall. Far away in the circumferential wall a little doorway looked like heaven, and he set off in a wild rush for it. He did not even look round at his pursuers until it was gained, and he had stumbled across the bridge, clambered a little way among the rocks, to the surprise and dismay of a young llama, who went leaping out of sight, and lay down sobbing for breath.

And so his *coup d'état* came to an end.

He stayed outside the wall of the valley of the Blind for two nights and days without food or shelter, and meditated upon the unexpected. During these meditations he repeated very frequently and always with a profounder note of derision the exploded proverb: "In the Country of the Blind the One-Eyed Man is King." He thought chiefly of ways of fighting and conquering these people, and it grew clear that for him no practicable way was possible. He had no weapons, and now it would be hard to get one.

The canker of civilisation had got to him even in Bogota, and he could not find it in himself to go down and assassinate a blind man.

Of course, if he did that, he might then dictate terms on the threat of assassinating them all. But—sooner or later he must sleep!…

He tried also to find food among the pine trees, to be comfortable under pine boughs while the frost fell at night, and—with less confidence—to catch a llama by artifice in order to try to kill it—perhaps by hammering it with a stone—and so finally, perhaps, to eat some of it. But the llamas had a doubt of him and regarded him with distrustful brown eyes, and spat when he drew near. Fear came on him the second day and fits of shivering. Finally he crawled down to the wall of the Country of the Blind and tried to make terms. He crawled along by the stream, shouting, until two blind men came out to the gate and talked to him.

"I was mad," he said. "But I was only newly made."

They said that was better.

He told them he was wiser now, and repented of all he had done.

Then he wept without intention, for he was very weak and ill now, and they took that as a favourable sign.

They asked him if he still thought he could *"see"*

"No," he said. "That was folly. The word means nothing—less than nothing!"

They asked him what was overhead.

"About ten times ten the height of a man there is a roof above the world—of rock—and very, very smooth." … He burst again into hysterical tears. "Before you ask me any more, give me some food or I shall die."

He expected dire punishments, but these blind people were capable of toleration. They regarded his rebellion as but one more proof of his general idiocy and inferiority; and after they had whipped him they appointed him to do the simplest and heaviest work they had for anyone to do, and he, seeing no other way of living, did submissively what he was told.

He was ill for some days, and they nursed him kindly. That refined his submission. But they insisted on his lying in the dark, and that was a great misery. And blind philosophers came and talked to him of the wicked levity of his mind, and reproved him so impressively for his doubts about the lid of rock that covered their cosmic casserole that he almost doubted whether indeed he was not the victim of hallucination in not seeing it overhead.

So Nunez became a citizen of the Country of the Blind, and these people ceased to be a generalised people and became individualities and familiar to him, while the world beyond the mountains became more and more remote and unreal. There was Yacob, his master, a kindly man when not annoyed; there was Pedro, Yacob's nephew; and there was Medina-saroté, who was the youngest daughter of Yacob. She was little esteemed in the world of the blind, because she had a clear-cut face, and lacked that satisfying, glossy smoothness that is the blind man's ideal of feminine beauty; but Nunez thought her beautiful at first, and presently the most beautiful thing in the whole creation. Her closed eyelids were not sunken and red after the common way of the valley, but lay as though they might open again at any moment; and she had long eyelashes, which were considered a grave disfigurement. And her voice was strong, and did not satisfy the acute hearing of the valley swains. So that she had no lover.

There came a time when Nunez thought that, could he win her, he would be resigned to live in the valley for all the rest of his days.

He watched her; he sought opportunities of doing her little services, and presently he found that she observed him. Once at a rest-day gathering they sat side by side in the dim starlight, and the music was sweet. His hand came upon hers and he dared to clasp it. Then very tenderly she returned his pressure. And one day, as they were at their meal in the darkness, he felt her hand very softly seeking him, and as it chanced the fire leapt then and he saw the tenderness of her face.

He sought to speak to her.

He went to her one day when she was sitting in the summer moonlight spinning. The light made her a thing of silver and mystery. He sat down at her feet and told her he loved her, and told her how beautiful she seemed to him. He had a lover's voice, he spoke with a tender reverence that came near to awe, and she had never before been touched by adoration. She made him no definite answer, but it was clear his words pleased her.

After that he talked to her whenever he could take an opportunity. The valley became the world for him, and the world beyond the mountains where men lived in sunlight seemed no more than a fairy tale he would some day pour into her ears. Very tentatively and timidly he spoke to her of sight.

Sight seemed to her the most poetical of fancies, and she listened to his description of the stars and the mountains and her own sweet white-lit beauty as though it was a guilty indulgence. She did not believe, she could only half understand, but she was mysteriously delighted, and it seemed to him that she completely understood.

His love lost its awe and took courage. Presently he was for demanding her of Yacob and the elders in marriage, but she became fearful and delayed. And it was one of her elder sisters who first told Yacob that Medina-saroté and Nunez were in love.

There was from the first very great opposition to the marriage of Nunez and Medina-saroté; not so much because they valued her as because they held him as a being apart, an idiot, incompetent thing below the permissible level of a man. Her sisters opposed it bitterly as bringing discredit on them all; and old Yacob, though he had formed a sort of liking for his clumsy, obedient serf, shook his head and said the thing could not be. The young men were all angry at the idea of corrupting the race, and one went so far as to revile and strike Nunez. He struck back. Then for the first time he found an advantage in seeing, even by twilight, and after that fight was over no one was disposed to raise a hand against him. But they still found his marriage impossible.

Old Yacob had a tenderness for his last little daughter, and was grieved to have her weep upon his shoulder.

"You see, my dear, he's an idiot. He has delusions; he can't do anything right."

"I know," wept Medina-saroté. "But he's better than he was. He's getting better. And he's strong, dear father, and kind—stronger and kinder than any I other man in the world. And he loves me—and, father, I love him."

Old Yacob was greatly distressed to find her inconsolable, and, besides—what made it more distressing—he liked Nunez for many things. So he went and sat in the windowless council-chamber with the other elders and watched the trend of the talk, and said, at the proper time, "He's better than he was. Very likely, some day, we shall find him as sane as ourselves."

Then afterwards one of the elders, who thought deeply, had an idea. He was the great doctor among these people, their medicine-man, and he had a very philosophical and inventive mind, and the idea of curing Nunez of his peculiarities appealed to him. One day when Yacob was present he returned to the topic of Nunez.

"I have examined Bogota," he said, "and the case is clearer to me. I think very probably he might be cured."

"That is what I have always hoped," said old Yacob.

"His brain is affected," said the blind doctor.

The elders murmured assent.

"Now, *what* affects it?"

"Ah!" said old Yacob.

"*This*," said the doctor, answering his own question. "Those queer things that are called the eyes, and which exist to make an agreeable soft depression in the face, are diseased, in the case of Bogota, in such a way as to affect his brain. They are greatly distended, he has eyelashes, and his eyelids move, and consequently his brain is in a state of constant irritation and distraction."

"Yes?" said old Yacob. "Yes?"

"And I think I may say with reasonable certainty that, in order to cure him completely, all that we need do is a simple and easy surgical operation—namely, to remove these irritant bodies."

"And then he will be sane?"

"Then he will be perfectly sane, and a quite admirable citizen."

"Thank Heaven for science!" said old Yacob, and went forth at once to tell Nunez of his happy hopes.

But Nunez's manner of receiving the good news struck him as being cold and disappointing.

"One might think," he said, "from the tone you take, that you did not care for my daughter."

It was Medina-saroté who persuaded Nunez to face the blind surgeons.

"*You* do not want me," he said, "to lose my gift of sight?"

She shook her head.

"My world is sight."

Her head drooped lower.

"There are the beautiful things, the beautiful little things—the flowers, the lichens among the rocks, the lightness and softness on a piece of fur, the far sky with its drifting down of clouds, the sunsets and the stars. And there is *you*. For you alone it is good to have sight, to see your sweet, serene face, your kindly lips, your dear, beautiful hands folded together... It is these eyes of mine you won, these eyes that hold me to you, that these idiots seek. Instead, I must touch you, hear you, and never see you again. I must come under that roof of rock and stone and darkness, that horrible roof under which your imagination stoops... No; you would not have me do that?"

A disagreeable doubt had arisen in him. He stopped, and left the thing a question.

"I wish," she said, "sometimes—" She paused.

"Yes," said he, a little apprehensively.

"I wish sometimes—you would not talk like that."

"Like what?"

"I know it's pretty—it's your imagination. I love it, but *now*—"

He felt cold. "*Now*?" he said faintly.

She sat quite still.

"You mean—you think—I should be better, better perhaps—"

He was realising things very swiftly. He felt anger, indeed, anger at the dull course of fate, but also sympathy for her lack of understanding—a sympathy near akin to pity.

"*Dear*," he said, and he could see by her whiteness how intensely her spirit pressed against the things she could not say. He put his arms about her, he kissed her ear, and they sat for a time in silence.

"If I were to consent to this?" he said at last, in a voice that was very gentle.

She flung her arms about him, weeping wildly. "Oh, if you would," she sobbed, "if only you would!"

~

For a week before the operation that was to raise him from his servitude and inferiority to the level of a blind citizen, Nunez knew nothing of sleep, and all through the warm sunlit hours, while the others slumbered happily, he sat brooding or wandered aimlessly, trying to bring his mind to bear on his dilemma. He had given his answer, he had given his consent, and still he was not sure. And at last work-time was over, the sun rose in splendour over the golden crests, and his last day of vision began for him. He had a few minutes with Medina-saroté before she went apart to sleep.

"Tomorrow," he said, "I shall see no more."

"Dear heart!" she answered, and pressed his hands with all her strength.

"They will hurt you but little," she said; "and you are going through this pain—you are going through it, dear lover, for *me*... Dear, if a woman's heart and life can do it, I will repay you. My dearest one, my dearest with the tender voice, I will repay."

He was drenched in pity for himself and her.

He held her in his arms, and pressed his lips to hers, and looked on her sweet face for the last time. "goodbye!" he whispered at that dear sight, "goodbye!"

And then in silence he turned away from her.

She could hear his slow retreating footsteps, and something in the rhythm of them threw her into a passion of weeping.

He had fully meant to go to a lonely place where the meadows were beautiful with white narcissus, and there remain until the hour of his sacrifice should come, but as he went he lifted up his eyes and saw the morning, the morning like an angel in golden armour, marching down the steeps...

It seemed to him that before this splendour he, and this blind world in the valley, and his love, and all, were no more than a pit of sin.

He did not turn aside as he had meant to do, but went on, and passed through the wall of the circumference and out upon the rocks, and his eyes were always upon the sunlit ice and snow.

He saw their infinite beauty, and his imagination soared over them to the things beyond he was now to resign for ever.

He thought of that great free world he was parted from, the world that was his own, and he had a vision of those further slopes, distance beyond distance, with Bogota, a place of multitudinous stirring beauty, a glory by day, a luminous mystery by night, a place of palaces and fountains and statues and white houses, lying beautifully in the middle distance. He thought how for a day or so one might come down through passes, drawing ever nearer and nearer to its busy streets and ways. He thought of the river journey, day by day, from great Bogota to the still vaster world beyond, through towns and villages, forest and desert places, the rushing river day by day, until its banks receded and the big steamers came splashing by, and one had reached the sea—the limitless sea, with its thousand islands, its thousands of islands, and its ships seen dimly far away in their incessant journeyings round and about that greater world. And there, unpent by mountains, one saw the sky—the sky, not such a disc as one saw it here, but an arch of immeasurable blue, a deep of deeps in which the circling stars were floating…

His eyes scrutinised the great curtain of the mountains with a keener inquiry.

For example, if one went so, up that gully and to that chimney there, then one might come out high among those stunted pines that ran round in a sort of shelf and rose still higher and higher as it passed above the gorge. And then? That talus might be managed. Thence perhaps a climb might be found to take him up to the precipice that came below the snow; and if that chimney failed, then another farther to the east might serve his purpose better. And then? Then one would be out upon the amber-lit snow there, and half-way up to the crest of those beautiful desolations.

He glanced back at the village, then turned right round and regarded it steadfastly.

He thought of Medina-saroté, and she had become small and remote.

He turned again towards the mountain wall, down which the day had come to him.

Then very circumspectly he began to climb.

When sunset came he was no longer climbing, but he was far and high. He had been higher, but he was still very high. His clothes were torn, his limbs were blood-stained, he was bruised in many places, but he lay as if he were at his ease, and there was a smile on his face.

From where he rested the valley seemed as if it were in a pit and nearly a mile below. Already it was dim with haze and shadow, though the mountain summits around him were things of light and fire. The mountain summits around him were things of light and fire, and the little details of the rocks near at hand were drenched with subtle beauty—a vein of green mineral piercing the grey, the flash of crystal faces here and there, a minute, minutely-beautiful orange lichen close beside his face. There were deep mysterious shadows in the gorge, blue deepening into purple, and purple into a luminous darkness, and overhead was the illimitable vastness of the sky. But he heeded these things no longer, but lay quite inactive there, smiling as if he were satisfied merely to have escaped from the valley of the Blind in which he had thought to be King.

The glow of the sunset passed, and the night came, and still he lay peacefully contented under the cold clear stars.

Eve's Diary

Mark Twain

Samuel Langhorne Clemens (1835-1910), popularly known as Mark Twain, was one of America's most beloved authors. An accomplished humorist, travel writer, journalist and lecturer, he was best known for *The Adventures of Tom Sawyer* (1876) and its sequel *The Adventures of Huckleberry Finn* (1885). Among Twain's other seminal works are travelogues—*The Innocents Abroad* (1869) and *Roughing It* (1872). His sense of humour was a unifying factor in all his works. 'Eve's Diary' (1905), written for Twain's wife, is also comic in nature.

SATURDAY.—I am almost a whole day old, now. I arrived yesterday. That is as it seems to me. And it must be so, for if there was a day-before-yesterday I was not there when it happened, or I should remember it. It could be, of course, that it did happen, and that I was not noticing. Very well; I will be very watchful now, and if any day-before-yesterdays happen I will make a note of it. It will be best to start right and not let the record get confused, for some instinct tells me that these details are going to be important to the historian some day. For I feel like an experiment, I feel exactly like an experiment; it would be impossible for a person to feel more like an experiment than I do, and so I am coming to feel convinced that that is what I AM—an experiment; just an experiment, and nothing more.

Then if I am an experiment, am I the whole of it? No, I think not; I think the rest of it is part of it. I am the main part of it, but I think the rest of it has its share in the matter. Is my position assured, or do I have to watch it and take care of it? The latter, perhaps. Some instinct tells me that eternal vigilance is the price of supremacy. (That is a good phrase, I think, for one so young.)

Everything looks better today than it did yesterday. In the rush of finishing up yesterday, the mountains were left in a ragged condition, and some of the plains were so cluttered with rubbish and remnants that the aspects were quite distressing. Noble and beautiful works of art should not be subjected to haste; and this majestic new world is indeed a most noble and beautiful work. And certainly marvelously near to being perfect, notwithstanding the shortness of the time. There are too many stars in some places and not enough in others, but that can be remedied presently, no doubt. The moon got loose last night, and slid down and fell out of the scheme—a very great loss; it breaks my heart to think of it. There isn't another thing among the ornaments and decorations that is comparable to it for beauty and finish. It should have been fastened better. If we can only get it back again—

But of course there is no telling where it went to. And besides, whoever gets it will hide it; I know it because I would do it myself.

I believe I can be honest in all other matters, but I already begin to realize that the core and center of my nature is love of the beautiful, a passion for the beautiful, and that it would not be safe to trust me with a moon that belonged to another person and that person didn't know I had it. I could give up a moon that I found in the daytime, because I should be afraid some one was looking; but if I found it in the dark, I am sure I should find some kind of an excuse for not saying anything about it. For I do love moons, they are so pretty and so romantic. I wish we had five or six; I would never go to bed; I should never get tired lying on the moss-bank and looking up at them.

Stars are good, too. I wish I could get some to put in my hair. But I suppose I never can. You would be surprised to find how far off they are, for they do not look it. When they first showed, last night, I tried to knock some down with a pole, but it didn't reach, which astonished me; then I tried clods till I was all tired out, but I never got one. It was because I am left-handed and cannot throw good. Even when I aimed at the one I wasn't after I couldn't hit the other one, though I did make some close shots, for I saw the black blot of the clod sail right into the midst of the golden clusters forty or fifty times, just barely missing them, and if I could have held out a little longer maybe I could have got one. So I cried a little, which was natural, I suppose, for one of my age, and after I was rested I got a basket and started for a place on the extreme rim of the circle, where the stars were close to the ground and I could get them with my hands, which would be better, anyway, because I could gather them tenderly then, and not break them. But it was farther than I thought, and at last I had go give it up; I was so tired I couldn't drag my feet another step; and besides, they were sore and hurt me very much.

I couldn't get back home; it was too far and turning cold; but I found some tigers and nestled in among them and was most adorably comfortable, and their breath was sweet and pleasant, because they live on strawberries. I had never seen a tiger before, but I knew them in a minute by the stripes. If I could have one of those skins, it would make a lovely gown.

Today I am getting better ideas about distances. I was so eager to get hold of every pretty thing that I giddily grabbed for it, sometimes when it was too far off, and sometimes when it was but six inches away but seemed a foot—alas, with thorns between! I learned a lesson; also I made an axiom, all out of my own head—my very first one; THE SCRATCHED EXPERIMENT SHUNS THE THORN. I think it is a very good one for one so young.

I followed the other Experiment around, yesterday afternoon, at a distance, to see what it might be for, if I could. But I was not able to make out. I think it is a man. I had never seen a man, but it looked like one, and I feel sure that that is what it is. I realize that I feel more curiosity about it than about any of the other reptiles. If it is a reptile, and I suppose it is; for it has frowzy hair and blue eyes, and looks like a reptile. It has no hips; it tapers like a carrot; when it stands, it spreads itself apart like a derrick; so I think it is a reptile, though it may be architecture.

I was afraid of it at first, and started to run every time it turned around, for I thought it was going to chase me; but by and by I found it was only trying to get away, so after that I was not timid any more, but tracked it along, several hours, about twenty yards behind, which made it nervous and unhappy. At last it was a good deal worried, and climbed a tree. I waited a good while, then gave it up and went home.

Today the same thing over. I've got it up the tree again.

SUNDAY.—It is up there yet. Resting, apparently. But that is a subterfuge: Sunday isn't the day of rest; Saturday is appointed for that. It looks to me like a creature that is more interested in resting than it anything else. It would tire me to rest so much. It tires me just to sit around and watch the tree. I do wonder what it is for; I never see it do anything.

They returned the moon last night, and I was SO happy! I think it is very honest of them. It slid down and fell off again, but I was not distressed; there is no need to worry when one has that kind of neighbors; they will fetch it back. I wish I could do something to show my appreciation. I would like to send them some stars, for we have more than we can use. I mean I, not we, for I can see that the reptile cares nothing for such things.

It has low tastes, and is not kind. When I went there yesterday evening in the gloaming it had crept down and was trying to catch the little speckled fishes that play in the pool, and I had to clod it to make it go up the tree again and let them alone. I wonder if THAT is what it is for? Hasn't it any heart? Hasn't it any compassion for those little creature? Can it be that it was designed and manufactured for such ungentle work? It has the look of it. One of the clods took it back of the ear, and it used language. It gave me a thrill, for it was the first time I had ever heard speech, except my own. I did not understand the words, but they seemed expressive.

When I found it could talk I felt a new interest in it, for I love to talk; I talk, all day, and in my sleep, too, and I am very interesting, but if I had another to talk to I could be twice as interesting, and would never stop, if desired.

If this reptile is a man, it isn't an IT, is it? That wouldn't be grammatical, would it? I think it would be HE. I think so. In that case one would parse it thus: nominative, HE; dative, HIM; possessive, HIS'N. Well, I will consider it a man and call it he until it turns out to be something else. This will be handier than having so many uncertainties.

NEXT WEEK SUNDAY.—All the week I tagged around after him and tried to get acquainted. I had to do the talking, because he was shy, but I didn't mind it. He seemed pleased to have me around, and I used the sociable "we" a good deal, because it seemed to flatter him to be included.

WEDNESDAY.—We are getting along very well indeed, now, and getting better and better acquainted. He does not try to avoid me any more, which is a good sign, and shows that he likes to have me with him. That pleases me, and I study to be useful to him in every way I can, so as to increase his regard.

During the last day or two I have taken all the work of naming things off his hands, and this has been a great relief to him, for he has no gift in that line, and is evidently very grateful. He can't think of a rational name to save him, but I do not let him see that I am aware of his defect. Whenever a new creature comes along I name it before he has time to expose himself by an awkward silence. In this way I have saved him many embarrassments. I have no defect like this. The minute I set eyes on an animal I know what it is. I don't have to reflect a moment; the right name comes out instantly, just as if it were an inspiration, as no doubt it is, for I am sure it wasn't in me half a minute before.

I seem to know just by the shape of the creature and the way it acts what animal it is. When the dodo came along he thought it was a wildcat—I saw it in his eye. But I saved him. And I was careful not to do it in a way that could hurt his pride. I just spoke up in a quite natural way of pleasing surprise, and not as if I was dreaming of conveying information, and said, "Well, I do declare, if there isn't the dodo!" I explained—without seeming to be explaining—how I know it for a dodo, and although I thought maybe he was a little piqued that I knew the creature when he didn't, it was quite evident that he admired me. That was very agreeable, and I thought of it more than once with gratification before I slept. How little a thing can make us happy when we feel that we have earned it!

THURSDAY.—My first sorrow. Yesterday he avoided me and seemed to wish I would not talk to him. I could not believe it, and thought there was some mistake, for I loved to be with him, and loved to hear him talk, and so how could it be that he could feel unkind toward me when I had not done anything? But at last it seemed true, so I went away and sat lonely in the place where I first saw him the morning that we were made and I did not know what he was and was indifferent about him; but now it was a mournful place, and every little thing spoke of him, and my heart was very sore. I did not know why very clearly, for it was a new feeling; I had not experienced it before, and it was all a mystery, and I could not make it out.

But when night came I could not bear the lonesomeness, and went to the new shelter which he has built, to ask him what I had done that was wrong and how I could mend it and get back his kindness again; but he put me out in the rain, and it was my first sorrow.

SUNDAY.—It is pleasant again, now, and I am happy; but those were heavy days; I do not think of them when I can help it.

I tried to get him some of those apples, but I cannot learn to throw straight. I failed, but I think the good intention pleased him. They are forbidden, and he says I shall come to harm; but so I come to harm through pleasing him, why shall I care for that harm?

MONDAY.—This morning I told him my name, hoping it would interest him. But he did not care for it. It is strange. If he should tell me his name, I would care. I think it would be pleasanter in my ears than any other sound.

He talks very little. Perhaps it is because he is not bright, and is sensitive about it and wishes to conceal it. It is such a pity that he should feel so, for brightness is nothing; it is in the heart that the values lie. I wish I could make him understand that a loving good heart is riches, and riches enough, and that without it intellect is poverty.

Although he talks so little, he has quite a considerable vocabulary.

This morning he used a surprisingly good word. He evidently recognized, himself, that it was a good one, for he worked in in twice afterward, casually. It was good casual art, still it showed that he possesses a certain quality of perception. Without a doubt that seed can be made to grow, if cultivated.

Where did he get that word? I do not think I have ever used it.

No, he took no interest in my name. I tried to hide my disappointment, but I suppose I did not succeed. I went away and sat on the moss-bank with my feet in the water. It is where I go when I hunger for companionship, some one to look at, some one to talk to. It is not enough—that lovely white body painted there in the pool—but it is something, and something is better than utter loneliness. It talks when I talk; it is sad when I am sad; it comforts me with its sympathy; it says, "Do not be downhearted, you poor friendless girl; I will be your friend." It IS a good friend to me, and my only one; it is my sister.

That first time that she forsook me! Ah, I shall never forget that —never, never. My heart was lead in my body! I said, "She was all I had, and now she is gone!" In my despair I said, "Break, my heart; I cannot bear my life any more!" and hid my face in my hands, and there was no solace for me. And when I took them away, after a little, there she was again, white and shining and beautiful, and I sprang into her arms!

That was perfect happiness; I had known happiness before, but it was not like this, which was ecstasy. I never doubted her afterward. Sometimes she stayed away—maybe an hour, maybe almost the whole day, but I waited and did not doubt; I said, "She is busy, or she is gone on a journey, but she will come." And it was so: she always did. At night she would not come if it was dark, for she was a timid little thing; but if there was a moon she would come. I am not afraid of the dark, but she is visits I have paid her; she is my comfort and my refuge when my life is hard—and it is mainly that.

TUESDAY.—All the morning I was at work improving the estate; and I purposely kept away from him in the hope that he would get lonely and come. But he did not.

At noon I stopped for the day and took my recreation by flitting all about with the bees and the butterflies and reveling in the flowers, those beautiful creatures that catch the smile of God out of the sky and preserve it! I gathered them, and made them into wreaths and garlands and clothed myself in them while I ate my luncheon—apples, of course; then I sat in the shade and wished and waited. But he did not come.

But no matter. Nothing would have come of it, for he does not care for flowers. He called them rubbish, and cannot tell one from another, and thinks it is superior to feel like that. He does not care for me, he does not care for flowers, he does not care for the painted sky at eventide—is there anything he does care for, except building shacks to coop himself up in from the good clean rain, and thumping the melons, and sampling the grapes, and fingering the fruit on the trees, to see how those properties are coming along?

I laid a dry stick on the ground and tried to bore a hole in it with another one, in order to carry out a scheme that I had, and soon I got an awful fright. A thin, transparent bluish film rose out of the hole, and I dropped everything and ran! I thought it was a spirit, and I WAS so frightened! But I looked back, and it was not coming; so I leaned against a rock and rested and panted, and let my limbs go on trembling until they got steady again; then I crept warily back, alert, watching, and ready to fly if there was occasion; and when I was come near, I parted the branches of a rose-bush and peeped through—wishing the man was about, I was looking so cunning and pretty—but the sprite was gone.

I went there, and there was a pinch of delicate pink dust in the hole. I put my finger in, to feel it, and said OUCH! and took it out again. It was a cruel pain. I put my finger in my mouth; and by standing first on one foot and then the other, and grunting, I presently eased my misery; then I was full of interest, and began to examine.

I was curious to know what the pink dust was. Suddenly the name of it occurred to me, though I had never heard of it before. It was FIRE! I was as certain of it as a person could be of anything in the world. So without hesitation I named it that—fire. I had created something that didn't exist before; I had added a new thing to the world's uncountable properties; I realized this, and was proud of my achievement, and was going to run and find him and tell him about it, thinking to raise myself in his esteem—but I reflected, and did not do it. No—he would not care for it. He would ask what it was good for, and what could I answer? for if it was not GOOD for something, but only beautiful, merely beautiful—

So I sighed, and did not go. For it wasn't good for anything; it could not build a shack, it could not improve melons, it could not hurry a fruit crop; it was useless, it was a foolishness and a vanity; he would despise it and say cutting words. But to me it was not despicable; I said, "Oh, you fire, I love you, you dainty pink creature, for you are BEAUTIFUL—and that is enough!" and was going to gather it to my breast. But refrained. Then I made another maxim out of my head, though it was so nearly like the first one that I was afraid it was only a plagiarism:

"THE BURNT EXPERIMENT SHUNS THE FIRE."

I wrought again; and when I had made a good deal of fire-dust I emptied it into a handful of dry brown grass, intending to carry it home and keep it always and play with it; but the wind struck it and it sprayed up and spat out at me fiercely, and I dropped it and ran. When I looked back the blue spirit was towering up and stretching and rolling away like a cloud, and instantly I thought of the name of it—SMOKE!—though, upon my word, I had never heard of smoke before.

Soon brilliant yellow and red flares shot up through the smoke, and I named them in an instant—FLAMES—and I was right, too, though these were the very first flames that had ever been in the world. They climbed the trees, then flashed splendidly in and out of the vast and increasing volume of tumbling smoke, and I had to clap my hands and laugh and dance in my rapture, it was so new and strange and so wonderful and so beautiful!

He came running, and stopped and gazed, and said not a word for many minutes. Then he asked what it was. Ah, it was too bad that he should ask such a direct question. I had to answer it, of course, and I did.

I said it was fire. If it annoyed him that I should know and he must ask; that was not my fault; I had no desire to annoy him. After a pause he asked:

"How did it come?"

Another direct question, and it also had to have a direct answer. "I made it."

The fire was traveling farther and farther off. He went to the edge of the burned place and stood looking down, and said:

"What are these?"

"Fire-coals."

He picked up one to examine it, but changed his mind and put it down again. Then he went away. NOTHING interests him.

But I was interested. There were ashes, gray and soft and delicate and pretty—I knew what they were at once. And the embers;

I knew the embers, too. I found my apples, and raked them out, and was glad; for I am very young and my appetite is active. But I was disappointed; they were all burst open and spoiled. Spoiled apparently; but it was not so; they were better than raw ones. Fire is beautiful; some day it will be useful, I think.

FRIDAY.—I saw him again, for a moment, last Monday at nightfall, but only for a moment. I was hoping he would praise me for trying to improve the estate, for I had meant well and had worked hard. But he was not pleased, and turned away and left me. He was also displeased on another account: I tried once more to persuade him to stop going over the Falls. That was because the fire had revealed to me a new passion —quite new, and distinctly different from love, grief, and those others which I had already discovered—FEAR. And it is horrible!—I wish I had never discovered it; it gives me dark moments, it spoils my happiness, it makes me shiver and tremble and shudder. But I could not persuade him, for he has not discovered fear yet, and so he could not understand me.

Extract From Adam's Diary

Perhaps I ought to remember that she is very young, a mere girl and make allowances. She is all interest, eagerness, vivacity, the world is to her a charm, a wonder, a mystery, a joy; she can't speak for delight when she finds a new flower, she must pet it and caress it and smell it and talk to it, and pour out endearing names upon it. And she is color-mad: brown rocks, yellow sand, gray moss, green foliage, blue sky; the pearl of the dawn, the purple shadows on the mountains, the golden islands floating in crimson seas at sunset, the pallid moon sailing through the shredded cloud-rack, the star-jewels glittering in the wastes of space — none of them is of any practical value, so far as I can see, but because they have color and majesty, that is enough for her, and she loses her mind over them. If she could quiet down and keep still a couple minutes at a time, it would be a reposeful spectacle. In that case I think I could enjoy looking at her; indeed I am sure I could, for I am coming to realize that she is a quite remarkably comely creature — lithe, slender, trim, rounded, shapely, nimble, graceful; and once when she was standing marble-white and sun-drenched on a boulder, with her young head tilted back and her hand shading her eyes, watching the flight of a bird in the sky, I recognized that she was beautiful.

MONDAY noon.—If there is anything on the planet that she is not interested in it is not in my list. There are animals that I am indifferent to, but it is not so with her. She has no discrimination, she takes to all of them, she thinks they are all treasures, every new one is welcome.

When the mighty brontosaurus came striding into camp, she regarded it as an acquisition, I considered it a calamity; that is a good sample of the lack of harmony that prevails in our views of things. She wanted to domesticate it, I wanted to make it a present of the homestead and move out. She believed it could be tamed by kind treatment and would be a good pet; I said a pet twenty-one feet high and eighty-four feet long would be no proper thing to have about the place, because, even with the best intentions and without meaning any harm, it could sit down on the house and mash it, for any one could see by the look of its eye that it was absent-minded.

Still, her heart was set upon having that monster, and she couldn't give it up. She thought we could start a dairy with it, and wanted me to help milk it; but I wouldn't; it was too risky. The sex wasn't right, and we hadn't any ladder anyway. Then she wanted to ride it, and look at the scenery. Thirty or forty feet of its tail was lying on the ground, like a fallen tree, and she thought she could climb it, but she was mistaken; when she got to the steep place it was too slick and down she came, and would have hurt herself but for me.

Was she satisfied now? No. Nothing ever satisfies her but demonstration; untested theories are not in her line, and she won't have them. It is the right spirit, I concede it; it attracts me; I feel the influence of it; if I were with her more I think I should take it up myself. Well, she had one theory remaining about this colossus: she thought that if we could tame it and make him friendly we could stand in the river and use him for a bridge. It turned out that he was already plenty tame enough—at least as far as she was concerned—so she tried her theory, but it failed: every time she got him properly placed in the river and went ashore to cross over him, he came out and followed her around like a pet mountain. Like the other animals. They all do that.

Tuesday—Wednesday—Thursday—and today: all without seeing him. It is a long time to be alone; still, it is better to be alone than unwelcome.

FRIDAY.—I had to have company—I was made for it, I think—so I made friends with the animals. They are just charming, and they have the kindest disposition and the politest ways; they never look sour, they never let you feel that you are intruding, they smile at you and wag their tail, if they've got one, and they are always ready for a romp or an excursion or anything you want to propose. I think they are perfect gentlemen. All these days we have had such good times, and it hasn't been lonesome for me, ever.

Lonesome! No, I should say not. Why, there's always a swarm of them around—sometimes as much as four or five acres—you can't count them; and when you stand on a rock in the midst and look out over the furry expanse it is so mottled and splashed and gay with color and frisking sheen and sun-flash, and so rippled with stripes, that you might think it was a lake, only you know it isn't; and there's storms of sociable birds, and hurricanes of whirring wings; and when the sun strikes all that feathery commotion, you have a blazing up of all the colors you can think of, enough to put your eyes out.

We have made long excursions, and I have seen a great deal of the world; almost all of it, I think; and so I am the first traveler, and the only one. When we are on the march, it is an imposing sight—there's nothing like it anywhere. For comfort I ride a tiger or a leopard, because it is soft and has a round back that fits me, and because they are such pretty animals; but for long distance or for scenery I ride the elephant. He hoists me up with his trunk, but I can get off myself; when we are ready to camp, he sits and I slide down the back way.

The birds and animals are all friendly to each other, and there are no disputes about anything. They all talk, and they all talk to me, but it must be a foreign language, for I cannot make out a word they say; yet they often understand me when I talk back, particularly the dog and the elephant. It makes me ashamed. It shows that they are brighter than I am, for I want to be the principal Experiment myself—and I intend to be, too. I have learned a number of things, and am educated, now, but I wasn't at first. I was ignorant at first. At first it used to vex me because, with all my watching, I was never smart enough to be around when the water was running uphill; but now I do not mind it. I have experimented and experimented until now I know it never does run uphill, except in the dark. I know it does in the dark, because the pool never goes dry, which it would, of course, if the water didn't come back in the night.

It is best to prove things by actual experiment; then you KNOW; whereas if you depend on guessing and supposing and conjecturing, you never get educated.

Some things you CAN'T find out; but you will never know you can't by guessing and supposing: no, you have to be patient and go on experimenting until you find out that you can't find out. And it is delightful to have it that way, it makes the world so interesting. If there wasn't anything to find out, it would be dull. Even trying to find out and not finding out is just as interesting as trying to find out and finding out, and I don't know but more so. The secret of the water was a treasure until I GOT it; then the excitement all went away, and I recognized a sense of loss.

By experiment I know that wood swims, and dry leaves, and feathers, and plenty of other things; therefore by all that cumulative evidence you know that a rock will swim; but you have to put up with simply knowing it, for there isn't any way to prove it—up to now. But I shall find a way—then THAT excitement will go. Such things make me sad; because by and by when I have found out everything there won't be any more excitements, and I do love excitements so! The other night I couldn't sleep for thinking about it.

At first I couldn't make out what I was made for, but now I think it was to search out the secrets of this wonderful world and be happy and thank the Giver of it all for devising it. I think there are many things to learn yet—I hope so; and by economizing and not hurrying too fast I think they will last weeks and weeks. I hope so. When you cast up a feather it sails away on the air and goes out of sight; then you throw up a clod and it doesn't. It comes down, every time. I have tried it and tried it, and it is always so. I wonder why it is? Of course it DOESN'T come down, but why should it SEEM to? I suppose it is an optical illusion. I mean, one of them is. I don't know which one. It may be the feather, it may be the clod; I can't prove which it is, I can only demonstrate that one or the other is a fake, and let a person take his choice.

By watching, I know that the stars are not going to last. I have seen some of the best ones melt and run down the sky. Since one can melt, they can all melt; since they can all melt, they can all melt the same night. That sorrow will come—I know it. I mean to sit up every night and look at them as long as I can keep awake; and I will impress those sparkling fields on my memory, so that by and by when they are taken away I can by my fancy restore those lovely myriads to the black sky and make them sparkle again, and double them by the blur of my tears.

After The Fall

When I look back, the Garden is a dream to me. It was beautiful, surpassingly beautiful, enchantingly beautiful; and now it is lost, and I shall not see it any more.

The Garden is lost, but I have found HIM, and am content. He loves me as well as he can; I love him with all the strength of my passionate nature, and this, I think, is proper to my youth and sex. If I ask myself why I love him, I find I do not know, and do not really much care to know; so I suppose that this kind of love is not a product of reasoning and statistics, like one's love for other reptiles and animals. I think that this must be so. I love certain birds because of their song; but I do not love Adam on account of his singing—no, it is not that; the more he sings the more I do not get reconciled to it. Yet I ask him to sing, because I wish to learn to like everything he is interested in. I am sure I can learn, because at first I could not stand it, but now I can. It sours the milk, but it doesn't matter; I can get used to that kind of milk.

It is not on account of his brightness that I love him—no, it is not that. He is not to blame for his brightness, such as it is, for he did not make it himself; he is as God make him, and that is sufficient. There was a wise purpose in it, THAT I know. In time it will develop, though I think it will not be sudden; and besides, there is no hurry; he is well enough just as he is.

It is not on account of his gracious and considerate ways and his delicacy that I love him. No, he has lacks in this regard, but he is well enough just so, and is improving.

It is not on account of his industry that I love him—no, it is not that. I think he has it in him, and I do not know why he conceals it from me. It is my only pain. Otherwise he is frank and open with me, now. I am sure he keeps nothing from me but this. It grieves me that he should have a secret from me, and sometimes it spoils my sleep, thinking of it, but I will put it out of my mind; it shall not trouble my happiness, which is otherwise full to overflowing.

It is not on account of his education that I love him—no, it is not that. He is self-educated, and does really know a multitude of things, but they are not so.

It is not on account of his chivalry that I love him—no, it is not that. He told on me, but I do not blame him; it is a peculiarity of sex, I think, and he did not make his sex. Of course I would not have told on him, I would have perished first; but that is a peculiarity of sex, too, and I do not take credit for it, for I did not make my sex.

Then why is it that I love him? MERELY BECAUSE HE IS MASCULINE, I think.

At bottom he is good, and I love him for that, but I could love him without it. If he should beat me and abuse me, I should go on loving him. I know it. It is a matter of sex, I think.

He is strong and handsome, and I love him for that, and I admire him and am proud of him, but I could love him without those qualities. If he were plain, I should love him; if he were a wreck, I should love him; and I would work for him, and slave over him, and pray for him, and watch by his bedside until I died.

Yes, I think I love him merely because he is MINE and is MASCULINE. There is no other reason, I suppose. And so I think it is as I first said: that this kind of love is not a product of reasonings and statistics. It just COMES—none knows whence—and cannot explain itself. And doesn't need to.

It is what I think. But I am only a girl, the first that has examined this matter, and it may turn out that in my ignorance and inexperience I have not got it right.

Forty Years Later

It is my prayer, it is my longing, that we may pass from this life together—a longing which shall never perish from the earth, but shall have place in the heart of every wife that loves, until the end of time; and it shall be called by my name.

But if one of us must go first, it is my prayer that it shall be I; for he is strong, I am weak, I am not so necessary to him as he is to me —life without him would not be life; how could I endure it? This prayer is also immortal, and will not cease from being offered up while my race continues. I am the first wife; and in the last wife I shall be repeated.

At Eve's Grave

ADAM: Wheresoever she was, THERE was Eden.

The Sculptor's Funeral

Willa Cather

Willa Cather (1873-1947) was an American editor, author and winner of the Pulitzer Prize in 1923 for *One of Ours* (1922). Her novels and stories explored the lives of European immigrants and the American frontier life in Nebraska. Other important themes that dominated her works were the constricted life and hampered creativity in the small towns of the prairies. This was amply reflected in 'The Sculptor's Funeral', published as part of the collection *The Troll Garden* (1905).

A group of the townspeople stood on the station siding of a little Kansas town, awaiting the coming of the night train, which was already twenty minutes overdue. The snow had fallen thick over everything; in the pale starlight the line of bluffs across the wide, white meadows south of the town made soft, smoke-colored curves against the clear sky. The men on the siding stood first on one foot and then on the other, their hands thrust deep into their trousers pockets, their overcoats open, their shoulders screwed up with the cold; and they glanced from time to time toward the southeast, where the railroad track wound along the river shore. They conversed in low tones and moved about restlessly, seeming uncertain as to what was expected of them. There was but one of the company who looked as though he knew exactly why he was there, and he kept conspicuously apart, walking to the far end of the platform, returning to the station door, then pacing up the track again, his chin sunk in the high collar of his overcoat, his burly shoulders drooping forward, his gait heavy and dogged. Presently he was approached by a tall, spare, grizzled man clad in a faded Grand Army suit, who shuffled out from the group and advanced with a certain deference, craning his neck forward until his back made the angle of a jack-knife three-quarters open.

"I reckon she's a-goin' to be pretty late agin tonight, Jim," he remarked in a squeaky falsetto. "S'pose it's the snow?"

"I don't know," responded the other man with a shade of annoyance, speaking from out an astonishing cataract of red beard which grew fiercely and thickly in all directions.

The spare man shifted the quill toothpick he was chewing to the other side of his mouth. "It ain't likely that anybody from the East will come with the corpse, I s'pose?" he went on reflectively.

"I don't know," responded the other, more curtly than before.

"It's too bad he didn't belong to some lodge or other. I like an order funeral myself. They seem more appropriate for people of some repytation," the spare man continued, with an ingratiating concession in his shrill voice, as he carefully placed his toothpick in his vest pocket. He always carried the flag at the G.A.R. funerals in the town.

The heavy man turned on his heel without replying, and walked up the siding. The spare man shuffled back to the uneasy group. "Jim's ez full ez a tick, ez ushel," he commented commiseratingly.

Just then a distant whistle sounded, and there was a shuffling of feet on the platform. A number of lanky boys of all ages appeared as suddenly and slimily as eels wakened by the crack of thunder; some came from the waiting-room, where they had been warming themselves by the red stove, or half asleep on the slat benches; others uncoiled themselves from baggage trucks or slid out of express wagons. Two clambered down from the driver's seat of a hearse that stood backed up against the siding. They straightened their stooping shoulders and lifted their heads, and a flash of momentary animation kindled their dull eyes at that cold, vibrant scream, the world-wide call for men. It stirred them like the note of a trumpet; just as it had often stirred in his boyhood the man who was coming home tonight.

The night express shot, red as a rocket, out of the eastward marsh lands, and wound along the river shore under the long lines of shivering poplars that sentineled the meadows, the escaping steam hanging in gray masses against the pale sky and blotting out the Milky Way. In a moment the red glare from the headlight streamed up the snow-covered track before the siding and glittered on the wet, black rails. The burly man with the disheveled red beard walked swiftly up the platform toward the approaching train, uncovering his head as he went. The group of men behind him hesitated, glanced questioningly at one another, and awkwardly followed his example. The train stopped, and the crowd shuffled up to the express car just as the door was thrown open, the spare man in the G.A.R. suit thrusting his head forward with curiosity. The express messenger appeared in the doorway, accompanied by a young man in a long ulster and traveling-cap.

"Are Mr. Merrick's friends here?" inquired the young man.

The group on the platform swayed and shuffled uneasily. Philip Phelps, the banker, responded with dignity: "We have come to take charge of the body. Mr. Merrick's father is very feeble and can't be about."

"Send the agent out here," growled the express messenger, "and tell the operator to lend a hand."

The coffin was got out of its rough box and down on the snowy platform. The townspeople drew back enough to make room for it and then formed a close semicircle about it, looking curiously at the palm-leaf which lay across the black cover. No one said anything. The baggageman stood by his truck, waiting to get at the trunks. The engine panted heavily, and the fireman dodged in and out among the wheels with his yellow torch and long oil-can, snapping the spindle boxes. The young Bostonian, one of the dead sculptor's pupils, who had come with the body, looked about him helplessly. He turned to the banker, the only one of that black, uneasy, stoop-shouldered group who seemed enough of an individual to be addressed.

"None of Mr. Merrick's brothers are here?" he asked uncertainly.

The man with the red beard for the first time stepped up and joined the group. "No, they have not come yet; the family is scattered. The body will be taken directly to the house." He stooped and took hold of one of the handles of the coffin.

"Take the long hill road up, Thompson; it will be easier on the horses," called the liveryman, as the undertaker snapped the door of the hearse and prepared to mount to the driver's seat.

Laird, the red-bearded lawyer, turned again to the stranger: "We didn't know whether there would be any one with him or not," he explained. "It's a long walk, so you'd better go up in the hack." He pointed to a single battered conveyance, but the young man replied stiffly: "Thank you, but I think I will go up with the hearse. If you don't object," turning to the undertaker, "I'll ride with you."

They clambered up over the wheels and drove off in the starlight up the long, white hill toward the town. The lamps in the still village were shining from under the low, snow-burdened roofs; and beyond, on every side, the plains reached out into emptiness, peaceful and wide as the soft sky itself, and wrapped in a tangible, white silence.

When the hearse backed up to a wooden sidewalk before a naked, weather-beaten frame house, the same composite, ill-defined group that had stood upon the station siding was huddled about the gate. The front yard was an icy swamp, and a couple of warped planks, extending from the sidewalk to the door, made a sort of rickety foot-bridge. The gate hung on one hinge, and was opened wide with difficulty. Steavens, the young stranger, noticed that something black was tied to the knob of the front door.

The grating sound made by the casket, as it was drawn from the hearse, was answered by a scream from the house; the front door was wrenched open, and a tall, corpulent woman rushed out bareheaded into the snow and flung herself upon the coffin, shrieking: "My boy, my boy! And this is how you've come home to me!"

As Steavens turned away and closed his eyes with a shudder of unutterable repulsion, another woman, also tall, but flat and angular, dressed entirely in black, darted out of the house and caught Mrs. Merrick by the shoulders, crying sharply: "Come, come, mother; you musn't go on like this!" Her tone changed to one of obsequious solemnity as she turned to the banker: "The parlor is ready, Mr. Phelps."

The bearers carried the coffin along the narrow boards, while the undertaker ran ahead with the coffin-rests. They bore it into a large, unheated room that smelled of dampness and disuse and furniture polish, and set it down under a hanging lamp ornamented with jingling glass prisms and before a "Rogers group" of John Alden and Priscilla, wreathed with smilax. Henry Steavens stared about him with the sickening conviction that there had been some horrible mistake, and that he had somehow arrived at the wrong destination. He looked painfully about over the clover-green Brussels, the fat plush upholstery; among the hand-painted china plaques and panels and vases, for some mark of identification, for something that might once conceivably have belonged to Harvey Merrick. It was not until he recognized his friend in the crayon portrait of a little boy in kilts and curls, hanging above the piano, that he felt willing to let any of these people approach the coffin.

"Take the lid off, Mr. Thompson; let me see my boy's face," wailed the elder woman between her sobs. This time Steavens looked fearfully, almost beseechingly, into her face, red and swollen under its masses of strong, black, shiny hair. He flushed, dropped his eyes, and then, almost incredulously, looked again. There was a kind of power about her face—a kind of brutal handsomeness, even; but it was scarred and furrowed by violence, and so colored and coarsened by fiercer passions that grief seemed never to have laid a gentle finger there. The long nose was distended and knobbed at the end, and there were deep lines on either side of it; her heavy, black brows almost met across her forehead, her teeth were large and square, and set far apart—teeth that could tear. She filled the room; the men were obliterated, seemed tossed about like twigs in an angry water, and even Steavens felt himself being drawn into the whirlpool.

The daughter—the tall, raw-boned woman in crêpe, with a mourning comb in her hair which curiously lengthened her long face—sat stiffly upon the sofa, her hands, conspicuous for their large knuckles, folded in her lap, her mouth and eyes drawn down, solemnly awaiting the opening of the coffin. Near the door stood a mulatto woman, evidently a servant in the house, with a timid bearing and an emaciated face pitifully sad and gentle. She was weeping silently, the corner of her calico apron lifted to her eyes, occasionally suppressing a long, quivering sob. Steavens walked over and stood beside her.

Feeble steps were heard on the stairs, and an old man, tall and frail, odorous of pipe smoke, with shaggy, unkempt gray hair and a dingy beard, tobacco-stained about the mouth, entered uncertainly. He went slowly up to the coffin and stood rolling a blue cotton handkerchief between his hands, seeming so pained and embarrassed by his wife's orgy of grief that he had no consciousness of anything else.

"There, there, Annie, dear, don't take on," he quavered timidly, putting out a shaking hand and awkwardly patting her elbow. She turned with a cry, and sank upon his shoulder with such violence that he tottered a little. He did not even glance toward the coffin, but continued to look at her with a dull, frightened, appealing expression, as a spaniel looks at the whip. His sunken cheeks slowly reddened and burned with miserable shame. When his wife rushed from the room, her daughter strode after her with set lips. The servant stole up to the coffin, bent over it for a moment, and then slipped away to the kitchen, leaving Steavens, the lawyer, and the father to themselves. The old man stood trembling and looking down at his dead son's face. The sculptor's splendid head seemed even more noble in its rigid stillness than in life. The dark hair had crept down upon the wide forehead; the face seemed strangely long, but in it there was not that beautiful and chaste repose which we expect to find in the faces of the dead. The brows were so drawn that there were two deep lines above the beaked nose, and the chin was thrust forward defiantly. It was as though the strain of life had been so sharp and bitter that death could not at once wholly relax the tension and smooth the countenance into perfect peace—as though he were still guarding something precious and holy which might even yet be wrested from him.

The old man's lips were working under his stained beard. He turned to the lawyer with timid deference: "Phelps and the rest are comin' back to set up with Harve, ain't they?" he asked. "Thank 'ee, Jim, thank 'ee." He brushed the hair back gently from his son's forehead. "He was a good boy, Jim; always a good boy. He was ez gentle ez a child and the kindest of 'em all—only we didn't none of us ever onderstand him." The tears trickled slowly down his beard and dropped upon the sculptor's coat.

"Martin, Martin—Oh, Martin! Come here," his wife wailed from the top of the stairs. The old man started timorously: "Yes, Annie, I'm coming." He turned away, hesitated, stood for a moment in miserable indecision; then reached back and patted the dead man's hair softly, and stumbled from the room.

"Poor old man, I didn't think he had any tears left. Seems as if his eyes would have gone dry long ago. At his age nothing cuts very deep," remarked the lawyer.

Something in his tone made Steavens glance up. While the mother had been in the room the young man had scarcely seen any one else; but now, from the moment he first glanced into Jim Laird's florid face and blood-shot eyes, he knew that he had found what he had been heart-sick at not finding before—the feeling, the understanding, that must exist in some one, even here.

The man was red as his beard, with features swollen and blurred by dissipation, and a hot, blazing blue eye. His face was strained—that of a man who is controlling himself with difficulty—and he kept plucking at his beard with a sort of fierce resentment. Steavens, sitting by the window, watched him turn down the glaring lamp, still its jangling pendants with an angry gesture, and then stand with his hands locked behind him, staring down into the master's face. He could not help wondering what link there could have been between the porcelain vessel and so sooty a lump of potter's clay.

From the kitchen an uproar was sounding; when the dining-room door opened, the import of it was clear. The mother was abusing the maid for having forgotten to make the dressing for the chicken salad which had been prepared for the watchers. Steavens had never heard anything in the least like it; it was injured, emotional, dramatic abuse, unique and masterly in its excruciating cruelty, as violent and unrestrained as had been her grief of twenty minutes before. With a shudder of disgust, the lawyer went into the dining-room and closed the door into the kitchen.

"Poor Roxy's getting it now," he remarked when he came back. "The Merricks took her out of the poor-house years ago; and if her loyalty would let her, I guess the poor old thing could tell tales that would curdle your blood. She's the mulatto woman who was standing in here a while ago, with her apron to her eyes. The old woman is a fury; there never was anybody like her for demonstrative piety and ingenious cruelty. She made Harvey's life a hell for him when he lived at home; he was so sick ashamed of it. I never could see how he kept himself so sweet."

"He was wonderful," said Steavens slowly, "wonderful; but until tonight I have never known how wonderful."

"That is the true and eternal wonder of it, anyway; that it can come even from such a dung-heap as this," the lawyer cried, with a sweeping gesture which seemed to indicate much more than the four walls within which they stood.

"I think I'll see whether I can get a little air. The room is so close I am beginning to feel rather faint," murmured Steavens, struggling with one of the windows. The sash was stuck, however, and would not yield, so he sat down dejectedly and began pulling at his collar. The lawyer came over, loosened the sash with one blow of his red fist, and sent the window up a few inches. Steavens thanked him, but the nausea which had been gradually climbing into his throat for the last half hour left him with but one desire—a desperate feeling that he must get away from this place with what was left of Harvey Merrick. Oh, he comprehended well enough now the gentle bitterness of the smile that he had seen so often on his master's lips!

He remembered that once, when Merrick returned from a visit home, he brought with him a singularly feeling and suggestive bas-relief of a thin, faded old woman, sitting and sewing something pinned to her knee; while a full-lipped, full-blooded little urchin, his trousers sustained by a single gallows, stood beside her impatiently twitching her gown to call her attention to a butterfly he had caught. Steavens, impressed by the tender and delicate modelling of the thin, tired face, had asked him if it were his mother. He remembered the dull flush that had burned up in the sculptor's face.

The lawyer was sitting in a rocking-chair beside the coffin, his head thrown back and his eyes closed. Steavens looked at him earnestly, puzzled at the line of the chin, and wondering why a man should conceal a feature of such distinction under that disfiguring shock of beard. Suddenly, as though he felt the young sculptor's keen glance, he opened his eyes.

"Was he always a good deal of an oyster?" he asked abruptly. "He was terribly shy as a boy."

"Yes, he was an oyster, since you put it so," rejoined Steavens. "Although he could be very fond of people, he always gave one the impression of being detached. He disliked violent emotion; he was reflective, and rather distrustful of himself—except, of course, as regarded his work. He was sure-footed enough there. He distrusted men pretty thoroughly, and women even more, yet somehow without believing ill of them. He was determined, indeed, to believe the best, but he seemed afraid to investigate."

"A burnt dog dreads the fire," said the lawyer grimly, and closed his eyes.

Steavens went on and on, reconstructing that whole miserable boyhood. All this raw, biting ugliness had been the portion of the man whose tastes were refined beyond the limits of the reasonable—whose mind was an exhaustless gallery of beautiful impressions, and so sensitive that the mere shadow of a poplar leaf flickering against a sunny wall would be etched and held there forever. Surely, if ever a man had the magic wand in his fingertips, it was Merrick. Whatever he touched, he revealed its holiest secret; liberated it from enchantment and restored it to its pristine loveliness, like the Arabian prince who fought the enchantress, spell for spell. Upon whatever he had come in contact with, he had left a beautiful record of the experience—a sort of ethereal signature; a scent, a sound, a color that was his own.

Steavens understood now the real tragedy of his master's life; neither love nor wine, as many had conjectured, but a blow which had fallen earlier and cut deeper than these could have done—a shame not his, and yet so unescapably his, to hide in his heart from his very boyhood. And without, the frontier warfare; the yearning of a boy, cast ashore upon a desert of newness and ugliness and sordidness, for all that is chastened and old, and noble with traditions.

At eleven o'clock the tall, flat woman in black crêpe entered and announced that the watchers were arriving, and asked them "to step into the dining-room." As Steavens rose, the lawyer said dryly: "You go on—it'll be a good experience for you, doubtless; as for me, I'm not equal to that crowd tonight; I've had twenty years of them."

As Steavens closed the door after him, he glanced back at the lawyer, sitting by the coffin in the dim light, with his chin resting on his hand.

The same misty group that had stood before the door of the express-car shuffled into the room. In the light of the kerosene lamp they separated and became individuals. The minister, a pale, feeble-looking man with white hair and blond chin-whiskers, took his seat beside a small side table, and placed his Bible upon it. The Grand Army man took a seat behind the stove and tilted his chair back comfortably against the wall, fishing his quill toothpick from his waistcoat pocket. The two bankers, Phelps and Elder, sat off in a corner behind the dinner-table, where they could finish their discussion of the new usury law and its effect on chattel security loans. The real estate agent, an old man with a smiling, hypocritical face, soon joined them. The coal and lumber dealer and the cattle shipper sat on opposite sides of the hard coal burner, their feet on the nickel-work. Steavens took a book from his pocket and began to read. The talk around him ranged through various topics of local interest while the house was quieting down. When it was clear that the members of the family were in bed, the Grand Army man hitched his shoulders, and untangling his long legs, caught his heels on the rounds of his chair.

"S'pose there'll be a will, Phelps?" he queried in his weak falsetto.

The banker laughed disagreeably, and began trimming his nails with a pearl-handled pocket-knife.

"There'll scarcely be any need for one, will there?" he queried in his turn.

The restless Grand Army man shifted his position again, getting his knees still nearer his chin. "Why, the ole man says Harve's done right well lately," he chirped.

The other banker spoke up. "I reckon he means by that Harve ain't asked him to mortgage any more farms lately so as he could go on with his education."

"Seems like my mind don't reach back to a time when Harve wasn't bein' edycated," tittered the Grand Army man.

There was a general chuckle. The minister took out his handkerchief and blew his nose sonorously. Banker Phelps closed his knife with a snap. "It's too bad the old man's sons didn't turn out better," he remarked, with reflective authority. "They never hung together. He spent money enough on Harve to stock a dozen cattle-farms, and he might as well have poured it into Sand Creek. If Harve had stayed at home and helped nurse what little they had, and gone into stock on the old man's bottom farm, they might all have been well fixed. But the old man had to trust everything to tenants and was cheated right and left."

"Harve never could have handled stock none," interposed the cattleman. "He hadn't it in him to be sharp. Do you remember when he bought Sander's mules for eight-year olds, when everybody in town knew that Sander's father-in-law give 'em to his wife for a wedding present eighteen years before, an' they was full-grown mules then."

Everyone chuckled, and the Grand Army man rubbed his knees with a spasm of childish delight.

"Harve never was much account for anything practical, and he shore was never fond of work," began the coal and lumber dealer. "I mind the last time he was home; the day he left, when the old man was out to the barn helpin' his hand hitch up to take Harve to the train, and Cal Moots was patchin' up the fence, Harve, he come out on the step and sings out, in his ladylike voice: 'Cal Moots, Cal Moots! Please come cord my trunk.'"

"That's Harve for you," approved the Grand Army man gleefully. "I kin hear him howlin' yet, when he was a big feller in long pants, and his mother used to whale him with a rawhide in the barn for lettin' the cows git foundered in the cornfield when he was drivin' 'em home from pasture. He killed a cow of mine that-a-way onct—a pure Jersey and the best milker I had, an' the ole man had to put up for her. Harve, he was watchin' the sun set acrost the marshes when the anamile got away; he argued that sunset was oncommon fine."

"Where the old man made his mistake was in sending the boy East to school," said Phelps, stroking his goatee and speaking in a deliberate, judicial tone. "There was where he got his head full of trapseing to Paris and all such folly. What Harve needed, of all people, was a course in some first-class Kansas City business college."

The letters were swimming before Steaven's eyes. Was it possible that these men did not understand, that the palm on the coffin meant nothing to them? The very name of their town would have remained forever buried in the postal guide, had it not been now and again mentioned in the world in connection with Harvey Merrick's. He remembered what his master had said to him on the day of his death, after the congestion of both lungs had shut off any probability of recovery, and the sculptor had asked his pupil to send his body home. "It's not a pleasant place to be lying while the world is moving and doing and bettering," he had said, with a feeble smile: "but it rather seems as though we ought to go back to the place we came from in the end. The townspeople will come in for a look at me; and after they have had their say, I shan't have much to fear from the judgment of God. The wings of the Victory, in there"—with a weak gesture toward his studio—"will not shelter me."

The cattleman took up the comment. "Forty's young for a Merrick to cash in; they usually hang on pretty well. Probably he helped it along with whisky."

"His mother's people were not long-lived, and Harvey never had a robust constitution," said the minister mildly. He would have liked to say more. He had been the boy's Sunday-school teacher, and had been fond of him; but he felt that he was not in a position to speak. His own sons had turned out badly, and it was not a year since one of them had made his last trip home in the express-car, shot in a gambling-house in the Black Hills.

"Nevertheless, there is no disputin' that Harve frequently looked upon the wine when it was red, also variegated, and it shore made an oncommon fool of him," moralized the cattleman.

Just then the door leading into the parlor rattled loudly, and everyone started involuntarily, looking relieved when only Jim Laird came out. His red face was convulsed with anger, and the Grand Army man ducked his head when he saw the spark in his blue, blood-shot eye. They were all afraid of Jim; he was a drunkard, but he could twist the law to suit his client's needs as no other man in all western Kansas could do; and there were many who tried. The lawyer closed the door gently behind him, leaned back against it, and folded his arms, cocking his head a little to one side. When he assumed this attitude in the court-room, ears were always pricked up, as it usually foretold a flood of withering sarcasm.

"I've been with you gentlemen before," he began in a dry, even tone, "when you've sat by the coffins of boys born and raised in this town; and, if I remember rightly, you were never any too well satisfied when you checked them up. What's the matter, anyhow? Why is it that reputable young men are as scarce as millionaires in Sand City? It might almost seem to a stranger that there was some way something the matter with your progressive town. Why did Reuben Sayer, the brightest young lawyer you ever turned out, after he had come home from the university as straight as a die, take to drinking and forge a check and shoot himself? Why did Bill Merrit's son die of the shakes in a saloon in Omaha? Why was Mr. Thomas's son, here, shot in a gambling-house? Why did young Adams burn his mill to beat the insurance companies, and go to the pen?"

The lawyer paused and unfolded his arms, laying one clenched fist quietly on the table. "I'll tell you why. Because you drummed nothing but money and knavery into their ears from the time they wore knickerbockers; because you carped away at them as you've been carping here tonight, holding our friends Phelps and Elder up to them for their models, as our grandfathers held up George Washington and John Adams. But the boys, worse luck, were young, and raw at the business you put them to; and how could they match coppers with such artists as Phelps and Elder? You wanted them to be successful rascals; they were only unsuccessful ones—that's all the difference. There was only one boy ever raised in this borderland between ruffianism and civilization who didn't come to grief, and you hated Harvey Merrick more for winning out than you hated all the other boys who got under the wheels. Lord, Lord, how you did hate him! Phelps, here, is fond of saying that he could buy and sell us all out any time he's a mind to; but he knew Harve wouldn't have given a tinker's damn for his bank and all his cattle-farms put together; and a lack of appreciation, that way, goes hard with Phelps.

"Old Nimrod, here, thinks Harve drank too much; and this from such as Nimrod and me!

"Brother Elder says Harve was too free with the old man's money—fell short in filial consideration, maybe. Well, we can all remember the very tone in which brother Elder swore his own father was a liar, in the county court; and we all know that the old man came out of that partnership with his son as bare as a sheared lamb. But maybe I'm getting personal, and I'd better be driving ahead at what I want to say."

The lawyer paused a moment, squared his heavy shoulders, and went on: "Harvey Merrick and I went to school together, back East. We were dead in earnest, and we wanted you all to be proud of us some day. We meant to be great men. Even I, and I haven't lost my sense of humour, gentlemen, I meant to be a great man. I came back here to practise, and I found you didn't in the least want me to be a great man. You wanted me to be a shrewd lawyer—oh, yes! Our veteran here wanted me to get him an increase of pension, because he had dyspepsia; Phelps wanted a new county survey that would put the widow Wilson's little bottom farm inside his south line; Elder wanted to lend money at 5 per cent a month and get it collected; old Stark here wanted to wheedle old women up in Vermont into investing their annuities in real-estate mortgages that are not worth the paper they are written on. Oh, you needed me hard enough, and you'll go on needing me; and that's why I'm not afraid to plug the truth home to you this once.

"Well, I came back here and became the damned shyster you wanted me to be. You pretend to have some sort of respect for me; and yet you'll stand up and throw mud at Harvey Merrick, whose soul you couldn't dirty and whose hands you couldn't tie. Oh, you're a discriminating lot of Christians! There have been times when the sight of Harvey's name in some Eastern paper has made me hang my head like a whipped dog; and, again, times when I liked to think of him off there in the world, away from all this hog-wallow, doing his great work, and climbing the big, clean upgrade he'd set for himself.

"And we? Now that we've fought and lied and sweated and stolen and hated as only the disappointed strugglers in a bitter, dead little Western town know how to do, what have we got to show for it? Harvey Merrick wouldn't have given one sunset over your marshes for all you've got put together, and you know it. It's not for me to say why, in the inscrutable wisdom of God, a genius should ever have been called from this place of hatred and bitter waters; but I want this Boston man to know that the drivel he's been hearing here tonight is the only tribute any truly great man could ever have from such a lot of sick, side-tracked, burnt-dog, land-poor sharks as the here-present financiers of Sand City—upon which town may God have mercy!"

The lawyer thrust out his hand to Steavens as he passed him, caught up his overcoat in the hall, and had left the house before the Grand Army man had found time to lift his ducked head and crane his long neck about at his fellows.

Next day Jim Laird was drunk and unable to attend the funeral services. Steavens called twice at his office, but was compelled to start East without seeing him. He had a presentiment that he would hear from him again, and left his address on the lawyer's table; but if Laird found it, he never acknowledged it. The thing in him that Harvey Merrick had loved must have gone underground with Harvey Merrick's coffin; for it never spoke again, and Jim got the cold he died of driving across the Colorado mountains to defend one of Phelps's sons, who had got into trouble out there by cutting government timber.

After Twenty Years

O. Henry

William Sydney Porter (1862-1910), popularly known as O. Henry, was a famous American short story writer. His writings were marked by ironic humour and surprise endings, a literary technique which increasingly came to be associated with O. Henry. Most of his stories were based in New York and dealt with the lives of common people. One such story, 'After Twenty Years', was first published in the collection *The Four Million* (1906).

The cop moved along the street, looking strong and important. This was the way he always moved. He was not thinking of how he looked. There were few people on the street to see him. It was only about ten at night, but it was cold. And there was a wind with a little rain in it.

He stopped at doors as he walked along, trying each door to be sure that it was closed for the night. Now and then he turned and looked up and down the street. He was a fine-looking cop, watchful, guarding the peace.

People in this part of the city went home early. Now and then you might see the lights of a shop or of a small restaurant. But most of the doors belonged to business places that had been closed hours ago.

Then the cop suddenly slowed his walk. Near the door of a darkened shop a man was standing. As the cop walked toward him, the man spoke quickly.

"It's all right, officer," he said. "I'm waiting for a friend. Twenty years ago we agreed to meet here tonight. It sounds strange to you, doesn't it? I'll explain if you want to be sure that everything's all right. About twenty years ago there was a restaurant where this shop stands. 'Big Joe' Brady's restaurant."

"It was here until five years ago," said the cop.

The man near the door had a colorless square face with bright eyes, and a little white mark near his right eye. He had a large jewel in his necktie.

"Twenty years ago tonight," said the man, "I had dinner here with Jimmy Wells. He was my best friend and the best fellow in the world. He and I grew up together here in New York, like two brothers. I was eighteen and Jimmy was twenty. The next morning I was to start for the West. I was going to find a job and make a great success. You couldn't have pulled Jimmy out of New York. He thought it was the only place on earth.

"We agreed that night that we would meet here again in twenty years. We thought that in twenty years we would know what kind of men we were, and what future waited for us."

"It sounds interesting," said the cop. "A long time between meetings, it seems to me. Have you heard from your friend since you went West?"

"Yes, for a time we did write to each other," said the man. "But after a year or two, we stopped. The West is big. I moved around everywhere, and I moved quickly. But I know that Jimmy will meet me here if he can. He was as true as any man in the world. He'll never forget. I came a thousand miles to stand here tonight. But I'll be glad about that, if my old friend comes too."

The waiting man took out a fine watch, covered with small jewels. "Three minutes before ten," he said. "It was ten that night when we said goodbye here at the restaurant door."

"You were successful in the West, weren't you?" asked the cop.

"I surely was! I hope Jimmy has done half as well. He was a slow mover. I've had to fight for my success. In New York a man doesn't change much. In the West you learn how to fight for what you get."

The cop took a step or two.

"I'll go on my way," he said. "I hope your friend comes all right. If he isn't here at ten, are you going to leave?"

"I am not!" said the other. "I'll wait half an hour, at least. If Jimmy is alive on earth, he'll be here by that time. Good night, officer."

"Good night," said the cop, and walked away, trying doors as he went.

There was now a cold rain falling and the wind was stronger. The few people walking along that street were hurrying, trying to keep warm. And at the door of the shop stood the man who had come a thousand miles to meet a friend. Such a meeting could not be certain. But he waited.

About twenty minutes he waited, and then a tall man in a long coat came hurrying across the street. He went directly to the waiting man.

"Is that you, Bob?" he asked, doubtfully.

"Is that you, Jimmy Wells?" cried the man at the door.

The new man took the other man's hands in his. "It's Bob! It surely is. I was certain I would find you here if you were still alive. Twenty years is a long time. The old restaurant is gone, Bob. I wish it were here, so that we could have another dinner in it. Has the West been good to you?"

"It gave me everything I asked for. You've changed, Jimmy. I never thought you were so tall."

"Oh, I grew a little after I was twenty." "Are you doing well in New York, Jimmy?"

"Well enough. I work for the city. Come on, Bob, We'll go to a place I know, and have a good long talk about old times."

The two men started along the street, arm in arm. The man from the West was beginning to tell the story of his life. The other, with his coat up to his ears, listened with interest.

At the corner stood a shop bright with electric lights. When they came near, each turned to look at the other's face.

The man from the West stopped suddenly and pulled his arm away. "You're not Jimmy Wells," he said. "Twenty years is a long time, but not long enough to change the shape of a man's nose."

"It sometimes changes a good man into a bad one," said the tall man. "You've been under arrest for ten minutes, Bob. Chicago cops thought you might be coming to New York. They told us to watch for you. Are you coming with me quietly? That's wise. But first here is something I was asked to give you. You may read it here at the window. It's from a cop named Wells."

The man from the West opened the little piece of paper. His hand began to shake a little as he read.

"Bob: I was at the place on time. I saw the face of the man wanted by Chicago cops. I didn't want to arrest you myself. So I went and got another cop and sent him to do the job.

JIMMY."

To Build A Fire

Jack London

Jack London (1876-1916), an American novelist and short story writer, was considered one of the most famous American authors of the 20th century. Best-known for novels such as *The Call of the Wild* (1903) and *White Fang* (1906), London's short stories also explored the theme of survival amidst natural calamities. 'To Build A Fire' (1908), London's most famous short story, has at its crux mankind's struggle to overcome elemental predicament.

Day had dawned cold and gray when the man turned aside from the main Yukon trail. He climbed the high earth-bank where a little-traveled trail led east through the pine forest. It was a high bank, and he paused to breathe at the top. He excused the act to himself by looking at his watch. It was nine o'clock in the morning. There was no sun or promise of sun, although there was not a cloud in the sky. It was a clear day. However, there seemed to be an indescribable darkness over the face of things. That was because the sun was absent from the sky. This fact did not worry the man. He was not alarmed by the lack of sun. It had been days since he had seen the sun.

The man looked along the way he had come. The Yukon lay a mile wide and hidden under three feet of ice. On top of this ice were as many feet of snow. It was all pure white. North and south, as far as his eye could see, it was unbroken white. The one thing that relieved the whiteness was a thin dark line that curved from the pine-covered island to the south. It curved into the north, where it disappeared behind another pine-covered island. This dark line was the trail—the main trail. It led south 500 miles to the Chilcoot Pass, and salt water. It led north 75 miles to Dawson, and still farther on to the north a thousand miles to Nulato, and finally to St. Michael, on Bering Sea, a thousand miles and half a thousand more.

But all this—the distant trail, no sun in the sky, the great cold, and the strangeness of it all—had no effect on the man. It was not because he was long familiar with it. He was a newcomer in the land, and this was his first winter.

The trouble with him was that he was not able to imagine. He was quick and ready in the things of life, but only in the things, and not in their meanings. Fifty degrees below zero meant 80 degrees of frost. Such facts told him that it was cold and uncomfortable, and that was all. It did not lead him to consider his weaknesses as a creature affected by temperature. Nor did he think about man's general weakness, able to live only within narrow limits of heat and cold. From there, it did not lead him to thoughts of heaven and the meaning of a man's life.

Fifty degrees below zero meant a bite of frost that hurt and that must be guarded against by the use of mittens, ear coverings, warm moccasins, and thick socks. Fifty degrees below zero was to him nothing more than 50 degrees below zero. That it should be more important than that was a thought that never entered his head.

As he turned to go, he forced some water from his mouth as an experiment. There was a sudden noise that surprised him. He tried it again. And again, in the air, before they could fall to the snow, the drops of water became ice that broke with a noise. He knew that at 50 below zero water from the mouth made a noise when it hit the snow. But this had done that in the air. Undoubtedly it was colder than 50 below. But exactly how much colder he did not know. But the temperature did not matter.

He was headed for the old camp on Henderson Creek, where the boys were already. They had come across the mountain from the Indian Creek country. He had taken the long trail to look at the possibility of floating logs from the islands in the Yukon down the river when the ice melted. He would be in camp by six o'clock that evening. It would be a little after dark, but the boys would be there, a fire would be burning, and a hot supper would be ready. As he thought of lunch, he pressed his hand against the package under his jacket. It was also under his shirt, wrapped in a handkerchief, and lying for warmth against the naked skin. Otherwise, the bread would freeze. He smiled contentedly to himself as he thought of those pieces of bread, each of which enclosed a generous portion of cooked meat.

He plunged among the big pine trees. The trail was not well marked here. Several inches of snow had fallen since the last sled had passed. He was glad he was without a sled. Actually, he carried nothing but the lunch wrapped in the handkerchief. He was surprised, however, at the cold. It certainly was cold, he decided, as he rubbed his nose and face with his mittened hand. He had a good growth of hair on his face, but that did not protect his nose or the upper part of his face from the frosty air.

Following at the man's heels was a big native dog. It was a wolf dog, gray-coated and not noticeably different from its brother, the wild wolf. The animal was worried by the great cold. It knew that this was no time for traveling. Its own feeling was closer to the truth than the man's judgment. In reality, it was not merely colder than 50 below zero; it was colder than 60 below, than 70 below. It was 75 below zero. Because the freezing point is 32 above zero, it meant that there were 107 degrees of frost.

The dog did not know anything about temperatures. Possibly in its brain there was no understanding of a condition of very cold, such as was in the man's brain. But the animal sensed the danger. Its fear made it question eagerly every movement of the man as if expecting him to go into camp or to seek shelter somewhere and build a fire. The dog had learned about fire, and it wanted fire. Otherwise, it would dig itself into the snow and find shelter from the cold air.

The frozen moistness of its breathing had settled on its fur in a fine powder of frost. The hair on the man's face was similarly frosted, but more solidly. It took the form of ice and increased with every warm, moist breath from his mouth. Also, the man had tobacco in his mouth. The ice held his lips so tightly together that he could not empty the juice from his mouth. The result was a long piece of yellow ice hanging from his lips. If he fell down it would break, like glass, into many pieces. He expected the ice formed by the tobacco juice, having been out twice before when it was very cold. But it had not been as cold as this, he knew.

He continued through the level forest for several miles. Then he went down a bank to the frozen path of a small stream. This was Henderson Creek and he knew he was ten miles from where the stream divided. He looked at his watch. It was ten o'clock. He was traveling at the rate of four miles an hour. Thus, he figured that he would arrive where the stream divided at half-past twelve. He decided he would eat his lunch when he arrived there.

The dog followed again at his heels, with its tail hanging low, as the man started to walk along the frozen stream. The old sled trail could be seen, but a dozen inches of snow covered the marks of the last sleds. In a month no man had traveled up or down that silent creek. The man went steadily ahead. He was not much of a thinker. At that moment he had nothing to think about except that he would eat lunch at the stream's divide and that at six o'clock he would be in camp with the boys. There was nobody to talk to; and, had there been, speech would not have been possible because of the ice around his mouth.

Once in a while the thought repeated itself that it was very cold and that he had never experienced such cold. As he walked along he rubbed his face and nose with the back of his mittened hand. He did this without thinking, frequently changing hands. But, with all his rubbing, the instant he stopped, his face and nose became numb. His face would surely be frozen. He knew that and he was sorry that he had not worn the sort of nose guard Bud wore when it was cold. Such a guard passed across the nose and covered the entire face. But it did not matter much, he decided. What was a little frost? A bit painful, that was all. It was never serious.

Empty as the man's mind was of thoughts, he was most observant. He noticed the changes in the creek, the curves and the bends. And always he noted where he placed his feet. Once, coming around a bend, he moved suddenly to the side, like a frightened horse. He curved away from the place where he had been walking and retraced his steps several feet along the trail. He knew the creek was frozen to the bottom. No creek could contain water in that winter. But he knew also that there were streams of water that came out from the hillsides and ran along under the snow and on top of the ice of the creek. He knew that even in the coldest weather these streams were never frozen, and he also knew their danger. They hid pools of water under the snow that might be three inches deep, or three feet. Sometimes a skin of ice half an inch thick covered them, and in turn was covered by the snow. Sometimes there was both water and thin ice, and when a man broke through he could get very wet.

That was why he had jumped away so suddenly. He had felt the ice move under his feet. He had also heard the noise of the snow-covered ice skin breaking. And to get his feet wet in such a temperature meant trouble and danger. At the very least it meant delay, because he would be forced to stop and build a fire. Only under its protection could he bare his feet while he dried his socks and moccasins.

He stood and studied the creek bottom and its banks. He decided that the flowing stream of water came from the right side. He thought a while, rubbing his nose and face. Then he walked to the left. He stepped carefully and tested the ice at each step. Once away from the danger, he continued at his four-mile pace.

During the next two hours he came to several similar dangers. Usually the snow above the pools had a sunken appearance. However, once again he came near to falling through the ice. Once, sensing danger, he made the dog go ahead. The dog did not want to go. It hesitated until the man pushed it forward. Then it went quickly across the white, unbroken surface. Suddenly it fell through the ice, but climbed out on the other side, which was firm. It had wet its feet and legs. Almost immediately the water on them turned to ice. The dog made quick efforts to get the ice off its legs. Then it lay down in the snow and began to bite out the ice that had formed between the toes. The animal knew enough to do this. To permit the ice to remain would mean sore feet. It did not know this. It merely obeyed the commands that arose from the deepest part of its being.

But the man knew these things, having learned them from experience. He removed the mitten from his right hand and helped the dog tear out the pieces of ice. He did not bare his fingers more than a minute, and was surprised to find that they were numb. It certainly was cold. He pulled on the mitten quickly and beat the hand across his breast.

At twelve o'clock the day was at its brightest. Yet the sun did not appear in the sky. At half-past twelve, on the minute, he arrived at the divide of the creek. He was pleased at his rate of speed. If he continued, he would certainly be with the boys by six o'clock that evening.

He unbuttoned his jacket and shirt and pulled forth his lunch. The action took no more than a quarter of a minute, yet in that brief moment the numbness touched his bare fingers. He did not put the mitten on, but instead, struck the fingers against his leg. Then he sat down on a snow-covered log to eat. The pain that followed the striking of his fingers against his leg ceased so quickly that he was frightened. He had not had time to take a bite of his lunch. He struck the fingers repeatedly and returned them to the mitten. Then he bared the other hand for the purpose of eating. He tried to take a mouthful, but the ice around his mouth prevented him.

Then he knew what was wrong. He had forgotten to build a fire and warm himself. He laughed at his own foolishness. As he laughed, he noted the numbness in his bare fingers. Also, he noted that the feeling which had first come to his toes when he sat down was already passing away. He wondered whether the toes were warm or whether they were numb. He moved them inside the moccasins and decided that they were numb.

He pulled the mitten on hurriedly and stood up. He was somewhat frightened. He stamped forcefully until the feeling returned to his feet. It certainly was cold, was his thought. That man from Sulphur Creek had spoken the truth when telling how cold it sometimes got in this country. And he had laughed at him at the time! That showed one must not be too sure of things. There was no mistake about it, it was cold. He walked a few steps, stamping his feet and waving his arms, until reassured by the returning warmth. Then he took some matches and proceeded to make a fire. In the bushes, the high water had left a supply of sticks. From here he got wood for his fire. Working carefully from a small beginning, he soon had a roaring fire.

Bending over the fire, he first melted the ice from his face. With the protection of the fire's warmth he ate his lunch. For the moment, the cold had been forced away. The dog took comfort in the fire, lying at full length close enough for warmth and far enough away to escape being burned. When the man had finished eating, he filled his pipe with tobacco and had a comfortable time with a smoke. Then he pulled on his mittens, settled his cap firmly about his ears, and started along the creek trail toward the left.

The dog was sorry to leave and looked toward the fire. This man did not know cold. Possibly none of his ancestors had known cold, real cold. But the dog knew and all of its family knew. And it knew that it was not good to walk outside in such fearful cold. It was the time to lie in a hole in the snow and to wait for this awful cold to stop. There was no real bond between the dog and the man. The one was the slave of the other. The dog made no effort to indicate its fears to the man. It was not concerned with the well-being of the man. It was for its own sake that it looked toward the fire. But the man whistled, and spoke to it with the sound of the whip in his voice. So the dog started walking close to the man's heels and followed him along the trail.

The man put more tobacco in his mouth and started a new growth of yellow ice on his face. Again his moist breath quickly powdered the hair on his face with white. He looked around him. There did not seem to be so many pools of water under the snow on the left side of Henderson Creek, and for half an hour the man saw no signs of any.

And then it happened. At a place where there were no signs, the man broke through. It was not deep. He was wet to the knees before he got out of the water to the firm snow.

He was angry and cursed his luck aloud. He had hoped to get into camp with the boys at six o'clock, and this would delay him an hour. Now he would have to build a fire and dry his moccasins and socks. This was most important at that low temperature. He knew that much.

So he turned aside to the bank, which he climbed. On top, under several small pine trees, he found some firewood which had been carried there by the high water of last year. There were some sticks, but also larger branches, and some dry grasses. He threw several large branches on top of the snow. This served for a foundation and prevented the young flame from dying in the wet snow. He made a flame by touching a match to a small piece of tree bark that he took from his pocket. This burned even better than paper. Placing it on the foundation, he fed the young flame with pieces of dry grass and with the smallest dry sticks.

He worked slowly and carefully, realizing his danger. Gradually, as the flame grew stronger, he increased the size of the sticks with which he fed it. He sat in the snow, pulling the sticks from the bushes under the trees and feeding them directly to the flame. He knew he must not fail. When it is 75 below zero, a man must not fail in his first attempt to build a fire. This is especially true if his feet are wet. If his feet are dry, and he fails, he can run along the trail for half a mile to keep his blood moving. But the blood in wet and freezing feet cannot be kept moving by running when it is 75 degrees below. No matter how fast he runs, the wet feet will freeze even harder.

All this the man knew. The old man on Sulphur Creek had told him about it, and now he was grateful for the advice. Already all feeling had gone from his feet. To build the fire he had been forced to remove his mittens, and the fingers had quickly become numb. His pace of four miles an hour had kept his heart pushing the blood to all parts of his body. But the instant he stopped, the action of the heart slowed down. He now received the full force of the cold. The blood of his body drew back from it. The blood was alive, like the dog. Like the dog, it wanted to hide and seek cover, away from the fearful cold. As long as he walked four miles an hour, the blood rose to the surface. But now it sank down into the lowest depths of his body. His feet and hands were the first to feel its absence. His wet feet froze first. His bare fingers were numb, although they had not yet begun to freeze. Nose and face were already freezing, while the skin of all his body became cold as it lost its blood.

But he was safe. Toes and nose and face would be only touched by the frost, because the fire was beginning to burn with strength. He was feeding it with sticks the size of his finger. In another minute he would be able to feed it with larger branches. Then he could remove his wet moccasins and socks. While they dried, he could keep his naked feet warm by the fire, rubbing them first with snow. The fire was a success. He was safe.

He remembered the advice of the old man on Sulphur Creek, and smiled. The man had been very serious when he said that no man should travel alone in that country after 50 below zero. Well, here he was; he had had the accident; he was alone; and he had saved himself. Those old men were rather womanish, he thought. All a man must do was to keep his head, and he was all right. Any man who was a man could travel alone. But it was surprising, the rapidity with which his face and nose were freezing. And he had not thought his fingers could lose their feeling in so short a time. Without feeling they were, because he found it very difficult to make them move together to grasp a stick. They seemed far from his body and from him. When he touched a stick, he had to look to see whether or not he was holding it.

All of which mattered little. There was the fire, promising life with every dancing flame. He started to untie his moccasins. They were coated with ice. The thick socks were like iron almost to the knees. The moccasin's strings were like ropes of steel. For a moment he pulled them with his unfeeling fingers. Then, realizing the foolishness of it, he grasped his knife.

But before he could cut the strings, it happened. It was his own fault, or instead, his mistake. He should not have built the fire under the pine tree. He should have built it in an open space. But it had been easier to pull the sticks from the bushes and drop them directly on the fire.

Now the tree under which he had done this carried a weight of snow on its branches. No wind had been blowing for weeks and each branch was heavy with snow. Each time he pulled a stick he shook the tree slightly. There had been just enough movement to cause the awful thing to happen. High up in the tree one branch dropped its load of snow. This fell on the branches beneath. This process continued, spreading through the whole tree. The snow fell without warning upon the man and the fire, and the fire was dead. Where it had burned was a pile of fresh snow.

The man was shocked. It was like hearing his own judgment of death. For a moment he sat and stared at the spot where the fire had been. Then he grew very calm. Perhaps the old man on Sulphur Creek was right. If he had a companion on the trail he would be in no danger now. The companion could have built the fire. Now, he must build the fire again, and this second time he must not fail. Even if he succeeded, he would be likely to lose some toes. His feet must be badly frozen by now, and there would be some time before the second fire was ready.

Such were his thoughts, but he did not sit and think them. He was busy all the time they were passing through his mind. He made a new foundation for a fire, this time in the open space, where no tree would be above it. Next, he gathered dry grasses and tiny sticks. He could not bring his fingers together to pull them out of the ground, but he was able to gather them by the handful. In this way he also got many pieces that were undesirable, but it was the best he could do. He worked carefully, even collecting an armful of the larger branches to be used later when the fire gathered strength. And all the while the dog sat and watched him. There was an anxious look in its eyes, because it depended upon him as the fire provider, and the fire was slow in coming.

When all was ready, the man reached in his pocket for the second piece of tree bark. He knew the bark was there, although he could not feel it with his fingers. He tried again and again, but he could not grasp it. And all the time, in his mind, he knew that each instant his feet were freezing. This thought alarmed him, but he fought against it and kept calm.

He pulled on his mittens with his teeth, and began swinging his arms. Then he beat his hands with all his strength against his sides. He did this while he was sitting down. Then he stood up to do it. All the while the dog sat in the snow, its tail curled warmly over its feet and its sharp wolf ears bent forward as it looked at the man. And the man, as he waved his arms and hands, looked with longing at the creature that was warm and secure in the covering provided by nature.

After a time, he began to notice some feeling in his beaten fingers. The feeling grew stronger until it became very painful, but the man welcomed the pain. He pulled the mitten from his right hand and grasped the tree bark from his pocket. The bare fingers were quickly numb again. Next, he brought out his pack of matches. But the awful cold had already driven the life out of his fingers. In his effort to separate one match from the others, the whole pack fell in the snow. He tried to pick it out of the snow, but failed. The dead fingers could neither touch nor hold.

Now he was very careful. He drove the thought of his freezing feet, and nose, and face, from his mind. He devoted his whole soul to picking up the matches. He followed the movement of his fingers with his eyes, using his sense of sight instead of that of touch. When he saw his fingers on each side of the pack, he closed them. That is, he willed to close them, because the fingers did not obey. He put the mitten on the right hand again, and beat it fiercely against his knee. Then, with both mittened hands, he lifted up the pack of matches, along with much snow, to the front of his jacket. But he had gained nothing.

After some struggling he managed to get the pack between his mittened hands. In this manner he carried it to his mouth. The ice broke as he opened his mouth with a fierce effort. He used his upper teeth to rub across the pack in order to separate a single match. He succeeded in getting one, which he dropped on his jacket. His condition was no better. He could not pick up the match. Then he thought how he might do it. He picked up the match in his teeth and drew it across his leg. Twenty times he did this before he succeeded in lighting it. As it flamed he held it with his teeth to the tree bark. But the burning smell went up his nose, causing him to cough. The match fell into the snow and the flame died.

The old man on Sulphur Creek was right, he thought in the moment of controlled despair that followed. After 50 below zero, a man should travel with a companion. He beat his hands, but failed to produce any feeling in them. Suddenly he bared both hands, removing the mittens with his teeth. He caught the whole pack of matches between his hands. His arm muscles were not frozen and he was able to press the hands tightly against the matches. Then he drew the whole pack along his leg. It burst into flame, 70 matches at once!

There was no wind to blow them out. He kept his head to one side to escape the burning smell, and held the flaming pack to the tree bark. As he so held it, he noticed some feeling in his hand. His flesh was burning. He could smell it. The feeling developed into pain. He continued to endure it. He held the flame of the matches to the bark that would not light readily because his own burning hands were taking most of the flame.

Finally, when he could endure no more, he pulled his hands apart. The flaming matches fell into the snow, but the tree bark was burning. He began laying dry grasses and the tiniest sticks on the flame. He could not choose carefully because they must be pieces that could be lifted between his hands. Small pieces of green grass stayed on the sticks, and he bit them off as well as he could with his teeth. He treated the flame carefully. It meant life, and it must not cease.

The blood had left the surface of his body and he now began to shake from the cold. A large piece of a wet plant fell on the little fire. He tried to push it out with his fingers. His shaking body made him push it too far and he scattered the little fire over a wide space. He tried to push the burning grasses and sticks together again. Even with the strong effort that he made, his trembling fingers would not obey and the sticks were hopelessly scattered. Each stick smoked a little and died. The fire provider had failed. As he looked about him, his eyes noticed the dog sitting across the ruins of the fire from him. It was making uneasy movements, slightly lifting one foot and then the other.

The sight of the dog put a wild idea into his head. He remembered the story of the man, caught in a storm, who killed an animal and sheltered himself inside the dead body and thus was saved. He would kill the dog and bury his hands in the warm body until feeling returned to them. Then he could build another fire.

He spoke to the dog, calling it to him. But in his voice was a strange note of fear that frightened the animal. It had never known the man to speak in such a tone before. Something was wrong and it sensed danger. It knew not what danger, but somewhere in its brain arose a fear of the man. It flattened its ears at the sound of the man's voice; its uneasy movements and the liftings of its feet became more noticeable. But it would not come to the man. He got down on his hands and knees and went toward the dog. But this unusual position again excited fear and the animal moved away.

The man sat in the snow for a moment and struggled for calmness. Then he pulled on his mittens, using his teeth, and then stood on his feet. He glanced down to assure himself that he was really standing, because lack of feeling in his feet gave him no relation to the earth. His position, however, removed the fear from the dog's mind.

When he commanded the dog with his usual voice, the dog obeyed and came to him. As it came within his reach, the man lost control. His arms stretched out to hold the dog and he experienced real surprise when he discovered that his hands could not grasp. There was neither bend nor feeling in the fingers. He had forgotten for the moment that they were frozen and that they were freezing more and more. All this happened quickly and before the animal could escape, he encircled its body with his arms. He sat down in the snow, and in this fashion held the dog, while it barked and struggled.

But it was all he could do: hold its body encircled in his arms and sit there. He realized that he could not kill the dog. There was no way to do it. With his frozen hands he could neither draw nor hold his knife. Nor could he grasp the dog around the throat. He freed it and it dashed wildly away, still barking. It stopped 40 feet away and observed him curiously, with ears sharply bent forward.

The man looked down at his hands to locate them and found them hanging on the ends of his arms. He thought it curious that it was necessary to use his eyes to discover where his hands were. He began waving his arms, beating the mittened hands against his sides. He did this for five minutes. His heart produced enough blood to stop his shaking. But no feeling was created in his hands.

A certain fear of death came upon him. He realized that it was no longer a mere problem of freezing his fingers and toes, or of losing his hands and feet. Now it was a problem of life and death with the circumstances against him. The fear made him lose control of himself and he turned and ran along the creek bed on the old trail. The dog joined him and followed closely behind. The man ran blindly in fear such as he had never known in his life. Slowly, as he struggled through the snow, he began to see things again—the banks of the creek, the bare trees, and the sky.

The running made him feel better. He did not shake any more. Maybe, if he continued to run, his feet would stop freezing. Maybe if he ran far enough, he would find the camp and the boys. Without doubt, he would lose some fingers and toes and some of his face. But the boys would take care of him and save the rest of him when he got there. And at the same time, there was another thought in his mind that said he would never get to the camp and the boys. It told him that it was too many miles away, that the freezing had too great a start and that he would soon be dead. He pushed this thought to the back of his mind and refused to consider it. Sometimes it came forward and demanded to be heard. But he pushed it away and tried to think of other things.

It seemed strange to him that he could run on feet so frozen that he could not feel them when they struck the earth and took the weight of his body. He seemed to be flying along above the surface and to have no connection with the earth.

His idea of running until he arrived at the camp and the boys presented one problem: he lacked the endurance. Several times he caught himself as he was falling. Finally, he dropped to the ground, unable to stop his fall. When he tried to rise, he failed. He must sit and rest, he decided. Next time he would merely walk and keep going.

As he sat and regained his breath, he noted that he was feeling warm and comfortable. He was not shaking, and it even seemed that a warm glow had come to his body. And yet, when he touched his nose or face, there was no feeling. Running would not bring life to them. Nor would it help his hands and feet. Then the thought came to him that the frozen portions of his body must be increasing. He tried to keep this thought out of his mind and to forget it. He knew that such thoughts caused a feeling of fright in him and he was afraid of such feelings. But the thought returned and continued, until he could picture his body totally frozen. This was too much, and again he ran wildly along the trail. Once he slowed to a walk, but the thought that the freezing of his body was increasing made him run again.

And all the time the dog ran with him, at his heels. When he fell a second time, the dog curled its tail over its feet and sat in front of him, facing him, curiously eager. The warmth and security of the animal angered him. He cursed it until it flattened its ears. This time the shaking because of the cold began more quickly. He was losing his battle with the frost. It was moving into his body from all sides. This thought drove him forward. But he ran no more than 100 feet, when he fell head first.

It was his last moment of fear. When he had recovered his breath and his control, he sat and thought about meeting death with dignity. However, the idea did not come to him in exactly this manner. His idea was that he had been acting like a fool. He had been running around like a chicken with its head cut off. He was certain to freeze in his present circumstances, and he should accept it calmly. With this newfound peace of mind came the first sleepiness. A good idea, he thought, to sleep his way to death. Freezing was not as bad as people thought. There were many worse ways to die.

He pictured the boys finding his body the next day. Suddenly he saw himself with them, coming along the trail and looking for himself. And, still with them, he came around a turn in the trail and found himself lying in the snow. He did not belong with himself any more. Even then he was outside of himself, standing with the boys and looking at himself in the snow. It certainly was cold, was his thought. When he returned to the United States he could tell the folks what real cold was.

His mind went from this to the thought of the old man of Sulphur Creek. He could see him quite clearly, warm and comfortable, and smoking a pipe.

"You were right, old fellow. You were right," he murmured to the old man of Sulphur Creek.

Then the man dropped into what seemed to him the most comfortable and satisfying sleep he had ever known. The dog sat facing him and waiting. The brief day ended in a long evening. There were no signs of a fire to be made. Never in the dog's experience had it known a man to sit like that in the snow and make no fire. As the evening grew darker, its eager longing for the fire mastered it. With much lifting of its feet, it cried softly. Then it flattened its ears, expecting the man's curse. But the man remained silent. Later, the dog howled loudly. And still later it moved close to the man and caught the smell of death. This made the animal back away. A little longer it delayed, howling under the stars that leaped and danced and shone brightly in the cold sky. Then it turned and ran along the trail toward the camp it knew, where there were the other food providers and fire providers.

The Story Of Wisdom

Cornelia Sorabji

Cornelia Sorabji (1866-1954) was an Indian lawyer, social reformer and writer who was the first female to graduate from Bombay University and the first woman to study Law at Oxford University. Later, she became the first woman to practice Law in India and Britain. 'The Story Of Wisdom' is from the enlightening collection *Between the Twilights: Being Studies of Indian Women by One of Themselves* (1908).

She comes with the Spring—a two days' guest in an Indian household. Nor has frequency bred either carelessness or coolness of reception. Early on the morning of her arrival you will see the women hastening from the Bathing Ghat, their garments clinging about their supple limbs, their long hair drying in the wind. They bear full water-pots, for nought but Gunga-Mai today suffices—no slothful backsliding to nearby pump.

In the house of my friend, it was Parvati, the oldest serving-woman who undertook to make ready the guest chamber. I watched her as she crossed the courtyard—a handful of the precious liquid for Dharti-Mai the Earth Mother, and the rest—a generous swob, for the black marble veranda. Soon had she helpers, and to spare—the most practised among them made the white chalk marks of good luck—tridents, fishes, flames of fire; and the tidiest made the little inclosure—white cotton "railings," the posts being balls of Ganges mud, in which were buried swiftly flying arrows—threat for daring devil.

But the centre of interest was naturally the Altar. This was just a plain raised platform of wood, carrying bravely its variety of offering. Great mountains of yellow and white flowers, with fruits, chiefly the cocoanut, fruit of healing, old Sanskrit manuscripts, lettered palm-leaves, thumbed and blotted copybooks and tattered primers—the prayers of children—the pointed reed, and ink-horns, glass ink pots and steel pens from the 'Europe' shop across the way; a school edition of "The Vicar of Wakefield," Ganot's Physics, quaint combs and mirrors, powder-boxes, and perfumes, "the tears of scented grass," or that more subtle "scent of red rose leaves." Why not? Is she not woman, even though a Goddess and learned ? The "Europe" products, I notice, carry milk in place of ink. "Sanctify to us this Western Education, "—is that what it means in this country, where deepest feeling finds outlet other than through doors of speech? So her worshippers made ready, not in private chapel but here where the life of the days pulsed and languished through the years; here, where friend or passing stranger might alike turn to greet her; for Wisdom is one, though her hosts be many. Moreover, She who is called Wisdom loves the voices of little children, and nothing is hushed, or ordered otherwise for her coming. The most unregenerate rogue romps at her feet, the most thriftless housewife, the most rebellious daughter-in-law has access to her Altar, and through the day one after another will come bearing her gift; and, lingering a while, will go away softly even as she came. Sometimes, by no means generally, there will be an image of the Goddess. One such I have seen in the house of a rich merchant. It was a life-sized figure dancing on a lotus, the full bloom, pink-edged, in her hand she bore a *bina,* for the Goddess of Wisdom is also Queen of Harmony; and the rich man's friends had honoured her as was meet, with priceless gifts of *Kincab,* of gem, of trinket. Now Wisdom of necessity has yet one more aspect, she is Goddess of Perfect Speech. It is of her that the tongue-tied prays eloquence, the scholar success; and the offering to her in this capacity you will find absent from no Altar, rich or poor. To omit this would mean the curse of the dumb for ever. It is a little cake of rice and milk, this oblation for lapses from accuracy, for "benevolent falsehood."

"Oh Guest of the hours, remember the past, the puzzling need of the tangled moments, remember—and forgive."

A list of benevolent falsehoods must needs vary with the age. Manu includes, "The giver of false evidence for a pious motive, for such an one shall not lose a seat in heaven," his lapses being called the "Speech of the Gods."

"To save a life," To protect a cow," "To counteract the thriftless ways of husbands," have added Hindu women of my acquaintance.

Simple is the ritual of the worship of Wisdom. "With folded hands I bow before he Goddess, the Goddess who provides all wealth, and vouchsafes the power of speech!"

"May the Goddess of Wisdom protect me, the Mother of the Vedas, who from the crimson lotus of her hands pours radiance on the implements of writing, and on the works produced by her power."

"May the Goddess of Wisdom protect me—she who robed in white, sets far all ignorance. She who abides with the Creator may she abide with me ...;" and the rest of the prayers are either said by the Priest, or found in the heart of the worshipper. The battered lesson book, the oft-used pen, are these not prayers in themselves?

The last time I saw the Goddess was at the Children's Festival. Wisdom danced on her lotus flower, in a little bower of bamboos and marigolds, out in the open courtyard. At her feet sat children, row upon row, ranging in age from three years to twelve. I watched them come so happily, tripping hand in hand with some friend or comrade. They wore their best gay little saree, gold-spangled and bordered, in their hair thread of gold, or great heavy ornament, or just some flower among the light close braidings. And, as they took their seats in the Great Cathedral roofed by God's sky, the Priests n1oved among them anointing each little forehead with oil of sandal wood from off the altar of her who is named Wisdom.

Then the musicians beat their drums and rang the bell of worship, and every single forehead was on the ground before the Goddess. The worship had begun... First be consecrate, then bring your offering—is the creed ... I heard no prayers, but there after, one by one, the Babies passed before her, throwing at her feet sweet-scented wreaths of Jasmine. I needed not then to hear their prayers ... And that was all the Service. The play of the children at the feet of Wisdom.

Thus then the Hindu honours his Guest. And, on the second day—for even Wisdom must share at length the waters of oblivion—

with music and singing with the happy laughter of children and a gay following of the faithful, her image is taken to the Ganges; and with love and much injunction as to next year's journey from the Mounts of Blessing, is it set afloat on that sacred river whose bourne is the Eternal Sea.

Wisdom, in Sanskrit story, is Creative Power to the Great God himself, his energy—without her he is but a great incommunicable passive force.

"I make strong whom I choose—originating all things I pass even as a breeze. Above the Heavens am I, beyond the Earth, and what is the Great One, *that* am I. I make holy the Great God Himself. For the Great Archer it is I bend the bow; it is I who stay evil in the name of the Destroyer. Few know me, yet near to all alike am I. God is he from whom Wisdom and Speech—after reaching Him—return."

Unravelling it all, what quaint teaching may we not piece together? That is true wisdom which puts man in touch with God creature with Creator. And the same power of God refrains not from blessing the things that are of value to the Earth—the written, the spoken word, all arts and harmonies and science.

Then, is it not a parable that the Goddess of Speech is primarily the Goddess of all Learning,? Let the ignorant keep silence.

The *Tulsi* spirals stirred in the hot wind, and the great white red-throated Sarus flapped his wings as he walked about the women's courtyard. The men of the house had taken the Image to the water, and we sat by the empty altar in the hour between the Twilights. "Tell me more about Wisdom," said I to my Wisest of the Wise, and she told me of how Vishnu gave her as wife to Brahma, and how Brahma put a slight upon the Lady of Wisdom—a slight which she never forgave.

A great sacrifice was going forward, and the Priest bade Brahma call his Lady. For is it not the wife, and she alone who must hold the sacred grass, must sprinkle the offerings. "But Saraswati is engaged in dressing," was the answer.

Then the Priest "without a wife what blessing can come?"

So Brahma turned to Indra, and bade him find a substitute in hedge or highway.

Indra soon returned, leading by the hand a n1ilkmaid, beautiful and happy. She bore a jar of butter on her head. "She shall become the Mother of the Vedas," said the Priest; and that is how Gayatri, the Milkmaid, was wed to the Great God Himself.

Then came forth Saraswati all unconscious, and very gorgeous, attended by the wives of Vishnu, Rudra, and other of the Gods—a worthy train.

When she heard what had happened, she was wroth beyond power of words to tell.

Said the Great God, shamefaced, "The Priest did this thing; the Priest and Indra."

But Saraswati said, "By the powers I have obtained, may Brahma never be worshipped in Temple or Sacred Place—except one day in each year—and since Indra, thou didst bring that Milkmaid to my Lord, thou shalt be bound in chains by all thine enemies and prisoned in a strange and distant country, thy power over the winds and thy station on high, given to others. Cursed also be ye—Priests. Henceforth shall ye perform sacrifices solely for the desire of obtaining the usual gifts, and for love of gain alone shall ye serve Temples and holy places; satisfied only shall ye be with the food of others, and dissatisfied with that of your own houses. And in quest of riches shall ye unduly perform rites and ceremonies."...

In great wrath she called for her peacock, to leave the assembly, but the Goddess of Wealth refused to accompany her; and her also did she curse.

"May you always abide with the vile and the inconstant, the contemptible and foolish, the sinful, cruel and vulgar."

After her departure Gayatri modifies all the curses; so neither need all Priests nor all the wealthy be base and contemptible.

When the youngest daughter-in-law in the house is listening to the storytelling my Wisest of the Wise adds a variation—Saraswati is appeased, and Brahma says he will do with the Milkmaid what the Goddess commands, while the Milkmaid herself falls at the feet of Wisdom, who, raising her, says, "Let be—let you and me both serve my Lord!"

~

And now for a year her Altar is empty but she is not forgotten, and in the practice and devotion of the faithful still does the third watch of the night belong to Wisdom.

"Let the home-keeping ones wake in the time sacred to Saraswati, the Goddess of Speech; let them reflect: on virtue and virtuous emoluments; and on the whole meaning and essence of the words of Wisdom."

~

"So desirable, and yet she may be only a two days' Guest in a Hindu household," I mused aloud.

"Ah, but," answered she who worshipped Wisdom, "were Wisdom always with us, how should we live among the sons of men!"

The Sisters

James Joyce

James Joyce (1882-1941) was an Irish writer known for seminal works such as *A Portrait of the Artist as a Young Man* (1916) and *Ulysses* (1922). He was notable for his mastery of the English language and the skilful use of literary devices. Besides writing novels, Joyce also wrote a collection of short stories *Dubliners* (1914) under the pseudonym Stephen Dedalus, of which 'The Sisters' is a part.

There was no hope for him this time: it was the third stroke. Night after night I had passed the house (it was vacation time) and studied the lighted square of window: and night after night I had found it lighted in the same way, faintly and evenly. If he was dead, I thought, I would see the reflection of candles on the darkened blind for I knew that two candles must be set at the head of a corpse. He had often said to me: "I am not long for this world," and I had thought his words idle. Now I knew they were true. Every night as I gazed up at the window I said softly to myself the word paralysis. It had always sounded strangely in my ears, like the word gnomon in the Euclid and the word simony in the Catechism. But now it sounded to me like the name of some maleficent and sinful being. It filled me with fear, and yet I longed to be nearer to it and to look upon its deadly work.

Old Cotter was sitting at the fire, smoking, when I came downstairs to supper. While my aunt was ladling out my stirabout he said, as if returning to some former remark of his:

"No, I wouldn't say he was exactly...but there was something queer...there was something uncanny about him. I'll tell you my opinion..."

He began to puff at his pipe, no doubt arranging his opinion in his mind. Tiresome old fool! When we knew him first he used to be rather interesting, talking of faints and worms; but I soon grew tired of him and his endless stories about the distillery.

"I have my own theory about it," he said. "I think it was one of those ... peculiar cases... But it's hard to say..."

He began to puff again at his pipe without giving us his theory. My uncle saw me staring and said to me:

"Well, so your old friend is gone, you'll be sorry to hear."

"Who?" said I.

"Father Flynn."

"Is he dead?"

"Mr Cotter here has just told us. He was passing by the house."

I knew that I was under observation so I continued eating as if the news had not interested me. My uncle explained to old Cotter.

"The youngster and he were great friends. The old chap taught him a great deal, mind you; and they say he had a great wish for him."

"God have mercy on his soul," said my aunt piously.

Old Cotter looked at me for a while. I felt that his little beady black eyes were examining me but I would not satisfy him by looking up from my plate. He returned to his pipe and finally spat rudely into the grate.

"I wouldn't like children of mine," he said, "to have too much to say to a man like that."

"How do you mean, Mr Cotter?" asked my aunt.

"What I mean is," said old Cotter, "it's bad for children. My idea is: let a young lad run about and play with young lads of his own age and not be... Am I right, Jack?"

"That's my principle, too," said my uncle. "Let him learn to box his corner. That's what I'm always saying to that Rosicrucian there: take exercise. Why, when I was a nipper every morning of my life I had a cold bath, winter and summer. And that's what stands to me now. Education is all very fine and large... Mr Cotter might take a pick of that leg mutton," he added to my aunt.

"No, no, not for me," said old Cotter.

My aunt brought the dish from the safe and put it on the table.

"But why do you think it's not good for children, Mr Cotter?" she asked.

"It's bad for children," said old Cotter, "because their minds are so impressionable. When children see things like that, you know, it has an effect..."

I crammed my mouth with stirabout for fear I might give utterance to my anger. Tiresome old red-nosed imbecile!

It was late when I fell asleep. Though I was angry with old Cotter for alluding to me as a child, I puzzled my head to extract meaning from his unfinished sentences. In the dark of my room I imagined that I saw again the heavy grey face of the paralytic. I drew the blankets over my head and tried to think of Christmas. But the grey face still followed me. It murmured; and I understood that it desired to confess something. I felt my soul receding into some pleasant and vicious region; and there again I found it waiting for me. It began to confess to me in a murmuring voice and I wondered why it smiled continually and why the lips were so moist with spittle. But then I remembered that it had died of paralysis and I felt that I too was smiling feebly as if to absolve the simoniac of his sin.

The next morning after breakfast I went down to look at the little house in Great Britain Street. It was an unassuming shop, registered under the vague name of *Drapery*. The drapery consisted mainly of children's bootees and umbrellas; and on ordinary days a notice used to hang in the window, saying: *Umbrellas Re-covered*. No notice was visible now for the shutters were up. A crape bouquet was tied to the door-knocker with ribbon. Two poor women and a telegram boy were reading the card pinned on the crape. I also approached and read:

July 1st, 1895
The Rev. James Flynn (formerly of S. Catherine's Church,
Meath Street), aged sixty-five years.
R. I. P.

The reading of the card persuaded me that he was dead and I was disturbed to find myself at check. Had he not been dead I would have gone into the little dark room behind the shop to find him sitting in his armchair by the fire, nearly smothered in his great-coat. Perhaps my aunt would have given me a packet of High Toast for him and this present would have roused him from his stupefied doze. It was always I who emptied the packet into his black snuff-box for his hands trembled too much to allow him to do this without spilling half the snuff about the floor. Even as he raised his large trembling hand to his nose little clouds of smoke dribbled through his fingers over the front of his coat. It may have been these constant showers of snuff which gave his ancient priestly garments their green faded look for the red handkerchief, blackened, as it always was, with the snuff-stains of a week, with which he tried to brush away the fallen grains, was quite inefficacious.

I wished to go in and look at him but I had not the courage to knock. I walked away slowly along the sunny side of the street, reading all the theatrical advertisements in the shop-windows as I went. I found it strange that neither I nor the day seemed in a mourning mood and I felt even annoyed at discovering in myself a sensation of freedom as if I had been freed from something by his death. I wondered at this for, as my uncle had said the night before, he had taught me a great deal. He had studied in the Irish college in Rome and he had taught me to pronounce Latin properly. He had told me stories about the catacombs and about Napoleon Bonaparte, and he had explained to me the meaning of the different ceremonies of the Mass and of the different vestments worn by the priest. Sometimes he had amused himself by putting difficult questions to me, asking me what one should do in certain circumstances or whether such and such sins were mortal or venial or only imperfections. His questions showed me how complex and mysterious were certain institutions of the Church which I had always regarded as the simplest acts. The duties of the priest towards the Eucharist and towards the secrecy of the confessional seemed so grave to me that I wondered how anybody had ever found in himself the courage to undertake them; and I was not surprised when he told me that the fathers of the Church had written books as thick as the *Post Office Directory* and as closely printed as the law notices in the newspaper, elucidating all these intricate questions. Often when I thought of this I could make no answer or only a very foolish and halting one upon which he used to smile and nod his head twice or thrice. Sometimes he used to put me through the responses of the Mass which he had made me learn by heart; and, as I pattered, he used to smile pensively and nod his head, now and then pushing huge pinches of snuff up each nostril alternately. When he smiled he used to uncover his big discoloured teeth and let his tongue lie upon his lower lip—a habit which had made me feel uneasy in the beginning of our acquaintance before I knew him well.

As I walked along in the sun I remembered old Cotter's words and tried to remember what had happened afterwards in the dream. I remembered that I had noticed long velvet curtains and a swinging lamp of antique fashion. I felt that I had been very far away, in some land where the customs were strange—in Persia, I thought... But I could not remember the end of the dream.

In the evening my aunt took me with her to visit the house of mourning. It was after sunset; but the windowpanes of the houses that looked to the west reflected the tawny gold of a great bank of clouds. Nannie received us in the hall; and, as it would have been unseemly to have shouted at her, my aunt shook hands with her for all. The old woman pointed upwards interrogatively and, on my aunt's nodding, proceeded to toil up the narrow staircase before us, her bowed head being scarcely above the level of the banister-rail. At the first landing she stopped and beckoned us forward encouragingly towards the open door of the dead-room. My aunt went in and the old woman, seeing that I hesitated to enter, began to beckon to me again repeatedly with her hand.

I went in on tiptoe. The room through the lace end of the blind was suffused with dusky golden light amid which the candles looked like pale thin flames. He had been coffined. Nannie gave the lead and we three knelt down at the foot of the bed. I pretended to pray but I could not gather my thoughts because the old woman's mutterings distracted me. I noticed how clumsily her skirt was hooked at the back and how the heels of her cloth boots were trodden down all to one side. The fancy came to me that the old priest was smiling as he lay there in his coffin.

But no. When we rose and went up to the head of the bed I saw that he was not smiling. There he lay, solemn and copious, vested as for the altar, his large hands loosely retaining a chalice. His face was very truculent, grey and massive, with black cavernous nostrils and circled by a scanty white fur. There was a heavy odour in the room—the flowers.

We blessed ourselves and came away. In the little room downstairs we found Eliza seated in his armchair in state. I groped my way towards my usual chair in the corner while Nannie went to the sideboard and brought out a decanter of sherry and some wine-glasses. She set these on the table and invited us to take a little glass of wine. Then, at her sister's bidding, she filled out the sherry into the glasses and passed them to us. She pressed me to take some cream crackers also but I declined because I thought I would make too much noise eating them. She seemed to be somewhat disappointed at my refusal and went over quietly to the sofa where she sat down behind her sister. No one spoke: we all gazed at the empty fireplace.

My aunt waited until Eliza sighed and then said:

"Ah, well, he's gone to a better world."

Eliza sighed again and bowed her head in assent. My aunt fingered the stem of her wine-glass before sipping a little.

"Did he...peacefully?" she asked.

"Oh, quite peacefully, ma'am," said Eliza. "You couldn't tell when the breath went out of him. He had a beautiful death, God be praised."

"And everything...?"

"Father O'Rourke was in with him a Tuesday and anointed him and prepared him and all."

"He knew then?"

"He was quite resigned."

"He looks quite resigned," said my aunt.

"That's what the woman we had in to wash him said. She said he just looked as if he was asleep, he looked that peaceful and resigned. No one would think he'd make such a beautiful corpse."

"Yes, indeed," said my aunt.

She sipped a little more from her glass and said:

"Well, Miss Flynn, at any rate it must be a great comfort for you to know that you did all you could for him. You were both very kind to him, I must say."

Eliza smoothed her dress over her knees.

"Ah, poor James!" she said. "God knows we done all we could, as poor as we are—we wouldn't see him want anything while he was in it."

Nannie had leaned her head against the sofa-pillow and seemed about to fall asleep.

"There's poor Nannie," said Eliza, looking at her, "she's wore out. All the work we had, she and me, getting in the woman to wash him and then laying him out and then the coffin and then arranging about the Mass in the chapel. Only for Father O'Rourke I don't know what we'd have done at all. It was him brought us all them flowers and them two candlesticks out of the chapel and wrote out the notice for the *Freeman's General* and took charge of all the papers for the cemetery and poor James's insurance."

"Wasn't that good of him?" said my aunt.

Eliza closed her eyes and shook her head slowly.

"Ah, there's no friends like the old friends," she said, "when all is said and done, no friends that a body can trust."

"Indeed, that's true," said my aunt. "And I'm sure now that he's gone to his eternal reward he won't forget you and all your kindness to him."

"Ah, poor James!" said Eliza. "He was no great trouble to us. You wouldn't hear him in the house any more than now. Still, I know he's gone and all to that..."

"It's when it's all over that you'll miss him," said my aunt.

"I know that," said Eliza. "I won't be bringing him in his cup of beef-tea any more, nor you, ma'am, sending him his snuff. Ah, poor James!"

She stopped, as if she were communing with the past and then said shrewdly:

"Mind you, I noticed there was something queer coming over him latterly. Whenever I'd bring in his soup to him there I'd find him with his breviary fallen to the floor, lying back in the chair and his mouth open."

She laid a finger against her nose and frowned: then she continued:

"But still and all he kept on saying that before the summer was over he'd go out for a drive one fine day just to see the old house again where we were all born down in Irishtown and take me and Nannie with him. If we could only get one of them new-fangled carriages that makes no noise that Father O'Rourke told him about, them with the rheumatic wheels, for the day cheap—he said, at Johnny Rush's over the way there and drive out the three of us together of a Sunday evening. He had his mind set on that… Poor James!"

"The Lord have mercy on his soul!" said my aunt.

Eliza took out her handkerchief and wiped her eyes with it. Then she put it back again in her pocket and gazed into the empty grate for some time without speaking.

"He was too scrupulous always," she said. "The duties of the priesthood was too much for him. And then his life was, you might say, crossed."

"Yes," said my aunt. "He was a disappointed man. You could see that."

A silence took possession of the little room and, under cover of it, I approached the table and tasted my sherry and then returned quietly to my chair in the corner. Eliza seemed to have fallen into a deep revery. We waited respectfully for her to break the silence: and after a long pause she said slowly:

"It was that chalice he broke... That was the beginning of it. Of course, they say it was all right, that it contained nothing, I mean. But still... They say it was the boy's fault. But poor James was so nervous, God be merciful to him!"

"And was that it?" said my aunt. "I heard something..."

Eliza nodded.

"That affected his mind," she said. "After that he began to mope by himself, talking to no one and wandering about by himself. So one night he was wanted for to go on a call and they couldn't find him anywhere. They looked high up and low down; and still they couldn't see a sight of him anywhere. So then the clerk suggested to try the chapel. So then they got the keys and opened the chapel and the clerk and Father O'Rourke and another priest that was there brought in a light for to look for him... And what do you think but there he was, sitting up by himself in the dark in his confession-box, wide-awake and laughing-like softly to himself?"

She stopped suddenly as if to listen. I too listened; but there was no sound in the house: and I knew that the old priest was lying still in his coffin as we had seen him, solemn and truculent in death, an idle chalice on his breast.

Eliza resumed:

"Wide-awake and laughing-like to himself... So then, of course, when they saw that, that made them think that there was something gone wrong with him..."

Mary Postgate

Rudyard Kipling

Rudyard Kipling (1865-1936) was an English novelist, poet and short story writer who received the Nobel Prize for Literature in 1907. He wrote tales for children as well as stories and novels that reflected his imperialist attitude. Some of his major works include *The Jungle Book* (1894), *Stalky and Co.* (1899) and *Kim* (1901). 'Mary Postgate' was first published in the September issue of *Nash's and Pall Mall Magazine* (1915), and is considered one of Kipling's finest short stories.

Of Miss Mary Postgate, Lady McCausland wrote that she was "thoroughly conscientious, tidy, companionable, and ladylike. I am very sorry to part with her, and shall always be interested in her welfare."

Miss Fowler engaged her on this recommendation, and to her surprise, for she had had experience of companions, found that it was true. Miss Fowler was nearer sixty than fifty at the time, but though she needed care she did not exhaust her attendant's vitality. On the contrary, she gave out, stimulatingly and with reminiscences. Her father had been a minor Court official in the days when the Great Exhibition of 1851 had just set its seal on Civilisation made perfect. Some of Miss Fowler's tales, none the less, were not always for the young. Mary was not young, and though her speech was as colourless as her eyes or her hair, she was never shocked. She listened unflinchingly to every one; said at the end, "How interesting!" or "How shocking!" as the case might be, and never again referred to it, for she prided herself on a trained mind, which "did not dwell on these things." She was, too, a treasure at domestic accounts, for which the village tradesmen, with their weekly books, loved her not.

Otherwise she had no enemies; provoked no jealousy even among the plainest; neither gossip nor slander had ever been traced to her; she supplied the odd place at the Rector's or the Doctor's table at half an hour's notice; she was a sort of public aunt to very many small children of the village street, whose parents, while accepting everything, would have been swift to resent what they called "patronage"; she served on the Village Nursing Committee as Miss Fowler's nominee when Miss Fowler was crippled by rheumatoid arthritis, and came out of six months' fortnightly meetings equally respected by all the cliques.

And when Fate threw Miss Fowler's nephew, an unlovely orphan of eleven, on Miss Fowler's hands, Mary Postgate stood to her share of the business of education as practised in private and public schools. She checked printed clothes-lists, and unitemised bills of extras; wrote to Head and House masters, matrons, nurses and doctors, and grieved or rejoiced over half-term reports. Young Wyndham Fowler repaid her in his holidays by calling her "Gatepost," "Postey," or "Packthread," by thumping her between her narrow shoulders, or by chasing her bleating, round the garden, her large mouth open, her large nose high in air, at a stiff-necked shamble very like a camel's. Later on he filled the house with clamour, argument, and harangues as to his personal needs, likes and dislikes, and the limitations of "you women," reducing Mary to tears of physical fatigue, or, when he chose to be humorous, of helpless laughter. At crises, which multiplied as he grew older, she was his ambassadress and his interpretress to Miss Fowler, who had no large sympathy with the young; a vote in his interest at the councils on his future; his sewing-woman, strictly accountable for mislaid boots and garments; always his butt and his slave.

And when he decided to become a solicitor, and had entered an office in London; when his greeting had changed from "Hullo, Postey, you old beast," to Mornin', Packthread,' there came a war which, unlike all wars that Mary could remember, did not stay decently outside England and in the newspapers, but intruded on the lives of people whom she knew. As she said to Miss Fowler, it was "most vexatious." It took the Rector's son who was going into business with his elder brother; it took the Colonel's nephew on the eve of fruit-farming in Canada; it took Mrs. Grant's son who, his mother said, was devoted to the ministry; and, very early indeed, it took Wynn Fowler, who announced on a postcard that he had joined the Flying Corps and wanted a cardigan waistcoat.

"He must go, and he must have the waistcoat," said Miss Fowler. So Mary got the proper-sized needles and wool, while Miss Fowler told the men of her establishment—two gardeners and an odd man, aged sixty—that those who could join the Army had better do so. The gardeners left. Cheape, the odd man, stayed on, and was promoted to the gardener's cottage. The cook, scorning to be limited in luxuries, also left, after a spirited scene with Miss Fowler, and took the housemaid with her. Miss Fowler gazetted Nellie, Cheape's seventeen-year-old daughter, to the vacant post; Mrs. Cheape to the rank of cook, with occasional cleaning bouts; and the reduced establishment moved forward smoothly.

Wynn demanded an increase in his allowance. Miss Fowler, who always looked facts in the face, said, "He must have it. The chances are he won't live long to draw it, and if three hundred makes him happy—"

Wynn was grateful, and came over, in his tight-buttoned uniform, to say so. His training centre was not thirty miles away, and his talk was so technical that it had to be explained by charts of the various types of machines. He gave Mary such a chart.

"And you'd better study it, Postey," he said. "You'll be seeing a lot of "em soon." So Mary studied the chart, but when Wynn next arrived to swell and exalt himself before his womenfolk, she failed badly in cross-examination, and he rated her as in the old days.

"You *look* more or less like a human being," he said in his new Service voice. "You *must* have had a brain at some time in your past. What have you done with it? Where d'you keep it? A sheep would know more than you do, Postey. You're lamentable. You are less use than an empty tin can, you dowey old cassowary."

"I suppose that's how your superior officer talks to *you*?" said Miss Fowler from her chair.

"But Postey doesn't mind," Wynn replied. "Do you, Packthread?"

"Why? Was Wynn saying anything? I shall get this right next time you come," she muttered, and knitted her pale brows again over the diagrams of Taubes, Farmans, and Zeppelins.

In a few weeks the mere land and sea battles which she read to Miss Fowler after breakfast passed her like idle breath. Her heart and her interest were high in the air with Wynn, who had finished "rolling" (whatever that might be) and had gone on from a "taxi" to a machine more or less his own. One morning it circled over their very chimneys, alighted on Vegg's Heath, almost outside the garden gate, and Wynn came in, blue with cold, shouting for food. He and she drew Miss Fowler's bath-chair, as they had often done, along the Heath footpath to look at the bi-plane. Mary observed that "it smelt very badly."

"Postey, I believe you think with your nose," said Wynn. "I know you don't with your mind. Now, what type's that?"

"I'll go and get the chart," said Mary.

"You're hopeless! You haven't the mental capacity of a white mouse," he cried, and explained the dials and the sockets for bomb-dropping till it was time to mount and ride the wet clouds once more.

"Ah!" said Mary, as the stinking thing flared upward. "Wait till our Flying Corps gets to work! Wynn says it's much safer than in the trenches."

"I wonder," said Miss Fowler. "Tell Cheape to come and tow me home again."

"It's all downhill. I can do it," said Mary, "if you put the brake on." She laid her lean self against the pushing-bar and home they trundled.

"Now, be careful you aren't heated and catch a chill," said overdressed Miss Fowler.

"Nothing makes me perspire," said Mary. As she bumped the chair under the porch she straightened her long back. The exertion had given her a colour, and the wind had loosened a wisp of hair across her forehead. Miss Fowler glanced at her.

"What do you ever think of, Mary?" she demanded suddenly.

"Oh, Wynn says he wants another three pairs of stockings—as thick as we can make them."

"Yes. But I mean the things that women think about. Here you are, more than forty—"

"Forty-four," said truthful Mary.

"Well?"

"Well?" Mary offered Miss Fowler her shoulder as usual.

"And you've been with me ten years now."

"Let's see," said Mary. "Wynn was eleven when he came. He's twenty now, and I came two years before that. It must be eleven."

"Eleven! And you've never told me anything that matters in all that while. Looking back, it seems to me that *I've* done all the talking."

"I'm afraid I'm not much of a conversationalist. As Wynn says, I haven't the mind. Let me take your hat."

Miss Fowler, moving stiffly from the hip, stamped her rubber-tipped stick on the tiled hall floor. "Mary, aren't you *anything* except a companion? Would you *ever* have been anything except a companion?"

Mary hung up the garden hat on its proper peg. "No," she said after consideration. "I don't imagine I ever should. But I've no imagination, I'm afraid."

She fetched Miss Fowler her eleven-o'clock glass of Contrexéville.

That was the wet December when it rained six inches to the month, and the women went abroad as little as might be. Wynn's flying chariot visited them several times, and for two mornings (he had warned her by postcard) Mary heard the thresh of his propellers at dawn. The second time she ran to the window, and stared at the whitening sky. A little blur passed overhead. She lifted her lean arms towards it.

That evening at six o'clock there came an announcement in an official envelope that Second Lieutenant W. Fowler had been killed during a trial flight. Death was instantaneous. She read it and carried it to Miss Fowler.

"I never expected anything else," said Miss Fowler; "but I'm sorry it happened before he had done anything."

The room was whirling round Mary Postgate, but she found herself quite steady in the midst of it.

"Yes," she said. "It's a great pity he didn't die in action after he had killed somebody."

"He was killed instantly. That's one comfort," Miss Fowler went on.

"But Wynn says the shock of a fall kills a man at once—whatever happens to the tanks," quoted Mary.

The room was coming to rest now. She heard Miss Fowler say impatiently, "But why can't we cry, Mary?" and herself replying, "There's nothing to cry for. He has done his duty as much as Mrs. Grant's son did."

"And when he died, *she* came and cried all the morning," said Miss Fowler. "This only makes me feel tired—terribly tired. Will you help me to bed, please, Mary?—And I think I'd like the hot-water bottle."

So Mary helped her and sat beside, talking of Wynn in his riotous youth.

"I believe," said Miss Fowler suddenly, "that old people and young people slip from under a stroke like this. The middle-aged feel it most."

"I expect that's true," said Mary, rising. "I'm going to put away the things in his room now. Shall we wear mourning?"

"Certainly not," said Miss Fowler. "Except, of course, at the funeral. I can't go. You will. I want you to arrange about his being buried here. What a blessing it didn't happen at Salisbury!"

Every one, from the Authorities of the Flying Corps to the Rector, was most kind and sympathetic. Mary found herself for the moment in a world where bodies were in the habit of being despatched by all sorts of conveyances to all sorts of places. And at the funeral two young men in buttoned-up uniforms stood beside the grave and spoke to her afterwards.

"You're Miss Postgate, aren't you?" said one. "Fowler told me about you. He was a good chap—a first-class fellow—a great loss."

"Great loss!" growled his companion. "We're all awfully sorry."

"How high did he fall from?" Mary whispered.

"Pretty nearly four thousand feet, I should think, didn't he? You were up that day, Monkey?"

"All of that," the other child replied. "My bar made three thousand, and I wasn't as high as him by a lot."

"Then *that's* all right," said Mary. "Thank you very much."

They moved away as Mrs. Grant flung herself weeping on Mary's flat chest, under the lych-gate, and cried, "*I* know how it feels! *I* know how it feels!"

"But both his parents are dead," Mary returned, as she fended her off. "Perhaps they've all met by now," she added vaguely as she escaped towards the coach.

"I've thought of that too," wailed Mrs. Grant; "but then he'll be practically a stranger to them. Quite embarrassing!"

Mary faithfully reported every detail of the ceremony to Miss Fowler, who, when she described Mrs. Grant's outburst, laughed aloud.

"Oh, how Wynn would have enjoyed it! He was always utterly unreliable at funerals. D'you remember—" And they talked of him again, each piecing out the other's gaps. "And now," said Miss Fowler, "we'll pull up the blinds and we'll have a general tidy. That always does us good. Have you seen to Wynn's things?"

"Everything—since he first came," said Mary. "He was never destructive—even with his toys."

They faced that neat room.

"It can't be natural not to cry," Mary said at last. "I'm *so* afraid you'll have a reaction."

"As I told you, we old people slip from under the stroke. It's you I'm afraid for. Have you cried yet?"

"I can't. It only makes me angry with the Germans."

"That's sheer waste of vitality," said Miss Fowler. "We must live till the war's finished." She opened a full wardrobe. "Now, I've been thinking things over. This is my plan. All his civilian clothes can be given away—Belgian refugees, and so on."

Mary nodded. "Boots, collars, and gloves?"

"Yes. We don't need to keep anything except his cap and belt."

"They came back yesterday with his Flying Corps clothes"—Mary pointed to a roll on the little iron bed.

"Ah, but keep his Service things. Some one may be glad of them later. Do you remember his sizes?"

"Five feet eight and a half; thirty-six inches round the chest. But he told me he's just put on an inch and a half. I'll mark it on a label and tie it on his sleeping-bag."

"So that disposes of *that*," said Miss Fowler, tapping the palm of one hand with the ringed third finger of the other. "What waste it all is! We'll get his old school trunk tomorrow and pack his civilian clothes."

"And the rest?" said Mary. "His books and pictures and the games and the toys—and—and the rest?"

"My plan is to burn every single thing," said Miss Fowler. "Then we shall know where they are and no one can handle them afterwards. What do you think?"

"I think that would be much the best," said Mary. "But there's such a lot of them."

"We'll burn them in the destructor," said Miss Fowler.

This was an open-air furnace for the consumption of refuse; a little circular four-foot tower of pierced brick over an iron grating. Miss Fowler had noticed the design in a gardening journal years ago, and had had it built at the bottom of the garden. It suited her tidy soul, for it saved unsightly rubbish-heaps, and the ashes lightened the stiff clay soil.

Mary considered for a moment, saw her way clear, and nodded again. They spent the evening putting away well-remembered civilian suits, underclothes that Mary had marked, and the regiments of very gaudy socks and ties. A second trunk was needed, and, after that, a little packing-case, and it was late next day when Cheape and the local carrier lifted them to the cart. The Rector luckily knew of a friend's son, about five feet eight and a half inches high, to whom a complete Flying Corps outfit would be most acceptable, and sent his gardener's son down with a barrow to take delivery of it. The cap was hung up in Miss Fowler's bedroom, the belt in Miss Postgate's; for, as Miss Fowler said, they had no desire to make tea-party talk of them.

"That disposes of *that*," said Miss Fowler. "I'll leave the rest to you, Mary. I can't run up and down the garden. You'd better take the big clothes-basket and get Nellie to help you."

"I shall take the wheel-barrow and do it myself," said Mary, and for once in her life closed her mouth.

Miss Fowler, in moments of irritation, had called Mary deadly methodical. She put on her oldest waterproof and gardening-hat and her ever-slipping goloshes, for the weather was on the edge of more rain. She gathered fire-lighters from the kitchen, a half-scuttle of coals, and a faggot of brushwood. These she wheeled in the barrow down the mossed paths to the dank little laurel shrubbery where the destructor stood under the drip of three oaks. She climbed the wire fence into the Rector's glebe just behind, and from his tenant's rick pulled two large armfuls of good hay, which she spread neatly on the fire-bars. Next, journey by journey, passing Miss Fowler's white face at the morning-room window each time, she brought down in the towel-covered clothes-basket, on the wheel-barrow, thumbed and used Hentys, Marryats, Levers, Stevensons, Baroness Orczys, Garvices, schoolbooks, and atlases, unrelated piles of the *Motor Cyclist*, the *Light Car*, and catalogues of Olympia Exhibitions; the remnants of a fleet of sailing-ships from ninepenny cutters to a three-guinea yacht; a prep-school dressing-gown; bats from three-and-sixpence to twenty-four shillings; cricket and tennis balls; disintegrated steam and clockwork locomotives with their twisted rails; a grey and red tin model of a submarine; a dumb gramophone and cracked records; golf-clubs that had to be broken across the knee, like his walking-sticks, and an assegai; photographs of private and public school cricket and football elevens, and his O.T.C. on the line of march; kodaks, and film-rolls; some pewters, and one real silver cup, for boxing competitions and Junior Hurdles; sheaves of school photographs; Miss Fowler's photograph; her own which he had borne off in fun and (good care she took not to ask!) had never returned; a playbox with a secret drawer; a load of flannels, belts, and jerseys, and a pair of spiked shoes unearthed in the attic; a packet of all the letters that Miss Fowler and she had ever written to him, kept for some absurd reason through all these years; a five-day attempt at a diary; framed pictures of racing motors in full Brooklands career, and load upon load of undistinguishable wreckage of tool-boxes, rabbit-hutches, electric batteries, tin soldiers, fret-saw outfits, and jig-saw puzzles.

Miss Fowler at the window watched her come and go, and said to herself, "Mary's an old woman. I never realised it before."

After lunch she recommended her to rest.

"I'm not in the least tired," said Mary. "I've got it all arranged. I'm going to the village at two o'clock for some paraffin. Nellie hasn't enough, and the walk will do me good."

She made one last quest round the house before she started, and found that she had overlooked nothing. It began to mist as soon as she had skirted Vegg's Heath, where Wynn used to descend—it seemed to her that she could almost hear the beat of his propellers overhead, but there was nothing to see. She hoisted her umbrella and lunged into the blind wet till she had reached the shelter of the empty village. As she came out of Mr. Kidd's shop with a bottle full of paraffin in her string shopping-bag, she met Nurse Eden, the village nurse, and fell into talk with her, as usual, about the village children. They were just parting opposite the "Royal Oak," when a gun, they fancied, was fired immediately behind the house. It was followed by a child's shriek dying into a wail.

"Accident!" said Nurse Eden promptly, and dashed through the empty bar, followed by Mary. They found Mrs. Gerritt, the publican's wife, who could only gasp and point to the yard, where a little cart-lodge was sliding sideways amid a clatter of tiles. Nurse Eden snatched up a sheet drying before the fire, ran out, lifted something from the ground, and flung the sheet round it. The sheet turned scarlet and half her uniform too, as she bore the load into the kitchen. It was little Edna Gerritt, aged nine, whom Mary had known since her perambulator days.

"Am I hurted bad?" Edna asked, and died between Nurse Eden's dripping hands. The sheet fell aside and for an instant, before she could shut her eyes, Mary saw the ripped and shredded body.

"It's a wonder she spoke at all," said Nurse Eden. "What in God's name was it?"

"A bomb," said Mary.

"One o' the Zeppelins?"

"No. An aeroplane. I thought I heard it on the Heath, but I fancied it was one of ours. It must have shut off its engines as it came down. That's why we didn't notice it."

"The filthy pigs!" said Nurse Eden, all white and shaken. "See the pickle I'm in! Go and tell Dr. Hennis, Miss Postgate." Nurse looked at the mother, who had dropped face down on the floor. "She's only in a fit. Turn her over."

Mary heaved Mrs. Gerritt right side up, and hurried off for the doctor. When she told her tale, he asked her to sit down in the surgery till he got her something.

"But I don't need it, I assure you," said she. "I don't think it would be wise to tell Miss Fowler about it, do you? Her heart is so irritable in this weather."

Dr. Hennis looked at her admiringly as he packed up his bag.

"No. Don't tell anybody till we're sure," he said, and hastened to the "Royal Oak," while Mary went on with the paraffin. The village behind her was as quiet as usual, for the news had not yet spread. She frowned a little to herself, her large nostrils expanded uglily, and from time to time she muttered a phrase which Wynn, who never restrained himself before his womenfolk, had applied to the enemy. "Bloody pagans! They *are* bloody pagans. But," she continued, falling back on the teaching that had made her what she was, "one mustn't let one's mind dwell on these things."

Before she reached the house Dr. Hennis, who was also a special constable, overtook her in his car.

"Oh, Miss Postgate," he said, "I wanted to tell you that that accident at the "Royal Oak" was due to Gerritt's stable tumbling down. It's been dangerous for a long time. It ought to have been condemned."

"I thought I heard an explosion too," said Mary.

"You might have been misled by the beams snapping. I've been looking at "em. They were dry-rotted through and through. Of course, as they broke, they would make a noise just like a gun."

"Yes?" said Mary politely.

"Poor little Edna was playing underneath it," he went on, still holding her with his eyes, "and that and the tiles cut her to pieces, you see?"

"I saw it," said Mary, shaking her head. "I heard it too."

"Well, we cannot be sure." Dr. Hennis changed his tone completely. "I know both you and Nurse Eden (I've been speaking to her) are perfectly trustworthy, and I can rely on you not to say anything—yet at least. It is no good to stir up people unless—"

"Oh, I never do—anyhow," said Mary, and Dr. Hennis went on to the county town.

After all, she told herself, it might, just possibly, have been the collapse of the old stable that had done all those things to poor little Edna. She was sorry she had even hinted at other things, but Nurse

Eden was discretion itself. By the time she reached home the affair seemed increasingly remote by its very monstrosity. As she came in, Miss Fowler told her that a couple of aeroplanes had passed half an hour ago.

"I thought I heard them," she replied, "I'm going down to the garden now. I've got the paraffin."

"Yes, but—what *have* you got on your boots? They're soaking wet. Change them at once."

Not only did Mary obey but she wrapped the boots in a newspaper, and put them into the string bag with the bottle. So, armed with the longest kitchen poker, she left.

"It's raining again," was Miss Fowler's last word, "but—I know you won't be happy till that's disposed of."

"It won't take long. I've got everything down there, and I've put the lid on the destructor to keep the wet out."

The shrubbery was filling with twilight by the time she had completed her arrangements and sprinkled the sacrificial oil. As she lit the match that would burn her heart to ashes, she heard a groan or a grunt behind the dense Portugal laurels.

"Cheape?" she called impatiently, but Cheape, with his ancient lumbago, in his comfortable cottage would be the last man to profane the sanctuary. "Sheep," she concluded, and threw in the fusee. The pyre went up in a roar, and the immediate flame hastened night around her.

"How Wynn would have loved this!" she thought, stepping back from the blaze.

By its light she saw, half hidden behind a laurel not five paces away, a bareheaded man sitting very stiffly at the foot of one of the oaks. A broken branch lay across his lap—one booted leg protruding from beneath it. His head moved ceaselessly from side to side, but his body was as still as the tree's trunk. He was dressed—she moved sideways to look more closely—in a uniform something like Wynn's, with a flap buttoned across the chest. For an instant, she had some idea that it might be one of the young flying men she had met at the funeral. But their heads were dark and glossy. This man's was as pale as a baby's, and so closely cropped that she could see the disgusting pinky skin beneath. His lips moved.

"What do you say?" Mary moved towards him and stooped.

"Laty! Laty! Laty!" he muttered, while his hands picked at the dead wet leaves. There was no doubt as to his nationality. It made her so angry that she strode back to the destructor, though it was still too hot to use the poker there. Wynn's books seemed to be catching well. She looked up at the oak behind the man; several of the light upper and two or three rotten lower branches had broken and scattered their rubbish on the shrubbery path. On the lowest fork a helmet with dependent strings, showed like a bird's nest in the light of a long-tongued flame. Evidently this person had fallen through the tree. Wynn had told her that it was quite possible for people to fall out of aeroplanes. Wynn told her too, that trees were useful things to break an aviator's fall, but in this case the aviator must have been broken or he would have moved from his queer position. He seemed helpless except for his horrible rolling head. On the other hand, she could see a pistol case at his belt—and Mary loathed pistols. Months ago, after reading certain Belgian reports together, she and Miss Fowler had had dealings with one—a huge revolver with flat-nosed bullets, which latter, Wynn said, were forbidden by the rules of war to be used against civilised enemies. "They're good enough for us," Miss Fowler had replied. "Show Mary how it works." And Wynn, laughing at the mere possibility of any such need, had led the craven winking Mary into the Rector's disused quarry, and had shown her how to fire the terrible machine. It lay now in the top-left-hand drawer of her toilet-table—a memento not included in the burning. Wynn would be pleased to see how she was not afraid.

She slipped up to the house to get it. When she came through the rain, the eyes in the head were alive with expectation. The mouth even tried to smile. But at sight of the revolver its corners went down just like Edna Gerritt's. A tear trickled from one eye, and the head rolled from shoulder to shoulder as though trying to point out something.

"Cassée. Tout cassée," it whimpered.

"What do you say?" said Mary disgustedly, keeping well to one side, though only the head moved.

"Cassée," it repeated. "Che me rends. Le médicin! Toctor!"

"Nein!" said she, bringing all her small German to bear with the big pistol. "Ich haben der todt Kinder gesehn."

The head was still. Mary's hand dropped. She had been careful to keep her finger off the trigger for fear of accidents. After a few moments' waiting, she returned to the destructor, where the flames were falling, and churned up Wynn's charring books with the poker. Again the head groaned for the doctor.

"Stop that!" said Mary, and stamped her foot. "Stop that, you bloody pagan!"

The words came quite smoothly and naturally. They were Wynn's own words, and Wynn was a gentleman who for no consideration on earth would have torn little Edna into those vividly coloured strips and strings. But this thing hunched under the oak-tree had done that thing. It was no question of reading horrors out of newspapers to Miss Fowler. Mary had seen it with her own eyes on the "Royal Oak" kitchen table. She must not allow her mind to dwell upon it. Now Wynn was dead, and everything connected with him was lumping and rustling and tinkling under her busy poker into red black dust and grey leaves of ash. The thing beneath the oak would die too. Mary had seen death more than once. She came of a family that had a knack of dying under, as she told Miss Fowler, "most distressing circumstances." She would stay where she was till she was entirely satisfied that It was dead—dead as dear papa in the late "eighties; aunt Mary in eighty-nine; mamma in "ninety-one; cousin Dick in ninety-five; Lady McCausland's housemaid in "ninety-nine; Lady McCausland's sister in nineteen hundred and one; Wynn buried five days ago; and Edna Gerritt still waiting for decent earth to hide her. As she thought—her underlip caught up by one faded canine, brows knit and nostrils wide—she wielded the poker with lunges that jarred the grating at the bottom, and careful scrapes round the brick-work above. She looked at her wrist-watch. It was getting on to half-past four, and the rain was coming down in earnest. Tea would be at five. If It did not die before that time, she would be soaked and would have to change. Meantime, and this occupied her, Wynn's things were burning well in spite of the hissing wet, though now and again a book-back with a quite distinguishable title would be heaved up out of the mass. The exercise of stoking had given her a glow which seemed to reach to the marrow of her bones. She hummed—Mary never had a voice—to herself. She had never believed in all those advanced views—though Miss Fowler herself leaned a little that way—of woman's work in the world; but now she saw there was much to be said for them. This, for instance, was *her* work—work which no man, least of all Dr. Hennis, would ever have done. A man, at such a crisis, would be what Wynn called a "sportsman"; would leave everything to fetch help, and would certainly bring It into the house. Now a woman's business was to make a happy home for—for a husband and children. Failing these—it was not a thing one should allow one's mind to dwell upon—but—

"Stop it!" Mary cried once more across the shadows. "Nein, I tell you! Ich haben der todt Kinder gesehn."

But it was a fact. A woman who had missed these things could still be useful—more useful than a man in certain respects. She thumped like a pavior through the settling ashes at the secret thrill of it. The rain was damping the fire, but she could feel—it was too dark to see—that her work was done. There was a dull red glow at the bottom of the destructor, not enough to char the wooden lid if she slipped it half over against the driving wet. This arranged, she leaned on the poker and waited, while an increasing rapture laid hold on her. She ceased to think. She gave herself up to feel. Her long pleasure was broken by a sound that she had waited for in agony several times in her life. She leaned forward and listened, smiling. There could be no mistake. She closed her eyes and drank it in. Once it ceased abruptly.

"Go on," she murmured, half aloud. "That isn't the end."

Then the end came very distinctly in a lull between two rain-gusts. Mary Postgate drew her breath short between her teeth and shivered from head to foot. "*That's* all right," said she contentedly, and went up to the house, where she scandalised the whole routine by taking a luxurious hot bath before tea, and came down looking, as Miss Fowler said when she saw her lying all relaxed on the other sofa, "quite handsome!"

The Spider's Thread

Ryunosuke Akutagawa

Ryunosuke Akutagawa (1892-1927) was a celebrated Japanese writer who drew inspiration from Japanese and Chinese history for his stories and gave them a modern psychological flavour. Widely acclaimed for his creative twists, his stories have been translated into several languages. 'The Spider's Thread' was first published in the children's magazine *Akai Tori* (1918).

One day, the Buddha was strolling along the brink of the lotus pond of Paradise. His eyes fell on a man named Kandata who was squirming with the other sinners in the bottom of hell. This Kandata had done so many evil things his lifeline but he had to his credit one good action. Once, while on his way through a deep forest, he had noticed a little spider creeping along beside the road. He was about to trample it to death when he suddenly changed his mind and spared the spider's life.

Now, as he looked down into hell, the Buddha remembered this good deed and thought he would like to deliver Kandata out of hell. Looking around he saw a spider of Paradise spinning a beautiful silvery thread on the lotus leaves. The Buddha took up the spider's thread in his hand and let it straight down to the bottom of hell which held Kandata securely with the other sinners in the Pool of Blood on the floor of hell.

On this day, Kandata lifted his head by chance and saw a silver spider's thread slipping down toward him from the high heavens. Kandata grasped the thread tightly in his two hands and began to climb up and up with all his might.

After climbing for a while, he was finally exhausted and could not ascend an inch higher. He stopped to rest and looked below him. What he saw filled him with fear. For, below on the thread, countless sinners were climbing eagerly after him up and up, like a procession of ants.

Kandata blinked his eyes at them with his big mouth hanging foolishly open in surprise and terror. How could that slender spider spider's thread which seemed as if it must break with him alone, ever support the weight of all those people? If it would break in mid air, even he himself would have to fall headlong back to Hell.

So Kandata cried out in loud voice. "Hey, you sinners! This thread is mine. Who gave you permission to come up it? Get down! Get down!"

At that moment, the spider's thread broke with a snap t the point where Kandata was hanging. Without even time to utter a cry, Kandata shot down and fell headlong into the darkness, spinning swiftly around and around like a top.

Bliss

Katherine Mansfield

Kathleen Mansfield Beauchamp (1888-1923), popularly known as Katherine Mansfield, was a New Zealand-born English writer considered a master of the short story genre. Her stories are notable for the interiority of the characters, brilliant observation and subtlety of narration. Mansfield played a pivotal role in the development of the short story. 'Bliss' (1918) is the epitome of Mansfield's unique style.

Although Bertha Young was thirty she still had moments like this when she wanted to run instead of walk, to take dancing steps on and off the pavement, to bowl a hoop, to throw something up in the air and catch it again, or to stand still and laugh at–nothing–at nothing, simply.

What can you do if you are thirty and, turning the corner of your own street, you are overcome, suddenly by a feeling of bliss–absolute bliss!–as though you'd suddenly swallowed a bright piece of that late afternoon sun and it burned in your bosom, sending out a little shower of sparks into every particle, into every finger and toe? ...

Oh, is there no way you can express it without being "drunk and disorderly"? How idiotic civilisation is! Why be given a body if you have to keep it shut up in a case like a rare, rare fiddle?

"No, that about the fiddle is not quite what I mean," she thought, running up the steps and feeling in her bag for the key–she'd forgotten it, as usual–and rattling the letter-box. "It's not what I mean, because–Thank you, Mary"–she went into the hall. "Is nurse back?"

"Yes, M'm."

"And has the fruit come?"

"Yes, M'm. Everything's come."

"Bring the fruit up to the dining-room, will you? I'll arrange it before I go upstairs."

It was dusky in the dining-room and quite chilly. But all the same Bertha threw off her coat; she could not bear the tight clasp of it another moment, and the cold air fell on her arms.

But in her bosom there was still that bright glowing place–that shower of little sparks coming from it. It was almost unbearable. She hardly dared to breathe for fear of fanning it higher, and yet she breathed deeply, deeply. She hardly dared to look into the cold mirror–but she did look, and it gave her back a woman, radiant, with smiling, trembling lips, with big, dark eyes and an air of listening, waiting for something…divine to happen…that she knew must happen…infallibly.

Mary brought in the fruit on a tray and with it a glass bowl, and a blue dish, very lovely, with a strange sheen on it as though it had been dipped in milk.

"Shall I turn on the light, M'm?"

"No, thank you. I can see quite well."

There were tangerines and apples stained with strawberry pink. Some yellow pears, smooth as silk, some white grapes covered with a silver bloom and a big cluster of purple ones. These last she had bought to tone in with the new dining-room carpet. Yes, that did sound rather far-fetched and absurd, but it was really why she had bought them. She had thought in the shop: "I must have some purple ones to bring the carpet up to the table." And it had seemed quite sense at the time.

When she had finished with them and had made two pyramids of these bright round shapes, she stood away from the table to get the effect–and it really was most curious. For the dark table seemed to melt into the dusky light and the glass dish and the blue bowl to float in the air. This, of course, in her present mood, was so incredibly beautiful… She began to laugh.

"No, no. I'm getting hysterical." And she seized her bag and coat and ran upstairs to the nursery.

Nurse sat at a low table giving Little B her supper after her bath. The baby had on a white flannel gown and a blue woollen jacket, and her dark, fine hair was brushed up into a funny little peak. She looked up when she saw her mother and began to jump.

"Now, my lovey, eat it up like a good girl," said nurse, setting her lips in a way that Bertha knew, and that meant she had come into the nursery at another wrong moment.

"Has she been good, Nanny?"

"She's been a little sweet all the afternoon," whispered Nanny. "We went to the park and I sat down on a chair and took her out of the pram and a big dog came along and put its head on my knee and she clutched its ear, tugged it. Oh, you should have seen her."

Bertha wanted to ask if it wasn't rather dangerous to let her clutch at a strange dog's ear. But she did not dare to. She stood watching them, her hands by her side, like the poor little girl in front of the rich girl with the doll.

The baby looked up at her again, stared, and then smiled so charmingly that Bertha couldn't help crying:

"Oh, Nanny, do let me finish giving her her supper while you put the bath things away.

"Well, M'm, she oughtn't to be changed hands while she's eating, said Nanny, still whispering. "It unsettles her; it's very likely to upset her."

How absurd it was. Why have a baby if it has to be kept–not in a case like a rare, rare fiddle–but in another woman's arms?

"Oh, I must!" said she.

Very offended, Nanny handed her over.

"Now, don't excite her after her supper. You know you do, M'm. And I have such a time with her after!"

Thank heaven! Nanny went out of the room with the bath towels.

"Now I've got you to myself, my little precious," said Bertha, as the baby leaned against her.

She ate delightfully, holding up her lips for the spoon and then waving her hands. Sometimes she wouldn't let the spoon go; and sometimes, just as Bertha had filled it, she waved it away to the four winds.

When the soup was finished Bertha turned round to the fire. "You're nice–you're very nice!" said she, kissing her warm baby. "I'm fond of you. I like you."

And indeed, she loved Little B so much–her neck as she bent forward, her exquisite toes as they shone transparent in the firelight–that all her feeling of bliss came back again, and again she didn't know how to express it–what to do with it.

"You're wanted on the telephone," said Nanny, coming back in triumph and seizing *her* Little B.

Down she flew. It was Harry.

"Oh, is that you, Ber? Look here. I'll be late. I'll take a taxi and come along as quickly as I can, but get dinner put back ten minutes–will you? All right?"

"Yes, perfectly. Oh, Harry!"

"Yes?"

What had she to say? She'd nothing to say. She only wanted to get in touch with him for a moment. She couldn't absurdly cry: "Hasn't it been a divine day!"

"What is it?" rapped out the little voice.

"Nothing. *Entendu*," said Bertha, and hung up the receiver, thinking how much more than idiotic civilisation was.

They had people coming to dinner. The Norman Knights–a very sound couple–he was about to start a theatre, and she was awfully keen on interior decoration, a young man, Eddie Warren, who had just published a little book of poems and whom everybody was asking to dine, and a "find" of Bertha's called Pearl Fulton. What Miss Fulton did, Bertha didn't know. They had met at the club and Bertha had fallen in love with her, as she always did fall in love with beautiful women who had something strange about them.

The provoking thing was that, though they had been about together and met a number of times and really talked, Bertha couldn't make her out. Up to a certain point Miss Fulton was rarely, wonderfully frank, but the certain point was there, and beyond that she would not go.

Was there anything beyond it? Harry said, "No." Voted her dullish, and "cold like all blonde women, with a touch, perhaps, of anaemia of the brain." But Bertha wouldn't agree with him; not yet, at any rate.

"No, the way she has of sitting with her head a little on one side, and smiling, has something behind it, Harry, and I must find out what that something is."

"Most likely it's a good stomach," answered Harry.

He made a point of catching Bertha's heels with replies of that kind ... "liver frozen, my dear girl," or "pure flatulence," or "kidney disease," ... and so on. For some strange reason Bertha liked this, and almost admired it in him very much.

She went into the drawing-room and lighted the fire; then, picking up the cushions, one by one, that Mary had disposed so carefully, she threw them back on to the chairs and the couches. That made all the difference; the room came alive at once. As she was about to throw the last one she surprised herself by suddenly hugging it to her, passionately, passionately. But it did not put out the fire in her bosom. Oh, on the contrary!

The windows of the drawing-room opened on to a balcony overlooking the garden. At the far end, against the wall, there was a tall, slender pear tree in fullest, richest bloom; it stood perfect, as though becalmed against the jade-green sky. Bertha couldn't help feeling, even from this distance, that it had not a single bud or a faded petal. Down below, in the garden beds, the red and yellow tulips, heavy with flowers, seemed to lean upon the dusk. A grey cat, dragging its belly, crept across the lawn, and a black one, its shadow, trailed after. The sight of them, so intent and so quick, gave Bertha a curious shiver.

"What creepy things cats are!" she stammered, and she turned away from the window and began walking up and down....

How strong the jonquils smelled in the warm room. Too strong? Oh, no. And yet, as though overcome, she flung down on a couch and pressed her hands to her eyes.

"I'm too happy–too happy!" she murmured.

And she seemed to see on her eyelids the lovely pear tree with its wide open blossoms as a symbol of her own life.

Really–really–she had everything. She was young. Harry and she were as much in love as ever, and they got on together splendidly and were really good pals. She had an adorable baby. They didn't have to worry about money. They had this absolutely satisfactory house and garden. And friends–modern, thrilling friends, writers and painters and poets or people keen on social questions–just the kind of friends they wanted. And then there were books, and there was music, and she had found a wonderful little dressmaker, and they were going abroad in the summer, and their new cook made the most superb omelettes…

"I'm absurd. Absurd!" She sat up; but she felt quite dizzy, quite drunk. It must have been the spring.

Yes, it was the spring. Now she was so tired she could not drag herself upstairs to dress.

A white dress, a string of jade beads, green shoes and stockings. It wasn't intentional. She had thought of this scheme hours before she stood at the drawing-room window.

Her petals rustled softly into the hall, and she kissed Mrs. Norman Knight, who was taking off the most amusing orange coat with a procession of black monkeys round the hem and up the fronts.

"…Why! Why! Why is the middle-class so stodgy–so utterly without a sense of humour! My dear, it's only by a fluke that I am here at all–Norman being the protective fluke. For my darling monkeys so upset the train that it rose to a man and simply ate me with its eyes. Didn't laugh–wasn't amused–that I should have loved. No, just stared–and bored me through and through."

"But the cream of it was," said Norman, pressing a large tortoise-shell-rimmed monocle into his eye, "you don't mind me telling this, Face, do you?" (In their home and among their friends they called each other Face and Mug.) "The cream of it was when she, being full fed, turned to the woman beside her and said: 'Haven't you ever seen a monkey before?'"

"Oh, yes!" Mrs. Norman Knight joined in the laughter. "Wasn't that too absolutely creamy?"

And a funnier thing still was that now her coat was off she did look like a very intelligent monkey–who had even made that yellow silk dress out of scraped banana skins. And her amber earrings: they were like little dangling nuts.

"This is a sad, sad fall!" said Mug, pausing in front of Little B's perambulator. "When the perambulator comes into the hall–" and he waved the rest of the quotation away.

The bell rang. It was lean, pale Eddie Warren (as usual) in a state of acute distress.

"It *is* the right house, *isn't* it?" he pleaded.

"Oh, I think so–I hope so," said Bertha brightly.

"I have had such a *dreadful* experience with a taxi-man; he was *most* sinister. I couldn't get him to stop. The *more* I knocked and called the *faster* he went. And *in* the moonlight this *bizarre* figure with the *flattened* head *crouching* over the *lit-tle* wheel..."

He shuddered, taking off an immense white silk scarf. Bertha noticed that his socks were white, too–most charming.

"But how dreadful!" she cried.

"Yes, it really was," said Eddie, following her into the drawing-room. "I saw myself *driving* through Eternity in a *timeless* taxi."

He knew the Norman Knights. In fact, he was going to write a play for N.K. when the theatre scheme came off.

"Well, Warren, how's the play?" said Norman Knight, dropping his monocle and giving his eye a moment in which to rise to the surface before it was screwed down again.

And Mrs. Norman Knight: "Oh, Mr. Warren, what happy socks?"

"I *am* so glad you like them," said he, staring at his feet. "They seem to have got so *much* whiter since the moon rose." And he turned his lean sorrowful young face to Bertha. "There *is* a moon, you know."

She wanted to cry, "I am sure there is–often–often!"

He really was a most attractive person. But so was Face, crouched before the fire in her banana skins, and so was Mug, smoking a cigarette and saying as he flicked the ash: "Why doth the bridegroom tarry?"

"There he is, now."

Bang went the front door open and shut. Harry shouted: "Hullo, you people. Down in five minutes." And they heard him swarm up the stairs. Bertha couldn't knew how he loved doing things at high pressure. What, after all, help smiling; she did an extra five minutes matter? But he would pretend to himself that they mattered beyond measure. And then he would make a great point of coming into the drawing-room, extravagantly cool and collected.

Harry had such a zest for life. Oh, how she appreciated it in him. And his passion for fighting–for seeking in everything that came up against him another test of his power and of his courage–that, too, she understood. Even when it made him just occasionally, to other people, who didn't know him well, a little ridiculous perhaps... For there were moments when he rushed into battle where no battle was... She talked and laughed and positively forgot until he had come in (just as she had imagined) that Pearl Fulton had not turned up.

"I wonder if Miss Fulton has forgotten?"

"I expect so," said Harry. "Is she on the 'phone?"

"Ah! There's a taxi, now." And Bertha smiled with that little air of proprietorship that she always assumed while her women finds were new and mysterious. "She lives in taxis."

"She'll run to fat if she does," said Harry coolly, ringing the bell for dinner. "Frightful danger for blonde women "

"Harry–don't!" warned Bertha, laughing up at him.

Came another tiny moment, while they waited, laughing and talking, just a trifle too much at their ease, a trifle too unaware. And then Miss Fulton, all in silver, with a silver fillet binding her pale blonde hair, came in smiling, her head a little on one side.

"Am I late?"

"No, not at all," said Bertha. "Come along." And she took her arm and they moved into the dining-room.

What was there in the touch of that cool arm that could fan–fan–start blazing–blazing–the fire of bliss that Bertha did not know what to do with?

Miss Fulton did not look at her; but then she seldom did look at people directly. Her heavy eyelids lay upon her eyes and the strange half-smile came and went upon her lips as though she lived by listening rather than seeing. But Bertha knew, suddenly, as if the longest, most intimate look had passed between them–as if they had said to each other, "You too?"–that Pearl Fulton, stirring the beautiful red soup in the grey plate, was feeling just what she was feeling.

And the others? Face and Mug, Eddie and Harry, their spoons rising and falling–dabbing their lips with their napkins, crumbling bread, fiddling with the forks and glasses and talking.

"I met her at the Alpha show–the weirdest little person. She'd not only cut off her hair, but she seemed to have taken a dreadfully good snip off her legs and arms and her neck and her poor little nose as well."

"Isn't she very *liée* with Michael Oat?"

"The man who wrote *Love in False Teeth?*"

"He wants to write a play for me. One act. One man. Decides to commit suicide. Gives all the reasons why he should and why he shouldn't. And just as he has made up his mind either to do it or not to do it–curtain. Not half a bad idea."

"What's he going to call it–'Stomach Trouble' ?"

"I *think* I've come across the *same* idea in a little French review, *quite* unknown in England."

No, they didn't share it. They were dears–dears–and she loved having them there, at her table, and giving them delicious food and wine. In fact, she longed to tell them how delightful they were, and what a decorative group they made, how they seemed to set one another off and how they reminded her of a play by Tchekof!

Harry was enjoying his dinner. It was part of his–well, not his nature, exactly, and certainly not his pose–his–something or other–to talk about food and to glory in his "shameless passion for the white flash of the lobster" and "the green of pistachio ices–green and cold like the eyelids of Egyptian dancers."

When he looked up at her and said, "Bertha, this is a very admirable *soufflée!*" she almost could have wept with child-like pleasure.

Oh, why did she feel so tender towards the whole world tonight? Everything was good–was right. All that happened seemed to fill again her brimming cup of bliss.

And still, in the back of her mind, there was the pear tree. It would be silver now, in the light of poor dear Eddie's moon, silver as Miss Fulton, who sat there turning a tangerine in her slender fingers that were so pale a light seemed to come from them.

What she simply couldn't make out–what was miraculous–was how she should have guessed Miss Fulton's mood so exactly and so instantly. For she never doubted for a moment that she was right, and yet what had she to go on? Less than nothing.

"I believe this does happen very, very rarely between women. Never between men," thought Bertha. "But while I am making the coffee in the drawing-room perhaps she will 'give a sign'".

What she meant by that she did not know, and what would happen after that she could not imagine.

While she thought like this she saw herself talking and laughing. She had to talk because of her desire to laugh.

"I must laugh or die."

But when she noticed Face's funny little habit of tucking something down the front of her bodice–as if she kept a tiny, secret hoard of nuts there, too–Bertha had to dig her nails into her hands–so as not to laugh too much.

It was over at last. And: "Come and see my new coffee machine," said Bertha.

"We only have a new coffee machine once a fortnight," said Harry. Face took her arm this time; Miss Fulton bent her head and followed after.

The fire had died down in the drawing-room to a red, flickering "nest of baby phoenixes," said Face.

"Don't turn up the light for a moment. It is so lovely." And down she crouched by the fire again. She was always cold… "without her little red flannel jacket, of course," thought Bertha.

At that moment Miss Fulton "gave the sign."

"Have you a garden?" said the cool, sleepy voice.

This was so exquisite on her part that all Bertha could do was to obey. She crossed the room, pulled the curtains apart, and opened those long windows.

"There!" she breathed.

And the two women stood side by side looking at the slender, flowering tree. Although it was so still it seemed, like the flame of a candle, to stretch up, to point, to quiver in the bright air, to grow taller and taller as they gazed–almost to touch the rim of the round, silver moon.

How long did they stand there? Both, as it were, caught in that circle of unearthly light, understanding each other perfectly, creatures of another world, and wondering what they were to do in this one with all this blissful treasure that burned in their bosoms and dropped, in silver flowers, from their hair and hands?

For ever–for a moment? And did Miss Fulton murmur: "Yes. Just *that*." Or did Bertha dream it?

Then the light was snapped on and Face made the coffee and Harry said: "My dear Mrs. Knight, don't ask me about my baby. I never see her. I shan't feel the slightest interest in her until she has a lover," and Mug took his eye out of the conservatory for a moment and then put it under glass again and Eddie Warren drank his coffee and set down the cup with a face of anguish as though he had drunk and seen the spider.

"What I want to do is to give the young men a show. I believe London is simply teeming with first-chop, unwritten plays. What I want to say to 'em is: 'Here's the theatre. Fire ahead.'"

"You know, my dear, I am going to decorate a room for the Jacob Nathans. Oh, I am so tempted to do a fried-fish scheme, with the backs of the chairs shaped like frying-pans and lovely chip potatoes embroidered all over the curtains."

"The trouble with our young writing men is that they are still too romantic. You can't put out to sea without being seasick and wanting a basin. Well, why won't they have the courage of those basins?"

"A *dreadful* poem about a *girl* who was *violated* by a beggar *without* a nose in a little wood..."

Miss Fulton sank into the lowest, deepest chair and Harry handed round the cigarettes.

From the way he stood in front of her shaking the silver box and saying abruptly: "Egyptian? Turkish? Virginian? They're all mixed up," Bertha realised that she not only bored him; he really disliked her. And she decided from the way Miss Fulton said: "No, thank you, I won't smoke," that she felt it, too, and was hurt.

"Oh, Harry, don't dislike her. You are quite wrong about her. She's wonderful, wonderful. And, besides, how can you feel so differently about someone who means so much to me. I shall try to tell you when we are in bed tonight what has been happening. What she and I have shared."

At those last words something strange and almost terrifying darted into Bertha's mind. And this something blind and smiling whispered to her: "Soon these people will go. The house will be quiet–quiet. The lights will be out. And you and he will be alone together in the dark room–the warm bed..."

She jumped up from her chair and ran over to the piano.

"What a pity someone does not play!" she cried. "What a pity somebody does not play."

For the first time in her life Bertha Young desired her husband. Oh, she'd loved him–she'd been in love with him, of course, in every other way, but just not in that way. And equally, of course, she'd understood that he was different. They'd discussed it so often. It had worried her dreadfully at first to find that she was so cold, but after a time it had not seemed to matter. They were so frank with each other–such good pals. That was the best of being modern.

But now–ardently! Ardently! The word ached in her ardent body! Was this what that feeling of bliss had been leading up to? But then, then–"My dear," said Mrs. Norman Knight, "you know our shame. We are the victims of time and train. We live in Hampstead. It's been so nice."

"I'll come with you into the hall," said Bertha. "I loved having you. But you must not miss the last train. That's so awful, isn't it?"

"Have a whisky, Knight, before you go?" called Harry.

"No, thanks, old chap."

Bertha squeezed his hand for that as she shook it.

"Good night, goodbye," she cried from the top step, feeling that this self of hers was taking leave of them for ever.

When she got back into the drawing-room the others were on the move.

"... Then you can come part of the way in my taxi."

"I shall be *so* thankful *not* to have to face *another* drive *alone* after my *dreadful* experience."

"You can get a taxi at the rank just at the end of the street. You won't have to walk more than a few yards."

"That's a comfort. I'll go and put on my coat."

Miss Fulton moved towards the hall and Bertha was following when Harry almost pushed past.

"Let me help you."

Bertha knew that he was repenting his rudeness–she let him go. What a boy he was in some ways–so impulsive–so–simple.

And Eddie and she were left by the fire.

"I *wonder* if you have seen Bilks' *new* poem called *Table d'Hôte*," said Eddie softly. "It's *so* wonderful. In the last Anthology. Have you got a copy? I'd *so* like to *show* it to you. It begins with an *incredibly* beautiful line: 'Why Must it Always be Tomato Soup?'"

"Yes," said Bertha. And she moved noiselessly to a table opposite the drawing-room door and Eddie glided noiselessly after her. She picked up the little book and gave it to him; they had not made a sound.

While he looked it up she turned her head towards the hall. And she saw... Harry with Miss Fulton's coat in his arms and Miss Fulton with her back turned to him and her head bent. He tossed the coat away, put his hands on her shoulders and turned her violently to him. His lips said: "I adore you," and Miss Fulton laid her moonbeam fingers on his cheeks and smiled her sleepy smile. Harry's nostrils quivered; his lips curled back in a hideous grin while he whispered: "Tomorrow," and with her eyelids Miss Fulton said: "Yes."

"Here it is," said Eddie. "'Why Must it Always be Tomato Soup?' It's so *deeply* true, don't you feel? Tomato soup is so *dreadfully* eternal."

"If you prefer," said Harry's voice, very loud, from the hall, "I can phone you a cab to come to the door."

"Oh, no. It's not necessary," said Miss Fulton, and she came up to Bertha and gave her the slender fingers to hold.

"Goodbye. Thank you so much."

"Goodbye," said Bertha.

Miss Fulton held her hand a moment longer.

"Your lovely pear tree!" she murmured.

And then she was gone, with Eddie following, like the black cat following the grey cat.

"I'll shut up shop," said Harry, extravagantly cool and collected.

"Your lovely pear tree–pear tree–pear tree!"

Bertha simply ran over to the long windows.

"Oh, what is going to happen now?" she cried.

But the pear tree was as lovely as ever and as full of flower and as still.

The Mark On The Wall

Virginia Woolf

Virginia Woolf (1882-1941), an English writer, was one of the greatest modernists of the 20th century. She played a crucial role in the development of the novel as a form and stream-of-consciousness as a narrative mode. She was a prolific writer of novels, short stories and essays on women's rights, politics of power as well as anti-war pieces. 'The Mark On The Wall' (1919) is a typical stream-of-consciousness story, of which Woolf was a master.

Perhaps it was the middle of January in the present that I first looked up and saw the mark on the wall. In order to fix a date it is necessary to remember what one saw. So now I think of the fire; the steady film of yellow light upon the page of my book; the three chrysanthemums in the round glass bowl on the mantelpiece. Yes, it must have been the winter time, and we had just finished our tea, for I remember that I was smoking a cigarette when I looked up and saw the mark on the wall for the first time. I looked up through the smoke of my cigarette and my eye lodged for a moment upon the burning coals, and that old fancy of the crimson flag flapping from the castle tower came into my mind, and I thought of the cavalcade of red knights riding up the side of the black rock. Rather to my relief the sight of the mark interrupted the fancy, for it is an old fancy, an automatic fancy, made as a child perhaps. The mark was a small round mark, black upon the white wall, about six or seven inches above the mantelpiece.

How readily our thoughts swarm upon a new object, lifting it a little way, as ants carry a blade of straw so feverishly, and then leave it ... If that mark was made by a nail, it can't have been for a picture, it must have been for a miniature—the miniature of a lady with white powdered curls, powder-dusted cheeks, and lips like red carnations. A fraud of course, for the people who had this house before us would have chosen pictures in that way—an old picture for an old room. That is the sort of people they were—very interesting people, and I think of them so often, in such queer places, because one will never see them again, never know what happened next. They wanted to leave this house because they wanted to change their style of furniture, so he said, and he was in process of saying that in his opinion art should have ideas behind it when we were torn asunder, as one is torn from the old lady about to pour out tea and the young man about to hit the tennis ball in the back garden of the suburban villa as one rushes past in the train.

But as for that mark, I'm not sure about it; I don't believe it was made by a nail after all; it's too big, too round, for that. I might get up, but if I got up and looked at it, ten to one I shouldn't be able to say for certain; because once a thing's done, no one ever knows how it happened. Oh! Dear me, the mystery of life! The inaccuracy of thought! The ignorance of humanity! To show how very little control of our possessions we have—what an accidental affair this living is after all our civilization—let me just count over a few of the things lost in one lifetime, beginning, for that seems always the most mysterious of losses—what cat would gnaw, what rat would nibble—three pale blue canisters of book-binding tools? Then there were the bird cages, the iron hoops, the steel skates, the Queen Anne coal-scuttle, the bagatelle board, the hand organ—all gone, and jewels, too. Opals and emeralds, they lie about the roots of turnips. What a scraping paring affair it is to be sure! The wonder is that I've any clothes on my back, that I sit surrounded by solid furniture at this moment. Why, if one wants to compare life to anything, one must liken it to being blown through the Tube at fifty miles an hour—landing at the other end without a single hairpin in one's hair! Shot out at the feet of God entirely naked! Tumbling head over heels in the asphodel meadows like brown paper parcels pitched down a shoot in the post office! With one's hair flying back like the tail of a race-horse. Yes, that seems to express the rapidity of life, the perpetual waste and repair; all so casual, all so haphazard...

But after life. The slow pulling down of thick green stalks so that the cup of the flower, as it turns over, deluges one with purple and red light. Why, after all, should one not be born there as one is born here, helpless, speechless, unable to focus one's eyesight, groping at the roots of the grass, at the toes of the Giants? As for saying which are trees, and which are men and women, or whether there are such things, that one won't be in a condition to do for fifty years or so. There will be nothing but spaces of light and dark, intersected by thick stalks, and rather higher up perhaps, rose-shaped blots of an indistinct colour—dim pinks and blues—which will, as time goes on, become more definite, become—I don't know what ...

And yet that mark on the wall is not a hole at all. It may even be caused by some round black substance, such as a small rose leaf, left over from the summer, and I, not being a very vigilant housekeeper—look at the dust on the mantelpiece, for example, the dust which, so they say, buried Troy three times over, only fragments of pots utterly refusing annihilation, as one can believe.

The tree outside the window taps very gently on the pane ... I want to think quietly, calmly, spaciously, never to be interrupted, never to have to rise from my chair, to slip easily from one thing to another, without any sense of hostility, or obstacle. I want to sink deeper and deeper, away from the surface, with its hard separate facts. To steady myself, let me catch hold of the first idea that passes ... Shakespeare ... Well, he will do as well as another. A man who sat himself solidly in an armchair, and looked into the fire, so—A shower of ideas fell perpetually from some very high Heaven down through his mind. He leant his forehead on his hand, and people, looking in through the open door—for this scene is supposed to take place on a summer's evening—But how dull this is, this historical fiction! It doesn't interest me at all. I wish I could hit upon a pleasant track of thought, a track indirectly reflecting credit upon myself, for those are the pleasantest thoughts, and very frequent even in the minds of modest mouse-coloured people, who believe genuinely that they dislike to hear their own praises. They are not thoughts directly praising oneself; that is the beauty of them; they are thoughts like this:

"And then I came into the room. They were discussing botany. I said how I'd seen a flower growing on a dust heap on the site of an old house in Kingsway. The seed, I said, must have been sown in the reign of Charles the First. What flowers grew in the reign of Charles the First?" I asked—(but, I don't remember the answer). Tall flowers with purple tassels to them perhaps. And so it goes on. All the time I'm dressing up the figure of myself in my own mind, lovingly, stealthily, not openly adoring it, for if I did that, I should catch myself out, and stretch my hand at once for a book in self-protection.

Indeed, it is curious how instinctively one protects the image of oneself from idolatry or any other handling that could make it ridiculous, or too unlike the original to be believed in any longer. Or is it not so very curious after all? It is a matter of great importance. Suppose the looking glass smashes, the image disappears, and the romantic figure with the green of forest depths all about it is there no longer, but only that shell of a person which is seen by other people—what an airless, shallow, bald, prominent world it becomes! A world not to be lived in. As we face each other in omnibuses and underground railways we are looking into the mirror that accounts for the vagueness, the gleam of glassiness, in our eyes. And the novelists in future will realize more and more the importance of these reflections, for of course there is not one reflection but an almost infinite number; those are the depths they will explore, those the phantoms they will pursue, leaving the description of reality more and more out of their stories, taking a knowledge of it for granted, as the Greeks did and Shakespeare perhaps—but these generalizations are very worthless. The military sound of the word is enough. It recalls leading articles, cabinet ministers—a whole class of things indeed which as a child one thought the thing itself, the standard thing, the real thing, from which one could not depart save at the risk of nameless damnation. Generalizations bring back somehow Sunday in London, Sunday afternoon walks, Sunday luncheons, and also ways of speaking of the dead, clothes, and habits—like the habit of sitting all together in one room until a certain hour, although nobody liked it. There was a rule for everything. The rule for tablecloths at that particular period was that they should be made of tapestry with little yellow compartments marked upon them, such as you may see in photographs of the carpets in the corridors of the royal palaces. Tablecloths of a different kind were not real tablecloths. How shocking, and yet how wonderful it was to discover that these real things, Sunday luncheons, Sunday walks, country houses, and tablecloths were not entirely real, were indeed half phantoms, and the damnation which visited the disbeliever in them was only a sense of illegitimate freedom. What now takes the place of those things I wonder, those real standard things? Men perhaps, should you be a woman; the masculine point of view which governs our lives, which sets the standard, which establishes Whitaker's Table of Precedency, which has become, I suppose, since the war half a phantom to many men and women, which soon—one may hope, will be laughed into the dustbin where the phantoms go, the mahogany sideboards and the Landseer prints, Gods and Devils, Hell and so forth, leaving us all with an intoxicating sense of illegitimate freedom—if freedom exists ...

In certain lights that mark on the wall seems actually to project from the wall. Nor is it entirely circular. I cannot be sure, but it seems to cast a perceptible shadow, suggesting that if I ran my finger down that strip of the wall it would, at a certain point, mount and descend a small tumulus, a smooth tumulus like those barrows on the South Downs which are, they say, either tombs or camps. Of the two I should prefer them to be tombs, desiring melancholy like most English people, and finding it natural at the end of a walk to think of the bones stretched beneath the turf ... There must be some book about it. Some antiquary must have dug up those bones and given them a name ... What sort of a man is an antiquary, I wonder? Retired Colonels for the most part, I daresay, leading parties of aged labourers to the top here, examining clods of earth and stone, and getting into correspondence with the neighbouring clergy, which, being opened at breakfast time, gives them a feeling of importance, and the comparison of arrow-heads necessitates cross-country journeys to the county towns, an agreeable necessity both to them and to their elderly wives, who wish to make plum jam or to clean out the study, and have every reason for keeping that great question of the camp or the tomb in perpetual suspension, while the Colonel himself feels agreeably philosophic in accumulating evidence on both sides of the question. It is true that he does finally incline to believe in the camp; and, being opposed, indites a pamphlet which he is about to read at the quarterly meeting of the local society when a stroke lays him low, and his last conscious thoughts are not of wife or child, but of the camp and that arrowhead there, which is now in the case at the local museum, together with the foot of a Chinese murderess, a handful of Elizabethan nails, a great many Tudor clay pipes, a piece of Roman pottery, and the wine-glass that Nelson drank out of—proving I really don't know what.

No, no, nothing is proved, nothing is known. And if I were to get up at this very moment and ascertain that the mark on the wall is really—what shall we say?—the head of a gigantic old nail, driven in two hundred years ago, which has now, owing to the patient attrition of many generations of housemaids, revealed its head above the coat of paint, and is taking its first view of modern life in the sight of a white-walled fire-lit room, what should I gain?—Knowledge? Matter for further speculation? I can think sitting still as well as standing up. And what is knowledge? What are our learned men save the descendants of witches and hermits who crouched in caves and in woods brewing herbs, interrogating shrew-mice and writing down the language of the stars? And the less we honour them as our superstitions dwindle and our respect for beauty and health of mind increases ... Yes, one could imagine a very pleasant world. A quiet, spacious world, with the flowers so red and blue in the open fields. A world without professors or specialists or house-keepers with the profiles of policemen, a world which one could slice with one's thought as a fish slices the water with his fin, grazing the stems of the water-lilies, hanging suspended over nests of white sea eggs... How peaceful it is drown here, rooted in the centre of the world and gazing up through the grey waters, with their sudden gleams of light, and their reflections—if it were not for Whitaker's Almanack—if it were not for the Table of Precedency!

I must jump up and see for myself what that mark on the wall really is—a nail, a rose-leaf, a crack in the wood?

Here is nature once more at her old game of self-preservation. This train of thought, she perceives, is threatening mere waste of energy, even some collision with reality, for who will ever be able to lift a finger against Whitaker's Table of Precedency? The Archbishop of Canterbury is followed by the Lord High Chancellor; the Lord High Chancellor is followed by the Archbishop of York. Everybody follows somebody, such is the philosophy of Whitaker; and the great thing is to know who follows whom. Whitaker knows, and let that, so Nature counsels, comfort you, instead of enraging you; and if you can't be comforted, if you must shatter this hour of peace, think of the mark on the wall.

I understand Nature's game—her prompting to take action as a way of ending any thought that threatens to excite or to pain. Hence, I suppose, comes our slight contempt for men of action—men, we assume, who don't think. Still, there's no harm in putting a full stop to one's disagreeable thoughts by looking at a mark on the wall.

Indeed, now that I have fixed my eyes upon it, I feel that I have grasped a plank in the sea; I feel a satisfying sense of reality which at once turns the two Archbishops and the Lord High Chancellor to the shadows of shades. Here is something definite, something real. Thus, waking from a midnight dream of horror, one hastily turns on the light and lies quiescent, worshipping the chest of drawers, worshipping solidity, worshipping reality, worshipping the impersonal world which is a proof of some existence other than ours. That is what one wants to be sure of ... Wood is a pleasant thing to think about. It comes from a tree; and trees grow, and we don't know how they grow. For years and years they grow, without paying any attention to us, in meadows, in forests, and by the side of rivers—all things one likes to think about. The cows swish their tails beneath them on hot afternoons; they paint rivers so green that when a moorhen dives one expects to see its feathers all green when it comes up again. I like to think of the fish balanced against the stream like flags blown out; and of water-beetles slowly raiding domes of mud upon the bed of the river. I like to think of the tree itself:—first the close dry sensation of being wood; then the grinding of the storm; then the slow, delicious ooze of sap. I like to think of it, too, on winter's nights standing in the empty field with all leaves close-furled, nothing tender exposed to the iron bullets of the moon, a naked mast upon an earth that goes tumbling, tumbling, all night long. The song of birds must sound very loud and strange in June; and how cold the feet of insects must feel upon it, as they make laborious progresses up the creases of the bark, or sun themselves upon the thin green awning of the leaves, and look straight in front of them with diamond-cut red eyes … One by one the fibres snap beneath the immense cold pressure of the earth, then the last storm comes and, falling, the highest branches drive deep into the ground again. Even so, life isn't done with; there are a million patient, watchful lives still for a tree, all over the world, in bedrooms, in ships, on the pavement, lining rooms, where men and women sit after tea, smoking cigarettes. It is full of peaceful thoughts, happy thoughts, this tree. I should like to take each one separately—but something is getting in the way … Where was I? What has it all been about? A tree? A river? The Downs? Whitaker's Almanack? The fields of asphodel? I can't remember a thing. Everything's moving, falling, slipping, vanishing … There is a vast upheaval of matter. Someone is standing over me and saying—

"I'm going out to buy a newspaper."

"Yes?"

"Though it's no good buying newspapers ... Nothing ever happens. Curse this war; God damn this war!... All the same, I don't see why we should have a snail on our wall."

Ah, the mark on the wall! It was a snail.

War

Luigi Pirandello

Luigi Pirandello (1867-1936) was an Italian playwright, novelist and short story writer who won the Nobel Prize for Literature in 1934. A prominent innovator in modern drama, he wrote over 50 plays, of which *Six Characters in Search of an Author* (1921) was universally acclaimed. Pirandello's short stories follow the realist mode and are poignant in tone. 'War' (1918) is a reflection on the physical and psychological damages inflicted by World War I (1914-1918).

The passengers who had left Rome by the night express had had to stop until dawn at the small station of Fabriano in order to continue their journey by the small old-fashioned local joining the main line with Sulmona.

At dawn, in a stuffy and smoky second-class carriage in which five people had already spent the night, a bulky woman in deep mourning was hosted in—almost like a shapeless bundle. Behind her—puffing and moaning, followed her husband—a tiny man; thin and weakly, his face death-white, his eyes small and bright and looking shy and uneasy.

Having at last taken a seat he politely thanked the passengers who had helped his wife and who had made room for her; then he turned round to the woman trying to pull down the collar of her coat and politely inquired:

"Are you all right, dear?"

The wife, instead of answering, pulled up her collar again to her eyes, so as to hide her face. "Nasty world," muttered the husband with a sad smile.

And he felt it his duty to explain to his traveling companions that the poor woman was to be pitied for the war was taking away from her her only son, a boy of twenty to whom both had devoted their entire life, even breaking up their home at Sulmona to follow him to Rome, where he had to go as a student, then allowing him to volunteer for war with an assurance, however, that at least six months he would not be sent to the front and now, all of a sudden, receiving a wire saying that he was due to leave in three days' time and asking them to go and see him off.

The woman under the big coat was twisting and wriggling, at times growling like a wild animal, feeling certain that all those explanations would not have aroused even a shadow of sympathy from those people who—most likely—were in the same plight as herself. One of them, who had been listening with particular attention, said:

"You should thank God that your son is only leaving now for the front. Mine has been sent there the first day of the war. He has already come back twice wounded and been sent back again to the front."

"What about me? I have two sons and three nephews at the front," said another passenger. "Maybe, but in our case it is our *only* son," ventured the husband.

"What difference can it make? You may spoil your only son by excessive attentions, but you cannot love him more than you would all your other children if you had any. Parental love is not like bread that can be broken to pieces and split amongst the children in equal shares. A father gives *all* his love to each one of his children without discrimination, whether it be one or ten, and if I am suffering now for my two sons, I am not suffering half for each of them but double..."

"True...true..." sighed the embarrassed husband, "but suppose (of course we all hope it will never be your case) a father has two sons at the front and he loses one of them, there is still one left to console him...while..."

"Yes," answered the other, getting cross, "a son left to console him but also a son left for whom he must survive, while in the case of the father of an only son if the son dies the father can die too and put an end to his distress. Which of the two positions is worse? Don't you see how my case would be worse than yours?"

"Nonsense," interrupted another traveler, a fat, red-faced man with bloodshot eyes of the palest gray.

He was panting. From his bulging eyes seemed to spurt inner violence of an uncontrolled vitality which his weakened body could hardly contain.

"Nonsense, "he repeated, trying to cover his mouth with his hand so as to hide the two missing front teeth. "Nonsense. Do we give life to our own children for our own benefit?"

The other travelers stared at him in distress. The one who had had his son at the front since the first day of the war sighed: "You are right. Our children do not belong to us, they belong to the country..."

"Bosh," retorted the fat traveler. "Do we think of the country when we give life to our children? Our sons are born because...well, because they must be born and when they come to life they take our own life with them. This is the truth. We belong to them but they never belong to us. And when they reach twenty they are exactly what we were at their age. We too had a father and mother, but there were so many other things as well...girls, cigarettes, illusions, new ties...and the Country, of course, whose call we would have answered—when we were twenty—even if father and mother had said no. Now, at our age, the love of our Country is still great, of course, but stronger than it is the love of our children. Is there any one of us here who wouldn't gladly take his son's place at the front if he could?"

There was a silence all round, everybody nodding as to approve.

"Why then," continued the fat man, "should we consider the feelings of our children when they are twenty? Isn't it natural that at their age they should consider the love for their Country (I am speaking of decent boys, of course) even greater than the love for us? Isn't it natural that it should be so, as after all they must look upon us as upon old boys who cannot move any more and must sit at home? If Country is a natural necessity like bread of which each of us must eat in order not to die of hunger, somebody must go to defend it. And our sons go, when they are twenty, and they don't want tears, because if they die, they die inflamed and happy (I am speaking, of course, of decent boys). Now, if one dies young and happy, without having the ugly sides of life, the boredom of it, the pettiness, the bitterness of disillusion...what more can we ask for him? Everyone should stop crying; everyone should laugh, as I do...or at least thank God—as I do—because my son, before dying, sent me a message saying that he was dying satisfied at having ended his life in the best way he could have wished. That is why, as you see, I do not even wear mourning..."

He shook his light fawn coat as to show it; his livid lip over his missing teeth was trembling, his eyes were watery and motionless, and soon after he ended with a shrill laugh which might well have been a sob.

"Quite so...quite so..." agreed the others.

The woman who, bundled in a corner under her coat, had been sitting and listening had—for the last three months—tried to find in the words of her husband and her friends something to console her in her deep sorrow, something that might show her how a mother should resign herself to send her son not even to death but to a probable danger of life. Yet not a word had she found amongst the many that had been said...and her grief had been greater in seeing that nobody—as she thought—could share her feelings.

But now the words of the traveler amazed and almost stunned her. She suddenly realized that it wasn't the others who were wrong and could not understand her but herself who could not rise up to the same height of those fathers and mothers willing to resign themselves, without crying, not only to the departure of their sons but even to their death.

She lifted her head, she bent over from her corner trying to listen with great attention to the details which the fat man was giving to his companions about the way his son had fallen as a hero, for his King and his Country, happy and without regrets. It seemed to her that she had stumbled into a world she had never dreamt of, a world so far unknown to her, and she was so pleased to hear everyone joining in congratulating that brave father who could so stoically speak of his child's death.

Then suddenly, just as if she had heard nothing of what had been said and almost as if waking up from a dream, she turned to the old man, asking him:

"Then...is your son really dead?"

Everyone stared at her. The old man, too, turned to look at her, fixing his great, bulging, horribly watery light gray eyes, deep in her face. For some time he tried to answer, but words failed him. He looked and looked at her, almost as if only then—at that silly, incongruous question—he had suddenly realized at last that his son was really dead—gone for ever—for ever. His face contracted, became horribly distorted, then he snatched in haste a handkerchief from his pocket and, to the amazement of everyone, broke into harrowing, heart-breaking, uncontrollable sobs.

The Interlopers

Saki

Hector Hugh Munro (1870-1916), popularly known as Saki, was a Scottish journalist and writer notable for his wit and political satires. His stories critiqued vanity, cruelty and social disharmony through well-devised plots, surprise endings and irony. 'The Interlopers' was first published in the posthumous collection *The Toys of Peace and Other Papers* (1919).

In a forest of mixed growth somewhere on the eastern spurs of the Karpathians, a man stood one winter night watching and listening, as though he waited for some beast of the woods to come within the range of his vision, and, later, of his rifle. But the game for whose presence he kept so keen an outlook was none that figured in the sportsman's calendar as lawful and proper for the chase; Ulrich von Gradwitz patrolled the dark forest in quest of a human enemy. The forest lands of Gradwitz were of wide extent and well stocked with game; the narrow strip of precipitous woodland that lay on its outskirt was not remarkable for the game it harboured or the shooting it afforded, but it was the most jealously guarded of all its owner's territorial possessions. A famous law suit, in the days of his grandfather, had wrested it from the illegal possession of a neighbouring family of petty landowners; the dispossessed party had never acquiesced in the judgment of the Courts, and a long series of poaching affrays and similar scandals had embittered the relationships between the families for three generations. The neighbour feud had grown into a personal one since Ulrich had come to be head of his family; if there was a man in the world whom he detested and wished ill to it was Georg Znaeym, the inheritor of the quarrel and the tireless game-snatcher and raider of the disputed border-forest. The feud might, perhaps, have died down or been compromised if the personal ill-will of the two men had not stood in the way; as boys they had thirsted for one another's blood, as men each prayed that misfortune might fall on the other, and this wind-scourged winter night Ulrich had banded together his foresters to watch the dark forest, not in quest of four-footed quarry, but to keep a lookout for the prowling thieves whom he suspected of being afoot from across the land boundary. The roebuck, which usually kept in the sheltered hollows during a storm-wind, were running like driven things tonight, and there was movement and unrest among the creatures that were wont to sleep through the dark hours. Assuredly there was a disturbing element in the forest, and Ulrich could guess the quarter from whence it came.

He strayed away by himself from the watchers whom he had placed in ambush on the crest of the hill, and wandered far down the steep slopes amid the wild tangle of undergrowth, peering through the tree trunks and listening through the whistling and skirling of the wind and the restless beating of the branches for sight and sound of the marauders. If only on this wild night, in this dark, lone spot, he might come across Georg Znaeym, man to man, with none to witness – that was the wish that was uppermost in his thoughts. And as he stepped round the trunk of a huge beech he came face to face with the man he sought.

The two enemies stood glaring at one another for a long silent moment. Each had a rifle in his hand, each had hate in his heart and murder uppermost in his mind. The chance had come to give full play to the passions of a lifetime. But a man who has been brought up under the code of a restraining civilisation cannot easily nerve himself to shoot down his neighbour in cold blood and without word spoken, except for an offence against his hearth and honour. And before the moment of hesitation had given way to action, a deed of Nature's own violence overwhelmed them both. A fierce shriek of the storm had been answered by a splitting crash over their heads, and ere they could leap aside a mass of falling beech tree had thundered down on them. Ulrich von Gradwitz found himself stretched on the ground, one arm numb beneath him and the other held almost as helplessly in a tight tangle of forked branches, while both legs were pinned beneath the fallen mass. His heavy shooting-boots had saved his feet from being crushed to pieces, but if his fractures were not as serious as they might have been, at least it was evident that he could not move from his present position till some one came to release him. The descending twig had slashed the skin of his face, and he had to wink away some drops of blood from his eyelashes before he could take in a general view of the disaster. At his side, so near that under ordinary circumstances he could almost have touched him, lay Georg Znaeym, alive and struggling, but obviously as helplessly pinioned down as himself. All round them lay a thick-strewn wreckage of splintered branches and broken twigs.

Relief at being alive and exasperation at his captive plight brought a strange medley of pious thank-offerings and sharp curses to Ulrich's lips. Georg, who was early blinded with the blood which trickled across his eyes, stopped his struggling for a moment to listen, and then gave a short, snarling laugh.

"So you're not killed, as you ought to be, but you're caught, anyway," he cried; "caught fast. Ho, what a jest, Ulrich von Gradwitz snared in his stolen forest. There's real justice for you!" And he laughed again, mockingly and savagely.

"I'm caught in my own forest-land," retorted Ulrich. "When my men come to release us you will wish, perhaps, that you were in a better plight than caught poaching on a neighbour's land, shame on you." Georg was silent for a moment; then he answered quietly: "Are you sure that your men will find much to release? I have men, too, in the forest tonight, close behind me, and *they* will be here first and do the releasing. When they drag me out from under these damned branches it won't need much clumsiness on their part to roll this mass of trunk right over on the top of you. Your men will find you dead under a fallen beech tree. For form's sake I shall send my condolences to your family."

"It is a useful hint," said Ulrich fiercely. "My men had orders to follow in ten minutes time, seven of which must have gone by already, and when they get me out–I will remember the hint. Only as you will have met your death poaching on my lands I don't think I can decently send any message of condolence to your family."

"Good," snarled Georg, "good. We fight this quarrel out to the death, you and I and our foresters, with no cursed interlopers to come between us. Death and damnation to you, Ulrich von Gradwitz."

"The same to you, Georg Znaeym, forest-thief, game-snatcher."

Both men spoke with the bitterness of possible defeat before them, for each knew that it might be long before his men would seek him out or find him; it was a bare matter of chance which party would arrive first on the scene.

Both had now given up the useless struggle to free themselves from the mass of wood that held them down; Ulrich limited his endeavours to an effort to bring his one partially free arm near enough to his outer coat-pocket to draw out his wine-flask. Even when he had accomplished that operation it was long before he could manage the unscrewing of the stopper or get any of the liquid down his throat.

But what a Heaven-sent draught it seemed! It was an open winter, and little snow had fallen as yet, hence the captives suffered less from the cold than might have been the case at that season of the year; nevertheless, the wine was warming and reviving to the wounded man, and he looked across with something like a throb of pity to where his enemy lay, just keeping the groans of pain and weariness from crossing his lips.

"Could you reach this flask if I threw it over to you?" asked Ulrich suddenly; "there is good wine in it, and one may as well be as comfortable as one can.

Let us drink, even if tonight one of us dies."

"No, I can scarcely see anything; there is so much blood caked round my eyes," said Georg, "and in any case I don't drink wine with an enemy."

Ulrich was silent for a few minutes, and lay listening to the weary screeching of the wind. An idea was slowly forming and growing in his brain, an idea that gained strength every time that he looked across at the man who was fighting so grimly against pain and exhaustion. In the pain and languor that Ulrich himself was feeling the old fierce hatred seemed to be dying down.

"Neighbour," he said presently, "do as you please if your men come first. It was a fair compact. But as for me, I've changed my mind. If my men are the first to come you shall be the first to be helped, as though you were my guest. We have quarrelled like devils all our lives over this stupid strip of forest, where the trees can't even stand upright in a breath of wind. Lying here tonight thinking I've come to think we've been rather fools; there are better things in life than getting the better of a boundary dispute. Neighbour, if you will help me to bury the old quarrel I–I will ask you to be my friend."

Georg Znaeym was silent for so long that Ulrich thought, perhaps, he had fainted with the pain of his injuries. Then he spoke slowly and in jerks.

"How the whole region would stare and gabble if we rode into the market-square together. No one living can remember seeing a Znaeym and a von Gradwitz talking to one another in friendship. And what peace there would be among the forester folk if we ended our feud tonight. And if we choose to make peace among our people there is none other to interfere, no interlopers from outside ... You would come and keep the Sylvester night beneath my roof, and I would come and feast on some high day at your castle ... I would never fire a shot on your land, save when you invited me as a guest; and you should come and shoot with me down in the marshes where the wildfowl are. In all the countryside there are none that could hinder if we willed to make peace. I never thought to have wanted to do other than hate you all my life, but I think I have changed my mind about things too, this last half-hour. And you offered me your wineflask ... Ulrich von Gradwitz, I will be your friend."

For a space both men were silent, turning over in their minds the wonderful changes that this dramatic reconciliation would bring about. In the cold, gloomy forest, with the wind tearing in fitful gusts through the naked branches and whistling round the tree-trunks, they lay and waited for the help that would now bring release and succour to both parties. And each prayed a private prayer that his men might be the first to arrive, so that he might be the first to show honourable attention to the enemy that had become a friend. Presently, as the wind dropped for a moment, Ulrich broke silence. "Let's shout for help," he said; "in this lull our voices may carry a little way."

"They won't carry far through the trees and undergrowth," said Georg, "but we can try. Together, then." The two raised their voices in a prolonged hunting call.

"Together again," said Ulrich a few minutes later, after listening in vain for an answering halloo.

"I heard nothing but the pestilential wind," said Georg hoarsely. There was silence again for some minutes, and then Ulrich gave a joyful cry.

"I can see figures coming through the wood. They are following in the way I came down the hillside."

Both men raised their voices in as loud a shout as they could muster.

"They hear us! They've stopped. Now they see us. They're running down the hill towards us," cried Ulrich.

"How many of them are there?" asked Georg.

"I can't see distinctly," said Ulrich; "nine or ten,"

"Then they are yours," said Georg; "I had only seven out with me." "They are making all the speed they can, brave lads," said Ulrich gladly.

"Are they your men?" asked Georg. "Are they your men?" he repeated impatiently as Ulrich did not answer.

"No," said Ulrich with a laugh, the idiotic chattering laugh of a man unstrung with hideous fear.

"Who are they?" asked Georg quickly, straining his eyes to see what the other would gladly not have seen.

"Wolves."

Red

W. Somerset Maugham

William Somerset Maugham (1874-1965) was an English playwright, novelist and short story writer known for *Of Human Bondage* (1915) and *Cakes and Ale* (1930). His short stories were also marked by a concise style of writing, deep insight into human nature and cynicism that was also characteristic of his novels. First published in the magazine *Asia* (1921), 'Red' reflects the simplicity, disillusionment and skilful narration associated with Maugham.

The skipper thrust his hand into one of his trouser pockets and with difficulty, for they were not at the sides but in front and he was a portly man, pulled out a large silver watch. He looked at it and then looked again at the declining sun. The Kanaka at the wheel gave him a glance, but did not speak. The skipper's eyes rested on the island they were approaching. A white line of foam marked the reef. He knew there was an opening large enough to get his ship through, and when they came a little nearer he counted on seeing it. They had nearly an hour of daylight still before them. In the lagoon the water was deep and they could anchor comfortably. The chief of the village which he could already see among the coconut trees was a friend of the mate's, and it would be pleasant to go ashore for the night. The mate came forward at that minute and the skipper turned to him.

"We'll take a bottle of booze along with us and get some girls in to dance," he said.

"I don't see the opening," said the mate.

He was a Kanaka, a handsome, swarthy fellow, with somewhat the look of a later Roman emperor, inclined to stoutness; but his face was fine and clean-cut.

"I'm dead sure there's one right here," said the captain, looking through his glasses. "I can't understand why I can't pick it up. Send one of the boys up the mast to have a look."

The mate called one of the crew and gave him the order. The captain watched the Kanaka climb and waited for him to speak. But the Kanaka shouted down that he could see nothing but the unbroken line of foam. The captain spoke Samoan like a native, and he cursed him freely.

"Shall he stay up there?" asked the mate.

"What the hell good does that do?" answered the captain. "The blame fool can't see worth a cent. You bet your sweet life I'd find the opening if I was up there."

He looked at the slender mast with anger. It was all very well for a native who had been used to climbing up coconut trees all his life. He was fat and heavy.

"Come down," he shouted. "You're no more use than a dead dog. We'll just have to go along the reef till we find the opening."

It was a seventy-ton schooner with paraffin auxiliary, and it ran, when there was no head wind, between four and five knots an hour. It was a bedraggled object; it had been painted white a very long time ago, but it was now dirty, dingy, and mottled. It smelt strongly of paraffin and of the copra which was its usual cargo. They were within a hundred feet of the reef now and the captain told the steersman to run along it till they came to the opening. But when they had gone a couple of miles he realised that they had missed it. He went about and slowly worked back again. The white foam of the reef continued without interruption and now the sun was setting. With a curse at the stupidity of the crew the skipper resigned himself to waiting till next morning.

"Put her about," he said. "I can't anchor here."

They went out to sea a little and presently it was quite dark. They anchored. When the sail was furled the ship began to roll a good deal. They said in Apia that one day she would roll right over; and the owner, a German-American who managed one of the largest stores, said that no money was big enough to induce him to go out in her. The cook, a Chinese in white trousers, very dirty and ragged, and a thin white tunic, came to say that supper was ready, and when the skipper went into the cabin he found the engineer already seated at table. The engineer was a long, lean man with a scraggy neck. He was dressed in blue overalls and a sleeveless jersey which showed his thin arms tattooed from elbow to wrist.

"Hell, having to spend the night outside," said the skipper.

The engineer did not answer, and they ate their supper in silence. The cabin was lit by a dim oil lamp. When they had eaten the canned apricots with which the meal finished the Chink brought them a cup of tea. The skipper lit a cigar and went on the upper deck. The island now was only a darker mass against the night. The stars were very bright. The only sound was the ceaseless breaking of the surf. The skipper sank into a deck-chair and smoked idly. Presently three or four members of the crew came up and sat down. One of them had a banjo and another a concertina. They began to play, and one of them sang. The native song sounded strange on these instruments. Then to the singing a couple began to dance. It was a barbaric dance, savage and primeval, rapid, with quick movements of the hands and feet and contortions of the body; it was sensual, sexual even, but sexual without passion. It was very animal, direct, weird without mystery, natural in short, and one might almost say childlike. At last they grew tired. They stretched themselves on the deck and slept, and all was silent. The skipper lifted himself heavily out of his chair and clambered down the companion. He went into his cabin and got out of his clothes. He climbed into his bunk and lay there. He panted a little in the heat of the night.

But next morning, when the dawn crept over the tranquil sea, the opening in the reef which had eluded them the night before was seen a little to the east of where they lay. The schooner entered the lagoon. There was not a ripple on the surface of the water. Deep down among the coral rocks you saw little coloured fish swim. When he had anchored his ship the skipper ate his breakfast and went on deck. The sun shone from an unclouded sky, but in the early morning the air was grateful and cool. It was Sunday, and there was a feeling of quietness, a silence as though nature were at rest, which gave him a peculiar sense of comfort. He sat, looking at the wooded coast, and felt lazy and well at ease. Presently a slow smile moved his lips and he threw the stump of his cigar into the water.

"I guess I'll go ashore," he said. "Get the boat out."

He climbed stiffly down the ladder and was rowed to a little cove. The coconut trees came down to the water's edge, not in rows, but spaced out with an ordered formality. They were like a ballet of spinsters, elderly but flippant, standing in affected attitudes with the simpering graces of a bygone age. He sauntered idly through them, along a path that could be just seen winding its tortuous way, and it led him presently to a broad creek. There was a bridge across it, but a bridge constructed of single trunks of coconut trees, a dozen of them, placed end to end and supported where they met by a forked branch driven into the bed of the creek. You walked on a smooth, round surface, narrow and slippery, and there was no support for the hand. To cross such a bridge required sure feet and a stout heart. The skipper hesitated. But he saw on the other side, nestling among the trees, a white man's house; he made up his mind and, rather gingerly, began to walk. He watched his feet carefully, and where one trunk joined on to the next and there was a difference of level, he tottered a little. It was with a gasp of relief that he reached the last tree and finally set his feet on the firm ground of the other side. He had been so intent on the difficult crossing that he never noticed anyone was watching him, and it was with surprise that he heard himself spoken to.

"It takes a bit of nerve to cross these bridges when you're not used to them."

He looked up and saw a man standing in front of him. He had evidently come out of the house which he had seen.

"I saw you hesitate," the man continued, with a smile on his lips, "and I was watching to see you fall in."

"Not on your life," said the captain, who had now recovered his confidence.

"I've fallen in myself before now. I remember, one evening I came back from shooting, and I fell in, gun and all. Now I get a boy to carry my gun for me."

He was a man no longer young, with a small beard, now somewhat grey, and a thin face. He was dressed in a singlet, without arms, and a pair of duck trousers. He wore neither shoes nor socks. He spoke English with a slight accent.

"Are you Neilson?" asked the skipper.

"I am."

"I've heard about you. I thought you lived somewheres round here."

The skipper followed his host into the little bungalow and sat down heavily in the chair which the other motioned him to take. While Neilson went out to fetch whisky and glasses he took a look round the room. It filled him with amazement. He had never seen so many books. The shelves reached from floor to ceiling on all four walls, and they were closely packed. There was a grand piano littered with music, and a large table on which books and magazines lay in disorder. The room made him feel embarrassed. He remembered that Neilson was a queer fellow. No one knew very much about him, although he had been in the islands for so many years, but those who knew him agreed that he was queer. He was a Swede.

"You've got one big heap of books here," he said, when Neilson returned.

"They do no harm," answered Neilson with a smile.

"Have you read them all?" asked the skipper.

"Most of them."

"I'm a bit of a reader myself. I have the *Saturday Evening Post* sent me regler."

Neilson poured his visitor a good stiff glass of whisky and gave him a cigar. The skipper volunteered a little information.

"I got in last night, but I couldn't find the opening, so I had to anchor outside. I never been this run before, but my people had some stuff they wanted to bring over here. Gray, d'you know him?"

"Yes, he's got a store a little way along."

"Well, there was a lot of canned stuff that he wanted over, an' he's got some copra. They thought I might just as well come over as lie idle at Apia. I run between Apia and Pago-Pago mostly, but they've got smallpox there just now, and there's nothing stirring."

He took a drink of his whisky and lit a cigar. He was a taciturn man, but there was something in Neilson that made him nervous, and his nervousness made him talk. The Swede was looking at him with large dark eyes in which there was an expression of faint amusement.

"This is a tidy little place you've got here."

"I've done my best with it."

"You must do pretty well with your trees. They look fine. With copra at the price it is now. I had a bit of a plantation myself once, in Upolu it was, but I had to sell it."

He looked round the room again, where all those books gave him a feeling of something incomprehensible and hostile.

"I guess you must find it a bit lonesome here though," he said.

"I've got used to it. I've been here for twenty-five years."

Now the captain could think of nothing more to say, and he smoked in silence. Neilson had apparently no wish to break it. He looked at his guest with a meditative eye. He was a tall man, more than six feet high, and very stout. His face was red and blotchy, with a network of little purple veins on the cheeks, and his features were sunk into its fatness. His eyes were bloodshot. His neck was buried in rolls of fat. But for a fringe of long curly hair, nearly white, at the back of his head, he was quite bald; and that immense, shiny surface of forehead, which might have given him a false look of intelligence, on the contrary gave him one of peculiar imbecility. He wore a blue flannel shirt, open at the neck and showing his fat chest covered with a mat of reddish hair, and a very old pair of blue serge trousers. He sat in his chair in a heavy ungainly attitude, his great belly thrust forward and his fat legs uncrossed. All elasticity had gone from his limbs. Neilson wondered idly what sort of man he had been in his youth. It was almost impossible to imagine that this creature of vast bulk had ever been a boy who ran about. The skipper finished his whisky, and Neilson pushed the bottle towards him.

"Help yourself."

The skipper leaned forward and with his great hand seized it.

"And how come you in these parts anyways?" he said.

"Oh, I came out to the islands for my health. My lungs were bad and they said I hadn't a year to live. You see they were wrong."

"I meant, how come you to settle down right here?"

"I am a sentimentalist."

"Oh!"

Neilson knew that the skipper had not an idea what he meant, and he looked at him with an ironical twinkle in his dark eyes.

Perhaps just because the skipper was so gross and dull a man the whim seized him to talk further.

"You were too busy keeping your balance to notice, when you crossed the bridge, but this spot is generally considered rather pretty."

"It's a cute little house you've got here."

"Ah, that wasn't here when I first came. There was a native hut, with its beehive roof and its pillars, overshadowed by a great tree with red flowers; and the croton bushes, their leaves yellow and red and golden, made a pied fence around it. And then all about were the coconut trees, as fanciful as women, and as vain. They stood at the water's edge and spent all day looking at their reflections. I was a young man then—Good Heavens, it's a quarter of a century ago—and I wanted to enjoy all the loveliness of the world in the short time allotted to me before I passed into the darkness. I thought it was the most beautiful spot I had ever seen. The first time I saw it I had a catch at my heart, and I was afraid I was going to cry. I wasn't more than twenty-five, and though I put the best face I could on it, I didn't want to die. And somehow it seemed to me that the very beauty of this place made it easier for me to accept my fate. I felt when I came here that all my past life had fallen away, Stockholm and its University, and then Bonn: it all seemed the life of somebody else, as though now at last I had achieved the reality which our doctors of philosophy—I am one myself, you know—had discussed so much. 'A year,' I cried to myself. 'I have a year. I will spend it here and then I am content to die.'"

"We are foolish and sentimental and melodramatic at twenty-five, but if we weren't perhaps we should be less wise at fifty."

"Now drink, my friend. Don't let the nonsense I talk interfere with you."

He waved his thin hand towards the bottle, and the skipper finished what remained in his glass.

"You ain't drinking nothin," he said, reaching for the whisky.

"I am of a sober habit," smiled the Swede. "I intoxicate myself in ways which I fancy are more subtle. But perhaps that is only vanity. Anyhow, the effects are more lasting and the results less deleterious."

"They say there's a deal of cocaine taken in the States now," said the captain.

Neilson chuckled.

"But I do not see a white man often," he continued, "and for once I don't think a drop of whisky can do me any harm."

He poured himself out a little, added some soda, and took a sip.

"And presently I found out why the spot had such an unearthly loveliness. Here love had tarried for a moment like a migrant bird that happens on a ship in mid-ocean and for a little while folds its tired wings. The fragrance of a beautiful passion hovered over it like the fragrance of hawthorn in May in the meadows of my home. It seems to me that the places where men have loved or suffered keep about them always some faint aroma of something that has not wholly died. It is as though they had acquired a spiritual significance which mysteriously affects those who pass. I wish I could make myself clear." He smiled a little. "Though I cannot imagine that if I did you would understand."

He paused.

"I think this place was beautiful because here I had been loved beautifully." And now he shrugged his shoulders. "But perhaps it is only that my aesthetic sense is gratified by the happy conjunction of young love and a suitable setting."

Even a man less thick-witted than the skipper might have been forgiven if he were bewildered by Neilson's words. For he seemed faintly to laugh at what he said. It was as though he spoke from emotion which his intellect found ridiculous. He had said himself that he was a sentimentalist, and when sentimentality is joined with scepticism there is often the devil to pay.

He was silent for an instant and looked at the captain with eyes in which there was a sudden perplexity.

"You know, I can't help thinking that I've seen you before somewhere or other," he said.

"I couldn't say as I remember you," returned the skipper.

"I have a curious feeling as though your face were familiar to me. It's been puzzling me for some time. But I can't situate my recollection in any place or at any time."

The skipper massively shrugged his heavy shoulders.

"It's thirty years since I first come to the islands. A man can't figure on remembering all the folk he meets in a while like that."

The Swede shook his head.

"You know how one sometimes has the feeling that a place one has never been to before is strangely familiar. That's how I seem to see you." He gave a whimsical smile. "Perhaps I knew you in some past existence. Perhaps, perhaps you were the master of a galley in ancient Rome and I was a slave at the oar. Thirty years have you been here?"

"Every bit of thirty years."

"I wonder if you knew a man called Red?"

"Red?"

"That is the only name I've ever known him by. I never knew him personally. I never even set eyes on him. And yet I seem to see him more clearly than many men, my brothers, for instance, with whom I passed my daily life for many years. He lives in my imagination with the distinctness of a Paolo Malatesta or a Romeo. But I daresay you have never read Dante or Shakespeare?"

"I can't say as I have," said the captain.

Neilson, smoking a cigar, leaned back in his chair and looked vacantly at the ring of smoke which floated in the still air. A smile played on his lips, but his eyes were grave. Then he looked at the captain. There was in his gross obesity something extraordinarily repellent. He had the plethoric self-satisfaction of the very fat. It was an outrage. It set Neilson's nerves on edge. But the contrast between the man before him and the man he had in mind was pleasant.

"It appears that Red was the most comely thing you ever saw. I've talked to quite a number of people who knew him in those days, white men, and they all agree that the first time you saw him his beauty just took your breath away. They called him Red on account of his flaming hair. It had a natural wave and he wore it long. It must have been of that wonderful colour that the pre-Raphaelites raved over. I don't think he was vain of it, he was much too ingenuous for that, but no one could have blamed him if he had been. He was tall, six feet and an inch or two—in the native house that used to stand here was the mark of his height cut with a knife on the central trunk that supported the roof—and he was made like a Greek god, broad in the shoulders and thin in the flanks; he was like Apollo, with just that soft roundness which Praxiteles gave him, and that suave, feminine grace which has in it something troubling and mysterious. His skin was dazzling white, milky, like satin; his skin was like a woman's."

"I had kind of a white skin myself when I was a kiddie," said the skipper, with a twinkle in his bloodshot eyes.

But Neilson paid no attention to him. He was telling his story now and interruption made him impatient.

"And his face was just as beautiful as his body. He had large blue eyes, very dark, so that some say they were black, and unlike most red-haired people he had dark eyebrows and long dark lashes. His features were perfectly regular and his mouth was like a scarlet wound. He was twenty."

On these words the Swede stopped with a certain sense of the dramatic. He took a sip of whisky.

"He was unique. There never was anyone more beautiful. There was no more reason for him than for a wonderful blossom to flower on a wild plant. He was a happy accident of nature."

"One day he landed at that cove into which you must have put this morning. He was an American sailor, and he had deserted from a man-of-war in Apia. He had induced some good-humoured native to give him a passage on a cutter that happened to be sailing from Apia to Safoto, and he had been put ashore here in a dugout. I do not know why he deserted. Perhaps life on a man-of-war with its restrictions irked him, perhaps he was in trouble, and perhaps it was the South Seas and these romantic islands that got into his bones. Every now and then they take a man strangely, and he finds himself like a fly in a spider's web. It may be that there was a softness of fi bre in him, and these green hills with their soft airs, this blue sea, took the northern strength from him as Delilah took the Nazarite's. Anyhow, he wanted to hide himself, and he thought he would be safe in this secluded nook till his ship had sailed from Samoa."

"There was a native hut at the cove and as he stood there, wondering where exactly he should turn his steps, a young girl came out and invited him to enter. He knew scarcely two words of the native tongue and she as little English. But he understood well enough what her smiles meant, and her pretty gestures, and he followed her. He sat down on a mat and she gave him slices of pineapple to eat. I can speak of Red only from hearsay, but I saw the girl three years after he first met her, and she was scarcely nineteen then. You cannot imagine how exquisite she was. She had the passionate grace of the hibiscus and the rich colour. She was rather tall, slim, with the delicate features of her race, and large eyes like pools of still water under the palm trees; her hair, black and curling, fell down her back, and she wore a wreath of scented flowers. Her hands were lovely. They were so small, so exquisitely formed, they gave your heart-strings a wrench. And in those days she laughed easily. Her smile was so delightful that it made your knees shake. Her skin was like a field of ripe corn on a summer day. Good Heavens, how can I describe her? She was too beautiful to be real."

"And these two young things, she was sixteen and he was twenty, fell in love with one another at first sight. That is the real love, not the love that comes from sympathy, common interests, or intellectual community, but love pure and simple. That is the love that Adam felt for Eve when he awoke and found her in the garden gazing at him with dewy eyes. That is the love that draws the beasts to one another, and the Gods. That is the love that makes the world a miracle. That is the love which gives life its pregnant meaning. You have never heard of the wise, cynical French duke who said that with two lovers there is always one who loves and one who lets himself be loved; it is a bitter truth to which most of us have to resign ourselves; but now and then there are two who love and two who let themselves be loved. Then one might fancy that the sun stands still as it stood when Joshua prayed to the God of Israel."

"And even now after all these years, when I think of these two, so young, so fair, so simple, and of their love, I feel a pang. It tears my heart just as my heart is torn when on certain nights I watch the full moon shining on the lagoon from an unclouded sky. There is always pain in the contemplation of perfect beauty."

"They were children. She was good and sweet and kind. I know nothing of him, and I like to think that then at all events he was ingenuous and frank. I like to think that his soul was as comely as his body. But I daresay he had no more soul than the creatures of the woods and forests who made pipes from reeds and bathed in the mountain streams when the world was young, and you might catch sight of little fawns galloping through the glade on the back of a bearded centaur. A soul is a troublesome possession and when man developed it he lost the Garden of Eden."

"Well, when Red came to the island it had recently been visited by one of those epidemics which the white man has brought to the South Seas, and one third of the inhabitants had died. It seems that the girl had lost all her near kin and she lived now in the house of distant cousins. The household consisted of two ancient crones, bowed and wrinkled, two younger women, and a man and a boy. For a few days he stayed there. But perhaps he felt himself too near the shore, with the possibility that he might fall in with white men who would reveal his hiding-place; perhaps the lovers could not bear that the company of others should rob them for an instant of the delight of being together. One morning they set out, the pair of them, with the few things that belonged to the girl, and walked along a grassy path under the coconuts, till they came to the creek you see. They had to cross the bridge you crossed, and the girl laughed gleefully because he was afraid. She held his hand till they came to the end of the first tree, and then his courage failed him and he had to go back. He was obliged to take off all his clothes before he could risk it, and she carried them over for him on her head. They settled down in the empty hut that stood here. Whether she had any rights over it (land tenure is a complicated business in the islands), or whether the owner had died during the epidemic, I do not know, but anyhow no one questioned them, and they took possession. Their furniture consisted of a couple of grass-mats on which they slept, a fragment of looking-glass, and a bowl or two. In this pleasant land that is enough to start housekeeping on."

"They say that happy people have no history, and certainly a happy love has none. They did nothing all day long and yet the days seemed all too short. The girl had a native name, but Red called her Sally. He picked up the easy language very quickly, and he used to lie on the mat for hours while she chattered gaily to him. He was a silent fellow, and perhaps his mind was lethargic. He smoked incessantly the cigarettes which she made him out of the native tobacco and pandanus leaf, and he watched her while with deft fingers she made grass mats. Often natives would come in and tell long stories of the old days when the island was disturbed by tribal wars. Sometimes he would go fishing on the reef, and bring home a basket full of coloured fish. Sometimes at night he would go out with a lantern to catch lobster. There were plantains round the hut and Sally would roast them for their frugal meal. She knew how to make delicious messes from coconuts, and the bread-fruit tree by the side of the creek gave them its fruit. On feast-days they killed a little pig and cooked it on hot stones. They bathed together in the creek; and in the evening they went down to the lagoon and paddled about in a dugout, with its great outrigger. The sea was deep blue, wine-coloured at sundown, like the sea of Homeric Greece; but in the lagoon the colour had an infinite variety, aquamarine and amethyst and emerald; and the setting sun turned it for a short moment to liquid gold. Then there was the colour of the coral, brown, white, pink, red, purple; and the shapes it took were marvellous. It was like a magic garden, and the hurrying fish were like butterflies. It strangely lacked reality. Among the coral were pools with a floor of white sand and here, where the water was dazzling clear, it was very good to bathe. Then, cool and happy, they wandered back in the gloaming over the soft grass road to the creek, walking hand in hand, and now the mynah birds filled the coconut trees with their clamour. And then the night, with that great, sky shining with gold, that seemed to stretch more widely than the skies of Europe, and the soft airs that blew gently through the open hut, the long night again was all too short. She was sixteen and he was barely twenty. The dawn crept in among the wooden pillars of the hut and looked at those lovely children sleeping in one another's arms. The sun hid behind the great tattered leaves of the plantains so that it might not disturb them, and then, with playful malice, shot a golden ray, like the outstretched paw of a Persian cat, on their faces. They opened their sleepy eyes and they smiled to welcome another day. The weeks lengthened into months, and a year passed. They seemed to love one another as—I hesitate to say passionately, for passion has in it always a shade of sadness, a touch of bitterness or anguish, but as whole heartedly, as simply and naturally as on that first day on which, meeting, they had recognised that a god was in them."

"If you had asked them I have no doubt that they would have thought it impossible to suppose their love could ever cease. Do we not know that the essential element of love is a belief in its own eternity? And yet perhaps in Red there was already a very little seed, unknown to himself and unsuspected by the girl, which would in time have grown to weariness. For one day one of the natives from the cove told them that some way down the coast at the anchorage was a British whaling-ship."

"'Gee,' he said, 'I wonder if I could make a trade of some nuts and plantains for a pound or two of tobacco.'"

"The pandanus cigarettes that Sally made him with untiring hands were strong and pleasant enough to smoke, but they left him unsatisfied; and he yearned on a sudden for real tobacco, hard, rank, and pungent. He had not smoked a pipe for many, months. His mouth watered at the thought of it. One would have thought some premonition of harm would have made Sally seek to dissuade him, but love possessed her so completely that it never occurred to her any power on earth could take him from her. They went up into the hills together and gathered a great basket of wild oranges, green, but sweet and juicy; and they picked plantains from around the hut, and coconuts from their trees, and breadfruit and mangoes; and they carried them down to the cove. They loaded the unstable canoe with them, and Red and the native boy who had brought them the news of the ship paddled along outside the reef."

"It was the last time she ever saw him."

"Next day the boy came back alone. He was all in tears. This is the story he told. When after their long paddle they reached the ship and Red hailed it, a white man looked over the side and told them to come on board. They took the fruit they had brought with them and Red piled it up on the deck. The white man and he began to talk, and they seemed to come to some agreement. One of them went below and brought up tobacco. Red took some at once and lit a pipe. The boy imitated the zest with which he blew a great cloud of smoke from his mouth. Then they said something to him and he went into the cabin. Through the open door the boy, watching curiously, saw a bottle brought out and glasses. Red drank and smoked. They seemed to ask him something, for he shook his head and laughed. The man, the first man who had spoken to them, laughed too, and he filled Red's glass once more. They went on talking and drinking, and presently, growing tired of watching a sight that meant nothing to him, the boy curled himself up on the deck and slept. He was awakened by a kick; and, jumping to his feet, he saw that the ship was slowly sailing out of the lagoon. He caught sight of Red seated at the table, with his head resting heavily on his arms, fast asleep. He made a movement towards him, intending to wake him, but a rough hand seized his arm, and a man, with a scowl and words which he did not understand, pointed to the side. He shouted to Red, but in a moment he was seized and flung overboard. Helpless, he swam round to his canoe which was drifting a little way off, and pushed it on to the reef. He climbed in and, sobbing all the way, paddled back to shore."

"What had happened was obvious enough. The whaler, by desertion or sickness, was short of hands, and the captain when Red came aboard had asked him to sign on; on his refusal he had made him drunk and kidnapped him."

"Sally was beside herself with grief. For three days she screamed and cried. The natives did what they could to comfort her, but she would not be comforted. She would not eat. And then, exhausted, she sank into a sullen apathy. She spent long days at the cove, watching the lagoon, in the vain hope that Red somehow or other would manage to escape. She sat on the white sand, hour after hour, with the tears running down her cheeks, and at night dragged herself wearily back across the creek to the little hut where she had been happy. The people with whom she had lived before Red came to the island wished her to return to them, but she would not; she was convinced that Red would come back, and she wanted him to find her where he had left her. Four months later she was delivered of a still-born child, and the old woman who had come to help her through her confinement remained with her in the hut. All joy was taken from her life. If her anguish with time became less intolerable it was replaced by a settled melancholy. You would not have thought that among these people, whose emotions, though so violent, are very transient, a woman could be found capable of so enduring a passion. She never lost the profound conviction that sooner or later Red would come back. She watched for him, and every time someone crossed this slender little bridge of coconut trees she looked. It might at last be he."

Neilson stopped talking and gave a faint sigh.

"And what happened to her in the end?" asked the skipper.

Neilson smiled bitterly.

"Oh, three years afterwards she took up with another white man."

The skipper gave a fat, cynical chuckle.

"That's generally what happens to them," he said.

The Swede shot him a look of hatred. He did not know why that gross, obese man excited in him so violent a repulsion. But his thoughts wandered and he found his mind filled with memories of the past. He went back five and twenty years. It was when he first came to the island, weary of Apia, with its heavy drinking, its gambling and coarse sensuality, a sick man, trying to resign himself to the loss of the career which had fired his imagination with ambitious thoughts. He set behind him resolutely all his hopes of making a great name for himself and strove to content himself with the few poor months of careful life which was all that he could count on. He was boarding with a half-caste trader who had a store a couple of miles along the coast at the edge of a native village; and one day, wandering aimlessly along the grassy paths of the coconut groves, he had come upon the hut in which Sally lived. The beauty of the spot had filled him with a rapture so great that it was almost painful, and then he had seen Sally. She was the loveliest creature he had ever seen, and the sadness in those dark, magnificent eyes of hers affected him strangely. The Kanakas were a handsome race, and beauty was not rare among them, but it was the beauty of shapely animals. It was empty. But those tragic eyes were dark with mystery, and you felt in them the bitter complexity of the groping, human soul. The trader told him the story and it moved him.

"Do you think he'll ever come back?" asked Neilson.

"No fear. Why, it'll be a couple of years before the ship is paid off, and by then he'll have forgotten all about her. I bet he was pretty mad when he woke up and found he'd been shanghaied, and I shouldn't wonder but he wanted to fight somebody. But he'd got to grin and bear it, and I guess in a month he was thinking it the best thing that had ever happened to him that he got away from the island."

But Neilson could not get the story out of his head. Perhaps because he was sick and weakly, the radiant health of Red appealed to his imagination. Himself an ugly man, insignificant of appearance, he prized very highly comeliness in others. He had never been passionately in love, and certainly he had never been passionately loved. The mutual attraction of those two young things gave him a singular delight. It had the ineffable beauty of the Absolute. He went again to the little hut by the creek. He had a gift for languages and an energetic mind, accustomed to work, and he had already given much time to the study of the local tongue. Old habit was strong in him and he was gathering together material for a paper on the Samoan speech. The old crone who shared the hut with Sally invited him to come in and sit down. She gave him *kava* to drink and cigarettes to smoke. She was glad to have someone to chat with and while she talked he looked at Sally. She reminded him of the Psyche in the museum at Naples. Her features had the same dear purity of line, and though she had borne a child she had still a virginal aspect.

It was not till he had seen her two or three times that he induced her to speak. Then it was only to ask him if he had seen in Apia a man called Red. Two years had passed since his disappearance, but it was plain that she still thought of him incessantly.

It did not take Neilson long to discover that he was in love with her. It was only by an effort of will now that he prevented himself from going every day to the creek, and when he was not with Sally his thoughts were. At first, looking upon himself as a dying man, he asked only to look at her, and occasionally hear her speak, and his love gave him a wonderful happiness. He exulted in its purity. He wanted nothing from her but the opportunity to weave around her graceful person a web of beautiful fancies. But the open air, the equable temperature, the rest, the simple fare, began to have an unexpected effect on his health. His temperature did not soar at night to such alarming heights, he coughed less and began to put on weight; six months passed without his having a haemorrhage; and on a sudden he saw the possibility that he might live. He had studied his disease carefully, and the hope dawned upon him that with great care he might arrest its course. It exhilarated him to look forward once more to the future. He made plans. It was evident that any active life was out of the question, but he could live on the islands, and the small income he had, insufficient elsewhere, would be ample to keep him. He could grow coconuts; that would give him an occupation; and he would send for his books and a piano; but his quick mind saw that in all this he was merely trying to conceal from himself the desire which obsessed him.

He wanted Sally. He loved not only her beauty, but that dim soul which he divined behind her suffering eyes. He would intoxicate her with his passion. In the end he would make her forget. And in an ecstasy of surrender he fancied himself giving her too the happiness which he had thought never to know again, but had now so miraculously achieved.

He asked her to live with him. She refused. He had expected that and did not let it depress him, for he was sure that sooner or later she would yield. His love was irresistible. He told the old woman of his wishes, and found somewhat to his surprise that she and the neighbours, long aware of them, were strongly urging Sally to accept his offer. After all, every native was glad to keep house for a white man, and Neilson according to the standards of the island was a rich one. The trader with whom he boarded went to her and told her not to be a fool; such an opportunity would not come again, and after so long she could not still believe that Red would ever return. The girl's resistance only increased Neilson's desire, and what had been a very pure love now became an agonising passion. He was determined that nothing should stand in his way. He gave Sally no peace. At last, worn out by his persistence and the persuasions, by turns pleading and angry, of everyone around her, she consented. But the day after when, exultant, he went to see her he found that in the night she had burnt down the hut in which she and Red had lived together. The old crone ran towards him full of angry abuse of Sally, but he waved her aside; it did not matter; they would build a bungalow on the place where the hut had stood. A European house would really be more convenient if he wanted to bring out a piano and a vast number of books.

And so the little wooden house was built in which he had now lived for many years, and Sally became his wife. But after the first few weeks of rapture, during which he was satisfied with what she gave him he had known little happiness. She had yielded to him, through weariness, but she had only yielded what she set no store on. The soul which he had dimly glimpsed escaped him. He knew that she cared nothing for him. She still loved Red, and all the time she was waiting for his return. At a sign from him, Neilson knew that, notwithstanding his love, his tenderness, his sympathy, his generosity, she would leave him without a moment's hesitation. She would never give a thought to his distress. Anguish seized him and he battered at that impenetrable self of hers which sullenly resisted him. His love became bitter. He tried to melt her heart with kindness, but it remained as hard as before; he feigned indifference, but she did not notice it. Sometimes he lost his temper and abused her, and then she wept silently. Sometimes he thought she was nothing but a fraud, and that soul simply an invention of his own, and that he could not get into the sanctuary of her heart because there was no sanctuary there. His love became a prison from which he longed to escape, but he had not the strength merely to open the door—that was all it needed—and walk out into the open air. It was torture and at last he became numb and hopeless. In the end the fire burnt itself out and, when he saw her eyes rest for an instant on the slender bridge, it was no longer rage that filled his heart but impatience. For many years now they had lived together bound by the ties of habit and convenience, and it was with a smile that he looked back on his old passion. She was an old woman, for the women on the islands age quickly, and if he had no love for her any more he had tolerance. She left him alone. He was contented with his piano and his books.

His thoughts led him to a desire for words.

"When I look back now and reflect on that brief passionate love of Red and Sally, I think that perhaps they should thank the ruthless fate that separated them when their love seemed still to be at its height. They suffered, but they suffered in beauty. They were spared the real tragedy of love."

"I don't know exactly as I get you," said the skipper.

"The tragedy of love is not death or separation. How long do you think it would have been before one or other of them ceased to care? Oh, it is dreadfully bitter to look at a woman whom you have loved with all your heart and soul, so that you felt you could not bear to let her out of your sight, and realise that you would not mind if you never saw her again. The tragedy of love is indifference."

But while he was speaking a very extraordinary thing happened. Though he had been addressing the skipper he had not been talking to him, he had been putting his thoughts into words for himself, and with his eyes fixed on the man in front of him he had not seen him. But now an image presented itself to them, an image not of the man he saw, but of another man. It was as though he were looking into one of those distorting mirrors that make you extraordinarily squat or outrageously elongate, but here exactly the opposite took place, and in the obese, ugly old man he caught the shadowy glimpse of a stripling. He gave him now a quick, searching scrutiny. Why had a haphazard stroll brought him just to this place? A sudden tremor of his heart made him slightly breathless. An absurd suspicion seized him. What had occurred to him was impossible, and yet it might be a fact.

"What is your name?" he asked abruptly.

The skipper's face puckered and he gave a cunning chuckle. He looked then malicious and horribly vulgar.

"It's such a damned long time since I heard it that I almost forget it myself. But for thirty years now in the islands they've always called me Red."

His huge form shook as he gave a low, almost silent laugh. It was obscene. Neilson shuddered. Red was hugely amused, and from his bloodshot eyes tears ran down his cheeks.

Neilson gave a gasp, for at that moment a woman came in. She was a native, a woman of somewhat commanding presence, stout without being corpulent, dark, for the natives grow darker with age, with very grey hair. She wore a black Mother Hubbard, and its thinness showed her heavy breasts. The moment had come.

She made an observation to Neilson about some household matter and he answered. He wondered if his voice sounded as unnatural to her as it did to himself. She gave the man who was sitting in the chair by the window an indifferent glance, and went out of the room. The moment had come and gone.

Neilson for a moment could not speak. He was strangely shaken. Then he said:

"I'd be very glad if you'd stay and have a bit of dinner with me. Pot luck."

"I don't think I will," said Red. "I must go after this fellow Gray. I'll give him his stuff and then I'll get away. I want to be back in Apia tomorrow."

"I'll send a boy along with you to show you the way."

"That'll be fine."

Red heaved himself out of his chair, while the Swede called one of the boys who worked on the plantation. He told him where the skipper wanted to go, and the boy stepped along the bridge. Red prepared to follow him.

"Don't fall in," said Neilson.

"Not on your life."

Neilson watched him make his way across and when he had disappeared among the coconuts he looked still. Then he sank heavily in his chair. Was that the man who had prevented him from being happy? Was that the man whom Sally had loved all these years and for whom she had waited so desperately? It was grotesque. A sudden fury seized him so that he had an instinct to spring up and smash everything around him. He had been cheated. They had seen each other at last and had not known it. He began to laugh, mirthlessly, and his laughter grew till it became hysterical. The Gods had played him a cruel trick. And he was old now.

At last Sally came in to tell him dinner was ready. He sat down in front of her and tried to eat. He wondered what she would say if he told her now that the fat old man sitting in the chair was the lover whom she remembered still with the passionate abandonment of her youth. Years ago, when he hated her because she made him so unhappy, he would have been glad to tell her. He wanted to hurt her then as she hurt him, because his hatred was only love. But now he did not care. He shrugged his shoulders listlessly.

"What did that man want?" she asked presently.

He did not answer at once. She was old too, a fat old native woman. He wondered why he had ever loved her so madly. He had laid at her feet all the treasures of his soul, and she had cared nothing for them. Waste, what waste! And now, when he looked at her, he felt only contempt. His patience was at last exhausted. He answered her question.

"He's the captain of a schooner. He's come from Apia."

"Yes."

"He brought me news from home. My eldest brother is very ill and I must go back."

"Will you be gone long?"

He shrugged his shoulders.

The Attendant's Confession

Joaquim Maria Machado de Assis

Joaquim Maria Machado de Assis (1839-1908) was a Brazilian poet, novelist and short story writer who was the first president of the Brazilian Academy of Letters. Considered a master of Brazilian literature, he had a unique style of writing. *Dom Casmurro* (1899) by Machado de Assis is considered a masterpiece of Brazilian realist literature. His writings cloaked the grave and pessimistic under a veneer of flippancy and humour. 'The Attendant's Confession,' translated by Isaac Goldberg, was part of the collection *Brazilian Tales* (1921).

So it really seems to you that what happened to me in 1860 is worth while writing down? Very well. I'll tell you the story, but on the condition that you do not divulge it before my death. You'll not have to wait long—a week at most; I am a marked man.

I could have told you the story of my whole life, which holds many other interesting details: but for that there would be needed time, courage and paper. There is plenty of paper, indeed, but my courage is at low ebb, and as to the time that is yet left me, it may be compared to the life of a candle-flame. Soon tomorrow's sun will rise—a demon sun as impenetrable as life itself. So goodbye, my dear sir; read this and bear me no ill will; pardon me those things that will appear evil to you and do not complain too much if there is exhaled a disagreeable odor which is not exactly that of the rose. You asked me for a human document. Here it is. Ask me for neither the empire of the Great Mogul nor a photograph of the Maccabees; but request, if you will, my dead man's shoes, and I'll will them to you and no other.

You already know that this took place in 1860. The year before, about the month of August, at the age of forty-two, I had become a theologian—that is, I copied the theological studies of a priest at Nictheroy, an old college-chum, who thus tactfully gave me my board and lodging. In that same month of August, 1859, he received a letter from the vicar of a small town in the interior, asking if he knew of an intelligent, discreet and patient person who would be willing, in return for generous wages, to serve as attendant to the invalid Colonel Felisbert. The priest proposed that I take the place, and I accepted it eagerly, for I was tired of copying Latin quotations and ecclesiastic formulas. First I went to Rio de Janeiro to take leave of a brother who lived at the capital, and from there I departed for the little village of the interior.

When I arrived there I heard bad news concerning the colonel. He was pictured to me as a disagreeable, harsh, exacting fellow; nobody could endure him, not even his own friends. He had used more attendants than medicines. In fact he had broken the faces of two of them. But to all this I replied that I had no fear of persons in good health, still less of invalids. So, after first visiting the vicar, who confirmed all that I had heard and recommended to me charity and forbearance, I turned toward the colonel's residence.

I found him on the veranda of his house, stretched out on a chair and suffering greatly. He received me fairly well. At first he examined me silently, piercing me with his two feline eyes; then a kind of malicious smile spread over his features, which were rather hard. Finally he declared to me that all the attendants he had ever engaged in his service hadn't been worth a button, that they slept too much, were impudent and spent their time courting the servants; two of them were even thieves.

"And you, are you a thief?"

"No, sir."

Then he asked me my name. Scarcely had I uttered it when he made a gesture of astonishment.

"Your name is Colombo?"

"No, sir. My name is Procopio José Gomes Vallongo."

Vallongo?—He came to the conclusion that this was no Christian name and proposed thenceforth to call me simply Procopio. I replied that it should be just as he pleased.

If I recall this incident, it is not only because it seems to me to give a good picture of the colonel, but also to show you that my reply made a very good impression upon him. The next day he told the vicar so, adding that he had never had a more sympathetic attendant. The fact is, we lived a regular honeymoon that lasted one week.

From the dawn of the eighth day I knew the life of my predecessors—a dog's life. I no longer slept. I no longer thought of anything, I was showered with insults and laughed at them from time to time with an air of resignation and submission, for I had discovered that this was a way of pleasing him. His impertinences proceeded as much from his malady as from his temperament. His illness was of the most complicated: he suffered from aneurism, rheumatism and three or four minor affections. He was nearly sixty, and since he had been five years old had been accustomed to having everybody at his beck and call. That he was surly one could well forgive; but he was also very malicious. He took pleasure in the grief and the humiliation of others. At the end of three months I was tired of putting up with him and had resolved to leave; only the opportunity was lacking.

But that came soon enough. One day, when I was a bit late in giving him a massage, he took his cane and struck me with it two or three times. That was the last straw. I told him on the spot that I was through with him and I went to pack my trunk. He came later to my room; he begged me to remain, assured me that there wasn't anything to be angry at, that I must excuse the ill-humoredness of old age … He insisted so much that I agreed to stay.

"I am nearing the end, Procopio," he said to me that evening. "I can't live much longer. I am upon the verge of the grave. You will go to my burial, Procopio. Under no circumstances will I excuse you. You shall go, you shall pray over my tomb. And if you don't," he added, laughing, "my ghost will come at night and pull you by the legs. Do you believe in souls of the other world, Procopio?"

"Nonsense!"

"And why don't you, you blockhead?" he replied passionately, with distended eyes.

That is how he was in his peaceful intervals; what he was during his attacks of anger, you may well imagine!

He hit me no more with his cane, but his insults were the same, if not worse. With time I became hardened, I no longer heeded anything; I was an ignoramus, a camel, a bumpkin, an idiot, a loggerhead—I was everything! It must further be understood that I alone was favored with these pretty names. He had no relatives; there had been a nephew, but he had died of consumption. As to friends, those who came now and then to flatter him and indulge his whims made him but a short visit, five or ten minutes at the most. I alone was always present to receive his dictionary of insults. More than once I resolved to leave him; but as the vicar would exhort me not to abandon the colonel I always yielded in the end.

Not only were our relations becoming very much strained, but I was in a hurry to get back to Rio de Janeiro. At forty-two years of age one does not easily accustom himself to perpetual seclusion with a brutal, snarling old invalid, in the depths of a remote village. Just to give you an idea of my isolation, let it suffice to inform you that I didn't even read the newspapers; outside of some more or less important piece of news that was brought to the colonel, I knew nothing of what was doing in the world. I therefore yearned to get back to Rio at the first opportunity, even at the cost of breaking with the vicar. And I may as well add—since I am here making a general confession—that having spent nothing of my wages, I was itching to dissipate them at the capital.

Very probably my chance was approaching. The colonel was rapidly getting worse. He made his will, the notary receiving almost as many insults as did I. The invalid's treatment became more strict; short intervals of peace and rest became rarer than ever for me. Already I had lost the meagre measure of pity that made me forget the old invalid's excesses; within me there seethed a cauldron of aversion and hatred. At the beginning of the month of August I decided definitely to leave. The vicar and the doctor, finally accepting my explanations, asked me but a few days' more service.

I gave them a month. At the end of that time I would depart, whatever might be the condition of the invalid. The vicar promised to find a substitute for me.

You'll see now what happened. On the evening of the 24th of August the colonel had a violent attack of anger; he struck me, he called me the vilest names, he threatened to shoot me; finally he threw in my face a plate of porridge that was too cold for him. The plate struck the wall and broke into a thousand fragments.

"You'll pay me for it, you thief!" he bellowed.

For a long time he grumbled. Towards eleven o'clock he gradually fell asleep. While he slept I took a book out of my pocket, a translation of an old d'Arlincourt romance which I had found lying about, and began to read it in his room, at a small distance from his bed. I was to wake him at midnight to give him his medicine; but, whether it was due to fatigue or to the influence of the book, I, too, before reaching the second page, fell asleep. The cries of the colonel awoke me with a start; in an instant I was up. He, apparently in a delirium, continued to utter the same cries; finally he seized his water-bottle and threw it at my face. I could not get out of the way in time; the bottle hit me in the left cheek, and the pain was so acute that I almost lost consciousness. With a leap I rushed upon the invalid; I tightened my hands around his neck; he struggled several moments; I strangled him.

When I beheld that he no longer breathed, I stepped back in terror. I cried out; but nobody heard me. Then, approaching the bed once more, I shook him so as to bring him back to life. It was too late; the aneurism had burst, and the colonel was dead. I went into the adjoining room, and for two hours I did not dare to return. It is impossible for me to express all that I felt during that time. It was intense stupefaction, a kind of vague and vacant delirium. It seemed to me that I saw faces grinning on the walls; I heard muffled voices. The cries of the victim, the cries uttered before the struggle and during its wild moments continued to reverberate within me, and the air, in whatever direction I turned, seemed to shake with convulsions. Do not imagine that I am inventing pictures or aiming at verbal style. I swear to you that I heard distinctly voices that were crying at me: "Murderer; Murderer!"

All was quiet in the house. The tick-tick of the clock, very even, slow, dryly metrical, increased the silence and solitude. I put my ear to the door of the room, in hope of hearing a groan, a word, an insult, anything that would be a sign of life, that might bring back peace to my conscience; I was ready to let myself be struck ten, twenty, a hundred times, by the colonel's hand. But, nothing—all was silent. I began to pace the room aimlessly; I sat down, I brought my hands despairingly to my head; I repented ever having come to the place.

"Cursed be the hour in which I ever accepted such a position," I cried. And I flamed with resentment against the priest of Nichteroy, against the doctor, the vicar—against all those who had procured the place for me and forced me to remain there so long. They, too, I convinced myself, were accomplices in my crime.

As the silence finally terrified me, I opened a window, in the hope of hearing at least the murmuring of the wind. But no wind was blowing. The night was peaceful. The stars were sparkling with the indifference of those who remove their hats before a passing funeral procession and continue to speak of other things. I remained at the window for some time, my elbows on the sill, my gaze seeking to penetrate the night, forcing myself to make a mental summary of my life so that I might escape the present agony. I believe it was only then that I thought clearly about the penalty of my crime. I saw myself already being accused and threatened with dire punishment. From this moment fear complicated my feeling of remorse. I felt my hair stand on end. A few minutes later I saw three or four human shapes spying at me from the terrace, where they seemed to be waiting in ambush; I withdrew; the shapes vanished into the air; it had been an hallucination.

Before daybreak I bandaged the wounds that I had received in the face. Then only did I pluck up enough courage to return to the other room. Twice I started, only to turn back; but it must be done, so I entered. Even then, I did not at first go to the bed. My legs shook, my heart pounded. I thought of flight; but that would have been a confession of the crime ... It was on the contrary very important for me to hide all traces of it. I approached the bed. I looked at the corpse, with its widely distended eyes and its mouth gaping, as if uttering the eternal reproach of the centuries: "Cain, what hast thou done with thy brother?" I discovered on the neck the marks of my nails; I buttoned the shirt to the top, and threw the bed-cover up to the dead man's chin. Then I called a servant and told him that the colonel had died towards morning; I sent him to notify the vicar and the doctor.

The first idea that came to me was to leave as soon as possible under the pretext that my brother was ill; and in reality I had received, several days before, from Rio, a letter telling me that he was not at all well. But I considered that my immediate departure might arouse suspicion, and I decided to wait. I laid out the corpse myself, with the assistance of an old, near-sighted negro. I remained continually in the room of the dead. I trembled lest something out of the way should be discovered. I wanted to assure myself that no mistrust could be read upon the faces of the others; but I did not dare to look any person in the eye. Everything made me impatient; the going and coming of those who, on tip-toe crossed the room; their whisperings; the ceremonies and the prayers of the vicar… The hour having come, I closed the coffin, but with trembling hands, so trembling that somebody noticed it and commented upon it aloud, with pity.

"Poor Procopio! Despite what he has suffered from his master, he is strongly moved."

It sounded like irony to me. I was anxious to have it all over with. We went out. Once in the street the passing from semi-obscurity to daylight dazed me and I staggered. I began to fear that it would no longer be possible for me to conceal the crime. I kept my eyes steadily fixed upon the ground and took my place in the procession. When all was over, I breathed once more. I was at peace with man. But I was not at peace with my conscience, and the first nights, naturally, I spent in restlessness and affliction. Need I tell you that I hastened to return to Rio de Janeiro, and that I dwelt there in terror and suspense, although far removed from the scene of the crime? I never smiled; I scarcely spoke; I ate very little; I suffered hallucinations and nightmares...

"Let the dead rest in peace," they would say to me. "It is out of all reason to show so much melancholy."

And I was happy to find how people interpreted my symptoms, and praised the dead man highly, calling him a good soul, surly, in truth, but with a heart of gold. And as I spoke in such wise, I convinced myself, at least for a few moments at a time. Another interesting phenomenon was taking place within me—I tell it to you because you will perhaps make some useful deduction from it—and that was, although I had very little religion in me, I had a mass sung for the eternal rest of the colonel at the Church of the Blessed Sacrament. I sent out no invitations to it, I did not whisper a word of it to anybody; I went there alone. I knelt during the whole service and made many signs of the cross. I paid the priest double and distributed alms at the door, all in the name of the deceased.

I wished to deceive nobody. The proof of this lies in the fact that I did all this without letting any other know. To complete this incident, I may add that I never mentioned the colonel without repeating, "May his soul rest in peace!" And I told several funny anecdotes about him, some amusing caprices of his...

About a week after my arrival at Rio I received a letter from the vicar. He announced that the will of the colonel had been opened and that I was there designated as his sole heir. Imagine my stupefaction! I was sure that I had read wrongly; I showed it to my brother, to friends; they all read the same thing. It was there in black and white, I was really the sole heir of the colonel. Then I suddenly thought that this was a trap to catch me, but then I considered that there were other ways of arresting me, if the crime had been discovered. Moreover, I knew the vicar's honesty, and I was sure that he would not be a party to such a plan. I reread the letter five times, ten times, a hundred times; it was true. I was the colonel's sole heir!

"How much was he worth?" my brother asked me.

"I don't know, but I know that he was very wealthy."

"Really, he's shown that he was a very true friend to you."

"He certainly was—he was..."

Thus, by a strange irony of fate, all the colonel's wealth came into my hands. At first I thought of refusing the legacy. It seemed odious to take a sou of that inheritance; it seemed worse than the reward of a hired assassin. For three days this thought obsessed me; but more and more I was thrust against this consideration: that my refusal would not fail to awake suspicion. Finally I settled upon a compromise; I would accept the inheritance and would distribute it in small sums, secretly.

This was not merely scruple on my part, it was also the desire to redeem my crime by virtuous deeds; and it seemed the only way to recover my peace of mind and feel that accounts were straight.

I made hurried preparations and left. As I neared the little village the sad event returned obstinately to my memory. Everything about the place, as I looked at it once again, suggested tragic deeds. At every turn in the road I seemed to see the ghost of the colonel loom. And despite myself, I evoked in my imagination his cries, his struggles, his looks on that horrible night of the crime ...

Crime or struggle? Really, it was rather a struggle; I had been attacked, I had defended myself; and in self-defence ... It had been an unfortunate struggle, a genuine tragedy. This idea gripped me. And I reviewed all the abuse he had heaped upon me; I counted the blows, the names ... It was not the colonel's fault, that I knew well; it was his affliction that made him so peevish and even wicked. But I pardoned all, everything!... The worst of it was the end of that fatal night ... I also considered that in any case the colonel had not long to live. His days were numbered; did not he himself feel that? Didn't he say every now and then, "How much longer have I to live? Two weeks, or one, perhaps less?"

This was not life, it was slow agony, if one may so name the continual martyrdom of that poor man ... And who knows, who can say that the struggle and his death were not simply a coincidence? That was after all quite possible, it was even most probable; careful weighing of the matter showed that it couldn't have been otherwise. At length this idea, too, engraved itself upon my mind ...

Something tugged at my heart as I entered the village; I wanted to run back; but I dominated my emotions and I pressed forward. I was received with a shower of congratulations. The vicar communicated to me the particulars of the will, enumerated the pious gifts, and, as he spoke, praised the Christian forbearance and the faithfulness which I had shown in my care of the deceased, who, despite his temper and brutality, had so well demonstrated his gratitude.

"Certainly," I said, looking nervously around.

I was astounded. Everybody praised my conduct. Such patience, such devotion. The first formalities of the inventory detained me for a while; I chose a solicitor; things followed their course in regular fashion. During this time there was much talk of the colonel. People came and told me tales about him, but without observing the priest's moderation. I defended the memory of the colonel. I recalled his good qualities, his virtues; had he not been austere?...

"Austere!" they would interrupt. "Nonsense! He is dead, and it's all over now. But he was a regular demon!"

And they would cite incidents and relate the colonel's perversities, some of which were nothing less than extraordinary.

Need I confess it? At first I listened to all this talk with great curiosity; then, a queer pleasure penetrated my heart, a pleasure from which, sincerely, I tried to escape. And I continued to defend the colonel; I explained him, I attributed much of the fault-finding to local animosity; I admitted, yes, I admitted that he had been a trifle exacting, somewhat violent...

"Somewhat! Why he was as furious as a snake!" exclaimed the barber.

And all—the collector, the apothecary, the clerk—all were of the same opinion. And they would start to relate other anecdotes. They reviewed the entire life of the deceased. The old folks took particular delight in recalling the cruelties of his youth. And that queer pleasure, intimate, mute, insidious, grew within me—a sort of moral tapeworm whose coils I tore out in vain, for they would immediately form again and take firmer hold than ever.

The formalities of the inventory afforded me a little relief; moreover, public opinion was so unanimously unfavorable to the colonel that little by little the place lost the lugubrious aspect that had at first struck me. At last I entered into possession of the legacy, which I converted into land-titles and cash.

Several months had elapsed, and the idea of distributing the inheritance in charity and pious donations was by no means so strong as it had at first been; it even seemed to me that this would be sheer affectation. I revised my initial plan; I gave away several insignificant sums to the poor; I presented the village church with a few new ornaments; I gave several thousand francs to the Sacred

House of Mercy, etc. I did not forget to erect a monument upon the colonel's grave—a very simple monument, all marble, the work of a Neapolitan sculptor who remained at Rio until 1866, and who has since died, I believe, in Paraguay.

Years have gone by. My memory has become vague and unreliable. Sometimes I think of the colonel, but without feeling again the terrors of those early days. All the doctors to whom I have described his afflictions have been unanimous as regards the inevitable end in store for the invalid, and were indeed surprised that he should so long have resisted. It is just possible that I may have involuntarily exaggerated the description of his various symptoms; but the truth is that he was sure of sudden death, even had this fatality not occurred…

Goodbye, my dear sir. If you deem these notes not totally devoid of value reward me for them with a marble tomb, and place there for my epitaph this variant which I have made of the divine sermon on the mount:

"Blessed are they who possess, for they shall be consoled."

A Hunger Artist

Franz Kafka

Franz Kafka (1883-1924), a German-speaking Bohemian Jewish novelist, was one of the foremost writers of the 20th century. His novels *The Judgment* (1913) and *The Trial* (1925), cemented his reputation as a writer. Kafka had a concise style of writing and the themes of despair and alienation were recurrent in his works. Max Brod, friend, biographer and editor of Kafka, defied the latter's request to burn his manuscripts, and published his works after the author's death. 'A Hunger Artist' (1922) is existentialist in tone and one of Kafka's finest stories.

During these last decades the interest in professional fasting has markedly diminished. It used to pay very well to stage such great performances under one's own management, but today that is quite impossible. We live in a different world now. At one time the whole town took a lively interest in the hunger artist; from day to day of his fast the excitement mounted; everybody wanted to see him at least once a day; there were people who bought season tickets for the last few days and sat from morning till night in front of his small barred cage; even in the nighttime there were visiting hours, when the whole effect was heightened by torch flares; on fine days the cage was set out in the open air, and then it was the children's special treat to see the hunger artist; for their elders he was often just a joke that happened to be in fashion, but the children stood open-mouthed, holding each other's hands for greater security, marveling at him as he sat there pallid in black tights, with his ribs sticking out so prominently, not even on a seat but down among straw on the ground, sometimes giving a courteous nod, answering questions with a constrained smile, or perhaps stretching an arm through the bars so that one might feel how thin it was, and then again withdrawing deep into himself, paying no attention to anyone or anything, not even to the all-important striking of the clock that was the only piece of furniture in his cage, but merely staring into vacancy with half-shut eyes, now and then taking a sip from a tiny glass of water to moisten his lips.

Besides casual onlookers there were also relays of permanent watchers selected by the public, usually butchers, strangely enough, and it was their task to watch the hunger artist day and night, three of them at a time, in case he should have some secret recourse to nourishment. This was nothing but a formality, instigated to reassure the masses, for the initiates knew well enough that during his fast the artist would never in any circumstances, not even under forcible compulsion, swallow the smallest morsel of food; the honor of his profession forbade it. Not every watcher, of course, was capable of understanding this, there were often groups of night watchers who were very lax in carrying out their duties and deliberately huddled together in a retired corner to play cards with great absorption, obviously intending to give the hunger artist the chance of a little refreshment, which they supposed he would draw from some private hoard. Nothing annoyed the artist more than these watchers; they made him miserable; they made his fast seem unendurable; sometimes he mastered his feebleness sufficiently to sing during their watch for as long as he could keep going, to show them how unjust their suspicions were. But that was of little use; they only wondered at his cleverness in being able to fill his mouth even while singing. Much more to his taste were the watchers who sat close up to the bars, who were not content with the dim night lighting of the hall but focused him in the full glare of the electric pocket torch given them by the impresario. The harsh light did not trouble him at all, in any case he could never sleep properly, and he could always drowse a little, whatever the light, at any hour, even when the hall was thronged with noisy onlookers. He was quite happy at the prospect of spending a sleepless night with such watchers; he was ready to exchange jokes with them, to tell them stories out of his nomadic life, anything at all to keep them awake and demonstrate to them again that he had no eatables in his cage and that he was fasting as not one of them could fast. But his happiest moment was when the morning came and an enormous breakfast was brought for them, at his expense, on which they flung themselves with the keen appetite of healthy men after a weary night of wakefulness. Of course there were people who argued that this breakfast was an unfair attempt to bribe the watchers, but that was going rather too far, and when they were invited to take on a night's vigil without a breakfast, merely for the sake of the cause, they made themselves scarce, although they stuck stubbornly to their suspicions.

Such suspicions, anyhow, were a necessary accompaniment to the profession of fasting. No one could possibly watch the hunger artist continuously, day and night, and so no one could produce first-hand evidence that the fast had really been rigorous and continuous; only the artist himself could know that, he was therefore bound to be the sole completely satisfied spectator of his own fast. Yet for other reasons he was never satisfied; it was not perhaps mere fasting that had brought him to such skeleton thinness that many people had regretfully to keep away from his exhibitions, because the sight of him was too much for them, perhaps it was dissatisfaction with himself that had worn him down. For he alone knew, what no other initiate knew, how easy it was to fast. It was the easiest thing in the world. He made no secret of this, yet people did not believe him, at best they set him down as modest, most of them, however, thought he was out for publicity or else was some kind of cheat who found it easy to fast because he had discovered a way of making it easy, and then had the impudence to admit the fact, more or less. He had to put up with all that, and in the course of time had got used to it, but his inner dissatisfaction always rankled, and never yet, after any term of fasting—this must be granted to his credit—had he left the cage of his own free will. The longest period of fasting was fixed by his impresario at forty days, beyond that term he was not allowed to go, not even in great cities, and there was good reason for it, too. Experience had proven that for about forty days the interest of the public could be stimulated by a steadily increasing pressure of advertisement, but after that the town began to lose interest, sympathetic support began notably to fall off; there were of course local variations as between one town and another or one country and another, but as a general rule forty days marked the limit. So on the fortieth day the flower-bedecked cage was opened, enthusiastic spectators filled the hall, a military band played, two doctors entered the cage to measure the results of the fast, which were announced through a megaphone, and finally two young ladies appeared, blissful at having been selected for the honor, to help the hunger artist down the few steps leading to a small table on which was spread a carefully chosen invalid repast. And at this very moment the artist always turned stubborn. True, he would entrust his bony arms to the outstretched helping hands of the ladies bending over him, but stand up he would not. Why stop fasting at this particular moment, after forty days of it? He had held out for a long time, an illimitably long time, why stop now, when he was in his best fasting form, or rather, not yet quite in is bet fasting form? Why should he be cheated of the fame he would get for fasting longer, for being not only the record hunger artist of all time, which presumably he was already, but for beating his own record by a performance beyond human imagination, since he felt that there were no limits to his capacity for fasting? His public pretended to admire him so much, why should it have so little patience with him; if he could endure fasting longer, why shouldn't the public endure it? Besides, he was tired, he was comfortable sitting in the straw, and now he was supposed to lift himself to his full height and go down to a meal the very thought of which gave him a nausea that only the presence of the ladies kept him from betraying, and even that with an effort. And he looked up into the eyes of the ladies who were apparently so friendly and in reality so cruel, and shook his head, which felt too heavy on its strengthless neck. But then there happened again what always happened. The impresario came forward, without a word—for the band made speech impossible—lifted his arms in the air above the artist, as if inviting Heaven to look down upon this creature here in the straw, this suffering martyr, which indeed he was, although in quite another sense; grasped him around the emaciated waist, with exaggerated caution, so that the frail condition he was in might be appreciated; and committed him to the care of the blenching ladies, not without secretly giving him a shaking so that his legs and body tottered and swayed. The artist now submitted completely; his head lolled on his breast as if it had landed there by chance; his body was hollowed out; his legs in a spasm of self-preservation clung close to each other at the knees, yet scraped on the ground as if it were not really solid ground, as if they were only trying to find solid ground; and the whole weight of his body, a featherweight after all, relapsed onto one of the ladies, who, looking around for help and panting a little—this post of honor was not at all what she had expected it to be—first stretched her neck as far as she could to keep her face at least free from contact with the artist, then finding this impossible, and her more fortunate companion not coming to her aid but merely holding extended in her own trembling hand the little bunch of knucklebones that was the artist's, to the great delight of the spectators burst into tears and had to be replaced by an attendant who had long been stationed in readiness. Then came the food, a little of which the impresario managed to get between the artist's lips, while he sat in a kind of half-fainting trance, to the accompaniment of cheerful patter designed to distract to public's attention for the artist's condition; after that, a toast was drunk to the public, supposedly prompted by a whisper from the artist in the impresario's ear; the band confirmed it with a mighty flourish, the spectators melted away, and no one had any cause to be dissatisfied with the proceedings, no one except the hunger artist himself, he only, as always.

So he lived for many years, with small regular intervals of recuperation, in visible glory, honored by the world, yet in spite of that, troubled in spirit, and all the more troubled because no-one would take his trouble seriously. What comfort could he possibly need? What more could he possibly wish for? And if some good-natured person, feeling sorry for him, tried to console him by pointing out that his melancholy was probably caused by fasting, it could happen, especially when he had been fasting for some time, that he reacted with an outburst of fury and to the general alarm began to shake the bars of his cage like a wild animal. Yet the impresario had a way of punishing these outbreaks which he rather enjoyed putting into operation. He would apologize publicly for the artist's behaviour, which was only to be excused, he admitted, because of the irritability caused by fasting; a condition hardly to be understood by well-fed people; then by natural transition he went on to mention the artist's equally incomprehensible boast that he could fast for much longer than he was doing; he praised the high ambition, the good will, the great self-denial undoubtedly implicit in such a statement; and then quite simply countered it by bringing out photographs, which were also on sale to the public, showing the artist on the fortieth day of a fast lying in bed almost dead from exhaustion. This perversion of the truth, familiar to the artist though it was, always unnerved him afresh and proved too much for him. What was a consequence of the premature ending of his fast was here presented as the cause of it! To fight against this lack of understanding, against a whole world of non-understanding, was impossible. Time and again in good faith he stood by the bars listening to the impresario, but as soon as the photographs appeared he always let go and sank with a groan back onto his straw, and the reassured public could once more come close and gaze at him.

A few years later when the witnesses of such scenes called them to mind, they often failed to understand themselves at all. For meanwhile the aforementioned change in public interest had set in; it seemed to happen almost overnight; there may have been profound causes for it, but who was going to bother about that; at any rate the pampered hunger artist suddenly found himself deserted on fine day by the amusement-seekers, who went streaming past him to other more-favored attractions. For the last time the impresario hurried him over half Europe to discover whether the old interest might still survive here and there; all in vain; everywhere, as if by secret agreement, a positive revulsion from professional fasting was in evidence. Of course it could not really have sprung up so suddenly as all that, and many premonitory symptoms which had not been sufficiently remarked or suppressed during the rush and glitter of success now came retrospectively to mind, but it was now too late to take any countermeasures. Fasting would surely come into fashion again at some future date, yet that was no comfort for those living in the present. What, then, was the hunger artist to do? He had been applauded by thousands in his time and could hardly come down to showing himself in a street booth at village fairs, and as for adopting another profession, he was not only too old for that but too fanatically devoted to fasting. So he took leave of the impresario, his partner in an unparalleled career, and hired himself to a large circus; in order to spare his own feelings he avoided reading the conditions of his contract.

A large circus with its enormous traffic in replacing and recruiting men, animals, and apparatus can always find a use for people at any time, even for a hunger artist, provided of course that he does not ask too much, and in this particular case anyhow it was not only the artist who was taken on but his famous and long-known name as well, indeed considering the peculiar nature of his performance, which was not impaired by advancing age, it could not be objected that here was an artist past his prime, no longer at the height of his professional skill, seeking a refuge in some quiet corner of a circus; on the contrary, the hunger artist averred that he could fast as well as ever, which was entirely credible, he even alleged that if he were allowed to fast as he liked, and this was at once promised him without more ado, he could astound the world by establishing a record never yet achieved, a statement that certainly provoked a smile among the other professionals, since it left out of account the change in public opinion, which the hunger artist in his zeal conveniently forgot.

He had not, however, actually lost his sense of the real situation and took it as a matter of course that he and his cage should be stationed, not in the middle of the ring as a main attraction, but outside, near the animal cages, on a site that was after all easily accessible. Large and gaily painted placards made a frame for the cage and announced what was to be seen inside it. When the public came thronging out in the intervals to see the animals, they could hardly avoid passing the hunger artist's cage and stopping there for a moment, perhaps they might even have stayed longer, had not those pressing behind them behind them in the narrow gangway, who did not understand why they should be held up on their way towards the excitements of the menagerie, made it impossible for anyone to stand gazing for any length of time. And that was the reason why the hunger artist, who had of course been looking forward to these visiting hours as the main achievement of his life, began instead to shrink from them. At first he could hardly wait for the intervals;

it was exhilarating to watch the crowds come streaming his way, until only too soon—not even the most obstinate self-deception, clung to almost consciously, could hold out against the fact—the conviction was borne in upon him that these people, most of them, to judge from their actions, again and again, without exception, were all on their way to the menagerie. And the first sight of them from a distance remained the best. For when they reached his cage he was at once deafened by the storm of shouting and abuse that arose from the two contending factions, which renewed themselves continuously, of those who wanted to stop and stare at him—he soon began to dislike them more than the others—not out of real interest but only out of obstinate self-assertiveness, and those who wanted to go straight on to the animals. When the first great rush was past, the stragglers came along, and these, whom nothing could have prevented from stopping to look at him as long as they had breath, raced past with long strides, hardly even glancing at him, in their haste to get to the menagerie in time. And all too rarely did it happen that he had a stroke of luck, when some father of a family fetched up before him with his children, pointed a finger at the hunger artist, and explained at length what the phenomenon meant, telling stories of earlier years when he himself had watched similar but much more thrilling performances, and the children, still rather uncomprehending, since neither inside or outside school had they been sufficiently prepared for this lesson—what did they care about fasting?—yet showed by the brightness of their intent eyes that new and better times might be coming. Perhaps, said the hunger artist to himself, many a time, things would be a little better if his cage were set not quite so near the menagerie. That made it too easy for people to make their choice, to say nothing of what he suffered from the stench of the menagerie, the animals' restlessness by night, the carrying past of raw lumps of flesh for the beasts of prey, the roaring at feeding times, depressed him continually. But he did not dare to lodge a complaint with the management; after all, he had the animals to thank for the troops of people who passed his cage, among whom there might always be one here and there to take an interest in him, and who could tell where they might seclude him if he called attention to his existence and thereby to the fact that, strictly speaking, he was only an impediment on the way to the menagerie.

A small impediment, to be sure, one that grew steadily less. People grew familiar with the strange idea that they could be expected, in times like these, to take an interest in a hunger artist, and with this familiarity the verdict went out against him. He might fast as much as he could, and he did so; but nothing could save him now, people passed him by. Just try to explain to anyone the art of fasting! Anyone who has no feeling for it cannot be made to understand it. The fine placards grew dirty and illegible, they were torn down; the little notice board showing the number of fast days achieved, which at first was changed carefully every day, had long stayed at the same figure, for after the first few weeks even this small task seemed pointless to the staff; and so the artist simply fasted on and on, as he had once dreamed of doing, and it was no trouble to him, just as he had always foretold, but no one counted the days, no one, not even the artist himself, knew what records he was already breaking, and his heart became heavy. And when once in a while some leisurely passer-by stopped, made merry over the old figure on the board and spoke of swindling, that was in its way the stupidest lie ever invented by indifference and inborn malice, since it was not the hunger artist who was cheating, he was working honestly, but the world was cheating him of his reward.

Many more days went by, however, and that too came to an end. An overseer's eye fell on the cage one day and he asked the attendants why this perfectly good cage should be left standing there unused with dirty straw inside it; nobody knew, until one man, helped out by the notice board, remembered about the hunger artist. They poked into the straw with sticks and found him in it. "Are you still fasting?" asked the overseer, "when on earth do you mean to stop?" "Forgive me, everybody," whispered the hunger artist; only the overseer, who had his ear to the bars, understood him. "Of course," said the overseer, and tapped his forehead with a finger to let the attendants know what state the man was in, "we forgive you." "I always wanted you to admire my fasting," said the hunger artist. "We do admire it," said the overseer, affably. "But you shouldn't admire it," said the hunger artist. "Well then we don't admire it," said the overseer, "but why shouldn't we admire it?" "Because I have to fast, I can't help it," said the hunger artist. "What a fellow you are," said the overseer, "and why can't you help it?" "Because," said the hunger artist, lifting his head a little and speaking, with his lips pursed, as if for a kiss, right into the overseer's ear, so that no syllable might be lost, "because I couldn't find the food I liked. If I had found it, believe me, I should have made no fuss and stuffed myself like you or anyone else." These were his last words, but in his dimming eyes remained the firm though no longer proud persuasion that he was still continuing to fast.

"Well, clear this out now!" said the overseer, and they buried the hunger artist, straw and all. Into the cage they put a young panther. Even the most insensitive felt it refreshing to see this wild creature leaping around the cage that had so long been dreary. The panther was all right. The food he liked was brought to him without hesitation by the attendants; he seemed not even to miss his freedom; his noble body, furnished almost to the bursting point with all that it needed, seemed to carry freedom around with it too; somewhere in his jaws it seemed to lurk; and the joy of life streamed with such ardent passion from his throat that for the onlookers it was not easy to stand the shock of it. But they braced themselves, crowded around the cage, and did not ever want to move away.

The Curious Case Of Benjamin Button

F. Scott Fitzgerald

Francis Scott Key Fitzgerald (1896-1940) was one of the greatest American novelists and short story writers of the 20th century. A member of the 'Lost Generation' of the 1920s, Fitzgerald's work illustrated the Jazz Age. Some of his finest works include *The Beautiful and Damned* (1922) and *The Great Gatsby* (1925). 'The Curious Case Of Benjamin Button' was first published in the May edition of *Collier's* (1922) and made into an eponymous film in 2008.

I

As long ago as 1860 it was the proper thing to be born at home. At present, so I am told, the high gods of medicine have decreed that the first cries of the young shall be uttered upon the anesthetic air of a hospital, preferably a fashionable one. So young Mr. and Mrs. Roger Button were fifty years ahead of style when they decided, one day in the summer of 1860, that their first baby should be born in a hospital. Whether this anachronism had any bearing upon the astonishing history I am about to set down will never be known.

I shall tell you what occurred, and let you judge for yourself.

The Roger Buttons held an enviable position, both social and financial, in ante-bellum Baltimore. They were related to the This Family and the That Family, which, as every Southerner knew, entitled them to membership in that enormous peerage which largely populated the Confederacy. This was their first experience with the charming old custom of having babies—Mr. Button was naturally nervous. He hoped it would be a boy so that he could be sent to Yale College in Connecticut, at which institution Mr. Button himself had been known for four years by the somewhat obvious nickname of "Cuff."

On the September morning consecrated to the enormous event he arose nervously at six o'clock, dressed himself, adjusted an impeccable stock, and hurried forth through the streets of Baltimore to the hospital, to determine whether the darkness of the night had borne in new life upon its bosom.

When he was approximately a hundred yards from the Maryland Private Hospital for Ladies and Gentlemen he saw Doctor Keene, the family physician, descending the front steps, rubbing his hands together with a washing movement—as all doctors are required to do by the unwritten ethics of their profession.

Mr. Roger Button, the president of Roger Button & Co., Wholesale Hardware, began to run toward Doctor Keene with much less dignity than was expected from a Southern gentleman of that picturesque period. "Doctor Keene!" he called. "Oh, Doctor Keene!"

The doctor heard him, faced around, and stood waiting, a curious expression settling on his harsh, medicinal face as Mr. Button drew near.

"What happened?" demanded Mr. Button, as he came up in a gasping rush. "What was it? How is she? A boy? Who is it? What—"

"Talk sense!" said Doctor Keene sharply, He appeared somewhat irritated.

"Is the child born?" begged Mr. Button.

Doctor Keene frowned. "Why, yes, I suppose so—after a fashion." Again he threw a curious glance at Mr. Button.

"Is my wife all right?" "Yes."

"Is it a boy or a girl?"

"Here now!" cried Doctor Keene in a perfect passion of irritation," I'll ask you to go and see for yourself. Outrageous!" He snapped the last word out in almost one syllable, then he turned away muttering: "Do you imagine a case like this will help my professional reputation? One more would ruin me—ruin anybody."

"What's the matter?" demanded Mr. Button appalled. "Triplets?"

"No, not triplets!" answered the doctor cuttingly. "What's more, you can go and see for yourself. And get another doctor. I brought you into the world, young man, and I've been physician to your family for forty years, but I'm through with you! I don't want to see you or any of your relatives ever again! Goodbye!"

Then he turned sharply, and without another word climbed into his phaeton, which was waiting at the curbstone, and drove severely away.

Mr. Button stood there upon the sidewalk, stupefied and trembling from head to foot. What horrible mishap had occurred? He had suddenly lost all desire to go into the Maryland Private Hospital for Ladies and Gentlemen—it was with the greatest difficulty that, a moment later, he forced himself to mount the steps and enter the front door.

A nurse was sitting behind a desk in the opaque gloom of the hall. Swallowing his shame, Mr. Button approached her.

"Good morning," she remarked, looking up at him pleasantly.

"Good morning. I—I am Mr. Button."

At this a look of utter terror spread itself over the girl's face. She rose to her feet and seemed about to fly from the hall, restraining herself only with the most apparent difficulty.

"I want to see my child," said Mr. Button.

The nurse gave a little scream. "Oh—of course!" she cried hysterically. "Upstairs. Right upstairs. Go—*up!*"

She pointed the direction, and Mr. Button, bathed in a cool perspiration, turned falteringly, and began to mount to the second floor. In the upper hall he addressed another nurse who approached him, basin in hand. "I'm Mr. Button," he managed to articulate. "I want to see my—"

Clank! The basin clattered to the floor and rolled in the direction of the stairs. Clank! Clank! It began a methodical descent as if sharing in the general terror which this gentleman provoked.

"I want to see my child!" Mr. Button almost shrieked. He was on the verge of collapse.

Clank! The basin had reached the first floor. The nurse regained control of herself, and threw Mr. Button a look of hearty contempt.

"All *right*, Mr. Button," she agreed in a hushed voice. "Very *well!* But if you *knew* what a state it's put us all in this morning! It's perfectly outrageous! The hospital will never have the ghost of a reputation after—"

"Hurry!" he cried hoarsely. "I can't stand this!" "Come this way, then, Mr. Button."

He dragged himself after her. At the end of a long hall they reached a room from which proceeded a variety of howls—indeed, a room which, in later parlance, would have been known as the "crying-room." They entered. Ranged around the walls were half a dozen white-enameled rolling cribs, each with a tag tied at the head.

"Well," gasped Mr. Button, "which is mine?" "There!" said the nurse.

Mr. Button's eyes followed her pointing finger, and this is what he saw. Wrapped in a voluminous white blanket, and partly crammed into one of the cribs, there sat an old man apparently about seventy years of age. His sparse hair was almost white, and from his chin dripped a long smoke-coloured beard, which waved absurdly back and forth, fanned by the breeze coming in at the window. He looked up at Mr. Button with dim, faded eyes in which lurked a puzzled question.

"Am I mad?" thundered Mr. Button, his terror resolving into rage. "Is this some ghastly hospital joke?

"It doesn't seem like a joke to us," replied the nurse severely. "And I don't know whether you're mad or not—but that is most certainly your child."

The cool perspiration redoubled on Mr. Button's forehead. He closed his eyes, and then, opening them, looked again. There was no mistake—he was gazing at a man of threescore and ten—a *baby* of threescore and ten, a baby whose feet hung over the sides of the crib in which it was reposing.

The old man looked placidly from one to the other for a moment, and then suddenly spoke in a cracked and ancient voice. "Are you my father?" he demanded.

Mr. Button and the nurse started violently.

"Because if you are," went on the old man querulously, "I wish you'd get me out of this place—or, at least, get them to put a comfortable rocker in here,"

"Where in God's name did you come from? Who are you?" burst out Mr. Button frantically.

"I can't tell you *exactly* who I am," replied the querulous whine, "because I've only been born a few hours—but my last name is certainly Button."

"You lie! You're an impostor!"

The old man turned wearily to the nurse. "Nice way to welcome a new-born child," he complained in a weak voice. "Tell him he's wrong, why don't you?"

"You're wrong. Mr. Button," said the nurse severely. "This is your child, and you'll have to make the best of it. We're going to ask you to take him home with you as soon as possible—some time today."

"Home?" repeated Mr. Button incredulously.

"Yes, we can't have him here. We really can't, you know?"

"I'm right glad of it," whined the old man. "This is a fine place to keep a youngster of quiet tastes. With all this yelling and howling, I haven't been able to get a wink of sleep. I asked for something to eat"—here his voice rose to a shrill note of protest — "and they brought me a bottle of milk!"

Mr. Button sank down upon a chair near his son and concealed his face in his hands. "My heavens!" he murmured, in an ecstasy of horror. "What will people say? What must I do?"

"You'll have to take him home," insisted the nurse—"immediately!"

A grotesque picture formed itself with dreadful clarity before the eyes of the tortured man—a picture of himself walking through the crowded streets of the city with this appalling apparition stalking by his side. "I can't. I can't," he moaned.

People would stop to speak to him, and what was he going to say? He would have to introduce this—this septuagenarian: "This is my son, born early this morning." And then the old man would gather his blanket around him and they would plod on, past the bustling stores, the slave market—for a dark instant Mr. Button wished passionately that his son was black—past the luxurious houses of the residential district, past the home for the aged....

"Come! Pull yourself together," commanded the nurse.

"See here," the old man announced suddenly, "if you think I'm going to walk home in this blanket, you're entirely mistaken."

"Babies always have blankets."

With a malicious crackle the old man held up a small white swaddling garment. "Look!" he quavered. "*This* is what they had ready for me."

"Babies always wear those," said the nurse primly.

"Well," said the old man, "this baby's not going to wear anything in about two minutes. This blanket itches. They might at least have given me a sheet."

"Keep it on! Keep it on!" said Mr. Button hurriedly. He turned to the nurse. "What'll I do?"

"Go down town and buy your son some clothes."

Mr. Button's son's voice followed him down into the hall: "And a cane, father. I want to have a cane."

Mr. Button banged the outer door savagely…

II

"Good morning," Mr. Button said, nervously, to the clerk in the Chesapeake Dry Goods Company. "I want to buy some clothes for my child."

"How old is your child, sir?"

"About six hours," answered Mr. Button, without due consideration. "Babies' supply department in the rear."

"Why, I don't think—I'm not sure that's what I want. It's—he's an unusually large-size child. Exceptionally—ah—large."

"They have the largest child's sizes."

"Where is the boys' department?" inquired Mr. Button, shifting his ground desperately. He felt that the clerk must surely scent his shameful secret.

"Right here."

"Well—" He hesitated. The notion of dressing his son in men's clothes was repugnant to him. If, say, he could only find a *very* large boy's suit, he might cut off that long and awful beard, dye the white hair brown, and thus manage to conceal the worst, and to retain something of his own self-respect—not to mention his position in Baltimore society.

But a frantic inspection of the boys' department revealed no suits to fit the new-born Button. He blamed the store, of course—in such cases it is the thing to blame the store.

"How old did you say that boy of yours was?" demanded the clerk curiously.

"He's—sixteen."

"Oh, I beg your pardon. I thought you said six *hours*. You'll find the youths' department in the next aisle."

Mr. Button turned miserably away. Then he stopped, brightened, and pointed his finger toward a dressed dummy in the window display. "There!" he exclaimed. "I'll take that suit, out there on the dummy."

The clerk stared. "Why," he protested, "that's not a child's suit. At least it *is*, but it's for fancy dress. You could wear it yourself!"

"Wrap it up," insisted his customer nervously. "That's what I want." The astonished clerk obeyed.

Back at the hospital Mr. Button entered the nursery and almost threw the package at his son. "Here's your clothes," he snapped out.

The old man untied the package and viewed the contents with a quizzical eye.

"They look sort of funny to me," he complained, "I don't want to be made a monkey of—"

"You've made a monkey of me!" retorted Mr. Button fiercely. "Never you mind how funny you look. Put them on—or I'll—or I'll *spank* you." He swallowed uneasily at the penultimate word, feeling nevertheless that it was the proper thing to say.

"All right, father"—this with a grotesque simulation of filial respect—"you've lived longer; you know best. Just as you say."

As before, the sound of the word "father" caused Mr. Button to start violently. "And hurry."

"I'm hurrying, father."

When his son was dressed Mr. Button regarded him with depression. The costume consisted of dotted socks, pink pants, and a belted blouse with a wide white collar. Over the latter waved the long whitish beard, drooping almost to the waist. The effect was not good.

"Wait!"

Mr. Button seized a hospital shears and with three quick snaps amputated a large section of the beard. But even with this improvement the ensemble fell far short of perfection. The remaining brush of scraggly hair, the watery eyes, the ancient teeth, seemed oddly out of tone with the gayety of the costume. Mr. Button, however, was obdurate—he held out his hand. "Come along!" he said sternly.

His son took the hand trustingly. "What are you going to call me, dad?" he quavered as they walked from the nursery—"just 'baby' for a while, till you think of a better name?"

Mr. Button grunted. "I don't know," he answered harshly. "I think we'll call you Methuselah."

III

Even after the new addition to the Button family had had his hair cut short and then dyed to a sparse unnatural black, had had his face shaved so close that it glistened, and had been attired in small-boy clothes made to order by a flabbergasted tailor, it was impossible for Button to ignore the fact that his son was a poor excuse for a first family baby. Despite his aged stoop, Benjamin Button—for it was by this name they called him instead of by the appropriate but invidious Methuselah—wasfive feet eight inches tall. His clothes did not conceal this, nor did the clipping and dyeing of his eyebrows disguise the fact that the eyes under—were faded and watery and tired. In fact, the baby-nurse who had been engaged in advance left the house after one look, in a state of considerable indignation.

But Mr. Button persisted in his unwavering purpose. Benjamin was a baby, and a baby he should remain. At first he declared that if Benjamin didn't like warm milk he could go without food altogether, but he was finally prevailed upon to allow his son bread and butter, and even oat-meal by way of a compromise. One day he brought home a rattle and, giving it to Benjamin, insisted in no uncertain terms that he should "play with it," whereupon the old man took it with a weary expression and could be heard jingling it obediently at intervals throughout the day.

There can be no doubt, though, that the rattle bored him, and that he found other and more soothing amusements when he was left alone. For instance, Mr. Button discovered one day that during the preceding week he had smoked more cigars than ever before—a phenomenon, which was explained a few days later when, entering the nursery unexpectedly, he found the room full of faint blue haze and Benjamin, with a guilty expression on his face, trying to conceal the butt of a dark Havana. This, of course, called for a severe spanking, but Mr. Button found that he could not bring himself to administer it. He merely warned his son that he would "stunt his growth."

Nevertheless he persisted in his attitude. He brought home lead soldiers, he brought toy trains, he brought large pleasant animals made of cotton, and, to perfect the illusion which he was creating—for himself at least—he passionately demanded of the clerk in the toy-store whether "the paint would come oft the pink duck if the baby put it in his mouth." But, despite all his father's efforts, Benjamin refused to be interested. He would steal down the back stairs and return to the nursery with a volume of the Encyclopaedia Britannica, over which he would pore through an afternoon, while his cotton cows and his Noah's ark were left neglected on the floor. Against such a stubbornness Mr. Button's efforts were of little avail.

The sensation created in Baltimore was, at first, prodigious. What the mishap would have cost the Buttons and their kinsfolk socially cannot be determined, for the outbreak of the Civil War drew the city's attention to other things. A few people who were unfailingly polite racked their brains for compliments to give to the parents—and finally hit upon the ingenious device of declaring that the baby resembled his grandfather, a fact which, due to the standard state of decay common to all men of seventy, could not be denied. Mr. and Mrs. Roger Button were not pleased, and Benjamin's grandfather was furiously insulted.

Benjamin, once he left the hospital, took life as he found it. Several small boys were brought to see him, and he spent a stiff-jointed afternoon trying to work up an interest in tops and marbles—he even managed, quite accidentally, to break a kitchen window with a stone from a sling shot, a feat which secretly delighted his father.

Thereafter Benjamin contrived to break something every day, but he did these things only because they were expected of him, and because he was by nature obliging.

When his grandfather's initial antagonism wore off, Benjamin and that gentleman took enormous pleasure in one another's company. They would sit for hours, these two, so far apart in age and experience, and, like old cronies, discuss with tireless monotony the slow events of the day. Benjamin felt more at ease in his grandfather's presence than in his parents'—they seemed always somewhat in awe of him and, despite the dictatorial authority they exercised over him, frequently addressed him as "Mr."

He was as puzzled as any one else at the apparently advanced age of his mind and body at birth. He read up on it in the medical journal, but found that no such case had been previously recorded. At his father's urging he made an honest attempt to play with other boys, and frequently he joined in the milder games—football shook him up too much, and he feared that in case of a fracture his ancient bones would refuse to knit.

When he was five he was sent to kindergarten, where he initiated into the art of pasting green paper on orange paper, of weaving colored maps and manufacturing eternal cardboard necklaces. He was inclined to drowse off to sleep in the middle of these tasks, a habit which both irritated and frightened his young teacher. To his relief she complained to his parents, and he was removed from the school. The Roger Buttons told their friends that they felt he was too young.

By the time he was twelve years old his parents had grown used to him. Indeed, so strong is the force of custom that they no longer felt that he was different from any other child—except when some curious anomaly reminded them of the fact. But one day a few weeks after his twelfth birthday, while looking in the mirror, Benjamin made, or thought he made, an astonishing discovery. Did his eyes deceive him, or had his hair turned in the dozen years of his life from white to iron-gray under its concealing dye? Was the network of wrinkles on his face becoming less pronounced? Was his skin healthier and firmer, with even a touch of ruddy winter color? He could not tell. He knew that he no longer stooped, and that his physical condition had improved since the early days of his life.

"Can it be—?" he thought to himself, or, rather, scarcely dared to think.

He went to his father. "I am grown," he announced determinedly. "I want to put on long trousers."

His father hesitated. "Well," he said finally, "I don't know. Fourteen is the age for putting on long trousers—and you are only twelve."

"But you'll have to admit," protested Benjamin, "that I'm big for my age."

His father looked at him with illusory speculation. "Oh, I'm not so sure of that," he said. "I was as big as you when I was twelve."

This was not true—it was all part of Roger Button's silent agreement with himself to believe in his son's normality.

Finally a compromise was reached. Benjamin was to continue to dye his hair. He was to make a better attempt to play with boys of his own age. He was not to wear his spectacles or carry a cane in the street. In return for these concessions he was allowed his first suit of long trousers…

IV

Of the life of Benjamin Button betweenhis twelfth and twenty-first year I intend to say little. Suffice to record that they were years of normal ungrowth. When Benjamin was eighteen he was erect as a man of fifty; he had more hair and it was of a dark gray; his step was firm, his voice had lost its cracked quaver and descended to a healthy baritone. So his father sent him up to Connecticut to take examinations for entrance to Yale College. Benjamin passed his examination and became a member of the freshman class.

On the third day following his matriculation he received a notification from Mr. Hart, the college registrar, to call at his office and arrange his schedule. Benjamin, glancing in the mirror, decided that his hair needed a new application of its brown dye, but an anxious inspection of his bureau drawer disclosed that the dye bottle was not there. Then he remembered—he had emptied it the day before and thrown it away.

He was in a dilemma. He was due at the registrar's in five minutes. There seemed to be no help for it—he must go as he was. He did.

"Good morning," said the registrar politely. "You've come to inquire about your son."

"Why, as a matter of fact, my name's Button—" began Benjamin, but Mr. Hart cut him off.

"I'm very glad to meet you, Mr. Button. I'm expecting your son here any minute."

"That's me!" burst out Benjamin. "I'm a freshman."

"What!"

"I'm a freshman."

"Surely you're joking."

"Not at all."

The registrar frowned and glanced at a card before him. "Why, I have Mr. Benjamin Button's age down here as eighteen."

"That's my age," asserted Benjamin, flushing slightly.

The registrar eyed him wearily. "Now surely, Mr. Button, you don't expect me to believe that."

Benjamin smiled wearily. "I am eighteen," he repeated.

The registrar pointed sternly to the door. "Get out," he said. "Get out of college and get out of town. You are a dangerous lunatic."

"I am eighteen."

Mr. Hart opened the door. "The idea!" he shouted. "A man of your age trying to enter here as a freshman. Eighteen years old, are you? Well, I'll give you eighteen minutes to get out of town."

Benjamin Button walked with dignity from the room, and half a dozen undergraduates, who were waiting in the hall, followed him curiously with their eyes. When he had gone a little way he turned around, faced the infuriated registrar, who was still standing in the doorway, and repeated in a firm voice: "I am eighteen years old."

To a chorus of titters which went up from the group of undergraduates, Benjamin walked away.

But he was not fated to escape so easily. On his melancholy walk to the railroad station he found that he was being followed by a group, then by a swarm, and finally by a dense mass of undergraduates. The word had gone around that a lunatic had passed the entrance examinations for Yale and attempted to palm himself off as a youth of eighteen. A fever of excitement permeated the college. Men ran hatless out of classes, the football team abandoned its practice and joined the mob, professors' wives with bonnets awry and bustles out of position, ran shouting after the procession, from which proceeded a continual succession of remarks aimed at the tender sensibilities of Benjamin Button.

"He must be the wandering Jew!"

"He ought to go to prep school at his age!"

"Look at the infant prodigy!"

"He thought this was the old men's home."

"Go up to Harvard!"

Benjamin increased his gait, and soon he was running. He would show them! He *would* go to Harvard, and then they would regret these ill-considered taunts!

Safely on board the train for Baltimore, he put his head from the window. "You'll regret this!" he shouted.

"Ha-ha!" the undergraduates laughed. "Ha-ha-ha!" It was the biggest mistake that Yale College had ever made…

V

In 1880 Benjamin Button was twenty years old, and he signalised his birthday by going to work for his father in Roger Button & Co., Whole-sale Hardware. It was in that same year that he began "going out socially"—that is, his father insisted on taking him to several fashionable dances. Roger Button was now fifty, and he and his son were more and more companionable—in fact, since Benjamin had ceased to dye his hair (which was still grayish) they appeared about the same age, and could have passed for brothers.

One night in August they got into the phaeton attired in their full-dress suits and drove out to a dance at the Shevlins' country house, situated just outside of Baltimore. It was a gorgeous evening. A full moon drenched the road to the lustreless colour of platinum, and late-blooming harvest flowers breathed into the motionless air aromas that were like low, half-heard laughter. The open country, carpeted for rods around with bright wheat, was translucent as in the day. It was almost impossible not to be affected by the sheer beauty of the sky—almost.

"There's a great future in the dry-goods business," Roger Button was saying. He was not a spiritual man—his aesthetic sense was rudimentary.

"Old fellows like me can't learn new tricks," he observed profoundly. "It's you youngsters with energy and vitality that have the great future before you."

Far up the road the lights of the Shevlins' country house drifted into view, and presently there was a sighing sound that crept persistently toward them—it might have been the fine plaint of violins or the rustle of the silver wheat under the moon.

They pulled up behind a handsome brougham whose passengers were disembarking at the door. A lady got out, then an elderly gentleman, then another young lady, beautiful as sin. Benjamin started; an almost chemical change seemed to dissolve and recompose the very elements of his body. A rigour passed over him, blood rose into his cheeks, his forehead, and there was a steady thumping in his ears. It was first love.

The girl was slender and frail, with hair that was ashen under the moon and honey-coloured under the sputtering gas-lamps of the porch. Over her shoulders was thrown a Spanish mantilla of softest yellow, butterflied in black; her feet were glittering buttons at the hem of her bustled dress.

Roger Button leaned over to his son. "That," he said, "is young Hildegarde Moncrief, the daughter of General Moncrief."

Benjamin nodded coldly. "Pretty little thing," he said indifferently. But when the negro boy had led the buggy away, he added: "Dad, you might introduce me to her."

They approached a group, of which Miss Moncrief was the centre. Reared in the old tradition, she curtsied low before Benjamin. Yes, he might have a dance. He thanked her and walked away—staggered away.

The interval until the time for his turn should arrive dragged itself out interminably. He stood close to the wall, silent, inscrutable, watching with murderous eyes the young bloods of Baltimore as they eddied around Hildegarde Moncrief, passionate admiration in their faces. How obnoxious they seemed to Benjamin; how intolerably rosy! Their curling brown whiskers aroused in him a feeling equivalent to indigestion.

But when his own time came, and he drifted with her out upon the changing floor to the music of the latest waltz from Paris, his jealousies and anxieties melted from him like a mantle of snow. Blind with enchantment, he felt that life was just beginning.

"You and your brother got here just as we did, didn't you?" asked Hildegarde, looking up at him with eyes that were like bright blue enamel.

Benjamin hesitated. If she took him for his father's brother, would it be best to enlighten her? He remembered his experience at Yale, so he decided against it. It would be rude to contradict a lady; it would be criminal to mar this exquisite occasion with the grotesque story of his origin. Later, perhaps. So he nodded, smiled, listened, was happy.

"I like men of your age," Hildegarde told him. "Young boys are so idiotic. They tell me how much champagne they drink at college, and how much money they lose playing cards. Men of your age know how to appreciate women."

Benjamin felt himself on the verge of a proposal—with an effort he choked back the impulse. "You're just the romantic age," she continued—"fifty. Twenty-five is too wordly-wise; thirty is apt to be pale from overwork; forty is the age of long stories that take a whole cigar to tell; sixty is—oh, sixty is too near seventy; but fifty is the mellow age. I love fifty."

Fifty seemed to Benjamin a glorious age. He longed passionately to be fifty.

"I've always said," went on Hildegarde, "that I'd rather marry a man of fifty and be taken care of than many a man of thirty and take care of *him*."

For Benjamin the rest of the evening was bathed in a honey-coloured mist. Hildegarde gave him two more dances, and they discovered that they were marvellously in accord on all the questions of the day. She was to go driving with him on the following Sunday, and then they would discuss all these questions further.

Going home in the phaeton just before the crack of dawn, when the first bees were humming and the fading moon glimmered in the cool dew, Benjamin knew vaguely that his father was discussing wholesale hardware.

"... And what do you think should merit our biggest attention after hammers and nails?" the elder Button was saying.

"Love," replied Benjamin absent-mindedly.

"Lugs?" exclaimed Roger Button, "Why, I've just covered the question of lugs."

Benjamin regarded him with dazed eyes just as the eastern sky was suddenly cracked with light, and an oriole yawned piercingly in the quickening trees...

VI

When, six months later, the engagement of Miss Hildegarde Moncrief to Mr. Benjamin Button was made known (I say "made known," for General Moncrief declared he would rather fall upon his sword than announce it), the excitement in Baltimore society reached a feverish pitch. The almost forgotten story of Benjamin's birth was remembered and sent out upon the winds of scandal in picaresque and incredible forms. It was said that Benjamin was really the father of Roger Button, that he was his brother who had been in prison for forty years, that he was John Wilkes Booth in disguise—and, finally, that he had two small conical horns sprouting from his head.

The Sunday supplements of the New York papers played up the case with fascinating sketches which showed the head of Benjamin Button attached to a fish, to a snake, and, finally, to a body of solid brass. He became known, journalistically, as the Mystery Man of Maryland. But the true story, as is usually the case, had a very small circulation.

However, every one agreed with General Moncrief that it was "criminal" for a lovely girl who could have married any beau in Baltimore to throw herself into the arms of a man who was assuredly fifty. In vain Mr. Roger Button published his son's birth certificate in large type in the Baltimore *Blaze*. No one believed it. You had only to look at Benjamin and see.

On the part of the two people most concerned there was no wavering. So many of the stories about her fiancé were false that Hildegarde refused stubbornly to believe even the true one. In vain General Moncrief pointed out to her the high mortality among men of fifty—or, at least, among men who looked fifty; in vain he told her of the instability of the wholesale hardware business. Hildegarde had chosen to marry for mellowness, and marry she did…

VII

In one particular, at least, the friends of Hildegarde Moncrief were mistaken. The wholesale hardware business prospered amazingly. In the fifteen years between Benjamin Button's marriage in 1880 and his father's retirement in 1895, the family fortune was doubled—and this was due largely to the younger member of the firm.

Needless to say, Baltimore eventually received the couple to its bosom. Even old General Moncrief became reconciled to his son-in-law when Benjamin gave him the money to bring out his "History of the Civil War" in twenty volumes, which had been refused by nine prominent publishers.

In Benjamin himself fifteen years had wrought many changes. It seemed to him that the blood flowed with new vigor through his veins. It began to be a pleasure to rise in the morning, to walk with an active step along the busy, sunny street, to work untiringly with his shipments of hammers and his cargoes of nails. It was in 1890 that he executed his famous business coup: he brought up the suggestion that *all nails used in nailing up the boxes in which nails are shipped are the property of the shippee*, a proposal which became a statute, was approved by Chief Justice Fossile, and saved Roger Button and Company, Wholesale Hardware, more than *six hundred nails every year*.

In addition, Benjamin discovered that he was becoming more and more attracted by the gay side of life. It was typical of his growing enthusiasm for pleasure that he was the first man in the city of Baltimore to own and run an automobile. Meeting him on the street, his contemporaries would stare enviously at the picture he made of health and vitality.

"He seems to grow younger every year," they would remark. And if old Roger Button, now sixty-five years old, had failed at first to give a proper welcome to his son he atoned at last by bestowing on him what amounted to adulation.

And here we come to an unpleasant subject which it will be well to pass over as quickly as possible. There was only one thing that worried Benjamin Button; his wife had ceased to attract him.

At that time Hildegarde was a woman of thirty-five, with a son, Roscoe, fourteen years old. In the early days of their marriage Benjamin had worshipped her. But, as the years passed, her honey-colored hair became an unexciting brown, the blue enamel of her eyes assumed the aspect of cheap crockery—moreover, and, most of all, she had become too settled in her ways, too placid, too content, too anemic in her excitements, and too sober in her taste. As a bride it had been she who had "dragged" Benjamin to dances and dinners—now conditions were reversed. She went out socially with him, but without enthusiasm, devoured already by that eternal inertia which comes to live with each of us one day and stays with us to the end.

Benjamin's discontent waxed stronger. At the outbreak of the Spanish-American War in 1898 his home had for him so little charm that he decided to join the army. With his business influence he obtained a commission as captain, and proved so adaptable to the work that he was made a major, and finally a lieutenant-colonel just in time to participate in the celebrated charge up San Juan Hill. He was slightly wounded, and received a medal.

Benjamin had become so attached to the activity and excitement of army life that he regretted to give it up, but his business required attention, so he resigned his commission and came home. He was met at the station by a brass band and escorted to his house.

VIII

Hildegarde, waving a large silk flag, greeted him on the porch, and even as he kissed her he felt with a sinking of the heart that these three years had taken their toll. She was a woman of forty now, with a faint skirmish line of gray hairs in her head. The sight depressed him.

Up in his room he saw his reflection in the familiar mirror—he went closer and examined his own face with anxiety, comparing it after a moment with a photograph of himself in uniform taken just before the war.

"Good Lord!" he said aloud. The process was continuing. There was no doubt of it—he looked now like a man of thirty. Instead of being delighted, he was uneasy—he was growing younger. He had hitherto hoped that once he reached a bodily age equivalent to his age in years, the grotesque phenomenon which had marked his birth would cease to function. He shuddered. His destiny seemed to him awful, incredible.

When he came downstairs Hildegarde was waiting for him. She appeared annoyed, and he wondered if she had at last discovered that there was something amiss. It was with an effort to relieve the tension between them that he broached the matter at dinner in what he considered a delicate way.

"Well," he remarked lightly, "everybody says I look younger than ever."

Hildegarde regarded him with scorn. She sniffed. "Do you think it's anything to boast about?"

"I'm not boasting," he asserted uncomfortably.

She sniffed again. "The idea," she said, and after a moment: "I should think you'd have enough pride to stop it."

"How can I?" he demanded.

"I'm not going to argue with you," she retorted. "But there's a right way of doing things and a wrong way. If you've made up your mind to be different from everybody else, I don't suppose I can stop you, but I really don't think it's very considerate."

"But, Hildegarde, I can't help it."

"You can too. You're simply stubborn. You think you don't want to be like any one else. You always have been that way, and you always will be. But just think how it would be if every one else looked at things as you do—what would the world be like?"

As this was an inane and unanswerable argument Benjamin made no reply, and from that time on a chasm began to widen between them. He wondered what possible fascination she had ever exercised over him.

To add to the breach, he found, as the new century gathered headway, that his thirst for gayety grew stronger. Never a party of any kind in the city of Baltimore but he was there, dancing with the prettiest of the young married women, chatting with the most popular of the debutantes, and finding their company charming, while his wife, a dowager of evil omen, sat among the chaperons, now in haughty disapproval, and now following him with solemn, puzzled, and reproachful eyes.

"Look!" people would remark. "What a pity! A young fellow that age tied to a woman of forty-five. He must be twenty years younger than his wife." They had forgotten—as people inevitably forget—that back in 1880 their mammas and papas had also remarked about this same ill-matched pair.

Benjamin's growing unhappiness at home was compensated for by his many new interests. He took up golf and made a great success of it. He went in for dancing: in 1906 he was an expert at "The Boston," and in 1908 he was considered proficient at the "Maxixe," while in 1909 his "Castle Walk" was the envy of every young man in town.

His social activities, of course, interfered to some extent with his business, but then he had worked hard at wholesale hardware for twenty-five years and felt that he could soon hand it on to his son, Roscoe, who had recently graduated from Harvard.

He and his son were, in fact, often mistaken for each other. This pleased Benjamin—he soon forgot the insidious fear which had come over him on his return from the Spanish-American War, and grew to take a naïve pleasure in his appearance. There was only one fly in the delicious ointment—he hated to appear in public with his wife. Hildegarde was almost fifty, and the sight of her made him feel absurd...

IX

One September day in 1910—a few years after Roger Button & Co., Wholesale Hardware, had been handed over to young Roscoe

Button—a man, apparently about twenty years old, entered himself as a freshman at Harvard University in Cambridge. He did not make the mistake of announcing that he would never see fifty again, nor did he mention the fact that his son had been graduated from the same institution ten years before.

He was admitted, and almost immediately attained a prominent position in the class, partly because he seemed a little older than the other freshmen, whose average age was about eighteen.

But his success was largely due to the fact that in the football game with Yale he played so brilliantly, with so much dash and with such a cold, remorseless anger that he scored seven touchdowns and fourteen field goals for Harvard, and caused one entire eleven of Yale men to be carried singly from the field, unconscious. He was the most celebrated man in college.

Strange to say, in his third or junior year he was scarcely able to "make" the team. The coaches said that he had lost weight, and it seemed to the more observant among them that he was not quite as tall as before. He made no touchdowns—indeed, he was retained on the team chiefly in hope that his enormous reputation would bring terror and disorganisation to the Yale team.

In his senior year he did not make the team at all. He had grown so slight and frail that one day he was taken by some sophomores for a freshman, an incident which humiliated him terribly. He became known as something of a prodigy—a senior who was surely no more than sixteen—and he was often shocked at the worldliness of some of his classmates. His studies seemed harder to him—he felt that they were too advanced. He had heard his classmates speak of St. Midas', the famous preparatory school, at which so many of them had prepared for college, and he determined after his graduation to enter himself at St. Midas', where the sheltered life among boys his own size would be more congenial to him.

Upon his graduation in 1914 he went home to Baltimore with his Harvard diploma in his pocket. Hildegarde was now residing in Italy, so Benjamin went to live with his son, Roscoe. But though he was welcomed in a general way there was obviously no heartiness in Roscoe's feeling toward him—there was even perceptible a tendency on his son's part to think that Benjamin, as he moped about the house in adolescent mooniness, was somewhat in the way. Roscoe was married now and prominent in Baltimore life, and he wanted no scandal to creep out in connection with his family.

Benjamin, no longer persona grata with the débutantes and younger college set, found himself left much alone, except for the companionship of three or four fifteen-year-old boys in the neighborhood. His idea of going to St. Midas school recurred to him.

"Say," he said to Roscoe one day, "I've told you over and over that I want to go to prep school."

"Well, go, then," replied Roscoe shortly. The matter was distasteful to him, and he wished to avoid a discussion.

"I can't go alone," said Benjamin helplessly. "You'll have to enter me and take me up there."

"I haven't got time," declared Roscoe abruptly. His eyes narrowed and he looked uneasily at his father. "As a matter of fact," he added, "you'd better not go on with this business much longer. You better pull up short. You better—you better"—he paused and his face crimsoned as he sought for words—"you better turn right around and start back the other way. This has gone too far to be a joke. It isn't funny any longer. You—you behave yourself!"

Benjamin looked at him, on the verge of tears.

"And another thing," continued Roscoe, "when visitors are in the house I want you to call me 'Uncle'—not 'Roscoe,' but 'Uncle,' do you understand? It looks absurd for a boy of fifteen to call me by my first name. Perhaps you'd better call me 'Uncle' *all* the time, so you'll get used to it."

With a harsh look at his father, Roscoe turned away…

X

At the termination of this interview, Benjamin wandered dismally upstairs and stared at himself in the mirror. He had not shaved for three months, but he could find nothing on his face but a faint white down with which it seemed unnecessary to meddle. When he had first come home from Harvard, Roscoe had approached him with the proposition that he should wear eye-glasses and imitation whiskers glued to his cheeks, and it had seemed for a moment that the farce of his early years was to be repeated. But whiskers had itched and made him ashamed. He wept and Roscoe had reluctantly relented.

Benjamin opened a book of boys' stories, "The Boy Scouts in Bimini Bay," and began to read. But he found himself thinking persistently about the war. America had joined the Allied cause during the preceding month, and Benjamin wanted to enlist, but, alas, sixteen was the minimum age, and he did not look that old. His true age, which was fifty-seven, would have disqualified him, anyway.

There was a knock at his door, and the butler appeared with a letter bearing a large official legend in the corner and addressed to Mr. Benjamin Button. Benjamin tore it open eagerly, and read the enclosure with delight. It informed him that many reserve officers who had served in the Spanish-American War were being called back into service with a higher rank, and it enclosed his commission as brigadier-general in the United States army with orders to report immediately.

Benjamin jumped to his feet fairly quivering with enthusiasm. This was what he had wanted. He seized his cap, and ten minutes later he had entered a large tailoring establishment on Charles Street, and asked in his uncertain treble to be measured for a uniform.

"Want to play soldier, sonny?" demanded a clerk casually.

Benjamin flushed. "Say! Never mind what I want!" he retorted angrily. "My name's Button and I live on Mt. Vernon Place, so you know I'm good for it."

"Well," admitted the clerk hesitantly, "if you're not, I guess your daddy is, all right."

Benjamin was measured, and a week later his uniform was completed. He had difficulty in obtaining the proper general's insignia because the dealer kept insisting to Benjamin that a nice Y. W. C. A. badge would look just as well and be much more fun to play with.

Saying nothing to Roscoe, he left the house one night and proceeded by train to Camp Mosby, in South Carolina, where he was to command an infantry brigade. On a sultry April day he approached the entrance to the camp, paid off the taxicab which had brought him from the station, and turned to the sentry on guard.

"Get some one to handle my luggage!" he said briskly.

The sentry eyed him reproachfully. "Say," he remarked, "where you goin' with the general's duds, sonny?"

Benjamin, veteran of the Spanish-American War, whirled upon him with fire in his eye, but with, alas, a changing treble voice.

"Come to attention!" he tried to thunder; he paused for breath—then suddenly he saw the sentry snap his heels together and bring his rifle to the present. Benjamin concealed a smile of gratification, but when he glanced around his smile faded. It was not he who had inspired obedience, but an imposing artillery colonel who was approaching on horseback.

"Colonel!" called Benjamin shrilly.

The colonel came up, drew rein, and looked coolly down at him with a twinkle in his eyes. "Whose little boy are you?" he demanded kindly.

"I'll soon darn well show you whose little boy I am!" retorted Benjamin in a ferocious voice. "Get down off that horse!"

The colonel roared with laughter. "You want him, eh, general?"

"Here!" cried Benjamin desperately. "Read this." And he thrust his commission toward the colonel.

The colonel read it, his eyes popping from their sockets.

"Where'd you get this?" he demanded, slipping the document into his own pocket.

"I got it from the Government, as you'll soon find out!"

"You come along with me," said the colonel with a peculiar look. "We'll go up to headquarters and talk this over. Come along."

The colonel turned and began walking his horse in the direction of headquarters. There was nothing for Benjamin to do but follow with as much dignity as possible—meanwhile promising himself a stern revenge.

But this revenge did not materialize. Two days later, however, his son Roscoe materialized from Baltimore, hot and cross from a hasty trip, and escorted the weeping general, *sans* uniform, back to his home.

XI

In 1920 Roscoe Button's first child was born. During the attendant festivities, however, no one thought it "the thing" to mention, that the little grubby boy, apparently about ten years of age who played around the house with lead soldiers and a miniature circus, was the new baby's own grandfather.

No one disliked the little boy whose fresh, cheerful face was crossed with just a hint of sadness, but to Roscoe Button his presence was a source of torment. In the idiom of his generation Roscoe did not consider the matter "efficient." It seemed to him that his father, in refusing to look sixty, had not behaved like a "red-blooded he-man"—this was Roscoe's favorite expression—but in a curious and perverse manner. Indeed, to think about the matter for as much as a half an hour drove him to the edge of insanity. Roscoe believed that "live wires" should keep young, but carrying it out on such a scale was—was—was inefficient. And there Roscoe rested.

Five years later Roscoe's little boy had grown old enough to play childish games with little Benjamin under the supervision of the same nurse. Roscoe took them both to kindergarten on the same day, and Benjamin found that playing with little strips of colored paper, making mats and chains and curious and beautiful designs, was the most fascinating game in the world. Once he was bad and had to stand in the corner—then he cried—but for the most part there were gay hours in the cheerful room, with the sunlight coming in the windows and Miss Bailey's kind hand resting for a moment now and then in his tousled hair.

Roscoe's son moved up into the first grade after a year, but Benjamin stayed on in the kindergarten. He was very happy. Sometimes when other tots talked about what they would do when they grew up a shadow would cross his little face as if in a dim, childish way he realized that those were things in which he was never to share.

The days flowed on in monotonous content. He went back a third year to the kindergarten, but he was too little now to understand what the bright shining strips of paper were for. He cried because the other boys were bigger than he, and he was afraid of them. The teacher talked to him, but though he tried to understand he could not understand at all.

He was taken from the kindergarten. His nurse, Nana, in her starched gingham dress, became the centre of his tiny world. On bright days they walked in the park; Nana would point at a great gray monster and say "elephant," and Benjamin would say it after her, and when he was being undressed for bed that night he would say it over and over aloud to her: "Elyphant, elyphant, elyphant." Sometimes Nana let him jump on the bed, which was fun, because if you sat down exactly right it would bounce you up on your feet again, and if you said "Ah" for a long time while you jumped you got a very pleasing broken vocal effect.

He loved to take a big cane from the hatrack and go around hitting chairs and tables with it and saying: "Fight, fight, fight." When there were people there the old ladies would cluck at him, which interested him, and the young ladies would try to kiss him, which he submitted to with mild boredom. And when the long day was done at five o'clock he would go upstairs with Nana and be fed oatmeal and nice soft mushy foods with a spoon.

There were no troublesome memories in his childish sleep; no token came to him of his brave days at college, of the glittering years when he flustered the hearts of many girls. There were only the white, safe walls of his crib and Nana and a man who came to see him sometimes, and a great big orange ball that Nana pointed at just before his twilight bed hour and called "sun." When the sun went his eyes were sleepy—there were no dreams, no dreams to haunt him.

The past—the wild charge at the head of his men up San Juan Hill; the first years of his marriage when he worked late into the summer dusk down in the busy city for young Hildegarde whom he loved; the days before that when he sat smoking far into the night in the gloomy old Button house on Monroe Street with his grandfather—all these had faded like unsubstantial dreams from his mind as though they had never been.

He did not remember. He did not remember clearly whether the milk was warm or cool at his last feeding or how the days passed—there was only his crib and Nana's familiar presence. And then he remembered nothing. When he was hungry he cried—that was all. Through the noons and nights he breathed and over him there were soft mumblings and murmurings that he scarcely heard, and faintly differentiated smells, and light and darkness.

Then it was all dark, and his white crib and the dim faces that moved above him, and the warm sweet aroma of the milk, faded out altogether from his mind.

Disorder And Early Sorrow

Thomas Mann

Thomas Mann (1875-1955), considered the greatest German writer of the 20th century, received the Nobel Prize for Literature in 1929. Some of his best works include *Buddenbrooks* (1900), *Death in Venice* (1912) and *The Magic Mountain* (1924). His engagement with the political and social issues of his time added to his imaginative, subtle and multi-layered works. 'Disorder And Early Sorrow' (1925) first appeared in English in the American magazine *The Dial* (1926).

The principal dish at dinner had been croquettes made of turnip greens. So there follows a trifle, concocted out of those dessert powders we use nowadays, that taste like almond soap. Xaver, the youthful manservant, in his outgrown striped jacket, white woollen gloves, and yellow sandals, hands it round, and the "big folk" take this opportunity to remind their father, tactfully, that company is coming today.

The "big folk" are two, Ingrid and Bert. Ingrid is brown-eyed, eighteen, and perfectly delightful. She is on the eve of her exams, and will probably pass them, if only because she knows how to wind masters, and even headmasters, round her finger. She the stage, on the ground of her ingratiating smile, her equally ingratiating voice, and a marked and irresistible talent for burlesque. Bert is blond and seventeen. He intends to get done with school somehow, anyhow, and fling himself into the arms of life. He will be a dancer, or a cabaret actor, possibly even a waiter, but not a waiter anywhere else save at Cairo, the night-club, whither he has once already taken flight, at five in the morning, and been brought back crestfallen. Bert bears a strong resemblance to the youthful manservant,

Xaver Kleinsgutl, of about the same age as himself; not because he looks common-in features he is strikingly like his father, Professor Cornelius—but by reason of an approximation of types, due in its turn to far-reaching compromises in matters of dress and bearing generally. Both lads wear their heavy hair very long on top, with a cursory parting in the middle, and give their heads the same characteristic toss to throw it off the forehead. When one of them leaves the house, by the garden gate, bareheaded in all weathers, in a blouse rakishly girt with a leather strap, and sheers off bent well over with his head on one side; or else mounts his push-bike—Xaver makes free with his employers', of both sexes, or even, in acutely irresponsible mood, with the Professor's own—Dr. Cornelius from his bedroom window cannot, for the life of him, tell whether he is looking at his son or his servant. Both, he thinks, look like young moujiks. And both are impassioned cigarette-smokers, though Bert has not the means to compete with Xaver, who smokes as many as thirty a day, of a brand named after a popular cinema star. The big folk call their father and mother the "old folk"—not behind their backs, but as a form of address and in all affection: "Hullo, old folks," they will say; though Cornelius is only forty-seven years old and his wife eight years younger. And the Professor's parents, who lead in his household the humble and hesitant life of the really old, are on the big folk's lips the "ancients." As for the "little folk," Ellie and Snapper, who take their meals upstairs with blue-faced Ann—so-called because of her prevailing facial hue—Ellie and Snapper follow their mother's example and address their father by his first name, Abel. Unutterably comic it sounds, in its pert, confiding familiarity; particularly on the lips, in the sweet accents, of five-year-old Eleanor, who is the image of Frau Cornelius's baby pictures and whom the Professor loves above everything else in the world.

"Darling old thing," says Ingrid affably, laying her large but shapely hand on his, as he presides in proper middle-class style over the family table, with her on his left and the mother opposite: "Parent mine, may I ever so gently jog your memory, for you have probably forgotten: this is the afternoon we were to have our little jollification, our turkey-trot with eats to match. You haven't a thing to do but just bear up and not funk it; everything will be over by nine o'clock."

"Oh, ah!" says Cornelius, his face falling. "Good!" he goes on, and nods his head to show himself in harmony with the inevitable. "I only meant, is this really the day? Thursday, yes. How time flies! Well, what time are they coming?"

"Half past four they'll be dropping in, I should say," answers Ingrid, to whom her brother leaves the major role in all dealings with the father. Upstairs, while he is resting, he will hear scarcely anything, and from seven to eight he takes his walk. He can slip out by the terrace if he likes.

"Tut!" says Cornelius deprecatingly, as who should say: "You exaggerate." But Bert puts in: "It's the one evening in the week Wanja doesn't have to play. Any other night he'd have to leave by half past six, which would be painful for all concerned."

Wanja is Ivan Herzl, the celebrated young leading man at the Stadttheater. Bert and Ingrid are on intimate terms with him, they often visit him in his dressing-room and have tea. He is an artist of the modern school, who stands on the stage in strange and, to the Professor's mind, utterly affected dancing attitudes, and shrieks lamentably. To a professor of history, all highly repugnant; but Bert has entirely succumbed to Herzl's influence, blackens the lower rim of his eyelids—despite painful but fruitless scenes with the father—and with youthful carelessness of the ancestral anguish declares that not only will he take Herzl for his model if he becomes a dancer, but in case he turns out to be a waiter at the Cairo he means to walk precisely thus.

Cornelius slightly raises his brows and makes his son a little bow—indicative of the unassumingness and self-abnegation that befits his age. You could not call it a mocking bow or suggestive in any special sense. Bert may refer it to himself or equally to his so talented friend.

"Who else is coming?" next inquires the master of the house. They mention various people, names all more or less familiar, from the city, from the suburban colony, from Ingrid's school. They still have some telephoning to do, they say. They have to phone Max. This is Max Hergesell, an engineering student;

Ingrid utters his name in the nasal drawl which according to her is the traditional intonation of all the Hergesells. She goes on to parody it in the most abandonedly funny and lifelike way, and the parents laugh until they nearly choke over the wretched trifle. For even in these times when something funny happens people have to laugh.

From time to time the telephone bell rings in the Professor's study, and the big folk run across, knowing it is their affair. Many people had to give up their telephones the last time the price rose, but so far the Corneliuses have been able to keep theirs, just as they have kept their villa, which was built before the war, by dint of the salary Cornelius draws as professor of history—a million marks, and more or less adequate to the chances and changes of post-war life. The house is comfortable, even elegant, though sadly in need of repairs that cannot be made for lack of materials, and at present disfigured by iron stoves with long pipes. Even so, it is still the proper setting of the upper middle class, though they themselves look odd enough in it, with their worn and turned clothing and altered way of life. The children, of course, know nothing else; to them it is normal and regular, they belong by birth to the "villa proletariat." The problem of clothing troubles them not at all. They and their like have evolved a costume to fit the time, by poverty out of taste for innovation: in summer it consists of scarcely more than a belted linen smock and sandals. The middle-class parents find things rather more difficult.

The big folk's table-napkins hang over their chair-backs, they talk with their friends over the telephone. These friends are the invited guests who have rung up to accept or decline or arrange; and the conversation is carried on in the jargon of the clan, full of slang and high spirits, of which the old folk understand hardly a word. These consult together meantime about the hospitality to be offered to the impending guests. The Professor displays a middle-class ambitiousness: he wants to serve a sweet or something that looks like a sweet—after the Italian salad and brown bread sandwiches. But Frau Cornelius says that would be going too far. The guests would not expect it, she is sure—and the big folk, returning once more to their trifle, agree with her.

The mother of the family is of the same general type as Ingrid, though not so tall. She is languid; the fantastic difficulties of the housekeeping have broken and worn her.

She really ought to go and take a cure, but feels incapable; the floor is always swaying under her feet, and everything seems upside down. She speaks of what is uppermost in her mind: the eggs, they simply must be bought today. Six thousand marks apiece they are, and just so many are to be had on this one day of the week at one single shop fifteen minutes' journey away. Whatever else they do, the big folk must go and fetch them immediately after luncheon, with Danny, their neighbour's son, who will soon be calling for them; and Xaver Kleinsgutl will don civilian garb and attend his young master and mistress. For no single household is allowed more than five eggs a week; therefore the young people will enter the shop singly, one after another, under assumed names, and thus wring twenty eggs from the shopkeeper for the Cornelius family. This enterprise is the sporting event of the week for all participants, not excepting the moujik Kleinsgutl, and most of all for Ingridand Bert, who delight in misleading and mystifying their fellow-men and would revel in the performance even if it did not achieve one single egg. They adore impersonating fictitious characters; they love to sit in a bus and carry on long lifelike conversations in a dialect which they otherwise never speak, the most commonplace dialogue about politics and people and the price of food, while the whole bus listens open-mouthed to this incredibly ordinary prattle, though with a dark suspicion all the while that something is wrong somewhere. The conversation waxes ever more shameless, it enters into revolting detail about these people who do not exist. Ingrid can make her voice sound ever so common and twittering and shrill as she impersonates a shop-girl with an illegitimate child, said child being a son with sadistic tendencies, who lately out in the country treated a cow with such unnatural cruelty that no Christian could have borne to see it. Bert nearly explodes at her twittering, but restrains himself and displays a grisly sympathy; he and the unhappy shop-girl entering into a long, stupid, depraved, and shuddery conversation over the particular morbid cruelty involved, until an old gentleman opposite, sitting with his ticket folded between his index finger and his seal ring, can bear it no more and makes public protest against the nature of the themes these young folk are discussing with such particularity. He uses the Greek plural: "themata." Whereat Ingrid pretends to be dissolving in tears, and Bert behaves as though his wrath against the old gentleman was with difficulty being held in check and would probably burst out before long. He clenches his fists, he gnashes his teeth, he shakes from head to foot; and the unhappy old gentleman, whose intentions had been of the best, hastily leaves the bus at the next stop.

Such are the diversions of the big folk. The telephone plays a prominent part in them: they ring up any and everybody—members of government, opera singers, dignitaries of the Church—in the character of shop assistants, or perhaps as Lord or Lady Doolittle. They are only with difficulty persuaded that they have the wrong number. Once they emptied their parents' card-tray and distributed its contents among the neighbours' letter-boxes, wantonly, yet not without enough impish sense of the fitness of things to make it highly upsetting. God only knowing why certain people should have called where they did.

Xaver comes in to clear away, tossing the hair out of his eyes. Now that he has taken off his gloves you can see the yellow chain-ring on his left hand. And as the Professor finishes his watery eight-thousand-mark beer and lights a cigarette, the little folk can be heard scrambling down the stair, coming, by established custom, for their after-dinner call on Father and Mother. They storm the dining-room, after a struggle with the latch, clutched by both pairs of little hands at once; their clumsy small feet twinkle over the carpet, in red felt slippers with the socks falling down on them. With prattle and shoutings each makes for his own place: Snapper to Mother, to climb on her lap, boast of all he has eaten, and thump his fat little turn; Ellie to her Abel, so much hers because she is so very much his; because she consciously luxuriates in the deep tenderness—like all deep feeling, concealing a melancholy strain—with which he holds her small form embraced; in the love in his eyes as he kisses her little fairy hand or the sweet brow with its delicate tracery of tiny blue veins.

The little folk look like each other, with the strong undefined likeness of brother and sister. In clothing and haircut they are twins. Yet they are sharply distinguished after all, and quite on sex lines. It is a little Adam and a little Eve. Not only is Snapper the sturdier and more compact, he appears consciously to emphasize his four-year-old masculinity in speech, manner, and carriage, lifting his shoulders and letting the little arms hang down quite like a young American athlete, drawing down his mouth when he talks and seeking to give his voice a gruff and forthright ring. But all this masculinity is the result of effort rather than natively his. Born and brought up in these desolate, distracted times, he has been endowed by them with an unstable and hypersensitive nervous system and suffers greatly under life's disharmonies. He is prone to sudden anger and outbursts of bitter tears, stamping his feet at every trifle; for this reason he is his mother's special nursling and care. His round, round eyes are chestnut brown and already inclined to squint, so that he will need glasses in the near future. His little nose is long, the mouth small—the father's nose and mouth they are, more plainly than ever since the Professor shaved his pointed beard and goes smooth-faced. The pointed beard had become impossible—even professors must make some concession to the changing times.

But the little daughter sits on her father's knee, his Eleonorchen, his little Eve, so much more gracious a little being, so much sweeter-faced than her brother—and he holds his cigarette away from her while she fingers his glasses with her dainty wee hands. The lenses are divided for reading and distance, and each day they tease her curiosity afresh.

At bottom he suspects that his wife's partiality may have a firmer basis than his own; that Snapper's refractory masculinity perhaps is solider stuff than his own little girl's more explicit charm and grace. But the heart will not be commanded, that he knows; and once and for all his heart belongs to the little one, as it has since the day she came, since the first time he saw her.

Almost always when he holds her in his arms he remembers that first time: remembers the sunny room in the Women's Hospital, where Ellie first saw the light, twelve years after Bert was born. He remembers how he drew near, the mother smiling the while, and cautiously put aside the canopy of the diminutive bed that stood beside the large one. There lay the little miracle among the pillows: so well formed, so encompassed, as it were, with the harmony of sweet proportions, with little hands that even then, though so much tinier, were beautiful as now; with wide-open eyes blue as the sky and brighter than the sunshine—and almost in that very second he felt himself captured and held fast. This was love at first sight, love everlasting: a feeling unknown, unhoped for, unexpected—in so far as it could be a matter of conscious awareness; it took entire possession of him, and he understood, with joyous amazement, that this was for life.

But he understood more. He knows, does Dr. Cornelius, that there is something not quite right about this feeling, so unaware, so undreamed of, so involuntary. He has a shrewd suspicion that it is not by accident it has so utterly mastered him and bound itself up with his existence; that he had—even subconsciously been preparing for it, or, more precisely, been prepared for it. There is, in short, something in him which at a given moment was ready to issue in such a feeling; and this something, highly extraordinary to relate, is his essence and quality as a professor of history. Dr. Cornelius, however, does not actually say this, even to himself; he merely realizes it, at odd times, and smiles a private smile. He knows that history professors do not love history because it is something that comes to pass, but only because it is something that has come to pass; that they hate a revolution like the present one because they feel it is lawless, incoherent, irrelevant—in a word, unhistoric; that their hearts belong to the coherent, disciplined, historic past. For the temper of timelessness, the temper of eternity—thus the scholar communes with himself when he takes his walk by the river before supper—that temper broods over the past; and it is a temper much better suited to the nervous system of a history professor than are the excesses of the present. The past is immortalized; that is to say, it is dead; and death is the root of all godliness and all abiding significance. Dr. Cornelius, walking alone in the dark, has a profound insight into this truth. It is this conservative instinct of his, his sense of the eternal, that has found in his love for his little daughter a way to save itself from the wounding inflicted by the times. For father love, and a little child on its mother's breast—are not these timeless, and thus very, very holy and beautiful? Yet Cornelius, pondering there in the dark, descries something not perfectly right and good in his love. Theoretically, in the interests of science, he admits it to himself. There is something ulterior about it, in the nature of it; that something is hostility, hostility against the history of today, which is still in the making and thus not history at all, in behalf of the genuine history that has already happened—that is to say, death. Yes, passing strange though all this is, yet it is true; true in a sense, that is. His devotion to this priceless little morsel of life and new growth has something to do with death, it clings to death as against life; and that is neither right nor beautiful—in a sense. Though only the most fanatical asceticism could be capable, on no other ground than such casual scientific perception, of tearing this purest and most precious of feelings out of his heart.

He holds his darling on his lap and her slim rosy legs hang down. He raises his brows as he talks to her, tenderly, with a half-teasing note of respect, and listens enchanted to her high, sweet little voice calling him Abel. He exchanges a look with the mother, who is caressing her Snapper and reading him a gentle lecture. He must be more reasonable, he must learn self-control; today again, under the manifold exasperations of life, he has given way to rage and behaved like a howling dervish. Cornelius casts a mistrustful glance at the big folk now and then, too; he thinks it not unlikely they are not unaware of those scientific preoccupations of his evening walks. If such be the case they do not show it. They stand there leaning their arms on their chairbacks and with a benevolence not untinctured with irony look on at the parental happiness.

The children's frocks are of a heavy, brick-red stuff, embroidered in modern "arty" style. They once belonged to Ingrid and Bert and are precisely alike, save that little knickers come out beneath Snapper's smock. And both have their hair bobbed. Snapper's is a streaky blond, inclined to turn dark. It is bristly and sticky and looks for all the world like a droll, badly fitting wig. But Ellie's is chestnut brown, glossy and fine as silk, as pleasing as her whole little personality. It covers her ears—and these ears are not a pair, one of them being the right size, the other distinctly too large. Her father will sometimes uncover this little abnormality and exclaim over it as though he had never noticed it before, which both makes Ellie giggle and covers her with shame. Her eyes are now golden brown, set far apart and with sweet gleams in them—such a clear and lovely look! The brows above are blond; the nose still unformed, with thick nostrils and almost circular holes; the mouth large and expressive, with a beautifully arching and mobile upper lip. When she laughs, dimples come in her cheeks and she shows her teeth like loosely strung pearls. So far she has lost but one tooth, which her father gently twisted out with his handkerchief after it had grown very wobbling. During this small operation she had paled and trembled very much. Her cheeks have the softness proper to her years, but they are not chubby; indeed, they are rather concave, due to her facial structure, with its somewhat prominent jaw. On one, close to the soft fall of her hair, is a downy freckle.

Ellie is not too well pleased with her looks—a sign that already she troubles about such things. Sadly she thinks it is best to admit it once for all, her face is "homely"; though the rest of her, "on the other hand," is not bad at all. She loves expressions like "on the other hand"; they sound choice and grown-up to her, and she likes to string them together, one after the other: "very likely," "probably," "after all." Snapper is self-critical too, though more in the moral sphere: he suffers from remorse for his attacks of rage and considers himself a tremendous sinner. He is quite certain that heaven is not for such as he; he is sure to go to "the bad place" when he dies, and no persuasions will convince him to the contrary—as that God sees the heart and gladly makes allowances. Obstinately he shakes his head, with the comic, crooked little peruke, and vows there is no place for him in heaven. When he has a cold he is immediately quite choked with mucus; rattles and rumbles from top to toe if you even look at him; his temperature flies up at once and he simply puffs. Nursy is pessimistic on the score of his constitution: such fat-blooded children as he might get a stroke any minute. Once she even thought she saw the moment at hand: Snapper had been in one of his berserker rages, and in the ensuing fit of penitence stood himself in the corner with his back to the room. Suddenly Nursy noticed that his face had gone all blue, far bluer, even, than her own.

She raised the alarm, crying out that the child's all too rich blood had at length brought him to his final hour; and Snapper, to his vast astonishment, found himself, so far from being rebuked for evil-doing, encompassed in tenderness and anxiety—until it turned out that his colour was not caused by apoplexy but by the distempering on the nursery wall, which had come off on his tear-wet face.

Nursy has come downstairs too, and stands by the door, sleekhaired, owl-eyed, with her hands folded over her white apron, and a severely dignified manner born of her limited intelligence. She is very proud of the care and training she gives her nurslings and declares that they are "enveloping wonderfully." She has had seventeen suppurated teeth lately removed from her jaws and been measured for a set of symmetrical yellow ones in dark rubber gums; these now embellish her peasant face. She is obsessed with the strange conviction that these teeth of hers are the subject of general conversation, that, as it were, the sparrows on the housetops chatter of them. "Everybody knows I've had a false set put in," she will say; "there has been a great deal of foolish talk about them." She is much given to dark hints and veiled innuendo: speaks, for instance, of a certain Dr. Bleifuss, whom every child knows, and "there are even some in the house who pretend to be him."

All one can do with talk like this is charitably to pass it over in silence. But she teaches the children nursery rhymes: gems like: "Puff, puff, here comes the train! Puff, puff, toot, toot, Away it goes again."

Or that gastronomical jingle, so suited, in its sparseness, to the times, and yet seemingly with a blitheness of its own: "Monday we begin the week, Tuesday there's a bone to pick. Wednesday we're half way through, Thursday what a great to-do! Friday we eat what fish we're able, Saturday we dance round the table. Sunday brings us pork and greens. Here's a feast for kings and queens!"

Also a certain four-line stanza with a romantic appeal, unutterable and unuttered: "Open the gate, open the gate And let the carriage drive in. Who is it in the carriage sits? A lordly sir with golden hair."

Or, finally that ballad about golden-haired Marianne who sat on a, sat on a, sat on a stone, and combed out her, combed out her, combed out her hair; and about blood-thirsty Rudolph, who pulled out a, pulled out a, pulled out a knife—and his ensuing direful end. Ellie enunciates all these ballads charmingly, with her mobile little lips, and sings them in her sweet little voice—much better than Snapper. She does everything better than he does, and he pays her honest admiration and homage and obeys her in all things except when visited by one of his attacks. Sometimes she teaches him, instructs him upon the birds in the picture-book and tells him their proper names: "This is a chaffinch, Buddy, this is a bullfinch, this is a cowfinch." He has to repeat them after her. She gives him medical instruction too, teaches him the names of diseases, such as inflammation of the lungs, inflammation of the blood, inflammation of the air. If he does not pay attention and cannot say the words after her, she stands him in the corner. Once she even boxed his ears, but was so ashamed that she stood herself in the corner for a long time. Yes, they are fast friends, two souls with but a single thought, and have all their adventures in common. They come home from a walk and relate as with one voice that they have seen two moolies and a teenty-weenty baby calf. They are on familiar terms with the kitchen, which consists of Xaver and the ladies Hinterhofer, two sisters once of the lower middle class who, in these evil days, are reduced to living "au pair" as the phrase goes and officiating as cook and housemaid for their board and keep. The little ones have a feeling that Xaver and the Hinterhofers are on much the same footing with their father and mother as they are themselves. At least sometimes, when they have been scolded, they go downstairs and announce that the master and mistress are cross. But playing with the servants lacks charm compared with the joys of playing upstairs. The kitchen could never rise to the height of the games their father can invent. For instance, there is "four gentlemen taking a walk." When they play it Abel will crook his knees until he is the same height with themselves and go walking with them, hand in hand. They never get enough of this sport; they could walk round and round the dining-room a whole day on end, five gentlemen in all, counting the diminished Abel.

Then there is the thrilling cushion game. One of the children, usually Ellie, seats herself, unbeknownst to Abel, in his seat at table. Still as a mouse she awaits his coming. He draws near with his head in the air, descanting in loud, clear tones upon the surpassing comfort of his chair; and sits down on top of Ellie. "What's this, what's this?" says he.

And bounces about, deaf to the smothered giggles exploding behind him. "Why have they put a cushion in my chair? And what a queer, hard, awkward-shaped cushion it is!" he goes on. "Frightfully uncomfortable to sit on!" And keeps pushing and bouncing about more and more on the astonishing cushion and clutching behind him into the rapturous giggling and squeaking, until at last he turns round, and the game ends with a magnificent climax of discovery and recognition. They might go through all this a hundred times without diminishing by an iota its power to thrill.

Today is no time for such joys. The imminent festivity disturbs the atmosphere, and besides there is work to be done, and, above all, the eggs to be got. Ellie has just time to recite "Puff, puff," and Cornelius to discover that her ears are not mates, when they are interrupted by the arrival of Danny, come to fetch Bert and Ingrid. Xaver, meantime, has exchanged his striped livery for an ordinary coat, in which he looks rather rough-and-ready, though as brisk and attractive as ever. So then Nursy and the children ascend to the upper regions, the Professor withdraws to his study to read, as always after dinner, and his wife bends her energies upon the sandwiches and salad that must be prepared. And she has another errand as well. Before the young people arrive she has to take her shopping-basket and dash into town on her bicycle, to turn into provisions a sum of money she has in hand, which she dares not keep lest it lose all value.

Cornelius reads, leaning back in his chair, with his cigar between his middle and index fingers. First he reads Macaulay on the origin of the English public debt at the end of the seventeenth century; then an article in a French periodical on the rapid increase in the Spanish debt towards the end of the sixteenth. Both these for his lecture on the morrow. He intends to compare the astonishing prosperity which accompanied the phenomenon in England with its fatal effects a hundred years earlier in Spain, and to analyse the ethical and psychological grounds of the difference in results. For that will give him a chance to refer back from the England of William III, which is the actual subject in hand, to the time of Philip II and the

Counter-Reformation, which is his own special field. He has already written a valuable work on this period; it is much cited and got him his professorship. While his cigar burns down and gets strong, he excogitates a few pensive sentences in a key of gentle melancholy, to be delivered before his class next day: about the practically hopeless struggle carried on by the belated Philip against the whole trend of history: against the new, the kingdom-disrupting power of the Germanic ideal of freedom and individual liberty. And about the persistent, futile struggle of the aristocracy, condemned by God and rejected of man, against the forces of progress and change. He savours his sentences; keeps on polishing them while he puts back the books he has been using; then goes upstairs for the usual pause in his day's work, the hour with drawn blinds and closed eyes, which he so imperatively needs. But today, he recalls, he will rest under disturbed conditions, amid the bustle of preparations for the feast. He smiles to find his heart giving a mild flutter at the thought. Disjointed phrases on the theme of black-clad Philip and his times mingle with a confused consciousness that they will soon be dancing down below. For five minutes or so he falls asleep.

As he lies and rests he can hear the sound of the garden gate and the repeated ringing at the bell. Each time a little pang goes through him, of excitement and suspense, at the thought that the young people have begun to fill the floor below. And each time he smiles at himself again—though even his smile is slightly nervous, is tinged with the pleasurable anticipations people always feel before a party. At half past four, it is already dark, he gets up and washes at the wash-stand. The basin has been out of repair for two years. It is supposed to tip, but has broken away from its socket on one side and cannot be mended because there is nobody to mend it; neither replaced because no shop can supply another. So it has to be hung up above the vent and emptied by lifting in both hands and pouring out the water. Cornelius shakes his head over this basin, as he does several times a day—whenever, in fact, he has occasion to use it. He finishes his toilet with care, standing under the ceiling light to polish his glasses till they shine. Then he goes downstairs.

On his way to the dining-room he hears the gramophone already going, and the sound of voices. He puts on a polite, society air; at his tongue's end is the phrase he means to utter: "Pray don't let me disturb you," as he passes directly into the dining-room for his tea. "Pray don't let me disturb you"—it seems to him precisely the *mot juste*; towards the guests cordial and considerate, for himself a very bulwark.

The lower floor is lighted up, all the bulbs in the chandelier are burning save one that has burned out. Cornelius pauses on a lower step and surveys the entrance hail. It looks pleasant and cosy in the bright light, with its copy of Marées over the brick chimney-piece, its wainscoted walls-wainscoted in soft wood and red-carpeted floor, where the guests stand in groups, chatting, each with his tea-cup and slice of bread-and-butter spread with anchovy paste. There is a festal haze, faint scents of hair and clothing and human breath come to him across the room, it is all characteristic and familiar and highly evocative. The door into the dressing-room is open, guests are still arriving.

A large group of people is rather bewildering at first sight. The Professor takes in only the general scene. He does not see Ingrid, who is standing just at the foot of the steps, in a dark silk frock with a pleated collar falling softly over the shoulders, and bare arms. She smiles up at him, nodding and showing her lovely teeth.

"Rested?" she asks, for his private ear. With a quite unwarranted start he recognizes her, and she presents some of her friends.

"May I introduce Herr Zuber?" she says. "And this is Fräulein Plaichinger."

Herr Zuber is insignificant. But Fräulein Piaichinger is a perfect Germania, blond and voluptuous, arrayed in floating draperies. She has a snub nose, and answers the Professor's salutation in the high, shrill pipe so many stout women have.

"Delighted to meet you," he says. "How nice of you to come! A classmate of Ingrid's, I suppose?"

And Herr Zuber is a golfing partner of Ingrid's. He is in business; he works in his uncle's brewery. Cornelius makes a few jokes about the thinness of the beer and professes to believe that Herr Zuber could easily do something about the quality if he would. "But pray don't let me disturb you," he goes on, and turns towards the dining-room.

"There comes Max," says Ingrid. "Max, you sweep, what do you mean by rolling up at this time of day?" For such is the way they talk to each other, offensively to an older ear; of social forms, of hospitable warmth, there is no faintest trace. They all call each other by their first names.

A young man comes up to them out of the dressing-room and makes his bow; he has an expanse of white shirt-front and a little black string tie. He is as pretty as a picture, dark, with rosy cheeks, clean-shaven of course, but with just a sketch of sidewhisker. Not a ridiculous or flashy beauty, not like a gypsy fiddler, but just charming to look at, in a winning, well-bred way, with kind dark eyes. He even wears his dinner-jacket a little awkwardly.

"Please don't scold me, Cornelia," he says; "it's the idiotic lectures." And Ingrid presents him to her father as Herr Hergesell.

Well, and so this is Herr Hergesell. He knows his manners, does Herr Hergesell, and thanks the master of the house quite ingratiatingly for his invitation as they shake hands. "I certainly seem to have missed the bus," says he jocosely. "Of course I have lectures today up to four o'clock; I would have; and after that I had to go home to change." Then he talks about his pumps, with which he has just been struggling in the dressing-room.

"I brought them with me in a bag," he goes on. "Mustn't tramp all over the carpet in our brogues—it's not done. Well, I was ass enough not to fetch along a shoe-horn, and I find I simply can't get in! What a sell! They are the tightest I've ever had, the numbers don't tell you a thing, and all the leather today is just cast iron. It's not leather at all. My poor finger,"—he confidingly displays a reddened digit and once more characterizes the whole thing as a "sell," and a putrid sell into the bargain. He really does talk just as Ingrid said he did, with a peculiar nasal drawl, not affectedly in the least, but merely because that is the way of all the Hergesells.

Dr. Cornelius says it is very careless of them not to keep a shoe-horn in the cloak-room and displays proper sympathy with the mangled finger. "But now you really must not let me disturb you any longer," he goes on. "Auf wiedersehen!" And he crosses the hall into the dining-room.

There are guests there too, drinking tea; the family table is pulled out. But the Professor goes at once to his own little upholstered corner with the electric light bulb above it—the nook where he usually drinks his tea. His wife is sitting there talking with Bert and two other young men, one of them Herzl, whom Cornelius knows and greets; the other a typical "Wandervogel" named Möller, a youth who obviously neither owns nor cares to own the correct evening dress of the middle classes (in fact, there is no such thing any more), nor to ape the manners of a gentleman (and, in fact, there is no such thing any more either). He has a wilderness of hair, horn spectacles, and a long neck, and wears golf stockings and a belted blouse. His regular occupation, the Professor learns, is banking, but he is by way of being an amateur folklorist and collects folk-songs from all localities and in all languages. He sings them, too, and at Ingrid's command has brought his guitar; it is hanging in the dressing-room in an oilcloth case. Herzl, the actor, is small and slight, but he has a strong growth of black beard, as you can tell by the thick coat of powder on his cheeks. His eyes are larger than life, with a deep and melancholy glow. He has put on rouge besides the powder—those dull carmine highlights on the cheeks can be nothing but a cosmetic. "Queer," thinks the Professor. "You would think a man would be one thing or the other—not melancholic and use face paint at the same time. It's a psychological contradiction. How can a melancholy man rouge? But here we have a perfect illustration of the abnormality of the artist soul-form. It can make possible a contradiction like this—perhaps it even consists in the contradiction. All very interesting—and no reason whatever for not being polite to him. Politeness is a primitive convention—and legitimate... Do take some lemon, Herr Hofschauspieler!"

Court actors and court theatres—there are no such things any more, really. But Herzl relishes the sound of the title, notwithstanding he is a revolutionary artist. This must be another contradiction inherent in his soul-form; so, at least, the Professor assumes, and he is probably right. The flattery he is guilty of is a sort of atonement for his previous hard thoughts about the rouge.

"Thank you so much, it's really too good of you, sir," says Herzl, quite embarrassed. He is so overcome that he almost stammers;

only his perfect enunciation saves him. His whole bearing towards his hostess and the master of the house is exaggeratedly polite. It is almost as though he had a bad conscience in respect of his rouge; as though an inward compulsion had driven him to put it on, but now, seeing it through the Professor's eyes, he disapproves of it himself, and thinks, by an air of humility towards the whole of unrouged society, to mitigate its effect.

They drink their tea and chat: about Möller's folk-songs, about Basque folk-songs and Spanish folk-songs; from which they pass to the new production of Don Carlos at the Stadttheater, in which Herzl plays the title-role. He talks about his own rendering of the part and says he hopes his conception of the character has unity. They go on to criticize the rest of the cast, the setting, and the production as a whole; and Cornelius is struck, rather painfully, to find the conversation trending towards his own special province, back to Spain and the Counter-Reformation. He has done nothing at all to give it this turn, he is perfectly innocent, and hopes it does not look as though he had sought an occasion to play the professor. He wonders, and falls silent, feeling relieved when the little folk come up to the table. Ellie and Snapper have on their blue velvet Sunday frocks; they are permitted to partake in the festivities up to bed-time. They look shy and large-eyed as they say how-do-you-do to the strangers and, under pressure, repeat their names and ages. Herr Möller does nothing but gaze at them solemnly, but Herzl is simply ravished. He rolls his eyes up to heaven and puts his hands over his mouth; he positively blesses them. It all, no doubt, comes from his heart, but he is so addicted to theatrical methods of making an impression and getting an effect that both words and behavior ring frightfully false. And even his enthusiasm for the little folk looks too much like part of his general craving to make up for the rouge on his cheeks.

The tea-table has meanwhile emptied of guests, and dancing is going on in the hail. The children run off, the Professor prepares to retire. "Go and enjoy yourselves," he says to Möller and Herzl, who have sprung from their chairs as he rises from his. They shake hands and he withdraws into his study, his peaceful kingdom, where he lets down the blinds, turns on the desk lamp, and sits down to his work.

It is work which can be done, if necessary, under disturbed conditions: nothing but a few letters and a few notes. Of course, Cornelius's mind wanders. Vague impressions float through it: Herr Hergesell's refractory pumps, the high pipe in that plump body of the Plaichinger female. As he writes, or leans back in his chair and stares into space, his thoughts go back to Herr Möller's collection of Basque folk-songs, to Herzl's posings and humility, to "his" Carlos and the court of Philip II. There is something strange, he thinks, about conversations. They are so ductile, they will flow of their own accord in the direction of one's dominating interest. Often and often he has seen this happen. And while he is thinking, he is listening to the sounds next door—rather subdued, he finds them. He hears only voices, no sound of footsteps. The dancers do not glide or circle round the room; they merely walk about over the carpet, which does not hamper their movements in the least. Their way of holding each other is quite different and strange, and they move to the strains of the gramophone, to the weird music of the new world. He concentrates on the music and makes out that it is a jazz-band record, with various percussion instruments and the clack and clatter of castanets, which, however, are not even faintly suggestive of Spain, but merely jazz like the rest. No, not Spain... His thoughts are back at their old round.

Half an hour goes by. It occurs to him it would be no more than friendly to go and contribute a box of cigarettes to the festivities next door. Too bad to ask the young people to smoke their own—though they have probably never thought of it. He goes into the empty dining-room and takes a box from his supply in the cupboard: not the best ones, nor yet the brand he himself prefers, but a certain long, thin kind he is not averse to getting rid of—after all, they are nothing but youngsters. He takes the box into the hall, holds it up with a smile, and deposits it on the mantel-shelf. After which he gives a look round and returns to his own room.

There comes a lull in dance and music. The guests stand about the room in groups or round the table at the window or are seated in a circle by the fireplace. Even the built-in stairs, with their worn velvet carpet, are crowded with young folk as in an amphitheatre: Max Hergesell is there, leaning back with one elbow on the step above and gesticulating with his free hand as he talks to the shrill, voluptuous Plaichinger. The floor of the hail is nearly empty, save just in the centre: there, directly beneath the chandelier, the two little ones in their blue velvet frocks clutch each other in an awkward embrace and twirl silently round and round, oblivious of all else. Cornelius, as he passes, strokes their hair, with a friendly word; it does not distract them from their small solemn preoccupation. But at his own door he turns to glance round and sees young Hergesell push himself off the stair by his elbow—probably because he noticed the Professor. He comes down into the arena, takes Ellie out of her brother's arms, and dances with her himself. It looks very comic, without the music, and he crouches down just as Cornelius does when he goes walking with the four gentlemen, holding the fluttered Ellie as though she were grown up and taking little "shimmying" steps. Everybody watches with huge enjoyment, the gramophone is put on again, dancing becomes general. The Professor stands and looks, with his hand on the door-knob. He nods and laughs; when he finally shuts himself into his study the mechanical smile still lingers on his lips.

Again he turns over pages by his desk lamp, takes notes, attends to a few simple matters. After a while he notices that the guests have forsaken the entrance ball for his wife's drawing-room, into which there is a door from his own study as well. He hears their voices and the sounds of a guitar being tuned. Herr Möller, it seems, is to sing—and does so. He twangs the strings of his instrument and sings in a powerful bass a ballad in a strange tongue, possibly Swedish. The Professor does not succeed in identifying it, though he listens attentively to the end, after which there is great applause. The sound is deadened by the portière that hangs over the dividing door. The young bank clerk begins another song. Cornelius goes softly in.

It is half-dark in the drawing-room; the only light is from the shaded standard lamp, beneath which Möller sits, on the divan, with his legs crossed, picking his strings. His audience is grouped easily about; as there are not enough seats, some stand, and more, among them many young ladies, are simply sitting on the floor with their hands clasped round their knees or even with their legs stretched out before them. Hergesell sits thus, in his dinner-jacket, next the piano, with Fräulein Plaichinger beside him. Frau Cornelius is holding both children on her lap as she sits in her easy-chair opposite the singer. Snapper, the Baeotian, begins to talk loud and clear in the middle of the song and has to be intimidated with hushings and finger-shakings. Never, never would Ellie allow herself to be guilty of such conduct. She sits there daintily erect and still on her mother's knee. The Professor tries to catch her eye and exchange a private signal with his little girl; but she does not see him. Neither does she seem to be looking at the singer. Her gaze is directed lower down.

Möller sings the "joli tambour": "Sire, mon roi, donnez-moi votre flue—"

They are all enchanted. "How good!" Hergesell is heard to say, in the odd, nasally condescending Hergesell tone. The next one is a beggar ballad, to a tune composed by young Möller himself; it elicits a storm of applause: "Gypsy lassie a-goin' to the fair, Huzza! Gypsy laddie a-goin' to be there—Huzza, diddlety umpty dido!"

Laughter and high spirits, sheer reckless hilarity, reigns after this jovial ballad. "Frightfully good!" Hergesell comments again, as before. Follows another popular song, this time a Hungarian one; Möller sings it in its own outlandish tongue, and most effectively. The Professor applauds with ostentation. It warms his heart and does him good, this outcropping of artistic, historic, and cultural elements all amongst the shimmying. He goes up to young Möller and congratulates him, talks about the songs and their sources, and Möller promises to lend him a certain annotated book of folk-songs. Cornelius is the more cordial because all the time, as fathers do, he has been comparing the parts and achievements of this young stranger with those of his own son, and being gnawed by envy and chagrin. This young Möller, he is thinking, is a capable bank-clerk (though about Möller's capacity he knows nothing whatever) and has this special gift besides, which must have taken talent and energy to cultivate. "And here is my poor Bert, who knows nothing and can do nothing and thinks of nothing except playing the clown, without even talent for that!" He tries to be just; he tells himself that, after all, Bert has innate refinement; that probably there is a good deal more to him than there is to the successful Möller; that perhaps he has even something of the poet in him, and his dancing and table-waiting are due to mere boyish folly and the distraught times. But paternal envy and pessimism win the upper hand; when Möller begins another song, Dr. Cornelius goes back to his room: He works as before, with divided attention, at this and that, while it gets on for seven o'clock. Then he remembers a letter he may just as well write, a short letter and not very important, but letter-writing is wonderful for the way it takes up the time, and it is almost half past when he has finished. At half past eight the Italian salad will be served; so now is the prescribed moment for the Professor to go out into the wintry darkness to post his letters and take his daily quantum of fresh air and exercise. They are dancing again, and he will have to pass through the hail to get his hat and coat; but they are used to him now, he need not stop and beg them not to be disturbed. He lays away his papers, takes up the letters he has written, and goes out. But he sees his wife sitting near the door of his room and pauses a little by her easy-chair.

She is watching the dancing. Now and then the big folk or some of their guests stop to speak to her; the party is at its height, and there are more onlookers than these two: blue-faced Ann is standing at the bottom of the stairs, in all the dignity of her limitations. She is waiting for the children, who simply cannot get their fill of these unwonted festivities, and watching over Snapper, lest his all too rich blood be churned to the danger-point by too much twirling round. And not only the nursery but the kitchen takes an interest: Xaver and the two ladies Hinterhofer are standing by the pantry door looking on with relish. Fräulein Walburga, the elder of the two sunken sisters (the culinary section—she objects to being called a cook), is a whimsical, good-natured sort, brown-eyed, wearing glasses with thick circular lenses; the nose-piece is wound with a bit of rag to keep it from pressing on her nose. Fräulein Cecilia is younger, though not so precisely young either. Her bearing is as self-assertive as usual, this being her way of sustaining her dignity as a former member of the middle class. For Fräulein Cecilia feels acutely her descent into the ranks of domestic service. She positively declines to wear a cap or other badge of servitude, and her hardest trial is on the Wednesday evening when she has to serve the dinner while

Xaver has his afternoon out. She hands the dishes with averted face and elevated nose—a fallen queen; and so distressing is it to behold her degradation that one evening when the little folk happened to be at table and saw her they both with one accord burst into tears. Such anguish is unknown to young Xaver. He enjoys serving and does it with an ease born of practice as well as talent, for he was once a "piccolo." But otherwise he is a thorough-paced good-for-nothing and windbag—with quite distinct traits of character of his own, as his long-suffering employers are always ready to concede, but perfectly impossible and a bag of wind for all that. One must just take him as he is, they think, and not expect figs from thistles. He is the child and product of the disrupted times, a perfect specimen of his generation, follower of the revolution, Boishevist sympathizer. The Professor's name for him is the "minuteman," because he is always to be counted on in any sudden crisis, if only it address his sense of humour or love of novelty, and will display therein amazing readiness and resource. But he utterly lacks a sense of duty and can as little be trained to the performance of the daily round and common task as some kinds of dog can be taught to jump over a stick. It goes so plainly against the grain that criticism is disarmed. One becomes resigned. On grounds that appealed to him as unusual and amusing he would be ready to turn out of his bed at any hour of the night. But he simply cannot get up before eight in the morning, he cannot do it, he will not jump over the stick. Yet all day long the evidence of this free and untrammelled existence, the sound of his mouth-organ, his joyous whistle, or his raucous but expressive voice lifted in song, rises to the hearing of the world above-stairs; and the smoke of his cigarettes fills the pantry. While the Hinterhofer ladies work he stands and looks on. Of a morning while the Professor is breakfasting, he tears the leaf off the study calendar—but does not lift a finger to dust the room. Dr. Cornelius has often told him to leave the calendar alone, for he tends to tear off two leaves at a time and thus to add to the general confusion. But young Xaver appears to find joy in this activity, and will not be deprived of it.

Again, he is fond of children, a winning trait. He will throw himself into games with the little folk in the garden, make and mend their toys with great ingenuity, even read aloud from their books—and very droll it sounds in his thick-lipped pronunciation. With his whole soul he loves the cinema; after an evening spent there he inclines to melancholy and yearning and talking to himself. Vague hopes stir in him that some day he may make his fortune in that gay world and belong to it by rights—hopes based on his shock of hair and his physical agility and daring. He likes to climb the ash tree in the front garden, mounting branch by branch to the very top and frightening everybody to death who sees him. Once there he lights a cigarette and smokes it as he sways to and fro, keeping a lookout for a cinema director who might chance to come along and engage him.

If he changed his striped jacket for mufti, he might easily dance with the others and no one would notice the difference. For the big folk's friends are rather anomalous in their clothing: evening dress is worn by a few, but it is by no means the rule. There is quite a sprinkling of guests, both male and female, in the same general style as Möller the ballad-singer. The Professor is familiar with the circumstances of most of this young generation he is watching as he stands beside his wife's chair; he has heard them spoken of by name. They are students at the high school or at the School of Applied Art; they lead, at least the masculine portion, that precarious and scrambling existence which is purely the product of the time. There is a tall, pale, spindling youth, the son of a dentist, who lives by speculation. From all the Professor hears, he is a perfect Aladdin. He keeps a car, treats his friends to champagne suppers, and showers presents upon them on every occasion, costly little trifles in mother-of-pearl and gold. So today he has brought gifts to the young givers of the feast: for Bert a gold lead-pencil, and for Ingrid a pair of earrings of barbaric size, great gold circlets that fortunately do not have to go through the little earlobe, but are fastened over it by means of a clip. The big folk come laughing to their parents to display these trophies; and the parents shake their heads even while they admire—Aladdin bowing over and over from afar.

The young people appear to be absorbed in their dancing—if the performance they are carrying out with so much still concentration can be called dancing. They stride across the carpet, slowly, according to some unfathomable prescript, strangely embraced; in the newest attitude, tummy advanced and shoulders high, waggling the hips. They do not get tired, because nobody could. There is no such thing as heightened colour or heaving bosoms. Two girls may dance together or two young men—it is all the same. They move to the exotic strains of the gramophone, played with the loudest needles to procure the maximum of sound: shimmies, foxtrots, one-steps, double foxes, African shimmies, Java dances, and Creole polkas, the wild musky melodies follow one another, now furious, now languishing, a monotonous Negro programme in unfamiliar rhythm, to a clacking, clashing, and strumming orchestral accompaniment.

"What is that record?" Cornelius inquires of Ingrid, as she passes him by in the arms of the pale young speculator, with reference to the piece then playing, whose alternate languors and furies he finds comparatively pleasing and showing a certain resourcefulness in detail.

"Prince of Pappenheim: 'Console thee, dearest child,'" she answers, and smiles pleasantly back at him with her white teeth.

The cigarette smoke wreathes beneath the chandelier. The air is blue with a festal haze compact of sweet and thrilling ingredients that stir the blood with memories of green-sick pains and are particularly poignant to those whose youth-like the Professor's own has been over-sensitive... The little folk are still on the floor. They are allowed to stay up until eight, so great is their delight in the party. The guests have got used to their presence; in their own way, they have their place in the doings of the evening. They have separated, anyhow: Snapper revolves all alone in the middle of the carpet, in his little blue velvet smock, while Ellie is running after one of the dancing couples, trying to hold the man fast by his coat. It is Max Hergesell and Fräulein Plaichinger. They dance well, it is a pleasure to watch them. One has to admit that these mad modern dances, when the right people dance them, are not so bad after all—they have something quite taking. Young Hergesell is a capital leader, dances according to rule, yet with individuality. So it looks. With what aplomb can he walk backwards—when space permits! And he knows how to be graceful standing still in a crowd. And his partner supports him well, being unsuspectedly lithe and buoyant, as fat people often are. They look at each other, they are talking, paying no heed to Ellie, though others are smiling to see the child's persistence. Dr. Cornelius tries to catch up his little sweetheart as she passes and draw her to him. But Ellie eludes him, almost peevishly; her dear Abel is nothing to her now. She braces her little arms against his chest and turns her face away with a persecuted look. Then escapes to follow her fancy once more.

The Professor feels an involuntary twinge. Uppermost in his heart is hatred for this party, with its power to intoxicate and estrange his darling child. His love for her—that not quite disinterested, not quite unexceptionable love of his—is easily wounded. He wears a mechanical smile, but his eyes have clouded, and he stares fixedly at a point in the carpet, between the dancers' feet.

"The children ought to go to bed," he tells his wife. But she pleads for another quarter of an hour; she has promised already, and they do love it so! He smiles again and shakes his head, stands so a moment and then goes across to the cloak-room, which is full of coats and hats and scarves and overshoes. He has trouble in rummaging out his own coat, and Max Hergesell comes out of the hail, wiping his brow.

"Going out, sir?" he asks, in Hergesellian accents, dutifully helping the older man on with his coat. "Silly business this, with my pumps," he says. "They pinch like hell. The brutes are simply too tight for me, quite apart from the bad leather. They press just here on the ball of my great toe,"—he stands on one foot and holds the other in his hand—"it's simply unbearable. There's nothing for it but to take them off; my brogues will have to do the business... Oh, let me help you, sir."

"Thanks," says Cornelius. "Don't trouble. Get rid of your own tormentors... Oh, thanks very much!" For Hergesell has gone on one knee to snap the fasteners of his snow-boots.

Once more the Professor expresses his gratitude; he is pleased and touched by so much sincere respect and youthful readiness to serve. "Go and enjoy yourself," he counsels. "Change your shoes and make up for what you have been suffering. Nobody can dance in shoes that pinch. Goodbye, I must be off to get a breath of fresh air."

"I'm going to dance with Ellie now," calls Hergesell after him. "She'll be a first-rate dancer when she grows up, and that I'll swear to."

"Think so?" Cornelius answers, already half out. "Well, you are a connoisseur, I'm sure. Don't get curvature of the spine with stooping."

He nods again and goes. "Fine lad," he thinks as he shuts the door. "Student of engineering. Knows what he's bound for, got a good clear head, and so well set up and pleasant too." And again paternal envy rises as he compares his poor Bert's status with this young man's, which he puts in the rosiest light that his son's may look the darker. Thus he sets out on his evening walk.

He goes up the avenue, crosses the bridge, and walks along the bank on the other side as far as the next bridge but one. The air is wet and cold, with a little snow now and then. He turns up his coat-collar and slips the crook of his cane over the arm behind his back. Now and then he ventilates his lungs with a long deep breath of the night air. As usual when he walks, his mind reverts to his professional preoccupations, he thinks about his lectures and the things he means to say tomorrow about Philip's struggle against the Germanic revolution, things steeped in melancholy and penetratingly just. Above all just, he thinks. For in one's dealings with the young it behoves one to display the scientific spirit, to exhibit the principles of enlightenment—not only for purposes of mental discipline, but on the human and individual side, in order not to wound them or indirectly offend their political sensibilities; particularly in these days, when there is so much tinder in the air, opinions are so frightfully split up and chaotic, and you may so easily incur attacks from one party or the other, or even give rise to scandal, by taking sides on a point of history. "And taking sides is unhistoric anyhow," so he muses. "Only justice, only impartiality is historic." And could not, properly considered, be otherwise... For justice can have nothing of youthful fire and blithe, fresh, loyal conviction. It is by nature melancholy. And, being so, has secret affinity with the lost cause and the forlorn hope rather than with the fresh and blithe and loyal—perhaps this affinity is its very essence and without it it would not exist at all!... "And is there then no such thing as justice?" the Professor asks himself, and ponders the question so deeply that he absently posts his letters in the next box and turns round to go home. This thought of his is unsettling and disturbing to the scientific mind—but is it not after all itself scientific, psychological, conscientious, and therefore to be accepted without prejudice, no matter how upsetting?

In the midst of which musings Dr. Cornelius finds himself back at his own door.

On the outer threshold stands Xaver, and seems to be looking for him.

"Herr Professor," says Xaver, tossing back his hair, "go upstairs to Ellie straight off. She's in a bad way."

"What's the matter?" asks Cornelius in alarm. "Is she ill?"

"No-o, not to say ill," answers Xaver. "She's just in a bad way and crying fit to bust her little heart. It's along o' that chap with the shirt-front that danced with her—Herr Hergesell. She couldn't be got to go upstairs peaceably, not at no price at all, and she's Wen crying bucketfuls."

"Nonsense," says the Professor, who has entered and is tossing off his things in the cloak-room. He says no more; opens the glass door and without a glance at the guests turns swiftly to the stairs. Takes them two at a time, crosses the upper hail and the small room leading into the nursery. Xaver follows at his heels, but stops at the nursery door.

A bright light still burns within, showing the gay frieze that runs all round the room, the large row of shelves heaped with a confusion of toys, the rocking-horse on his swaying platform, with red-varnished nostrils and raised hoofs. On the linoleum lie other toys-building blocks, railway trains, a little trumpet. The two white cribs stand not far apart, Ellie's in the window corner, Snapper's out in the room.

Snapper is asleep. He has said his prayers in loud, ringing tones, prompted by Nurse, and gone off at once into vehement, profound, and rosy slumber—from which a cannon-ball fired at close range could not rouse him. He lies with both fists flung back on the pillows on either side of the tousled head with its funny crooked little slumber-tossed wig.

A circle of females surrounds Ellie's bed: not only blue-faced Ann is there, but the Hinterhofer ladies too, talking to each other and to her. They make way as the Professor comes up and reveal the child sitting all pale among her pillows, sobbing and weeping more bitterly than he has ever seen her sob and weep in her life. Her lovely little hands lie on the coverlet in front of her, the nightgown with its narrow lace border has slipped down from her shoulder—such a thin, birdlike little shoulder—and the sweet head Cornelius loves so well, set on the neck like a flower on its stalk, her head is on one side, with the eyes rolled up to the corner between wall and ceiling above her head. For there she seems to envisage the anguish of her heart and even to nod to it—either on purpose or because her head wobbles as her body is shaken with the violence of her sobs. Her eyes rain down tears. The bow-shaped lips are parted, like a little mater dolorosa's, and from them issue long, low wails that in nothing resemble the unnecessary and exasperating shrieks of a naughty child, but rise from the deep extremity of her heart and wake in the Professor's own a sympathy that is well-nigh intolerable. He has never seen his darling so before. His feelings find immediate vent in an attack on the ladies Hinterhofer.

"What about the supper?" he asks sharply. "There must be a great deal to do. Is my wife being left to do it alone?"

For the acute sensibilities of the former middle class this is quite enough. The ladies withdraw in righteous indignation, and Xaver Kleingutl jeers at them as they pass out. Having been born to low life instead of achieving it, he never loses a chance to mock at their fallen state.

"Childie, childie," murmurs Cornelius, and sitting down by the crib enfolds the anguished Ellie in his arms. "What is the trouble with my darling?"

She bedews his face with her tears.

"Abel... Abel..." she stammers between sobs. "Why—isn't Max my brother? Max ought to be—my brother!"

Alas, alas! What mischance is this? Is this what the party has wrought, with its fatal atmosphere? Cornelius glances helplessly up at blue-faced Ann standing there in all the dignity of her limitations with her hands before her on her apron. She purses up her mouth and makes a long face. "It's pretty young," she says, "for the female instincts to be showing up."

"Hold your tongue," snaps Cornelius, in his agony. He has this much to be thankful for, that Ellie does not turn from him now; she does not push him away as she did downstairs, but clings to him in her need, while she reiterates her absurd, bewildered prayer that Max might be her brother, or with a fresh burst of desire demands to be taken downstairs so that he can dance with her again. But Max, of course, is dancing with Fraulein Plaichinger, that behemoth who is his rightful partner and has every claim upon him; whereas Ellie—never, thinks the Professor, his heart torn with the violence of his pity, never has she looked so tiny and birdlike as now, when she nestles to him shaken with sobs and all unaware of what is happening in her little soul. No, she does not know. She does not comprehend that her suffering is on account of Fräulein Plaichinger, fat, overgrown, and utterly within her rights in dancing with Max Hergesell, whereas Ellie may only do it once, by way of a joke, although she is incomparably the more charming of the two. Yet it would be quite mad to reproach young Hergesell with the state of affairs or to make fantastic demands upon him. No, Ellie's suffering is without help or healing and must be covered up. Yet just as it is without understanding, so it is also without restraint—and that is what makes it so horribly painful. Xaver and blue-faced Ann do not feel this pain, it does not affect them—either because of native callousness or because they accept it as the way of nature. But the Professor's fatherly heart is quite torn by it, and by a distressful horror of this passion, so hopeless and so absurd.

Of no avail to hold forth to poor Ellie on the subject of the perfectly good little brother she already has. She only casts a distraught and scornful glance over at the other crib, where Snapper lies vehemently slumbering, and with fresh tears calls again for Max. Of no avail either the promise of a long, long walk tomorrow, all five gentlemen, round and round the dining-room table; or a dramatic description of the thrilling cushion games they will play. No, she will listen to none of all this, nor to lying down and going to sleep. She will not sleep, she will sit bolt upright and suffer... But on a sudden they stop and listen, Abel and Ellie; listen to something miraculous that is coming to pass, that is approaching by strides—two strides, to the nursery door, that now overwhelmingly appears...

It is Xaver's work, not a doubt of that. He has not remained by the door where he stood to gloat over the ejection of the Hinterhofers. No, he has bestirred himself, taken a notion; likewise steps to carry it out. Downstairs he has gone, twitched Herr Hergesell's sleeve, and made a thick-lipped request. So here they both are. Xaver, having done his part, remains by the door; but Max Hergesell comes up to Ellie's crib; in his dinner-jacket, with his sketchy side-whisker and charming black eyes; obviously quite pleased with his role of swan knight and fairy prince, as one who should say: "See, here am I, now all losses are restored and sorrows end!"

Cornelius is almost as much overcome as Ellie herself.

"Just look," he says feebly, "look who's here. This is uncommonly good of you, Herr Hergesell."

"Not a bit of it," says Hergesell. "Why shouldn't I come to say good night to my fair partner?"

And he approaches the bars of the crib, behind which Ellie sits struck mute. She smiles blissfully through her tears. A funny, high little note that is half a sigh of relief comes from her lips, then she looks dumbly up at her swan knight with her golden brown eyes—tear-swollen though they are, so much more beautiful than the fat Plaichinger's. She does not put up her arms. Her joy, like her grief, is without understanding; but she does not do that. The lovely little hands lie quiet on the coverlet, and Max Hergesell stands with his arms leaning over the rail as on a balcony.

"And now," he says smartly, "she need not 'sit the livelong night and weep upon her bed'!" He looks at the Professor to make sure he is receiving due credit for the quotation. "Ha ha!" he laughs, "she's beginning young. 'Console thee, dearest child!' Never mind, you're all right! Just as you are you'll be wonderful! You've only got to grow up... And you'll lie down and go to sleep like a good girl, now I've come to say good night? And not cry any more, little Lorelei?"

Ellie looks up at him, transfigured. One birdlike shoulder is bare; the Professor draws the lace-trimmed nighty over it. There comes into his mind a sentimental story he once read about a dying child who longs to see a clown he had once, with unforgettable ecstasy, beheld in a circus. And they bring the clown to the bedside marvellously arrayed, embroidered before and behind with silver butterflies; and the child dies happy. Max Hergesell is not embroidered, and Ellie, thank God, is not going to die, she has only been "in a bad way." But, after all, the effect is the same. Young Hergesell leans over the bars of the crib and rattles on, more for the father's ear than the child's, but Ellie does not know that—and the father's feelings towards him are a most singular mixture of thankfulness, embarrassment, and hatred.

"Good night, little Lorelei," says Hergesell, and gives her his hand through the bars. Her pretty, soft, white little hand is swallowed up in the grasp of his big, strong, red one. "Sleep well," he says, "and sweet dreams! But don't dream about me—God forbid! Not at your age—ha ha!" And then the fairy clown's visit is at an end. Cornelius accompanies him to the door. "No, no, positively, no thanks called for, don't mention it," he large-heartedly protests; and Xaver goes downstairs with him, to help serve the Italian salad.

But Dr. Cornelius returns to Ellie, who is now lying down, with her cheek pressed into her flat little pillow.

"Well, wasn't that lovely?" he says as he smooths the covers. She nods, with one last little sob. For a quarter of an hour he sits beside her and watches while she falls asleep in her turn, beside the little brother who found the right way so much earlier than she. Her silky brown hair takes the enchanting fall it always does when she sleeps; deep, deep lie the lashes over the eyes that late so abundantly poured forth their sorrow; the angelic mouth with its bowed upper lip is peacefully relaxed and a little open. Only now and then comes a belated catch in her slow breathing.

And her small hands, like pink and white flowers, lie so quietly, one on the coverlet, the other on the pillow by her face. Dr. Cornelius, gazing, feels his heart melt with tenderness as with strong wine.

"How good," he thinks, "that she breathes in oblivion with every breath she draws! That in childhood each night is a deep wide gulf between one day and the next. Tomorrow, beyond all doubt, young Hergesell will be a pale shadow, powerless to darken her little heart. Tomorrow, forgetful of all but present joy, she will walk with Abel and Snapper, all five gentlemen, round and round the table, will play the ever-thrilling cushion game."

Heaven be praised for that!

The Rocking-Horse Winner

D.H. Lawrence

David Herbert Lawrence (1885-1930), an English poet, novelist, playwright, essayist, travelogue and short story writer, was one of the most important writers of the 20th century. The use of psychoanalysis in his works was unique. He broke away from Victorian morality to write freely about sexuality, sexual passion and instincts, something that also made his novels like *Sons and Lovers* (1913) and *Women in Love* (1920) highly controversial. Lawrence was also a short story writer, as is evident in 'The Rocking-Horse Winner' (1926).

There was a woman who was beautiful, who started with all the advantages, yet she had no luck. She married for love, and the love turned to dust. She had bonny children, yet she felt they had been thrust upon her, and she could not love them. They looked at her coldly, as if they were finding fault with her. And hurriedly she felt she must cover up some fault in herself. Yet what it was that she must cover up she never knew. Nevertheless, when her children were present, she always felt the centre of her heart go hard. This troubled her, and in her manner she was all the more gentle and anxious for her children, as if she loved them very much. Only she herself knew that at the centre of her heart was a hard little place that could not feel love, no, not for anybody. Everybody else said of her: "She is such a good mother. She adores her children." Only she herself, and her children themselves, knew it was not so. They read it in each other's eyes.

There were a boy and two little girls. They lived in a pleasant house, with a garden, and they had discreet servants, and felt themselves superior to anyone in the neighbourhood.

Although they lived in style, they felt always an anxiety in the house. There was never enough money. The mother had a small income, and the father had a small income, but not nearly enough for the social position which they had to keep up. The father went into town to some office. But though he had good prospects, these prospects never materialised. There was always the grinding sense of the shortage of money, though the style was always kept up.

At last the mother said: "I will see if I can't make something." But she did not know where to begin. She racked her brains, and tried this thing and the other, but could not find anything successful. The failure made deep lines come into her face. Her children were growing up, they would have to go to school. There must be more money, there must be more money. The father, who was always very handsome and expensive in his tastes, seemed as if he never would be able to do anything worth doing. And the mother, who had a great belief in herself, did not succeed any better, and her tastes were just as expensive.

And so the house came to be haunted by the unspoken phrase: There must be more money! There must be more money! The children could hear it all the time though nobody said it aloud. They heard it at Christmas, when the expensive and splendid toys filled the nursery. Behind the shining modern rocking-horse, behind the smart doll's house, a voice would start whispering: "There must be more money! There must be more money!" And the children would stop playing, to listen for a moment. They would look into each other's eyes, to see if they had all heard. And each one saw in the eyes of the other two that they too had heard. "There must be more money! There must be more money!"

It came whispering from the springs of the still-swaying rocking-horse, and even the horse, bending his wooden, champing head, heard it. The big doll, sitting so pink and smirking in her new pram, could hear it quite plainly, and seemed to be smirking all the more self-consciously because of it. The foolish puppy, too, that took the place of the teddy-bear, he was looking so extraordinarily foolish for no other reason but that he heard the secret whisper all over the house: "There must be more money!"

Yet nobody ever said it aloud. The whisper was everywhere, and therefore no one spoke it. Just as no one ever says: "We are breathing!" in spite of the fact that breath is coming and going all the time.

"Mother," said the boy Paul one day, "why don't we keep a car of our own? Why do we always use uncle's, or else a taxi?"

"Because we're the poor members of the family," said the mother. "But why are we, mother?"

"Well, I suppose," she said slowly and bitterly, "it's because your father has no luck."

The boy was silent for some time.

"Is luck money, mother?" he asked, rather timidly.

"No, Paul. Not quite. It's what causes you to have money."

"Oh!" said Paul vaguely. "I thought when Uncle Oscar said filthy lucker, it meant money."

"Filthy lucre does mean money," said the mother.

"But it's lucre, not luck."

"Oh!" said the boy. "Then what is luck, mother?"

"It's what causes you to have money. If you're lucky you have money.

That's why it's better to be born lucky than rich. If you're rich, you may lose your money. But if you're lucky, you will always get more money."

"Oh! Will you? And is father not lucky?"

"Very unlucky, I should say," she said bitterly. The boy watched her with unsure eyes.

"Why?" he asked.

"I don't know. Nobody ever knows why one person is lucky and another unlucky."

"Don't they? Nobody at all? Does nobody know?"

"Perhaps God. But He never tells."

"He ought to, then. And aren't you lucky either, mother?"

"I can't be, it I married an unlucky husband."

"But by yourself, aren't you?"

"I used to think I was, before I married. Now I think I am very unlucky indeed."

"Why?"

"Well, never mind! Perhaps I'm not really," she said.

The child looked at her to see if she meant it. But he saw, by the lines of her mouth, that she was only trying to hide something from him.

"Well, anyhow," he said stoutly, "I'm a lucky person."

"Why?" said his mother, with a sudden laugh.

He stared at her. He didn't even know why he had said it. "God told me," he asserted, brazening it out.

"I hope He did, dear!", she said, again with a laugh, but rather bitter. "He did, mother!"

"Excellent!" said the mother, using one of her husband's exclamations.

The boy saw she did not believe him; or rather, that she paid no attention to his assertion. This angered him somewhere, and made him want to compel her attention.

He went off by himself, vaguely, in a childish way, seeking for the clue to 'luck'. Absorbed, taking no heed of other people, he went about with a sort of stealth, seeking inwardly for luck. He wanted luck, he wanted it, he wanted it.

When the two girls were playing dolls in the nursery, he would sit on his big rocking-horse, charging madly into space, with a frenzy that made the little girls peer at him uneasily. Wildly the horse careered, the waving dark hair of the boy tossed, his eyes had a strange glare in them. The little girls dared not speak to him.

When he had ridden to the end of his mad little journey, he climbed down and stood in front of his rocking-horse, staring fixedly into its lowered face. Its red mouth was slightly open, its big eye was wide and glassy-bright.

"Now!" he would silently command the snorting steed. "Now take me to where there is luck! Now take me!"

And he would slash the horse on the neck with the little whip he had asked Uncle Oscar for. He knew the horse could take him to where there was luck, if only he forced it. So he would mount again and start on his furious ride, hoping at last to get there.

"You'll break your horse, Paul!" said the nurse.

Joan.

"He's always riding like that! I wish he'd leave off!" said his elder sister But he only glared down on them in silence. Nurse gave him up. She could make nothing of him. Anyhow, he was growing beyond her.

One day his mother and his Uncle Oscar came in when he was on one of his furious rides. He did not speak to them.

"Hallo, you young jockey! Riding a winner?" said his uncle.

"Aren't you growing too big for a rocking-horse? You're not a very little boy any longer, you know," said his mother.

But Paul only gave a blue glare from his big, rather close-set eyes. He would speak to nobody when he was in full tilt. His mother watched him with an anxious expression on her face.

At last he suddenly stopped forcing his horse into the mechanical gallop and slid down.

"Well, I got there!" he announced fiercely, his blue eyes still flaring, and his sturdy long legs straddling apart.

"Where did you get to?" asked his mother. "Where I wanted to go," he flared back at her.

"That's right, son!" said Uncle Oscar. "Don't you stop till you get there. What's the horse's name?"

"He doesn't have a name," said the boy. "Gets on without all right?" asked the uncle.

"Well, he has different names. He was called Sansovino last week."

"Sansovino, eh? Won the Ascot. How did you know this name?"

"He always talks about horse-races with Bassett," said Joan.

The uncle was delighted to find that his small nephew was posted with all the racing news. Bassett, the young gardener, who had been wounded in the left foot in the war and had got his present job through Oscar Cresswell, whose batman he had been, was a perfect blade of the 'turf'. He lived in the racing events, and the small boy lived with him.

Oscar Cresswell got it all from Bassett.

"Master Paul comes and asks me, so I can't do more than tell him, sir," said Bassett, his face terribly serious, as if he were speaking of religious matters.

"And does he ever put anything on a horse he fancies?"

"Well, I don't want to give him away, he's a young sport, a fine sport, sir. Would you mind asking him himself? He sort of takes a pleasure in it, and perhaps he'd feel I was giving him away, sir, if you don't mind. asked.

Bassett was serious as a church.

The uncle went back to his nephew and took him off for a ride in the car. "Say, Paul, old man, do you ever put anything on a horse?" the uncle The boy watched the handsome man closely. "Why, do you think I oughtn't to?" he parried.

"Not a bit of it! I thought perhaps you might give me a tip for the Lincoln."

The car sped on into the country, going down to Uncle Oscar's place in Hampshire.

"Honour bright?" said the nephew.

"Honour bright, son!" said the uncle. "Well, then, Daffodil."

"Daffodil! I doubt it, sonny. What about Mirza?"

"I only know the winner," said the boy.

"That's Daffodil." "Daffodil, eh?"

There was a pause. Daffodil was an obscure horse comparatively. "Uncle!"

"Yes, son?"

"You won't let it go any further, will you? I promised Bassett." "Bassett be damned, old man! What's he got to do with it?"

"We're partners. We've been partners from the first. Uncle, he lent me my first five shillings, which I lost. I promised him, honour bright, it was only between me and him; only you gave me that ten-shilling note I started winning with, so I thought you were lucky. You won't let it go any further, will you?"

The boy gazed at his uncle from those big, hot, blue eyes, set rather close together. The uncle stirred and laughed uneasily.

"Right you are, son! I'll keep your tip private. How much are you putting on him?"

"All except twenty pounds," said the boy. "I keep that in reserve." The uncle thought it a good joke.

"You keep twenty pounds in reserve, do you, you young romancer? What are you betting, then?"

"I'm betting three hundred," said the boy gravely. "But it's between you and me, Uncle Oscar! Honour bright?"

"It's between you and me all right, you young Nat Gould," he said, laughing. "But where's your three hundred?"

"Bassett keeps it for me. We're partners."

"You are, are you! And what is Bassett putting on Daffodil?"

"He won't go quite as high as I do, I expect. Perhaps he'll go a hundred and fifty."

"What, pennies?" laughed the uncle.

"Pounds," said the child, with a surprised look at his uncle. "Bassett keeps a bigger reserve than I do."

Between wonder and amusement Uncle Oscar was silent. He pursued the matter no further, but he determined to take his nephew with him to the Lincoln races.

"Now, son," he said, "I'm putting twenty on Mirza, and I'll put five on for you on any horse you fancy. What's your pick?"

"Daffodil, uncle."

"No, not the fiver on Daffodil!"

"I should if it was my own fiver," said the child.

"Good! Good! Right you are! A fiver for me and a fiver for you on Daffodil."

The child had never been to a race-meeting before, and his eyes were blue fire. He pursed his mouth tight and watched. A Frenchman just in front had put his money on Lancelot. Wild with excitement, he flayed his arms up and down, yelling "Lancelot!, Lancelot!" in his French accent.

Daffodil came in first, Lancelot second, Mirza third. The child, flushed and with eyes blazing, was curiously serene. His uncle brought him four five-pound notes, four to one.

"What am I to do with these?" he cried, waving them before the boys eyes. "I suppose we'll talk to Bassett," said the boy. "I expect I have fifteen hundred now; and twenty in reserve; and this twenty."

His uncle studied him for some moments.

"Look here, son!" he said. "You're not serious about Bassett and that fifteen hundred, are you?"

"Yes, I am. But it's between you and me, uncle. Honour bright?"

"Honour bright all right, son! But I must talk to Bassett."

"If you'd like to be a partner, uncle, with Bassett and me, we could all be partners. Only, you'd have to promise, honour bright, uncle, not to let it go beyond us three. Bassett and I are lucky, and you must be lucky, because it was your ten shillings I started winning with..."

Uncle Oscar took both Bassett and Paul into Richmond Park for an afternoon, and there they talked.

"It's like this, you see, sir," Bassett said. "Master Paul would get me talking about racing events, spinning yarns, you know, sir. And he was always keen on knowing if I'd made or if I'd lost. It's about a year since, now, that I put five shillings on Blush of Dawn for him: and we lost. Then the luck turned, with that ten shillings he had from you: that we put on Singhalese. And since that time, it's been pretty steady, all things considering. What do you say, Master Paul?"

"We're all right when we're sure," said Paul. "It's when we're not quite sure that we go down."

"Oh, but we're careful then," said Bassett.

"But when are you sure?" smiled Uncle Oscar.

"It's Master Paul, sir," said Bassett in a secret, religious voice. "It's as if he had it from heaven. Like Daffodil, now, for the Lincoln. That was as sure as eggs."

"Did you put anything on Daffodil?" asked Oscar Cresswell. "Yes, sir, I made my bit."

"And my nephew?"

Bassett was obstinately silent, looking at Paul.

"I made twelve hundred, didn't I, Bassett? I told uncle I was putting three hundred on Daffodil."

"That's right," said Bassett, nodding.

"But where's the money?" asked the uncle.

"I keep it safe locked up, sir. Master Paul he can have it any minute he likes to ask for it."

"What, fifteen hundred pounds?"

"And twenty! And forty, that is, with the twenty he made on the course." "It's amazing!" said the uncle.

"If Master Paul offers you to be partners, sir, I would, if I were you: if you'll excuse me," said Bassett.

Oscar Cresswell thought about it. "I'll see the money," he said.

They drove home again, and, sure enough, Bassett came round to the garden-house with fifteen hundred pounds in notes. The twenty pounds reserve was left with Joe Glee, in the Turf Commission deposit.

"You see, it's all right, uncle, when I'm sure! Then we go strong, for all we're worth, don't we, Bassett?"

"We do that, Master Paul."

"And when are you sure?" said the uncle, laughing.

"Oh, well, sometimes I'm absolutely sure, like about Daffodil," said the boy; "and sometimes I have an idea; and sometimes I haven't even an idea, have I, Bassett? Then we're careful, because we mostly go down."

"You do, do you! And when you're sure, like about Daffodil, what makes you sure, sonny?"

"Oh, well, I don't know," said the boy uneasily. "I'm sure, you know, uncle; that's all."

"It's as if he had it from heaven, sir," Bassett reiterated. "I should say so!" said the uncle.

But he became a partner. And when the Leger was coming on Paul was 'sure' about Lively Spark, which was a quite inconsiderable horse. The boy insisted on putting a thousand on the horse, Bassett went for five hundred, and Oscar Cresswell two hundred. Lively Spark came in first, and the betting had been ten to one against him. Paul had made ten thousand.

"You see," he said. "I was absolutely sure of him." Even Oscar Cresswell had cleared two thousand.

"Look here, son," he said, "this sort of thing makes me nervous."

"It needn't, uncle! Perhaps I shan't be sure again for a long time."

"But what are you going to do with your money?" asked the uncle.

"Of course," said the boy, "I started it for mother. She said she had no luck, because father is unlucky, so I thought if I was lucky, it might stop whispering."

"What might stop whispering?"

"Our house. I hate our house for whispering."

"What does it whisper?"

"Why, why," the boy fidgeted, "why, I don't know. But it's always short of money, you know, uncle."

"I know it, son, I know it."

"You know people send mother writs, don't you, uncle?" "I'm afraid I do," said the uncle.

"And then the house whispers, like people laughing at you behind your back. It's awful, that is! I thought if I was lucky..."

"You might stop it," added the uncle.

The boy watched him with big blue eyes, that had an uncanny cold fire in them, and he said never a word.

"Well, then!" said the uncle. "What are we doing?"

"I shouldn't like mother to know I was lucky," said the boy. "Why not, son?"

"She'd stop me."

"I don't think she would."

"Oh!" and the boy writhed in an odd way, "I don't want her to know, uncle."

"All right, son! We'll manage it without her knowing."

They managed it very easily. Paul, at the other's suggestion, handed over five thousand pounds to his uncle, who deposited it with the family lawyer, who was then to inform Paul's mother that a relative had put five thousand pounds into his hands, which sum was to be paid out a thousand pounds at a time, on the mother's birthday, for the next five years.

"So she'll have a birthday present of a thousand pounds for five successive years," said Uncle Oscar. "I hope it won't make it all the harder for her later."

Paul's mother had her birthday in November. The house had been 'whispering' worse than ever lately, and, even in spite of his luck, Paul could not bear up against it. He was very anxious to see the effect of the birthday letter, telling his mother about the thousand pounds.

When there were no visitors, Paul now took his meals with his parents, as he was beyond the nursery control. His mother went into town nearly every day. She had discovered that she had an odd knack of sketching furs and dress materials, so she worked secretly in the studio of a friend who was the chief 'artist' for the leading drapers. She drew the figures of ladies in furs and ladies in silk and sequins for the newspaper advertisements. This young woman artist earned several thousand pounds a year, but Paul's mother only made several hundreds, and she was again dissatisfied. She so wanted to be first in something, and she did not succeed, even in making sketches for drapery advertisements.

She was down to breakfast on the morning of her birthday. Paul watched her face as she read her letters. He knew the lawyer's letter. As his mother read it, her face hardened and became more expressionless. Then a cold, determined look came on her mouth. She hid the letter under the pile of others, and said not a word about it.

"Didn't you have anything nice in the post for your birthday, mother?" said Paul.

"Quite moderately nice," she said, her voice cold and hard and absent. She went away to town without saying more.

But in the afternoon Uncle Oscar appeared. He said Paul's mother had had a long interview with the lawyer, asking if the whole five thousand could not be advanced at once, as she was in debt.

"What do you think, uncle?" said the boy. "I leave it to you, son."

"Oh, let her have it, then! We can get some more with the other," said the boy.

"A bird in the hand is worth two in the bush, laddie!" said Uncle Oscar. "But I'm sure to know for the Grand National; or the Lincolnshire; or else the Derby. I'm sure to know for one of them," said Paul.

So Uncle Oscar signed the agreement, and Paul's mother touched the whole five thousand. Then something very curious happened. The voices in the house suddenly went mad, like a chorus of frogs on a spring evening. There were certain new furnishings, and Paul had a tutor. He was really going to Eton, his father's school, in the following autumn. There were flowers in the winter, and a blossoming of the luxury Paul's mother had been used to. And yet the voices in the house, behind the sprays of mimosa and almond-blossom, and from under the piles of iridescent cushions, simply trilled and screamed in a sort of ecstasy: "There must be more money! Oh-h-h; there must be more money. Oh, now, now-w! Now-w-w...there must be more money! More than ever! More than ever!"

It frightened Paul terribly. He studied away at his Latin and Greek with his tutor. But his intense hours were spent with Bassett. The Grand National had gone by: he had not 'known', and had lost a hundred pounds. Summer was at hand. He was in agony for the Lincoln. But even for the Lincoln he didn't 'know', and he lost fifty pounds. He became wild-eyed and strange, as if something were going to explode in him.

"Let it alone, son! Don't you bother about it!" urged Uncle Oscar. But it was as if the boy couldn't really hear what his uncle was saying.

"I've got to know for the Derby! I've got to know for the Derby!" the child reiterated, his big blue eyes blazing with a sort of madness.

His mother noticed how overwrought he was.

"You'd better go to the seaside. Wouldn't you like to go now to the seaside, instead of waiting? I think you'd better," she said, looking down at him anxiously, her heart curiously heavy because of him.

But the child lifted his uncanny blue eyes.

"I couldn't possibly go before the Derby, mother!" he said. "I couldn't possibly!"

"Why not?" she said, her voice becoming heavy when she was opposed. "Why not? You can still go from the seaside to see the Derby with your Uncle Oscar, if that that's what you wish. No need for you to wait here. Besides, I think you care too much about these races. It's a bad sign. My family has been a gambling family, and you won't know till you grow up how much damage it has done. But it has done damage. I shall have to send Bassett away, and ask Uncle Oscar not to talk racing to you, unless you promise to be reasonable about it: go away to the seaside and forget it. You're all nerves!"

"I'll do what you like, mother, so long as you don't send me away till after the Derby," the boy said.

"Send you away from where? Just from this house?"

"Yes," he said, gazing at her.

"Why, you curious child, what makes you care about this house so much, suddenly? I never knew you loved it."

He gazed at her without speaking. He had a secret within a secret, something he had not divulged, even to Bassett or to his Uncle Oscar.

But his mother, after standing undecided and a little bit sullen for some moments, said: "Very well, then! Don't go to the seaside till after the Derby, if you don't wish it. But promise me you won't think so much about horse-racing and events as you call them!"

"Oh no," said the boy casually. "I won't think much about them, mother. You needn't worry. I wouldn't worry, mother, if I were you."

"If you were me and I were you," said his mother, "I wonder what we should do!"

"But you know you needn't worry, mother, don't you?" the boy repeated. "I should be awfully glad to know it," she said wearily.

"Oh, well, you can, you know. I mean, you ought to know you needn't worry," he insisted.

"Ought I? Then I'll see about it," she said.

Paul's secret of secrets was his wooden horse, that which had no name. Since he was emancipated from a nurse and a nursery-governess, he had had his rocking-horse removed to his own bedroom at the top of the house.

"Surely you're too big for a rocking-horse!" his mother had remonstrated. "Well, you see, mother, till I can have a real horse, I like to have some sort of animal about," had been his quaint answer.

"Do you feel he keeps you company?" she laughed.

"Oh yes! He's very good, he always keeps me company, when I'm there," said Paul.

So the horse, rather shabby, stood in an arrested prance in the boy's bedroom.

The Derby was drawing near, and the boy grew more and more tense. He hardly heard what was spoken to him, he was very frail, and his eyes were really uncanny. His mother had sudden strange seizures of uneasiness about him. Sometimes, for half an hour, she would feel a sudden anxiety about him that was almost anguish. She wanted to rush to him at once, and know he was safe.

Two nights before the Derby, she was at a big party in town, when one of her rushes of anxiety about her boy, her first-born, gripped her heart till she could hardly speak. She fought with the feeling, might and main, for she believed in common sense. But it was too strong. She had to leave the dance and go downstairs to telephone to the country. The children's nursery-governess was terribly surprised and startled at being rung up in the night.

"Are the children all right, Miss Wilmot?" "Oh yes, they are quite all right."

"Master Paul? Is he all right?"

"He went to bed as right as a trivet. Shall I run up and look at him?"

"No," said Paul's mother reluctantly. "No! Don't trouble. It's all right. Don't sit up. We shall be home fairly soon." She did not want her son's privacy intruded upon.

"Very good," said the governess.

It was about one o'clock when Paul's mother and father drove up to their house. All was still. Paul's mother went to her room and slipped off her white fur cloak. She had told her maid not to wait up for her. She heard her husband downstairs, mixing a whisky and soda.

And then, because of the strange anxiety at her heart, she stole upstairs to her son's room. Noiselessly she went along the upper corridor. Was there a faint noise? What was it?

She stood, with arrested muscles, outside his door, listening. There was a strange, heavy, and yet not loud noise. Her heart stood still. It was a soundless noise, yet rushing and powerful. Something huge, in violent, hushed motion. What was it? What in God's name was it? She ought to know. She felt that she knew the noise. She knew what it was.

Yet she could not place it. She couldn't say what it was. And on and on it went, like a madness.

Softly, frozen with anxiety and fear, she turned the door-handle.

The room was dark. Yet in the space near the window, she heard and saw something plunging to and fro. She gazed in fear and amazement.

Then suddenly she switched on the light, and saw her son, in his green pyjamas, madly surging on the rocking-horse. The blaze of light suddenly lit him up, as he urged the wooden horse, and lit her up, as she stood, blonde, in her dress of pale green and crystal, in the doorway.

"Paul!" she cried. "Whatever are you doing?"

"It's Malabar!" he screamed in a powerful, strange voice. "It's Malabar!" His eyes blazed at her for one strange and senseless second, as he ceased urging his wooden horse. Then he fell with a crash to the ground, and she, all her tormented motherhood flooding upon her, rushed to gather him up.

But he was unconscious, and unconscious he remained, with some brain-fever. He talked and tossed, and his mother sat stonily by his side.

"Malabar! It's Malabar! Bassett, Bassett, I know! It's Malabar!"

So the child cried, trying to get up and urge the rocking-horse that gave him his inspiration.

"What does he mean by Malabar?" asked the heart-frozen mother. "I don't know," said the father stonily.

"What does he mean by Malabar?" she asked her brother Oscar. "It's one of the horses running for the Derby," was the answer.

And, in spite of himself, Oscar Cresswell spoke to Bassett, and himself put a thousand on Malabar: at fourteen to one.

The third day of the illness was critical: they were waiting for a change. The boy, with his rather long, curly hair, was tossing ceaselessly on the pillow. He neither slept nor regained consciousness, and his eyes were like blue stones. His mother sat, feeling her heart had gone, turned actually into a stone.

In the evening Oscar Cresswell did not come, but Bassett sent a message, saying could he come up for one moment, just one moment? Paul's mother was very angry at the intrusion, but on second thoughts she agreed. The boy was the same. Perhaps Bassett might bring him to consciousness.

The gardener, a shortish fellow with a little brown moustache and sharp little brown eyes, tiptoed into the room, touched his imaginary cap to Paul's mother, and stole to the bedside, staring with glittering, smallish eyes at the tossing, dying child.

"Master Paul!" he whispered. "Master Paul! Malabar came in first all right, a clean win. I did as you told me. You've made over seventy thousand pounds, you have; you've got over eighty thousand. Malabar came in all right, Master Paul."

"Malabar! Malabar! Did I say Malabar, mother? Did I say Malabar? Do you think I'm lucky, mother? I knew Malabar, didn't I? Over eighty thousand pounds! I call that lucky, don't you, mother? Over eighty thousand pounds! I knew, didn't I know I knew? Malabar came in all right. If I ride my horse till I'm sure, then I tell you,

Bassett, you can go as high as you like. Did you go for all you were worth, Bassett?"

"I went a thousand on it, Master Paul."

"I never told you, mother, that if I can ride my horse, and get there, then I'm absolutely sure, oh, absolutely! Mother, did I ever tell you? I am lucky!"

"No, you never did," said his mother. But the boy died in the night.

And even as he lay dead, his mother heard her brother's voice saying to her, "My God, Hester, you're eighty-odd thousand to the good, and a poor devil of a son to the bad. But, poor devil, poor devil, he's best gone out of a life where he rides his rocking-horse to find a winner."

Buchmendel

Stefan Zweig

Stefan Zweig (1881-1942) was an Austrian essayist, poet and short story writer known for his work *Three Masters* (1920) and the psychological novel *Beware of Pity* (1938). Zweig's study of psychology, and specifically of Freud, contributed to the development of complex yet subtle characterisation in his writings. 'Buchmendel' (1929) is one of Zweig's most poignant stories.

Having just got back to Vienna, after a visit to an out-of-the-way part of the country, I was walking home from the station when a heavy shower came on, such a deluge that the passers-by hastened to take shelter in doorways, and I myself felt it expedient to get out of the downpour. Luckily there is a cafe at almost every street corner in the metropolis, and I made for the nearest, though not before my hat was dripping wet and my shoulders were drenched to the skin. An old-fashioned suburban place, lacking the attractions (copied from Germany) of music and a dancing-floor to be found in the centre of the town; full of small shopkeepers and working folk who consumed more newspapers than coffee and rolls. Since it was already late in the evening, the air, which would have been stuffy anyhow, was thick with tobacco-smoke. Still, the place was clean and brightly decorated, had new satin-covered couches, and a shining cash-register, so that it looked thoroughly attractive. In my haste to get out of the rain I had not troubled to read its name, but what matter? There I rested, warm and comfortable, though looking rather impatiently through the blue-tinted windowpanes to see when the shower would be over, and I should be able to get on my way. Thus I sat unoccupied, and began to succumb to that inertia which results from the narcotic atmosphere of the typical Viennese cafe. Out of this void, I scanned various individuals whose eyes, in the murky room, had a greyish look in the artificial light; I mechanically contemplated the young woman at the counter as, like an automaton, she dealt out sugar and a teaspoon to the waiter for each cup of coffee; with half an eye and a wandering attention I read the uninteresting advertisements on the walls, and there was something agreeable about these dull occupations. But suddenly, and in a peculiar fashion, I was aroused from what had become almost a doze. A vague internal movement had begun; much as a toothache sometimes begins, without one's being able to say whether it is on the right side or the left, in the upper jaw or the lower. All I became aware of was a numb tension, an obscure sentiment of spiritual unrest. Then, without knowing why, I grew fully conscious. I must have been in this cafe once before, years ago, and random associations had awakened memories of the walls, the tables, the chairs, the seemingly unfamiliar smoke-laden room.

The more I endeavoured to grasp this lost memory, the more obstinately did it elude me; a sort of jellyfish glistening in the abysses of consciousness, slippery and unseizable. Vainly did I scrutinize every object within the range of vision. Certainly when I had been here before the counter had had neither marble top nor cash register; the walls had not been panelled with imitation rosewood; these must be recent acquisitions. Yet I had indubitably been here, more than twenty years back. Within these four walls, as firmly fixed as a nail driven up to the head in a tree, there slung a part of my ego, long since overgrown. Vainly I explored, not only the room, but my own inner man, to grapple the lost links. Curse it all, I could not plumb the depths!

It will be seen that I was becoming vexed, as one is always out of humour when one's grip slips in this way, and reveals the inadequacy, the imperfections, of one's spiritual powers. Yet I still hoped to recover the clue. A slender thread would suffice, for my memory is of a peculiar type, both good and bad; on the one hand stubbornly untrustworthy, and on the other incredibly dependable. It swallows the most important details, whether in concrete happenings or in faces, and no voluntary exertion will induce it to regurgitate them from the gulf. Yet the most trifling indication, a picture postcard, the address on an envelope, a newspaper cutting, will suffice to hook up what is wanted as an angler who has made a strike and successfully embedded his hook reels in a lively, struggling, and reluctant fish. Then I can recall the features of a man seen once only, the shape of his mouth and the gap to the left where he had an upper eye-tooth knocked out, the falsetto tone of his laugh, and the twitching of the moustache when he chooses to be merry, the entire change of expression which hilarity effects in him. Not only do these physical traits rise before my mind's eye, but I remember, years afterwards, every word the man said to me, and the tenor of my replies. But if I am to see and feel the past thus vividly, there must be some material link to start the current of associations. My memory will not work satisfactorily on the abstract plane.

I closed my eyes to think more strenuously, in the attempt to forge the hook which would catch my fish. In vain! In vain! There was no hook, or the fish would not bite. So fierce waxed my irritation with the inefficient and mulish thinking apparatus between my temples that I could have struck myself a violent blow on the forehead, much as an irascible man will shake and kick a penny-in-the-slot machine which when he has inserted his coin, refuses to render him his due.

So exasperated did I become at my failure, that I could no longer sit quiet, but rose to prowl about the room. The instant I moved, the glow of awakening memory began. To the right of the cash-register, I recalled, there must be a doorway leading into a windowless room, where the only light was artificial. Yes, the place actually existed. The decorative scheme was different, but the proportions were unchanged. A square box of a place, behind the bar, the card room. My nerves thrilled as I contemplated the furniture, for I was on the track, I had found the clue, and soon I should know all. There were two small billiard-tables, looking like silent ponds covered with green scum. In the corners, card-tables, at one of which two bearded men of professorial type were playing chess. Beside the iron stove, close to a door labelled "Telephone," was another small table. In a flash, I had it! That was Mendel's place, Jacob Mendel's. That was where Mendel used to hang out, Buchmendel. I was in the Cafe Gluck! How could I have forgotten Jacob Mendel. Was it possible that I had not thought about him for ages, a man so peculiar as well nigh to belong to the Land of Fable, the eighth wonder of the world, famous at the university and among a narrow circle of admirers, magician of book-fanciers, who had been wont to sit there from morning till night, an emblem of bookish lore, the glory of the Cafe Gluck? Why had I had so much difficulty in hooking my fish? How could I have forgotten Buchmendel?

I allowed my imagination to work. The man's face and form pictured themselves vividly before me. I saw him as he had been in the flesh, seated at the table with its grey marble top, on which books and manuscripts were piled. Motionless he sat, his spectacled eyes fixed upon the printed page. Yet not altogether motionless, for he had a habit (acquired at school in the Jewish quarter of the Galician town from which he came) of rocking his shiny bald pate backwards and forwards and humming to himself as he read, There he studied catalogues and tomes, crooning and rocking, as Jewish boys are taught to do when reading the Talmud. The rabbis believe that, just as a child is rocked to sleep in its cradle, so are the pious ideas of the holy text better instilled by this rhythmical and hypnotizing movement of head and body. In fact, as if he had been in a trance, Jacob Mendel saw and heard nothing while thus occupied. He was oblivious to the click of billiard-balls, the coming and going of waiters, the ringing of the telephone bell; he paid no heed when the floor was scrubbed and when the stove was refilled. Once a red-hot coal fell out of the latter, and the flooring began to blaze a few inches from Mendel's feet; the room was full of smoke, and one of the guests ran for a pail of water to extinguish the fire. But neither the smoke, the bustle, nor the stench diverted his attention from the volume before him. He read as others pray, as gamblers follow the spinning of the roulette board, as drunkards stare into vacancy; he read with such profound absorption that ever since I first watched him the reading of ordinary mortals has seemed a pastime. This Galician second-hand book dealer, Jacob Mendel, was the first to reveal to me in my youth the mystery of absolute concentration which characterizes the artist and the scholar, the sage and the imbecile; the first to make me acquainted with the tragical happiness and unhappiness of complete absorption.

A senior student introduced me to him. I was studying the life and doings of a man who is even today too little known, Mesmer the magnetizer. My researches were bearing scant fruit, for the books I could lay my hands on conveyed sparse information, and when I applied to the university librarian for help he told me, uncivilly, that it was not his business to hunt up references for a freshman. Then my college friend suggested taking me to Mendel.

"He knows everything about books, and will tell you where to find the information you want. The ablest man in Vienna, and an original to boot. The man is a saurian of the book-world, an antediluvian survivor of an extinct species."

We went, therefore, to the Cafe Gluck, and found Buchmendel in his usual place, bespectacled, bearded, wearing a rusty black suit, and rocking as I have described. He did not notice our intrusion, but went on reading, looking like a nodding mandarin. On a hook behind him hung his ragged black overcoat, the pockets of which bulged with manuscripts, catalogues, and books. My friend coughed loudly, to attract his attention, but Mendel ignored the sign. At length Schmidt rapped on the table-top, as if knocking at a door, and at this Mendel glanced up, mechanically pushed his spectacles on to his forehead, and from beneath his thick and untidy ashen-grey brows there glared at us two dark, alert little eyes. My friend introduced me, and I explained my quandary, being careful (as Schmidt had advised) to express great annoyance at the librarian's unwillingness to assist me. Mendel leaned back, laughed scornfully, and answered with a strong Galician accent:

"Unwillingness, you think? Incompetence, that's what's the matter with him. He's a jackass. I've known him (for my sins) twenty years at least, and he's learned nothing in the whole of that time. Pocket their wages that's all such fellows can do. They should be mending the road, instead of sitting over books."

This outburst served to break the ice, and with a friendly wave of the hand the bookworm invited me to sit down at his table. I reiterated my object in consulting him; to get a list of all the early works on animal magnetism, and of contemporary and subsequent books and pamphlets for and against Mesmer. When I had said my say, Mendel closed his left eye for an instant, as if excluding a grain of dust. This was, with him, a sign of concentrated attention. Then, as though reading from an invisible catalogue, he reeled out the names of two or three dozen titles, giving in each case place and date of publication and approximate price. I was amazed, though Schmidt had warned me what to expect. His vanity was tickled by my surprise, for he went on to strum the keyboard of his marvellous memory, and to produce the most astounding bibliographical marginal notes. Did I want to know about sleepwalkers, Perkins's metallic tractors, early experiments in hypnotism, Braid, Gassner, attempts to conjure up the devil, Christian Science, theosophy, Madame Blavatsky? In connexion with each item there was a hailstorm of book-names, dates and appropriate details. I was beginning to understand that Jacob Mendel was a living lexicon, something like the general catalogue of the British Museum Reading Room, but able to walk about on two legs. I stared dumbfounded at this bibliographical phenomenon, which masqueraded in the sordid and rather unclean domino of a Galician second-hand book dealer, who after rattling off some eighty titles (with assumed indifference but really with the satisfaction of one who plays an unexpected trump), proceeded to wipe his spectacles with a handkerchief which might long before have been white.

Hoping to conceal my astonishment, I inquired:

"Which among these works do you think you could get for me without too much trouble?"

"Oh, I'll have a look round," he answered. "Come here tomorrow and I shall certainly have some of them. As for the others, it's only a question of time, and of knowing where to look."

"I'm greatly obliged to you," I said; and, then, wishing to be civil, I put my foot in it, proposing to give him a list of the books I wanted. Schmidt nudged me warningly, but too late. Mendel had already flashed a look at me such a look, at once triumphant and affronted, scornful and overwhelmingly superior, the royal look with which Macbeth answers Macduff when summoned to yield without a blow. He laughed curtly. His Adam's apple moved excitedly. Obviously he had gulped down a choleric, an insulting epithet.

Indeed he had good reason to be angry. Only a stranger, an ignoramus, could have proposed to give him, Jacob Mendel, a memorandum, as if he had been a bookseller's assistant or an underling in a public library. Not until I knew him better did I fully understand how much my would-be politeness must have galled this aberrant genius, for the man had and knew himself to have, a titanic memory wherein, behind a dirty and undistinguished-looking forehead, was indelibly recorded a picture of the title-page of every book that had been printed. No matter whether it had issued from the press yesterday or hundreds of years ago, he knew its place of publication, its author's name and its price. From his mind, as if from the printed page, he could read off the contents, could reproduce the illustrations; could visualize, not only what he had actually held in his hands, but also what he had glanced at in a bookseller's window; could see it with the same vividness as an artist sees the creations of fancy which he has not yet reproduced upon canvas. When a book was offered for six marks by a Regensburg dealer, he could remember that, two years before, a copy of the same work had changed hands for four crowns at a Viennese auction and he recalled the name of the purchaser. In a word: Jacob Mendel never forgot a title or a figure; he knew every plant, every infusorian, every star, in the continually revolving and incessantly changing cosmos of the book-universe. In each literary speciality, he knew more than the specialists; he knew the contents of the libraries better than the librarians; he knew the book-lists of most publishers better than the heads of the firms concerned, though he had nothing to guide him except the magical powers of his inexplicable but invariably accurate memory.

True this memory owed its infallibility to the man's limitations, to his extraordinary power of concentration. Apart from books, he knew nothing of the world. The phenomena of existence did not begin to become real for him until they had been set in type, arranged upon a composing stick, collected and, so to say, sterilized in a book. Nor did he read books for their meaning, to extract their spiritual or narrative substance. What aroused his passionate interest, what fixed his attention, was the name, the price, the format, the title-page Though in the last analysis unproductive and uncreative, this specifically antiquarian memory of Jacob Mendel, since it was not a printed book-catalogue but was stamped upon the grey matter of a mammalian brain, was, in its unique perfection, no less remarkable a phenomenon than Napoleon's gift for physiognomy, Mezzofanti's talent for languages, Lasker's skill at chess-openings, Busoni's musical genius. Given a public position as teacher, this man with so marvellous a brain might have taught thousands and hundreds of thousands of students, have trained others to become men of great learning and of incalculable value to those communal treasure-houses we call libraries. But to him, a man of no account, a Galician Jew, a book-pedlar whose only training had been received in a Talmudic school, this upper world of culture was a fenced precinct he could never enter; and his amazing faculties could only find application at the marble-topped table in the inner room of the Cafe Gluck. When, some day, there arises a great psychologist who shall classify the types of that magical power we term memory as effectively as Buffon classified the genera and species of animals, a man competent to give a detailed description of all the varieties, he will have to find a pigeon-hole for Jacob Mendel, forgotten master of the lore of book-prices and book-titles, the ambulatory catalogue alike of incunabula and the modern commonplace.

In the book-trade and among ordinary persons, Jacob Mendel was regarded as nothing more than a secondhand book dealer in a small way of business. Sunday after Sunday, his stereotyped advertisement appeared in the "Neue Freie Presse" and the "Neues Wiener Tagblatt." It ran as follows: "Best prices paid for old books, Mendel, Obere Alserstrasse." A telephone number followed, really that of the Cafe Gluck. He rummaged every available corner for his wares, and once a week, with the aid of a bearded porter, conveyed fresh booty to his headquarters, and got rid of old stock, for he had no proper bookshop. Thus he remained a petty trader, and his business was not lucrative. Students sold him their textbooks, which year by year passed through his hands from one "generation" to another; and for a small percentage on the price he would procure any additional book that was wanted. He charged little or nothing for advice. Money seemed to have no standing in his world. No one had ever seen him better dressed than in the threadbare black coat. For breakfast and supper he had a glass of milk and a couple of rolls, while at midday a modest meal was brought him from a neighbouring restaurant. He did not smoke; he did not play cards; one might almost say he did not live, were it not that his eyes were alive behind his spectacles, and unceasingly fed his enigmatic brain with words, titles, names. The brain, like a fertile pasture, greedily sucked in this abundant irrigation. Human beings did not interest him, and of all human passions perhaps one only moved him, the most universal-vanity.

When someone, wearied by a futile hunt in countless other places, applied to him for information, and was instantly put on the track, his self-gratification was overwhelming; and it was unquestionably a delight to him that in Vienna and elsewhere there existed a few dozen persons who respected him for his knowledge and valued him for the services he could render. In every one of these monstrous aggregates we call towns, there are here and there facets which reflect one and the same universe in miniature, unseen by most, but highly prized by connoisseurs, by brethren of the same craft, by devotees of the same passion. The fans of the book-market knew Jacob Mendel. Just as anyone encountering a difficulty in deciphering a score would apply to Eusebius Mandyczewski of the Musical Society, who would be found wearing a grey skull-cap and seated among multifarious musical MSS., ready, with a friendly smile, to solve the most obstinate crux; and just as, today, anyone in search of information about the Viennese theatrical and cultural life of earlier times will unhesitatingly look up the polyhistor Father Glossy; so, with equal confidence did the bibliophiles of Vienna, when they had a particularly hard nut to crack, make a pilgrimage to the Cafe Gluck and lay their difficulty before Jacob Mendel.

To me, young and eager for new experiences, it became enthralling to watch such a consultation. Whereas ordinarily, when a would-be seller brought him some ordinary book, he would contemptuously clap the cover to and mutter, "Two crowns"; if shown a rare or unique volume, he would sit up and take notice, lay the treasure upon a clean sheet of paper; and, on one such occasion, he was obviously ashamed of his dirty, ink-stained fingers and mourning fingernails. Tenderly, cautiously, respectfully, he would turn the pages of the treasure. One would have been as loath to disturb him at such a moment as to break in upon the devotions of a man at prayer; and in very truth there was a flavour of solemn ritual and religious observance about the way in which contemplation, palpation, smelling, and weighing in the hand followed one another in orderly succession. His rounded hack waggled while he was thus engaged, he muttered to himself, exclaimed "Ah" now and again to express wonder or admiration, or "Oh, dear" when a page was missing or another had been mutilated by the larva of a book-beetle. His weighing of the tome in his hand was as circumspect as if books were sold by the ounce, and his snuffling at it as sentimental as a girl's smelling of a rose. Of course it would have been the height of bad form for the owner to show impatience during this ritual of examination.

When it was over, he willingly, nay enthusiastically, tendered all the information at his disposal, not forgetting relevant anecdotes, and dramatized accounts of the prices which other specimens of the same work had fetched at auctions or in sales by private treaty. He looked brighter, younger, more lively at such times, and only one thing could put him seriously out of humour. This was when a novice offered him money for his expert opinion. Then he would draw back with an affronted air, looking for all the world like the skilled custodian of a museum gallery to whom an American traveller has offered a tip, for to Jacob Mendel contact with a rare book was something sacred, as is contact with a woman to a young man who has not had the bloom rubbed off. Such moments were his platonic love-nights. Books exerted a spell on him, never money. Vainly, therefore, did great collectors (among them one of the notables of Princeton University) try to recruit Mendel as librarian or book-buyer. The offer was declined with thanks. He could not forsake his familiar headquarters at the Cafe Gluck. Thirty-three years before, an awkward youngster with black down sprouting on his chin and black ringlets hanging over his temples, he had come from Galicia to Vienna, intending to adopt the calling of rabbi; but ere long he forsook the worship of the harsh and jealous Jehovah to devote himself to the more lively and polytheistic cult of books. Then he happened upon the Cafe Gluck, by degrees making it his workshop, headquarters, post-office his world. Just as an astronomer, alone in an observatory, watches night after night through a telescope the myriads of stars, their mysterious movements, their changeful medley, their extinction and their flaming-up anew, so did Jacob Mendel, seated at his table in the Cafe Gluck, look through his spectacles into the universe of books, a universe that lies above the world of our everyday life, and, like the stellar universe, is full of changing cycles.

It need hardly be said that he was highly esteemed in the Cafe Gluck, whose fame seemed to us to depend far more upon his unofficial professorship than upon the godfathership of the famous musician, Christoph Willibald Gluck, composer of *Alcestis* and *Iphigenia*. He belonged to the outfit quite as much as did the old cherry wood counter, the two billiard-tables with their cloth stitched in many places, and the copper coffee-urn. His table was guarded as a sanctuary. His numerous clients and customers were expected to take a drink "for the good of the house," so that most of the profit of his far-flung knowledge flowed into the big leathern pouch slung round the waist of Deubler, the waiter. In return for being a centre of attraction, Mendel enjoyed many privileges. The telephone was at his service for nothing. He could have his letters directed to the cafe, and his parcels were taken in there. The excellent old woman who looked after the toilet brushed his coat, sewed on buttons, and carried a small bundle of underlinen every week to the wash. He was the only guest who could have a meal sent in from the restaurant; and every morning Herr Standhartner, the proprietor of the cafe, made a point of coming to his table and saying "Good morning!" though Jacob Mendel, immersed in his books, seldom noticed the greeting. Punctually at half-past seven he arrived, and did not leave till the lights were extinguished. He never spoke to the other guests, never read a newspaper, noticed no changes; and once, when Herr Standhartner civilly asked him whether he did not find the electric light more agreeable to read by than the malodorous and uncertain kerosene lamps they had replaced, he stared in astonishment at the new incandescent bulbs. Although the installation had necessitated several days' hammering and bustle, the introduction of the glow-lamps had escaped his notice. Only through the two round apertures of the spectacles, only through these two shining and sucking lenses, did the milliards of black infusorians which were the letters filter into his brain. Whatever else happened in his vicinity was disregarded as unmeaning noise. He had spent more than thirty years of his waking life at this table, reading, comparing, calculating, in a continuous waking dream, interrupted only by intervals of sleep.

A sense of horror overcame me when, looking into the inner room behind the bar of the Cafe Gluck, I saw that the marble-top of the table where Jacob Mendel used to deliver his oracles was now as bare as a tombstone. Grown older since those days, I understood how much disappears when such a man drops out of his place in the world, were it only because, amid the daily increase in hopeless monotony, the unique grows continually more precious. Besides, in my callow youth a profound intuition had made me exceedingly fond of Buchmendel. It was through the observation of him that I had first become aware of the enigmatic fact that supreme achievement and outstanding capacity are only rendered possible by mental concentration, by a sublime monomania that verges on lunacy. Through the living example of this obscure genius of a second-hand book dealer, far more than through the flashes of insight in the works of our poets and other imaginative writers, had been made plain to me the persistent possibility of a pure life of the spirit, of complete absorption in an idea, an ecstasy as absolute as that of an Indian yogi or a medieval monk; and I had learned that this was possible in an electric-lighted cafe and adjoining a telephone box. Yet I had forgotten him, during the war years, and through a kindred immersion in my own work. The sight of the empty table made me ashamed of myself, and at the same time curious about the man who used to sit there.

What had become of him? I called the waiter and inquired.

"No, Sir," he answered, "I'm sorry, but I never heard of Herr Mendel. There is no one of that name among the frequenters of the Cafe Gluck. Perhaps the head-waiter will know."

"Herr Mendel?" said the head-waiter dubiously, after a moment's reflection. "No, Sir, never heard of him. Unless you mean Herr Mandl, who has a hardware store in the Florianigasse?"

I had a bitter taste in the mouth, the taste of an irrecoverable past. What is the use of living, when the wind obliterates our footsteps in the sand directly we have gone by? Thirty years, perhaps forty, a man had breathed, read, thought, and spoken within this narrow room; three or four years had elapsed, and there had arisen a new king over Egypt, which knew not Joseph. No one in the Cafe Gluck had ever heard of Jacob Mendel, of Buchmendel. Somewhat pettishly I asked the headwaiter whether I could have a word with Herr Standhartner, or with one of the old Staff.

"Herr Standhartner, who used to own the place? He sold it years ago, and has died since ... The former head-waiter? He saved up enough to retire, and lives upon a little property at Krems. No, Sir, all of the old lot are scattered. All except one, indeed, Frau Sporschil, who looks after the toilet. She's been worked under the late owner, I know. But she's not likely to remember your Herr Mendel. Such as she hardly know one guest from another."

I dissented in thought.

"One does not forget a Jacob Mendel so easily!" What I said was:

"Still, I should like to have a word with Frau Sporschil, if she has a moment to spare."

The "Toilettenfrau" (known in the Viennese vernacular as the "Schocoladefrau") soon emerged from the basement, white-haired, run to seed, heavy-footed wiping her chapped hands upon a towel as she came. She had been called away from her task of cleaning up, and was obviously uneasy at being summoned into the strong light of the guest-rooms, for common folk in Vienna, where an authoritative tradition has lingered on after the revolution, always think it must be a police matter when their "superiors" want to question them. She eyed me suspiciously, though humbly. But as soon as I asked her about Jacob Mendel, she braced up, and at the same time her eyes filled with tears.

"Poor Herr Mendel ... so there's still someone who bears him in mind?"

Old people are commonly much moved by anything which recalls the days of their youth and revives the memory of past companionships. I asked if he was still alive.

"Good Lord, no. Poor Herr Mendel must have died five or six years ago. Indeed, I think it's fully seven since he passed away. Dear, good man that he was; and how long I knew him, more than twenty-five years; he was already sitting every day at his table when I began to work here. It was a shame, it was the way they let him die."

Growing more and more excited, she asked if I was a relative. Didn't I know what had happened to him?

"No," I replied, "and I want you to be good enough to tell me all about it."

She looked at me timidly, and continued to wipe her damp hands. It was plain to me that she found it embarrassing, with her dirty apron and her tousled white hair, to be standing in the full glare of the cafe. She kept looking round anxiously, to see if one of the waiters might be listening.

"Let's go into the card-room," I said, "Mendel's old room. You shall tell me your story there." She nodded appreciatively, thankful that I understood and led the way to the inner room, a little shambling in her gait. As I followed, I noticed that the waiters and the guests were staring at us as a strangely assorted pair. We sat down opposite one another at the marble topped table, and there she told me the story of Jacob Mendel's ruin and death. I will give the tale as nearly as may be in her own words, supplemented here and there by what I learned afterwards from other sources.

"Down to the outbreak of war, and after the war had begun, he continued to come here every morning at half past seven, to sit at this table and study all day just as before. We had the feeling that the fact of a war going on had never entered his mind. Certainly didn't read the newspapers, and didn't talk to anyone except about books. He paid no attention when (in the early days of the war, before the authorities put a stop to such things) the newspaper-vendors ran through the streets shouting, 'Great Battle on the Eastern Front' (or wherever it might be), 'Horrible Slaughter,' and so on; when people gathered in knots to talk things over, he kept himself to himself; he did not know that Fritz, the billiard-marker, who fell in one of the first battles, had vanished from this place; he did not know that Herr Standhartner's son had been taken prisoner by the Russians at Przemysl; never said a word when the bread grew more and more uneatable and when he was given bean-coffee to drink at breakfast and supper instead of hot milk. Once only did he express surprise at the changes, wondering why so few students came to the cafe. There was nothing in the world that mattered to him except his books.

"Then disaster befell him. At eleven one morning, two policemen came, one in uniform, and the other a plainclothes man. The latter showed the red rosette under the lapel of his coat and asked whether there was a man named Jacob Mendel in the house. They went straight to Herr Mendel's table. The poor man, in his innocence, supposed they had books to sell, or wanted some information; but they told him he was under arrest, and took him away at once. It was a scandal for the cafe. All the guests flocked round Herr Mendel, as he stood between the two police officers, his spectacles pushed up under his hair, staring from each to the other bewildered. Some ventured a protest, saying there must be a mistake, that Herr Mendel was a man who wouldn't hurt a fly; but the detective was furious, and told them to mind their own business. They took him away, and none of us at the Cafe Gluck saw him again for two years. I never found out what they had against him, but I would take my dying oath that they must have made a mistake. Herr Mendel could never have done anything wrong. It was a crime to treat an innocent man so harshly."

The excellent Frau Sporschil was right. Our friend Jacob Mendel had done nothing wrong. He had merely (as I subsequently learned) done something incredibly stupid, only explicable to those who knew the man's peculiarities. The military censorship board, whose function it was to supervise correspondence passing into and out of neutral lands, one day got its clutches upon a postcard written and signed by a certain Jacob Mendel, properly stamped for transmission abroad. This postcard was addressed to Monsieur Jean Labourdaire, Librairie, Quai de Grenelle, Paris to an enemy country, therefore. The winter complained that the last eight issues of the monthly "Bulletin bibliographique de la France" had failed to reach him, although his annual subscription had been duly paid in advance. The jack-in-office who read this missive (a high-school teacher with a bent for the study of the Romance languages, called up for "war-service" and sent to employ his talents at the censorship board instead of wasting them in the trenches) was astonished by its tenor. "Must be a joke," he thought. He had to examine some two thousand letters and postcards every week, always on the alert to detect anything that might savour of espionage, but never yet had he chanced upon anything so absurd as that an Austrian subject should unconcernedly drop into one of the imperial and royal letter-boxes a postcard addressed to someone in an enemy land, regardless of the trifling detail that since August 1914 the Central Powers had been cut off from Russia on one side and from France on the other by barbed-wire entanglements and a network of ditches in which men armed with rifles and bayonets, machine-guns and artillery, were doing their utmost to exterminate one another like rats. Our schoolmaster enrolled in the Landsturm did not treat this first postcard seriously, but pigeon-holed it as a curiosity not worth talking about to his chief. But a few weeks later there turned up another card, again from Jacob Mendel, this time to John Aldridge, Bookseller, Golden Square, London, asking whether the addressee could send the last few numbers of the "Antiquarian" to an address in Vienna which was clearly stated on the card, The censor in the blue uniform began to feel uneasy. Was his "class" trying to trick the schoolmaster? Were the cards written in cipher? Possible, anyhow; so the subordinate went over to the major's desk, clicked his heels together, saluted, and laid the suspicious documents before "properly constituted authority." A strange business, certainly. The police were instructed by telephone to see if there actually was a Jacob Mendel at the specified address, and, if so, to bring the fellow along. Within the hour, Mendel had been arrested, and (still stupefied by the shock) brought before the major, who showed him the postcards, and asked him with drill sergeant roughness whether he acknowledged their authorship. Angered at being spoken to so sharply, and still more annoyed because his perusal of an important catalogue had been interrupted, Mendel answered tartly:

"Of course I wrote the cards. That's my handwriting and signature. Surely one has a right to claim the delivery of a periodical to which one has subscribed?"

The major swung half-round in his swivel-chair and exchanged a meaning glance with the lieutenant seated at the adjoining desk.

"The man must be a double-distilled idiot," was what they mutely conveyed to one another. Then the chief took counsel within himself whether he should discharge the offender with a caution, or whether he should treat the case more seriously. In all offices, when such doubts arise, the usual practice is, not to spin a coin, but to send in a report. Thus Pilate washes his hands of responsibility. Even if the report does no good, it can do no harm, and is merely one useless manuscript or typescript added to a million others.

In this instance, however, the decision to send in a report did much harm, alas, to an inoffensive man of genius, for it involved asking a series of questions, and the third of them brought suspicious circumstances to light.

"Your full name?"

"Jacob Mendel."

"Occupation?"

"Book-pedlar" (for, as already explained, Mendel had no shop, but only a pedlar's licence).

"Place of birth?"

Now came the disaster. Mendel's birthplace was not far from Petrikau. The major raised his eyebrows. Petrikau, or Piotrkov, was across the frontier, in Russian Poland.

"You were born a Russian subject. When did you acquire Austrian nationality? Show me your papers."

Mendel gazed at the officer uncomprehendingly through his spectacles. "Papers? Identification papers? I have nothing but my hawker's licence."

"What's' your nationality, then? Was your father Austrian or Russian?" Undismayed, Mendel answered:

"A Russian, of course."

"What about yourself?"

"Wishing to evade Russian military service, I slipped across the frontier thirty-three years ago, and ever since I have lived in Vienna."

The matter seemed to the major to be growing worse and worse.

"But didn't you take steps to become an Austrian subject?"

"Why should I?" countered Mendel. "I never troubled my head about such things."

"Then you are still a Russian subject?"

Mendel, who was bored by this endless questioning, answered simply, "Yes, I suppose I am."

The startled and indignant major threw himself back in his chair with such violence that the wood cracked protestingly. So this was what it had come to! In Vienna, the Austrian capital, at the end of 1915, after Tarnow, when the war was in full blast, after the great offensive, a Russian could walk about unmolested, could write letters to France and England, while the police ignored his machinations. And then the fools who wrote in the newspapers wondered why Conrad von Hotzendorf had not advanced in seven-leagued boots to Warsaw, and the general staff was puzzled because every movement of the troops was immediately blabbed to the Russians.

The lieutenant had sprung to his feet and crossed the room to his chief's table. What had been an almost friendly conversation took a new turn, and degenerated into a trial.

"Why didn't you report as an enemy alien directly the war began?"

Mendel, still failing to realize the gravity of his position, answered in his singing Jewish jargon: "Why should I report? I don't understand."

The major regarded this inquiry as a challenge, and asked threateningly: "Didn't you read the notices that were posted up everywhere ?"

"No."

"Didn't you read the newspapers?"

"No."

The two officers stared at Jacob Mendel (now sweating with uneasiness) as if the moon had fallen from the sky into their office. Then the telephone buzzed, the typewriters clacked, orderlies ran hither and thither, and Mendel was sent under guard to the nearest barracks, where he was to await transfer to a concentration camp. When he was ordered to follow the two soldiers, he was frankly puzzled, but not seriously perturbed. What could the man with the gold-lace collar and the rough voice have against him? In the upper world of books, where Mendel lived and breathed and his being, there was no warfare, there were no misunderstandings, only an ever-increasing knowledge of words and figures, of book-titles and authors' names. He walked good-humouredly enough downstairs between the soldiers, whose first charge was to take him to the police station. Not until, there, the books were taken out of his overcoat pockets, and the police impounded the portfolio containing a hundred important memoranda and customers' addresses, did he lose his temper, and begin to resist and strike blows. They had to tie his hands. In the struggle, his spectacles fell off, and those magical telescopes, without which he could not see into the wonder world of books, were smashed into a thousand pieces. Two days later, insufficiently clad (for his only wrap was a light summer cloak), he was sent to the internment camp for Russian civilians at Komorn.

I have no information as to what Jacob Mendel suffered during these two years of internment, cut off from his beloved books, penniless, among roughly nurtured men, few of whom could read or write, in a huge human dunghill. This must be left to the imagination of those who can grasp the torments of a caged eagle. By degrees, however, our world, grown sober after its fit of drunkenness, has become aware that, of all the cruelties and wanton abuses of power during the war, the most needless and therefore the most inexcusable was this herding together behind barbed-wire fences of thousands upon thousands of persons who had outgrown the age of military service, who had made homes for themselves in a foreign land, and who (believing in the good faith of their hosts) had refrained from exercising the sacred right of hospitality granted even by the Tunguses and Araucanians the right to flee while time permits. This crime against civilization was committed with the same unthinking hardihood in France, Germany, and Britain, in every belligerent country of our crazy Europe.

Probably Jacob Mendel would, like thousands as innocent as he, have perished in this cattle-pen, have gone stark mad, have succumbed to dysentery, asthenia, softening of the brain, had it not been that, before the worst happened, a chance (typically Austrian) recalled him to the world in which a spiritual life became again possible. Several times after his disappearance, letters from distinguished customers were delivered for him at the Cafe Gluck. Count Schonberg, sometime lord lieutenant of Styria, an enthusiastic collector of works on heraldry; Siegenfeld, the former dean of the theological faculty, who was writing a commentary on the works of St. Augustine; Edler von Pisek, an octogenarian admiral on the retired list, engaged in writing his memoirs, these and other persons of note, wanting information from Buchmendel, had repeatedly addressed communications to him at his familiar haunt, and some of these were duly forwarded to the concentration camp at Komorn. There they fell into the hands of the commanding officer, who happened to be a man of humane disposition, and was astonished to find what notables were among the correspondents of this dirty little Russian Jew, who, half-blind now that his spectacles were broken and he had no money to buy new ones, crouched in a corner like a mole, grey, eyeless, and dumb. A man who had such patrons must be a person of importance, whatever he looked like. The C.O. therefore read the letters to the short-sighted Mendel, and penned answers for him to sign, answers which were mainly requests that influence should be exercised on his behalf. The spell worked, for these correspondents had the solidarity of collectors. Joining forces and pulling strings they were able (giving guarantees for the "enemy alien's" good behaviour) to secure leave for Buchmendel's return to Vienna in 1917, after more than two years at Komorn on the condition that he should report daily to the police. The proviso mattered little. He was a free man once more, free to take up his quarters in his old attic, free to handle books again, free (above all) to return to his table in the Cafe Gluck. I can describe the return from the underworld of the camp in the good Frau Sporschil's own words:

"One day, Jesus, Mary, Joseph; I could hardly believe my eyes, the door opened (you remember the way he had) little wider than a crack, and through this opening he sidled, poor Herr Mendel. He was wearing a tattered and much-darned military cloak, and his head was covered by what had perhaps once been a hat thrown away by the owner as past use. No collar. His face looked like a death's head, so haggard it was, and his hair was pitifully thin. But he came in as if nothing had happened, went straight to his table, and took off his cloak, not briskly as of old, for he panted with the exertion. Nor had he any books with him. He just sat there without a word, staring straight in front of him with hollow, expressionless eyes. Only by degrees, after we had brought him the big bundle of printed matter which had arrived for him from Germany, did he begin to read again: But he was never the same man."

No, he was never the same man, not now the miraculum mundi, the magical walking book-catalogue. All who saw him in those days told me the same pitiful story. Something had gone irrecoverably wrong; he was broken; the blood-red comet of the war had burst into the remote, calm atmosphere of his bookish world. His eyes, accustomed for decades to look at nothing but print, must have seen terrible sights in the wire-fenced human stockyard, for the eyes that had formerly been so alert and full of ironical gleams were now almost completely veiled by the inert lids, and looked sleepy and red-bordered behind the carefully repaired spectacle-frames. Worse still, a cog must have broken somewhere in the marvellous machinery of his memory, so that the working of the whole was impaired; for so delicate is the structure of the brain (a sort of switchboard made of the most fragile substances, and as easily jarred as are all instruments of precision) that a blocked arteriole, a congested bundle of nerve-fibres, a fatigued group of cells, even a displaced molecule, may put the apparatus out of gear and make harmonious working impossible. In Mendel's memory, the keyboard of knowledge, the keys were stiff, or to use psychological terminology the associations were impaired. When, now and again, someone came to ask for information, Jacob stared blankly at the inquirer, failing to understand the question, and even forgetting it before he had found the answer. Mendel was no longer Buchmendel, just as the world was no longer the world. He could not now become wholly absorbed in his reading, did not rock as of old when he read, but sat bolt upright, his glasses turned mechanically towards the printed page, but perhaps not reading at all, and only sunk in a reverie. Often, said Frau Sporschil, his head would drop on to his book and he would fall asleep in the daytime, or he would gaze hour after hour at the stinking acetylene lamp which (in the days of the coal famine) had replaced the electric lighting. No, Mendel was no longer Buchmendel, no longer the eighth wonder of the world, but a weary, worn-out, though still breathing, useless bundle of beard and ragged garments, which sat, as futile as a potato-bogle, where of old the Pythian oracle had sat; no longer the glory of the Cafe Gluck, but a shameful scarecrow, evil-smelling, a parasite.

That was the impression he produced upon the new proprietor, Florian Gurtner from Retz, who (a successful profiteer in flour and butter) had cajoled Standhartner into selling him the Cafe Gluck for eighty thousand rapidly depreciating paper crowns. He took everything into his hard peasant grip, hastily arranged to have the old place redecorated, bought fine-looking satin-covered seats, installed a marble porch, an was in negotiation with his next-door neighbour to buy a place where he could extend the cafe into a dancing-hall. Naturally while he was making these embellishments, he was not best pleased by the parasitic encumbrance of Jacob Mendel, a filthy old Galician Jew, who had been in trouble with the authorities during the war, was still to be regarded as an "enemy alien," and, while occupying a table from morning till night, consumed no more than two cups of coffee and four or five rolls. Standhartner, indeed, had put in a word for this guest of long standing, had explained that Mendel was a person of note, and, in the stock-taking, had handed him over as having a permanent lien upon the establishment, but as an asset rather than a liability. Florian Gurtner, however, had brought into the cafe, not only new furniture, and an up-to-date cash register, but also the profit-making and hard temper of the post-war era, and awaited the first pretext for ejecting from his smart coffee-house the last troublesome vestige of suburban shabbiness.

A good excuse was not slow to present itself. Jacob Mendel was impoverished to the last degree. Such banknotes as had been left to him had crumbled away to nothing during the inflation period; his regular clientele had been killed, ruined, or dispersed. When he tried to resume his early trade of book-pedlar, calling from door to door to buy and to sell, he found that he lacked strength to carry books up and down stairs. A hundred little signs showed him to be a pauper. Seldom, now, did he have a midday meal sent in from the restaurant, and he began to run up a score at the Cafe Gluck for his modest breakfast and supper. Once his payments were as much as three weeks overdue. Were it only for this reason, the head-waiter wanted Gurtner to "give Mendel the sack." But Frau Sporschil intervened, and stood surety for the debtor. What was due could be stopped out of her wages!

This staved off disaster for a while, but worse was to come. For some time the head-waiter had noticed that rolls were disappearing faster than the tally would account for. Naturally suspicion fell upon Mendel, who was known to be six months in debt to the tottering old porter whose services he still needed. The head-waiter, hidden behind the stove, was able, two days later, to catch Mendel red-handed. The unwelcome guest had stolen from his seat in the card-room, crept behind the counter in the front room, taken two rolls from the bread basket, returned to the card-room, and hungrily devoured them. When settling-up at the end of the day, he said he had only had coffee; no rolls. The source of wastage had been traced, and the waiter reported his discovery to the proprietor. Herr Gurtner, delighted to have so good an excuse for getting rid of Mendel, made a scene, openly accused him of theft, and declared that nothing but the goodness of his own heart prevented his sending for the police.

"But after this," said Florian, "you'll kindly take yourself off for good and all. We don't want to see your face again at the Cafe Gluck."

Jacob Mendel trembled, but made no reply. Abandoning his poor belongings, he departed without a word.

"It was ghastly," said Frau Sporschil. "Never shall I forget the sight. He stood up, his spectacles pushed on to his forehead, and his face white as a sheet. He did not even stop to put on his cloak, although it was January, and very cold. You'll remember that severe winter, just after the war. In his fright, he left the book he was reading open upon the table. I did not notice it at first, and then, when I wanted to pick it up and take it after him, he had already stumbled out through the doorway. I was afraid to follow him into the street, for Herr Gurtner was standing at the door and shouting at him, so that a crowd had gathered. Yet I felt ashamed to the depths of my soul. Such a thing would never have happened under the old master. Herr Standhartner would not have driven Herr Mendel away for pinching one or two rolls when he was hungry, but would have let him have as many as he wanted for nothing, to the end of his days. Since the war, people seem to have grown heartless. Drive away a man who had been a guest daily for so many, many years. Shameful! I should not like to have to answer before God for such cruelty!"

The good woman had grown excited, and, with the passionate garrulousness of old age, she kept on repeating how shameful it was, and that nothing of the sort would have happened if Herr Standhartner had not sold the business. In the end I tried to stop the flow by asking her what had happened to Mendel, and whether she had ever seen him again. These questions excited her yet more.

"Day after day, when I passed his table, it gave me the creeps, as you will easily understand. Each time I thought to myself: 'Where can he have got to, poor Herr Mendel?' Had I known where he lived, I would have called and taken him something nice and hot to eat for where could he get the money to cook food and warm his room? As far as I knew, he had no kinsfolk in the wide world. When, after a long time, I had heard nothing about him, I began to believe that it must be all up with him, and that I should never see him again. I had made up my mind to have a mass said for the peace of his soul, knowing him to be a good man, after twenty-five years' acquaintance.

"At length one day in February, at half-past seven in the morning, when I was cleaning the windows, the door opened, and in came Herr Mendel. Generally, as you know, he sidled in, looking confused, and not 'quite all there' but this time, somehow, it was different. I noticed at once the strange look in his eyes; they were sparkling, and he rolled them this way and that, as if to see everything at once; as for his appearance, he seemed nothing but beard and skin and bone. Instantly it crossed my mind: 'He's forgotten all that happened last time he was here; it's his way to go about like a sleepwalker noticing nothing; he doesn't remember about the rolls, and how shamefully Herr Gurtner ordered him out of the place, half in mind to set the police on him.' Thank goodness, Herr Gurtner hadn't come yet, and the head-waiter was drinking coffee. I ran up to Herr Mendel, meaning to tell him he'd better make himself scarce, for otherwise that ruffian," she looked round timidly to see if we were overheard, and hastily amended her phrase, "Herr Gurtner, I mean, would only have him thrown into the street once more. 'Herr Mendel,' I began. He started, and looked at me. In that very moment (it was dreadful), he must have remembered the whole thing, for he almost collapsed, and began to tremble, not his fingers only, but to shiver and shake from head to foot. Hastily he stepped back into the street, and fell in a heap on the pavement as soon as he was outside the door. We telephoned for the ambulance, and they carried him off to hospital, the nurse who came saying he had high fever directly she touched him. He died that evening. 'Double pneumonia,' the doctor said, and that he never recovered consciousness, could not have been fully conscious when he came to the Cafe Gluck. As I said, he had entered like a man walking in his sleep. The table where he had sat day after day for thirty-six years drew him back to it like a home."

Frau Sporschil and I went on talking about him for a long time, the two last persons to remember this strange creature, Buchmendel: I to whom in youth the book-pedlar from Galicia had given the first revelation of a life wholly devoted to the things of the spirit; she, the poor old woman who was caretaker of a cafe-toilet, who had never read a book in her life, and whose only tie with this strangely matched comrade in her subordinate, poverty-stricken world had been that for twenty-five years she had brushed his overcoat and had sewn on buttons for him. We, too, might have been considered strangely assorted, but Frau Sporschil and I got on very well together, linked, as we sat at the forsaken marble topped table, by our common memories of the shade our talk had conjured up, for joint memories, and above all loving memories, always establish a tie. Suddenly, while in the full stream of talk, she exclaimed:

"Lord Jesus, how forgetful I am. I still have the book he left on the table the evening Herr Gurtner gave him the key of the street. I didn't know where to take it. Afterwards, when no one appeared to claim it, I ventured to keep it as a souvenir. You don't think it wrong of me, Sir?"

She went to a locker where she stored some of the requisites for her job: and produced the volume for my inspection. I found it hard to repress a smile, for I was face to face with one of life's little ironies. It was the second volume of Hayn's *Bibliotheca Germanorum erotica et curiosa*, a compendium of gallant literature known to every book-collector. "Habent sua fata libelli!" This scabrous publication, as legacy of the vanished magician had fallen into toil worn hands which had perhaps never held any other printed work than a prayer-book. Maybe I was not wholly successful in controlling my mirth, for the expression on my race seemed to perplex the worthy soul, and once more she said:

"You don t think it wrong of me to keep it, Sir?"

I shook her cordially by the hand.

"Keep it, and welcome," I said. "I am absolutely sure that our old friend Mendel would be only too delighted to know that someone among the many thousands he has provided with books, cherishes his memory."

Then I took my departure, feeling a trifle ashamed when I compared myself with this excellent old woman, who, so simply and so humanely, had fostered the memory of the dead scholar. For she, uncultured though she was, had at least preserved a book as a memento; whereas I, a man of education and a writer, had completely forgotten Buchmendel for years I, who at least should have known that one only makes books in order to keep in touch with one's fellows after one has ceased to breathe, and thus to defend oneself against the inexorable fate of all that lives transitoriness and oblivion.

The Deceiver

Ashapurna Debi

Prominent Bengali novelist, short story writer and poet, Ashapurna Debi (1909-1995) was one of the first women writers to claim a position in a literary canon, otherwise, dominated by the standards set by male writers. In her career spanning 70 years, Ashapurna wrote extensively about the private lives of her characters within middle-class Bengali households. Her short story 'The Deceiver' has been translated by twice-winner of the Crossword translation award, Arunava Sinha.

The taxi sped past the two people standing there, gaping. Gazing bitterly in the direction in which the vehicle disappeared, while the dust it had raised settled back on the road, they marched off with a "To hell with it, what do we care."

After a long journey with several turns, the taxi stopped in front of a building where a wedding ceremony was underway. It was one of those thirty-thousand-rupee weddings, with corresponding grandeur in light arrangements, stage decorations and gate ornamentation.

Dressed to match such splendour, Anindita Sen and her married daughter Ajanta Bose got out of the taxi.

Anindita Sen was brimming with regret for having to arrive in a taxi on such an occasion. But what could she do, for fate was against her. Today, of all days her husband had had to take the car on official work to Barasat or Sonarpur or some such place.

The wedding was taking place in Anindita Sen's brother's house, her niece was getting married. She had been visiting regularly for the past few days, and even that morning, although in less ostentatious garments. Now she got out of the taxi with her daughter, glinting in silk and embroidery and sequins and beads.

She got out laughing and talking at the same time. Had the groom arrived? Had the first of the guests been disposed of in terms of dinner? Anindita Sen became voluble with such questions as soon as she had arrived.

Her daughter, Ajanta Bose, was not as loquacious, but she had dressed to dazzle. She had had a rather innovative outfit made for her dearest friend and cousin's wedding—she had dressed, not as a Bengali woman, but as a courtesan from Lucknow. The combination of a dupatta, ghagra, choli and matching jewellery was undoubtedly a novelty.

But people began to exchange glances the moment they got out of the taxi. Was it because they were overdressed, perhaps excessively so?

Were their clothes and appearance so abhorrent to everyone?

It wasn't as though no one else had overdone things. There was Mandira Roy, the bouffant on her head resembling a Sikh's turban. There was Hena Haldar, who had grown her nails to a point where they looked longer than her fingers. Who knew how many months she had been growing them, all for this wedding. She had painted them in three different shades.

But no one was staring at them.

Certainly not with such strange, confused looks.

And what about the soft murmurs of uneasiness that could be heard beneath the sounds of happiness and laughter at the wedding?

Whom was it for?

People seemed to be exchanging covert whispers everywhere. About what?

No one had actually singled them out, but the eyes of all the people who had gathered for the wedding seemed to have become a collective finger pointing in their direction. At Anindita Sen and her daughter.

But the funny thing was, bubbling over as they were with their own joy, they weren't aware of any of this. Anindita Sen was uniting the universe with a constant stream of observations, and Ajanta Bose was sitting like a queen bee amidst a circle of women, spreading her radiance in all directions.

And yet—

Ajanta was wondering, why aren't the stars in my eyes? Somewhere the melody had been interrupted, the rhythm had broken. Ajanta's fingers were not doing magic with the strings.

Was it her dressing as a courtesan from Lucknow that had appeared unseemly to people? But why? At her own wedding just the other day, her cousin had won everyone's heart by dressing as a fruitseller from Kashmir and singing and dancing. How much everyone had enjoyed it! Had Ajanta become too old for this sort of thing in the year and a half that had passed?

Anyway, let the groom take his place after the ceremonies, Ajanta would show them. With song and laughter and her sparkling sense of humour, she would ensure the poor man realised what a gem of a sister-in-law he had acquired.

Anindita wasn't thinking of any of this.

Anindita was just blazing a trail wherever she went.

"Well, ladies, I hope you can do the rituals properly. However modern we are, weddings are no fun without the rituals."

"Oh my, I didn't see you all this time, where have you been? Is that a new necklace you're wearing?... Oh my god Ushashi, what a murderously beautiful sari that is! Where'd you buy it ... You boys there, you're gobbling the fish fry yourself instead of serving it, think I can't see?... Who's handing out the paan? Give me one ... Where's the bride's mother? Haven't seen her all evening. What's this, are you going to hide now that you're a mother-in-law?"

No rest for the tongue. Anindita Sen seemed to have vowed not to rest her faculty of speech.

"The groom's here, the groom's here."

A commotion began, like a mighty torrent. The more the people, the stronger it was. And those who were celebrating the groom's arrival were not behaving strangely, their music had not been interrupted. They were men.

Here, though—

A string broke with a twang. It happened when the married women were gathering to welcome the groom. Ajanta was rushing to join in, after all, she had personally decorated some of the trays that morning.

Ajanta's aunt, the bride's mother, swooped like a hawk to snatch the tray from her hands, saying, "Never mind, you can't do all this in a ghagra and dupatta ..."

Tears of humiliation welled up in Ajanta's eyes. "Why didn't you tell me earlier, Maami?" she said. "I'd have dressed in a sari."

Her aunt said sulkily, "No need. No dearth of married women here. We have seventy-seven where we need seven."

This was true.

Seventy-seven.

But was Ajanta supposed to be one in a crowd?

A rich man's daughter, a rich man's wife, the pretty Ajanta had always been the centre of attraction at her uncle and aunt's house.

Biting her lips, Ajanta decided, "The ghagra was a mistake."

But how strange!

Everyone had known, after all. Ajanta's aunt had been with her when she had bought the dupatta.

It must be the thousand-and-odd women gathered here who were at the root of all this. Never mind, she wouldn't try to welcome the groom, she would just light up the gathering after the ceremonies with the bride and groom and friends and family.

But even that didn't seem acceptable to anyone.

The mild opposition and the suppressed buzz of discontent was neither mild nor suppressed now.

They were about to swell into sharp anger and furious condemnation. A meeting had been summoned downstairs in the room where the glasses were stored.

Two of Anindita Sen's sisters were present, as were the bride's mother and her elder sister. Even the bride's father himself had been asked to join, he would arrive at any moment.

The agitated voices were becoming more and more aggressive. "Does she mean to continue this way? What if she starts games with the married couple? She's already ensconced herself where the bride and groom will go. Send for Ani. Get her to come to her senses. Is this any way to behave on such a day? We can't even make a fuss, no one wants the festivities to be marred. But ..."

The bride's elder bother arrived. A distressed, beleaguered look on his face, along with a frown.

"Well? What have you decided?"

"Whatever all of you say. We've sent for him, where is he?"

"On his way. My colleagues are eating ..."

The bride's father arrived.

He looked flustered. His expression suggested pressure, not sorrow.

"What I'm saying is, why not let things be as they are. Since Ani doesn't know. Whatever Sen Moshai thinks is right ..."

"Ohhh, so clever!" The bride's mother barked. "I have just the one daughter, and you're suggesting ..."

The incomplete sentence carries more weight. Scratching his pate, the bride's father said, "Well then, here's an idea. You can say Sen Moshai couldn't make it here after returning from Barasat, he sent word that he isn't well, so Anindita and Ajanta should ..."

They approved of this.

After all, a man's brain. This wouldn't lead to an uproar among the wedding guests, but the mother and daughter would leave as quickly as they could.

Meanwhile Ajanta was sitting with the bride, whispering her artificial regret into her cousin's ear, "See what a horrible man he is? Didn't come. You won't believe how I entreated him in the letter. Your parents did too. People travel all the way from England for a wedding, and he's just a few hours away in Durgapur ... Tell me, Mr Groom, isn't this cruelty on the part of your gender?"

Who knew what the groom would have said, but the bride's brother summoned her gravely, "Just a minute, Ajanta."

Ajanta missed a heartbeat. The summons was ominous. She rose to ask him, "What is it, Ranga-da?"

"It's er just that your father is um not well, it would be best if you went home."

Ajanta paled. "Did Baba leave because he was unwell, Ranga-da?"

"No, he didn't even come."

"Didn't come? Ma? Where's Ma?"

"She's somewhere downstairs."

Her cousin hurried away.

The heart cannot tarry when calamity looms large.

It was he who went off to inform Anindita.

Anindita was astonished at first. "What, you mean your uncle didn't even come? I thought he had eaten and left without telling us..."

Anindita's effusiveness deflated suddenly, running up against the wall of silence around her.

She rushed into a car with her daughter. Someone had volunteered a vehicle from the two rows parked on the road.

Ajanta was distraught. "How is Baba? If he couldn't even come on Runu's wedding night, it means he's not strong enough."

But it was impossible to tell Anindita's thoughts from her face. Perhaps she had turned to stone out of fury with her husband for choosing this particular day to turn hostile. Why were her eyes looking like glass?

Jumping out of the car, still resplendent in her silk and embroidery and sequins and beads, Ajanta was taken aback. Her father wasn't ill at all. He was pacing up and down in front of the house.

What was it?

She ran up to him. "What's happened to you, Baba?"

"Go inside," said Mr Sen, sounding like thunder.

Tears sprang to Ajanta's eyes at his tone.

What was all this?

Why was everyone humiliating her in unison today?

Covering her eyes with her silk dupatta, Ajanta entered the house.

Anindita was about to follow her in.

Without a word to her husband, possibly to announce the intensity of her anger.

"Wait," said Sen.

Anindita turned towards him.

The gaudy end of her white Benarasi silk sari flashed. And she wrinkled her nose in contempt. "Well, is this a trial for my crime?" she said. "A court martial?"

Sen lost his patience.

"Quiet," he exclaimed. "Answer my question first. Did two people from Durgapur come here before you left?"

Anindita stood stock still. "They did," she said.

"What did they tell you?"

Anindita said even more steadily, "Nothing. I didn't let them."

"You didn't let them?"

"No."

This was true, Anindita had indeed not allowed them to speak.

They had said, "We're coming from Durgapur..."

Anindita had looked at them. Anindita had read their faces. So, Anindita had pretended to be busy. "If you could come tomorrow please, I don't have time right now, I'm about to go out ..."

They had pleaded desperately, "You don't understand, it's very important. Nishith Bose is your son-in-law, isn't he? In Durgapur today..."

"Yes, I understand, he can't make it. I knew he wouldn't come. There was no need to send word ceremonially ..."

Shepherding her daughter into a taxi, Anindita had got in behind her.

The men had been so frantic that they had practically jumped in front of the vehicle. "Please listen to what we have to say, at eleven this morning Mr Bose ..."

"At eleven?" Anindita had said. "He's arriving at eleven? There's no train at that time. Is he coming by road? That's something. Nomoshkar. Please don't mind, I'm very busy."

The taxi had sped past the two people standing there, gaping.

A worried Ajanta had asked, "What were they saying, Ma?"

Anindita had dismissed the question.

She had dismissed it airily.

She had said, "The poor dear can't make it, so now he's sent word to absolve himself, saying he'll come by road if he can."

Ajanta had looked glum. "I knew he wouldn't. Right from the beginning he's been saying, take two days off to attend your cousin's wedding, are you mad?"

Anindita remembered all this clearly.

Sen roared like an enraged tiger, "Were you in such a hurry to attend the wedding that you couldn't even hear them out?"

Looking her husband in the eye, Anindita articulated her words clearly. "There was no need to hear what they had to say. It was written on their faces."

"What do you mean?" Sen gripped his plump, ornamented wife by the arms and shook her like a child. "What are you trying to say?

You knew from their faces? And knowing that Nishith was dead you still ..."

"Yes, knowing that he was dead. But can you tell me what harm this has caused in this huge, wide world? Just when Ajanta was on her way to a wedding celebration, so cheerful and happy, if I had dragged her down to the road and told her, it's all over for you, your life has ended, you don't belong to this world anymore—how would that have benefited anyone?"

"Never mind all the poetry. There's a limit to pretence. Don't you know one of Nishith's uncle is related to your sister-in-law's family? Everyone at the wedding was scandalised. While the two of you were dressed as dancers ..."

Anindita was not perturbed at this condemnation. She seemed to have forgotten how to be distressed. So, she said calmly, "I knew someone in Boudi's family is Nishith's uncle. All I didn't know was that the news would travel so quickly through all these family connections. I thought, the girl has been waiting six months for a wonderful evening at Runu's wedding, let her have one. The last time she'll be able to celebrate. After this, there will be a lifetime wrapped in ice. I had thought of stealing three hours from the ocean of eternity, hoping that no one would notice. But I see it didn't work. The entire world was up in arms against the theft ..."

Gazing for a minute or so at the tears coursing over Anindita's rouged cheeks, Sen rebuked her indignantly, "I get the argument. But how *could* you? She didn't know, but you did. How could you still have a good time at the wedding?"

"I had thought that was what would fool people. Stupidity. And as for how I could get myself to do it, maybe human beings shouldn't be able to do such a thing, but you just did, too. You found it easy to demand an explanation for why I stole three hours from your daughter's eternal widowhood."

you knew. Even their faces. And knowing that Nishith was dead you still—"

"Yes, knowing that he was dead. But can you tell me what harm this has caused in this big, wide world? That when Amrita was on her way to a wedding celebration, [illegible] happened to [illegible] dragged her down to the road and told her lies all over for you, your life has ended, you don't belong to this world anymore—how would she have [illegible]?"

"Never mind all the poetry. There's a limit to pretence. Don't you know one of Nishith's uncles is related to your sister-in-law's family? Everyone at the wedding was scandalised! While the two of you were dressed as [illegible]."

Amrita was not [illegible] at this condemnation. She seemed to have forgotten how to be distressed. She said calmly, "I knew someone at [illegible] family is Nishith's uncle. All I didn't know was that the news would travel so quickly through all these family [illegible]. [illegible] the girl had been with me [illegible] for a wonderful evening at [illegible] wedding. [illegible] have one. The last time she'll be able to [illegible]. After this, [illegible] on a [illegible] [illegible]. That the [illegible] the [illegible] world [illegible] that no one would [illegible]. But [illegible] didn't work. The [illegible] was up [illegible] the [illegible]."

[illegible] for a minute or so at the [illegible] Amrita's [illegible] check. [illegible] with [illegible]. [illegible] the argument [illegible] she didn't know [illegible]. How could you [illegible] have a good time at the wedding?"

"I [illegible] that was what [illegible] people. [illegible] [illegible] [illegible] [illegible] human beings [illegible] be able to do such [illegible] for you [illegible] [illegible] to [illegible] [illegible] [illegible] three [illegible] your [illegible] widowhood."

you know. Everything. Yes. And knowing that Nikhil was dead you still...'

'Yes, knowing that he was dead. But can you tell me what harm this has caused in this big, wide world? That when Amrita was on her way to a wedding celebration, so excited and happy, if I had dragged her down to the road and told her [illegible] over for you, your life has [illegible], you don't belong to this world any more—how would that have helped anybody?'

'Never mind all the poetry. There's a limit to pretence. Don't you know one of Amrita's uncles is [illegible] family? Everyone at the wedding was scandalised. While the two of you were dressed [illegible].'

Anandita was not perturbed at this condemnation. She seemed to have forgotten how to be distressed any more. She said calmly, 'I knew someone [illegible] family [illegible] Nikhil's [illegible]. All I didn't know was that the news would travel so quickly through all these [illegible] [illegible] the girl has been [illegible] for a wonderful evening at [illegible] wedding [illegible]. The last time she'll be able to [illegible]. After this [illegible] [illegible] [illegible] But [illegible] didn't work [illegible] the [illegible].'

[illegible]

[illegible] thought [illegible] was what [illegible] people [illegible] [illegible] [illegible] [illegible] [illegible] [illegible] [illegible].'